Buck and Petal

Chill the Anthropocene

Also by John Mickey

Poisoned Medicine

Ultimatum Day

Buck and Petal

Chill the Anthropocene

A Novel

John Mickey

PINAOULA PRESS

Manoa • New York • Portland

BUCK AND PETAL

CHILL THE ANTHROPOCENE

Published in the United States of America
Pinaoula Press, Honolulu, Hawaii 96822
ISBN-13 : 978-0-615-30106-8
ISBN-10: 0615301061

Cover Design by the author from the painting:
Sphinx Albedo

This is a work of fiction. All characters, incidents,
organizations, and dialogue used in this novel
are either the products of the author's imagination
or are used fictitiously.

ANTHROPOCENE

The geologic era during which the fate of the Earth was
determined by the actions of Man.

CHAPTER 1

CONSCRIPTION

"First off, get rid of your save-the-world fantasies."

He was obviously talking to Buck now. No one would ever accuse Petal Steele of harboring such mundane figments in her imagination.

Petal nodded politely, distancing herself from this male hierarchy ritual by pretending to regard her nails—a gesture all the more powerful when a woman is wearing gloves. But then, hat and gloves had been *de rigueur* ever since the Queen's visit and would be for another seventy-two hours at least, in Petal's professional opinion.

Planck took no offense at Ferret's tone. It was one of his major failings. Buck Planck was one of those exasperating people who thinks that everybody, deep down, has a heart.

"You folks against saving the world?" he asked. "Or is it just the fantasizing part?"

Planck had spent his life dealing with disasters. Kosovo, Darfur, Katrina. Earthquakes, tidal waves, epidemics. He was universally recognized as The Disaster Guy. But Planck had never actually fantasized about saving the world, per se. He had been too busy patching up little pieces of it, one fragment at a time.

Richard Ferret leaned back in his massive chair, its intricate array of sensors and struts silently anticipating every gravitational need. He pondered the ceiling for a while, as if waiting for some helpful text to be projected there. None forthcoming, he begrudgingly conceded to Planck's demand for literalness. Subtle would have been so much more comfortable. Overt leaves so little room for deniability. Concrete can be so hard when you hit it head on.

"Planck, you're a smart guy. You know as well as anyone that the jig is up. Only the fossil fools still deny it in public, but even they admit it to each other. How many Exxon execs own beachfront anymore? Check it out. Zero.

"Let's face it. It's over. The point has been tipped. The pooch, skewered. The planet is boiling in its own oil and no amount of do-gooder hand wringing will slow the inevitable one iota. Not any more. Did you see the 'casts today? We're at 500 parts per million and accelerating. A red letter day. A day you would have told your grandchildren about if they hadn't been baked before they were born.

"Saving the world is a fool's mission, anyway," said Ferret, now pacing the huge office, itself a high distillate of an obscene expanse of endangered rainforest. "The world will do just fine burnt up. Look at Mars. It's still spinning merrily along. The Earth will cope. And life will adapt. Hell, they've even got germs that live in volcanoes, for God's sake. I saw it on T.V.

"And I'm not even saying that there won't be any people left, necessarily. The species is hardy enough. Humans are great breeders and do fine hiding in holes. It's just their societies that are so fragile. Civilization is on its way out and people like us will just have to make the best of it."

Petal Steele did not share Buck's obliviousness to slights, even those unintended.

"Just whom do you think you are including in your 'like us', Mr. Ferret?" she asked, arching her back and smoothing her Queen-Mother-by-Wang. Certainly none of *her* people would be caught dead in this venue of commerce, albeit palatial, high above Wall Street.

Ferret had thought this would be easier. He wasn't used to talking to people who didn't know enough to cower. He sat on the edge of his desk and leaned toward the two, as if lecturing truants.

"Look, none of this is my idea. Personally, I've got better things to do than to talk you two into this project. But the Publisher specifically stipulated that it be Petal Steele and Buck Planck and no one else."

"What publisher?" asked Buck.

"He means *The* Publisher," Petal hissed from the corner of her mouth.

"There is only one Publisher nowadays," agreed Ferret.

"Oh, him," nodded Buck, suddenly feeling trapped. "Why us? What project?" He had thought that this appointment had been for some kind of media interview. The afternoon had just turned from annoying to ominous.

Ferret stood up and stretched. How much nicer to be in charge. No one challenged the authority of The Publisher. Not if they wanted to continue to live among other people.

"We here at *Hedge Insider Daily* take pride in the exclusivity of our readership," he began in his usual expansive manner.

"Ten thousand per subscription," whispered Petal in Buck's direction.

"Per year?" Planck assumed.

"Per issue," offered Ferret. "But there aren't any ads."

"Unless you consider the whole thing an ad," said Petal, eager to assure all present that those of her class may worship nothing more than the possession of money, but disdained nothing more than the making of it.

"We do not advertise, my dear, we advise," Ferret continued. "And our subscribers are eager to know how to position their assets when the Earth itself finally assumes the position, if you follow my metaphor."

"Your people want to know how to make money off of the end of the world?" Petal may not know much about metaphors, but she knew everything about rich people. She had been the Czarina of the *Times* society page for a decade, after all.

"Why choose us for this? We're not business people," Buck protested. He may not have much else in common with Petal, but he was sure about this one.

"The Publisher does not explain his decisions to anyone, even to me," admitted Ferret. "But it's obvious, really. Planck, you're the disaster guy. No one knows more about disasters than you do. And has there ever been a more complete and devastating disaster in all of human history? The plagues? The ice ages? Wars? Famines? Not even close. Who better than you to predict how the dominoes will fall, how people will react, what governments and NGOs and millions of refugees will do? You're the man, Planck."

"And why me?" asked Petal, in a voice that begged to be excused.

"Our readership may care deeply, as individuals, about the starving and dispossessed of the world, but it is their fiduciary responsibility to themselves to know how the money is going to move. And rich people are the ones who control the money, both their money and the government's money. And no one knows rich people like Petal Steele. And besides, Mr. Planck's personality makes him susceptible to certain sentimental leanings. The Publisher needs someone with your world view to keep him out of the political deep end, if you get my drift.

"You two are the perfect team. Steele and Planck. Planck and Steele. I don't care which way it is. You work it out.

"This is how it comes down. You have ninety days to research this thing. Here is the number of your Swiss account, call me if you need more. Cost is no object. Bribe anybody. Go anywhere. Do anything. Just get the data, bulletproof your case, and distill it down for dummies in time for the Christmas issue."

"And what exactly is in it for us?" sulked Petal, inappropriately.

"You and your condemned descendants may yet escape the Publisher's wrath," offered Ferret, magnanimously.

She looked to Buck, fuming. He was the man. He should be the one to stand up to this bully.

"Well, then, what more could we ask for?" beamed Buck, flashing them both the guileless grin that Petal knew would drive her to mayhem, long before the Christmas issue.

CHAPTER 2

IMELDA

"You sure this is the best place to talk?" asked Buck, trying to stuff himself into a sadistic booth built for someone six inches shorter and sixty pounds lighter.

"Where else? This is the hottest place in town," assured Petal, making little nods of contact around the room. "And even if you eat in a different hottest place every day, you still end up conspicuously absent from way too many hottest places by the end of the month. Then you have to make up that you've been in rehab or something so you don't look like you're out of the loop."

Marcos's Mesopotamia was indeed hot. Imelda had installed special humidifiers that precisely recreated the atmosphere of her Persian Tapas Palace in Manila. In August. All the beautiful people considered it quite authentic. Though not too many Persians there, for some reason.

"And besides," she continued, stripping down to her blouse, "We've got nothing to hide. Or do we?"

"Only that we are about to perform the most despicable act of vulturism in the history of mankind on behalf of the world's sleaziest weasel and his money-lusting disciples. I can't think of half as vile an atrocity that can be mentioned in a restaurant. Other than that, we've got nothing to be ashamed of."

Buck had given up on the booth and was perched on a spindly chair in the aisle. Wait staff in their burkhas glared at him invisibly.

"Yeah, but we don't have to let on why we are researching the climate debate, do we? Everybody else is doing a book about it. Why shouldn't we?"

If there was one thing that those of Petal's station excelled at, it was viewing their own misbehavior in the most flattering light.

"Climate debate," said Buck, mopping his neck with his napkin. "Do people still use that euphemism?"

"What else?" said Petal, antennae up for an impending unintended slight. "The people I talk to at parties—"

"At parties?" winced Buck, tearing off his tie.

"Yes, at parties. Where else do people talk?" Petal picked up a bottle of iodine tablets from the table and dropped a couple into her water glass. Another of Imelda's authentic touches. "The people that I talk to at parties say that all this brouhaha about climate change is just so much mass hysteria. So, the earth is getting hotter. So what? That's because the sun is getting hotter. Apparently the weather is hotter on Jupiter, too. All to do with sunspots and eccentric orbits. Nothing to do with business—I mean, nothing to do with human beings."

"And scientists blame greenhouse gases because they're jealous of CEO salaries and would gladly destroy the economy just to get back at them." Buck was careful to avoid the slightest hint of sarcasm.

"Yeah, that's what they say," she agreed. "But even in the liberal media you'll find plenty of scientists with opposing views."

"The Publisher is nothing if not fair and balanced," allowed Buck. "Equal time for every opinion. Fifty-fifty. Truth just a coin toss away."

Buck didn't know how much more of Petal Steele he could take. Getting her head on straight was more than a ninety-day project in itself. Nine hundred days wouldn't be long enough, given where her head was starting. Maybe they could collaborate on this project at a distance.

"Petal, let's sketch out a plan for the next three months," he said, clearing a space on the table. Tiny plates of Black Dog in Frankincense and Monitor Lizard with Sand piled up to one side. "Here's a stack of three by five cards for you." Buck was never without plenty of three by fives. "And a stack for me. Let's write down every source of information we can think of that might shed light on the collapse of civilization, or the climate debate, if you prefer. Then we'll just divide them up, gather the data, and get together for an all-nighter before the report is due."

Some women are hard to read. Not Petal. It was one of her greatest strengths. Easy readability.

"What's wrong?" he asked, noting the push of the lip, the tilt of the head, the flare of the nostrils. Hurt. Angry. Suspicious. Stubborn.

6

"I'm supposed to be keeping an eye on you. That's what he said. Make sure your cannon doesn't get loose or something. We're a team, and you'd better get used to it. And if you think I'm going to let you get me in trouble with the Publisher, you don't know the first thing about disasters. So, you want a plan, do you? Well, I've got a plan. I assume you own a tux."

"Of course I do," he replied, a little hurt himself. What did she take him for, some kind of hick? "L. L. Bean. Top of the line."

"Sounds like a real disaster," she said, putting on her hat and gloves. "Meet me at Lincoln Center in three hours. Pick up your ticket at Will Call. I'll be chatting with Al and Leonardo until you get there." She was halfway out the door already, sticking him with the check.

"And Buck," she said, back-lit by the last rich rays of autumn sunlight, her smile now benevolent, almost warm. "Try not to be such a Buck."

CHAPTER 3

NGUYEN

As usual, it took Buck longer than anticipated to schlep uptown to his place in Harlem. With all this rain, the Six had been flooded for weeks, and the only way to get a cab these days was through the right of primogeniture. Buses always had room for one more, but since Buck was the size of one and a half (and obviously soaked), he got the wave from the first six drivers who passed. Always the optimist, Buck waved back with a smile—hoping to bank some good will and improve his chances for the trip to Lincoln Center in his tux.

Buck's apartment was a not-exactly-kosher space carved out of the totally-illegal living quarters of Xuyen Nguyen and his fourteen family members—owners and operators of Beulah's Soul Food Kitchen and Wigs, which packed 'em in 24/7 on the floor below. Recently, Xuyen had been arriving at Buck's door within minutes of his arrival, carrying a steaming plate of chittlins and okra in hopes of bartering for advice about his (Xuyen's, that is) upcoming IPO on the NASDAQ—Beulah's having already spun off into a dozen cities run by more of Xuyen's relatives and now ready to go international.

Xuyen refused to believe that Buck, as such a major player in international disaster circles and all, didn't know the first thing about financial shenanigans, and figured that he was just holding out for some real Vietnamese delicacies—the kind that were consumed under Rosicrucian-grade secrecy in the Nguyen's apartment just down the hall. So tonight, in desperation, Xuyen showed up with a potent potion of mambo snake pho, double dosed with contraband Phu Quoc XXO fish sauce, its anchovies fermented an additional decade or two in barrels once thought lost in the sweltering jungles of Southeast Asia.

But Buck, now in a major time bind, was making so much noise tearing his apartment apart in a desperate attempt to locate something approximating a cummerbund (SCUBA weight belt, ATV inner tube, amphibious-lander escape slide, Tibetan prayer rug—) that he failed to hear Xuyen's exquisitely polite footfalls behind him. And then, in a flash of memory, the vision of the missing garment (wrapped around a radiator pipe that had hissed all last winter) popped into Buck's mind, whirling him around and directly into a tray of steaming fish and reptile soup.

Buck's first reaction (the one right after he realized that he had not actually fallen into the putrefying hold of an overdue herring trawler, drifting crewless for generations through the mists of the Bermuda Triangle) was concern for the wellbeing of his friend, who, despite being spared the pungent scalding that Buck's tuxedo had sustained, had nonetheless been knocked largely senseless by the momentum of a man who was one point eight five times his mass.

Buck, his old paramedic training kicking into automatic, began assessment of the injured party. Breathing—okay. Heartbeat—regular. Pupils—equal. Mental status—out cold. Fearing that he could have broken the poor guy's neck, Buck painstakingly stabilized Xuyen's cervical spine using the tray as a splint, to which he bound the patient's shoulders with the cummerbund and his head with a belt. Barely taking time to admire the elegance of his first-responder improvisation, Buck began dialing 911.

However, the sound of exploding soup bowls had triggered a wave of second responders from down the hall, led by Xuyen's wife Thanh, who, despite multiple U.S. administrations' pronouncements of remorse for the inconsiderate bombing of her native country back to the Stone Age (as expressed through decades of economic subversion and good-natured CIA pranks) had never completely grown to trust Green-Beret-looking white guys.

To Thanh it was immediately obvious that her unconscious husband, bound head and shoulders to a tray, had been the victim of some extraordinary-rendition water-boarding interrogation perpetrated by this despicable covert operative who had burrowed like a maggot into the sanctity of their home and then tortured their beloved patriarch to the brink of death with his own fish sauce.

Accustomed to commanding platoons of young Nguyens, honed in the kitchens and hardened in the streets of Harlem,

Thanh needed to shriek only a few sharp syllables to set loose a veritable Tet upon the fishy but otherwise unprotected body of Buck Planck. Within an instant, Buck's position had been rendered completely Gulliverian, pinned to the floor by a dozen men half his size, each who had dreamed all of his testosterone-marinated adolescence of such a perfect, guilt-free, honor-bound, low-risk orgy of mindless violence.

To Thanh, however, it was clear that merely ripping out Buck's gizzard was way too good for him, and so, with a wave of her hand, she arrested the trajectories of the score of switchblades that threatened the integrity of Planck's already-distressed formal wear. In addition, it had become clear to her that the reason for her husband's inquisition must have something to do with the details of Beulah's Soul Food Kitchen and Wigs' upcoming debut in the financial markets (there being no other valuable secret in the family besides the name of their Phu Quoc sauce dealer) and that this information must be very valuable indeed for the infiltrator to have moled the last ten years away in this dump of an apartment waiting for his time to strike.

Thanh, who herself had favored an off-shore, private-equity, multi-level-marketing structure for the new, multinational Beulah's, over Xuyen's IPO leveraged derivatives buyback approach, was now completely swayed by this incontrovertible validation of her husband's corporate vision by Buck, an agent of a country which, while admittedly totally incapable of balancing its own checkbook, did lead the world in the invention of these kinds of Escherian financial construction.

As if in a flash (which in actuality was a flash—since all embarrassing moments of human experience were now being captured by cell phone cameras and instantly delivered to billions of scandal thirsty internet voyeurs) Thanh saw her husband in a totally new light. She had overlooked his intellect, underestimated his potency, and completely misapprehended his valor. She realized that, for the sake of his family, this courageous man had resisted the intruder's 'wet work,' and, ironically, may now be on the brink of taking his now-clearly-brilliant business plan to the grave.

The other people in the room became invisible to Thanh. There were just the two of them now, childhood sweethearts, desperately holding each other in the tunnels, the smell of napalm sharp in the evening air, the beat of helicopters fading into distance. Tears streaming from her eyes, she struggled to free her one true love from his bonds, and smothered his face with kisses. She ripped open his shirt, to feel his heartbeat, to staunch a wound that may be hidden by his clothes. She clamped her mouth on his, if not to breathe life back in, at least to claim one final ecstasy before goodbye.

Xuyen's consciousness was slowly reconstituting itself under the influence of Thanh's tightly focused erotic field. Out of the ethereal void emerged the archetypal seductress of the male Id, baring his chest, ravishing his lips. Determined not to let this perfect apparition slip away, as she had done in so many other dreams, Xuyen clasped her to his chest in an embrace that threatened to crush them both. He would finally have this woman and it would be now.

For Thanh, the joy of feeling her husband returned to life was now overwhelmed by the joy of feeling her husband returned to youth, a feeling more insistent every minute she straddled him there on the floor. Not one to waste precious natural resources, especially previously dwindling ones, Thanh shifted her skirts and his pajamas just so in one deft wiggle, and right there in front of God and everybody, dreams became reality, death was turned to life, and love was born anew.

Which, luckily for Buck and the kids, did not take all that long. In fact, all of them had been holding their breath throughout the entire drama, and on the signal of the couple's ultimate gasp of unification, the room, too, gasped in unison. So loud a collective inspiration it was that it startled all those present completely out of whatever individual brain states had possessed them theretofore, leaving them blinking at one another in disbelief at the improbable tableau they now composed.

"I love you, Thanh," sighed Xuyen, gazing into her eyes.

"I love you too, my little monkey thymus," she cooed, using a term of endearment that had made him blush all those decades before. If he didn't care who was watching, then neither would she.

"Thanks to our friend Buck, I have just had the most remarkable experience," he said, rising up on one elbow. "It was like I was a bird, flying above our lives, all the years condensed into minutes. I saw us there in the rice paddies of Viet Nam, everything we loved sacrificed to violence. I saw us escaping to America with nothing but determination and each other. I watched as we hid our real selves away with our history and our culture so that we would be tolerated among those who had no right to hate us. I watched as we worked, tirelessly and with no complaint, to follow what everyone said was the American dream.

"And I watched as we succeeded, ever so slowly, in building an empire of soul food and wigs that stretched from sea to shining sea. And I was proud. Proud not only to be selling the crispiest catfish, the most succulent hush puppies, and the most bodacious hairpieces in or outside of Birmingham, but to have done it without a Mammy or a Pappy or an Aunt Jemima or even a Beulah, not to mention an uncle in banking, a father in Skull and Bones, or even a formal education, for God's sake.

"And that vision made me realize how proud we really ought to be. Why are we hiding our heritage under our beds? Why do we have South Vietnam in our apartment and South Alabama in our restaurants? Why do we perpetuate this segregation? Why can't we come out of the closet and be proud of everything that we love?

"I'm not talking about just another Vietnamese restaurant. That would only perpetuate our cultural polarization. I'm talking about a totally new cuisine! I'm talking okra in coconut milk, grits with Phu Quoc, possum with basil! Saigon Soul! Isn't this exhilarating? I feel like a young man again! Quick, Thanh, to the kitchen! We have a whole new world to create!" He was on his feet now, embracing his wife.

"So Buck was actually helping your creative process with all these belts and trays and fish sauce?" she mulled, almost ready to believe anything.

"We owe him a great debt of gratitude," assured Xuyen. "Buck, my friend, how can we ever repay you?"

The young Nguyens helped Buck to his feet, secretly relieved that there wasn't going to be some huge bloody mess to clean up, and that Buck, who had always been like an uncle to them, wasn't really an embedded assassin after all.

"A ride to Lincoln Center would be nice," said Buck, knowing that it would have to be on the back of the family moped. "And a little help with this bow tie. I never can get the ends right."

So within minutes, Buck was clinging to the bony back of Tyrone Nguyen, a moped pilot whose skill was only exceeded by his bravery, as they flew down Broadway's dark and rain-swept center line, waving at the bus drivers who sat stalled in a gridlock stretching miles in both directions.

CHAPTER 4

LINCOLN

The cause of Broadway's gridlock became apparent blocks above Lincoln Center. Thousands of ordinary citizens, clearly motivated by something other than immediate personal gain, were enduring the rain and dark and autumn chill to do something—if only mill and churn—to make a statement. The streets and sidewalks were clogged with people plodding silently south, hooded against the ever-present drizzle, their spirits sodden, their hopes melted, and their energies spent.

With so many people so desperate to be heard, you would think that their message would be pretty clear to the outside observer. But there were no placards, no bullhorns, no chants— not even a squirt of graffiti or a multiply-Xeroxed handbill. This was a mob that was too discouraged to be unruly, too depressed to be rude.

At a light, Buck called to a dude on the corner, "Wassup?"

"Carbon Life. At the Center," he shouted back over the din of stalled traffic. This meant nothing to Buck, and before he could call back "Wazzat?" Tyrone had jumped the light and was roaring down the narrow slot between oncoming cars.

The demonstration in front of the Center may not have been communicating a coherent message, but it was in fact accomplishing something—it was making it tough for the tuxedo class to get close to the entrance. But no one in evening wear except for Buck had the benefit of a fearless driver of an urban all-terrain vehicle, who, with maximum use of horn and bumper, could slice through the human gridlock like a bayonet through Cool Whip.

The Will Call clerks were busy watching a reality show on TV that appeared to be about Will Call clerks having a really hard time of it, and were overtly resentful to be asked to do some real Will Call kind of work. So resentful, in fact, that their designated representative seemed eager to expend more energy denying Buck his ticket than it would have taken just to fork the damn thing over. But then, this is how people acted in reality shows, didn't they, so, why not in reality?

"You sure you're Kurt Platt, honey?" she said, filling her side of the window.

"I'm actually not so sure about that," he answered, rifling his pockets for his mandatory Homeland Security American Citizen Identification and MasterCharge Card, which apparently was still back in his apartment with his wallet. "You see, that sounds like a name that someone would have written down while taking instructions through a poor cell phone connection from a caller in a noisy public place while simultaneously trying to fulfill several other duties required by their most demanding Will Call position, when in fact, the caller meant to say Buck Planck, which is actually my name. But Kurt Platt will do, if that's all you've got."

"Your card is in your other tux, right darlin'?" she said, the voice of experience.

"No, this is actually my only tux," asserted Buck, intuiting that in this situation his *bona fides* as a pretend member of the tux-ready class were somewhat less valuable than his actual solidarity with the ticket-granting class.

Both of them were now suddenly and painfully conscious of the state of his attire. Usually Buck was a meticulous dresser, albeit one for whom form was always trumped by function. But maybe 'trumped' is too kind a word, implying a contest in which the losing party is at least acknowledged. Buck's relationship to style was neither agnostic or atheistic as much as amnestic or obliviistic. But then, as expected from the oblivious, he would never have admitted it.

Buck's bow tie was actually pretty well done, and had withstood the rainy moped ride from Harlem quite admirably. And had the jacket and pants not been of LL Bean's finest Kevlar and Poly blend, they might have been quite wrinkled from spending the last year at the bottom of a duffel. It was his shirt that bore the legacy of its history most legibly. But perhaps legibly is not rich enough a word either, since it omits the entire complex realm of the olfactory senses.

A thick glass barrier (bullet-proofed against Puccini partisans gone postal) denied the Will Call clerk access to these vital gustatory clues, but even through her seemingly opaque sunglasses (an indispensable evening fashion accessory this season) she couldn't help but spot the unmistakable visual evidence of a massive collision with mambo snake pho, doped heavily with high octane Phu Quoc. Looking askance can be quite difficult through black lenses, so it was over hot-pink frames that she rolled her eyes once, looked Buck straight in the chest, and jerked her gaze heavenward.

"Tie dyed," he assured her, "Arch, yet naïve. Retro to the last time it was retro. Petal says to watch for it in Paris next month."

"You the one with Miss Steele, then," she said, relaxing back into her chair. "Why didn't you say so? She told us to make sure you don't get lost. Come round to the door there, sweetheart, and I'll take care of you. We'll go the back way."

Ms. Pearl turned out to be a regular at Beulah's as well as an ardent fan of Petal's column. These sorts of coincidences might at first seem highly unlikely given the staggeringly huge number of people now piling up on Earth, but in the self-conscious and self-referential ecology of New York City above 60th Street it was almost to be expected. Ms. Pearl was quite impressed with Buck's intimate connection with both of her revered institutions, and thus was polite enough not to inquire, when they met face to face in the hallway, why Buck smelled like the tuna fish sandwich you forgot in your locker before summer vacation.

"Mint?" she offered as she escorted him through a labyrinth of passageways, bustling with all the frantic ancillary personnel needed to give such an enormous formal occasion the illusion of calm.

"No thanks," said Buck. "Wouldn't want to ruin my dinner."

Buck, like most colonoscopists and disaster professionals, tended not to have such an acute sense of smell to begin with, but the massive overdose of fish sauce delivered straight up his nose had totally Phu Quoc'd his olfactory lobe. He, of course, was unaware of this because the phenomenon of olfactory fatigue is quite specific to the stimulus that has been down-regulated. In other words, except for the scent of rotting anchovies, he could smell all the aromas around him just fine.

"Where are we?" he asked as they entered a dark and cavernous space the size of an airplane hangar.

17

"Why, under the stage, of course, precious," answered Pearl. These tuxedo people don't know nothin' about how things work.

He could identify multiple platforms controlled by thousands of tons of hydraulic equipment, hundreds of cables pulled by high speed winches, hundreds of lights on electronically operated cranes and scores of wind machines, smoke generators, and flame throwers. Every piece of equipment had a dozen operators. Throw in the couple hundred performers and their entourage and you had a moon-shot-grade production in progress.

"Is it like this here every night?" he asked. This was the kind of equipment that he always needed after an earthquake, but never could seem to find.

"Don't be silly, chile'," said Pearl. "This is just for tonight. Took them a month to install it all, but everything comes out in the morning. Next month it'll be some other crazy stunt; *Circle Jerk Do So Lay* I think they said."

Pearl positioned him over an X on the floor and stood back. "Have fun, now, y'hear?" she said pumping her arm like a trucker and nodding to a guy in a control booth.

A pedestal not much wider than Buck accelerated him up toward a manhole that was now opening in the ceiling. In a few seconds he would be delivered to the exact center of the stage.

This might have gone largely unnoticed by the rippling sea of Armani-and-Wang-adorned ticket-holders in the hall above, furiously networking and getting sloshed before dinner, had it not been for the fact that just then Mrs. Daphne Rose-Glasse, heiress to the inspirational plaque fortune, had stepped up to the microphone and, as is the usual custom, began blowing a deafening roar into it.

The elevator Buck was riding was intended to deliver the event's master of ceremonies to this very microphone in about an hour hence, when, at a signal of trumpets, a mist would drift across the stage, within which the emcee would magically appear and address the astonished crowd. Mrs. Rose-Glasse, however, had felt compelled to call attention to her important role in the proceedings by taking it upon herself to make some helpful unscheduled announcement about cell phone ringers or parking validation or some other such nonsense—she hadn't yet decided exactly. Luckily for all concerned, Mrs. Rose-Glasse's upstaging urge was so intense that she had actually pushed the microphone forward about a foot before the trap door opened in the stage floor right where she would have been standing.

As was the case with most of the female attendees, Mrs. Rose-Glasse was wearing a gown with an enormous hoop skirt of the *Way Beyond Gone with the Wind* style. This fashion statement was an obvious progression from the Queen Mother era of last week, and was being hailed by critics as the final step in the long-awaited liberation of womankind from ten millennia of exploitation and oppression.

The hemispheric construction of Mrs. Rose-Glasse's skirt, some ten feet in diameter at the equator, was the product of extensive collaboration between teams from Chanel and Michelin, employing a concentric series of circular inflatable battens that supported the superstructure with a minimum of weight and rotational inertia. Matrons with the big bucks could opt for voice-activated pneumatic controls that would allow discretionary sectional deflations to facilitate passage through doorways, entry into vehicles, or merely sitting down. Daphne, never one to be outdone by some upstart matron, had gone the whole way by electing for the newest, designer helium-argon blend as her inflational gas of choice.

But, as early adopters of technology know all too well, the perfection of a product depends on the many lessons learned in the 'after market.' One particular lesson to be learned tonight (one actually theorized by Jacques Charles in 1787, but, mind you, just a theory, and to be taught to schoolchildren only in conjunction with competing theories) concerned the expansion of gases subjected to increasing temperatures.

As it turned out, the guys in the lab had totally underestimated how hot it could get under Mrs. Rose-Glasse's pneumo-petticoats when she was pumping herself up for a vigorous spasm of self-aggrandizing *regardez-moi*. The resultant ballooning of her already buoyant support structures had the effect (consistent with, but in no way proof of, a hypothesis proposed by the flagrant theorizer Archimedes, whose opinion, to this day, on the relationship between the volume of an object and the amount of fluid displaced by it remains no better than anyone else's) of rendering her entire garment, below the bodice, considerably lighter than air.

Of course, the magnitude of this upward force was not even remotely sufficient to actually levitate Mrs. Rose-Glasse off the floor in her entirety. Such a physical impossibility is so absurd that any account of a woman being carried off by the buoyancy of her dress can out of hand be considered ludicrous and unworthy of further attention. But she did get enough lift to make her truly light on her feet, which in turn buoyed her spirits, and in turn swelled her confidence. So, it was with an inappropriately loud and authoritarian voice that she commanded the assembled masses below her.

"May I have your attention! May I please have all of your attentions, please!" And for emphasis she stamped her foot, which did actually levitate her a little bit, but not enough to be ludicrous.

By this time Buck had reached his maximum vertical velocity in his escape from the underworld. However, in the milliseconds prior to his passage through the orifice, clues began to accumulate that made him doubt that this would be an uncomplicated delivery.

First was the distinctly un-motherly tone of Daphne's "your attentions, please!" The second was the view, through the approaching portal, of Mrs. Rose-Glasse's *haute couture* from the inside out, an image that included elements of the familiar (chase-me pumps, personal-trainer calves, lipo-sucked thighs, and stockings supported by some unnecessarily complicated garter belt contraption) but also the completely foreign (a rubber bull's eye inside a pink parachute?)

But when you are talking milliseconds, it doesn't really matter how many clues you accumulate. You are going through the hole in the floor and that is all there is to it. Even if it means that your entire two hundred and fifty pound frame (with hardly an ounce of fat), held in its most cylindrical posture, is headed at warp speed up the dress of Mrs. Daphne Rose-Glasse.

It is understandable that the guys in the Chanel-Michelin lab, in their rush to market, had not planned well for this particular contingency. But, nonetheless, their product performed with admirable predictability, no loss of life or limb, and only intangible morbidity. Detailed reconstruction of the event by their investigation team using high-speed, x-ray cameras demonstrated how the head of Mr. Planck (P) must have made contact with the inner aspect of the skirt of Mrs. Rose-Glasse (RG) at about the level of her knees. The transfer of kinetic energy (from P to RG) that thus ensued was enough to propel RG to a height of approximately five feet, at which time the hemispheric shape of the

20

garment under analysis suffered an abrupt transition from its intended stable configuration (A) to its secondary, but unintended configuration (V).

Lay persons may find it helpful to visualize this process by imagining an umbrella turning inside-out in a high wind, and mentally substituting the umbrella's handle with a woman's legs (LRG). Those with advanced imagination skills might attempt to replace the imaginary hand that would be holding said umbrella with an imaginary P hugging the legs of an imaginary RG like a bear.

For Buck, as well, the chain of causation was understandable only in retrospect. At the moment, the experience was similar to one of the random deployments of his Yugo's airbag—a sudden discontinuity in the flow of time in which a tranquil prelude is spliced, like broken celluloid, onto a tumultuous aftermath, without benefit of transition. One moment you are innocently riding a piston toward a hole in the ceiling, the next moment you are on stage in front of thousands of New York's moneyed elite, bear-hugging the legs of a screaming woman whose lower half seems to be sticking out of the bottom of a huge rubber mixing bowl.

Of the many questions that were lining up in Buck's brain queue, a couple elbowed their way to the front. One was, "Why is this woman so light?" Another was, "How am I supposed to find Petal in this crowd?"

The answer to the first obviously must have something to do with the bizarre dress that was stuck up over this woman's head. So did the second.

"Pardon me, folks," said Buck into the mike. "We seem to have a fashion emergency here. Is there a fashion editor in the house? Petal Steele, please report to the stage, stat!"

CHAPTER 5

VERITAS

Meanwhile, the two cinematographers, Truman and McKinley (not their real names) were lurking in the kitchen.

"[sic] Truman, I have a feeling that this is going to turn out to be a very bad idea," said [sic] McKinley, sweating because his waiter's uniform was jammed with hot recording equipment.

"Don't be silly," answered [sic] Truman, sweating because his sweat glands were being pounded like anvils from the inside. "This is not only the idea of the century, it's the best idea we have ever had. And vice-versa. People who remember things will remember this one longer than they will remember the name of the Great Sectarian Originator's (not his real name) brother-in-law. I wouldn't be surprised if our exploits tonight inspire the Supreme Mother-May-I (close, but not his official position) to publish a supplement to the Holy Book of South Hampton Escrow Archives (title modified, with all due respect) sort of like they do with encyclopedias, when, before you have actually looked anything up in them, you have accumulated a dozen of yearly updates, each of which might contain a crucial bit of information that would totally negate an assertion in the original work, so that before you could pin down the capital of, say, North Dakota, for example, you would have to scour your twelve yearly supplements for "Capitals, State, USA," and "Dakota, North, Cities, Noteworthy," and "North, States designated by, Government, Seats of—"

"This is exactly what I am talking about, Truman," said McKinley, now sick of saying [sic]. "I don't care what the stoners in the lab say; this so-called truth serum is just your same old bullshit serum with a make over."

"—and Names, Forgotten, Cold Places—"

"Granted, it is High Concept, as our Most Learned Sour Gummy Bear (not far off) would say. And I am as tired as you are of those Speak-Truth-to-Power documentaries the Americans make, where the oppressed people in baseball caps end up looking pathetic and shrill out in the rain with their posters while the CEO shrugs his shoulders and goes back inside for another martini. And lo, great has been our yearning to have a real truth serum—as if such a thing were possible—and to be there to film it when the Powerful Finally Speak the Truth."

"—Secessions, Union from, Semi-Canadian States—"

"But who wants to see a documentary where the Powerful Speak Bullshit? It's what they do already! But I guess with the right editing we might be able make truth out of bullshit. It's been done before."

McKinley found it necessary to splash water in Truman's face to get him reset. "Will you snap out of it and focus, for the sake of Allan?"

"Sorry," apologized Truman. "But this seems to be one of your 'whole truth' kind of truth serums. Some of your more primitive truth sera would be good for a yes or no answer under polygraph conditions, and later generation formulations might get you a 'I did not have sex with that woman' if you were lucky and the guy couldn't keep his mouth shut anyway. But with your state-of-the-art truth sera it can be an all or nothing kind of thing, with a spontaneous and exuberant outpouring of all of the truth in all of its elegant detail, all of its ramifications, its implications, its assumptions, its necessary and sufficient—"

"Will you stop? I'm warning you, Truman, if you don't keep your mouth shut I'm going to pour soup down your tux and electrocute you. So just keep filming and don't get started talking under any circumstances. Do you hear me? Just nod. Don't speak. Okay?"

He had never seen Truman this stoned before. He had never seen anyone standing up this stoned before.

Carts loaded with appetizers started rolling out of the kitchen. All were identical: a small plate on which a bite-sized puff pastry squatted in a puddle of he/she-crab bisque while supporting a dollop of melamine mousse and three truth-serum-soaked Beluga caviar eggs with a sprig of foxglove.

"Start filming!" hissed McKinley, adjusting his equipment to get the authentic rumble of the cart wheels. Truman flipped a switch on the frame of his glasses and panned the scene like a pro.

"Now act like a waiter and grab a tray. We're off to the VIP table," he added, but then stopped in mid stride after a few feet.

"Truman, I don't want you to start talking, but I do want to know one thing. How many of those caviar eggs did you swallow, anyway?"

Truman's eyes bulged, his pupils filling his orbits, as he struggled to contain an overwhelmingly explosive compulsion to speak. He motioned downward with a nod of his head toward his foot, where he prepared to paw out the count, as would Trigger.

And with the exaggerated precision of the fully baked, he drew his leg up at the knee and threw his foot out, stamping his foot down like a horse.

Once.

CHAPTER 6

VIPS

"I am *not* a fashion editor, I am a society columnist!"

"Sorry, Petal, I figured you could cross cover in a pinch. Besides, you did a great job up there. If Mrs. Rose-Glasse doesn't have Lincoln Center bulldozed under, it will be because of your heroic work."

Buck figured he had gotten off light. Good thing that the emergency fashion technicians had not been able to reconstitute Mrs. Rose-Glasse's skirt into the downward-opening orientation or she would have surely been able to pick his face out of a lineup. As it was, they had to get a running start to get her through the double doors feet first and back to the Chanel showroom on a flatbed.

Buck had come out of the incident looking pretty good (while not exactly smelling like a rose) because even though no one had actually seen him cause Mrs. Rose-Glasse's *Jupe Catastrophe*, he clearly had had something to do with shutting her up. His celebrity mojo was not quite as powerful as his Phu Quoc cologne, however, so he and Petal enjoyed an uncrowded ten-foot no-man's-land perimeter wherever they went in the jammed ballroom.

Petal, fortunately for both of them, was a great fan of esoteric Asian condiments and found Buck's aroma quite captivating. After years of subsisting entirely on rubber-chicken banquet dinners, she had learned to smuggle jars of hot sauces, chutneys, pimentos, wasabis, horseradishes, tzatzikis, and remoulades into the most formal of occasions. As with most of the hard core, her gateway garnish had been a seemingly innocent Worcestershire, but soon she found herself "experimenting" with jalapeño, only to find herself caught in that inevitable downward spiral of degradation and self-loathing that ends in an orgy of pure, unadulterated Phu Quoc.

Buck, being a man and all, could manage to be oblivious to almost everything in his surroundings without being oblivious to

Petal's sudden attraction to him. This, he had to admit, was not an entirely unwelcome development, not even counting the practical aspect of having an ally and interpreter in the alien world where he was presently stranded. And, now that he thought of it, Petal did seem to have a certain tenderness about her, at least when she wasn't actively busting your chops.

For Petal, the attraction remained entirely subliminal, for she, as with all slaves to substance, could not afford to reveal to her conscious self that her affinity to a man might be inextricably entangled with her curiosity about the name of his dealer. Thus veiled to the complex paths of causation within her inner self (as are we all, with the possible exception of Truman at this point in the evening) she had to admit that Mr. Planck, while still a buffoon, must be a very accomplished one indeed and, what's more, didn't seem to have an ounce of fat on his dangerously cute ass.

"Petal," he whispered into her ear, taking her by the arm. "May I admit something kind of personal?"

"Of course, Buck," she said, her smile quizzical but supportive.

"I'm not sure what is happening here." His eyes left hers briefly, but perhaps it was his boyish reticence.

"I feel it, too, Buck," she said, blushing a little.

Buck, of course, had been referring to the fact that the purported purpose of this formal occasion was still a mystery to him, and he was counting on her to clue him in without pointing out what an idiot he was. However, when a woman says to you, apropos of nothing, 'I feel it, too,' you can be pretty sure that, unless you are extremely careful, your idiocy will be widely advertised and very soon.

"You do?" was the best he could do, trying for an earnest, but all-purpose expression.

Petal was not prepared for such a show of sensitivity from this rugged, disaster-hardened man. Perhaps he had suffered loss, somewhere in the fires of Tangiers, the floods of Rangupoon, the eruption of Pantaluna. There must have been one that he couldn't rescue, try as he might, clawing through the rubble, calling her exotic name, so rich in clicks and diphthongs. Petal could see him kneeling in the smoldering ruins, head in hands, vowing never to love again.

How could she have judged him so harshly in the beginning? She turned to face him now, taking both of his hands.

"Buck, I didn't think that this would ever happen to me again, either. But here we are, thrown together by fate, on a secret mission for The Publisher himself, among the most important people in the civilized world, with seats at the VIP table, and by the smell of it, something to eat that you can actually taste, for God's sake. These things don't just happen by accident. There is synchronicity here."

He could tell that, to her, this meant something.

"I am so glad you feel that way, too," said Buck, sincerely believing that with a little time and attention, the 'too' would grow to be as true as the rest. Because he was glad. Glad to be trading accidents for synchronicities. Glad not to be alone on this insane mission. Glad that she was glad. The only thing that would have made him gladder would be to know what the hell was going on here.

"Petal," he asked with both respect and affection, "Maybe you could give me a little background about our dinner partners, so I don't, you know, stick my foot in it?"

"Of course, Buck," she said, her shoulder now against his, pointing out people in the room with subtle nods of her head.

"At the head of the VIP table will be Vice President Chiezie and his lovely wife, Amphora. That's them over there with all the SS guys. He looks taller in his pictures. You'll do fine if you stick to politics and avoid the weather. Ever since the Prez started pretending to be aware of the climate debate, he's had to hold up the die-hard deniers all by himself."

Buck nodded, trying not to ogle too obviously. Chiezie looked happier in his pictures, too.

"Then there's Hiram Kelvin and his lovely wife, Sublimé. CEO of MotherEarth Reverence Corporation, which used to be Exxon Mobil before the name change. Reminisce about the great Indy 500 races of yesteryear and you'll do fine with him."

Buck spotted a swarthy little guy in a shiny tux. He probably looked quite reverent under his shades.

"Next to him will be Saul Flare and his lovely wife, Methené . He's CEO of Gaia Family Services, or what they used to call Shell Oil. In the world of collecting, the Flares are widely acknowledged to be two of the most accomplished collectors of goods and services in the world today."

"Inspiring," acknowledged Buck, gliding her around the ballroom.

"Okay, then on my right will be Rex Clinker and his lovely current life-partner Solphie. He runs Heartland Hearth and Home. They dig coal. All of it. Her medical research foundation was the first to recognize how good acid rain was for your acne."

"Dandruff, too, I'll bet," said Buck."

"Right. Now, who's next? Oh yeah, Otto Wiremeter and his lovely soon-to-be ex-wife Rita. Cuddle-Poo Creations. Electric power. They make it, they move it, they trade it. Don't like it? See you off the grid. I wouldn't shake hands with him—he's always got one of those buzzer things."

"Any more?" asked Buck as they approached their table.

"One more. Bruno Uberpipe and his lovely escort Vapor. He's got what used to be Daimler-Chrysler-GM-Ford. You'll find them on the NASDAQ under Precious Devotions, LLC. He is the one who endowed the big pain center downtown. Not the one that treats pain—that's the one uptown."

"Admirable," said Buck. "And finally, Petal, what is this event all about? I mean, why are all these people here?"

"Why, it's the annual Carbon Life Celebration, silly. They're here to eat, drink, and be seen. And most of all, for the award."

"What award?"

"The award to the company that in the last year has returned the most life-giving carbon dioxide back to the hungry plants of the earth. The coveted Green Giant Cup!"

CHAPTER 7

DINNER

Buck was the only one who needed introductions, and Petal shot through these at lightning speed. She knew VIPs only pay attention to be polite, and none of these VIPs were all that polite. The women were mildly curious about whether Buck was Petal's date, associate, friend, companion, partner, stepbrother, bodyguard, food-taster, personal trainer, or what. The men couldn't give a rip.

Luckily for Buck, conversation was abruptly made impossible by the astonishing appearance of the emcee out of a dry-ice mist in the middle of an empty stage. After a few opening comments (during which he pantomimed difficulty keeping his jacket from flying up over his head, a routine that would be downloaded split-screen beside Mrs. Rose-Glasse's on YouTube some 400 million times before finally being used as evidence in her lawsuit against him, claiming damages of a dollar per download) he introduced a series of heartwarming videos prepared by the companies in competition for the Green Giant Cup.

Methenè Flare had been the creative genius behind the first one, which portrayed a beleaguered oil-drilling executive whose emotional life is rent asunder by two simultaneous psychic traumas: on one hand, his son is a petulant teenager with obnoxious eating habits, and on the other hand, there is still oil down there. This dramatic tension is brought to deft resolution when he realizes that there is not a damn thing you can do about teenagers, but that if you bend your drill a little, like a straw, you can get every last drop of that oil up to the surface where it can be burned fast and cheap, just like God intended.

Solphie Clinker had produced the second, which, through time-lapse animation, portrayed the natural history of coal, starting with billions of acres of prehistoric forest, each tiny leaflet capturing a ray of the sun's energy and using it to break apart a CO_2 molecule, releasing the oxygen and using its carbon to make more leafy stuff. And so on, over and over for millions of years, with one forest growing up upon the remains of the last, the bodies of dead trees getting squashed by time and heat and pressure into this thing called coal, which festered in the dermis of the Earth like a nasty blackhead, until, with surgical strip-mining precision, it could be excised by Heartland Hearth and Home's terrestrial cosmeticians, thus restoring the Earth's complexion to a healthy glow and the CO_2 to its rightful place in the atmosphere, not to mention a little zit-busting sulfur dioxide thrown in as a bonus.

While Vapor had played no role in the production of the next film (having just been introduced to Bruno Uberpipe earlier that day at the Pain Center's Executive Dungeon) her spirit nonetheless perfused it—MTV would have filed the video in the *Albert Speer does Death Metal* bin. Buffeted by a soundtrack of peri-orgasmic Wagner and unsimulated explosions, the visuals depicted an early Earth, infested with sniveling vermin of every species, clawing over each other in the chaotic and purposeless horror sometimes referred to as "life."

Then, just as it seemed that our planet might be lost to this madness forever, from the fiery bowels of the Earth itself burst forth, like the Four Hundred Horsepower of the Apocalypse, an immense, fume-belching internal combustion engine, blackening the sky as it churned across the land, inhaling into its huge metallic maw all manner of unclean things that scuttle or fly or writhe upon their bellies, and leaving in its wake a crisp, smooth ribbon of interstate, as pure and impeccable as a Zen chopstick. And soon peace and order and discipline reigned, as the Earth's fetid nakedness was entirely replaced by the pristine precision of asphalt.

And then there were a bunch of other documentaries that, while perhaps not up to the artistic excellence of the first three, were moving nonetheless for their straightforward depiction of the facts. For example, greenhouses, as it turns out, all have heaters in them. It is amazing that no one ever looked before. It would have saved everybody a lot of tongue wagging.

Also, humans have boundless ingenuity. A few years ago when there were only three billion of them, climate change might have been a problem, but now that there are seven billion it is a statistical certainty that at least one of them will figure out a solution that doesn't involve lurching off half-cocked into some half-baked, hair-brained boondoggle that loses everybody a ton of money.

In another video it was indisputably proven beyond a shadow of a doubt that the "climate" was definitely not changing, and even if it were, it would definitely not be because of anything people had done, and even if it did, there was definitely nothing that anybody could do about it, and even if there were, it would definitely be too late anyway, and even if it weren't, it would likely be too exhausting even to think about.

As fascinating as all of this was, it wasn't dinner. Buck had found precious little edible at Imelda's earlier and he was getting a little giddy from hunger. He had fished the cherry out of Petal's Manhattan, a gambit that she considered both virile and lascivious, and was trying to flag down a waiter to send out for a pizza.

It was obvious that the interminable videos had been scheduled before dinner to assure that there was at least someone left in the room when the projector went on. However, this strategy had the unintended but predictable effect of assuring that most attendees soon "had had too little to eat," (which is French for "self-inflicted alcoholic stupor")—an effect which could have been attained slightly more quickly by injecting gin directly into the brain with a basting bulb.

Buck had had a problem with alcohol once. It was an Old Mr. Boston Sloe Gin Fizz mixed with Sprite behind the bleachers at his high school prom. He could still taste it when the seas got rough. Since then, purloined maraschinos were about as wild as it got for Buck Planck.

Petal's relationship with alcohol was purely professional, and her professionalism was legendary. She was perky when others were hung over and lucid when others were smashed. The level of liquid in her glass always seemed to match that of the host or guest of honor, whoever was most important. Close observers would swear that there was no sleight of hand betwixt the cup and the lip, but rumors still circulated about mysterious hidden appliances—complex arrangements of invisible tubes and rubber bladders sewn into her corsets—that would account for her immunity to the toxin. But she would laugh off such accusations as obvious occupational jealousies or latent latex fantasies.

So, apart from Buck and Petal (and the Lincoln employees, who actually had to work for a living) everyone at the Carbon Life was getting a little too looped. A huge cheer rang up from the back of the hall when one intrepid veteran of the Grenada conflict stormed the control booth and decommissioned the video projector. The emcee declared the competition closed (to resounding applause) and cued the kitchen to start moving chicken.

In a twinkling there appeared in front of each VIP a puff pastry surprise. Buck, still gun shy from Imelda's, was suspicious of unidentifiable larval forms that lacked a certifiable plant pedigree. In his book, fish eggs were bad enough (since people consumed them only to demonstrate that they were rich enough to do so) but the eggs of just about any other non-chicken creature were worse.

Unobtrusively as possible, he lifted his three doses of truth-serum-laden caviar off of his pitiful appetizer and set them aside on his plate. Petal, thinking this was a continuation of Buck's Tom-Jones-style food foreplay, demurely did the same with hers, but managed to sneak in a nostril flare in his direction.

The only VIP to notice this little drama was Vice President Chiezie, whose prodigious powers of observation rarely missed any detail in his field of view. He figured, largely due to his prodigious powers of malevolence, that Buck and Petal must either be a couple of those vegetarian wusses or were mocking him for having so many stents in his arteries. Either way, they pissed him off, and so with exaggerated bravado he popped his appetizer into his mouth and swallowed it whole. This peri-presidential gesture was a clear message to the rest of the VIPs to do the same, which, of course, they did without question.

The effects of truth serum on someone who always tells the truth can, in theory, be difficult to detect. An analogous statement can be made about bullshit serum. Anyway, Truman and McKinley (who, by this time, really didn't know what kind of serum they had just given to five thousand people) couldn't see that the drug was doing anything to these VIPs, but were filming madly away, nonetheless.

The ambient noise level in the ballroom was steadily rising and people were having difficulty understanding what the person right next to them was saying. Nonetheless, Truman and McKinley had no trouble piecing it all together later with the help of modern video editing technology:

DICK CHIEZIE (VP)
So you're one of those wussy vegetarians, then?

DIRK PLANCK (Our Hero)
Low Episcopalian, actually. Lapsed.

VAPOR (Escort)
Lashed? And paddled, too? Make me smile, eh?

BRUNO UBERPIPE (Cars)
Mileage? We'll have that down to 5mpg in time for next season!

SAUL FLARE (Oil)
Reason? Because we give you billions to keep it down, that's why!

BRUNER UBERPIPE (Cars)
Buy? They'll buy what we tell them to buy. Sheep!

OTTO WIREMETER (Electricity)
Cheap? Make power cheap with dirty coal and old technology. Cost of clean is way too high!

REX CLINKER (Coal)
Sky? Who cares if you can see the sky? What's up there to see anyway? Just asking.

DICK CHIEZIE (VP)
Taxing? We're not taxing! If we taxed you what you cost this country, there'd be nothing cheaper than alternative energy.

ALL THE VIPS

           (in unison)
           Alternative energy! We told you not to
           use those words! Why else would we give
           so much money to your stupid party?

       PETAL STEELE (Our Heroine)
           They're right. This really is a stupid party.
           Hey, Buck! Want to bust out of here and
           get some soul food?

       DIRK PLANCK (OH)
           To tell you the truth, that's best thing I've
           heard all night. Like yours with fish
           sauce?

       PETAL STEELE (OH)
           (unintelligible)

CUT TO VIEW FROM CEILING CAM

The lovely couple makes their way to the exit among a pandemonium of food fighters in eveningwear, rubber chicken filling the air, the Green Giant's Cup all but forgotten.

CHAPTER 8

EPA

"That was fun last night," she said, buckling in for the shuttle to D.C.

Buck understood that there was no minefield more treacherous than a simple declarative statement made by a woman about the previous evening. Or about anything, for that matter. Give me that tangential circumlocution about the sister's wedding dress, IRS audit, and lost puppy any day.

"Wonderful," replied Buck, turning to face her with a smile. He knew that he would be in big trouble if he failed to raise the ante from 'fun,' but figured that at this stage in their relationship 'beautiful' might leave him little room to move.

"Shame about the tear gas, though," she said.

"Good thing we were at Beulah's by then."

"Never saw CEOs actually throw food before."

"Things are different now," he said. "Everything's heating up."

"I'll say," she said.

They had decided that everyone had pretty much lost their minds in New York and that they should go to D.C. where cooler heads always prevailed. There they would cut through all the red tape and go straight to the director of the Agency in Charge of Doing Something about the Climate Crisis. He/She would be able to explain to them the objective scientific facts about global warming, the official predictions about its effects, and what the government was planning to do about it all. Their report to The Publisher would then be indisputably off the ground.

Not immediately finding a listing for the ACDSACC, they settled for the Environmental Protection Agency as a reasonable approximation. Within two hours of landing at Dulles (Reagan still under water) they were being ushered into the office of Horace Tick who had held the director's post for eight days, a new record.

Horace seemed a little peeved at having this urgent meeting
forcibly inserted into the day he was counting on to hang all the
pictures of Horace Tick shaking hands with other equally
prestigious members of the administration and all his old friends in
the uranium tailings disposal industry, with whom he had not a
single millicurie of conflict of interest.

"Used to take three months for reporters to get interviews
with directors in this town," muttered Tick, largely to himself, in
the manner of resentful old men wondering what happened to the
good old days when a boy could pick up a pole and a can of worms
and just wander on down to the pond and dump uranium tailings
all afternoon without a bunch of big city lawyers getting their
shorts in a bunch about it.

"And we really appreciate you making time for us at this short
notice," said Buck. "Especially with the urgency of the current
situation."

"Yeah? And which particular urgent situation would you two
be referring to today?" Other directors might lack the courage it
took to stand up and bear witness to the fact that they didn't find
anything all that urgent, but not Horace Tick.

"We were counting on you to clear that up for us," said Petal.
"With all the debate and the politicization of science these days."

Horace had never heard the word before, but figured it must
have something to do with the police, and if there was any debate
about arresting any damn scientists, there was no debate about
which side he was on.

"No problem clearing that one up. The ones that stick to their
knittin', you leave 'em be. The ones that make all the fuss where it's
none of their business, then I say forget about politicizing 'em, you
just take 'em out back and shoot 'em. That'd cut down on them
whiny thousand page reports, I'll tell you right now." Horace was
warming to this interview.

"But what is the agency planning to do about carbon?" said
Buck, trying to get back on track.

"Carmen is none of that agency's business. She don't work for
no agency anymore. Strictly free-lance. And I don't know her
anyway. And she's none of your business either."

"Carbon, not Carmen."

"I should know the girl's name, for God's sake. If I knew her,
that is."

"We're talking about carbon dioxide, the gas in the air. What's the EPA planning to do about it?"

"Listen, sonny, I don't know what they teach you-all in school nowadays, but back when they made you take tests it was pretty well accepted that carbon dioxide was supposed to be in the air. Where do you think that they get carbonated water, anyway? You got your oxygen and you got your carbon dioxide and you got your whatever else is in there. That's the natural order of things. You can't improve on that. The EPA is here to protect the damn environment, not to tell God how to make air, for God's sake. You got a funny little snail gone missing? Then you call us. You got a beef with God? Well, I don't know what you do, call the Pope, I guess." Tick was starting to get tired of these ignorant reporter types.

"Director Tick," said Petal, stepping on Buck's foot under the table. "You've been most gracious and we hate to impose further on your busy day." She stood and shook his hand. "Thank you for this most informative interview."

"Yes, and keep up the good work," said Buck, now hustling after her and closing the door behind them.

Tick's administrative assistant, Ms. Brushmeat, was busy with the interior decorator who was re-doing the reception area. She clearly was the brains of the team and was what made Tick tick. She glared at Buck and Petal as they let themselves out into the hall.

"I think we aimed a little too high that time," Petal said. "Let's try closer to the ground. Follow me."

Soon Petal was working her reporter's wiles with the youngest looking secretary in Human Resources.

"Hi. We're with Internal Census. Just a couple quick ones. First, a list of all the employees in the building." Petal was peering over the girl's shoulder at her screen. "Now just the scientists. Good. Now the ten who have been with the EPA longest. That's it. Now the one with the fewest promotions. Perfect. Now, how to find his office. Thanks, you're a dear."

Within minutes they were following a map through the building's sub-basement.

"If there is anyone in a bureaucracy who knows what's going on and is willing to talk about it, you can bet he is pissing off his superiors," said Petal. "But since they can't really fire the guy, that means he gets stuck forever in some windowless office next to an obnoxious mechanical room. I think we are getting close."

They pulled up in front of a door with a cardboard name plate, attached with yellowed tape. "Loudon Stillwright, PhD. Please Knock Without Entering."

"That's an old one," said Buck.

"Must be our guy," she said.

Stillwright's office was huge, and would have looked hugher if there had not been some monstrous length of the building's guts running right through it. Tattered asbestos insulation was wound around the pipes and pumps, but still the mechanical intestines ground and gurgled like an airliner sunk in the mud.

The rest of the space was crammed with duct-tape-crafted prototypes of survival equipment for a dystopic future. In one corner was a paddle-wheeled outrigger kayak outfitted with collapsible mast (or maybe clothesline) and a solar something. An inflatable yurt made of what appeared to be shredded energy-bar wrappers and dryer hoses was baking under buzzing bulbs in another. And an outhouse made entirely from crushed cell phones sat charging at an outlet nearby.

Wrinkled maps of every part of the world from every perspective covered every wall. Half-dissected PCs swapped buckets of bytes with banks of disfigured mates through tangles of cables festooned from coat hangers hooked into the ceiling. A teletype machine pounded out already-faded pages in competition with two laser printers purring near by. And everywhere were piles of paper—leaning, crumbling, decaying piles of print, covering every inch of floor and reaching to waist if not shoulder. Even the narrow paths between piles were littered with paper. And still the printers pumped away.

Stillwright himself was on his knees performing some back-alley obscenity on an old Coke machine with one of his coat hangers. His ears were plugged into an iPod and his back to the door. There was no way to get the man's attention without touching him, but neither Buck nor Petal wanted to get that close. So after a respectful interval, Petal balled up a trodden-on scrap and bounced it off of the fellow's head.

This got the old guy's attention, all right, but before looking back to identify the origin of the missile, he scrambled to retrieve the ball of paper and quickly smoothed it out, with a show of

40

affection one uses when apologizing to pets. Only then did he stand and turn to greet his guests—or assailants—as the case may be.

Stillwright was a grizzled, old environmentalist of the Teddy Roosevelt school—in fact, he looked like he might have been a classmate. Buck expected to see a revolver stuck in his belt to dispatch rattlers caught nesting among the printouts. He was wearing a shirt that probably had been white once and pants that likely would have been black. Now, they were a pretty good match. On his feet were tire-tread huaraches in need of a retread. In fact, almost everything about Stillwright needed a retread.

Except his face. You couldn't get more tread on a face if you used both sides. Stillwright had the kind of face that begged for a large format Hasselblad and a fresh roll of black and white. Buck wondered if it took special equipment to wash a face like that, perhaps some sort of long-haired, ultrasonic, terrycloth gizmo on a power hose. It was a face that provided its own shade, a face that made short work of clocks, dogs, and babies—one that only mothers would love but everyone would befriend.

Except maybe those in a bureaucratic hierarchy beholden to their appointers. Those for whom power must always trump truth. Every visitor that Stillwright had entertained in the last decade had come with ominous incentives to retirement, offers only the most stubborn could refuse.

"You must be a couple of Horace Tick's!" he said with suspicion, shouting above the background noise.

Ordinarily, such an accusation would have justified a snappy rejoinder such as, "And you must be a rhinoceros willie!" but Buck and Petal, instinctively striving for a more conciliatory tone, stuck with the familiar "That's what she said!" delivered in unison with the theatrical wink and nudge designed to cement Stillwright into their conspiratorial bond.

"I can't hear a thing you're saying!" Stillwright yelled over the din. "Here, put these on." He produced a couple of battered iPods from a file cabinet and fiddled with the dials. The room became almost silent when the ear buds were in place.

"Now, you two part of that Horace Tick infestation?" Stillwright's voice was clear and strong. He had converted the music players into noise cancellation, blue tooth transmitter/receivers. Sharp guy. Buck hadn't even figured how to change the battery in his.

"No, Dr. Stillwright," Petal said, "We're from outside the Agency. As part of an important mission whose details I am not authorized to reveal, we need to determine the truth about what is happening with the climate. And we need to know what is going to happen in the foreseeable quarter—I mean future."

"Right," echoed Buck. "We need to cut through all the rhetoric and propaganda and get to the bottom line on global warming so we can get the word out to all the right people." Buck imagined how proud these words might have made him under the right circumstances. Like if they were true, for example.

"That's a big topic," said Stillwright, sitting them down on milk crates scattered around his desk. "Where should we start? You two climatologists?"

"No, not exactly," admitted Petal.

"Meteorologists?"

"No, but I am a big fan," tried Buck.

"Oceanographers, then?"

"Well, no," said Petal, shaking her head.

"Environmental scientists of any sort?"

"Unh Unh."

"Science majors?"

"Sorry."

"Ever heard of a ball point pen?"

"Why, sure," Petal perked up. Buck nodded in agreement, producing the exact item from his pocket.

"Well, it's a start, anyway. Let me see that thing." Stillwright scribbled a few lines on a small scrap of paper and then unscrewed the pen, rolled up the note inside its barrel and reassembled it.

"Thanks," he said, handing it back to Petal, who was closer. She frowned distastefully at the "Jack's Wenches" logo and tossed it to Buck.

"What?" he whispered. How did it get to this? Now he was explaining himself to this woman! Where else should he get winches? Frank's?

"I'm afraid I'm not gonna be able to help you kids today," said Stillwright, looking genuinely sorry.

"But, Dr. Stillwright, if it's the money, we are prepared to offer a generous—"

"It's not that," he cut her off. "It's them." He nodded toward the door behind them. There stood Ms. Brushmeat and a phalanx of security guards.

"This area is off limits to visitors, as you well know from all the signs," she said. "And Dr. Stillwright is not a designated spokesperson for the Agency. Liability constraints prohibit anyone in the Agency other than designated spokespersons from conversing about Agency issues with non-Agency personnel. And since this is the Environmental Protection Agency and there is nothing in the world that is not part of the environment, then obviously there is no conceivable topic which is legal for Dr. Stillwright to discuss with you.

"Therefore, Mr. Planck and Ms. Steele, you are currently violating at least two federal statutes and probably a dozen. Please come quietly with us now and the Agency will consider not pressing charges."

Buck and Petal stood and took off their iPods, looking at Stillwright's face one last time. In it, among the residue of years of frustration, was a faint smile of conspiratorial satisfaction. They hoped that it was meant for them.

CHAPTER 9

STARBUCKS

Buck and Petal needed a place to talk, so they took a cab to the nearest Starbucks across the street. Cabs were not that easy to get in D.C. since, due to heightened security, pedestrian traffic had been limited to travel along the short axis of sidewalks. Thankfully, enforcement was lenient, so that if one's cab couldn't stop directly in front of one's destination, one could usually traverse a few feet along the sidewalk's long axis, but only if one adopted the exaggerated tip-toe gait of mischievous cartoon mice hurrying by sleeping cartoon cats and the National Guardsmen were pretending not to notice. It was rarely a problem, anyway, because nobody wanted to walk outside on account of all the blowing sand.

"I'm afraid that you are on our suspended list, Mr. Planck," the cashierista informed him after a twenty minute wait in line.

"Do I know you?" asked Buck, searching his face.

"No, I don't think so," he said scanning his computer. "Your Homeland Security card says you live in New York. I've never been there. Your file says you've never been in this store before either."

"Did I just show you my card?" asked Buck. Maybe he had been sleepwalking. Weirder things have happened in Starbucks.

"No, we scan its chip when you walk in. You don't have to take it out of your wallet. All the stores do that now as a convenience for their customers." The crowd behind Buck was becoming more desperate for their fix.

"No kidding? But why am I suspended, whatever that means?"

"You are behind on your lattes," he said. "You get a warning first, but then if you don't make up your lack of lattes then you're suspended. Everybody knows that."

"I can't buy a cup of coffee here?" Buck was having trouble with this.

"Usually something can be worked out with our Director of Indulgences. He'll take it all into consideration—extenuating circumstances, evidence of intent, expressions of remorse, demonstration of rehabilitation, net worth, liquidity of assets—"

"Why don't I just buy," said Petal, cutting in line. "Two coffees, black, small, for here."

"I'm sorry, Ms. Steele," he said, searching his screen. "We don't seem to carry that item any more."

"Two no-milk lattes, then," she said. "With double no-milk."

"Excellent," he said. "Coming right up. That will be thirty dollars. On your card?"

"Of course," she said, putting her thumb on the scanner. "You think I'd carry cash in this city? Silly boy."

Holding up a Starbucks line is guaranteed to make you plenty of new enemies-for-life in an already cutthroat urban environment, but it will occasionally increase the chances of getting a table by shaking loose the more timid, over-caffeinated squatters who split at the first hint of impending mayhem. Thus, Buck and Petal were able to snatch a prime piece of window-front real estate next to a homeless derelict who was day-trading forged-art futures on his laptop.

"Let me see that pen from the cathouse," said Petal daintily.

"Disaster supply house. Jack's a great guy but he can't spell. Or maybe he's a sadistic guy who spells great. Anyway, despite the logo, you can only get winches there, not wenches. As far as I know, anyway." Buck realized he should have just handed her the damn thing and kept his mouth shut.

Petal fished Stillwright's note out of the pen's barrel with an eyebrow tweezers (made of carbon fiber composite for smuggling onto airplanes) and spread it out on the table.

"Ephraim Endgame 208-522-3861 Password: Pooch," she read. "That's all it says. Idaho's area code is 208. I recognize it because all the celebs go there to act as if they are fishing, except for the ones who just act as if they are going there. They like Idaho because it's an honest, straightforward kind of place where they can let down their pretenses and just be themselves, acting as if they are fishing."

"Should we flip to see who calls?" asked Buck.

He knew that you would never ask a woman 'Should we flip to see who opens the door?' or 'Should we flip to see if your mother comes for Christmas.' But in general, Buck was the kind of guy who considered egalitarianism to be a respectful form of eroticism and subservience to protocol an antidote to intimacy. But, then again, maybe he was just a guy.

"Fair enough," said Petal. She knew that whatever kind of guy Buck was, that's the kind of guy he would be, and that the only thing to be gained in taking offense would be the sheer pleasure of a good scold. Besides, she was beginning to think Buck Planck was kind of intriguing, in a kind of out of it kind of way.

Neither of them could find a coin (or remember when they had last seen one) so Buck just made the call because he was the man.

"Mr. Endgame, this is Buck Planck. You don't know me but we just met with Loudon Stillwright and he gave us your name and the password 'Pooch,' and—Yeah, he wrote it down. I have it in front of me—Yes, he wrote it in his own handwriting—No, nobody but me and my partner knows—No, not that kind of partner. She's a woman—No, of course you're not—Sure, plenty of my friends, too—Listen, we were hoping—Sure, I have a pen—Okay, shoot."

Buck scribbled a couple of three by five's worth and repeated back a few high points.

"All right, tomorrow then—Don't worry, we'll make sure no one follows us."

"Well?" Petal said when Buck had put down the phone. "We going to Idaho?"

Buck nodded. "And I get the feeling that we may be getting into something we don't know anything about," he said, choosing his words carefully.

"This is just a feeling for you?" she said. "For me, I would call the proposition that we don't know what we are doing more like an immutable truth. Maybe even an axiom. Certainly a certainty. I am prepared to stipulate that our ignorance of what we are getting into is without equal. However, the real question is whether we want to chase this lead or get back to interviewing a bunch of Horace Ticks."

"I don't know if I can take any more Horace Ticks," he said.

She smiled and refused to swing. Some lobs were just too easy.

47

"And Endgame sounded like it was real important that we get there right away," he said. "I think we were the first people that Stillwright ever gave that password to. Usually people don't get so excited at the prospect of doing reporters a favor. He has to be expecting something of us—something that he assumes Stillwright has told us about." Buck was drawing arrows between boxes on a three by five.

"But we hardly spent a minute with Stillwright, and, frankly, I think we blew our first impression," she said. "Why would he trust us with anything that is obviously so secret?"

"I think Stillwright is a very smart man," said Buck.

"And I think he knows that time is running out," said Petal.

"So he's desperate and will settle for us because he can tell in a minute that we are competent and honorable and our hearts are in the right place," he said, putting his hand on her hand.

A compliment shared can sometimes be the warmest kind. Especially when it raises one's expectation of oneself.

"Then we mustn't disappoint them," she said. "Once we're sure their hearts are in the right place."

"That's always the trick, isn't it?" said Buck. "Finding the heart."

"That's really what she said," she said, looking down at their hands.

"Yeah, she wouldn't have said all those other things," agreed Buck.

They sat a while longer at Starbucks, watching the dunes pile up on K Street in the blowing sand. It was beautiful, really. Like snow. Only warmer.

CHAPTER 10

EDEN

Their instructions had been quite specific. Endgame would be wearing an orchid in his lapel. Buck would be pretending to take a leak behind the Hattie's House of Lard billboard on I-70 south of Coeur d'Alene, while Petal sat in the rental car pretending to read *Rich People* magazine. But since Buck was a guy who was perpetually early and Endgame was a guy who was perpetually late, Buck had plenty of time to question his note-taking, wave to oncoming traffic, and get an embarrassing sunburn. Petal, who had already studied this month's *Rich People*, had secretly hidden a copy of *Flagrant Squanderer* under its cover. But, other than some trouble mastering the fine points of chewing tobacco, she, too, was in perfect compliance with the meeting's protocol.

The Idaho countryside was almost too bucolic for such film-noir espionage. Here, under the broken shade of the palms, with the sweet calls of the conure, caique, and kakariki from the canopy nearby, all seemed right with the world. Maybe the Carbon Life guys were right after all, and Buck and Petal had been sent off on some Chinese Chicken Little fire drill for the amusement of a soon-to-be-revealed reality show audience. Then everybody could have a good laugh and Buck could get back to the disaster business and Petal to her desperate fans.

Endgame finally showed up in a truck full of orchids. Plucking one for his lapel, he ambled over to Buck and recited the code, without offering to shake hands.

"Hi there, citizen. Nice day. Who's screwed?"

"The pooch," replied Buck, without referring to notes.

"Ephraim Endgame," he whispered. "Follow me. It's about ten miles. Stay close. Keep this on your dash. Show it to anyone who tries to pull you over."

Buck put the "Ephraim's Orchids for Every Occasion" sign in plain sight and pulled out onto the highway behind Endgame's truck. Soon, they had turned onto a dirt road into the forest and their speed was down to ten. The vehicles lurched over ruts and roots, passing unmarked trails disappearing off to either side every mile or two. Flashes of scarlets and hyacinths broke across the narrow patch of sky above the slot the road had etched through the jungle.

Abruptly, the truck turned onto an even more primitive path to the left, and after another fifteen minutes of reflux-inducing jolts, the caravan entered a clearing in the vegetation. A twenty foot chain link fence topped with razor wire was just ahead. A man with a shotgun waved them through the gate. A dozen other armed men watched suspiciously as they drove through the orchid fields and up to a group of structures deep within the compound.

Ephraim's architect had clearly been a native of the New Guinea highlands who had been deeply influenced by an acid trip in the Mexico City dump. There was a heavy reliance on native Idaho bamboo coercively conjoined with the picked-over detritus of obsolete technology. Stairs might be lashed together by woven frond ropes or discarded electrical wires. Windows might be covered by oiled papyrus or by reclaimed computer screens. Rooms were divided by woven mats or stacks of plastic bottles, tied in place with twine spun from plastic grocery bags or wild hemp. And everywhere tires. Tough, heavy, round and impervious to wear and weather, tires would be part of everything short of dinner at Ephraim's.

Ephraim himself looked like an aging Amish basketball player. At nearly seven feet, he was one of the few people in memory that Buck had ever had to look up at. His beard was full, his scalp stubble, and his upper lip shorn. His overalls were cut off below the knee, just above the tops of his combat boots. He wore no insignia, but the demeanor of his men implied that 'Commandant' might be a safer form of address than 'Bubba.' With a nod a table was cleared and drinks delivered for the three, orchid tea in cut-down plastic Evian bottles.

"Welcome to New Eden Mr. Planck and Ms. Steele," he said, raising his cup. "You should know that it is quite an honor to be selected by Loudon Stillwright. There are few people he trusts any more."

"I don't think he gets out much these days," offered Buck, immediately regretting attempts at modesty with so many shotguns at parade rest all around the room.

"So much the better for honing one's judgment of one's fellow man," hastened Petal, stepping on his foot. "Loudon is still at the top of his game. Very perceptive."

"Right-O," agreed Buck. "The old boy is sharper than ever."

"Excellent to hear it, but I'm afraid that time is too short for pleasantries. If you don't mind, let me get on with your briefing." A large topographical map of northern Idaho was spread out on the table. "How much detail did Loudon give you?"

"We were under constant surveillance," said Petal. "Better start from the beginning. Like, for example, where are we?"

"Okay, here's Northern Idaho," he said, spreading open a map. "More survival organizations here than the rest of the world combined." He tapped a well-worn spot with the tip of a bayonet. "And this is us, New Eden. Unfortunately, that compound you see nearest to us is the DE's." He looked up to see if she needed further explanation.

Petal raised her eyebrows and nodded encouragingly.

"Deep Doo Doo Ecologists," he elaborated. "They believe that the Earth's ecosystem, evolved to perfection over billions of years, was able to adapt to one global crisis after another—ice ages, volcanic winters, asteroid impacts, mass extinctions—until it met with a force so overpoweringly evil, so wantonly destructive, so willfully contemptuous of the Creator that it would bring life on Earth to within its last breath, and stand arrogantly by, twisting the blade and drowning out its final cries with a continuous drone of self-aggrandizing babble. And the only way to cure this terminal disease, if it is not already too late, is to expunge the cause, to cut out the cancer, to eradicate the contagion."

"By?" she prompted.

"By eliminating the human race. Entirely. The DE's wouldn't even keep a few in zoos, for fear they would get out and start the whole thing over again. Just as countless species have done before them, the human species will join the list of expired DNA, retired forever, another genetic experiment that proved to be a near fatal mistake for Mother Earth."

"But how? When?" asked Buck.

51

"This next massive area belongs to the Doms," Endgame continued, as if not hearing the question. "For Dominionites, as in 'God gave Man dominion over the Earth.' They figure that whatever humans have done to the planet must be okay, humans obviously being God's favorite and the recipient of the gift of limitless intelligence. So just as we have used the divine gift of reasoning to indulge in one slash-and-burn, nest-fouling civilization after another, we can now use our technological prowess to survive as everything else crashes around us—or at least the richest of us, anyway. The Dom's are heavily invested in self-contained, underground bunkers, run on nuclear power. For every billionaire's berth they need a score of mercenary technicians to keep the place running and replace worn out parts."

"What are they going to do after they use up their last computer chip?" asked Buck.

Endgame ignored the question and continued, "This small area is the Cryo Creeps facility. There you can get yourself frozen until some later civilization emerges from the ashes or arrives from outer space. They've got the same problem as the Dom's, running out of quarters to feed the meter during that long dry spell. Oh, and here is the Cyber Corps place. They figure you can be digitized and reconstituted later, or at least run on a Mac, which would get you into some cool video games if not a new body."

"And in New Eden?" Petal asked, open-ended and coy.

"We will be the only true survivors," he said without bravado. "Because we have perfected the art of adaptation. We find the utility in everything around us—what grows without our meddling and what others have cast away. Human societies have spent the last ten thousand years converting Earth's bounty into trash, so we have a lot to work with—at least another ten thousand years' worth. And we are mobile. As the great American desert moves toward the poles, as are the African and Asian deserts, we move, too, staying in the zone hospitable to life."

"And when that zone is gone, too?" asked Buck.

Endgame spread his hands open like a book. "Then Man will be no more. But we are counting on a reversal. The ecosystem may heal once there is no more carbon going into the atmosphere. There may be a handful of others around the world that makes it through the collapse, but they won't last long. The engines of pollution will be shut off forever. It could take a thousand years, maybe many thousands, but equilibrium will be restored." He rocked back in his chair.

"There was a time in the past when the population of our species had dwindled down to a hundred mating pairs," he continued. "That's the number we have at New Eden," he stood up for added emphasis, "now that you two have joined us. We begin the final phase at dawn. Guards, please escort our final mating pair to their quarters."

Petal had hoped that it would have been a little more romantic. Buck had hoped that there wouldn't have been so many shotguns involved. But sometimes when the irresistible hand of fate thrusts two lovers together it is best to embrace the moment joyfully.

At least until it is dark enough to run like hell.

CHAPTER 11

BUNK

Dark enough came soon enough, but running like hell would obviously remain a luxury enjoyed exclusively by those on the other side of that razor wire fence. Not that there wouldn't be running. Or digging. Or carrying sacks of manure. There would be plenty of that here at New Eden where the mission statement included both the creation of a new human civilization and the production of the best darn orchids in Northern Idaho. What was kind of disappointing, though, was that, despite all that romantic talk about breeding pairs, Buck and Petal found themselves bunked down in same-sex (always a euphemism for no-sex) dormitories.

"How'd you come to join this outfit?" Buck whispered to the guy on the next cot, who seemed to be having as much trouble sleeping on shredded tires and orchid droppings as Buck was.

"Kind of inevitable, in a way," he replied, pulling at a pesky piece of steel belted radial that had been poking him in the ribs. "Come from a long line of survivalists—can't think of any of my people who weren't, now that I try. You'd even have to say that all them pioneers who opened up this part of the country were survivalists, and good ones too. And their kids and their kids— though some tended to get soft after a while after a few generations, I guess. But not my pappy and his pappy either. They were tough and smart to the end.

"My grandpappy was the one who discovered that those bar codes on the backs of stop signs are really instructions for the United Nations World Government troops. Blew the cover right off of that one. And you remember when that vote came up about concealed bazookas in the public schools? Well you have my very own pappy and his Krugerrands to thank for protecting your freedom there.

"So it was just natural that I would step right into their boots when I was grown enough. But, you know how kids get at a certain age, kind of rebellious and all? Somehow, the thought of waiting for the Korean EMP attack in our bunker watching Kurt Saxon duck and cover videos just seemed so old school to me, you know, like beyond stodgy. Okay, sure, the mongrel races were down-breeding the kleptocracy and the Hollywood homosexuals were going to take away our mamas, but I needed something bigger in *my* life to survive. Something huge, like the heat death of the universe, only a little more imminent.

"My family thought I was reckless of course, risking everything in search of the ever more pernicious and egregious menace to survive when there were plenty of much safer and reliable dangers right at home. But how is civilization to advance, if not through the impulsivity of youth?

"So I traveled the world in search of a calamity of my own. And the farther and wider that I looked, the more it eluded me. Everywhere I went all I found were the same old petty genocides, fabricated famines, and mechanized mass murder. Nothing a boy could sink his teeth into. Nothing really worth surviving for.

"It became an obsession really. I couldn't eat. I couldn't sleep. I became desperate and then depressed. So one night in a bar in Darfur I was moping over my glass of khat when one of the Burmese sex slaves there came by collecting for the snail darters. One look at her brochure and it was like the heavens had opened up for me. Hallelujah! It was the happiest day of my life."

"Darfur will do that for you," agreed Buck.

"Ironic how you can search the world over and not see what is right in front of your face." The guy heaved a great sigh as if to conclude his remarks.

"Snail darters?" coaxed Buck. "Sex slaves?"

"No, man. The world. The world itself. My people have always spent their lives surviving some imagined malevolence that some imagined malefactor might be imagining, when all the while we and them and everyone everyone knows were busy ignoring the fact that the whole planet was coming down like a house of cards. No, worse than ignoring it. When you try to keep other people from seeing something, then it is definitely worse than ignoring it.

"The snail darter is just a metaphor. Hell, it's not even on the endangered list any more, and I personally wouldn't know a snail darter from a bug-eyed sprite. But the critters that eat snail darters care a lot if they all go extinct, and those critters' kids care a real lot. And then you got the slimy guys that snail darters would have eaten piling up all over the place and clogging up the real estate where a dozen other unsuspecting bystanders are trying to eke out a living, not to mention all the folks that depend on those guys. And then you multiply that by thousands of species going extinct with no other creature quite filling each of their shoes and what have you got?

"But the real pisser about the snail darter, the pisser that makes you realize that this disaster is completely hopeless, my proof positive that I had found the most insoluble catastrophe of all time is this—that among humans, this little fish became famous, not as symbolic of the obvious unraveling of the web of life—the safety net of life, really—but as a weapon of ridicule. Those who wanted to hide the roadside bomb of ecological destruction would ridicule those who wanted to sound the alarm. They would ridicule them as people who would care about a snail darter.

"I know. I know. If it were fiction, no one would believe it. But to care about the extinction of life, to love a snail darter, was made to seem more embarrassing than picking your nose with the wrong fork or dragging the toilet-seat protector behind you like a train. And this did not happen by accident. People did it to make sure that no one would rescue a dying little fish." The guy's voice was choked up now.

"And, mister, this is why human civilization will die. And why it deserves to die."

Buck heard the guy roll over and pretend to sleep. But sleep wouldn't come to them that night. Not to either of them.

CHAPTER 12

LOUISE

Petal had every right to a bad mood. Prisoner in some apocalyptic death spa. Gang shower with forty-nine girls and no conditioner. Designerless overalls. Orchid smoothie breakfast. Confiscated purse. World ending. Problem was, though, she just couldn't get it going.

She tried her usual, fail-proof mental disciplines. Huge zit before TV spot. Whiny ex suing for herpes. Looming spinsterhood. Roots showing. She strained at her visualizations. She chanted her disaffirmations. Nothing.

Maybe it was that great night's sleep. It was the first time in years that she hadn't taken the little pink Oblivien tablet, just to be sure. How could she have slept without it? Probably was that divine mattress. Or the soothing snores and snorts of her dorm sisters. Or how the moon shone so softly through the mosquito netting.

She decided to put up with her euphoria. It would pass. And no one she knew was around to call her on it. None of the girls here seemed embarrassed about having a good time. She might just fit right in.

In the meantime she figured she would milk a cow. If there was ever going to be a time in her life to do it, it would be now. The girls at her breakfast table were all going to and they said she could come along. Just don't let Mother General see. She might have other plans for you.

Cows are bigger in person than on TV, even a really big TV. And thicker, too. Like you have to reach way under there to get any tit at all, and by that time your nose is all smashed up against its belly and you are sneezing your brains out if you can even breathe at all.

It's obvious that you should just wait for the cow to lie down for a nap. Its undercarriage would be way more approachable in that position. But it would be pushy to start changing all the operating procedures around the first day on the job, so she kept her mouth shut and tried a one handed approach not unlike the Stance of the Incorrigibly Rude Cobra that her yoga teacher had gotten stuck in last year.

"I think we had better find another chore for you, Ms. Steele," said a voice behind her, "before your nails get us all killed. Cows flip for rhinestones. You wouldn't want to see it."

Petal loosened her grip and looked up at Mother General, who didn't look much like either. Instead, she looked like your usual Fortune 500 CEO's executive assistant. Except for the overalls. And not counting the aura. Maybe she was forty, but with some faces wisdom seems to accumulate independently from age, and it was possible that she was twice that, or half that. Actually, it was hard to see her face distinctly. Maybe it was the light.

"Louise Akrittok," she said, shaking Petal's hand, never mind the milk. "Love your column, when I can get it. Unfortunately, Ephraim thinks that we won't be ready to do without civilization if we enjoy it while it lasts. But we girls think that starting a new one would be easier if it wasn't entirely from scratch. And where better to learn civilization than from gossip? So, we often seek forgiveness rather than permission and sneak in a few of your pieces. Besides, the girls are young. It can't be all work for them."

Louise was about the most mellow authority figure Petal had ever met. In New York they would have locked her up, just on suspicion. In the City it was subversive to be competent without being frantic. Fomenting mellowness in a public place was *de facto* sedition. To be mellow is to be unafraid. Lack of fear is disrespect of hierarchy. Worse, it is the fearless who act. The fearful don't. Louise would never have been tolerated near the seat of power. Her peace would have been too threatening.

"Thanks, Louise," said Petal studying her. Was there light coming out of this woman? There didn't seem to be any shadows around her. "I should learn to do something other than society gossip anyway. It's probably the first thing to go when society collapses."

"Always be gossip, Petal," she said smiling. "And society, too. Let's walk a while."

Petal followed, schussing along the muddy path on bamboo clogs, sprinkled with twinkling wisps of the aura that wafted behind

Louise. Louise spoke the precise, sharply enunciated diction of someone for whom English was one of several second languages, but perhaps not the favorite. Her voice was so soft that you could have easily missed something, but for its cadence anticipating the rhythm of ambient noises, her words politely waiting for lulls between calls of the birds and crickets and frogs.

The voices of these creatures became part of her voice in that way, and you wondered if sometimes she was addressing them in their language as she talked to you, just to keep everyone reassured and connected. She called their names as they passed—names with consonants hard and sibilant, vowels resonant and sad. Names Petal had never heard before. Names that bore both long familiarity and deep respect. Names that lifted beetles to the peerage, chipmunks to the aristocracy.

They were in a clearing now, where dragonflies chased butterflies and even a honeybee or two soldiered on. They sat on a log, soft with moss, listening to the morning get itself going. It was a place so veiled from the intrusive industry of Man that you could pretend that it was untouched, unthreatened, uncondemned.

"How do you know what to believe, Louise?" asked Petal after a long silence. It was not a rhetorical question. It was the crux. And Petal was surprised that she could ask it. Louise's aura must be getting in her eyes, going to her head.

"Don't you mean whom to believe, Petal," said Louise, without a hint of criticism.

"I guess you're right," she admitted. "How much do we ever really discover for ourselves, anyway?"

"Most everything we know we learn from someone else," said Louise. "And when we test it for truth in our own lives, we only see the answers that fit, the evidence that supports our mental model of the world, the one we accept as a place to start and then cling to forever for fear of being cut adrift."

"But then someone comes along with proof that everything is different from what you believe," said Petal. "And someone else with what looks like proof of the opposite. And they both appeal to your reasoning, your fears, your faith. What if you just can't choose?"

"There is no not choosing any more." Louise looked down at the ground. Her answer would not come by rote.

"You have chosen," said Petal.

"It is easier for me than for you," she said looking up, directly into Petal's eyes. "We started in different places. We have seen different things. We see different things now, even if we look in the same place. There is no way for either of us to start over, to construct the world in our heads with different assumptions, different variables, and different unknowns."

"But it can't be hopeless. We can learn. We can change our minds. We can be open."

"You and Mr. Planck are looking for answers to questions that don't matter to us anymore. Who did what when? How much of this accounts for that? What if this thing didn't or won't happen? What if people stop doing this or start doing that? We are not looking for blame. We are not looking for solutions, except for ourselves and those who come after us. Our task is difficult enough. We have given up on yours."

"But, Louise," said Petal. "Can't you just tell me what you believe is true? I'll understand if you can't tell me why you believe it. And I won't ask you to convince me of it. I just want to imagine seeing it as you do, despite all the reasons why I couldn't possibly."

"Okay, then imagine growing up in a place that is no longer there," she said. "I did. It was a place that had been there for hundreds of thousands of years, and my people had lived there for many thousands. It was a difficult place to make a home, far out in the Chukchi Sea, north of Siberia. But after so many generations, your people and your place become one. You anticipate the place's rhythms, you tolerate its rages, you wait out its changes until it changes back. And, of course, you become part of it, an important part. A part that knows its place.

"When I was young and knew nothing I would listen to those whom I believed. I can't tell you why I believed them, Petal, but I did. They were old and respected, but so were the ones that I ignored. And the ones I believed would say 'Look at the light, the color of it on the ice. It has come before its season. The seals will be afraid.' And then there would be no seals. And they would say, 'See those birds. There are too many for the sky to hold. They will make the snow too wet to cut.' And so it would be. It was like that season after season until one night the oldest one gathered us together and said 'The world has now caught fire inside. The ice will melt and our islands will sink and we will boil like fish in a pot. It is the time for our people to die.'

"Of course, most everybody had to argue about why which god must be angry with which of us and how to patch that up. Or they would argue about which old ones had achieved the greatest wisdom and which had achieved the greatest senility and how to tell the difference. The old ones sat around talking about the next world and the great hunters just sulked and refused to discuss it. There were a few of us, though, who were young enough not to be afraid of risking death but old enough to be terrified of waiting for it. We were the ones who left.

"All of us made it to Siberia. Some of us to school. A couple to college. For me, to Moscow in geophysics. I was lucky, but I was driven, too. It was personal for me. There was nothing abstract about it. My people were gone. My home was gone. They weren't an aberration, a fluke. They were just a few of the first. I had to know what was happening. And the answer was not in the gods. The answer had to be in science.

"I was with them at Kyoto, the most junior member of our scientific team. We were full of hope in those days. The cold war had ended. The dark days of Soviet isolation were over. It seemed like the rational people of the earth could at last cooperate, solve problems crucial to survival. It was as if mankind had finally grown up. No longer would stubborn bullies keep the world in conflict for their own selfish ends. We were proud of our motives. We were proud to be members of the world community. We were proud to be adults.

"But scientists were not making decisions at Kyoto. The world community was not making decisions at Kyoto. Men with agendas of their own, fashioned in meetings with money brokers, anonymous by executive privilege, were making decisions about the future of the planet. Instead of a universal acclamation of resolve to put aside our differences and save ourselves, we got another new business for businessmen. Their trading in carbon credits was as ghoulish as trading rats in a plague.

"And the leaders of the most powerful, the most advanced, and the most affluent country in the world thumbed their noses at the rest of us. The country that had done the most damage to the Earth refused to cooperate, for fear some poor country might get a break. Did you know that Senators of the United States voted down the treaty ninety-five to zero? The whole world was watching and not one of those men would stand up for the Earth. We learned that day how democracy worked.

"Not to mention that the most populous, the most ecologically irresponsible, and now the most self-destructively polluting country of all, China, managed to exempt itself from the whole thing on the grounds that they needed more money so that they could multiply their polluting power by ten, just to catch up.

"My colleagues shrugged it off and got back to work, seeing Kyoto as just another setback to be overcome. It was not the time to give up. It was time to renew our efforts. No worthwhile social change comes easily. The Suffragettes had been rejected for years before women finally got the vote. How can we feel their frustration from our perspective now? Who knows what would have happened if they had all decided their goal was futile. I told myself all these things. I tried to believe them. I just couldn't convince myself.

"Time was running out. The science was clear. The data was only disputed by those with a stake in the status quo, those paid to defend business as usual. And the business as usual scenario was grim indeed, with the tipping point looming near, in our lifetimes. Even the most hopeful scenarios only delayed the inevitable a little while. There is too much inertia in the system to reverse it quickly enough. I knew that humankind had lost its chance. I had seen it happen to my people in the Arctic. It would happen to the other seven billion too, even the ones who can read the light on the ice."

Petal let her sit in silence for a while before she spoke.

"You can be proud of what you are doing at New Eden, Louise. They really need you here."

"I know, Petal," she said. "It is the right thing, the only logical thing. But I had always hoped that when the time came I wouldn't again be running away. I wanted to be someone who would stand and fight."

Petal put her arm around Louise. It is what you should do for someone when their aura begins dripping from their eyes like tears.

CHAPTER 13

ARCHIE

Buck figured he would be forced to do hours of hard, back-breaking labor in the hot sun, abraded by grit, assaulted by insects, and abused by inertial masses.

If only. No doubt, though, he would run up against gatekeepers who would judge him unworthy. "Overqualified," would be their damning praise. He tried for his flakiest look, hoping to sneak past undetected.

The problem was that Buck was one of those obviously competent guys—somebody you call when you've really got a disaster. Word gets around about guys like this. Pretty soon they've got too many disasters on their plate by half. This is bad enough, but then the real disaster happens. They get promoted.

Or at least that's the euphemism. For Buck, a promotion was a pin-striped prison—an exile into the ether of abstraction. Only the flaky are allowed the freedom of tangible reality. The competent are all ultimately rounded up and locked inside the metaphysical compound of theory.

Where they invariably get into trouble. Unless you give these guys a wrench and a pipe they start constructing ever more arcane and labyrinthine intellectual systems that progressively bear less and less resemblance to the worldly structures they claim to represent. And inevitably, competitions break out to see who can baffle the rest with the most unintuitive, untestable, and unworkable conclusions.

This is okay as long as there isn't a disaster. String theorists have nothing to worry about. Critics, think-tankers, spiritualists, and advisors of all sub-types are also heavily insulated from face-on–asphalt reconciliations with the concrete world. Disaster guys are not. All the theories, principles, and protocols so carefully honed on white boards remain impeccable and unassailable until the hurricane actually hits and nature serves up another thousand ways for everything to go horribly wrong.

Not that thinking about things ahead of time isn't worth doing, even the thinking done by professional thinkers. If anything, there is way too little cash-up-front, let's-get-ready kind of activity going on. It's just that when the wrench is in your hand and you've got a valve that hasn't budged in forty years, you learn something in a minute that studying the schematic all day wouldn't tell you.

So Buck treasured these times that his arm would ache against the shovel, that his back would strain against the rope—not from some romantic fantasy about the honor of work, but because of the lessons in physics that could be learned nowhere else. Dirt was Buck's greatest teacher. After a certain number of conference room Power Points, he always needed a refresher course in a ditch. The hard part was getting permission to take one.

"Mr. Planck? Would you please come with me?" asked the guard, taking away his shovel. "The Commandant thinks your skills can be put to better use advising the Wizard."

Buck glanced back at all that wonderfully heavy dirt that was begging to be moved from here to there, but followed without objection. "The Wizard?" he felt obligated to ask.

"Dr. Medeiros, Director of Technology. Big job. Overwhelming, really. Maybe you can help."

Buck felt encouraged. This wouldn't take long. How much technology could these people have anyway? Or want anyway? They paused briefly at the door of a bamboo structure the size of a supermarket. Its interior looked like a warehouse for Loudon Stillwright's discarded nightmares.

"Archie?" the guard said gently to a bald guy, sitting with his head in his hands, staring at the table. "Mr. Planck is here. You remember, we mentioned—you agreed—Dr. Medeiros?"

Medeiros was one of those testosterone-poisoned fellows who sprout hair from everywhere except from where most people want it. It was hard to tell what color his hair used to be, largely because it was hard to tell what color it was now. As the hairs of his beard were born of his face they seemed to aspire to whiteness, but after only a few weeks in a hostile and multi-pigmented world, they would find their moral fiber tainted, their resolve dissolved, and their self-image tarnished. There was history in this beard, if only you knew how to read it.

Some men are meticulous and skilled at trimming their own facial hair. Others are content to delegate the chore to professionals. But a few, like Medeiros, entrust the task to random encounters with machines with unshielded moving parts. His beard, like the surface of the moon, bore witness to events of cataclysmic upheaval at various times in its history, each an artifact of such extreme human drama as to deserve naming, in the style of famous battles, plagues, and geologic catastrophes. "The Mix Master Mayhem of 2007" would be evident on his left cheek, "The Great Illinois InSinkErator Incident" on his right, and "The Crème Brûlée Torch Conflagration" easily identifiable on his chin.

Buck was not surprised to see that Medeiros had ignored the universal illegalization of tobacco. Archie had stuck a cigar in his mouth when he was twelve and there was one in there now. Not much time had passed in between without one. He had tried lighting one once, but found the practice appallingly wasteful. Cigars last longer if you just chewed on them. After a few hours they would eventually disappear, but not nearly as fast as when they were burning. Where they disappeared to was nobody's business except his, given that he wasn't producing a stink that makes babies cry two miles down the beach, another allegedly unintentional effect of lighting them up.

His skin color was clearly more Medeiros-like than Archie-like, tanned khaki by disdain of sunscreen and camouflaged by collateral damage from arc welders and blast furnaces. And there was a lot of it, too, for Archie had one of those spherical physiognomies that ignored the over-rated but under-powered interventions of diet and exercise. In times of famine, communities of Archies tend to remain immutably fat for months, until on one tragic day, all of them disintegrate at once into a fine aerosol of glistening lipid globules.

"Sorry, Mr. Planck, I don't get called upon to be polite very often," he said, finally aware of his visitors. "We're all family around here. When you're polite to your family they suspect your motives."

"I like being treated like family," said Buck with his family-style grin. "It would be interesting to be in a family as big as yours."

"God save you from anything that interesting," he said, motioning Buck to sit down in a leaking Naugahyde relic across from him. "Especially if it involves babysitting two hundred innocents chosen entirely for their aptitude in breeding. Actually, it's worse than babysitting. Babysitting would be easy compared with what I'm supposed to do with them."

"What are you supposed to do with them?" coaxed Buck after a respectful silence.

"Well, I'm glad that it's not obvious to you, because it sure as hell isn't obvious to me, either. It seems to be obvious to everyone else around here, until you try to pin them down about it. Then you get a lot of hand waving and nonsense like 'create a new civilization out of the ashes of the old,' and 'design technology for a sustainable post-apocalyptic society,' or 'just get us through this.'

"Even I thought the job was obvious before I took it," Medeiros continued. "But now that I have it, I haven't got a clue."

"How about Stillwright, can't he help?" suggested Buck, recalling how he and Petal had gotten into this mess.

"Stillwright? Help? Why do you think he's still in Washington? He may be a renegade, but he's still a regulator. That's even worse than being a consultant, as you well know. Whenever he gets close to a real problem he melts right down into a radioactive puddle."

"How about Endgame? He seems pretty sure of himself," Buck offered. Guys with shotguns always seemed sure of themselves.

"Endgame? Sure of himself? That's the problem, people who are so damn sure of themselves. Ideologues! They're the worst! Try asking one of them a question that's not on their play list. They stare at you like you've just lapsed into Chinese, for God's sake. Except for the Chinese ones, of course, who are even worse than the worst, but don't get me started on them."

"Well, what did you think the job was when you took it?" said Buck, trying not to sound too much like a fed-up psychiatrist.

"You sound like my mother," complained Medeiros. "According to her, nobody gets to complain about anything that they could have avoided. So where does that leave complaining? 'You could have always hung yourself, you know.' 'You knew what you were getting yourself into when you decided not to hang yourself.' What kind of argument is that?"

"What I meant was why don't we start from the beginning on this? I've done my share of disasters. I'm an on-the-ground kind of guy. Just tell me what the job looked like at first and we'll go from there." Being competent meant that you had to do your share of head shrinking, too.

"Okay, fair enough," said Medeiros, now pacing among contraptions covered with tarps. "Back to first principles it is. How far back do you want to start? Five hundred thousand years? Twice that? Half that? Sometime in there people figure out that they don't like freezing their furry bums off. Nobel Prize piece of work, that. Then they figure out that burning stuff gets them hot, and they've been hot about burning stuff ever since. Problem is, keeping yourself warm for a day burns up more stuff than a tree can make in a century. And we're not just talking about the wood. Oxygen ain't free either—it took the trees millions of years to make the stuff. But, hey, who gives a damn? There's plenty trees. There's plenty oxygen. And it's not like nature has done you any favors, with this nasty, brutish, and short shrift she's given you.

"So that's how it starts. Innocently enough. No Big Coal. No Big Oil. No secret Energy Task Forces. Just a bunch of freezing hominids trying to keep warm. Can't blame them. They didn't even invent fire anyway. It was there all along. But you can trace the whole problem back to them, huddled around that fire. Pumping CO_2 into the sky.

"Think of CO_2 as trash that never gets picked up. Sure, after a couple hundred years a bunch of it gets soaked up by the ocean. Good thing, too, because if it didn't our prissy, health-club asses would have been burnt up long ago. But the stuff is trash in the air and trash in the ocean. Makes the water more acid. Ocean critters don't complain when that happens, they just croak. You want details with that? We got plenty. And there aren't too many people stupid enough to think that we could survive with a dead ocean.

"So then, a couple hundred years ago we as a species get real good at burning up stuff, and not just stuff that is growing now, but stuff that grew millions of years ago, stuff that took hundreds of thousands of years to grow. The only thing that we seem to be just as good at is making babies, and every one of them hot to burn as much carbon as the most glamorous celebrity in Hollywood, because there is obviously nothing in the world sexier than oxidizing massive quantities of carbon while everyone watches.

"Of course we know there is nothing wrong with being a celebrity and making tons of money as long as you spend tons of money and keep it all trickling down. The problem is with all the

CO_2 trickling up. And just about every dollar you spend making yourself more glamorous—unless you are very, very careful about it—trickles more and more CO_2 into everybody else's air.

"And did everybody else give you permission to do that? Did you offer to pay them to allow it? Are you going to object when they ask you to stop? Or better yet, when they demand that you pay for the damage you have done to them? If you dumped your sewage in your neighbor's house the courts would make you pay. You expect the judge to care less about the sewage you dumped in your neighbor's air?

"But it is too late to be angry at the glamour seekers. They can't do a damn thing about it now. No one can. It's because of inertia.

"The Earth system is so huge that it takes a huge push for a long time to get it to budge. For centuries, we acted like God had told us that it couldn't be budged, so we leaned on it like it was the proverbial immovable object, piling up our irresistible billions of tons of CO_2 until, big surprise, it became clear that we had been making it move all along, just too slowly at first for us to see. But now any fool can see (with the exception of those fools paid not to see and those fools fooled by them) that it is moving a lot, and faster all the time.

"So that's why it's too late. Because now that we've got it moving with all those years of pushing, it would take just as big a pull to get it to stop, and a whole lot more to move it back. And who is pulling? Nobody. Everybody is still pushing in the wrong direction, some just harder than others. And with a billion more of us getting born every time you turn around—"

"Maybe we need to narrow our focus a little—" tried Buck. "New Eden?'

"Right," he said, mopping his brow and taking a breath. "New Eden. Well, we're your basic lunatic fringe survivor outfit, but with heavy utopian overtones, a touch of pastoralism, the standard dollop of paranoia, a twist of artificial anti-authoritarianism, deist-free, but reeking with an overpowering bouquet of technological ambivalence. Hence, the trouble with my job. Director of Technology. Get it?"

"Technology. You love it and you hate it," said Buck, trying for simplification.

"No, not me, personally. I have no romantic involvement whatsoever with technology. I'm just the guy that is supposed to know something about it. When something big needs to get done, they are all at my door expecting some magical solution. At the same time, we are supposed to be creating the new, sustainable, post-apocalyptic society. So do you want the back hoe in here belching diesel smoke or not? Maybe at night, when no one will see it? Or maybe we should check if the Pharaoh is done with the Israelites? Whoops! Even they are breathing out CO_2.

"And we haven't even started agreeing on what we are supposed to do after the crash. Are we going to preserve all of mankind's accumulated knowledge so far, or just the parts that won't get us in trouble the next time around? And how are we going to preserve knowledge, anyway? Books, I guess. They last longer than anything if you take care of them. But that's a lot of books, any way you look at it. Forget about disks and tapes. All that recorded stuff is only good for time capsules. After a generation, nothing electronic is going to work and it will take a thousand years before we are making chips again."

"And this rap that Endgame and Stillwright do about recycling the leftovers of the dead society. It's like they are imagining some sci-fi movie set where all the world's people were whisked off by aliens, leaving their breakfasts half-eaten, and the good people of New Eden go in and borrow their mittens for the winter. What do they think is going to happen in the end?"

"I'd like to know that, too," said Buck, with the recollection that he too had a job description that eluded him. "How is it going to end?"

"That I can tell you. Imagine the goriest zombie movie of all time and then multiply by seven billion. When there is no food, states fail or go to war. Either way, they bring their neighbor states down with them. The social order disintegrates and people are left to claw at each other over the rubble. Warlords with the most violent tribes will last the longest. We are hoping we can outlast all of them."

"And you have technologies to make that happen?" asked Buck.

"Sadly, only one. We aren't smart enough to have invented another," Medeiros said, moving to a curtain that partitioned off

71

half of the room. With a quick jerk he opened it wide and stood back, a look of embarrassment on his face.

There sat hundreds of crates. Here were enough automatic weapons to wage a war. A very long war. A war against the rest of humanity.

CHAPTER 14

REEPUR

Petal was sitting quietly in the dim room when Buck was rushed in, breathless from urgency. The guard bowed respectfully and left them alone.

"You okay?" he asked, taking her hands in his, sitting close.

"I'm fine," she whispered. "A little scared, I guess." Her eyes were more resigned than afraid. She was being brave, but would not stoop to staged joviality or affected swagger. There was nothing to say, but it warmed her to have Buck there with whom not to say it.

"What happened?" Buck ventured as gently as he could. He had to know, even if it would be hard for her to tell it. He could feel his evolutionary imperative as protector welling up in his chest, obscuring rational connections, making his tenderness clumsy. How easy it is to injure an already suffering person with one's spontaneous and poorly focused rage. How hard it is to be a man when your heart and your gut are at war and your mind is powerless to intervene.

"He said it was going to be routine, but then he looked all worried and walked out of the room. Then after a long time they brought me out here to wait. Nobody is telling me anything, but I know it's bad, that's all." She stared at their hands in her lap.

"Nobody hurt you?" Buck's hands were shaking.

"No, Buck. Nothing like that," she said looking up quickly, realizing she must summon the strength needed to extinguish any accidental hostility that might divert him from dealing with this real crisis. "Everyone's been grand. Up until now."

Buck felt his heart rate coasting down. He sat back a little and looked up, the fog of imagined violence clearing, details of his surroundings sharpening their focus. The room was more finished than others in New Eden, with seamless floor and double-wall construction. There was even a counter with a window across from them, now shuttered. The place was silent but for their breathing.

"What is this place?" he asked.

"Why, the doctor's office, of course!" How could he be so dense?

Of course! How could he be so dense? Where else is uncertainty suffered so intensely? Where else are the minutes between points of anchor so dark and vertiginous? And where else is the imagination goaded into such intricate despair? Remote but still potent associations stirred whiffs of ether, ripplets of nausea, and flushes of humiliation up into Buck's awareness. The Doctor's Office. His spirits sank again.

"You okay?" he asked.

"How would I know? Do I look like some kind of doctor?" she chafed.

"But you feel okay?" he persisted.

"I thought I did at first. They said everybody has to get a physical when they come to New Eden. It's part of the routine. Not to worry. So they brought me here and I filled out all their forms—I swear I hardly fibbed at all—and then the doctor barely spent five seconds with me before he discovered whatever it was and rushed out like he'd seen a ghost.

"And now I realize that I have been kind of tired lately and every now and then I get this sudden twitching in my eyelid for no reason. And my memory. I'll find myself in a room going after something, but can't remember for the life of me what it was. What's worse is seeing someone on the street and not being able to recall if their absence at the Toidy-Haupt nuptials was because the Toidy-Haupts were snubbing them or because they were snubbing the Toidy-Haupts. Not to mention how sore my back gets after only three or four hours of Pilates. Plus all the gas, but you must have noticed that. What could it be, Buck?"

"I don't know, Petal. But I'm sure the doctor can find out. I'll bet they have the most up to date medical facility here, and everyone I've met so far has been a real professional. New Eden is not your everyday, fly-by-night, trans-Armageddon delivery service. It's got to be right up there in the Fringe 500." Buck could at least be reassuring, if he could do nothing more.

"You're right," she said. "I've never met more accomplished and inspiring people in any lunatic doomsday cult, including that

Outdoor Circle coven on the Upper West Side. But medical science can't cure everything, and if you had seen that look on the doctor's face you'd be worried, too."

Buck was worried, more worried than he could dare let on. So he held her gently, but not provocatively, in his quiet but not taciturn and strong but not overbearing way. He thought.

"Is Mr. Buck Planck here?" said the woman now sitting behind the window.

"Yes, I'm Buck Planck," he answered, jumping up and rushing to her.

"Hello, Mr. Planck. We'll need to complete a little paperwork before we get started. Now, first a few questions. Name?" She paused with her pen over the form.

"Still Buck Planck," he said, regretting it immediately.

"Is 'Still' your first name or a professional or military title, and if so, which profession or military entity, and if military, para or non-para?" she recited.

"No, I'm sorry, there is no Still. It's just first name Buck and last name Planck. No titles." He tried to look contrite.

"No middle?"

"Essentially no middle. Never use it," Buck squirmed.

"Does your birth certificate use it?" she said, looking over her glasses.

"Okay, it's Sweetcheeks," he whispered. "It was my mother's first child and my father's first drink."

"Is that Sweet Cheeks two words or all run together Sweetcheeks?" she asked, a little too loudly.

"One word. Listen, I'm not here for me. I'm here for my," his hesitation barely noticeable, "partner, Ms. Steele. We are both quite concerned and need to speak to the doctor immediately. It really is quite urgent."

"Sex?" she asked, pen over form.

"Maybe it would be faster if I just filled out the form myself. Save you the trouble?"

She was happy to get out of this chore and professional enough not to show it. She pushed the stack of papers over to him and shuttered the window, leaving Buck wondering if he would ever see her again. He sat down next to Petal and got to work.

"Hurry up," she said. "She's not going to let us see the doctor until you're done with those forms and I'm starting to feel sweaty and my mouth is really dry. Maybe she could have done it faster by herself."

"I'm really good at forms," he lied, having just made it past "sex," thinking that he was in the true or false section rather than the multiple choice part of the test.

"Social Security number, phone number, credit card number," he mumbled to himself. "Homeland Security number, health insurance number—what good are all these numbers at the end of civilization? We're hiding in an outlaw encampment, for God's sake. Did Che Guevera send bills to Medicare? I doubt it—tax identification number, Publisher's Clearinghouse number—"

"Gimme some of that," said Petal grabbing a handful of pages. "We've got to pick up the pace here. My electrolytes are fading. I can feel it."

"Mandatory Patient Satisfaction Survey," she read. "All questions must be answered truthfully. Answers judged to be ironic will void the questionnaire and result in summary expulsion of the patient from the facility. Literal or concrete interpretations will be considered ironic, *de facto*. Answers with awkward construction or tiresome alliterations may be revised after one warning (see Chicago Manual of Style, section10.102, regarding use of apostrophes in Romanized Chinese place names). Shallow characterization and inauthentic dialog will not be tolerated.

"The first question is: 'How long did it take you to make this appointment?'" she continued. "Is it okay if I answer 'None of your damn business'?"

"No."

"How about 'I'm out here dying in your waiting room and if you don't get the doctor back off the golf course pretty soon all you're going to find of me is a smelly puddle of electrolytes that one of you will have to clean up'?" she asked.

"Slightly less abusive but still unresponsive."

"Okay, 'four months'."

"Perfect."

"Would you recommend this facility to friends or family for their next dehumanizing and torturous interaction with America's For-Profit Healthcare Delivery System®?" she read.

"That's a 'yes,'" he advised.

"How about this one. 'Did you know that the poorest person in America gets better medical care than the richest person in Canada?'" she read.

"Tell them you knew," counseled Buck. "But in an appreciative and humble way."

"There's just a tiny box for 'yes' or 'no,'" she said.

"Write small."

"Okay. But what about this one. 'You don't want a bunch of government bureaucrats in the exam room with you, poking their noses into decisions that should be left to you and your doctor (not counting anything about sex or fertilized ova about which the state has an insatiable and God-given curiosity) like in those socialist countries where the lines are so long and everyone smells of garlic, do you?'"

"Well, duh!" answered Buck. Why was she bugging him with these simple ones when he still hadn't finished the first page?

"Help me with this one," he said. "'Have you ever, knowingly or unknowingly, on a date prior to your initial application for health insurance, experienced signs or symptoms of a nature that would lead a reasonable person to believe that they might in fact be experiencing the first inkling of a condition, that, no matter how incipient, how tentative, might someday have the potential of possibly developing into some horrendous disease that would cost us money, while it eats you alive?'"

"Yours are so easy!" complained Petal. "Let's trade pages."

Their struggle over the stack of paper had nearly degenerated into hair pulling, horse biting, and wedgie pulling when the doctor appeared in the doorway looking grim.

"Mr. Planck?" he said, pulling up a chair across from them. "I am Dr. Reepur."

"Yes, doctor," was all he could muster.

"Thank you for coming. It can be of great comfort for patients to have their loved ones near when life's major upheavals must be faced," he said slowly, choosing his words to be kind, but unambiguous.

Petal held Buck's arm so tightly that her nails pierced his skin. Only later would he feel their sting.

"As you know, New Eden is a very special place, but it is not magical. We cannot do the impossible," he spread his hands as if to show his honesty, his humility, his compassion.

"In the crudest sense, it is all about resources. This place is like a space ship, escaping a world which has exhausted its resources. And on that ship it must carry enough resources to sustain its crew until it can establish itself on a new world, however hostile and far away that might be. And each of the crew must be capable of surviving the ordeal of transition and making a heroic contribution to the survival of the group. We have made the calculations. There is no leeway. Everyone must be ready for maximum effort. Otherwise we will fail. The human race itself will fail. Our species will wither and die out. It is a great responsibility that all of us here share.

"It saddens me to have to tell you what I must, but you deserve to know the truth and the truth will become obvious to you soon enough." He stared at the floor as if not knowing how to proceed.

"Tell me, Dr. Reepur," she pleaded. "I'm ready to hear it."

"Well, our examination revealed that at most you only have eight left." His voice was dry, near cracking.

"Months? Years?" she prompted.

"God, no!" he looked up, startled. "We're talking about babies here. You have to be good for a dozen to qualify for New Eden. Even with a little hormone help I think that nine would be a stretch for you, Ms. Steele, with all due respect." He handed her a Kleenex.

"You mean I'm going to live?" she asked.

"No more than a hundred years or until the end of the world, whichever comes first," he said, doing the calculations in his head.

"But I'm afraid you'll have to do it outside of New Eden," he said standing up. "The guards will escort you both to the gate. We'll make sure you have a new set of overalls and a hundred dollars." He shook their hands in the limp way that consolation prize winners' hands get shaken.

"Oh, one last thing," he said as Buck and Petal walked out the door, arm in arm. "You might try one of the warlord outfits down the road. If you can handle an assault rifle they might not be so strict on the fertility requirements. Good luck!"

And as they left, Dr. Reepur was inspired by how bravely the two seemed to be taking the news.

CHAPTER 15

GRANDMA

"Let's face it, Buck," said Petal, walking backward with her thumb out. "The New Eden folks were awfully nice and they made some good points, but do they really represent mainstream America?"

"Way left," said Buck, walking forward on the other side of the road with his thumb out. "Or right. Hard to tell." Either way, they had ended up with the couple's cash, clothes, and rental car. Now Buck and Petal were reduced to team hitching in both directions.

"Maybe we should talk to someone with a more centrist position," she said, showing a little ankle to a car speeding past. Ankle was as good as it gets out here in overall country, but, somehow, still not good enough. Buck was amazed. He would have stopped.

"Among polarizing issues, I think this may be one of the more polar," ventured Buck. "Although it is hard to think of a non-polarizing issue these days. The flag? Nope. Apple pie? No, no, no. Motherhood? Are you kidding? Kindness to children? As long as it doesn't discourage them from buying their own health insurance, maybe. Kittens on bubbles? That may be it! Can we all agree about kittens on bubbles?"

"I have never admitted it to anyone before," Petal confided. "But any image that has to do with the combination of kittens and bubbles immediately makes me want to puke. I have no particular political position on either, actually, and when pressed, I have nothing but good things to say about each of them individually. It's just that, juxtaposed, they create an immediate and overwhelming compulsion to blow lunch. Not as bad as those nostalgic paintings of cottages in forests, though. Especially the ones at dusk with lights in the windows. Uggh! I think I'm going to be sick. How could you bring this up?"

"Sorry, Petal," he said, adding this conversation to his growing collection of evidence that Petal was, at times, pulling his leg. Not that this bothered him, as long as he was aware of it. Or not aware of it, by definition. Either way, he reasoned, hanging out with someone whose sense of humor is more subtle than yours should be an opportunity for growth. Or humiliation. Depending.

Buck's metaphysical musings were cut short by a vehicle skidding to a stop between them.

"Trade a lift for some muscle, sonny?" said the grandmotherly driver, leaning toward him.

"Why sure, ma'am. If you have room for two of us," he said nodding to Petal.

"You're not going the other way, honey?" she asked Petal.

"Since we don't know where we are, we figure we can go in either direction," explained Petal.

"So where are you-all headed, then?"

"We're not exactly sure of that, either," admitted Buck.

"You kids aren't on drugs, are ya?" she asked.

"Absolutely not!" Petal stamped indignantly.

"We're just kind of lost," said Buck, trying not to sound too pathetic.

"Well, come on with Grandma, we'll set you right."

They pried themselves into the VW Minivan through a door that didn't seem to open very often or very much. This was a vehicle that if it had been newer could have been in a museum. That it was still running on its own was a tribute to either superior German engineering or to a worm hole in the time-space continuum.

Its body seemed to be held together by its psychedelic paint job, inside and out, tires and windows, upholstery and floor. On its side, if you squinted and shook your eyes back and forth, you could make out the logo "Be Nice to Mother" woven into the paisley floral motif.

From its tailpipe burped a pungent purple haze that reminded you of high school and that bet about the fifty bags of French fries. The three of them crowded into the front seat since it was the only seat, and since the rest of the interior was crammed with bales of pamphlets, smelling fresh from the printer.

"Gertrude Bootstrap," she said, shaking hands with a grip of iron. "Call me Grandma. What are you kids doing out here in the country?"

"We were trying to interview Ephraim Endgame for an article we're writing about climate change," said Petal, who had immediately felt a flush of filial affection for Gertrude, who was just as she had imagined her own lost Grandma Gertrude, who had run off with the drummer of the *Changing Tyres* the night after Petal's mother was born. The sudden association punctured an aerosol can of bottled up emotions that bounced wildly around inside Petal's cranium, spewing artificial nostalgia for a relationship she had never had but had always wanted.

"But then we were kind of kidnapped until they found out I only had eight babies left in me!" she blubbered, her eyes welling up with tears.

"Awww, don't cry, darlin'. That Ephraim Endgame don't know nothin' about nothin'. You two stay away from those people. They're what we call 'poisoned with pessimism' over at Grandma's. They got the wrong idea about everything with all that end-of-the-world boo-hooing. No wonder you two are so confused. You-all come with me and I'll show you how to make it better."

She fished around with the shift knob until she found a gear with some teeth left on it and the van lurched off in a fog of McDonald's effluent.

Buck comforted Petal as best he could over the deafening borborygmal rumblings of Grandma's fry-o-diesel and studied the old lady as she drove. Gertrude may have been too short to see over the steering wheel, but she looked tough enough to bite a nickel in half and just as determined. She was dressed like she had just come off a pancake syrup label with her calico dress, white apron, sensible shoes, and a bun done up with a yellow pencil. She didn't seem to be wearing any jewelry except for a small "Be Nice" button on her collar and a wedding band that was as black as rubber.

They had made pretty good time in the foothills, but as the grade steepened into the mountains, Grandma's van strained to keep up walking speed. Buck was about to offer to get out and push when she reached under the dash and pulled on a rope. They were slammed back into their seats as if on a rocket sled.

"Nitrous," Gertrude said, grinning. "Love the stuff."

81

The van vaulted a quarter mile uphill in three great leaps, just rejoining the pavement as the road leveled off and the jet assist ran out. From the crest of the hill the view was spectacular, as the setting sun lit the region's sulfur dioxide haze into a rich brocade of pinks and orange.

Petal, still recalling her imagined childhood, could see herself lying on her back on such a hillside, as the evening waned and the stars winked on, one at a time at first, but then rushing in together, filling the sky with light in a way you now only see looking down, as your plane approaches L.A. at midnight.

And just below them in a valley of conifers next to a stream they could glimpse Grandma's place, yellow lights in its gingerbread windows and a wisp of smoke from its red brick chimney. Thatch spilled over its pitched eves almost down to its exposed Black Forest beams.

Buck silently began scanning the van for what stewardesses call a "New York Bag," (named in reference to the fact that no one wants to york into an old york bag). But Petal (whose secret lust for Thomas Kinkade fantasies was known only to her mother, who had found sticky stacks of his brochures under Petal's bed well after the girl should have grown out of such things, but who had never summoned the parental courage to confront her with the evidence, rationalizing that at least she wasn't driving around with her tasteless friends doing gazebos and lighthouses and who knows what late at night) was transfixed by the scene, mouth open and gurgling a little bit, but not the slightest bit green in the gills.

Seeing this look in Petal's eyes (and so ironically soon after she professed such profound aversion to the love object that now consumed her entire consciousness) invoked great warring emotional contradictions in Buck, not unlike those of the settled-for bridegroom who foolishly had expected silence after "If anyone here present knows why these two people should not be joined—" And yet, Buck reasoned, one should welcome into one's relationships diverse sources of mutual joy and fulfillment from all the richness the world has to offer (with the possible exception of those offered by one's local heroin dealer.)

So, Buck, incurable optimist and part-time romantic, gathered the rest of himself into his highest self and said, "Nice spot, Grandma. You get cable up here?"

"That ain't the half of it, sonny," she said. "You just wait."

For some women such male-typical deflationary spell-breaking would be grounds for a mandatory five days of stony silence followed by another two of failure to be amused. But for Petal, Buck's few words had shown that he could open his heart in a welcoming, relaxed, and nonjudgmental way to the possibility that they might someday share an intimacy that she had feared she could never entrust to another human being, an ecstatic experience that with two would be more than doubled in intensity, the joy of hiding under her bed with a box of tissues and her complete collection of Kinkade catalogues.

Of course, there was no way for Buck to comprehend the complexity (let alone the gist) of Petal's now obvious appreciation of him, which was now being made manifest in ways usually reserved for back seats of vans and almost never in the presence of grandmothers. He could only assume that at last, after so many once-promising potential life-partners had elected to drop the course in mid-semester, as it were, he had finally found someone who would accept him for who he was, and, better yet, who appreciated the subtle beauty of cable.

"You see, Grandma's got you kids feeling better already," she beamed as they stopped at the path to her cottage. "Come on in for some cocoa. We can carry in those bundles later."

She led them through an arbor of rose, bordered by delphinium, daylily, and holly. The air was chilly at this altitude, and Gertrude shooed them inside quickly to gather in front of a fireplace that, while large for a cottage, only contained a small but steadily burning fire.

"When this place was built everybody thought you had to build a big fire and sit far away," she said, handing them mugs of hot chocolate. "Now we know that we should all be building small fires and sitting close. In a way, that sums up what we are doing here."

"We?" asked Petal.

"All the Grandmas at Be Nice to Mother. There are quite a lot of us who care about Mother Earth and what centuries of not-so-nice people have done to her. But we aren't blaming anybody for what they did when they didn't know any better. We were all at fault in that way. What's important is that we all pull together and take care of her now that we know that we have to and now that we know how to do it. It's really not all that hard to do, if everybody does their part." She led them over to a rough-hewn but warn-smooth dining room table that was covered with books and papers.

"I know you young people take things kind of literally, so right off I want to assure you that we're not a bunch of superstitious old ladies. When we talk about Mother Earth it's just a metaphor. A figure of speech. Now, I'm not saying I'm down on anybody's religion or anything. If somebody wants to think that there is some supernatural spirit in the Earth or that the ecosystem is one big living organism then that's fine with us. As long as what you do to the world leaves her better, then you're on our side.

"Be Nice to Mother is a strictly pragmatic, hard-science outfit," she said spreading out a large sheet of paper. "We promote everything that individual people can do at a grass roots level that will save the planet."

Grandma was one of those people who had to write while they talked, as if she had been in school so long that she couldn't help but take notes in a lecture, even if she was the one giving it. She had a stack of already-recycled brown paper bags next to her, which when cut into panels took a Number 2 pencil line quite well. Next to the fireplace was a gizmo made of dowels and coat hangers that rolled up used sheets of paper into logs. Buck knew that there must be another contraption just out of view that took the soot from the chimney and crammed it back into new pencils.

"We may be grandmas but we've got credentials. I was a professor of ecology at Princeton until it was bought by that investor group and sold for scrap. Which was kind of a shame, of course, with all those nostalgic buildings and lawns, but you have to admit that they were hopelessly energy-inefficient, and now there is a totally green shopping mall there which saves the local residents tons of time driving to the other mall down the street and, consequently, tons of CO_2. I don't have to tell you two about CO_2, do I?" she said, looking over her granny glasses.

Buck and Petal shook their heads 'No,' sensing that her question, like all questions raised by lecturers, was entirely rhetorical.

"So I don't have to tell you that CO_2's the name of the game. Mother Earth has got a fever, the kind that kills you when it gets too high. And CO_2 is the cause. Some people quibble about there being other causes too, and which are more important than others and quibble, quibble, quibble. But it boils down to this: Get that CO_2 down and Mother lives. Push it up and she dies. That's the choice.

"And that's what I'm talking about. Pragmatism. CO_2. Everybody pulling together. Power in numbers. Did you know that one compact fluorescent light bulb saves a half of a ton of CO_2 over its lifespan? One bulb! Multiply that by all the bulbs in all the cities of the world and what have you got?" she asked, furiously scribbling calculations. "You've got a decent first step, that's what."

"And biofuel. Could anything be more logical? Convert the power of the sun into a liquid that can run your cars and generate your electricity, all without adding more carbon from buried coal and oil into the atmosphere. Brazil has pretty much done it with sugar cane. So can the rest of the world. Just look at all that sunshine that's falling where plants could be growing but aren't. There's enough wasted energy just there to fill all the world's needs right now. And suck down CO_2 from the air to boot." She had filled another sheet with figures that balanced lumens, joules, and metric tons.

"Can't plant? At least don't waste. A new, vacuum-insulated refrigerator can run on an eighth of the power of that clunker in your den, the one with the rubber ice cube trays. Not to mention that your house leaks like a sieve. I'm talking heat, now. Another foot of insulation and a caulking gun can save tons of carbon a year." Those got added to a running tally she had going on a separate sheet.

"And if you can get up off your butt, you can get off the grid entirely, and make money doing it. Eight solar panels is all it takes to run your house—add a couple more and you're making money, selling clean power that would otherwise have been made with the world's dirtiest technology—coal-fired electric generators. Got a quarter acre? You could plant grass and pretend you are English aristocracy or plant corn and make $200, or you could put up a wind turbine and make $100,000. Actually, you could have the turbine and still grow more corn than you could eat." She had books open with charts of average wind speeds and cloudless days for every spot on the globe.

"And talking about butts, let's look at your toilet paper. Is it from recycled fiber or from a tree that died for your precious little tush? Switching one roll per family in this country is worth half a million trees.

"And we haven't even started talking about diapers. Your kid as smart as the average African kid? Then get him on the pot starting day one. Skip the cloth versus paper debate." She had added up cubic miles of landfill per Pamper-clad kid but was having trouble comparing that with laundry services' chlorine bleach pollution. "He'll thank you for it when he gets around to talking, which, by the way, is a lot less intuitive trick that he manages to figure out despite all your help."

"And talking about debates, get involved! Make your voices heard! Hydrogen fuel cells. Now we're talking! Green nuclear. It's here! Geothermal. Did you know that in Iceland—"

Gertrude's roll was suddenly cut short by the blasts of shotguns and the voices of men calling from outside.

"Grandma! We don't want no trouble, but you got our people in there and we aim to get them back! Now I'm leaving my gun outside and coming in, so put that little Derringer up on the table where I can see it. Okay?" It was the unmistakable voice of Ephraim Endgame.

"Okay, okay," she answered with a snarl, producing from her skirts not only the tiny pistol but also a hunting knife, two shuriken, blow darts, and a stun gun which clattered to the table in a pile.

The door swung open and Endgame ducked through the frame to approach them.

"Ms. Petal, Mr. Buck," he said nodding to them. "Grandma," he acknowledged grudgingly. No one answered.

"I'm sorry to have to barge in like this where I'm not welcome, but there's wrongs that need to be set right. First of all, Ms. Petal, I have to apologize for the grievous medical error made by our Dr. Reepur. When reanalyzed using algorithms not available until after your departure, your biometric data clearly shows that your initial projected fecundity of eight was grossly underestimated."

"It was?" said Petal, excitedly.

"It wasn't," said Buck, incredulously.

"So what?" asked Gertrude, disgustedly. "I mean, so what is it now?"

"Well, the new algorithm says fourteen," admitted Endgame.

"It does?" said Petal, clapping her hands.

"It doesn't," said Buck, holding his head.

"Who cares," said Gertrude. "More than one should be against the law anyway. But even if it were, the world's population would still—"

"But don't worry, we've taken care of everything," interrupted Endgame. "Dr. Reepur has been severely punished for this error, unavoidable as it was. His patient satisfaction survey category has been adjusted from 'Eerily Superhuman' to 'Pretty Good, I Guess' and a number of anonymous entries have been placed on his *Rateyourdoctor.com* site. I think that they will meet with your approval. We have, 'This bozo is a complete doo-doo head,' and 'His nails need a total make-over,' and 'He looked at my chart with an inappropriate expression'. Now, if you will be so kind as to sign this release of liability form here—and here—and here—and here—"

Petal's face was frozen into a stare of incomprehension.

"Of course," he added hastily, sensing her reluctance. "We are prepared to go so far as adding 'His stethoscope lightly brushed the swell of my bosom as his eyes locked with mine, the murmur of my heart now loud enough for both of us to hear above the straining of our—'"

"These kids ain't going to sue that quack Reepur!" protested Grandma. "He's just a vet anyway. I've known him since he was a kid."

"Being a vet is harder," said Endgame, reluctantly putting away his forms. "And I'm not just here to cover my—sorry, ma'am—I mean I'm not just here to apologize. I'm here to save these two innocent kids from being brainwashed by you and your Pseudo-Pollyanna grandma corporation." Endgame was now on the offensive, pointing his finger at Gertrude.

"I'll bet in the short time you have been here," he said, now pacing in front of Buck and Petal. "She has filled your heads with the subtle guilt trip that you as individuals have caused global warming and it is your individual responsibility to clean it up. And how are you supposed to do that, even if it would work? You're supposed to buy more stuff!

"That's right. You are supposed to schlep down to the store (burning fuel all the way) and plunk down ten bucks for a compact fluorescent bulb to replace a perfectly good incandescent one that might last another century in the guest room, all to save on pollution that's being caused by the power station! Never mind that the contraption is full of mercury which will poison your brain and your entire family's unborn children if it breaks, which it inevitably will. That's why it's against the law to put them in the trash in a lot of cities, even though none of those cities have figured out what else you are supposed to do with the dead ones, of which there are plenty, right out of the box. And why does it cost twenty times more than the old kind? Because it uses up twenty times more resources at the factory to make the damn thing. And we're not even counting the resources it takes to replace the fixtures that these things burn out from running so hot. And what are resources anyway but stuff that takes energy to get together at the factory.

So where are the savings? How is Mother better off with all this? She's not. It's another shell game that keeps the consumer spending and the polluters, in this case the power plant, off the hook.

"I'll bet Grandma gave you the same rap about all your appliances, too. Well, when will the ones you buy today be so offensively inefficient that you've got to use up all the resources necessary to replace them too? A year? Six months? And how are you going to get rid of the old ones? With friends like you, the Earth doesn't need enemies! But the stocks go up. That's some consolation.

"And biofuels! I bet you got an earful about that riding up here in Grandma's greasemobile. This has got to be the worst idea yet. You can always spot the worst ideas because they're the ones that get all the publicity, in this case lavishly funded by agribusiness giant Archer Daniels Midland. Here's how you do it. First you make sure that you parlay your phony image as a hard working family farmer into enough government subsidies, import tariffs, price supports, incentives, breaks, grants, barriers, exceptions, guarantees, waivers and contracts to assure enough room at the public trough for the enormous width of your 37 billion dollar snout.

"Then you convince the public that the answer to global warming is to take land that could be used for growing food and grow corn to be distilled into alcohol to burn in cars. This would be a bad idea even if it didn't take more oil to do all this than the amount of oil saved. It would be a bad idea even if all the fertilizers and pesticides involved didn't end up running into our rivers and water supplies. And it would be a bad idea even if it didn't end up in putting more carbon into the air than before the fraud was perpetrated. The main reason it is a bad idea is that it takes food that could have gone to feed poor, hungry people and uses it to make rich people feel less guilty while they drive around in their cars. It pays people who should be the stewards of the world's rainforests to burn them down to plant palm oil trees to fuel diesel engines.

"And all of this so that AMD's corporate buddies in Detroit won't have to give up on the internal combustion engine, the most sacred of the First World's religious relics. It wouldn't be hard for them—in fact they did it decades ago when some off-payroll government agency in California made them do it. That was the electric car of movie fame. Of course, they never allowed anyone to actually own one, so they could cancel the leases and crush them once the unruly regulators were taken out. Couldn't they make money on electric cars? Sure. Just not as much money. Electric cars have about a tenth as many parts that need to be replaced. And that's bad for business.

"And I'll bet Grandma had just gotten around to selling you—"

Endgame's voice was cut off in mid-rant by what at first seemed like a lightning bolt splitting the cottage in two, as the back wall suddenly was replaced by a gaping hole surrounded by spotlights. Squinting into the void Buck and Petal could make out a vast warehouse with dozens of forklift trucks ferrying green appliances, wind turbines, solar panels and the like into waiting trucks. Five Grandmas with rifles strode into the room through the open door and stood at attention, safeties off.

"Enough of your Commie subversion, Endgame," said Gertrude standing up and pulling off her wig. "That kind of talk is enough to get you twenty years in this state, and now we've got it all on tape."

She turned to Buck and Petal. Or maybe 'she' is the wrong pronoun. Without the disguise Gertrude was probably called Gus.

"Ms. Steele and Mr. Planck, we have you to thank for tonight's great success. I've been working with the authorities for years to bring this enemy of freedom to justice. We applaud the courage and patriotism it took for you two to lure him out of his lair. I'm sure our corporate partners will want to show their appreciation in some way. A nice Grandma's franchise in Wyoming maybe?"

Buck was too stunned to speak, but wouldn't have anyway. All of his attention was directed toward Petal, who had started to weep softly into her handkerchief.

"I don't want a Grandma's, Buck," she said. "I just want my grandma."

"Me too, Petal," he said. "Me too."

CHAPTER 16

DONUT

"Donut, Petal?" Buck asked, knowing the answer would be no, but hoping to elicit a brave chuckle of solidarity between two weary comrades pushed to the very limits of their endurance.

He realized, of course, that for her the most appropriate response would be to smash the greasy wad of stale dough right up his nose in a totally justified explosion of frustration and rage. But love and risk have always been inextricably linked—ever since Adam found himself thinking with his Australopithecine pecker instead of his nascent cortex and thereby queering the world's cushiest setup until CEOs learned to set their own salaries. And as an inveterate risk taker, Buck had two unwavering principles: that faint heart never won fair lady and that even a nose full of donut is better than an hour full of boredom.

"How long we been sitting here, Buck?" she asked, hefting the congealed torus of sugar and lard as if to estimate the combined weight of its innumerable anti-nutritional properties. And then, balancing the atheromatous bomb on her knee, she began unraveling a thread from the hem of her overalls.

"Hours, maybe days," he estimated. "Not a week, I don't think."

The Coeur d'Alene courthouse had been a sadly under-maintained, embarrassing reminder of a long-passed era of civic pride until the mayor had agreed to "partner" (which until then he had thought was a noun) with a corporate sponsor who promised to make the facility "A Showcase of Public and Private Consanguinity." This offer was as difficult to pass up as it was to understand, and soon the Krispy Kreme Korporation of Amerika had miraculously transformed the entire municipal complex into a sadly under-maintained, embarrassing reminder of rancid cooking oil.

There were plenty of donuts there, though. So many, in fact, that the community at large had largely become saturated with petty crime and hooliganism now that Coeur d'Alene's finest had lost their one and only incentive to actually get into a black and white and cruise down the street.

Petal had produced a ten foot length of overall-hem twine which she was tying to the glazed glob of empty calories, careful not to disturb its copyrighted surface pattern of fingerprints, insect parts, and atmospheric particulate matter. She then stealthily slipped the bait onto the counter of the window labeled "Wait Until Called" and snuck back to her chair, clutching the free end of the string.

Buck was shocked to see that, in her desperation, Petal had been reduced to the kind of person who would troll for clerks. This was not a pretty sight, but it was awesome to witness the raw power of the life force in its struggle to survive. The image of a mother bear protecting her cubs could not be more inspiring than that of Petal holding this last thread of hope in her determined grip.

With the patience of a bushman poised to snare the last remaining *kȴc-kȴc* bird or go extinct trying, Petal sat—frozen, breathless, silent. Minute after long minute failed to tick by on the dusty clock, hanging unplugged on the wall above. Faint stirrings in the dim unseen beyond the window seemed to grow more active, perhaps as the unholy scent of genetically engineered Krispy yeasts, still flatulently pumping CO_2 into their own sticky biosphere, wafted into the mouth of the lair.

And then, without warning and too quickly for all but high-speed cameras to detect, a hand shot out of the dark at the bloated slug of slimy sucrose. Without a nanosecond's delay Petal jerked deftly on the twine with just enough snap for the slip knot to slice through the gummy blob and find purchase on a distal phalanx of a now-impressed public servant.

"Excuse me, sir," Petal said, reeling him closer with the delicate touch necessary for landing obese prey on low-test line. "But can we go now?"

"Have you been called?" he asked with disdain.

"Not exactly."

"Well I'm afraid that—"

"She means, 'Not recently'," said Buck quickly, jumping to his feet. "We definitely were called, no doubt about it. We were just—"

"In the bathroom!" said Petal, rescuing him.

"Together?" said the clerk, scandalized and suspicious.

"Because of her contact lens!" interjected Buck.

"It was totally stuck," nodded Petal. "Took both of us to get it out."

"I'm sure if you check your records you'll find it clearly documented that we were in the bathroom when we were called," advised Buck.

"It will be all there in black and white," assured Petal. "In triplicate."

The clerk, painfully aware that record keeping in the courthouse had sort of gotten a little behind after thirty employees were replaced six months ago by a thirty million dollar computer system that no one had figured out how to plug in yet, now was certain that Buck and Petal were part of some organizational competence audit, and that he was in grave danger of an anonymously created and totally incontestable low performance rating that could easily hound him to his grave.

"Well, in that case, you had better go in right away," he said, with gracious efficiency.

"Go in where?" asked Petal, *sotto voce.*

"The courtroom, of course," he answered, buzzing open the door for them.

"Grandma said we were going to get some kind of commendation," whispered Buck to her, trying to sound convincing.

"Grandma could sell brimstone offsets to the devil," said Petal, still feeling jilted by Gertrude in some indefensible way.

"That's good for us, then, right?" said Buck failing to convince even himself.

"Shhhhh—" warned the sergeant at arms as they walked into the back of a huge hall.

Hundreds of people were crammed into the courtroom's pews as tight as Christmas and Easter. Portable fans stirred fetid air around a nodding jury, slumping in their box. Defendants in handcuffs stood, heads down, as their counselors cut deals with the judge, his hand over the microphone on his bench. Guys in Gucci suits conferred earnestly with guys in Budweiser tee shirts, each one mortified to be seen with the other. Proud hookers in their patent platforms towered over butch defenders in their sturdy brogues. Unpaid tradesmen glared back at unfulfilled consumers. And lovers by the dozen, stunned speechless by the unfair intrusion of bleak reality into their romantic fantasies, stood patiently in line, waiting for their money back.

"Let's leave," whispered Petal. "I've seen this movie." But there was only one way out, and the latch had already clicked.

"Names?" asked the officer.

"Buck Planck and Petal Steele," he answered, shaking with both hands. "We're here for a medal, which under ordinary circumstances we would cherish forever, we really would. But, with all due respect, I'm afraid we're just going to have to take a rain check on it, or them, if there are two, until after this very important deadline we have with some desperately needy billionaires who are literally on the verge of burning up, and—"

With a click, Buck found his wrists cuffed together. He looked over his shoulder to find Petal submitting to the same at the hands of a stern, uniformed matron, the kind for whom no hidden contraband would be too far up.

"You're late," said the officer. "Your case came up hours ago. You are both now automatically in contempt of court. And as you ought to know, we have mandatory sentencing for contempt in this state."

"Mandatory jail time?" said Petal. "How long?"

"Until you are no longer in contempt of court, of course," he answered. "A bit longer than that, actually. Until, in your heart, you no longer harbor the faintest trace of displeasure with the court, the slightest whiff of resentment, the tiniest frown of impatience, or the dimmest glimmer of wistfulness regarding the court whatsoever. When the thought of the court elicits nothing but a rosy glow of adoration, a heart-swelling of admiration, and a button-bursting pride that you personally had been part of this great system of justice, then, by definition, you will no longer be in contempt of court."

"And then?" they asked in unison.

"And then you will be eligible for parole—once they get people to sit on parole boards again—and eventually you will rejoin society as a rehabilitated and productive citizen, minus the ability to make a living, vote, borrow money, drive a car, or walk within two hundred yards of a church, school or public playground, of course."

"But how can our guilt and punishment depend on how we feel about the court? How can the state know how we feel about anything, when our inner emotional states are so complex and so often hidden even to ourselves," said Buck, slightly blushing as Petal looked up at him with newly piqued curiosity.

"Especially when our insecurities and shyness hold us back from risking commitment to a burgeoning affection at a time when it is most fragile and in need of nurturing?" she asked the officer, her eyes never leaving Buck's.

"And when these emotions are so dependent on the lightness of heart that comes from the youthful freedom to imagine a future of limitless possibility, shared with the one true soul mate who could never imagine a future without the other," beseeched Buck of the officer, while he gathered Petal into his manacled arms.

"And how can the state measure how these affections grow by infinitesimal increments into an enduring structure which entwines two separate lives while it enshrines two convergent dreams?" asked Petal of the officer, yielding to Buck's handcuffed, yet sensitive embrace.

"Even when the strength of these emotions has grown beyond that which can be contained, past the point of rational control, when they determine their own physical manifestations and demand their own realization—how does the state quantify these forces grown infinite from their own inner heat?" said Buck to the officer, now lifting Petal off the ground, burying his face in the burning redness of her neck.

"That's easy," said the policeman, loud enough for the couple to hear over their snuffling. "We contract with that Scientology outfit. They have a machine, you see, with handles that you grip and a needle that moves when they ask you a question that makes you squirm, so that they can keep at you until you cough up a secret that they can use on you in case you decide to quit giving them money. That's how they use it on each other, anyway, but it's the same basic principle for prisoners. They've got it all worked out. It's scientific. Hence the name."

"You are going to give us over to the Scientologists?" shrieked the couple in mid-grope. This was beyond cruel and unusual.

"How about the Taliban?" bargained Buck.

"Khmer Rouge?" offered Petal. "IRA?"

"IRS?" said Buck, now desperate.

"Tell it to the judge," said the policeman, signaling his counterpart at the front of the courtroom.

"The State and Its Corporate Partners versus Planck and Steele," boomed the loudspeaker.

And the two marched down the aisle—hand in handcuff, lurid visions of their imagined futures flashing in front of their eyes.

CHAPTER 17

WHIPLATCH

"Pssst! You two! Come here! Yes, you two!"

Buck felt himself being pulled unto a pew about half way down the aisle, Petal in tow.

"Keep your heads down!" the fellow hissed, hunkering them all to the floor in a squat, wedged into the tight and disgusting trench between benches. A row of huge dudes in ten-gallon hats provided cover from the front.

"Quiet! Now, where's your voucher?"

"Voucher?" asked Buck, as the guy rifled through his pockets.

"Here it is," said the guy, producing the coupon which had been wedged in the handcuff chain. "Good. Now I'm your court-appointed lawyer. William Whiplatch. Pleased to meet you. You can call me Mr. Whiplatch. Or William. Whichever. Just not Willie. Especially not Little Willie. Or even Big Willie. Or Whippie. Or anything like that. I hate that."

Buck could see that Willie really, really did hate that and had always hated that and had hated that with a depth of feeling that had surpassed every other feeling he had ever felt. This observation was so obvious that upon first meeting him, before words were spoken, any sensitive person could tell that a diminutive form of address, no matter how endearing, would grind Willie's heart right into the dirt.

And it was also obvious that Willie's life had been filled with people who, while perhaps sensitive, had not been kind. Children who had chanted, girls who had teased, rivals who had taunted, and peers who had jeered. Frat brothers found The Whipster not embraced by the moniker. Team mates found Whippet not flattered by the analogy. Dates found Willie Whipper too mortified to perform. Even Mother found her William Junior inexplicably petulant. The *sine qua non* was William. William was a necessity. Maybe not a sufficiency, but an absolute prerequisite.

But Willie had picked the wrong job to be William. It wasn't that he hadn't thought about it. Becoming a lawyer is not an easy accomplishment. It should command respect. And there is a certain formality afforded to the law, with all the stilted language and wigs and intimidation involved. Especially for judges. Since childhood, he had secretly dreamed of becoming Judge Whiplatch. Judges never had nicknames. Everyone else had nicknames, from atom bombs on down, but judges were exempt. Judgeship was his personal nirvana, shimmering in the distance.

Problem was, most judges start out as lawyers. And lawyers have to deal with people. And people are almost never considerate of other people's neuroses. Especially lawyers' neuroses.

People even think that they are doing you a favor by calling you on your neurosis. Let on that you are freaked by spiders and what do your so-called friends do next but wave one in your face, drop one on your sandwich, or leave one on your pillow. It's for your own good, they squeal in delight. They are helping you get over your fear by laughing their asses off at your suffering. They are making you strong. They are getting you ready for that cold, hard future when they won't be around to help you any more.

But it was too late for Willie to become an accounts receivable reconciliation auditor, passing day after blissful day interacting with his fellow man through laser-printed reports, spiral bound at Kinko's, signed W. Whiplatch, ARRA, with the worst to fear being an email addressed to "W" by a thoughtless superior in some distant time zone. Willie was stuck. He was a lawyer now. And he was desperate enough to make the best of it.

"Pleased to meet you, Mr. Whiplatch," said Buck, shaking hands as well as anyone in handcuffs could, squished into a narrow crack. He sized Willie up, which, because of his size, didn't take all that long. The word 'emaciated' wasn't quite apt for Whipo. Neither was 'gaunt' or even 'cadaveric,' actually. He was much skinnier than that. He was what you would call really, really skinny.

And Dickie had the look of someone getting skinnier all the time. Partially this was due to the Dick Whip's habit of buying clothes two sizes too big, so that they would fit once things settled down enough for him to get serious about diet and get his weight under control. But mostly it was because of the way he moved. Watching the Whipmeister was like watching an elementary particle as it jumped between quantum states. It was like viewing a movie with half the frames cut out. Dickola didn't move as much as he would flicker, a massless photon skittering across a discontinuous screen.

"Don't mention it," said the Latch Man, furiously filling out forms. "Worry not. I'll have you kids divorced in a nano-second. Mental cruelty, infidelity, impotence, nymphomania, irreconcilable pheromonic dissonance—"

"We're not getting divorced!" protested Petal, trying to get a peek at Billy around Buck's obscuring bulk. "We're not even married yet!"

"What did she say?" asked Dubya Dubya, darting around in a blur. "You're not married what?"

"Yet," answered Buck, swallowing hard.

"You can't get married here," said Double Dub. "This is a courthouse. Though now that you bring it up, it should be possible. I'll tell you what. For another grand I'll work it out with the judge. Maybe we can do something in the parking lot over lunch. But I'm telling you right off, I don't do flowers. You want flowers, you get them yourself."

"I'm not getting married in a parking lot!" protested Petal, who after years of journalistic voyeurism had developed a very clear image of her fantasy nuptial setting. In this tableau, society's finest floated over marble, swirling up cloudlets of confetti and blossoms with each effortless curtsy. Asphalt was intentionally absent.

"Mr. Whiplatch," said Buck, always searching for the third way, "we really appreciate your kind offers, but it would probably be best to put weddings and divorces and things like that off for a while until we take care of this contempt of court charge, if you don't mind."

"Contempt! My God, you won't be out for years!" said Wumpmunch, scrolling madly into the future on his iPlod. "And I don't think they let ex-cons get divorces or things like that anyway. But I'll tell you what, for a small retainer I can look into something in Mexico or maybe Vegas. I heard of an oil platform that declared sovereignty—"

"I'm not getting divorced in Las Vegas!" shrieked Petal, rattling her manacles in Wubyou's direction. Her fantasy divorce sequence had been shot in dim sepia tones from a low camera angle, the last wan rays of a dying sun casting long shadows on the paneled wall behind her betrayed but courageous profile.

"But Mr. Whiplatch," Buck intervened, "with all due respect, I know that this is your area of expertise, and we certainly wouldn't pretend to understand the complexities of legal arcana, but intuitively it would seem that, given the justice system's unerring and relentless pursuit of truth, and the fact that Petal and I are not guilty—"

"Not guilty?" said Whimplash, incredulity freezing his Brownian motion in mid-wiggle, his image for once in focus, his wave function collapsed. He had never had a client who wasn't guilty before. All of his professional reflexes, honed by years of diligent and exhausting practice, were now defeated, rendered impotent and irrelevant, much like those concert pianists who, in mid-concerto, find their Steinways suddenly replaced by bathtubs of borscht. He scanned the blankness of his experience for landmarks, waiting for inspiration from his inner core of being.

"You could lie," he suggested. "Plenty of innocent people plead guilty. It's easier on the court, it's easier on me, and it's easier on you. It's win-win-win all the way home. Lying about your guilt is one of the basic pillars of a free society—it's what separates us from the barbarians. Rule of law and all that. And nearly everyone does it, one way or another. You can, too, if you try."

"Don't listen to him, Buck," said Petal. "No way am I lying about anything. When they find out, it goes on your permanent record and then they cancel your insurance when you need chemo or CPR or something. I want you to march right up to that judge and just tell him the truth. We are not in contempt of court—we were just in the bathroom putting in my contact."

"Taking out your contact," corrected Buck. "And there was no bathroom and you don't even wear contacts. The question is, if we don't enter the court with clean hands, do we have a leg to stand on? Shouldn't we make a clean breast of it?"

"Get a grip," said Petal, suddenly squirmy in her seat. "There are certain intimacies that honorable men do not reveal in public. Even to special prosecutors."

"You're right, Petal," said Buck, pulling all three of them to their feet. "We are honorable people and we will do the honorable thing."

"You're pleading guilty?" asked Whupsnatch.

"You're pleading not guilty?" asked Petal.

"Mr. Whiplatch," announced Buck proudly. "Would you be so kind as to instruct the clerk that in answer to the charge of contempt of court, the defendants Planck and Steele enter a plea of "None of Your Business!"

CHAPTER 18

GLASHAUS

"Oyez, oyez, oyez. The Fifth District Court of the Proud State of Idaho, the Monarch Butterfly State, the Cutthroat Trout State, the Star Garnet State, the Mountain Bluebird State, and the Maple-Glazed Raspberry-Filled Cruller State is now in session. All rise! Judge Ernest Glashaus presiding. In the case State of Idaho and its Corporate Sponsors, *et al*, versus Mr. Buck No-Admitted-Middle-Name Planck of Harlem, New York and Petal Illegible-Smudged-Glob-of-Printer-Ink Steele of Elegant Pre-War Gem, 2BR, 1□ Bath, Stunning Views, Doorman, New York, how do you plead, so help you God?"

"Your honor, may I approach the bench?" pled counselor Wickless.

"You have to rise first," insisted the clerk.

"I am risen!" insisted Whipmee, approaching in a huff without waiting for 'Judge says, yes you may.'

"That must have been very hurtful for you," said Glashaus softly, motioning to the court electrician to bring over his stepladder.

"What do you mean," answered Lashmee, now at eye level with the judge.

"That callous reference to your height. When your fellow man so gratuitously causes you pain at every interaction, for no justification other than some y-axis normative prejudice, how can you, in your heart, sustain your love for him?" asked Glashaus, earnestly.

"Love for who?" puzzled WumYum, suspiciously.

"For your fellow man. Isn't the basis of each of our own personal philosophies how we conceptualize our fellow man? Do we begin from an innate belief in his goodness and trust in his humanity or do we start with an assumption of his selfishness and guard against his aggression?" asked Glashaus, really wanting to know.

"Hunh?" asked Ripratch.

"And isn't love of one's fellow man what distinguishes us in the helping professions from those who would exploit and objectify another living being? You must have an old and very wise soul, Counselor Whiplatch, that sustains your determination to carry mankind's burdens in face of the inexcusable unkindness of Man." Glashaus placed his hands on Ripplehatch's and nodded for a moment of silent appreciation.

"Well, thank you, sir. I do try."

"I know you do," said the Judge. "Now, let's see how we can help your two clients." He ruffled through some papers. "Why don't you have them come up here and we'll chat for a while about these charges?"

Buck and Petal shuffled up to the bench, hats in hand. Since they hadn't thought to bring hats, the sergeant at arms had to rent them a couple. These happened to be sombreros, which, despite their divisive iconic baggage, had become quite popular at higher latitudes. Petal, on the other hand, was mortified because there was just no way that her earrings would work in a Latin theme and you could always count on there being a photographer around when you as much as took out the trash in the wrong earrings.

"Why don't you two have a seat in the witness chair?" said the judge. "That's right, Ms. Steele, he won't mind if you sit in his lap, will you Mr. Planck?"

"Not at all, sir, Your Honor, Judge Glashaus, sir," said Buck.

"Call me Ernie, please," he said, opening his hands. "Can it be Buck? Petal?"

"You can call me William," said the Whippersnatcher, eagerly.

"Why, thank you, William, it would be an honor," said the judge. He turned to Buck and Petal, who were trying to make room for themselves, their handcuffs, and their sombreros in the wooden witness chair.

"Now why don't you tell me about yourselves, so we can get to know one another a little better?"

"Where would you like us to start?" asked Buck.

"Just start at the beginning," said the judge, settling back.

"Well, I, for one, was born at a very young age," began Petal, wistfully gazing at the ceiling.

"Maybe not that far back," the judge suggested gently.

"You see Ernie," volunteered Buck, "It all started when, through no fault of our own, The Publisher—"

"The Publisher—Oh my," intoned the Judge, templing his fingers.

"Right. The Publisher told us to find out what really was going to happen with the climate crisis so that the *Hedge Insider Daily* subscribers would know where to put their money."

"Right," continued Petal. "So we went to the EPA which led us to Mr. Endgame and then Grandma Gertrude."

"And that's how we happened to end up in the paddy wagon with all those guys with shotguns and muʻumuʻus," continued Buck.

"And we didn't hear our name called because we thought we were going to get a medal so we don't really have contempt of court even if I don't wear contacts," sniffled Petal. "I swear it, cross my heart."

"I see," said Glashaus, pulling at his goatee. "On the surface it does seem rather complicated. But I think that there is one pivotal question upon which everything depends. And that question is: Have you gotten in touch with your feelings about this?"

"Personally, I can say that I am quite concerned," admitted Buck.

"Deeply concerned," nodded Petal.

"Yes, I think that we all are," agreed the judge.

"And not a little disturbed, to be honest," granted Buck.

"Terribly distressed, really," expanded Petal.

"Understandably so," nodded Glashaus.

"And somewhat saddened by the whole thing," sighed Buck, shaking his head.

"A bit disappointed," admitted Petal. "We had such hopes."

"A little angry, too, perhaps?" suggested Glashaus, cocking his head.

"No," said Buck. "Finding blame would be counter-productive here. Now we need to seek reconciliation so that together we can move forward."

"Maybe a little bit angry," admitted Petal.

"What are we talking about?" interrupted Widdle Wawyer Whipwash, feeling left out.

"Why, we're talking about our feelings, William," said Glashaus. "And we care about your feelings, too. Very much. I'm sorry we got carried away and hogged the conversation. Go ahead, tell us how you feel."

"About what, exactly?" asked the Wimper Junior.

"Petal and Buck's situation, *vis à vis* their commission."

"They're not on commission," explained Whaplitch, "It's a voucher. I get paid either way. Though I do get a bonus if the trial lasts less than five minutes."

"No, we're talking about how they feel about being commissioned by The Publisher to help rich people make money off of global catastrophe."

"We are?" whispered Petal.

"Right, of course we are," agreed Buck.

"Exactly," said the judge. "And it's understandable that they are troubled by it. Despite the slogans of the absolutists, the moral lines here are not that easily drawn. For example, even if one grants the ultimate seriousness and even urgency of the environmental crisis, couldn't one argue that attention to the issue diverts resources away from even more pressing humanitarian problems? What about the billions who live in crushing poverty, tortured by disease, displaced by wars, their human rights violated? Is a cup of soup for them not worth its carbon footprint? Can we let their children starve or be sold into slavery so we can have more money for windmills?

"Or are we too horrified to look into the faces of real people who are suffering now from our neglect? Do their smells and their agony repel us too much, make us feel too guilty? Is that why we choose to concern ourselves with something as nebulous and impersonal as 'the environment,' something that shocks and alarms us only in an abstract way, like a scary movie that we know is make believe?

"And isn't it the most despicable hubris that the affluent pretend to be defending the earth to avoid spending what carbon it takes to lift fellow humans out of their hells on earth? We have squandered plenty of resources to attain our own luxurious ways of life. It will take resources to lift a third of our planet's people out of misery. Can we be so selfish as to deny them a tiny fraction of what we have spent on ourselves?"

"Gosh, I never looked at it—" started Petal.

"On the other hand," continued Glashaus, "Man's newfound concern for his poor planet might just bring with it an unintended miracle for the planet's poor.

"Let's face it, despite all the technologic progress and religious and intellectual posturing of the last five thousand years, people have done next to nothing to alleviate the suffering of anyone not immediately related to them. It would seem that compassion at a distance is just not in our collective make up.

"Evidently, the only hope for the world's disenfranchised is for human consciousness to make an abrupt and radical change. A consciousness-changing idea-virus is what we need, one that is so contagious and invasive that our very inner natures are transformed. Maybe the ecological movement has inadvertently brought us such a powerful, brain-expanding meme.

"To think environmentally is to admit that consequences of our actions extend beyond our own immediate gratification. It is to think of ourselves as a significant part of a greater network of interdependent living things. It is to extend our mental image of 'us' beyond our small number of family and friends, beyond our own homogeneous social class to include those who have nothing in common with us except for their humanity. This is a paradigm shift as radical for humans as deciding to walk on two legs.

"The modern market society has been constructed on the premise that everything will work out for the best if everyone just pursues his own self interest and doesn't bother anyone else. Selfishness is advertised as a guarantee of efficiency. Efficiency is held up as the only path to prosperity. And the claim is that everyone wins with prosperity, because the richer the winners get, the more riches trickle down to the losers.

"If only. If only this premise was something more than rationalization, something other than a way to keep the losers waiting and the winners from feeling guilty.

"Our global economy is built upon a blatantly dishonest premise. It is a premise that overnight could be replaced by an honest one. And when that change in human consciousness occurs, every human institution will be reborn. Destroying the environment for the sake of profit will become unthinkable. Destroying a family's livelihood for the sake of efficiency will become unimaginable. Tolerating atrocities will become an embarrassment of the past.

"And it will become unallowable for conscienceless corporate entities to hold shareholder's interests above the interest of humanity as a whole. Group selfishness will become as gauche as individual piggery.

"And this is why environmental thinking is so frightening to those who control the stream of status-quo dollars. They know that the institutions that have polluted the world are the same ones that have concentrated the wealth, that have impoverished the disenfranchised. They know that once they can no longer hide behind the fraud of *laissez faire*, their greed will no longer be a credential for celebrity, but will be evidence for their conviction. When it is the norm for individual and institutional actions to be judged on their effect on the world community, then those who have become powerful perfecting selfishness will find themselves more than disenfranchised.

"This is why the defenders of the status quo are so desperate to contain the spread of consciousness-changing ideas. It is why they have replaced the marketplace of ideas with engines of marketing. It is why their vehicles for advertising that pose as news media become ever more shrill in denouncing global warming as a fraud, humanitarianism as socialism, and environmentalism as too expensive.

"Well they are right on one point. It will be expensive for them. They may find that a populace with a new set of values would prefer for all of its people to live without misery rather than allow a handful of people to hoard unimaginable wealth.

"So, you see, William," said Glashaus leaning toward him. "Your clients are in a serious dilemma. They are lucky to have you as their counselor. So, how would you advise them to plea? Guilty? Not Guilty?"

"Maybe we can, you know, bargain a little?" he replied, finding himself in an area of the law he had previously not imagined to exist.

"Good suggestion," replied the judge. "As Buck said, we should be seeking reconciliation and not blame, after all."

Everyone took a much needed breath, but not a long one.

"On the other hand," Glashaus continued, "this is a very serious situation. In fact, this may be the most serious situation in the history of the world. There is no place here for excuses or equivocation. And there is no time to waste. Are we all agreed?"

"Yes, sir," said Buck and Petal, not really sure what they were agreeing to.

"Right on," said Lawyer Bill, looking at his watch.

"Excellent. Then let the record state: 'In the case of The State of Idaho and so on versus Buck and Petal et cetera, that final determination of guilt or innocence and subsequent sentencing to life in prison or worse, depending, will be held in abeyance for ninety days and be contingent upon successful performance of the remedial action prescribed by the court.'"

"Did we get off?" Petal asked, squiggling in her seat.

"Almost," said Buck, trying to be reassuring.

"Your honor," asked Willham, trying to tie this thing up, "for the record, what exactly must my clients do in the next ninety days to get their charges dismissed?"

"Why, solve this damn global warming problem, of course!" Glashaus declared, picking up his gavel. "This court is adjourned. See you back in ninety days. And you had better not need those sombreros by then, either."

And as all rose as ordered, Buck and Petal looked at each other trying to contain two brand new consciousnesses that were more than two sizes too big.

CHAPTER 19

HACK

"Buck, you have to admit that this puts a whole new complexion on the thing," she said, sawing furiously at his chain.

"I guess so," he agreed, caring less about what she was driving at than how she was driving the hacksaw. "A clearer complexion for sure. I hate those morally ambiguous complexions. Makes you look kind of gray. Give me a nice, simple black and white complexion any day."

"Clearer may be simpler, I suppose," she said, sweating like a politician on a polygraph, "but in our case, simpler is definitely not easier. In fact, our problem may have gotten so simple it could now be impossible. How are we going to fix global warming in ninety days, Buck?"

"We're not afraid of a little work," he said by way of encouragement. Her strokes per minute were down twenty percent. "And solving problems isn't really work anyway. What you are doing now is work. Building levees is work. Making beds is work. All we have to do is a little cognitive synthesis."

"Sounds like work to me," she said, finally breaking through the link with her blade. "Where do we start?"

Buck stretched his arms apart, savoring the delicious feeling of freedom. He felt that he could do anything now. Handcuffs, he realized, did more than immobilize your hands. They confined your spirit. They collapsed your sphere of self. No one could ever be an enemy of freedom—only an enemy of someone else's freedom.

"Well, we start by breaking the problem down into manageable parts," he said, filing smooth the sharp edges of Petal's dangly, half-handcuff chains. "Our problem has two parts. The first part is to figure out how to fix global warming. The second part is to actually fix it." He paused to see if she was still with him.

"Fair enough," she said, admiring her bracelets. Their audacity emboldened her. She loved their message of authority subverted, freedom reclaimed, and technology defied. Soon everyone would be trading their gumdrop-colored wrist aphorisms for locked rings of tempered steel; as hard as one's will, as permanent as one's resolve. This would signal society's coming of age. Adolescents can wear plastic. Adults will wear iron. Iron conceived in a machine but conquered by a human hand.

"But aren't we back to the question of whom to believe?" she asked. "A lot of very educated people have devoted their lives to solving this problem. Some of them passionately believe that they have the answer. And why wouldn't they be passionate about their answer, after spending all that time working on it? If I had spent my life working on Orgone boxes, I guess I would get pretty passionate about them, too. How are we going to decide who is right? How can we get an unbiased opinion?"

Buck chafed at his cuffs. He hated jewelry. He couldn't imagine wearing a statement made simple enough for broadcast from his body. The only thing he wanted to display in public was his anonymity. Being ignored was nice. Invisibility would be delicious. He tried to push the bondage bangles under his shirt sleeves, but his arms were too big.

"Tough to get an unbiased opinion out of a stakeholder," he said. "And tough to find expertise in someone who has no stake. Looks like we are about the most motivated impartial arbiters in this whole mess. If only we weren't so ignorant—about this one topic, that is.

"Let's look at it another way," he continued. "We seem to have plenty of experts who recognize that human survival is threatened by global warming. What we need is an expert whose own personal survival is threatened by the *solution* to global warming. That would be the guy with an impartial assessment. Find out what he fears most and, *voilà*, the best solution. Makes sense to me."

"People's fears are never rational, Buck," she said. "I think it's part of the definition. Otherwise people would happily take their cholesterol medicine but never get in a car. And what kind of experts are you talking about anyway? Air conditioner repairmen, hurricane lamp salesmen, disaster guys?"

"How about those oil and coal barons? The guys at the Carbon Life banquet. Kelvin. Clinker. Flare. They have a big stake in squelching alternative energy. I'm sure they've poured millions into figuring out which alternative is the greatest threat to them. Getting at their secrets might be tricky, but you know these guys, right Petal?"

"Not intimately enough for that," she started, "but there was this guy, once, a long time ago—" she stopped, eyes down, voice low, cheeks now red again.

Unlike some women, Petal would never talk about a past guy with a present guy. In her business, one came to understand the physics of relationships—time's arrow had good reason to be scared straight ahead. The present was messy enough with all of its undetected simultaneities and its unhealthy relationship with the future. Anyone who would purposefully complicate it with noncontextual bomblets from the past, with their preposterous pretense of immutability, must be suffering from an astonishing sense of boredom and a masochistic thirst for catastrophe.

"A guy?" asked Buck, struggling for a tone of voice that would allow her to continue. Rational but not uncaring. Realistic but not unromantic. Adult but not jaded. Guys knew that attractive women like Petal had likely not just turned attractive the minute before they walked in the door. They also knew, intellectually, that this attraction had summoned other men before them, using a call that, while more selective than bulk mail, was not exactly as choosy as a registered letter, either. And the fact that few had been chosen out of the many called was of little comfort to the guy who, zits and all, had to compete with memories whose complexions had become totally unblemished by the Clearasil of time.

"Yeah, kind of a guy," she said tentatively. "We were young. I was finishing at the *Institut Villa Pierrefeu* in the Alps. He was studying at the School of Banking in Zurich. The nights were darker then, the stars as sharp as points. It was a foolish and heady time.

"We spilled champagne from private cellars in the back of his limousine, racing sunrise to the chalet, motorcades of bodyguards struggling to keep us in sight. We skied off-piste with picnics to places only the Special Forces commandos could follow. And we gambled away fortunes at the Casino Monte Carlo, laughing at the indignation of the adults, so quick to judge those who couldn't care less.

"It didn't matter that a future between us was impossible. In fact, a possible future would have likely made the time we shared impossible. As adolescents, we saw our scandalous behavior as a sign of our courage and independence, but, of course, it was just a sign that we were being indulged. And soon enough, we were expected to grow up and put our relationship aside with other childish pastimes. We were brave that day we had to say goodbye. There were no tears. But we have never dared to correspond again, even after all these years."

"Why couldn't you have stayed together?" said Buck, trying to be a man rather than a guy.

"Race. Class. Family. Religion and the volumes of prohibitions it accumulates. Geo-political balance. War. Peace. The inexorable flow of history. And then there was that other little thing."

"What other little thing?" asked Buck, knowing that whatever gargantuan force of nature you could name, including the momenta of galaxies or the accumulated dark energy of the universe, it would pale in magnitude to anything a woman might refer to as 'other little.'

"You'll see," she said, standing up in the dim and empty courtroom. "Here's the plan. First we hightail it back to New York. We stop at Brioni for a couple of suits and then pick up our passports and some facial hair. The Publisher shouldn't have any problem with the visas. Flights permitting, we'll be in country in forty hours and have our answer in forty-eight. And then we can move on to phase two."

"Excellent," said Buck, in full agreement with her direction and enthusiasm. "And if you need any help with the details, I'm good at that sort of thing. Like remembering his name, for example."

"Don't be silly. Everyone in the world knows his name. At school we called him Hookah, but officially he is now Sultan Ali bin Said Andun, absolute ruler of the biggest oil producing country in the world, the Royal Arab Kingdom of Yomamah."

CHAPTER 20

ALI

No one else in the plane had kept their coats and hats on the entire flight from JFK to King Abdullah bin Gitn 'Ini International Airport. But then, people expected to see a rich variety of diverse local customs in this part of the world and were generally quite accepting of ethnic idiosyncrasies that didn't seem worth exterminating. The identically and impeccably dressed men (was it Kiton, Canali, Bottega Veneta?) had barely moved for eight hours except to accompany one another to the lavatory and to engage in mutual beard grooming rituals. Except for the fact that one of them was zero point seven five times the size of the other, they could have been twins. Probably diamond merchants deadheading home, given their handcuffs empty of valises.

But then again, mere diamond merchants would never have been whisked around customs by Arab men whose very presence could disable metal detectors and security doors. And not even foreign heads of state were usually hustled into convoys of monstrous Mercedes, ponderous with armor, their license plates as black as their windows, which sped directly south without regard to stoplights, sidewalks, or semi-permanent dwellings. Yes, thought the other passengers, these were no ordinary mortals we have flown with. They could only have been American rock stars.

In the back of the limo Petal was careful not to sit too close to Buck or to attempt any verbal communication. Even with her deepest stage voice she still sounded like a girl. Buck would have to do all the talking, but since he wasn't the one with the rusty bedroom Arabic (or even an approximate idea of what they were up to) she had to give him instructions every step of the way, transmitted from a microphone hidden in her beard to a receiver stuck in his ear. As a cover for her muttering, Petal constantly rocked back and forth, one hand rubbing the other, in a perfect rendition of a holy man meditating on his prayer beads or a slacker dude groovin' on his iPod.

Traveling by car gives one a far more intimate feel for a country than, say, flying over it at thirty thousand feet—and by camel, more intimate yet. However, as many a couple has discovered by the cold, gray light of dawn, more intimate is not necessarily more better. After an hour of watching the horizon sit unbroken and motionless out every window of the speeding car, Buck and Petal were ready to stipulate that the world was indeed flat and the sun indeed eternal just to get on with the proceedings. The tedium was occasionally relieved, sort of, by a series of checkpoints, each swarming with sun-stricken, khat-crazed teenagers, armed to the teeth with Uzis and to the feet with Nikes.

The security around Sheik Yobuti Palace became ever tighter during the last fifty miles of the journey. Razor wire, concertina wire, and barbed wire gave way to electrified wire and rusty wire with germs that could give you lockjaw if you weren't careful. Snarling dogs strained at their chains. Laser beams glowed red in the blowing sand. Landmines hunkered in their holes. Stern matrons x-rayed camel caravans for nail clippers. This was a country that was always on red alert. Petal had said that the national motto (*Utahk Inami?*) roughly translated into "Relax and Die." Buck sat on the edge of his seat. Petal prayed faster. Tensions mounted.

As the cars skidded to a stop, a platoon in traditional Yomamah regalia snapped to attention, lining either side of a gilded pathway to the Sultan's *Baahs Dihghs* (Most Expensive Publicly-Admitted Residence) extending their (largely) ceremonial swords to create a (hopefully) welcoming arbor for the arriving dignitaries, one of whom had to duck-walk under it to avoid decapitation. After a hike through a succession of ever more lush and sculpted courtyards, each guarded by a cadre of ever less ceremonial and ever more edgy militiamen, Buck and Petal were delivered, unchaperoned, into a rather unpretentious living room of marble and gold the size of a basketball court. There they stood, nodding together in silent prayer.

"So you and the Sultan parted on good terms," Buck reiterated, by way of reassurance.

"Maybe I exaggerated that part a teeny bit," Petal admitted. "I had a little problem with impulse control back then. But everybody has some childish behavior in their past that they would rather forget."

"I'm sure he has forgotten," said Buck. "Upper class types tend to be quite forgiving."

"Not this one," said Petal. "He always said that compassion made him look fat. In this part of the world, holding grudges is how people stay in touch. That's why they invented arithmetic, to keep track of grievances."

"No doubt he's mellowed over the years," said Buck, trying to ignore the overwhelming evidence to the contrary conspicuously displayed around him. "Dedicated his life to contemplation and asceticism."

Petal's opportunity to snort at this suggestion was cut short by the deep rumble of a huge brass gong across the expanse of opulence in front of them. There, lit by strategic spots, stood the imposing figure of Sultan Ali bin Said Andun, Supreme Potentate of the Holy Arab Kingdom of Yomamah and All of Its Future Conquered Territories, Commander in Chief of All Armies, Navies, Militias, and Everybody Else With a Gun or Something Sharp, And Lord Chief Baron of the Exchequer In Charge of Every Last Nickel. The Sultan cut an imposing figure. Ramrod posture, decisive jaw, powerful physique, exquisite mascara.

"Petal-pie, is that really you?" sang the Sultan as he swept across the parlor, yards of diaphanous chiffon billowing behind him. "You are so naughty to have kept all that luscious gossip all to yourself, year after year, when you know how I just live for gossip! I may just have to paddle your little bottom! But how could I when you are such a dear to dress up for me just like old times! This is your best beard yet! You are so stern looking with it trimmed like that. Sort of Sadistic Hassidic or is it Amish with a twist? You won't punish me too strictly will you Mr. Petal, sir? I just couldn't take it if you made me do the doggy thing again, I would blush my little cheeks off!

"And speaking of cute cheeks, who's the hunk under the other beard, Arnold Schwartswhatever, Prince of California? I don't suppose he's a housewarming present? Not! Oh, don't mind us, Mr. Planck—we get to have a little fun, don't we? It's Buck, isn't it? Very sexy but kind of short. No, no not that! I mean your name, silly. Needs a few more bins in it, don't you think. Bin Buck bin Planck at least. Why don't you sleep on it?

"Sleep on it! Oh what a fabulous idea! We'll have a slumber party just like at the chalet! And watch Judy movies! I still have them in Betamax if you want to be really retro, but you've got to see them in HD on the plasma. We can make popcorn! Actually, they won't let me make popcorn any more—the price of Sultanhood—but we can get someone else to make it, tons of it if we want.

"But listen to me, gushing on and on with no manners whatsoever. Come! Sit! Take your coats off. Take your shoes off. Take everything off! One good thing about being Sultan, they expect you to be nuts. Wouldn't want to disappoint them.

"You must be famished. I know I am! My new diet is the pits! I mean that literally. It's pits and more pits and pits all the way down. Date pit pâté, olive pit puree, avocado pit chops, prune pit power pudding. Super sadistic but worth it. I lost five pounds in the first four hours. But not tonight. Tonight we party. How about Chinese? We've got great Chinese in Yomamah. Of course there's Middle Eastern, but it's just so-so here. Go to Berlin if you want good Middle Eastern, take it from me. So it's Chinese? Okay I'll order."

The Sultan emoted into his cell phone as he ushered Buck and Petal into a smaller but still enormous living area decorated as if it were a New York penthouse waiting for the Architectural Digest photographer to arrive. Petal stopped short at the threshold and gasped.

"Oh, Petal, I know you must think me the little bitch for so shamelessly copying your décor. But that spread about your place in *Preen and Plunder* a couple of years ago just made me emerald with envy. Please don't be mad, darling—I could never upstage you. No photographers allowed in here, and how was I to know that you would ever show up, anyway? Sincerest form of flattery, too, right?"

Petal drifted slowly around the room as if in a dream. Items that had been visible to the camera in the magazine article were perfectly reproduced; those outside of its field of view were faithful extrapolated in taste if not in scale. No apartment in Manhattan could ever be this big, but still she felt as if she were back in her own cozy place. Even the view of Central Park was perfect, with muggers and joggers chasing one another fifty floors below.

"Hookie, it's wonderful. You are such a sweetheart to appreciate my taste. How could I ever be cross with you?" She curled up on the couch and blew him a kiss through her whiskers.

Buck had never seen Petal's apartment or any magazine article about Petal's apartment or any apartment belonging to anybody like Petal or any magazine about apartments at all. That such magazines might actually exist came as no great surprise to him, though. He was, after all, a man of the world. He had witnessed his share of bizarre and macabre human behavior in the seamier Oriental ports of call. He had even once come across a publication with nothing but photographs of emaciated young men who obviously had been abducted and sedated for days, denied access to combs or razors, and then forced to wear suit jackets two sizes too small, all to satisfy the voyeuristic lusts of nubile Italian girls in huge sunglasses lurking in the foreground.

However, in his most disturbing of nightmares, he had never imagined that anyone, no matter how rich, would, on purpose, choose to live in an environment in which every architectural detail, every utilitarian object, and every decorative flourish would bear the fetal feline visage of a hot-pink Hello Kitty. Hello's unnerving lidless stare followed him everywhere. Her mouthless cheeks, already stuffed with some unspeakable horror, seemed ready to pack in countless more innocent bodies. Spikes extruded from the flesh of her face, but she did not flinch, she did not grimace. And most bone chilling of all was the way she proudly displayed, stapled to her left ear, the bleeding thyroid gland of her last victim, freshly ripped from its throat.

"Do you think that it's too much?" she asked the Sultan.

"Definitely!" he assured her. "With a wide margin. Have you seen anything in the literature that comes even close to being as too much as your apartment, and now, by reflection, mine? Of course, week after week we must witness the pathetic failures of all the spineless decorators with their limp attempts at too much. Did you see how they snubbed Lars von Sewit's Fifth Avenue penthouse done entirely in frozen meat? Low concept poorly executed if you ask me. And not even very comfortable with everyone in parkas blowing on their hands all evening. And what about Nora Lumen's disaster with her *Loft Without Light*? I mean, why didn't she just use beanbags instead of glass and save herself all the liability? No, Petal. You've got nothing to worry about. Your place is way beyond too much and will hold that distinction as long as there are people with taste."

Buck nodded in agreement, squinting his eyes against the merciless wavelength of hot pink that could not have been part of any natural electromagnetic spectrum. Just as there are noises (made only by transistors) that take a hacksaw to your cochleas, there are colors (made only by former war-criminal chemists) that penetrate directly into your retinas (without regard to your eyelids) and bomb them with graffiti. The Petal/Hookie Palaces were created entirely of one such color. Walls, floors, ceilings and everything in between.

This is a color that was intended to be used as an accent hue in books for infants who are too young to express disgust. There are laws against it being sold in cans larger than a pint, and even then it has to carry a black box warning. Special protocols are in place in the event of industrial spills. And yet, here it was surrounding them like the walls of a furnace, blistering their skin.

"You really like it, Buck?" she asked, snuggling next to him.

"Well, oomp," he started, his answer cut short by the mouthpiece of one of the Sultan's eponymous hookahs being jammed between his lips.

"Pull hard, Buck," said the Sultan. "It's a long hose. These things have been around for three thousand years and still haven't been perfected. What's that tell you about the stuff in the bowl, then? Must ruin your brain. One day we'll quit. But not tonight! Tonight we celebrate! Here's the food, eat up!"

"Aw, Hookie, you shouldn't have!" giggled Petal through a cloud of smoke. The Sultan's cooks had delivered the Chinese in traditional cardboard boxes with the little wire handles. White cardboard, thank God.

And in the hours that followed, as well as can be determined given limitations of short-term memory, various crucial events transpired. Judy skipped down the yellow brick road on a hot pink plasma that had descended from the ceiling. Buck allowed himself a microbrew or two flown in from Hood River. The Sultan blew smoke all around. Petal made everybody do that embarrassing doggie thing. Somehow all the beards came off. They snuck into the kitchen and made popcorn while the cook snoozed in the corner. The Sultan tried to teach Buck belly dancing. Petal almost wet her pants. Everybody collapsed on a bottomless pile of fuzzy pink pillows.

"So, out with it," said the Sultan, passing them cups of coffee as black and thick as oil. "No more pretending you guys schlepped all the way to Yomamah just to party with Sultan Ali. Not that there is anyone else in the world even half as fun, of course. So what can I do for you? Need a couple million for a down payment on something? Letters of reference? Shoe box of hashish? Camel gossip?"

"Hookie, you are such a dear to be so wise and generous," said Petal, "It's true that we do have an ulterior motive for our visit. I wish it were as simple as just borrowing some money, but I'm afraid that we're here to ask a much bigger favor of you. And we will understand if you don't feel comfortable with it, we really will. But if you can find it in your heart to help us, we will be eternally grateful. It will mean more to us than you could ever know."

"We wouldn't ask this if we weren't in a real jam," added Buck. "But we don't want to put you on the spot or anything."

"Right," said Petal. "We don't want you to feel obligated, just because of our relationship and how important this is to Buck and me. We want you to grant us this favor only if you can guarantee that there is no chance whatsoever that sometime in the future you might think back upon it with regret."

"But we want to make it clear," said Buck, "that we mean no offense by implying that there might be a limit your generosity. It's just that we would hate to be presumptuous about it, for fear of causing offense."

"Exactly," said Petal. "We want you to grant us this favor understanding that we will be eternally grateful for your great sacrifice, yet at the same time we will avoid worrying about resentment by pretending that you have made no sacrifice at all."

"Right," said Buck. "The last thing we want to appear to have on our minds is exploiting friendship for personal gain."

"So, Hookie, how about it?" she said, sitting up to look him in the eye.

Which would have been easier if he hadn't been so profoundly and blissfully asleep. A sleep that was so contagious that within minutes it had sent Buck and Petal to dream worlds only slightly less bizarre than the one they had just left.

CHAPTER 21

CONSCIENCE

"So you came all this way because you were worried that I was worried?" said the Sultan, peering suspiciously at some unidentifiable pit product on his plate. At first, only awkward silence answered him. Awkward, conflicted silence.

A gauzy, artificial breeze rustled counterfeit leaves in the quaint but totally bogus arboretum where they were having breakfast. Soothing calls of phony birds lilted a cheerful insincerity in the distance. A brilliant, completely unconvincing sunrise filled the ersatz eastern sky. Buck and Petal were lulled by the peacefulness and calm of this fraudulent setting and reassured in an unauthentic kind of way. And so, even though their heads were hung over, their hearts were buoyed up by the kind of hope and optimism shared by airline passengers who catch their stewardess praying. It was that kind of ambiguous morning, the kind that inevitably follows an evening of euphoric certainty.

"Right," Petal jumped in, seeing that Buck was about to answer. Buck was one of those guys who could be a real liability when you are trying to get the truth spinning fast enough to slide past someone's bullshit detector. "Worry is a terrible thing. It eats at you day and night. Sleep evades you. Your libido droops. Your Botox crumbles. You age in dog years. And then—"

"Oh Petal, how did you know?" said Ali putting down his fork. "I thought I was putting up such a brave front that no one could tell—day after day soldiering on, doing my best to uphold the royal standards of ruthless obstinance and conspicuous consumption for the sake of the people of Yomamah, and yet having lost all enjoyment in beheadings and jihads and other inherently pleasurable duties of state.

"But somehow you could tell, my dear Petal-pudding, even across all the miles and years. This really proves that you are my last true friend. I should actually say 'friends' because I can tell that you, too, Buck, are a man true of heart and that through Petal we have become bonded as brothers."

Sultan Ali was beaming now, basking in the unconditional support of his loved ones, finally able to let down his protective shell of chiffon and reveal his most intimate vulnerabilities. Here, at last, were people he could trust, people who accepted him for himself, people without subversive or selfish agendas.

"You can talk to us, Hookie," said Petal. "That's what friends are for."

Buck was squirming in his seat now, in spite of rather than because of the extraordinary pressure Petal's heel was exerting on his big toe. She was trying to communicate something to him, this he could tell. Something important and subtle about pain and secrecy and grappling with inner turmoil in silence.

Buck was no stranger to pain. His occupation was largely a series of contests between human endurance and the overwhelming malevolence of environmental catastrophe. His body bore the scars of those battles, each with its own throbbing back story replayed with every fall of the barometer. And after every devastating world event, as all the disaster guys were packing up their muddy kits to go home, Buck would shake their hands in turn, knowing that even though there may have been disagreements among them, there had never been dishonesty. And though competition among men appeared to be inevitable, there had never been a man who had worked to make Buck fail, who had betrayed him for personal gain.

Buck and Petal had come to Yomamah on a mission that was crucial to the future of the planet, not just to their own immediate, personal futures. The situation was desperate. The goal was worthy. Desperate measures were called for. This was not the time for polite squeamishness. Sleeves would have to be rolled up. Collateral damage expected. Consciences bruised.

But even though he had willingly worn a disguise, Buck hadn't felt he was misrepresenting himself until now. They had come here to find out how to stop global warming. That meant finding the right alternative to fossil fuels and putting the oil grave robbers out of business. Buck could live with that. But now they were seducing a friend into opening his heart so that they might plunge their daggers straight through it. Buck hadn't wanted it to be this way.

124

He hadn't had any other idea about how it might play out exactly, but this felt all wrong.

But disaster guys must be realistic in their utilitarian calculations. They cannot allow themselves to favor the individual victim whose pleading eyes lock on theirs out of the thousands of others whose faces they cannot see. Triage is too cold a word for such a heartbreaking duty. But then, one must gather all of one's coldness to get it done. Buck squirmed, but he did not speak. A familiar wave of guilt washed over him.

"Where do I start?" asked the Sultan. "Life was good back when we were in school, Petal, not a care in the world. Sure, there was always the odd war or assassination that could sneak up on you, but I never gave them a moment's thought, even after the throne was passed to me.

"At first, being an oil sheik was the greatest job in the world. We were Emperors of the Universe. The future was all ours. Everybody in the world loved oil and we had more oil than anybody. Looking back on it, we should have just been good businessmen and let it play out, quietly buying up the planet with our profits a little bit at a time. Eventually we could have had it all. But, no, we had to let emotion and religion and politics and all that mushy stuff sneak in to bugger the whole thing up.

"What happened was that somewhere along the way one of our geologists got guts enough to point out that the earth wasn't actually making oil anymore. And once we really looked, the amount we had under our feet didn't seem all that huge after all, especially once it dawned on us that just about every kid in China and India would rather be cruising their 'hood in a Lexus than digging in the dirt with a stick. And every time we looked, there were about a jillion more of them, freshly flush with American bucks and looking around for a gas station.

"Initially, you'd think that nothing could make a bunch of sheiks happier. But upon further reflection, it made us kind of nervous. I mean, it was pretty clear that almost nobody in Kennebunkport and Sioux Falls really liked us, and once our oil was gone we would be just another bunch of wogs, good for nothing but Polish jokes. Something like that can really hurt your feelings, especially if you were born sensitive to begin with.

"And that's not even counting how the West was always acting like they owned the Middle East already, drawing straight lines on maps all over the place, setting up countries for people they felt guilty about, replacing one nasty situation with another, and generally bombing the doo doo out of everybody. All this and they don't even believe in Allah! Can you blame a sheik for getting a little crazy? So, somebody came up with The Plan. I can't say exactly which of us it was, but I went along with it so I'm as guilty as anyone."

"Guilt is as bad as worry," opined Petal, grinding on Buck's toe some more. "It wrenches your gut. It grays your hair. It perforates your spirit. Your ventricles wither—"

"The plan was devilishly simple," continued Ali. "First we set up OPEC, the club for oil-pumping countries. The story was that OPEC would use its monopoly to keep the price of oil high, thereby maximizing our profits. Everybody in the West believed this little ruse, because it is exactly what their businessmen do whenever they think they can get away with it. And every now and then OPEC would cut production a smidgen just to keep up the pretense. Nobody suspected a thing.

"But the cheap oil just kept flowing away, just like there was no tomorrow. And year after year, the OPEC countries reported that they had plenty left to pump. In fact, every year they reported that their reserves had miraculously grown bigger! The more they pumped, the more that seemed to be left! Praise Allah! If only it had been true. If only someone in the West hadn't been so drunk on cheap gas that they could have seen what was really going on. But no one wanted to see. They all wanted to believe that OPEC had centuries of oil left, even though it had taken less than a century for the West to pump all of its own wells dry."

"I still don't see—" started Petal.

"We were playing you, Petal. Classic East versus West. Kung Fu versus bare knuckles. Scimitar versus broad sword. Finesse versus brute strength. Century after century. We always win. And does the West ever learn? No. And why not, you ask? Because it would be against their religion to learn. And I'm not talking about the religion of the Crusaders now. I'm talking about the modern West's real religion.

"Let's face it, not counting your own fundamentalist fringe (who are too obsessed with not having sex to think about the fate of the world) the only true religion in the West is the Church of Market-Techno. And just about everyone in the West is a true

126

believer, as deeply convinced of his religion as any pilgrim in Mecca.

"According to this faith, the God of the Market is omniscient. He can see every need, large and small, present and future. And His partner, the God of Techno, can fill any need, just in time, when stroked the right way by the Market. It is all automatic, taken care of. The faithful needn't worry. They don't need to think, to plan, to anticipate. When the oil starts running out, then supply will fall, the price will rise and a Techno-Priest-Corporation will come up with an alternative source of energy, just in time. No need to speculate how they will do it. By then the technology would just have come along, just like it always has.

"The West never saw much advantage in understanding our religion, but we sheiks were not so arrogant—we intensely studied yours. We learned the catechisms of Market-Techno. We dissected its circular reasoning, and saw where all the gaps in logic had been filled with magical leaps of faith. And we knew our plan was safe when we saw how the Church dealt with its heretics, quickly dispatching the orthodoxy enforcers, talk-show inquisitors, and legitimacy assassins to silence anyone who would suggest the possibility of another world view. It was fine to preach religious tolerance, as long as the only religion to be tolerated was the Church of Market-Techno.

"Yes, it was obvious that our plan would succeed. We would get together for high-five sessions just to gloat and talk about how it was going to be, once The Plan came to its final conclusion. I was as giddy as the rest of them, at least at the start.

"But I hadn't anticipated the guilt that I would feel. When something is just an idea you can forgive yourself for thinking it. When it becomes a plan for some remote future action, you can put off taking responsibility for it, you can pretend to yourself that something irrevocable hasn't really been set in motion. But when the day of reckoning bears down upon you with a momentum that you couldn't resist if you tried, then there is no hiding from yourself. You must live with the reality of your cruelty and your vengefulness." The Sultan's eyes glistened in the artificial sunshine.

"But, Hookie, I still don't understand," said Petal, holding his hand. "If OPEC wasn't set up to keep the oil prices high, then it must have been set up—"

"Right. To keep the price low. Ridiculously low. So low that no Market-Techno country would ever develop an alternative to oil. They would just keep sending their armies all over the world on trumped up crusades against evil dictators who were supposed to have all of these pretend oil reserves sitting under their palaces, all the while burning it up ever faster with their war machines.

"Until the day of the Big Surprise. The day that OPEC would announce that it was just kidding about all those oil reserves. The day that all the wells go dry. We have it orchestrated to the minute. This time, the end of the world will be televised. All the sheiks in our finest sheik-duds shrugging for the cameras. 'Bomb us if you want,' we'll say. 'Look for yourselves,' we'll say. This time we'll be telling the truth. There will be no more oil. And the West and its wannabes in Asia will dissolve into chaos.

"All their talk about oil shale, Orinoko sludge, Canadian tar sand, coal gasification, and the Arctic Wildlife Refuge will remain just talk. The Techno-Market won't have time to invent ways to make use of them. It can't get going without its cappuccinos. And when there is rioting in the streets and people freezing in their homes, Western society will grind to a halt and cappuccinos will be no more.

"You know what your governments will do. What they have always done. Declare war on the guys they think have what they want. But nobody will have energy. They won't find one percent of what they need to keep their civilizations going, no matter how stealthy their bombers, how smart their bombs, and how bombastic their leaders.

"All your dabbling in wind and nuclear and corn and coal that your science-fair dilettantes have done won't be worth diddly squat when your cars are stuck in the driveway and the lights go off for the last time and all your food rots in the field.

"But we in the desert will be just fine. We did fine before anybody even knew about oil, and we'll do fine again. We've got all the money, remember, and we've been preparing for this day for a long time. And after what's left of the West and Asia settles back into the Stone Age, we will praise Allah for being on our side, like everyone should have known all along.

"I thought that I would welcome that day when it arrived, but as it grows close I find myself filled with nothing but anguish and dread. I know it is too late to do anything about it now, but it feels better just to get this load of guilt off my chest."

Buck stared at him. The question had been begged.

"When?" he finally asked.

"Christmas Day," said the Sultan. "It seemed appropriate at the time."

The saccharine breeze was chilling them now, in spite of the artificial sun. Or maybe it was the truth, coming out in the open for the first time, its reality so cold that it threatened to freeze them all.

CHAPTER 22

YASSER

Buck and Petal watched their friend dab his eyes with a napkin.

"You would let all those innocent people die? Millions, probably billions of them, all over the world?" asked Petal.

"It does sound kind of mean, doesn't it?" admitted Ali. "But remember, you folks started it. I think."

"Even still," insisted Petal.

"Please don't be mad, Petal, I feel bad enough already," he said, sniffling.

"You don't feel half as bad as you are going to once I'm done with you," said Petal, grabbing him by the ear. "Now quit whimpering and let's get to work fixing this mess. We've got ninety days. That includes an hour for you to tell us how and ninety days minus an hour to get it done. So spit it out, Hookie, or it's the doggie thing with a real—"

"There's no way to fix it!" he whined, flapping his hands to make her stop. "On Christmas Day the last barrel will be pumped out of the ground. You can't change that, Petal. Then you've got until maybe New Years before the pipelines and tankers and emergency reserves are all used up. Then you better be here with me, 'cause that's when all Hell freezes over and the mighty sword of Allah—"

"Will you stop with that phony piety?" she said, twisting harder. "I don't preach Zoroastrianism at you, do I? Do I skip work on Antonio Banderas's birthday? Do I wear my mask to class?"

"That's Zorroism," he said. "And don't make fun of religion. We're very sensitive about that."

"Well, get over it, Hookie, because you and your spoiled sultan buddies have just about violated every commandment of every Creator that anybody every heard of and then some.

Sensitive! I'll show you sensitive!" she torqued his other ear a good one.

"Okay, you two," said Buck. "There's no time for that. Let's get busy. We need to replace the world's energy supply in three months, or at least the oil part. So, Ali, you sultans must have studied this. What alternative to oil is the most feasible, the one you were most worried about? That's what we came to find out in the first place."

"You came to find out the best replacement for oil?" Ali said, searching their faces, back and forth. "You came to find out which of my competitors to side with? You came to put me out of business, throw me out on the street with no shoes? You pretended to be worried about my emotional health so that you could ruin me? How could you be so heartless, so sneaky, so cruel, so—"

"You should talk!" said Petal, her indignation a little more sheepish. "We were never going to murder all of your people!"

"As good as! Have you ever spent a summer here without air conditioning? Talk about murder!"

"Enough!" said Buck, taking out a stack of three by fives. "We'll decide who gets to be angrier later. First we have to solve this energy problem. So which is it Ali? Nuclear? Wind? Biomass?"

"What difference does it make?" said Ali. "It's too late now. Even if you found a limitless source of free energy you couldn't convert all the oil-burning engines in the world to something else in time. If you had ten years, maybe. But not three months.

"Look, you know when hydrogen fuel cells were invented? 1839! You've had all those years to get them going, and how many hydrogen cars do you see on the street? Zip! And your so-called hybrids? They won't go five miles an hour without the gas engine kicking in. Not to mention your electric cars, hauling a ton of batteries around that take all night to charge. How many of these do you see? Nada. And don't forget, pretty much all of their energy comes from fossil fuel that runs the power plants anyway. Let's face it; you're doomed when the oil runs out."

"We're doomed," said Petal, reminding him of the price of absolution by reaching for his ear.

"Yeah, okay. We're doomed," granted Ali. Somehow his confession hadn't made him feel less guilty. And he couldn't really blame Buck and Petal for wanting to save the world. It was a fantasy that had peeked out of his own subconscious from time to time, he was embarrassed to admit.

Thoughts like that would get you laughed right out of the Sultan Club. One had to guard against them. Keeping a clear focus on one's short-term self-interest was the best way to ward off such troublesome do-gooder delusions. You always got in trouble if your mind wandered too far from the bottom line. You learned that on Day One in Business 101. And not much else on Day 1+n in Business n.

"So if there is no more oil to dig up and we've got to have oil, at least for a while, then why don't we just make oil," reasoned Petal, her forty-weight coffee kicking in. "They can make every other damn thing you can think of. Hell, you can go to the mall and find a hundred kinds of pantyhose, and go back the next month and all of them are different! Who needs a hundred kinds of pantyhose a month? Who needs pantyhose at all? Who makes all this stuff? I bet they could make oil. And we haven't even started talking about lipstick. Don't get me started on lipstick! That's practically oil already. And what's oil made out of anyway? It's a hydrocarbon, right? What's that?"

"Well, it's got your hydrogen for one and your carbon for two," said Ali, counting on his fingers. "And then there's—" He looked up for help.

"I think that's about it," prompted Buck.

"What about the acid rain and smog and greenhouse whatevers. Oil's got to have those in there, too, doesn't it?" said Ali. Like every good CEO, he knew not to micromanage his enterprise. Most technical details were best left to competent specialists who could be counted on to stand there holding the bag. But sometimes plausible deniability requires an almost implausible degree of ignorance. Even Ali had trouble believing how little he really knew about anything. Except about money, of course.

"Nope. Just hydrogen and carbon. Strung together in chains. And not all that carefully, either. Oil is a messy gemish of molecules of different length and structure. Very crude stuff. High school kid could make it," said Buck.

"So is there some kind of shortage of hydrogen and carbon?" asked Petal. "All of it is worn out by now, right?"

"Hardly," said Buck. "Water is mostly hydrogen, and we have plenty of that. And the atmosphere is full of carbon, that's where we dumped it when we burned up all the oil."

"So tell me again why everybody is killing each other over this stuff? What makes it so great?" said Petal, knowing that Buck was bound to have one of his glib comebacks that would make the whole thing sound so-o obvious.

"Carbon would rather bind to oxygen, as in carbon dioxide or carbon monoxide. It takes a lot of energy to break them apart. That's what plants do, use sun energy to take the oxygen off of CO_2 and put hydrogen on instead. Then they have hydrocarbons, or carbohydrates to you."

"Carbs! I am so sick of hearing about carbs! You're telling me that all this is just about carbs?" Petal smelled a trick.

"So hydrocarbons are great at storing energy. All you have to do is mix them with a little oxygen—which we still have plenty of—and you get all your energy back, which you can use to either run your car or pad your butt. Your choice." Buck did not seem to be kidding about this.

"So if plants are so good at this, let them do it," she said, not wanting to dwell too long on padded butts.

"Too slow," said Buck. "Oil is the product of millions of years of stored sunlight, and we burnt it all in a hundred. The math is easy. If all the land in the world was covered in plants, the amount of sun energy captured wouldn't come close to satisfying even current human demand. That's why biodiesel is ultimately futile, not counting how badly people trash the environment producing it."

"Okay then, let your high school kids make it, Mr. Smartypants. We've got plenty of high school kids. What do they need to get started? Beakers? Hoses? Designer sneakers?" Petal was anxious to wrap this up.

"Energy, Petal," said Buck. "They need an absolutely huge source of energy. Preferably one that doesn't poison us all. Which leads us back to what brought us to Yomamah in the first place.

"So, Ali, let me ask you again. OPEC has hundreds of very smart scientists on payroll and a whole lot more smart businessmen. They had to know that they would have been ruined by a clean alternative to oil. I'll bet you and your buddies have it pinned down exactly and have been sabotaging its development for years. So now it's time to clear your conscience and become the hero of the world. Come clean, Ali. Where can we get the energy we need?"

Ali squared his shoulders and straightened his keffiyeh. His friends were right. It was time to do the right thing for his fellow man. It was time to be a man. It was time to save the world. And, who knows, maybe this was what Allah had been after all along.

"Buck and Petal, my dear friends," he started. "The time for deception is over. From now on there will be no secrets among us. I will tell you—"

"Shut up, Ali bin Said!" boomed a voice. They looked up to see armed men stepping out from behind every tree, dozens of them. Their leader, a huge Arab in jet black robes, jet black beard, and impossibly black sunglasses, strode to the table and towered over them.

"Yasser Ibahb!" cried Ali in alarm. "How did you get in here?"

"You forgot your key at my place, you little bitch. And you think you can dump me just like that for some blond pool boy? After all those things you said, too, and not even a note. I'm so mortified; I can't even show myself at the gym. You know how it makes me crazy when you look at other guys. I'm warning you, I'm not accountable for my actions when you get me this way. You don't have a Valium, do you?"

"No, I don't have a Valium. And it's over between us, Yasser. I can't take your smothering jealousy another minute. I've got to be me. And the new me is done with you and all of you other nut-case sultans who think that you can just murder half the people in the world anytime you want over some imagined slight from back before the Middle Ages—"

"Silence!" boomed Ibahb, crashing his meaty but carefully manicured fist right through the fake Louis XVI breakfast table. "I knew that you were just an oil-digging tramp all along. I wouldn't take you back now if you begged. Which you will, along with the rest of the pitiful scum of the earth who will pay the ultimate price for pissing me off. And I assure you that it will be more than half of the world, much more.

"You see, as delightful as it will be to watch the infidels claw at each other over their last remaining cans of gas, it would be horrible to think that the end of oil might somehow slow down the global warming disaster that they most richly deserve. So my real friends and I here have put together a little insurance policy of our own. One that we will make sure you take responsibility for."

"Yasser, you are seriously mental," said Ali. "You and your friends couldn't put together a birthday party. My mother warned me never to get mixed up with—"

"Enough!" he boomed some more, kicking the legs out from under Ali's reproduction Louis XVII loveseat and spilling him on the floor. "Tonight we fly to Greenland with every American nuclear device in the Middle East, stolen, it will seem, by Sultan Ali bin Said Andun. There, strategically placed, they will blow the entire Greenland Ice Sheet into the sea.

"Now, experts argue about how much this will raise worldwide sea levels. Some say seven meters. Some say twenty-three feet. Whatever. But what they all agree on is that this much fresh water in that part of the North Atlantic will immediately shut down the Thermohaline circulation."

"That's a magazine?" whispered Petal.

"That's the Gulf Stream," whispered Buck.

"That's bad, right?" whispered Petal.

"Only for living things," whispered Buck, "above the level of plankton. Actually, plankton probably wouldn't do so well, either. At least in the short term. After a few million years—"

"Quiet!" said Ibahb. "And on websites all over the world there will be pictures of you three despicable suicide bombers smiling at the cameras as you commit the most heinous act of eco-terrorism since—since—since—"

"Since what?" asked Petal.

"Since when?" asked Ali.

Yasser couldn't answer this one. Generally, he hated not having an answer to a question. This time it just made him smile.

CHAPTER 23

THERMOHALINE

"You'll never get away with this, Yasser," said Ali, straining against the straps that bound him to the cargo plane's bulkhead. "By the time we get there, Greenland will be crawling with American military."

Ibahb, now completely intoxicated by his own villainy, threw back his head and roared a nefarious laugh. "Fools! Everywhere fools! Why must I always match wits with morons? Why is there never a worthy opponent for my evil genius? At the end of my life I will have but one complaint for our Creator, that it was all too easy! Bwaah ha ha!"

"Is he always like this?" whispered Petal to Ali. As a matter of policy she avoided criticizing the romantic choices of others, especially in light of the embarrassing procession of bozos that marched back through her intimate history. "What were you thinking?"

"He's a total wuss. Afraid of the dark. Can't sleep without his blanket," answered Ali over the deafening roar of the engines. "Don't worry, he's just overtired. I'll get him calmed down. He'll be whimpering for his daddy in no time."

"The Americans don't know their nukes are going to Greenland!" bellowed Ibahb with delight. "They think that you've got them holed up in your palace. And if it weren't for the fact that they think that you are still sitting on a bottomless well of oil, they would have dropped the big one on it already. As it is, they've got Yomamah surrounded, its borders bristling with American firepower, the entire United State's military behemoth mobilized to that line in the sand, at least that part of the military not otherwise occupied in Iraq, Afghanistan, Korea, Pakistan, Manila, Lebanon, Indonesia, Myanmar, Columbia, Angola, Monte Carlo, New Caledonia, Decatur, Las Vegas—"

"They won't wait for long," insisted Ali. "Americans are very impatient. They'll call me up, get the answering machine, and then roll right in."

"We've got that covered. Right now they are on hold for the next Nuclear Hostage Customer Service Representative in Bangalore. These call center people are professionals. They can keep you chasing your tail forever. But we don't need forever. All we need is ninety days."

"What? Ninety days again!" said Petal. "Doesn't anybody do anything now any more? I swear, when I was a kid if I had said to my mother, 'Okay, I'll get that laundry done in the next ninety days,' why she would—"

Buck struggled in his straight jacket to get an elbow free for her ribs. "Will you please shut up?" hissed Ali.

"Timing is everything in the terror business," said Yasser. "We don't want to ruin the surprise of The Plan. Just to see the look on all those faces when the oil runs out will be worth the wait. And it will take about that long to get the nukes set up. You see, this is a very delicate piece of pyrotechnics. We don't want to just vaporize a lot of ice. We want to sweep it all off the south end of the land mass into the ocean." He drew an elongated Greenlandish blob on a crate with a marker and then a series of four parallel east-to-west lines through the country at even intervals of latitude.

"So we plant a series of explosives along each of these lines, buried deep in the ice. The northernmost ones go off first, and then at just the right time the next ones to the south detonate and then each line down in sequence. It will be like hosing the dirt off your driveway. This is the biggest piece of ice outside of Antarctica, three times the size of Texas and up to two miles thick. And all of it will end up all at once in the North Atlantic. Bwaah ha ha!" He high fived himself and did a little James Brown on one foot out of sheer exuberance.

"So who cares if you put ice in the ocean, you big doo-doo head!" sputtered Petal, now uncontainable. "It's too cold to swim there already, and while some people may have a weird thing about plankton, frankly, I don't give a damn. And if the Gulf Stream goes down then everybody will just go to one of the other streams, if they even give a damn about streams, which I certainly don't. In fact, for all I care you can shut them all down. I can't think of the last time I needed a stream for anything. You might not have noticed, but in America we are way beyond streams now. We have laundromats. Not like in your dismal country where you have to squat with a rock—"

"Blah, blah, blah," Yasser said, walking off with his fingers in his ears.

"Tell her again, Buck," groaned Ali. Actually, he wanted to know, too, but didn't want to let on.

"There is really only one ocean, Petal," started Buck, finding it hard to talk without waving his hands. Buck was one of those guys who thought that by drawing unidentifiable figures in the air he was somehow helping his audience to understand, when, in fact, he was just helping them imagine being caught in a propeller.

"All of the world's salt water is connected. And even though it looks like a washing machine a lot of the time, it is more like a river, with a defined and predictable circulation, a circulation that all of its inhabitants have come to depend on. In fact, I should say that because of its influence on the climate, all of the world's inhabitants are dependent on the ocean's stability as well.

"What we call the Gulf Stream is really part of a worldwide conveyor system that moves massive amounts of heat energy around the globe. Water absorbs just about all of the energy there is in sunlight; very little is reflected back out into space. So, near the equator the surface of the ocean is quite warm—you can swim in it all day and not feel chilled. But as you dive deeper, the water gets cold, real cold. In fact, if you go deep enough anywhere in the ocean the water temperature is just about freezing.

"This is because the warm layers on top don't mix much with the cold bottom layers. Water may flow horizontally at the surface or down deep, but water hardly ever circulates up and down, except in certain places. Water expands a lot when it is heated. It takes up more room and gets less dense. In other words, it gets lighter. This lighter, warm water floats like a thin skin on the cold, denser water below.

"With help from the wind, the warm surface water of the Caribbean flows north along the coast of North America and across the North Atlantic toward Europe, all the while evaporating and dumping heat into the air as it goes. The mild climate in Europe depends on all this heat being delivered from the tropics, without it London would be as cold as Moscow and Moscow colder yet.

"So as the ocean loses water from evaporation it gets saltier and as it loses heat it gets colder and denser. This salty, cold water is now heavier, and at a certain spot off the southwest tip of Greenland it starts to sink. This sinking becomes a gargantuan waterfall, sucking unimaginable amounts of ocean water from the surface to the great depths—more water than is contained in all of the rivers of the world. The enormous mass of this water plunging downward pushes the cold water on the bottom southward, where it flows as a monstrous river, with forks that go past Africa, around Antarctica and on into the Pacific and others that return to South America.

"And just like a river, the ocean's health depends on its movement. If it stagnates, it will putrefy and die. Everything in the ocean depends on this steady flow of nutrients and energy.

"But the circulation is fragile. It has stopped before in the geologic past, and took hundreds of thousands of years to get going again. And the most certain way to stop it is at its most vulnerable spot, right off the coast of Greenland where billions of tons of water are falling like countless Niagaras, driving the world's water like a pump. All you have to do is add enough fresh water to change the saltiness of the ocean water right there just a little, enough to make it less dense, light enough to float. Then the whole engine stops. The world's circulation shuts down. The planet has a cardiac arrest. It goes into shock."

"And the ice on Greenland? That's enough to stop the circulation?" asked Petal.

"A hundred times over, I'm afraid," he said. "Even if Yasser is only one percent as evil as he thinks he is then his plan will do us in."

"Right after *your* plan does us in," said Petal, pointedly in Ali's direction.

"Don't look at me," protested the Sultan. "I'm as tied up as you are."

"You can still bat your eyelashes," said Petal. "Or something."

"At this point, we might need a better plan than that," said Buck.

Unfortunately, though, at that point, no one could even come up with a worse one.

CHAPTER 24

SIVERTH

When one refers to the history of Greenland, it is conventionally understood that the topic at hand is actually the history of human beings in Greenland, which, like the history of human beings everywhere else, is cloaked in mystery and shrouded in bunk. It is also understood that one is referring to the history of the human beings who traveled to Greenland from the east (whom everyone called "Europeans," except for them) and not the history of the human beings who traveled there from the west (who called themselves "Non-Europeans" because they liked the sound of it and had apparently never gotten around to naming themselves before.) These diverse cultures brought with them their own deep traditions of bunk that, melded together, have produced the detailed historic record of hokum and baloney that we inherit today.

For example, in every dim-lit, low-ceilinged mead warren in Qasigiannguit, one could expect to be treated, over and over, to the colorful fable of Eric the Red being run out of Iceland in 982 for being not only a rogue and rapscallion but an incorrigible blackguard as well. Since every other country inhabited by Europeans had left him with a vague sense of ennui and the assurance that he would be summarily hanged, Eric and his frisky band of rascals decided to "settle" in a land that had no Europeans in it at all.

The only spot like this readily available turned out to be a nearly continent-sized island with so much ice on it that its center had actually sunk a thousand feet below sea level from the weight. A hundred years before, a fellow Norseman named Gunnbjörn Ulfsson had considered vacationing there and concluded that hanging would be preferable. In those days the place was called Kalaallit Nunaat, which is Norse for "Even Colder than Where You Live Now." Legend has it that Eric changed the name to

Greenland just to be cute and, with luck, attract some Nordic girls on their way to California.

While stories like this are almost universally bogus, people are desperate to have something in their lives that is certain and unchanging, and they foolishly turn to the past for such an anchor. But nothing, of course, is as fickle as the unverifiable past, and, as it turns out, nothing about the past makes it particularly amenable to verification. So, consider how adrift one can become when after a lifetime of repeating such legends, evidence emerges that it was really Eric In The Red who, from his teak-paneled office in Oslo, had done nothing so romantic or adventurous as package a typical pump-and-dump, sub-prime real estate swindle for The Gables on The Fjord, which, had the temperature ever gotten above thirty two, would have found itself a mile and a half under water.

It was this kind of blue-funk pall that had fallen upon the Greenland Semi-Autonomous Self-Governing Overseas Administrative Division of the Nominally-Christian Kingdom of Denmark, from Qaqortoq to Qaanaaq and every frigid habitation in between. The national sense of bravado had been deflated. Grizzled Greenlanders moped over their mead in brooding silence instead of regaling each other with nostalgic tales of murder, rape, and pillage from the turn of the century. (Not that century, the other century.) It was the feeling you might get in Ulaanbaatar at the Mongol Hoard Bar and Grill after it became known that Genghis Khan had actually been an actuary. The man in the street was in a sad state. His past had been cut from beneath his feet. He had nothing now in his life except for his present and his future.

Both of which kind of sucked. You see, life in Greenland had always depended critically on things being the way they were. For hundreds of generations Greenlanders had just barely hung on through sheer grit and an encyclopedic knowledge of the way things were. Actually, taken literally, the word 'encyclopedic' here is much too wimpy. 'Library of Congress' would be more like it.

When you are trying to feed your family and the blizzard looks like it will go on for another six weeks and the sun isn't due for at least that long and the only thing to eat is polar bear and you know that the polar bear is thinking the same thing about you and all you've got is a sharp stick, then you had better have a few things down pat. Like how things are, for starters. How things have been, how things are, and how things will be. These things, at least, you gotta know. Otherwise you might as well sit in your tent and read your encyclopedia until you starve.

But things in Greenland were definitely not the way they were. They were not the way anybody had ever known them to be. They were not the way anybody had ever imagined they could be. They were as if the Earth itself had turned against men, against seals, against bears. It was as if the Earth was striking back at life itself.

When you are sitting in your Manhattan apartment in February, reading a *Times* piece about how temperatures are slightly warmer in some unbearably cold place that you wouldn't ever dream of visiting, you are expected to turn to your significant other and say, "I'll take those five degrees Celsius any day," as if you could tell a Celsius from a BTU. But how your urban attitude would change if, as you nodded to the doorman on the way to the metro, the sidewalk suddenly collapsed in shards beneath your weight, plunging you into a black and airless sea of sub-freezing brine that swept you tumbling beneath the brownstones above. And how you might think again if, after calling down for some Chinese, you find that the price of delivery is to starve for two weeks and then have to rip the heart out of a ravenous monster ten times your size who is clawing at your door, a monster who might not have been all that hungry if things had just stayed the way they had been.

No such imaginary demonstrations were necessary for any of the patrons of the Nose Kiss Tavern underneath Mamarut's Propane and Lunch in downtown Kangerlussuaq. It's not that these individuals knew everything. They may not know, for example, exactly why their almost impossible lives had suddenly become even more dangerous and uncertain. They might not even be able to predict what treacherous traps their beloved arctic world would set for them in the future. And they certainly couldn't explain the sudden disappearance of their past. But they did know one thing for certain. They knew their connection had been lost.

Without connection, your spirit dries to dust. And without your spirit, fear replaces love. Courage becomes unreachable and faith a fragile pretense. Hope recedes into the distance, ever dimmer until your memory of it is finally black.

Except if you are Siverth Narup. In all of his twenty seven years, Siverth had never had a bad day. He had heard of them, of course, but really couldn't imagine what one would be like. For a while, he was worried that he was missing out on something, and resolved with determination to have at least one before he died. He would set out on ill-advised crusades, poorly prepared, courting frustration and defeat. And yet, faced with each unanticipated adversity, he would find only exhilaration, and with each reversal of fortune, only marvel. Finally he accepted his limitation and vowed to make the best of it. Someday, he believed (as you would expect), this defect would prove to be a gift, summoned into service by the higher power of circumstance.

And that day happened to be this day. The air in the Nose Kiss was thick with tobacco and resignation. Shadows of half-empty mead horns flickered in the light of a re-run Bulgarian soccer match, the Romanian commentary mercifully silenced on the black and white that clung to the wall behind its wire cage, a device required to protect Greenland bar TVs from the nearly continuous incoming barrage of herring and glass. Patrons sat sweating beneath their anoraks, dripping snow onto the wooden planks and tears into their drinks. Voices were scarce. There wasn't even joy enough for a fight.

Until the arrival of Siverth Narup and his orbiting cloud of ebullience and commotion. Siverth was the kind of guy who knows that it is only out of politeness that everyone doesn't cheer when he walks into a room. This never stopped him from cheering back, of course, giving special attention to people who seem to be hiding their heads out of shyness. He was one of those guys who knows that you secretly appreciate his leaving the door open, that you really weren't having a conversation when he arrived talking, that you can't wait to sign on for the misadventure of a lifetime. The kind of guy you want to strangle before he saves you. One of those one-of-a-kind kind of guys. Siverth Narup.

"I'm telling you Ole," he started, sitting down across from Ole Enoksen, one of Siverth's staunchest supporters, "you and I are going to be heroes this time, so get ready for flashbulbs and champagne and ticker tape and state dinners and girl reporters with microphones and—"

"I'm not supposed to be talking to you," said Ole, making as if to leave. "That's what the judge said. Ninety days. And then after that only 'in the presence of someone with the good sense that God gave them.' Those were his exact words. So if you will excuse me, I have some staying out of jail to do." Ole drained his glass and stood, pulling on his nasaq.

"You can't take this legalistic jargon too literally, Ole. It's obvious that he was speaking ironically. Or metaphorically. Or figuratively. Whatever. And you can't order someone not to talk can you? It's in the Constitution. We have a constitution, don't we? I know it's in somebody's constitution. And where are we going to find this hypothetical guy with good sense? In the Nose Kiss? Come on! Anyway, I'm sure he didn't really mean it. I can tell when he's serious. I've been before him lots of times."

Siverth pushed his inniikkilaq up on his forehead. Rarely was he seen without his traditional slit snow-goggles. His detractors accused him of affectation, but it was only in the dimmest places that he didn't need them. Siverth's pupils were always huge. A side effect of over-optimism, his doctor had said. As a result, no detail escaped Siverth Narup's notice. Even details that, in retrospect, might have been part of some other dimension.

"He sounded pretty literal to me," said Ole, sitting back down and waving for another drink. Ole was a good boy, but he was no match for peer pressure. "But nobody here will tell on us, I guess."

"Of course they won't. The Nose Kiss is the last bastion of Greenlandic manhood, the very font of the Inuit spirit, the stronghold of our national will!" he waved his arm to include every one of the disheveled morning-drinkers scattered around the dismal, windowless den. No one cheered. The only acknowledgment was a half-eaten herring launched their way from deep in the shadows.

"Here's the deal," said Siverth, leaning close now, "we're going to make a movie!" He spread his hands and grinned, as if the rest was obvious.

"A heroic movie," said Ole, relaxing a bit. He had been afraid that, like most of Siverth Narup's art, this one would involve municipal structures and oceans of paint or agricultural-waste storage facilities and home-made explosives, or diplomatic ceremonies and multi-species nudity, or regulatory agencies and—

"The most heroic of movies," Siverth expanded. "A documentary that will show the world what is happening to the arctic, what is happening to our people and to our way of life. A documentary about us, Ole! Imagine. In Hi Def on the big screen. You and I mushing and shoeing and paddling from Kangerlussuaq to the pole, fighting our way through a landscape ravaged by global climate disaster, suffering shoulder to shoulder with our brothers hanging tenuously to life itself, and finally exposing the villainy that is the cause of this entire catastrophe."

Ole knew that there would be villains involved. Siverth's art invariably conformed to certain thematic constraints. There was always the egregious social outrage to be righted (the Issue). There was the evil guilty party hiding in plain sight (the Villain). There was the unexpected materialization of some grand-scale offense against human sensibility (the Work). And then there were the arrests (the Sacrifice). Of course this was only the visual half of the performance piece. After that would come the mobilization of public opinion, the recruitment of legal defense teams, the release of media circus clowns, the stoking of editorial bombast masters, the incitement of human rights watchdogs, the massive street demonstrations (coincident with the unexplained arrival of massive quantities of free mead), the declaration of martial law, the sacking of scapegoated petty officials, and, finally, the dismissal of the case just to restore public order (the Triumph of Truth).

This kind of art doesn't come cheap. But part of Siverth's magic was to make it all levitate with no visible means of support. But there was support, plenty of it. With completion of each successive "Socio-Orgasmic Deconstruction," Siverth would find himself the recipient of staggering sums of grant money from the growing collection of curators in his thrall. This would be augmented by the fees and commissions and honoraria and endorsements from tours that would invariably follow his release on bail. Museums from Nagasaki to Nantucket clamored for Narup installations and personal narrations of the video records of each successive work.

Which was where Ole came in. He was the guy with the camera. "Retino-collaborator" as Siverth would put it. "Cameraman" was good enough for Ole. The pay was the same, and the last thing Ole wanted to be was a high-profile wunderkind in the world of over-the-edge art. Unlike Siverth, who always spent every krone he had on his projects, Ole lived frugally, satisfied with his modest apartment above Gedion's Day Old Shrimp and his quiet Nose Kiss social circle. Ole thought he probably was rich. No matter. Whatever he had he ended up lending to Siverth anyway.

"Are you sure it's just a movie?" asked Ole, suspicious. "No incitements to riot? No sedition? No violation of United Nations' resolutions?" After all, all of Siverth's works ultimately involved making a "movie" of the contrived social catastrophe.

"The most heroic movie of all time! Here we will document the innocent and peace-loving indigenous people of Greenland, who have been pushed to the limit of survival by the wanton devastation of their homeland by a cowardly and insidious enemy, finally striking back and reclaiming what is theirs, restoring nature to its balance, and thus, saving the world from environmental collapse." This was turning out to be something only Siverth could call a movie.

"These indigenous people being you and me, I suppose," asked Ole.

"There are fifty thousand more who will join us once they hear about it. Right now I have nine hundred sworn to secrecy. The internet is a wonderful thing, Ole. No one is too far north anymore."

Siverth didn't have to say it. Your average guy on the sled loved Siverth Narup. He was a celebrity, a national institution. There would be no shortage of volunteers, no matter how crazy the idea.

"And you are going to orchestrate some massive public action that solves global warming? I don't get it. We're all going to kayak to Washington?" Ole asked.

"Do you know what ice cores are, Ole?" said Siverth, opening up a map.

"Of course I do, but what does—"

"Then I'll tell you," continued Siverth. "In places of permanent cold like Greenland and Antarctica, the snow piles up from season to season without melting. Bits of air get trapped between the snowflakes, and as the weight from above compresses the snow into ice, the air is sealed inside as little bubbles, each a precious record of the atmosphere as is was at that year. And so, year after year these little frozen samples of another time stack up, like rings of a tree, waiting to be read. We have ice that is two miles thick here, Ole. You can get a sample of air from a hundred thousand years ago, and every year in between. Imagine!"

"Yes, but what—"

"And you know what they show? Carbon dioxide levels in the atmosphere varying between ice ages and warm periods, back and forth, with the levels around 200 parts per million when it's cold and 280 when it's hot. But never higher than that until now. Starting a couple hundred years ago the concentration starts to rise abruptly, shooting upward, to 300, 340, and in 2009 up to 380 parts of CO_2 per million. Soon it will be 500. The last time it was that high was a hundred and fifty million years ago. Everything about the earth was different then. There is not one species of life living then that is the same now."

"I didn't—"

"And you know where that extra carbon came from? Plant stuff that had been trapped underground that people dug up and burned. It's that simple. You know, Ole, it takes a lot of time for a carbon atom to get trapped underground. If you follow one around you'll see it reincarnated over and over as either plant stuff or animal stuff or CO_2. Carbon dioxide gets gobbled up by plants to make carbohydrate plant stuff which gets eaten by other critters to make dinner. Dinner gives you energy to get on with your life but turns the carbon right back into CO_2 gas.

"But after countless recyclings, an exceedingly rare event can occur—a critter doesn't finish its dinner! A bit of plant stuff gets stuck deep in the ocean floor or underground somewhere. Somewhere where even bacteria can't get at it. And if you know bacteria, you know how unlikely a place that must be. You would have to follow that carbon atom for a hundred and fifty thousand years before it got stuck where life couldn't get at it. It is amazing that it even happens at all.

"But the world has been around a long time. So long that it makes a hundred and fifty thousand years seem like no time at all. Life, after all, has been around for some three and half billion years. Back at the start, the atmosphere was almost all CO_2. It was plant life that pulled all that carbon out of the air, and it was the extremely rare piece of plant that got hidden underground that kept it from going right back into the air after somebody's dinner."

"Well then, why wasn't all the carbon in the atmosphere eventually trapped underground? Why was there any left at all by the time humans came along? What's a hundred and fifty thousand into three billion, anyway?" Ole tried the math on a napkin, but it was too wet.

"Volcanoes, Ole! You see, as the tectonic plates of the earth's crust get swept around by the heat underneath, the edge of one may get forced under the other where they crash together, pulling all the sediment with all that trapped plant carbon down to where it is hot enough to melt rock. Water is turned to steam and carbohydrate into CO_2 in an explosion that sends it all back into the atmosphere to start the carbon cycle of birth and rebirth again. The carbon atom that you had followed for a hundred and fifty thousand years before it got trapped in the sediment is now back in action, but it had to wait hundreds of millions of years to be released.

"And get this. The rate that this geologic process returns carbon to the air from the Earth's crust matches the rate that plants get trapped in the crust so closely that never has there been a time when life, even higher forms of life, became impossible because of too much or too little CO_2.

"Isn't it beautiful? Imagine, living organisms with life spans in days being intimately connected with continents moving at a pace measured in millions of years. And imagine the entire atmosphere of the planet, created by living things, in turn as sculptor of the continents and the oceans. And all of it, each part depending on the other, in this delicate balancing act, this ballet on the high wire, wavering a little, but never falling, never giving up.

"Sure, there have been good times and bad. There were ice ages so cold that oceans froze at the equator. And there were times so hot that there were ferns at the poles. But never did the Earth betray life. And never did life betray the Earth."

"Until now," finished Ole.

"Until now," nodded Siverth. "Man, first in his ignorance and now in his arrogance, has assumed the power of the volcano. For two hundred years he has been pulling the carbon out of where it is trapped and burning it for fuel, releasing it millions of years before its time, dumping twenty times the normal amount of CO_2 per year into a delicate system. A system that has never dealt with such an influx since the beginning of time. A system that will respond initially by heating up, but eventually in a way that will bring it crashing down."

Siverth swallowed deeply from his canteen. He only drank water he had melted from snow. He knew better, but it had become a thing for him. If the snows of Greenland were to kill him, then, he figured, it would be his time to go.

"And, Ole, not to be too racist about this, but these men who have done this unforgivable, self-destructive thing—who are doing it now, even though they know the consequences—none of them are arctic people. And why is that? Is it that we arctic people don't need heat up here? Is it because we are too stupid to drive a SUV? Because we don't like trinkets from the mall?"

"Well, I don't know. Actually, there's nothing in a mall that I would—" started Ole.

"I'll tell you why! It's because we arctic people have something that no other band of humans have. Why us and not them? I couldn't tell you. But it is a fact that is as undeniable and inescapable as anything you know for sure. It is what makes us special, Ole, and it is what gives us such a great responsibility, what makes it imperative that we act, together, and now."

"And that is?" asked Ole.

"We are connected to it, Ole. Our souls, our spirits, our bodies are fused to it. It is one with us. The turning of the Earth, the sun, the air, all of it has seeped through our histories for so long that we have senses others do not. We can hear it weeping. Our eyes tear when we see the sadness in its face. And we wander hopelessly in its discouragement. The Earth must be looking to us now, Ole. We are its only hope. We of the north have stood apart from men for all this time. Now we must be the ones who decide what Man is to do. It is our time, my friend. We must not fail."

Ole and Siverth sat in silence, marking the impact of this moment. Two men had made an unspoken pact. Art and life had merged again. The trajectory of history would change today.

"Which brings us back to the ice cores," said Siverth, getting down to details. He spread a map of Greenland out on the table. There was a score of circles drawn on it. From Ole's perspective most seemed to line up along four, evenly spaced lines of latitude. "This is big business now. Scientists from all over the world have come here to drill into our ice—look at them all—and these are just the ones that started this month! These are important people, valuable to their countries, sitting in their tents on the ice sheet, without so much as a bow and arrow."

"You are suggesting—?" asked Ole.

"The other countries of the world have bankrupted our planet. We will hold their scientists for the ransom they owe to the Earth. No harm will come to anyone if it is paid. All they need to do is what is in their own self-interest anyway. Stop carbon pollution now."

"And if they don't? If they laugh at us? Then what will we do?" Ole asked.

Siverth was quiet. They both knew this was the most probable outcome.

"The whole world will be watching. We will appeal to the people of the Earth," he said.

"And if they don't care?" asked Ole.

"Then they will watch as we join our captives, turn off the heat, and freeze."

And with that he drained his canteen and set it down. He was not smiling now. He was serious. Dead serious.

CHAPTER 25

NUCULAR

There is almost no one who doesn't work for the Speedo Corporation who will contend that the world is a prettier place because of its efforts. This is not to say that its products are inherently unaesthetic, or that exceptional examples of human physique were better appreciated in the beachwear of 1900. It's just that, overall, on the average, in general, exceptions aside, putting a regular guy into a Speedo does not exactly contribute to the beautification of the planet.

Now, of course, there will be those who will argue that one's visceral reaction to viewing one's vicar in a Speedo is a product of lifelong mass indoctrination by a perverse and pervasive corporate fashion industry, whose androgynous puppeteers have worked their media harpoons so deeply into our limbic systems that they can jerk us into ever more massive consumption of useless tokens of self-aggrandizement through increasingly grotesque manipulations of our mental image of the normal human form.

But even if we grant that this is the case, and throw in for good measure the corollary assertion that we are all beautiful in our own way, it does not automatically follow that our experience of life would be more sublime if the plumber showed up in a Speedo.

(Editor's note: Legal counsel has advised that the reader be reminded here that in works of fiction, the term "Speedo" is understood to refer to a sheer, thong garment worn with the intent of displaying the maximum amount of paunch, flab, body hair, and cellulite available. This imaginary construct is not to be confused with the elegant and high quality items of apparel marketed by the actual Speedo©®™ Corporation, which are hand-crafted by meticulous professionals, chained to their sewing machines in Sri Lanka in lieu of kindergarten.)

Aesthetics aside, however, the Speedo does have its functional value. Through laborious water-tunnel experiments, Speedo scientists have systematically reduced the hydrodynamic drag of their competitive swimwear (or now, because of its technical sophistication, more appropriately termed *swimware*), allowing crucial milliseconds to be shaved off of the elapsed time between the pop of the starting gun and the slurp of Uncle Bernie's first Mai Tai at the Tiki pool bar. But, ironically, for Buck and Petal and Ali, the intended utility of their Speedos was not to speed them up, but rather to slow them down.

Yasser Ibahb, seemingly stuck for good in his increasingly tedious, B-movie-villain persona, had calculated correctly that Speedos of nylon were stronger than chains of steel for prisoners on the Greenland ice sheet. So strong, in fact, that he had judged the posting of guards an unjustifiable personnel expense, especially given the anticipated overtime, workers comp, profit sharing, and 403b considerations. So it was with complete confidence that Yasser closed the lockless door to the prefab ice-coring hut and scurried, breath steaming, to his waiting helicopter, leaving his prisoners hundreds of miles from any name on the map, bound by their Speedos to the small halo of warmth emanating from a courageous but under-engineered Soviet-era space heater.

Yet, despite the desperate situation and humiliating couture, spirits were high and conversation brisk within the little cabin. The group had adopted this unnatural collective affect through tacit agreement when it appeared that the only alternative was to rip each other's throats out. Maintaining such an attitude required a certain amount of determination, especially for Buck, who had long harbored suspicions about colleagues whose euphoria seemed to increase with the ambient level of danger and physical discomfort. One could never be sure that they weren't purposefully maneuvering the group's collective ass into a crack just for another bracing round of competitive faux joviality. You shouldn't turn your back on people like that, but you might learn a few skills from them, just the same.

Nonetheless, because of Buck's underlying bedrock of optimism and aversion to dying, he had no trouble operating within these artificial constraints of equanimity. Petal, never one to be outdone, had picked up the challenge right away. Ali, always sensitive to accusations of being a weenie, had risen to the occasion. There was to be no whining in this hut until such time as there was nothing left to whine about.

"I think if we fashioned a reflective cone and suspended it, point down, over the heater, it would even things out better," said Buck. Suggestions were allowed, as long they were concrete, theoretically achievable, and didn't involve detonating the nuclear device that hunkered in the crate next to them.

Petal, embarrassed to admit her previous youthful indiscretions with tanning booths, understood the concept immediately. Their current technique of continuous rotation to keep their far sides from freezing while their near sides were thawing was flawed by the anatomic limitations of spinal curvature. While facing the heater it was possible to bend toward it in an arc, keeping most of your near surface equidistant from the sputtering heat source. But when your back was toward the heat, you had to stand up, moving your shoulders into the far reaches of space, where the tiny ember of energy was as dim as the sun as seen from Pluto.

Ali, who had been experimenting with a complex series of Hatha Yoga postures involving alternating headstands with Indignant Mambas, was currently less interested in the problem of thermal management than in the problem of taking a leak. The existing protocol involved a preliminary group hug to get the on-deck whizzer maximally warm, slipping into the single pair of Styrofoam clogs that had been nervously carved out of the atomic weapon's little nest, and running outside in your Speedo to do your business, all the while hugging your sides and screaming your bloody head off.

"I'm sure that one of these crates has an indoor toilet," said Ali, peering at their Cyrillic stenciling for clues. "Ice core teams drill for years before they get to the good stuff. You can bet they aren't running outside freezing their hooters off all the time."

The hut was indeed meant to appear to be just another ice core drilling site of one international scientific team or another. Except that in this hut, as in the other twenty that Yasser Ibahb had hastily commissioned, the drilling would be done to make a deposit rather than a withdrawal from the repository of history. Yasser's mad-scientist-in-chief, Husain Abd al-Yelo Qaake, had implied that, due to this particular hut's geographic position, drilling here might not be absolutely necessary, and certainly not worth the sacrifice of dramatic effect when the ceiling camera transmitted the face of the Sultan of Yomamah, startled by the bomb's detonator whirring into its final minute countdown, the recorded drawl of a mid-western farm boy recruit subtly cracking as the final digits inevitably must be pronounced, "Three, Two, One—Detonation!"

Therefore, it was possible that no drilling team would ever return to this hut to bury the bomb and uncrate the toilet and finish up the decorating. It was possible that the three of them would live out their last three months around this heater, subsisting on Soviet surplus Soyuz Sunrise, each faded packet sporting the grinning, gap-toothed image of Khrushchev toasting a just-ignited missile with a glass of clotting protein powder. It was possible that they would tire of flipping the bird to the camera with each of their spit rotations. It was possible that they would give up hope before their water and propane gave out. Possible, maybe, but not without a fight.

Buck had not given up trying to free up a piece of metal that could be used to free up a bigger piece of metal that could be used to pry open crates. Yasser's men, however, had done an excellent job of clearing out any loose pieces of stuff more durable than a paper cup. Buck was down to digging at rivets with his nails until the cold would force him back to the huddle around the heater. But toilets really didn't interest him much. It was clothes and a radio he was after, or maybe the raw materials he could use to make either. Until then, they were stuck sipping their Soyuz Sunrises and sunning themselves in their Speedos.

"It seems to me that we could get some heat out of that atomic thing," said Petal, nodding at the ominous crate in the corner. The others, following their unspoken protocol, didn't snort but couldn't stop their eyebrows from jumping. "I mean, it's not really *that* big, and we could just turn it on low."

Sensing that Petal was just pulling their chains (not that hard to do in Speedos), Buck sought to deflect the topic. "Ali, your people must have studied nuclear power as an alternative to oil. You can tell us, now that it's too late to do anything. That was your biggest worry, right? Cheap, safe, pollution-free nuclear energy that would cut our dependence on foreign oil and eliminate production of CO_2?"

Ali looked at Buck and Petal with equal measures of disbelief. It was hard for him to tell which of them was stupider.

156

"You know, that's what I love about you Americans. You are so good-hearted that you can't believe that someone could look you in the eye and lie to you. Let's not use the word gullible. Will you accept naïve? Let's just say over-generous. And the ones you choose to believe? Let's say they suffer from political scotomata, or maybe financial astigmatism. We won't call them liars and cheats. That would be intemperate. Shrill, even. Couldn't have that. That would make us look impassioned. And in the public arena looking impassioned is worse than being a liar.

"So let's start with the easy ones. First, the little white lie about eliminating your dependence on foreign oil. Now listen closely. This is pretty complicated. Ready? Number A: Cars run on oil. Number B: Nuclear plants make electricity. Number C: You don't have any electric cars. Got that? Still with me? So where is your escape from oil? You could put a nuclear power plant in every kid's backyard and still be just as stuck on oil as you are right now.

"So what do they mean by this jingoistic appeal to good old American self-reliance, this contention that nuclear power is key to energy independence? What they mean is that they think that you are too stupid to tell gas from electricity when you are standing at the pump.

"And let's say that you did manage to convert all your cars from gas to electricity overnight. Great. That would get you off of oil, all right. But you don't need nuclear power to do that. There are lots of safer, cheaper, and less polluting ways to make electricity than nuclear power. And not more than a couple of percent of your electricity is made by burning oil, anyway.

"In other words, the link between nuclear power and getting free of us nasty sheiks may make great theater, but it is theater of the absurd. But you can't blame the atomic power industry's marketing department for their youthful enthusiasm, can you? They are not actually lying, are they? Just a little sleight of hand juggling of a couple of phony choices.

"And what about this tiny fib that nuclear power doesn't put carbon dioxide into the atmosphere? This must be true, they say it often enough. And it is true, but only in an imaginary world where uranium pellets are delivered from outer space and nuclear plants appear out of hats and, what's harder, disappear back into hats when they get old, along with all their deadly, terrorist-tempting trash.

"Your mistake was thinking that the people who told you this fib might be referring to the real world that we live in, where huge quantities of CO_2 are generated by the thousands of massive oil-burning machines needed to crush mountains to get at the uranium, to purify it, move it, store it, and clean up after it. Not to mention all the oil-burning machines needed to build these massive and complex nuclear plants and all the oil-burning resources needed to deal with the mess they make. Not to mention all of the oil-burning military protection needed to keep some lunatic (we aren't saying any names here) from running an airplane into an atomic power plant, which, last time I looked you had wisely built in out-of-the-way spots like suburban Chicago and New York City.

"I know you two aren't much into math, but I think you can get this concept. Go ahead and convert all your power to nuclear and what will happen to CO_2? It will get worse, and just as fast as if you had never done it. Probably faster.

"And by the way, if you are so worried about CO_2 you ought to be ten thousand times more worried about CFCs. These are the ozone layer busters that you thought had been phased out by the Montreal Protocol, the one's that used to power your deodorant and hair sprays. But, surprise! They're *baack*! One of the little perks you get in the nuclear industry club is being allowed to leak tons of this illegal stuff into the air every year. And your legacy is secure, because each molecule lasts a hundred years, and is ten thousand times worse than CO2 as a greenhouse gas. But eventually it will break down in the stratosphere, taking the protective ozone layer with it. But you don't go outside much nowadays, anyway. And there's always sunscreen.

"And that brings us to the slight exaggeration (an excusable little slip, an understandable product of your leaders' exuberance and unquenchable optimism) that nuclear power will provide, and I quote, 'limitless energy that will be too cheap to meter.' Kind of hard to pass up, isn't it? Think of the things you could have done with your life if it just hadn't been for that damn electric meter! You could have been spraying electricity around the house like champagne! Hoo-haaah!

"Except for one little wrinkle. One that should the end the whole discussion right now. Ready? Here it is: there isn't that much uranium. Not in the whole world. The earth isn't that big, you see. People have been all over it. They know where the uranium is. It's no secret how much uranium is underground. And if you converted electric power production over to nuclear, you know how long the uranium would last? We're talking about all the uranium we could possibly dig up. And all the radioactive crap we have sitting around already, weapons and everything. Go ahead and guess. Come on! A thousand years? A hundred years? Sorry. The answer is nine years. And that's just for current electricity needs. That doesn't even count the energy we use from oil and natural gas. Or any increase in demand. Or any increase in population. Take those into account and you don't have enough uranium to last a Presidential term of office.

"Which is about all the time a patriotic political contributor would need to nail down his share of the tens of billions in federal subsidies, tax credits, research grants, loan guarantees, incentives, and free insurance that your government is dying to lavish on him. Mind you, these are the same guys who would call you a socialist if you wanted money for health care. Free markets are too important, it seems, to waste on nuclear power.

"You will note that I haven't even mentioned the fact that there is almost nothing more poisonous to the planet than digging up uranium from underground—where it isn't bothering anybody—and concentrating it in one place. Your current nuclear reactors use up about fifty thousand tons of highly refined uranium fuel a year. To make all this you need to leave lying around five million tons of radioactive tailings and a billion gallons of radioactive liquid full of arsenic and other toxic metals. And that's before you start making the fuel into even more poisonous waste in the reactor, which in the process, by the way, makes the reactor itself into a huge pile of poisonous waste.

"This stuff is the real problem. Nuclear power plants are really just big plutonium factories. Very hot ones. Turns out you can boil water on hot things. Then you can make steam. Which you can use to turn wheels. Which you can use to turn a generator and make electricity. Nuclear power, after all, is just another way to boil water. An incredibly expensive, wasteful, polluting, and hazardous way to boil water. So you can boil water in a plutonium factory. So what? You could boil water in the ovens at Auschwitz, but that wouldn't change what they were or excuse the damage they did.

"And what is plutonium good for, now that you have gone to all this trouble to make it? One thing and one thing only. Killing life dead. And keeping it dead. For hundreds of thousands of years. Great stuff, eh? Worth spending billions for. It used to be that if you wanted to wipe out every living thing for a hundred millennia you would have to come back every year or so and scorch the place all over again. Now, thanks to the nuclear power industry, all you have to do is sprinkle a few of their droppings around and you're done for another quarter million years. What a time saver! But don't tell this to any nut cases out there. They might not use the information responsibly. Let's just keep plutonium our little secret. Mum's the word.

"But that would be kind of tough, though. Nuclear plants have already piled up fifty four thousand tons of highly radioactive trash that you will have to deal with for the next quarter of a million years. If your Nevada politicians sell out completely and allow them to dump it in Yucca Mountain (which is still the only place anyone is even thinking of putting it) the place will be full the day it opens. Then what are you going to do? Should have thought of that before you made the stuff, shouldn't you? And tell me again why you didn't? Oh, but I forgot. You are the folks who like to pay for wars on your kids' credit cards. Can't expect you to make plans for taking out the trash.

"And don't start with those fantasies about 'next generation' plants that burn their own waste, perpetual-motion style. The only worse nightmare-posing-as-wishful-thinking is the notion of using nuclear fusion for power. Even in the most power-drunk CEO's wildest imaginations, these plants will operate at the temperature of the sun while they generate, leak, and turn themselves into massive quantities of highly radioactive junk that can never be used for anything or ever gotten rid of. Assuming one ever gets built. Which, thankfully, no one has managed to do in the last sixty years of trying.

"Now, I can see you two are wondering why you should believe what I say about anything, me being just your average sheik on the street and all, especially since you are probably still mad about how we will be destroying your entire culture in the next few months. You are no doubt saying to yourselves, 'If nuclear power is so awful, why has our government dumped hundreds of billions of dollars into it and almost nothing into renewable, sustainable, non-polluting energy technologies that are within easy reach?'

"I'm glad you asked that, my friends. I'll tell you. It has to do with the momentum of money and the fallacy of sunk costs. Remember the Manhattan Project? Think of the magnitude of the effort! Tens of thousands of people from the government, industry and the military. Dozens of communities. Years of work. Millions of dollars. All to make three atomic bombs and end a war. Worth it? That's not the question. And one not worth asking now.

"But there was one question that should have been asked after the war. And that was, 'How should we meet our energy needs in the future?' Instead the question became, 'Now that we have spent a ton of dough on this nuclear thing, how do we recoup our investment in peacetime?' Or, more accurately, 'How do we keep the money flowing into this huge military-industrial machine that cost us so much to build?'

"And make no mistake, the connection between making electricity for your refrigerator and making a planet-ending nuclear war has been there ever since. The deciders always knew that the only place you could get plutonium was from nuclear power plants. They always knew that there was nothing to do with plutonium but wage war. So plutonium has proven poisonous even on paper. It has poisoned the decisions about how we made electricity for the last fifty years.

"And year after year we fooled ourselves with the same fallacy of sunk costs, throwing good money after bad, telling ourselves that to re-evaluate, to change course, to make use of new knowledge, would mean that all the money spent before must have been wasted, and that somebody, somewhere, along the line must have made a mistake. And there is no society in the world that elects men who admit error. Never has been.

"Never mind that it would have been cheaper and better for us in every way just to have stepped back from nuclear power, taken a hard look and walked away. We could have done this every year for the last four generations. We knew enough, even then. But we didn't, because since we had already spent so much money on it, we were condemned by our natures to keep on spending more.

"And, let's face it, would the generals have opted for windmills? Would the energy barons have petitioned for efficiency? Would the captains of industry have picked the planet over profit? Would politicians have given up their vote-buying subsidies?

"So, put yourselves in their place, the leaders of the free-market free-world. When faced with the task of fueling your economy's future, would you pose the challenge to the ingenious and resourceful American people, open it up to every entrepreneur and inventor, tap into the wellspring of creativity and cooperation that has made America the most successful and productive society on Earth? Or would you construct an exclusive funnel for the maximum flow of public dollars to a select few corporate cronies and protect them from competition by the power of law under the guise of national security?

"I know, it is a silly question. No decider could pass up such a juicy contribution-laundering, patronage scheme. How could you control something that was open to everybody, that drew strength from diversity, that was truly democratic? No, it is much better to preach open markets to the subsistence farmer in Costa Rica and protect your own power monopolies at home."

Ali looked at his friends' faces for a moment. Their eyes never left his. No one was shivering now. The little room seemed hotter, somehow.

"You tell me. Are you surprised at how wrong things get started from right things and then never can get stopped? It doesn't surprise me at all. In fact, it surprises me that there are as many people as there are who still are trying to fix them, as futile as it is. But they never do, do they? One foolish idealist after another spends his life telling everyone what is obvious and expecting their leaders to do the right thing, once everyone agrees how obvious it is. But they never do, do they? No, they never do. Makes you want to give up on right things altogether, doesn't it? Well, it does me.

"But maybe this is what you tell yourself, late at night, when you are the leader of a little country waiting to be squashed by the big one, once your usefulness is over. Maybe this is what you tell yourself once you have decided that the only hope for the world is to start over, to get a new history, and, with luck, get it right this time. Maybe this is how you live with yourself once you have done something that you can't take back. When you are responsible for something you are ashamed of.

"Maybe you are right to look at me that way. Maybe you shouldn't listen to me about anything any more. I don't know. You tell me."

162

CHAPTER 26

ICE

They were Ole's dogs when it came to the chores, but they had run so often with Siverth that they went just as berserk when he came to wrestle and were just as disciplined when he assumed command. Ole didn't mind sharing their affections with Siverth. The rule in Greenland is that if one dog gets petted, they all get petted; so, when you have a harem of twenty, two-timing canines can save you a lot of time.

Twelve were in harness now, with all the heavy tools of survival and cinematography packed tightly onto one sled. The dogs had never pulled a load this massive before, but, as expected, they relished the extra weight as an opportunity to test their strength and show off their determination. And determination was always the overwhelming emotion out on the ice. The determination of the men reinforced the determination of the dogs, whose determination inspired the men, as it had been on every mush through every snowfield since the beginning of the love affair between dog and man.

To an observer who had lost track of time, this team in the wilderness could easily have been mistaken for one arriving from the west five thousand years before, bearing news of the strait and sweets from Siberia. This was important to Siverth. Modernity had provided his pulpit of notoriety and had propagated his voice around the world. But it was also the enemy of his culture, which was the source of everything his voice had to say. Siverth never admitted this contradiction. He parsed his ambivalence in private, careful never to give it the power of words for fear it might turn some unwanted logical conclusion back against him.

In the wild, Siverth insisted on doing things the traditional way, but Ole contended that no ancestor of his would be stupid enough to make runners out of wood when there was plenty of good Teflon around. So they compromised. Teflon where it didn't show. Harnesses with lower tug line angles, as long as they looked archaic. Doggie vitamins, as long as they were kept in bear-scrotum pouches. High def cameras, as long as they were camouflaged in fur. Satellite phones, but only for survival, or for the operation. Operation Hot Ice.

It had taken three weeks on the sled to get to the places they had needed to visit in person, but without their electronic link it would have taken years to talk with all the members of the strike force. Some they had to sit with for hours. Others just needed a nod. Many had questions. None had arguments. All were in agreement. They were trained. They were determined. They were ready.

And today was the day. Twenty Inuit teams poised near twenty ice core drilling huts, harpoons ready, waiting for the signal. Waiting to take twenty handfuls of scientists prisoner (in the most polite and courteous way possible) and hold them as collateral against the changing of the world.

They had their scripts in their hands. They had done their Prisoner Sensitivity Training on line. They had copies of *Seal Soup for the Hostage's Soul* ready for the frightened ones. They had Canadian Valium for the nervous ones. They had handcuffs for the rowdy ones. But they didn't have guns. That was Siverth's rule.

They all also carried a copy of the video that would be transmitted to the world via *everybodylistentothisrightnow.com*. Ole and Siverth had filmed it in one take. There was nothing fancy about it, only Siverth looking straight at the camera and explaining to the people of the world that they and their governments had a choice. Save six billion anonymous people or let a hundred specific ones die. Live video feeds from each of the captured huts would allow each of the prisoners and their captors to tell their individual life's stories, to become as intimate with the world as any family member, to create a reality show with the future of the world at stake.

Siverth knew how easy it was for people to let countless numbers of their own species suffer and die as long as they were kept anonymous and out of sight. He knew how easy it was for people to allow themselves to be abused, as long as they were made to fear the unknown alternatives more. And he knew how fiercely they would fight for their own families and friends, how many resources they would mobilize to rescue one of their perceived circle, how consumed and compelled they could become about some immediate, concrete, and isolated situation. As long as there was right and wrong, life and death, and someone they cared about, then people would respond. That was the difference between people and governments, people and corporations, people and groups of people.

What he didn't know was whether the people of the world would choose to care this time. Whether they would be too busy caring about something else to spare their attention this time. Whether the world-saving video would arrive the day after a co-ed went missing in the Bahamas, or a baby down a well, or a miner in a cave-in. These things he couldn't know. But he was willing to gamble his life and the lives of his followers on them. This is what made people follow people like Siverth Narup. His ability to gamble their lives.

The dogs stopped as one at Siverth's command. They stood panting, sniffing for bear. None whimpered, they knew their breathing was loud enough for predators to hear. It was hard for them to be still. They didn't like to rest like humans did. They felt vulnerable standing there. Their masters' unspoken anxiety had made them nervous. They wouldn't be happy until they were running again.

Ole was filming from the sled, propping the telephoto on one knee. The air was dry, the wind low. It was easy to see the little hut plopped onto the ice way off in the distance, casting a long autumn shadow even at noon. There were no vehicles around, no signs of life. He needn't waste much battery power filming here. Except for the smoothly gliding shadows, the scene could remain the same for months.

"Take a look," he said to Siverth, supporting the long lens for him. This was it. The last hut was now in view. All it would take was Siverth's satellite phone signal and the other nineteen teams would move on their targets, and the history of the world would be changed forever. One way or another.

Mushing across the ice had always been Siverth's passion. He could fill his mind with the details of survival, the grandeur of the scene, and the telepathy of the dogs. Balance, breathing, exertion, movement. That's all there would be. No other conscious thought could ever intrude. None could ever have fit.

Art was conceived in times like these, when his attention was maximally occupied. Everything great that he had ever imagined had come to him when he was totally consumed in the elsewhere of sledding. The truth had never showed itself when he had stared right at it. It was as if he had to look away hard before he could see what was right in front of him.

But not this time. Not this trip. This time his mind had raced so fast he could not escape it. Circles of interlocking calculations spiraled with tangles of branching contingencies in rabidly vicious cycles. He could no longer feel the ice or hear the dogs. There was nothing but self-amplifying anxiety, self-referential argument, and self-destructive doubt. Siverth was losing it. He had allowed his mind to think too much. It had paralyzed his brain.

He had never risked so much before. He had never asked so many others to risk their lives for his ideas before. In the beginning, it had seemed like the right thing to do. When he had been sitting in the Nose Kiss playing with the products of his imagination it had seemed so right. It had seemed that the rightness of it would silence whatever worries might come later, would blot out the images of his friends, setting off in their sleds, leaving their families waving from the doorways, trusting that Siverth Narup, the smartest man in Greenland, would never betray their trust.

He hadn't slept in days. He had barely eaten. All day he had ignored the thirst, the cold, the pain. Although he would never admit it, Siverth was thankful for the pain. He wanted to suffer in advance, to pre-pay the debt he owed to the men of Greenland who were to suffer because of him. He longed for the delirium of pain that would rescue him from the horror of his guilt. It was only the mission that kept him from succumbing to it.

Siverth's eyes could barely focus. He leaned against the sled's uprights to keep himself from falling. Ole said nothing, but steadied the camera for him. For long minutes Siverth could make out only whiteness and blur. But then he found the hut in the distance and zoomed slowly in.

The image wavered and rippled from magnification and thermal wavelets. Corkscrews of snow blew a ghostly haze around the hut, winking it in and out of view, as if it were a glimpse into some nearby universe, colliding briefly with ours on its way to a parallel destiny beyond the boundaries of human comprehension. Or as if time and history and myth and imagination and faith and hope had all folded upon themselves here at the top of the world, like lines of longitude piling up with nowhere else to go. It was as if the cold had crystallized the dreams of men, sweeping them to the pole like snow while they slept, and scooped them into drifts to be buried for the rest of geologic time. The camera was cutting through time now. It had opened a view into a place that could not be seen because it was too real. Siverth prayed the camera's batteries would last forever, because he knew that no man would ever see this again.

And then there she was, floating just above the ice, nude but for a wisp of cloth clinging to her body and broken shackles hanging from her wrists, her head thrown back, mouth open, beseeching the world beneath her to listen, to follow, to believe, and be saved.

This was the image he had never been able to imagine. This was the vision he had groped for, blindly, in his soul. Here was the answer to his life of questioning. He knew now that the Earth would not abandon Her people. That She would not betray them.

She had chosen this place and this time above all others in history. Today was to be either the Last of Days or the First of Days. It was up to him. This was not a sign. Not a message. This was a command.

And with a shudder the camera whirred to a stop, a flurry of snow engulfed them all, and she was gone.

Siverth reeled back off the runners, dropping the camera into Ole's hands. He couldn't breathe. His vision tilted and faded. He dropped to one knee, clawing at his throat for air. The phone was suddenly in his hands, screaming static, its *Send* button red as blood.

"I—we must—" Siverth's voice was as harsh as tearing metal. He squeezed the phone with frozen fingers and pressed it to his mouth. "She is—" His lips were moving but no sound would come. Without air, there can be no sound.

He looked up for Ole, but could not see him. He couldn't see anything now but the after image of Her, burned onto his retinas, all else obliterated by the white blankets of unconsciousness and blowing snow.

CHAPTER 27

KISS

Petal was particularly difficult to warm up in this last post-pee group hug. On these occasions, protocol called for a few minutes of group jumping up and down, which would usually start in perfect synchrony but, because of the widely different resonant frequencies of the individuals involved, would soon deteriorate into a mosh pit (or 'mush pit', as they say in Greenland) of bikini-clad, goose-pimpled, prisoners gone wild, without the sound track.

"Cold enough for ya?" asked Buck in his best Down East, staggering from a rebound off of Ali into Petal. It was easier for Petal to keep her balance because girl Speedos don't require the use of both hands to keep them up during group jumping up and downs. Good thing, too, because they sure didn't hide bruises, or anything else, all that well.

"I couldn't pee!" she said, agilely avoiding a major flattening in between the colliding guys. "There's something spooky out there. It felt like someone was watching me. And now I'm frozen and jumping around with a full bladder! Do you think my bladder's frozen, Buck? Does that happen?"

"I never can pee when somebody's watching me, either," confided Ali. "You two have it easy. No bodyguards or butlers or attendants or other sheiks trying to get a peek at your *ule* when all you want is a little privacy, and your bladder is so full you think that you—"

"Will you stop!" cried Petal. "You're doing it on purpose! Just shut up and jump!"

"No way is your bladder frozen, Petal," said Buck. "Your nose and fingers and toes would all freeze off long before your core temperature dropped to—"

"Not you, too!" she wailed. "I thought we agreed to be nice in our final—our final—our final—whatever time we have left before we die of frozen bladders or protein powder poisoning or Speedo strangulation or atomic Gulf Stream—"

"What's nicer than empathy, Petal?" protested Ali. "I think we are all being very supportive of your bladder. Girls aren't the only ones with bladders, you know. Besides, look on the bright side, it would be a good thing if someone really was watching you. Then they could come rescue us. Unless, of course, they were the really pervy types who wander aimlessly over thousands of miles of frozen wilderness on the off chance they will stumble across girls in Speedos out squatting—"

"Don't listen to him, Petal," interrupted Buck. "His argument is based entirely on licensed premises. Let's say we do stipulate that there must exist at least one example of every variety of pervy guy you can think of—and no doubt more than one, maybe even clubs of them, possibly even on-line communities of like-minded pervs with blogs and chat rooms and over-pixilated camera-phone photos—and even if we do grant that the kind of pervy guy Ali is postulating—the arctic, bladder-obsessed, nomadic type with an impaired sense of statistical probabilities—is more likely to be found lurking around here than, let's say, Crawdad, Texas—then, so what? What you have to remember is that it has been proven beyond a shadow of a doubt that the feeling that one gets of being watched while peeing has no basis in physics whatsoever and is pure superstition and all in one's head. With all due respect, of course."

Petal was in no mood for any reciprocal jerking of chains, if that was what was going on, and was getting ready to smack both of them a good one (not expressly prohibited by protocol) when the room exploded with light, noise, and cold.

Now, from the peaceful warmth of your easy chair you might indulge a fleeting smirk of superiority as you view the image of these three unfortunates immediately turning to look not at the bear-like monster back-lit in their doorway, but at the still-inert crate of plutonium planet-poison squatting at the opposite wall.

'Silly people,' you might think, sipping some chamomile, the music of distant crickets gliding in on the soft evening air, 'don't they know that if that bomb went off they wouldn't have time to look at it, and if they did, it certainly wouldn't feel cold, for God's sake, and even if it did, looking at it would be the last thing you would want to do, especially without OSHA-certified eye protection.' But, almost by definition, if you had been them you would have been pretty jumpy too. So jumpy in fact that, like them, had you not been otherwise terrified, you would have been amazed at the dizzying height you had attained on that last synchronous group jump just after your little world seemed to have blown itself apart.

This was one of those slow-motion kind of jumps that can ordinarily only be achieved by employing high-end, state-of-the-art athletic shoes, precision engineered by international consortia of homeys from the hood, schoolgirls from Shanghai, and confabulators from Nike. This was one of those time-gumming jumps that allow bullets to be dodged and fireballs outrun, falling damsels caught and flying kicks deflected. Absent these demands, this particular jump proved to be a leisurely ascent with all heads turning toward the crated instrument of politics-by-atomic-means at one end of the room followed by a two-beat double take at apex, followed by a floating, open-mouthed descent gaping at the snow-covered Yeti in the doorway.

Or more correctly, the two headed Yeti. For at that instant Ole had Siverth in a bear hug from behind and was straining to get their combined bulk through the narrow aperture of the hut's only door. Siverth's blood pressure had rallied briefly from Ole's inadvertent Heimlich maneuver, thus restoring a level of consciousness just sufficient to allow in the vision of She-Earth levitating with two consorts in attendance. Which, of course, was enough to knock anybody in his state of mind immediately back out cold.

Buck, his reflexes honed sharp by years of Hong Kong cinema, landed as lightly on his feet as a cat doing Kung Fu.

"Atsuk!" he barked at the intruders, which actually means "turn left" but was the only Greenlandic word he knew.

"We're saved, Allah be praised!" gushed Ali, who continued to jump up and down, clapping his hands and beaming good will and Godspeedo.

"Will you perverts please close that door?" said Petal. "Don't you know it's freezing out there? And is knocking too bourgeois anymore? We could have been indisposed or something. But you might as well come in, since you're here. At least now we can pee in peace, for God's sake."

Ole was only the cameraman. He had learned early on never to judge content. But years of suspending judgment had made it increasingly more difficult for him to tell whether what was happening around him was really reality or just part of another Siverth-contrived Socio-Orgasmic Deconstruction.

This was not entirely a bad thing. Ole's highly developed *laissez-faire* world view allowed him an admirable equanimity when dealing with nearly nude, flying apparitions and other presumed manifestations of Siverth's paranormal powers. For Ole, a gorilla would always be a guy in a gorilla suit, rivers of blood would always be Red Dye Number 4, and the end of the world just a well-done special effect. Or maybe it was the other way around.

While some might turn cynical or vertiginous from teetering on such a slippery perspective, Ole had become more polite and respectful (in a necessarily detached kind of way) of beings from other dimensions who just might believe (rightly or wrongly) that they were actually beings from other dimensions. But surely such beings, without abandoning persona, could take a break from levitations and dematerializations and whatever to lend a hand when the greatest artist in Greenland and probable author of their very existence lay dying at their feet.

"Siverth Narup is dying!" he cried, hauling his limp comrade into the room. "Do something!"

Buck immediately warmed to the familiar 'Do something!'— the customary greeting that an appreciative citizenry gives to disaster guys arriving at the scene. And with little fanfare, that's exactly what they would do, because doing something was what they did. It was what they were good at. It was why they had come. Buck marveled at how comforting it was to have a job whose expectations were so clear. What if you had to be an artist? Or a critic? Or a columnist? How could you stand it?

In a flash Buck had Siverth supine near the heater, just undressed enough to allow room for his well-honed paramedic exam. Semi-conscious Inuit male, twenty five to thirty five, with shallow respirations and thready pulse. Skin cool. Pupils dilated but equal. Extremities responsive to noxious stimuli. Chest clear. Abdomen soft. Bowel sounds hyperactive. Fingers artistic.

"Is this man an artist?" asked Buck, looking up at Ole.

"Of course he is! I told you he's Siverth Narup, the most famous artist in Greenland! Maybe even the world! What has that got to do with it?" Ole was worried that there might be an insurance issue here. This guy was obviously an American, and everybody knew Americans couldn't blow their nose without some insurance issue.

"When did he eat last or have some water?" Buck asked, more confident in his diagnosis.

"Siverth hardly ever eats. But he's been under stress lately and I don't think he has eaten in days. And I know he didn't drink any water today, because the first time we stopped was right out there where he fainted."

"Aha! I knew it," announced Buck. "What this man needs is a good, home-cooked meal!"

"Who doesn't?" asked Ali.

"Soyuz Sunrise?" offered Petal, stirring madly at the chalky suspension.

"Just the thing," agreed Buck, "Got any salt?" he asked Ole.

"We have a block that the dogs lick on."

"Drop a piece of it in here. Might make all the difference."

"Be right back," said Ole, careful to close the door behind him.

"Ali," said Buck. "Help me move that box over here. We can prop his legs up on it. That will help, too. And Petal, hold his head up and see if you can get him to drink anything. Careful now."

Petal cradled Siverth's head in her lap and coaxed some of the liquid onto his lips. Ali and Buck were straining in the shadows at a box and Ole was off rooting in the sled. Siverth was inert in her arms. She studied his young, gaunt face, moving closer than she would have dared had they not been essentially alone and he essentially asleep.

She had never seen such a sensitive, vulnerable expression on a grown man before. Even unconscious, he had the look of a visionary and charismatic leader but also of an innocent and naïve child. It was heartbreaking to feel his life ebbing away in her arms, all for lack of some life-giving sustenance that would only dribble down his cheek. There was only one thing to do, and only moments to do it in.

Petal filled her mouth with the drink and placed her lips on his, gently probing until she felt his resistance surrender and the warm fluid penetrate slowly into him. She was careful not to go too quickly, but was insistent, guiding, firm. She stroked the shaft of his throat, encouraging the muscles there to respond in their primordial, instinctive way. The blush of her breast burned his cheek, her racing heartbeat pounded in his ear. Her tongue guided the gift of life deep to where it needed to be, to where all needs meet and all needs are met in turn.

And as the gifted molecules found their crucial slots in the metabolic machinery that made up Siverth Narup, neurons flickered to life again, picking up pieces of consciousness where they had left off, booting subsystems into supersystems until, as if a button has been pushed, the world was back on again to find him enfolded in the bosom of She-Earth herself, deep in a kiss that had saved his life first among all of the world's lives to follow.

CHAPTER 28

OLE

"You boys from around here?" asked Buck, once everyone had finally settled down to dinner. Speedos were still *de rigueur*, but now thankfully covered by layers of insulating fur and fabric courtesy of Siverth and Ole. The seal jerky appetizer had been followed by the seal jerky entrée except for those whose delicate sensitivities had compelled them to call ahead so that a lot of trouble could be gone to providing them with the special vegetarian seal jerky plate. Because of the occasion everyone was drinking a little more water than was good for them, except for Siverth, who would drink nothing but Soyuz Sunrise for the next seventy years of his life.

Ole wasn't used to entire minutes going by without Siverth's voice filling all time and space available. It was distinctly unlike him to sit mute and catatonic, staring at an American woman without so much as blinking. On the other hand, whatever happened around Siverth was always distinctly unlike anything that you had previously imagined, and therefore was unsurprising, in a way. In any case, you could always be sure that however disastrous the situation, Siverth had set it in motion, right down to the last unintended, random, and unpredictable detail. Ole kept reminding himself how reassuring this was supposed to be; even now that Siverth himself had become zombified beyond recognition.

"Kangerlussuaq," answered Ole, amicably.

"Ahhh," nodded Buck. He chewed dessert for a few more minutes, hoping to encourage elaboration. None forthcoming, he tried, "That far?"

"Three weeks by sled, but we went the long way." Ole smiled at everyone in turn. He was doing great. Siverth would have been proud of him.

"You-all on business or pleasure?" prompted Buck.

Ole felt himself starting to sweat. This was getting harder. He shot a glance at Siverth, whose face was blank as Botox. His pupils were huge, but there was no other sign of anything getting through.

"Business, I guess," he said. "Mr. Narup's latest work. Art work. Art project. We're working on it. I'm the cameraman. Optical collaborator. I think."

"Wait a second!" said Ali, finally giving up on a particularly impenetrable hunk of after-dinner seal jerky and spitting it into the corner. "Are you telling us that this is S. Narup?" He waved his hand excitedly in front of Siverth's face.

"We say it nay-ROOP, not NAHR-up, but yeah, that's right. I guess most of the world says it NAHR-up. But then most of the world probably gets Kangerlussuaq wrong, too. You see, Greenlandic pronunciation, while heavily influenced by the Danish, is really—"

"Petal! This is Siverth Narup!" Ali was jumping up and down again. "I have one of his works! I was going to show it to you. Very powerful. *Polar Bears in Polartec Boiling Exxon in Oil.* Mixed media. Crude and hide on acetylene tempera."

If Petal was familiar with this particular piece, or with the work of S. Narup, or the concept of art in general, or with the convention of answering when spoken to, it could not be discerned from her face, which seemed to be frozen in an attentive but puzzled expression, not unlike that of the young artist with whom her gaze was locked.

In many such cases of Spontaneous Mutual Auto-Reciprocal Hypnosis (according to the earnestly clinical but subtly prurient solicitations of the SMARH foundation) it is the victims' friends or families that first pick up the early clues that something is amiss: furniture repossessions, property foreclosures, piled up text messages. And so it would have been with this case, had it not been for the more powerful forces of denial at work among the three as-yet-unstricken diners. Ole would never accept that there could be anything wrong with Siverth Narup that Siverth Narup had not specifically intended and, thus, could not be counted as something wrong. And as for Buck and Ali, well, they figured that Petal was a girl, after all.

In addition, there were some pretty heavy issues of social protocol up in the air just now. For example, in situations such as these, who is to be considered the "host" and who are to be considered the "guests"? And do heads of Arab states sit to the left or the right of *artistes provocateur* around the space heater? And at what point in the evening is it polite to reveal one's intent to freeze one's host/guests to death on internet TV? And is it considered good manners or bad to be part of a plan to sweep one's host/guests into the ocean with a nuclear broom right after you cut off their oil and freeze them solid?

Therefore, it is sometimes considered prudent—among the more refined members of civilized society, anyway—to steer the conversation at first onto such non-controversial topics as sex and religion before venturing into more contentious areas such as the weather and why so many of our friends have turned into zombies recently.

Knowing this instinctively, Buck smiled at Ole and said, "So you guys are artists? Wow, that's great! Personally, I think that art is swell. I mean, I don't consider myself a collector or anything like Ali, here, but you'd be hard pressed to find a bigger fan of a good piece of art than me. But don't get me wrong, now, I don't mean to say that it's just good art that I like. I don't have anything at all against bad art or even just so-so art, if that's what you guys do. What I mean is that, even though I wouldn't call myself an expert, I do know what I like, and that's the main thing, right? But that's not to say that I'm not a huge fan of art that I don't like either. I'm sure that plenty of important art has been made without the intention of pleasing Mr. Buck Planck! But I'm a huge fan of that, too. Huge."

"You really mean that?" asked Ole, touched.

"Absolutely!" assured Buck. "We'd love to hear about your project. Ice carvings? Snowscapes? Sun-almost-sets?"

Ole searched Siverth's face for a prompt, a clue. There was nothing but stare. This had to mean something. This had to be a communication in itself, an unequivocal statement, a direct order that could not be ignored. Clearly, it was Siverth's plan for Ole to become the prime mover now. Siverth had brought them to this place and time for this purpose, and it was not up to Ole to question it. It was up to Ole to act. It was up to him to make it all happen. Siverth must know something about Ole that Ole had never recognized in himself. He must know that it was Ole who possessed the hidden inner power needed at this pivotal moment in history that would determine the fate of the world. He must be telling Ole that he should trust his own instincts now, that he should be acting as Ole would act, straight from his heart, and not trying to mimic or please Siverth Narup.

"Well, you see, this is what we call a performance piece. We create a situation that challenges the status quo and then document it on film." Ole was finding his voice now. Direct. Truthful. Sincere.

"So you aren't exactly street performers, then." Buck should have known this already, given there were no streets here, but in his defense he was making conversation with only a small part of his attention, the rest being consumed by his growing concern for Petal's apparent mental disappearance.

"Sure we are," said Ole, taking no offense. "It's just a matter of scale. We have about three hundred people involved in this project so far. But once it is set in motion, every person on Earth will eventually become a participant. And, of course, with survival of the planet at stake, not to mention all of our own impending deaths, we aren't primarily interested in the entertainment value of the event."

Ali and Buck froze in mid-distraction and looked bug-eyed at each other. There were already too many players in play with peculiar plans for the planet. And bystander rescuers were supposed to be part-time Wal-Mart clerks who dive into the icy waters after you, collect their medals, and then get back to their lives of futile pursuit of decent health insurance. They weren't supposed to have grandiose and scary-sounding agendas of their own. Especially those involving your parenthetical inclusion in yet another impending-death club.

"Just whose impending deaths are we talking about, exactly?" asked Ali, in a tone that successfully hid the fact that whatever these artists had cooked up, it could hardly make matters worse.

"Well, there are our people, four or five per team, and then there are the scientists, like you, that they capture at the nineteen other ice-core huts."

"Scientists like us, eh?" said Ali, eyeing Buck.

"Right. No ethnic animosity intended, of course, but you scientists come from the leading countries of the world, the very countries that are destroying our country with your poisonously hot carbon dioxide. All of you are now hostages of the Inuit people.

"Your ransom will be the return of the Earth. Each of your countries will pay in proportion to its crime. And until they do, the whole world will watch us starve and freeze, captives and captors together."

Ole reached high on the wall and affixed a webcam on a magnetized mount. From its position it could see the whole room, including Yasser's camera on the other side.

"So we're your hostages now?" asked Buck without menace. He had learned that a cool demeanor could be a great asset in situations like this.

"Right. If that's okay with you, of course," said Ole, still a novice at hostage protocol.

"Ole, under ordinary circumstances that would be the least we could do, especially after all you two have done for us," said Buck. "But, Ole—it is Ole, right, like OH-lee—you see there is this little—"

"Yes, it is Ole," he said, eagerly, "Some people say it like they are starting in on Ole Man River, but it really is OH-lee. Personally, I find it super-tedious when ethnic types act offended over mispronunciation of their names. You go to Japan and the schoolgirls are chanting oh-LEE, oh-LEE, oh-LEE! What are you supposed to do? Scold them? Hey, I can't say ten words in Japanese. Not to mention Chinese! Forget it! I'll bet there's not one Greenlander in the country who can get Chinese right, even looking at the menu."

"Ole," said Ali gently, putting his hand on his arm, "Do you have a map of the ice core huts your people have captured?"

"Why sure. We have dozens of maps. This operation is very well planned. We've thought of everything. Siverth called it foolproof." He rifled through some papers, grease-stained from multiple handlings and storage next to the seal jerky.

"Here is an overview," he said, spreading one out on the floor. "We are here, and here are the other huts. We chose ones that had just been set up. We figured they wouldn't have really gotten started on any serious work yet. We're not anti-science, you know."

The map looked like a Xerox of the one Yasser had drawn on the crate: four lines of latitude, each with five circles evenly spaced across the girth of the island. Each circle revealing the precise location of a nuclear device stolen from the US government, disguised as a research station, waiting to play its role in the shutdown of Western civilization, and now unintentionally part of an Inuit art project intended to shame the world into saving itself.

Now, at this point in the narrative there are bound to be those readers who point to such "unlikely" intersections of historical threads as evidence of intervention by a higher power and nod in tacit support of whatever happens to be next in the unknowable script of time. And there also will be those who insist that all of existence is just one astronomically unlikely event after another, but, since the roulette ball of reality eventually has to fall somewhere, things are precisely as they are for no better reason than this is where the quantum energy states happened to be standing when the music stopped.

And, of course, let's not forget those who, with Zen certainty, would silently invoke the robin's nest with its perfect egg when debate becomes intractably tangled with words such as "coincidence," "contrived," "unrealistic," and "improbable." All of these people have valid, though incompatible, points. What they all agree on, however, is that truth is stranger than fiction and that you can't make this stuff up.

"Ole?" asked Buck gently. "This plan of yours, when is it supposed to go down?"

"Oh, it's already happened, I think. Siverth was giving the signal when he got—well, got this way." He looked at his friend for some sign of approval, validation, or consciousness.

"Do you think maybe you ought to check on things?" asked Ali. "Call the troops, drop them an email, something?"

"Yeah, maybe that would be a good idea," allowed Ole. "But I'm sure everything is okay. I mean, what could possibly have gone wrong?"

CHAPTER 29

REVIVAL

"Ole, where are—"

"It worked!" cried Ole to the others, who were too busy re-orienting Petal to pay any attention to him or Siverth. "He's back!"

Siverth pulled himself up on one elbow and tried to focus. "We're in the hut, right? Did you see her? I must have passed out. She was here, though. You saw her. Tell me you saw her."

"You talking about Petal? Sure I saw her. She's over there with Ali and Buck just waking up. You two were in some kind of hypnotic vapor lock or something. Buck knows the name of it, I forget. Doesn't matter, it's not supposed to be permanent."

"But the scientists, the captives, where—?"

"Siverth, Buck says you need to keep calm or PHF might set in. It's not an uncommon complication."

"Who the hell is Buck and what the hell is PHF and what the hell is going on?" Siverth was straining against Ole, trying to sit up

"Post Hypnotic Freakout. It doesn't sound good. Maybe you should just try and get some sleep."

"Sleep! Wasn't I just asleep? I'm supposed to go back to sleep?"

"Actually, it would make things a little easier, if you don't mind," said Ole. "See, it's gotten kind of complicated while you were out, and at this delicate stage of negotiations maybe it wouldn't be such a good idea for someone with PHF to come barging in—"

"Barging in! I'm in charge here! I'm the artist! This is my greatest—"

"And being comatose doesn't exactly count as sleep, does it? Not to mention hypnotic trances—what could be more exhausting? Siverth, you really do look tired. Sleepy, even. Like your eyes are getting heavier and heavier, and you can't hold your head up a minute longer because everything is getting so slow and dreamy and you are getting sleepier and sleepier—"

"Ole, will you knock it off! I am not going to sleep, I am going to stand up right now and pick up this operation where we left off. And quit trying to hypnotize me, it's freaking me out. Now, where were we? Outside the hut, getting ready to take our captives when—when—there she was, floating in the air, commanding the wind, stopping the sun, suspending time, beseeching the creatures of the Earth—"

Siverth considered Ole to be his truest friend. He had never imagined that there would be a thought that he couldn't share with him. He had watched Ole's face react to hundreds of thousands of his thoughts—thoughts embarrassing enough to get him blackmailed, incriminating enough to get him indicted, and short-sighted enough to get him elected. Ole's expression had always been respectful and encouraging. Siverth had grown to count on Ole's face. He knew that no matter how crazy the thought, Ole would see the kernel of wisdom hiding within.

Until this one. It only took a glimpse of Ole's expression to freeze Siverth in place, as if he had spotted a land mine inches under his foot. This was a look that told you that you were about to be locked in the loony bin forever. That you were about to give up your membership in the brotherhood of sentient beings. That no one would ever listen to another word you said.

Siverth's mouth was hanging open, his jaw unhinged. He knew that from now on he must partition his brain into two compartments, one that he could share with his most intimate confidants, and one that he must forever keep secret. He could no longer live his life with its previous abandon. Every word, every action would need to be examined ahead of time, scrubbed clean of clues that would betray the thing that no other person would understand. This was a shame, he thought, but worth it.

"In my dream, I mean," he said, watching his friend's face relax. "I must have been hallucinating before I fainted. Remind me to drink more water out there, will you, Ole?"

"Sure I will, Siverth," said Ole, hugging his friend as if he had just returned from the dead. "Your brains get mushy if you don't take care of them. Gotta watch out for that. Ready to meet our new friends?"

"Our captives?" Siverth asked cautiously. Nothing he was thinking was entirely free of craziness.

"Better than," said Ole, helping him up. "Just keep your mind open."

Siverth wasn't sure this was the safest approach, so he kept his mouth shut instead.

"Siverth, I'd like to present Sultan Ali bin Said Andun, Supreme Potentate of the Erstwhile Oil Rich Kingdom of Yomamah and one of your biggest fans," said Ole, bowing deeply to a guy who, with the right nose job, would have fit right in at the Nose Kiss. Until he opened his mouth, that is.

"I am so absolutely tickled pink to meet you in person, Mr. Narup," gushed Ali alternately bowing and hugging. "I have your *Polar Bears in Polartec*, as everyone who is anyone knows. And how absolutely fabulous of you and your loyal sidekick to rescue us from that dreadful Yasser Ibahb. He is such an ungrateful bitch, and you just won't believe what he was about to do to your country, not to mention the world, and not to mention us, with those totally scary nuclear exploding things like that one over there. And leaving us in this icebox in our Speedos, can you imagine? The man is seriously demented, I tell you. But now that you're here everything is going to be okay, I can just tell. At least until the oil runs out, but we can talk about that later. In the meantime I just have to hug you! And by the way, I love your beard. We will have to have the name of your hairdresser, just between you and me. I promise not to tell a soul."

Siverth glanced at Ole to see if this lunatic Ali was also getting 'that look,' but instead found him beaming like a parent at a spelling bee. It was becoming clearer to Siverth that somewhere out on the ice he had entirely screwed up his sanity detection system. This was not all that uncommon an affliction among creative geniuses to begin with and perhaps not much of a disadvantage either, but over the years Siverth had grown rather fond of his ability to pick the material world out of a lineup of bizarre hallucinations. No great loss, he reasoned to himself, especially given the sad state the material world found itself in these days.

"Buck Planck," said Buck, pumping his hand. "Disaster guy. Pleased to meet you. Good thing you're awake—we're going to need your help saving the planet. Pull up a box here and let's get our mission statement hammered down before we move into strategy and logistics. I understand you have command of two hundred armed men with satellite link—"

"Petal Steele," she said, taking his hand. "I think we've met." Petal's face was luminous, framed in white by the fur of her parka, which was actually his parka. She was smiling, but just barely, in a way that excluded the others and acknowledged their secret shared.

Her eyes darted once to either periphery and he nodded, but just barely, cementing their bond of silence. From her expression he could tell that she approved of these other mortals—she had chosen to walk among them, after all—but could not allow them to see through her disguise as Siverth had. She was not worried that he would betray her. She knew that he would take their secret to his grave, if that would be her will.

"Yes, we most certainly have," he answered, almost in a whisper. "Thank you for saving my life."

"And you, mine," she said. "I hope you don't mind me wearing your coat. They left us practically nude out here on the ice."

Siverth hadn't been prepared for the Fire of Kundalini to immolate his spinal cord, slamming every sphincter and squeezing his adrenals into nubbins. If these few words could do this to him, then conversations with her would have to be kept very short. Otherwise his brain would explode in front of everyone and give it all away.

"Not at all," he said, tearing his eyes away from her. "It suits you. Please keep it." It took all of his strength to keep from falling at her feet, but he would be masterful here. He would make her proud. Feigning indifference to her presence, he sat down with the other men. He could feel her nod of approval. He could sense her hovering there, outside their circle, pretending to be touching the ground.

"Ole," he said, "status report, please."

"Yes, sir," he answered, spreading a map out on a box in front of them. "I'm afraid all I have is bad news. Our plan to ransom ice-core scientists has failed. There wasn't a single scientist in any of the twenty huts our teams captured. You remember that we had chosen these particular huts because they were the newest ones to be set up in Greenland. What we didn't know was that these huts were all bogus, part of a nefarious plan by the evil Yasser Ibahb to blow the ice sheet into the ocean with nuclear devices stolen from the United States. So the only things our teams have captured are a bunch of Arab guys and twenty atomic bombs. Not much to work with. I guess we should all go home."

"So, you mean we just saved our country from nuclear annihilation?" asked Siverth. This might be bad news to some people, but the guys at the Nose Kiss wouldn't throw a herring at it.

"There's another problem you should know about," offered Buck. "The sheiks have pulled a fast one on the rest of the world by pretending that they were sitting on huge reserves of oil. Turns out that in three months all the oil will be gone, leaving the world with no time to switch over to anything else. This might not be as bad for business as an atomic bomb in your backyard, but it's right up there with the Black Death when it comes to keeping civilization civilized."

"So, you mean that all of a sudden there will be no more oil? All of a sudden cars and planes and furnaces will just stop spewing CO_2? And the so-called first world economies will grind to a halt, along with their noxious, planet-killing pollution? And the world will finally pare down its plague of people to some sustainable size? This is the bad news you are trying to break to me?"

It was all Siverth could do to keep from looking at Her. This had to be her doing. The Earth was standing up for Herself at last. Hallelujah!

"Mr. Narup," said her voice, sweet and soft near his ear, "the people of the Earth are part of the Earth now. You can't think of them as separate. Nature cannot be divided into human and non-human, master and subject, worthy and unworthy. All of the Earth's creatures are selfish and ignorant in their own way. Humans are no different. If we are to save the planet, we must save its people as well. They can learn. They can do better. None of them deserves to die before their time. There is not one creature on the Earth that deserves to suffer."

He turned to look at her, unable to restrain himself any longer. By that time her lips had stopped moving and only a wisp of her breath still hung in the air between them. Her cheeks were flushed, her eyes cast down. Had the others heard her, or had she spoken directly into his head? No matter. She had spoken. And what she had said he knew to be true by its absolute absence of hate. He should have expected no less from Her. Forgiveness, love, hope.

Suddenly he felt a lifetime of outrage lifted from him. He felt as if he, too, could float above the ice. He felt as if he could do anything—and, indeed, that he must do everything. Now there was more to save than the earth itself. Its people must be saved as well, and, harder yet, saved from themselves. She had chosen this place and this time for it to be done. And She had chosen him to do it.

He turned back to the men in the circle, looking at them each in turn. Together they could do this thing. Now that sanity was no constraint and hallucination counted as concrete, there was no reason that four men and an incarnation couldn't change the course of planetary history from within this metal box lost in the middle of frozen nowhere.

"So, it's unanimous, then," he said, raising a carton of Soyuz Sunrise. "We will save the planet and all of her people. When Ole and I created the Hot Ice project, we knew it had one serious flaw—it depended on our ability to make the people care. But now we cannot fail, for now we have the key into the heart of hearts of every person in the world."

They all stood, raising their cartons high, glancing nervously at the nuclear weapon in the corner, and wondering just how Siverth Narup might use it to open the heart of humanity.

All except for Siverth and Petal—they knew that he wasn't talking about atomic bombs at all. He was talking about something much more powerful than that. He was talking about the power of Her.

CHAPTER 30

PEARLS

"So let's get to work on this mission statement," said Buck, spreading home-made three by fives out on the box. "We need to be clear on our long and short term goals here."

"Shouldn't we just do what we can do and then go home?" asked Ole. "I mean, who could ask more of us than that?"

"Our friend is half right on that one," said Ali. "And I'm talking about the going home part. You might as well face it, there isn't a damn thing that anybody can do for the world at this point, so let's not waste a lot of time dreaming up cockamamie schemes and concentrate on getting the hell out of here. I favor someplace warm that nobody knows about. With the appropriate amenities, of course."

"We need to repair the Earth. We need to undo the damage we have done to Her, and we need to learn to nurture Her as She has us. We need to do this for Her and for all of Her people as well." Siverth gazed into middle distance as he spoke. The words seemed to flow through him, channeled from an entity that perfused all space.

Petal started to speak but then stopped herself. She was still a little embarrassed about all that had happened, or at least what she imagined to have happened. She consoled herself with the knowledge that suggestibility was correlated with intelligence, but it was still unsettling to have another post-hypnotic blank spot in her memory and wonder what kind of humiliating things she might have done in some zombie-like trance.

The first time it had happened was just before high school. The Great Maldini had been sawing women in half and guessing women's weights and otherwise displaying his scandalously erotic dominance over them for the benefit of the pre-pubescent matinee crowd when he declared that he would then hypnotize them all. The entire audience held their arms straight out, rapt in concentration on his syrupy yet penetrating accent as they eagerly offered their minds up for his control. Those who found that they could not lower their arms, try as they might, were ordered to the stage to be subjects of his will.

Later, giggling under a blanket with their flashlights, her girlfriends had confessed that they had just been playing along, all the way through the pantomimed scenes of cold showers, first kisses, and ants in their pants. Petal had confessed this, too, even though she was, as The Great Maldini had ordered, completely amnesic for the entire event. She knew then that from then on she had better steer clear of hypnotists and, just to be on the safe side, any guy from Rome with a saw.

This turned out to be not quite as easy as you might think. High society occasions could be expected to boast an aria by Pavarotti or an etude by Stern but not uncommonly would be found slumming a headbanger by Springsteen or a vanishing by Copperfield. And rarely, but much too often, there was a guy with an accent hypnotizing the crowd. Petal's friends would tell her later how surprised they had been by her uninhibited enthusiasm at the Ballet for Spoiled Princesses Benefit. Others would cattily compliment her good sportsmanship at the Annual In Lieu of Charity Ball. Given that she hadn't the slightest recollection of these events, Petal soon figured that the wisest course of action was to head for the loo whenever a top hat would appear on stage.

Now it was clear that it had happened again. One minute she was trying to revive an unconscious artist with a little mouth to mouth nutritional CPR and the next thing she knew she was deep in a kiss with Buck, eight hours later. Very disconcerting. At least there were no winks and nudges from her friends with oblique references to goldfish and hula hoops. In fact, everyone was acting as if nothing more significant than an afternoon nap had occurred. Maybe drooling in her sleep was as bad as it had gotten. This would explain everything, even the nice Mr. Narup's standoffish behavior. She had nothing to be embarrassed about. But still this feeling of pervasive shyness clung to her like a net. That and the nagging realization that there was not a top hat to be seen in the whole cabin. Or country, for that matter.

"I think you are all right," she said, "except for Ali, of course. No offense, Ali."

"Exactly," said Siverth, catching her insight. "Our goals must be as grand as our imaginations can envision but our strategies must be realistic, foolproof. We must work with what we have, but we must leverage it to move all of human society and the trajectory of geophysics itself."

"Are we agreed on a goal of 270 parts per million?" asked Buck. "That would take us back to pre-industrial CO_2 levels."

"Fine by me," said Ole.

"Okay, for a start," said Siverth. "But we must also reach into the very soul of mankind; reaffirm the cathexis between the spirit—"

"Dreamers," said Ali. "Do you know how much CO_2 people have dumped into the atmosphere in the last century and a half? It will take thousands of years for nature to clean this up, even if we stop putting more in right now, which you know we can't do without sending all seven billion of us back to the Stone Age. If you are as set on saving the people as you are on saving the planet then you obviously have a logical impossibility here."

"Why can't we just take the carbon dioxide back out of the air?" asked Petal. "Plants do it."

The men looked up from their three by fives. Every idea must be honored, no matter how fanciful. Siverth risked a conspiratorial nod.

"Yeah, what if every square inch of land was covered in plants," posed Ole. "Then how long would it take to pull all the CO_2 out?"

"That wouldn't work even if it weren't impossible," said Ali. "You would have to bury everything that grew in a place where bacteria couldn't get to it, otherwise it would be just like burning it or eating it—all the carbon would eventually go back into the atmosphere as CO_2 again. That's why all the plant-a-tree efforts are so ludicrous. Trees only tie up carbon temporarily. Oil and coal would have tied it up forever, if people had just had the good sense to leave it there."

"I mean why don't humans take it out of the air and put it somewhere?" Petal insisted. "I heard about power companies pumping CO_2 underground, into old oil wells I think."

"That's also a load of baloney, in my humble opinion," argued Ali. "What could be a bigger time bomb than a gigantic stash of CO_2 just waiting for the next earthquake to burp it up into the atmosphere all at once? Something like this happened at Lake Nyos in 1986, you know. Seventeen hundred people were smothered in their sleep by CO_2 bubbling up one night. Trying to keep a gas trapped under dirt forever makes about as much sense as trying to keep a rhinoceros trapped in a butterfly net."

"So we turn it into something easier to store," said Petal. "Lots of things must have carbon in them besides pasta and CO_2. How about diamonds and pearls. They've got carbon, right? People can make diamonds, right? They're not quite as nice as the real thing, of course, but I think we can make some compromises here, given the urgency of the situation."

"She may be onto something here," said Ole. "Anything we do on a worldwide scale is going to take a ton of money. So we use the money from selling diamonds to make diamonds until all that extra carbon is locked up in tiaras like it ought to be."

"Are you kidding?" said Ali. "Before you even made a dent in the huge amount of carbon piled up in the atmosphere you would have made so many diamonds that they would be as cheap as driveway gravel. Not that they wouldn't make good driveway gravel, now that I mention it, but it takes gigantic presses and lots of energy to make even a tiny diamond. People have been trying to make diamonds for as long as they have been trying to make anything, and no one has made more than a handful of them yet."

"Not so fast, Ali," said Siverth, knowing that Petal's every utterance must contain a hidden message that would be the key to everything. "She's right. Pearls are just calcium carbonate, the same thing as shells are made of, just lined up pretty. This stuff is easy to make, sea creatures do it all the time. All it takes is CO_2, calcium, and some water—and there's no shortage of these in the ocean. In fact, the CO_2 in the ocean is in equilibrium with the CO_2 in the air. Take some out of either and it reduces the amount in the other."

"He's right," said Buck. "Calcium carbonate would be a great place to store carbon. That's what limestone is made of, marble, too. And these don't bubble up and smother people when they aren't looking or get eaten and turned back into CO_2. They basically sit there happily for eons. And it can't be much trouble to make the stuff, every boat you put in the water is covered with barnacles before you know it, all made out of calcium carbonate."

"So you are going to save the world with barnacle farms? Wait until the venture capital guys hear that one. And you forget, the

190

world is out of oil. Any of your grandiose schemes will require mobilization of entire societies, unification of human effort toward some goal in the future. Civilization will be in chaos in ninety days. You won't be able to get anything done. And wait until your altruists at Greenplanet and Save the Krill find their families hungry. They'll be ripping at each other's throats like every other species in the food chain."

"How about changing all the cars to electric?" asked Ole, knowing it was a dumb idea.

"Good idea if we had the time," said Buck. "That would sure help with the CO_2 problem. But we need a quick fix that will keep traffic moving until we can make a switch like that."

"What about people making oil?" asked Petal. "Like we were talking about just before that dreadful Yasser person kidnapped us?"

"It's been done in the lab," said Buck. "In theory, it should be a simple proposition. Oil is nothing but carbon and hydrogen linked into little strings. CO_2 and water is all you need."

"And gigantic amounts of energy, is what he forgot to say," added Ali. "You'll need to put at least as much energy into making the oil as you plan to get out of it when you run your car, and probably ten times more. That gets you back to your original problem, finding a source of energy to power human civilization that won't run out and won't poison the planet.

"This is why you came to see me in Yomamah; to find out which alternative energy source the sultans were afraid would take over from fossil fuels. Well, because of a very rude interruption by the very rude Yasser Ibahb, we never got around to answering your question, but now is as good a time as any. Ready for it? Are you sitting down? Here it is, the best-kept secret of every government, every corporation, every think tank, and every advocacy group. The envelope please." He held up a make-shift three by five and leaned into an imaginary microphone.

"Nothing!" he shouted, grinning like he was about to kiss the new Mr. America. "That's right. Nothing. After thousands of years of looking, mankind has come up with nothing better than a campfire. In fact, every step after campfires has been a step in the wrong direction.

"Every other creature that has lived on this planet over the last three or four billion years has managed to keep itself going using the energy of the sun. The sun doles out a certain amount of energy to the Earth every day. If you are smart, like plants, you can capture some of it to run your plant machinery and keep your species going. If you are more rapacious than smart, like every critter who isn't a plant, then you are just stooping to steal energy from plants or from some other critter who has done the stealing for you. And as nasty and brutish as this sounds, at least the arrangement is sustainable. Energy is used no faster than it comes in from the sun. There is no energy debt. Every bill is paid in advance.

"But in the last infinitesimally small sliver of time in our planet's history, a species evolved to be the most rapacious of them all. This one was not content with consuming just enough energy to power its own muscles like every other living being had always done before. This one took pleasure in wasting vast quantities of plant-captured energy, throwing it away as heat and light and CO_2. The great forests were decimated by men and their energy-wasting orgies of fire. By all rights, this species should have gone extinct long ago after burning up all their trees, as did the vanished civilizations of Easter Island and all the others that left no trace.

"And they would have, too, and the Earth would have healed, but for one tragic event. This species discovered a treasure chest buried deep in the ground, one filled with plant energy that the Earth had buried millions of years before, its carbon safely bottled up for eons. And instead of quietly closing the lid of this Pandora's Box and walking away, this species did what it has become famous for. It had another orgy. And it convinced itself that the orgy could go on forever. Worse than that, it convinced itself that it couldn't live without the orgy, that it had a right to orgy, and that the entire universe had been created as a stage for its orgy. The orgy became the defining characteristic of the species. The orgy became its god.

"Until our species came along, life had always lived off of the interest generated by the wealth of the Earth. Humans, with their boundless capacity for self-deception in service of selfishness, saw nothing wrong in spending down the Earth's capital to fund it's trinkets of progress. Let's face it, the sum total of all of mankind's accomplishments, from scribbling on a cave to walking on the moon, were all funded through deficit spending, from plundering the past. And as everyone knows, the past can't go on forever.

"The treasure chest has a bottom on it. And when it is finally empty, humans will be left whining in the cold, acting shocked and petulant because their free ride has finally come to an end and all they have left is a dry well and a planet poisoned by their own excesses. Have they made plans to become responsible inhabitants of the planet? Have they been working as diligently on a new, sustainable way of life as they have been on killing each other over the last drops of oil? Have they come up with an alternative to going extinct? No. That would be too much trouble. That would be too expensive. That would be bad for business this fiscal year."

Everyone was speechless, but Ali was not done anyway.

"So that's why you can't make oil, Petal, at least not for very long," he said. "Every barrel of oil represents thousands of years of sun energy captured by vast quantities of plants, and your country alone uses over 20 million barrels a day. Where are you going to get the energy for that, Petal? The past just ran out. The future has always been just out of reach. You got a way to live in the present? You know that's not our style, Petal. Let's get out of this icebox and find a place to drink champagne and watch the ship go down. It's the only civilized thing to do."

Ali stood up and walked over to a crate at the other end of the room. The one with the nuclear genie trapped inside. He leaned on it, facing away from them. He didn't want anyone to see his face.

The others sat in silence, heads down, toying with their three by fives, except for Petal who cleared her throat loudly and slammed a hunk of seal jerky down on the box like a gavel.

"So it's unanimous," she declared brightly. "We're now in the oil making business. Sounds like this may cost some money. Anybody know where we can get some of that?"

Everyone looked up at her, expressions of disbelief turning into expressions of revelation. They all smiled. This they could do.

CHAPTER 31

EBAY

"So, who's got money?" said Petal. "Everybody ante up."

"My accountant says I'll have plenty to live on if I retire at 85 and don't spend anything until then," said Buck. "But I don't know what that means in real money. I do have a bank account, though, which, unless it's overdrawn, is all yours."

"Thanks Buck. Your heart's in the right place."

"My accountant says that I am fabulously wealthy occasionally, but not usually, and, unfortunately, not currently," admitted Siverth. "In fact, I am at this time in arrears to my optical collaborator here. Otherwise, what's mine is yours."

"Don't worry about me, Siverth," said Ole. "I never spend any of the money you give me. In fact, my accountant says that I need to drastically increase consumption or my estate will be in grave danger of a serious asset overload problem, with devastating tax consequences. I try my best, but as you know there's only so much one can consume at the Nose Kiss without devastating hangover consequences. It will be a relief to get rid of it. Anyway, I think there is about ten thousand in there."

"Dollars or Krone?" asked Buck, pen poised.

"Gold," he said. "Ounces, I believe."

"That's ten million dollars, Ole," said Siverth. "I'm broke and you have ten million dollars? What I could do with ten million dollars!"

"Okay, then, do it. The only thing I do with it is lend it to you anyway."

"How about you, Ali?" asked Buck. "How much are you worth, after all is said and done?"

"Put me down for a hundred billion, plus or minus, and that'll be in dollars. You've got to remember, though, that we sheiks don't really own anything—we're just caretakers for the wealth of our people, who are happy to live in abject poverty for the pure vicarious joy of watching us squander it. By all rights, I should ask them if it okay to give it to you, but since I never have asked them before, it seems a little silly now. And then, of course, I'll be out on the street with no shoes, if that matters to anybody."

"So is that a hundred billion or not," asked Buck.

"Plus or minus," answered. "And they're going to have a cow about this back home, you know."

"I've got about five hundred thousand in stocks that go worthless when the Street gets nervous," said Petal. "How much does that give us, Buck?"

"A hundred billion and change," he said, looking up. "Plus or minus. Are we in the ballpark?"

"Not by a long shot," said Petal. "We need to be solidly into the high trillions to pull this off. What else have we got to work with? Twenty surplus Soviet ice-core huts at a hundred dollars each, that's two thousand while the market holds."

"Don't forget the hostages," said Ole. "How much do you think their boss would pay for all those Arab guys?"

"Yasser Ibahb?" answered Ali. "That would be approximately zero knowing him. Whatever happened to that naughty boy, anyway? It's not like him to give up so easily."

"He didn't give up that easily," said Ole. "Made a mess of hut number eighteen before our guys could get a net over him."

"So we've got Yasser under a net! Put him down for ten billion," said Ali.

"Still not enough," said Petal. "What else have we got?"

"Well, there *are* the A-bombs," said Ole. He looked up to see Petal's eyes widen. She and Siverth were staring at each other again.

"But we wouldn't—" said Ole.

"We couldn't—" said Ali.

"We shouldn't—" said Buck.

"The hell we won't!" said Siverth. "Having the bomb is obviously worth trillions! Look at all the trillions the US spent to get the bomb, and all the trillions that every other country spent to get the bomb despite the US spending trillions to keep anybody else from getting the bomb. Trillions upon trillions! And even at this it must be cheap! The leaders of those countries aren't stupid. They have to know what the bomb is worth. They've done the math. There are only so many trillions to go around, after all.

Trillions for the bomb must be the best bargain in town. Otherwise why would they be so desperate to get it?

"This is the kind of desperation you only see at the Filene's Basement Five for One Queen Size Foundation Blowout Sale. Heads of state crawling over each other to get their fists into that pile of Double D Cup Multiple Re-entry Underwire Warheads. Stuffing their shopping bags full of those Tummy Tightening Jiggle Control Thermonuclear Derrière Detonators. Outta my way, girl! Don't get between me and my WMDs!"

"Are you nuts, Siverth?" said Ole. "We can't save the Earth by blowing up A-bombs!"

"That's the great part—you don't have to blow them up to use them. Nobody ever blows them up anymore, and that hasn't reduced their usefulness one iota, whatever the hell an iota is. In fact, it's obvious from the nightly news that they're getting more useful all the time—essential, even."

Siverth was pacing furiously. His creative engine was revving back up. Ole hadn't seen him this intense since they installed *Halliburton Eating Its Young* on top of the Lincoln Memorial under the cover of darkness.

"The only problem is that to make them useful you have to convince everybody else that you are nuts enough to blow them up. If you let them suspect that you are in actuality an intelligent and reasonable leader of a thoughtful and moral nation then that automatically renders your A-bombs useless and all your trillions are down the drain. This is why it is so important to elect stubborn, anti-intellectual leaders with strong convictions about the afterlife. They may screw up everything else in the country, but it's worth it to keep your A-bomb investment growing."

"There must be a better way to use these bombs than threatening people into acting right," said Petal. "You know how countries get when you scold them. It makes them feel bad about themselves and they get all sulky and act out in public. Or they have tantrums on the ground and hold their breaths until you finally apologize and buy them ice cream. We need to win their hearts. While we take their money, of course."

Nothing stoked Siverth's hyperinflationary imagination more than divine inspiration. His muse had materialized and it was She.

"Exactly! We will use these bombs to engage the people of the world in the common purpose of saving the planet! We will turn them from a symbol of man's destructive and belligerent nature into a medium of expression of humanity's goodness and unity. We will use them to create a global community of creative genius, to organize a worldwide effort that will dwarf that of the Manhattan Project, the Panama Canal, the Pyramids, the Moon Shot, the Gold Rush, the—"

"With all due respect, Mr. Narup," said Ali, jumping up to claim the floor. "These devices that we find in our possession represent the pinnacle of Man's achievement in the persuasive arts. They are the supreme expression of Man's godlike need to intimidate. They define the aesthetic of coercion. They allow Man to transcend his very mortality, to rise above his base instincts of self-preservation into higher planes of vengeance and spite. If you do not intend to use them in the proper fashion, as they were meant to be used, then stand aside and let someone who is not afraid to cut off his own nose to—"

"He's right!" interrupted Buck, standing up and pacing with the other two. "I mean Siverth, of course. What Ali is saying is a crock of dung—no offense, Ali. We need to get all the world's great minds together on this problem, and all the not so great ones, too. We need to get great minds who know how to get the most out of other great minds and other great minds who know how to organize it all. And we need more than just minds, we need hands and backs. We need bricks and mortar. We need to make ideas happen. We need action. Prototypes. Fast track, expedited implementation. Science! Industry! Workers, shoulder to shoulder. All working to repair the damage humankind has done to the biosphere. To reverse global warming. To cool down the Anthropocene. That's what we'll call it! Chill the Anthropocene! Our ancestors will look back on this as the geologic age in which mankind saved the biosphere, not ruined it. We can do it! All we need is—"

"What he's trying to say," said Ole, jumping onto the box to be as tall as the rest of them. "Is that we need cash! We need to get as many trillions as the world would waste on self-destruction and put it to work in an effort that rises above nationalism, capitalism, socialism, egoism, sexism, racism, pessimism—"

"eBay," said Petal softly.

The hut was suddenly silent, the four men frozen in mid rant. All eyes were on Petal. No one dared to move.

198

"We put them on eBay but we only allow two bidders, the US government and the people of the world. If the US wins, we give the bombs back. If the people of the world win, then we destroy them or hide them or rocket them into space or something." She blushed a little and looked down at her hands. She knew how history would recall this moment. It was appropriate to be humble.

"The US won't bid, they've got plenty of nukes," sniffed Ali. "So what if they lose a few."

"Sure they will," said Ole. "They're desperate to keep nukes out of the wrong hands. They would never believe that we wouldn't just sell them to the richest terrorist. That's just the way governments think. People, on the other hand, are not nearly as cynical as governments and will figure that if we were going to sell the bombs to the bad guys we would have just gone ahead and done it without drawing a lot of attention to ourselves."

"And who of you wouldn't pitch in a buck to repudiate nuclear madness?" said Buck. "Last I remember, no one ever asked me to vote on whether my hard-earned tax dollar should be spent on nuclear weapons. Any of you ever see that on the ballot?"

"And we'll let people know that the money they bid will be spent on saving the planet. No sense keeping that a secret," said Ali, finally coming around. "We'll publish how much everyone gives. For corporations, we'll match it up with how much they have cost the earth in carbon and other pollution. We'll steer consumers away from companies who haven't donated their fair share. That'll intimidate them!"

"We will welcome all people from all nations to join us, giving what they can in money, ideas, work," said Petal. "When we build—and build we will—the money will go back as jobs to do the most noble work that men have ever done."

"And Mankind will redeem itself," said Siverth quietly. "His abuse of the Earth repented, reconciled, forgiven. Her love, at last, returned in full. Man and the Earth will finally embrace one another. They will become one in bliss."

Siverth and Petal, against their better judgments, indulged their eyes in one brief brush of contact, but quickly looked away before a massive discharge of spiritual power had a chance to vaporize them all.

CHAPTER 32

VIRUS

"Anything I can do to help?" asked Buck, blowing on his hands and stamping his feet. He squinted off at the frozen sun.

"Move two feet to the left," said Siverth. "Your shadow is in the frame. And don't speak, it shows up in her face."

Buck figured he might as well go back inside. Siverth and Ole had been filming Petal for hours, just standing there and occasionally raising one arm or the other. When she got cold, they would do takes of her walking away from the cabin. Maybe it was none of his business, but Buck was starting to get curious about what was going on.

"Help with anything?" Buck asked, back inside and shaking the snow off.

"Were you born in a barn?" asked Ali, intently pecking away at Ole's field-hardened laptop. "You're freezing me to death. You don't know what it's like to have bolts through your nipples. They're not designed for sudden changes of temperature, you know. So make up your mind. Stay in or go out, but, either way, leave the damn door shut!"

"What are they doing out there, Ali?" asked Buck, sitting down next to him.

"Making a movie, obviously," he said, without looking up.

"What for? I don't get it," said Buck, getting up and walking back to the door to take a peek.

"Don't you dare open that door again!" warned Ali, ready to launch a carton of Soyuz Sunrise at him. No one would dare spill this stuff on themselves. Its bouquet, roughly translated from the label, was described as "The smell that never goes away!"

"This time I'm serious, Buck," he said, cocking his arm. "Get this stuff on you and you'll have to pay for friends. So sit down and make yourself useful. And quit obsessing about Petal. She's a big girl. She can take care of herself."

"She has her vulnerabilities," countered Buck, not sure he knew what he was talking about. "As do we all."

"Will you stop mooning? You straights are so pitiful and confused. No surprise, though. How could you hope to understand someone of a completely opposite sex? Their brains are different, you know. They've done scans on them. The best you can do is go with the flow and stay out of the blast zone." Ali pushed *Send* and sat back, rubbing his hands together.

"I am not mooning," protested Buck, getting up and putting his ear to the door. "And I am not trying to understand a member of the opposite sex. I'm just—just—concerned, that's all."

"You want some advice about women?" asked Ali. "Forget all the advice you have ever heard about women. It's a load of propaganda, superstition, and wishful thinking. And another thing. If a woman is trying to make you jealous then that's the last thing that you ought to be. And if she's not trying to make you jealous, then you'll only screw things up by feeling that way."

"What's the point of advice about involuntary emotions anyway?" objected Buck. "Aren't they involuntary, after all? 'Don't be afraid, don't be nervous, don't be sad, don't be jealous.' This sort of advice just makes the giver feel superior and the recipient feel angry."

"People who are angered by advice are the ones who need it most," said Ali. "Old Arab saying that I just made up. Anyway, take it from me; you've got nothing to worry about that a little more worrying won't take care of. All you need to get your mind off your worries is to get busy worrying about stuff that is really worth worrying about. Think you can think of any? This is not that hard, you know."

"What if the US tracks these A-bombs here?" worried Buck.

"Very good! Now you're trying!" congratulated Ali.

"What if nobody believes we really have them?"

"A little less visceral, but not bad."

"What if there really isn't any way to rescue the planet, after all?"

"Excellent! Keep it up," said Ali. "Feeling better?"

"Yeah, I guess I do," admitted Buck. "What if we run out of food?" he asked with a grin.

"Starvation! It's the worst," encouraged Ali, slapping him on the back. "Except for radiation sickness, I hear."

"Right. Do you think this A-bomb is leaking? It hasn't been treated very well recently. They say not to thaw and re-freeze them." Buck was feeling back to himself now, kneeling next to the crate, looking for its 'Best If Used By' date.

"See, what did I tell you? Just come to Uncle Ali if you start feeling punk again."

"Thanks, Ali," said Buck, shaking his hand. "I needed that."

"Any time," said the Sultan, pulling up his parka hood at the sound of the door opening again. This time it was the cinema contingent coming in from the cold.

"Did you set that virus loose?" asked Siverth, warming his hands over the heater.

"Piece of cake," said Ali. "You don't think it's too obnoxious, do you? People hate spam and pop-ups and stuff that messes with their computers. We have to be careful not to turn folks against us."

"No one will even guess that it's there, that's the beauty of it."

"What's this about a virus? You never said anything about a virus," said Buck.

"Sure we did. I don't think you were paying attention. Maybe you were mooning about something else," said Siverth. "So listen up now. My team in Nuuk worked for a year on this one. It was supposed to be part of the piece *Too Bad About Your Brain*, which had to do with how easy it is to control what goes into people's heads. The program isn't that complicated; it determines the context of the web page that you're reading and then makes a few helpful modifications and inserts hyperlinks that drive you to our website—"

"We have a website already?" asked Buck.

"Sure. We must have done that while you were out taking a leak. Here, I'll show you how this works. Now, just get on line and look up anything."

"Okay," said Buck, fingers on the keyboard. "Let's Google 'best recipes for seal ice cream.' Here we go—the first link is to Mama Larsen's Blubber Blog where she's making Flaming Seal Jubilee. Just looks like a recipe to me."

"Look closely."

"Ingredients:" he read. "Ten pound of fresh seal blubber—if you can find any, that is, since rising global temperatures have decimated the seal population through destruction of their habitat. Click *here* to fix this problem."

"And here takes them to our website. Try again," said Siverth.

"Okay, how about we search for 'Archimedes's Twelfth Proposition on the Properties of Conoids and Spheroids'?"

"Go ahead, it doesn't matter," said Siverth, looking confident.

"Here it is. Google has narrowed our search to a hundred million web pages. Let's pick number thirteen thousand."

"Read away."

"'If a paraboloid of revolution be cut by a plane neither parallel nor pendicular to the axis, and if the plane through the axis perpendicular to the cutting plane intersects it in a straight line of which the portion intercepted within the paraboloid is RR', the section of the paraboloid will be an ellipse whose major axis is RR' and whose minor axis is equal to the perpendicular distance between the lines through R, R' parallel to the axis of the paraboloid.' Seems pretty straightforward, but what does it have to do with us?" asked Buck.

"Keep going."

"'But why waste revolutions on paraboloids that will only end up getting cut by planes anyway when you can join a real revolution that cuts the CO_2 right out of planes? That would show 'em! If Archimedes were around he would click *here* before the world really gets screwed. Any geometer worth his protractor would, too, and so should you.'"

"What do you think?"

"Amazing! Let's try something more mainstream. What do you think the most common search question is?" Buck asked.

"Everybody knows that," answered Ali. "It's 'How do I get a bigger *ule*?'"

"Is that spelled 'O-O-L-I-E'?"

"What, are you completely illiterate? It's U-L-E, of course. Don't they have schools in America?"

"'How do I get a bigger *ule*?'" typed Buck obediently. "Looks like there are more web pages to choose from than there are elemental particles in the universe. I'll pick one at random. Oh my God, this is a big *ule*! Does this stuff really work?"

"'Hung Lo's Ancient Oriental *Ule* Enlarger,'" read Petal over Buck's shoulder. "'You get puny *ule*? Hung Lo get answer for you.

Five dollar. But careful, not use too much! Hung Lo not responsible for you get jaw dropping monster kind *ule*!'"

"Keep reading," urged Ali.

"Do you think this stuff really works?" she asked.

"Keep reading," agreed Siverth.

"And for extra no charge, Hung Lo offer you lucky boy (or whatever) Hung Lo Protection Plan for guarantee you get something to do with that hu-mongous *ule* of yours for years to come! Click *here* and do what man say so civilization not collapse from rotten air in sky. When that happen, nobody give a damn about your *ule*, even you."

"Amazing!" said Petal.

"Contextual semantic extrapolation," explained Siverth.

"Is it a cream or a pill?" asked Petal.

"Semiotic neural net coupling," Siverth expanded.

"Vacuums? Pulleys? Centrifugal forces?"

"Iterative cognition modeling," Siverth answered. "With sub-architectural redundancy."

"Mirrors? Struts? Collagen?"

"I think we can all agree that however it works, it's key to mankind's survival," said Buck, eager to be done with intimidating *ules*. "Shall we follow the link to our website? Here we go. Click!"

Long minutes passed with everyone looking over Buck's shoulder. The website had chosen the English version for them, having detected that they had most recently been using English rather than Greenlandic. There were very few written words, anyway, yet the message was clear, reasoned, and straight to the heart. It took a moment for them to realize that there was an audio track, a very soft recording of a forest at sunrise that grew progressively more poignant as species became silenced by their extinction, one by one.

And then they found themselves in the noisy confines of eBay, the global auction place of every good and service known to man, and, now, of mankind's life and death itself. The electronic auctioneer tipped his boater and shook his cane.

Step up and decide how you want it to be. You have come to bid, have you not? One way or another.

Any questions about the items? Their authenticity? Their potency? How about a testimonial or two? Maybe a demo? Some photos from Hiroshima? That one of the girl on the bridge, her clothes burned away, her skin in sheets. More? Or are you ready now?

Are you ready to join this world that you observe like a spectator from your insulated life? Are you ready to step up and take responsibility for it? Are you ready to quit hiding behind your selfishness, pretending that what you do doesn't matter?

Yes, I'm talking to you.

That's right, you.

It's your bid now.

What's it going to be?

CHAPTER 33

ESCAPE

"Siverth, we've got to get ready," said Ole. "They'll be here any minute."

"Okay, okay. I just need to finish this one thing," he said, inching through their last takes on the HD-Cam, frame by frame. "They'll want to rest for a while anyway."

"Are you kidding? This is the last place they'll want to rest! We've got to get as far from this hut as we can before anybody rests! You can edit all that stuff later. We've got to move!"

"Go help the others, Ole," he said. "It won't take me a minute."

"Ali, wrap that up, will you?" Ole said, walking across the room. "We've got to be ready when the teams arrive."

"Yeah, yeah, I hear you," said the Sultan, peering intently at the screen of Siverth's FlakMac Armored Ultra-Portable. "Just don't bug me for one more second. These laundering programs are real finicky and this one will choke up again if I don't get another thousand accounts opened pretty quick. Couldn't you guys have said something in the website about waiting a few days? This is ridiculous! I've never seen so much money moving so fast, and I don't mean to brag, but personally I've blown through a ton of—"

"Buck, Petal," said Ole. "We've really got to go. The teams will be here any time now and they are super freaked out. They say the Americans are going to bomb us back to the Stone Age—not that that would take much of a bomb. Something about the Grudge Report. Have you seen it?"

"No, what did he say this time? Here, move over," she said, nudging Buck away from the screen of Ole's GateCrasher Drop-Ready laptop. They had been cyber-coping with the avalanche of people volunteering for Chill the Anthropocene, trying to figure out how to organize something that they had just barely thought up that was already ballooning out of control.

"Yomamah Got Nothin'!" read Petal. "Uncle Sam Declares War on Filchers! Vows to Clean House from Pole to Pole! Warsaw files defamation complaint at wrong embassy!"

"Is that it?" asked Buck. "It was only a matter of time until they figured out that Yomamah's got no nukes. What makes us think they've tracked the bombs up here?"

"Stuff about the poles?" guessed Ole. "There are only two of them, last count. You know the Americans will start with the easier one and here we are sitting in these outhouses like in some video game for pre-school bomber pilots."

"Pole to pole is just an expression, Ole," said Buck. "Besides, they wouldn't bomb their own nukes. They would likely just drop in about a hundred SEALs who would paralyze us with gas and then slit our throats while we were struggling for air."

"Seals do that?" asked Petal. She had recently developed a deep sense of guilt about eating other sentient beings, especially ones that could balance balls on their noses better than she could. She looked down at her hands, still greasy from lunch. She wiped them on her parka, over and over, but the glistening evidence of her iniquity remained, mocking her, marking her. She knew that she should have chosen to starve until some wandering St. Bernard stumbled upon their cabin with a ration of Caesar's hanging from its collar. But, no, she had to cave to peer pressure and pig out on seal.

She vowed she would no longer consume beings who played joyfully with their siblings, who showed affection for their mates, and who honored rituals of social hierarchy. Even vegetarians looked like cannibals to her, blithely gobbling up beings intelligent enough to move with the sun, climb up wires, and recruit members of other kingdoms into their complex customs of procreation.

She would show her solidarity with the soy, kinship with the kale. She would consume only carbon, nitrogen, and hydrogen in their bare, elemental forms. It would be her penance, her atonement. The seals would be able to sense this, in their fairness and compassion. They would spare her, in spite of the telltale remnants of their brothers still dripping from her chin.

"Come on, Buck," pleaded Ole. "You know there's nobody better than the Americans at cleaning house from pole to pole! And when they decide to clean house they don't care how big a mess they make. So if you value your house at all you'll be ready when our boys get here, 'cause they're not waiting around for that big Hoover in the sky to start sucking up Greenlanders."

"Okay, Ole," said Petal, locking down the computer. "What do we do?"

"Just get dressed; I'll pack up the stuff. The under layer has the fur next to your skin, the outer layer has the fur outside. Then you pull the white nylon layer over everything—that way you will be invisible on the ice. And here, wear this transmitter in case you get separated from the others out there."

He strapped the device next to one of her Coeur d'Alene souvenir bracelets and looked at her, one eyebrow up. During all of their hours of filming, she had never offered an explanation for the manacles. Siverth had acted as if it was to be expected that all beings such as Petal would have chains hanging from their wrists. Ole figured that it was just one more thing he ought to learn about American women but would never have the nerve to ask.

"Handcuffs," she nodded. "Everybody's wearing them."

"Or will be. I can guarantee that. Give 'em ninety days. You just watch," he said over his shoulder as he carried a load of gear out to the sled.

Ninety days, she thought. No doubt it will be handcuffs for everyone by then. She could only hope for hacksaws enough to go around.

The sound of dogs rushed in as he opened the door. Men yelling orders, tension perfusing an ancient language few people had ever heard.

"They're here!" called Ole, "Let's go!"

Buck and Petal finished dressing one another. They were now entirely white except for the tiny slit of their goggles. They turned to see Siverth standing there, as invisibly white as they were.

"I look forward to the time that we may speak all that we know in our hearts," he said, bowing slightly. His voice was muffled. It was impossible to see his eyes.

"Is this goodbye?" asked Buck. "Aren't we leaving together?"

"My friends will take you north," he said. "It will be safer for you to go over the pole. The rest of us will move this horrible weapon to a more secure spot."

"Mr. Narup—" Petal started.

Siverth raised his hand. Even as bundled up as he was, the message was clear. They would not talk until—

"Now!" shouted Ole through the open doorway. They could hear the noise of dogs and men outside, but could see nothing there but thin, gray light.

Buck grasped Petal's hand and led her into the blowing snow. He felt Ole guide his arm, but still could make out only blurs.

"Let me introduce you to your traveling companions," he said. "Please meet Mr. One and Mr. Two and Mr. Three. Over there is Mr. Four and Mr. Five. They know you as Mr. A and Mr. B and Ms. C. Here, let me help you two onto your sled. Petal, squeeze in there in front of Buck. Ali, yours is that one over there. Mr. Three, why don't you show Mr. A how to get comfortable?"

Everything had been sprayed white, the sled, the baggage, the dogs. In the visual spectrum, at least, they were invisible. In the infrared and less human electromagnetic regions, probably not.

Buck had picked up Ole's paranoia. Why shouldn't there be planes circling overhead? Yasser Ibahb was clearly certifiable, so why assume that he could pull off the greatest larceny of all time without leaving any clues? Granted, it had taken a modicum of competence to steal all these nukes in the first place, but since the Americans outsourced just about everything, somebody had to get the contract for security. Actually, it was remarkable that anybody had ever noticed that the nukes had been filched since the contract for noticing had gone to Ibahb, too.

But notice they had, and now the predictable War on Filchers had been joined. How much suffering and money and carbon would be spent on this one before it was over, if ever that would be? What miracles could be worked by Chill the Anthropocene if only it had the resources poured into all the Wars on This's and the Wars on That's?

Buck wondered if he should just call the Feds and put an end to this one right now. If it hadn't been so obvious that all that saved money would immediately find itself funding the next War on The Other, he might have considered it. *Wars On* clearly trumped *Chill The* any day. Any day the boys with the big money were playing.

There was a shout, then motion. Somehow the dogs knew better than to bark this time. He pulled Petal tighter, her back to his chest, her ear close enough to hear him even through their parkas. But he didn't speak. There was too much he didn't know that filled his head and choked his heart.

CHAPTER 34

MUSH

Buck had always heard (from people with no particular place to go) that it was the journey, not the destination. Similarly, he was accustomed to being advised (from people who had already acquired way too much) how spiritually essential it was to abandon acquisitiveness. These seemed to be the same people who (having grown much too big for their own britches) argued so passionately for limits on (other people's) growth and who (from their defensive positions on the top of the ladder) urged all below to stop and smell the roses.

Buck's higher self slapped itself out of this brief cynical lapse and back to its baseline of boundless optimism. Well, sort of. And was that even better, or was optimism itself overrated?

Whom to believe? What to believe? Did others find these questions easy? Was easier better? There had to be a clue to this, but were there any first growth clues still left standing, ones that hadn't themselves been planted?

Advice was not necessarily bad advice just because it was self-serving, was it? Logical argument did not necessarily become propaganda merely by virtue of its proponent's motivation and allegiance, now did it? It was clear that the truth could not be parsed by party line. Especially these days, ever since the last remaining impartial observer had been caught on film with his hand in the till.

Therefore, it was with a mind eager to be open, a heart anxious to be trusting, and a nagging appreciation of his own species-defining capacity for self-delusion that Buck weighed the assertion, set forth by Mr. Two, that while ten Fahrenheit degrees below freezing might be unbearably chilly on the Scottish Highlands, thirty degrees colder on the Greenland ice sheet felt positively balmy. It was the humidity, you see.

Now, while the power of auto-suggestion might be potent enough to allow Mr. Two to mush with his gloves off and Mr. One to lounge around with his hood down, Buck himself couldn't eke a single erg of heat out of this particular article of faith. He wondered if his feet might finally get warm if he could just believe better. Maybe it was the wet blanket of doubt that was keeping his toes blue. It wasn't such an illogical concept, after all, this idea about humidity. He felt he might just be able to talk himself into it, if only he hadn't been so busy freezing his behind off.

Petal, on the other hand, had apparently incorporated the entire Greenlandic mindset into her more encompassing, gender-enhanced worldview. Astoundingly, she seemed to have no trouble believing anything that was demonstrably true. If a dog could smell a bear a mile away (which became indisputable on the third day out) then why doubt its ability to sniff the honesty of a man? If the ice buried beneath you could record weather reports by the millennia, then why doubt that its feel under your boot might foretell an impending global cataclysm? If the Inuit could cruise through an Ice Age while the occupying Norse (not exactly a tropical tribe themselves) went extinct, then why doubt their *bona fides* when preparing for the next planetary climactic disaster?

From Petal's perspective, there was no reason to doubt anything Messrs. One through Five might say about the divine origins of the Greenlandic fan hitch, the mischievousness of sea ice, the psychotropic effects of starlight, or the nutritional wastefulness of cooking. After all, their fluency in canine clairvoyance was undeniable and their navigation by means of squinting-at-the-sky was GPS verifiable. Petal, the hype-hardened media urbanite, was having no trouble with the truth. She found herself unencumbered from what now seemed to be weighing Buck down. Without the ballast of doubt, she had become enlightened.

Petal's powers of cultural assimilation were proving to be prodigious. She took to eating like they did, biting into a slab of flesh as big as a shoe and as tough as leather and then sawing off a hunk with a knife, the gleaming blade flashing alarmingly close to her eyes, sparkling in the firelight.

One day, Mr. One agreed to teach Petal to mush. By the next, he was happily snoozing in the sled, snuggled up to Buck, while she drove like she had been born to it.

212

"Huughauq!" she would command. "Haru!" "Atsuk!" The dogs would never question her authority, they never hesitated. Somehow they knew to obey this strange voice. They could tell instinctively, as Siverth had, that she was true.

She adopted Mr. Three's downhill technique, which required more finesse with the dogs, but less weight on the brake. Her hands chapped, her face burned, her muscles growled, and her hair shone with grease.

She used Mr. Four's musk ox oil on her blisters, Mr. Five's way of seeing a crevasse before it was visible, Mr. Two's squat in the bumps, and Mr. Three's dip in the turns. Soon she could take scariest drops without chipping her teeth. And when she did fall off the runners, one of them would scoop her up on the first bounce and have her back on the sled without missing a beat.

She could teach them nothing of value in return, of course, but that didn't keep them from hanging on her every word, rolling in laughter and snow at her enactments of Manhattan latte ordering, dog grooming, and ring tone tweaking. They howled together at the absurdities of modern life in the First World. How could people live in a city where there wasn't enough room for them all to go outside at the same time, they would wonder. How could people consider themselves educated if they couldn't survive a week without a credit card?

Petal took no offense. On the contrary, she found their bafflements more insightful and wise than any *Times* op-ed. Buck may be more facile with science and Ali with finance, but Messrs. One through Five clearly were the ones with an open line to the heartbeat of Gaia, the life-force of the Earth, the Giver of Dreams. By the twelfth day it was clear that the Inuit soul had fused with hers.

She could feel the depth of their unadmitted despair. She could feel their confusion at the destruction of their homeland, their inability to understand the assault on them by the uncaring and unknowing people of the south. She could feel their sadness, she could share their resolve. But above all, she could marvel at what she didn't feel through them—anger, resentment, doubt.

The pattern of their days entrained her biorhythms—ten hours of mushing through the flat, gray light of permanent dusk, gusting snow obliterating all of the world beyond the sled in front—two hours of setting camp, building snow walls against the

213

rising winds—an hour to eat and six to sleep, huddled together in their tent, the dogs circled around them—and then off again in a cycle which ignored the sun, a sun that day by day seemed itself to be slowly limping away to die.

The hours of concentration on the ice, the dogs, and the opaque wind were a meditation for her, a doorway into a place where all boundaries were blurred, where the limits to her conscious reach were abolished. Here there were no dark traps of disbelief. Here there was room for everything but doubt. The truth was there, clear and just ahead.

She could feel each dog through its connection to the sled. She could feel the ice through their paws. And she could feel the core of the Earth, turning restlessly like an unborn child, miles and miles below them all.

She had escaped from time. She would spend forever here in blissful oneness with creation distilled to its essence, frozen but always moving, growing ever purer as contaminants of cynicism were eluted away by the wind and snow, the truth becoming crystalline, its sharp facets shearing uncertainty away.

The journey and destination had become one. One fine and perfect thing. One she would never leave. Never.

CHAPTER 35

KNELSEN

They had watched the frozen river widen for hours, and now they could see children in the distance, running toward them, waving and shouting. Beyond them were glints of red and green, bits of houses peeking out of the drifts.

"The North Pole!" declared Ali, clapping his hands. "Elves! I knew it was true!"

"Ittoqqortoormiit," said Mr. Three, as if it were obvious.

"We've been going east for days, Ali," said Petal surprised that he hadn't yet picked up the global-positioning squint.

"We're not going to the North Pole?" He sounded disappointed. "Siverth said we were going over the pole."

"He didn't mean we would mush the whole way," said Buck. "You don't want another two month's of this, do you?"

Two more months of mushing! To Petal it sounded like a honeymoon in Maui.

"I bet we could do it in under two months," she said, nodding at the Messrs. "If we wanted to."

"Way under," agreed Mr. Four, who would mush on forever as long as the excuses held out. Just seeing how long it would take was excuse enough.

"No way," said Mr. Three. "Sea ice no good now. Last year, bad. This year, too bad. We end up swimming. You know that."

"Bad years can't last forever," said Mr. Four, looking at his feet and wishing it were true. It was worth a try just to find out.

The children were all around them now, jumping on the sleds, petting the dogs, and squealing with delight at the sight of whitened-out trekkers. Only the Danish army guys ever bothered to camouflage themselves, and they rarely ventured far from their bases. The children thought their friends, Messrs. One through Five, must be playing soldier, too. All the kids had been playing soldier ever since the American SEALs had come by helicopter three days before. No one had ever seen an American soldier in Ittoqqortoormiit before. They were even scarier than the Danish ones. Even scarier than the ones on TV.

"What are they saying?" asked Ali, hoping it had something to do with invitations to dinner and offers of a hot shower.

"American military," answered Mr. Two. "Three days ago. Asking questions. Apparently not a goodwill tour. These kids don't know much. Especially how to keep their mouths shut. We had better get you out of here before you show up on their Icebook pages."

He urged the dogs to run faster toward the ocean in the distance. Petal mushed closely after, her hood blowing back, her blond hair streaming behind her, a sight that would prove to be both indelible and uncontainable in the Ittoqqortoormiit adolescent imagination, which, of course, had become thoroughly intercalated into the frantic electronic cloud that made up the collective adolescent imagination of the planet.

"No hot shower?" whined Ali, picking up the gist if not the deeper implications of this turn of events.

"There's a shower on the boat," answered Mr. Two. "Or at least a sink. I think." Mr. Two was clearly bullshitting here, and the rest of the Messrs. knew it. All of them had spent plenty of time on the ocean, in vessels from kayaks to tankers. Messrs. Two and Three even would SCUBA dive under icebergs just for laughs from time to time. But none of them had ever had the nerve to set foot on Captain Knelsen's boat, a sentiment shared by all sober residents of Ittoqqortoormiit.

Siverth, while technically always sober, had no qualms about sailing with Captain Knelsen—or so he said anyway, never having exactly gotten around to doing so. Siverth remained a staunch supporter of the Captain despite all of his picaresque tribulations, as did the Captain of him, even though Captain Knelsen wouldn't know a piece of performance art from a bushel of boiled blubber.

Much of Siverth's expansive social network consisted of mutual-admiration-from-a-respectable-distance relationships such as this one. These connections proved indispensable to the production of large scale artistic high jinks, but were always a bit disconcerting to other FOS (Friends of Siverth) who found themselves in unintentional collusion with people they thought would be better off in jail. That it worked at all was a tribute to

Siverth's force of personality rather than any rational quid pro quo. If any FOS had become enriched from his association with Siverth, it was only in the satisfaction of knowing that he had helped make the world a more bizarre and unpredictable place—a worthy enough legacy for any man.

Captain Knelsen's boat, the Laaka Nuuke, sat listing slightly to port at a dock that seemed to be otherwise abandoned. Down the harbor about half a mile were a handful of fishing vessels that seemed actually to have paint left on them, moored to berths that hadn't yet been relinquished to nature. Apparently, most of the Ittoqqortoormiit fleet was already out to sea, pursuing productive endeavors that could only have been figments of the Laaka Nuuke's confabulatory imagination.

Captain Knelsen himself sat slightly listing to starboard with his feet on the ship's rail, rocked back precariously and apparently asleep in his plastic lawn chair. His used-to-be-high-visibility-yellow rain hat was pulled down over his face in a way that only his beard—a still high-visibility orange hemisphere—was exposed, which left the impression that his head had been replaced by a buoy. Not that that wouldn't have been an improvement, as would soon become apparent. The only signs of life were his foghorn snoring and a continuous but unconscious adjustments of the hand that kept his drink from sloshing with every roll of the boat.

When even the noise of the sled dogs didn't waken the Captain, Mr. Four, not willing to actually board the Laaka Nuuke, chucked a frozen herring at him. Knelsen, accustomed to this protocol, pulled himself upright, rubbing the knot on his noggin.

"Ahh, Søren, Jens, Kaus," he said. "You here already? Siverth said it would take—what time is it anyway?"

"Eleven thirty," said Mr. Two.

"And that would be eleven thirty of which day now?"

"Wednesday, Cap'n."

"Wednesday already. Are you sure?"

"No doubt about it Cap'n. Wednesday for sure."

"You wouldn't have the date with that, would you," asked Knelsen shaking his watch.

"Captain Knelsen," said Mr. One. "Did you tell Mr. Narup that you would be helping these friends of his?"

"Sure did. My pleasure. At your service. Out of the country right away. First thing. Not a minute to spare."

"So what difference does the date make?"

"Well, my relief gets deposited on the first, and if it's before the seventh then there's bound to be enough for gas. After that, no guarantees." Knelsen spread his hands and beamed his winning but gap-toothed smile. Not responsible for the calendar, now are we, mate?

"You guys got gas money?" asked Mr. One.

"Wallet's in my other Speedo," answered Ali.

"In theory," answered Buck.

"Ditto," said Petal. "But we're good for it in ninety days."

"Okay, okay," said Mr. Three. Everybody knew he had a trust fund. His father had made a bundle helping a Nigerian gentleman who had sent him an email about some kind of banking problem.

"Just don't forget," he said. Mr. Three wasn't stingy with money; in fact he had little use for it, day to day. It was just that all he knew about having money he had learned from American TV, and it was obvious that the richer you were the cheaper you were supposed to act.

"We will never forget any of you," said Petal, getting teary and hugging them all in turn.

"We could never repay you for saving our lives," said Buck, knowing how far a little thanks went with members of the rescuing professions. "Though when this is all over we certainly will try."

"You guys are greatest," said Ali, kissing them all on the cheeks. "We definitely will have you down to Yomamah for some sand mushing and camel blubber. Give us about ninety days to get this all straightened out first, though."

"Yeah, ninety days," agreed Petal.

"Ninety one at the most," assured Buck.

Petal petted all the dogs goodbye, calling them by name and promising to come back someday for a nice long mush. Buck and Ali waited patiently on board and Mr. Three fed the gas pump for the Captain. Fortunately, the departure was a pretty emotional scene for everyone; otherwise they might have realized just what they were getting themselves into. They weren't ten minutes from shore before they began to have a bad case of buyer's regret, or in their case, beggar's regret.

"Kind of rough out here today," observed Ali, holding on with both hands and just barely keeping his feet and his lunch. It was crowded with all four of them in the wheelhouse, but it was better than being out on the deck where the spray was like a Freon fire hose. The little boat was bucking like a horse with one short leg.

"We're still in the harbor, mate," said the Captain. "And a snug little harbor she is. Not a calmer place in all of East Greenland. Throw a baby in here to teach 'em how to swim." He wrestled with the wheel, which seemed to be kind of loose in between the places that it stuck.

"Really nice of you to help us out like this," said Buck. "Hate to take you out of your way."

"My way, my way," mused the Captain as if beginning to recount one of the many profound lessons of the sea which he couldn't quite remember. "Don't worry, son, I've had my way with every furlong of ocean above the Arctic Circle, from Nome to Nuuk, from Natchez to Mobile, the high seas and low—" He waved his arm in a great circle, still managing not to spill a drop.

"Captain Knelsen?" asked Petal, managing to look him in the eye by grabbing him by the collar. "You wouldn't mind telling us just where you are taking us, would you?"

"Out of the country, my dear. Straight away. Not a minute to spare. I hear you kids are in a pack of trouble. My specialty, that. Trouble, I mean."

"Well, I assure you that we have done nothing to be in trouble about, and in the end our good names will be totally vindicated," insisted Petal. "Though, I admit that the circumstances do make it appear, initially, on the surface—"

"Say no more, dear lady! No lesser man than I have found myself unjustly incarcerated against my will with entire holding cells of innocent victims of mistaken identity, administrative malfeasance, and teetotalling intolerance. Our mutual friend, Mr. Narup, has been insightful enough to vouch for my character countless times through small donations of bail and timely contributions to the constabulary pension fund. The least I can do is facilitate your repatriation to a more understanding municipality, along with a truly massive block of hashish entrusted to me by the local representative of the Afghani Rastafarian community who—"

"Your hold is full of hashish?" asked Ali. "Is that why the boat is listing?"

"Must have shifted," said the Captain. "You'll get used to it. Just face the stern when one leg gets tired. That's what I do."

"Does Mr. Narup know that you are a drug smuggler?" asked Ali, who personally had nothing against drug smugglers. In fact, some of his best friends were drug smugglers.

"Such an indelicate way to put it! I prefer to see myself as just a small link in the developing world's alternative economy. Certainly you don't want the World Bank to have a monopoly on hashish along with everything else, do you? Besides, their hash sucks. And no, I have not burdened Mr. Narup with the humdrum details of my daily toil. He's a busy man, you know. Art, I think."

"We're going over the pole with hashish?" asked Ali, trying to get this straight.

"Of course not, why would we do that? That's where it just came from. Afghanistan to Uzbekistan to Kazakhstan to Russia to Finland to Norway to the North Pole and then to here. The hashish superhighway. My piece is the hop between Ittoqqortoormiit and Isafjordur. A sleepy little sail, though getting a bit late in the season." The Captain rubbed at the windscreen with his sleeve, a gesture that did nothing to make it less opaque. Waves crashing over the bow could be felt—sort of like what a wrecking ball feels like—but not seen. Probably a good thing.

"What's he saying?" yelled Buck, over the thunderous wind.

"We're going south," said Petal, squinting at the charcoal sky.

"Iceland," declared the Captain. "You'll love it there. Practically in the tropics and a great place to chill out after the frantic pace of Ittoqqortoormiit."

Finally, a place to chill, thought the three refugees. Things could have been worse.

CHAPTER 36

REGATTA

Log more than an hour on a barstool in Lahaina and you are guaranteed to get stuck between two skippers who claim that their trips across the Molokai Channel had been the roughest in history. Their harrowing tales are sure to chill your spine and whiten your knuckles. Or is that your Mai Tai? Maybe it needs a fresh parasol. Okay, granted, it can get kind of hairy sailing among the Hawaiian Islands on a bad day, but, let's face it boys; it's not exactly the Greenland Sea, now is it?

The only thing mellow about the Greenland Sea is its name. Literally rolls off the tongue like the script off a Tolkien map—conjuring visions of a mythical mirrored lake, its swirling mists muffling the oar strokes of elven craft returning from a quest.

If only.

But call it what you want, this hellish piece of unsellable real estate is what gives the Arctic Ocean a bad name, a pinch point for unstoppable, sub-freezing gales and monstrous icebergs bearing down like freight trains from the pole, destined to collide with humongous speeding mountains of wet air and warm water catapulted up from the Equator by the Gulf Stream. Their meeting is about as rude as two dogs in a ditch, and a lot like whipping up a big batch of vinegar and baking soda Margaritas in your blender. Only bigger. And with you in it.

Captain Knelsen had made the crossing from Greenland to Iceland once when sober and had learned quickly enough not to try that again. But even properly anesthetized, the trip was still like having a prize fighter give you a root canal on a roller coaster. Towering swells from every direction would slam together, scrubbing the frostbitten Laaka Nuuke with saline slush and hurling her twenty feet skyward, only to slam her to the mat, punch-drunk, and stomp on her again. The gale turned spray into icy darts that splintered wood, stripped paint, and punctured skin.

The wheelhouse became a sadistic laundromat, tangling everyone's arms and legs into a knotted ball that, thankfully, was too big to fit out the door. It was a good thing that the Laaka Nuuke knew the way, because no one dared grab her wheel, which spun continuously like a finger-eating buzz-saw.

But within even the most chaotic maelstroms there will sometimes form tiny eddies, transient bubbles of paradoxical calm, where all the malevolent forces cancel each other out for a while. Or maybe such refuges are the rule rather than the exception, part of a law of nature that balances good and evil, violence and healing. Maybe there is a thermodynamics of peace, a conservation of kindness that guarantees that even in the worst of space-times there must be at least one concentrated granule of beauty hidden within the turbulence.

And it was with the sudden surety of a toggle switch that the Laaka Nuuke's universe flipped from negative to positive, from black to white, when the little boat popped through the conceptual membrane separating such a nugget of tranquility from the storm that surrounded it. Satellite photos of the event would be judged unremarkable—a continent-sized atmospheric disturbance that, at the macro scale, had the same geometric stereotypy as a whirling galaxy, each with its pale dot of inexplicable mystery at the center. But from within those geographic eyes, beholders would find a beauty beyond the mathematical and a sense of wonder beyond the predictable.

"Are we dead?" asked Ali, disengaging himself from the human pile that now had settled on the deck of the wheelhouse. The sun, while low, hung in a cloudless sky. The air was still, the ocean like an infinite pool spilling off the horizon. Everyone's ears rang in the silence; even the Laaka Nuuke's engines were still, having stalled hours before. Only a gentle tinkling of wavelets against the hull could be heard by those whose hearing had recovered.

"Eye of the storm, mate," answered the Captain, walking out on deck. Even he didn't believe it. It was too other-worldly for such a natural sounding explanation. Everything was weird here, temperature, humidity, barometric pressure, and, above all, the pervasive sense of immortality.

"Hope its eye is bigger than its stomach," said Buck, pulling off his wet parka. "I thought we were getting digested back there."

"Seems pretty big," said Petal, wringing out her hair and scanning the horizon. The sky and sea could have been made of construction paper for all their homogeneous regularity. "What are the coordinates for Isafjordur, Captain?"

"66° North, 23° West," Knelsen recited. He used to have a chart and sextant back before global positioning devices had been developed. On the other hand, he didn't exactly own a global positioning device himself, but wouldn't be caught dead with obsolete technology. That left him dead reckoning, which, thanks to the deity that protects drunks and hashish smugglers, had not rendered him dead yet.

"Not far," said Petal, squinting. "But do you think it wise for us to be receiving visitors just now?" She pointed north, where the sharp demarcation between sky and ocean was punctuated by a cluster of tiny, colored dots.

"Pirates or police," postulated Knelsen, firing up the Laaka Nuuke's engine. "Maybe some country's navy. Nobody we want to see. Especially nobody we want to see us. The damn arctic is getting too crowded these days. Used to be you could run contraband in peace all day and not see a soul. Now just when you think that you've gotten back to nature, some bozo with a gun is in your face ruining the view."

The little boat excelled in flat water, especially after about a ton of it had been pumped out of the hold. But with only the approaching boats as reference points, there was an eerie feeling that it was moving backwards, being sucked northward by its own wake.

"This thing go any faster?" asked Ali, now able to identify twenty or thirty craft closing behind them.

"Not unless you jump out and push," answered Knelsen testily. "Or just jump out. Either way."

"We could jettison cargo," offered Buck, not prepared for the horrified expressions of both the Captain and the Sultan. "In theory, I mean."

"Well, that's a mighty fine theory, that one. And I'll bet if you all work on it, you can think up dozens more just as good. But while you're busy thinking, why don't you make yourselves useful? There are paddles enough to go around right in that box."

Buck took the bow position with Petal to port and Ali to starboard.

"That's it. Stroke! Stroke! Stroke!" called the Captain, craning his neck to check on their pursuers. After a while he thought this might actually be helping.

"Land ahead!" cried Petal.

"Hooray!" cried the crew.

"And helicopters!" cried Petal. "With flashing blue lights!"

"Shee-it!" cried the crew.

"Now what?" asked Ali, pausing at the oar.

"Act natural," said the Captain. "And keep paddling. Helicopters can't hurt you. They're just big mosquitoes."

He ran a tattered Icelandic flag up, begrudging the additional aerodynamic drag. A Kevlar vest would be more appropriate right about now. He would add it to his Christmas list, right above the GPS.

The rowing team of Ali, Buck, and Petal would have made Oxford proud, and seemed to be slowing the rate of acceleration of the rate of change of the distance to the approaching boats. The warm air and the exertion had gotten the three of them sweating and eager to be rid of their wet, smelly mushing clothes. Down to their Speedos, they really got up to speed, the Laaka Nuuke surging ahead with every stroke, gliding on faces of following seas. Heads down, they pulled with all their strength, in perfect synchrony with the Captain's chanted cadence.

So focused they were on their task that for a time they became oblivious to all else, and when the sounds of horns and sirens jolted them alert, they were astounded to see the harbor of Isafjordur looming just ahead, crowded with boats of all sizes, all moving toward them under power of sail, engine, or muscle. Right behind them the pursuing flotilla was bearing down in their final push. Now there were a half dozen aircraft circling and hovering. Flares streaked through the air. Anything with a horn was blowing it. The sound of human voices swelled on the breeze.

It was as if the entire world had been chasing them and was now about to pounce. There was no escape. Their goose was cooked. But still they paddled. They paddled even harder than before, turning their growing panic into super-human exertion, their eyes wild, their muscles bulging, their Speedos clinging with sweat.

And then the gunfire. One loud and sharp and unmistakable explosion. The Captain clutched his chest. The paddlers froze in mid stroke. And then pandemonium.

Boats were all around them blocking their way. People screaming. Bullhorns blaring in Icelandic. A shining police cutter somehow cut through the crowd and clamped to their bow. The Laaka Nuuke's engine coughed and quit. It was the end. They were finished.

"And this year's winner of The Coors Invitational Isafjordur to Isafjordur Great Circle Around the World from Pole to Pole Regatta is the—the Laaka Nuuke!" announced a bullhorn, eventually in English. A camera crew complete with lights and spectacularly augmented news reportress was suddenly on board, attaching her wires and dabbing at her makeup. The statuesque investigatrix homed immediately in on Buck (for reasons too complex to go into here) and began the ritual post-athletic-victory blather-fest with an incisive "How does it feel to win this year's Coors Great Circle Mr.—Mr.—"

"Downe," he lied. "Hans."

"A pleasure, Mr. Downe. May I call you Hans?" Even her English was heavily siliconed. "How does it feel, Hans, to win this year's Coors Great Circle?"

"Actually, to be honest, I think that—"

"And is it true that your team paddled the entire way around the globe, the whole, like, what, thousands of miles?" she gushed, cupping her earphone, trying to hear what questions she was supposed to ask over the roaring of the crowd.

"That would be 24,859.82 miles," offered Buck, "not counting having to skirt around Antarctica. Of course, the equatorial route would have been slightly longer—24,901.55 miles to be exact— owing to the bulge caused by the planet's rotation—not counting all the continents in the way, of course, and discounting the effect of water temperature on hydrodynamic viscosity and hull buoyancy—"

"And did you train to painful exhaustion every day for decades to the exclusion of every other bodily and mental function, shunning any consideration of your family, your health and your future, blinded to any real issues confronting humanity by the single-minded obsession of winning the Coors Great Circle?" she cooed.

"Well, the truth of the matter is—"

"And what do you think about athletes taking steroids? I mean, obviously, these drugs do give you that luscious and powerful physique that women drool over and make the difference between winning and losing, obviously, but can't they also shrink down your?—your?—but I see, obviously, that this is not a problem in your particular—"

"I can assure you right now that the Laaka Nuuke team has never used any drug that improved its performance even a tiny bit, Miss—Miss—"

"Anderson," she said, extending her card. "Call me Hana. Any time."

"That would be just swell, Hana," he said looking back at the wheelhouse. The Captain was still down after a serious psychosomatic gunshot wound but holding his own thanks to the swift action of Petal and Ali who attended to his vital signs with their heads obscured in shadow.

Police were everywhere, crawling all over the boat, keeping fans from boarding, and opening a path in the gridlock so the sea ambulance could get through. Cameras pointed from every direction, whirring and snapping and flashing. He could imagine the face recognition programs at Interpol clicking toward their digital jackpots. He had better get the team out of there fast. Desperate measures were called for, whatever the risk to life or limb.

"Maybe we could do an in-depth exclusive, maybe back at your studio, where maybe there aren't so many people around?" suggested Buck, courageously.

"You would let me do an exclusive on you?" breathed Hana, her voice sizzling like a griddle beneath her professional persona.

"We could all do an exclusive together," he suggested, nodding to his friends. Ali and Petal gave her a little wave. Knelsen, fortunately, was below her line of sight. "My friends are really good at exclusives."

Hana seemed to be having a little trouble with both her antiperspirant and her power of speech. She mumbled something that sounded censorable in Icelandic and began groping in her blouse and wiggling in her skirt. Eventually she was able locate a little microphone that had grown slippery and plunged from her lapel into the Nordic darkness below. After a few urgent-sounding orders into it she looked to the sky, holding up four fingers. The unmistakable sound of helicopter rotors engulfed them and, within a minute, a cabin that looked like a ski gondola was being lowered to the deck. Buck signaled his friends to hurry.

"Let's go Captain," said Petal. "Our chariot awaits."

"You're not getting me on no helicopter," he replied. "Those things are dangerous. Terrible safety record. Why, I was reading recently that compared to food allergies and adulterated toothpaste, helicopter crashes are six times more—"

"But the police!" insisted Petal. "They're everywhere!"

"Don't worry about those boys. They're just the next cloverleaf in the Great Hashish Superhighway. And besides, I ain't never been famous before!"

CHAPTER 37

CHOPPER

Buck, of course, was no stranger to humongous helicopters. Need a couple hundred tons of men and materiel at an earthquake in Oaxaca or a typhoon in Chuuk? Then you had better have a fleet of these mamas gassed and greased with crews on standby—and about a million dollars a minute to keep their meters ticking. Monstrous helicopters like this were not for the faint of heart or light of wallet, and never was one in the air for a frivolous purpose.

Anyone who had ever been in Buck's business (or whose country had ever annoyed the American war deciders) could have spotted the KICE news chopper as a tarted up CH-47 Chinook, made over in pink and puce, gloss and glitter, looking like a drill sergeant in drag. Hoisting up the entire camera crew, their equipment, Buck, Petal, Ali, Hana, and the attendants for all of her various parts was nothing compared to its intended payload of tanks and bulldozers. While appreciative to be sure, Buck could still be appropriately appalled by this profligate display of technological excess. To him, a TV station with a Chinook was like a movie star with a moon rocket. But then, Buck was kind of a prude about Hummers, too.

As the dangling gondola approached the behemoth's belly in an unearthly display of airborne rebirthing, Buck anticipated that the mother ship's interior would also be done up like an entry in the Hello Kitty Emesis Through Architecture competition. It was a great relief, then, to be delivered into a cavernous utilitarian space painted the familiar olive drab shared by every military container, large and small, inside and out, since the color had been invented.

This particular ship was configured like a 47G or even a 47F with half its hold allotted to troops and half to cargo. When the ship jerked forward in a nose-down drive to a hundred and fifty knots, everyone in the party scrambled into seat belts except for Buck, who stretched like a cat and ambled up to the front. It was great to be in the air again. His heart warmed in his nostalgia, even as the rest of him shivered in his Speedo.

"Nice airplane," said Buck, leaning over the pilot's shoulder, gambling on the guy's English and sense of humor.

The pilot's initial expression of annoyance melted when he turned to see Buck's winning smile. "Nice tuxedo," he replied with the Midwestern-like accent they all have in Reykjavik.

"Planck," he said, extending his hand. "Buck."

"You were in Sudan after the ceasefire that time, right? Didn't like being shot at, as I remember," he said. "Arni Gunnarsson."

"Gunner. Sure, I remember. You were with that Swedish NGO, or was it Danish? Some Birkenstock outfit anyway."

"Flew for all of them. Strictly a mercenary do-gooder. Would have dropped pâté into Paris for Gourmands without Borders if it had fit in their budget. No good deed too small, you know, as long as you break even in the end."

"So what's with this gig, Gunner?" asked Buck. "You've got a mission-ready 47G on the inside and a powder puff derby, transvestite getup on the outside. Some sort of weird civilian camouflage or what?"

"Actually it's a 47J. Made for Boeing by Kawasaki in Kobe for the sole purpose of running American dollars through Japanese corporations to pay them back for doing the same, then leased to the Icelandic government at a steep discount in return for being late to a vote on sanctions against whaling, and then sub-let to a helicopter timeshare tax write-off broker out of Reykjavik to keep the cash flowing until the government figures out what it wants with a big helicopter in the first place.

"Right now it's KICE's month. In a few weeks we'll be running squid to the Vatican or nuns to the northern lights. It only takes a day to paint a ship like this, but sometimes the painter gets drunk and we have to fly nuns as squids or squids as nuns. Every now and then we get to do something useful in Darfur or Dhaka, but nowadays the only money around seems to be bound up in one or another amusement for the affluent. Honest work and nothing to be embarrassed about, but not exactly stuff you'd be proud to tell your grandchildren."

"Gunner, my friends and I are involved in something that every grandkid in the future will be proud of, and we could sure use a guy with your experience—once we get our current situation stabilized a little bit, that is."

"Do I get to wear a Speedo?"

"It's kind of a long story, Gunner—"

"Where do you keep your wallet, anyway?"

"Our wallets, unfortunately, have become temporarily—"

"And the half sawed-off handcuffs? My grandkids are gonna love me in handcuffs."

"Sometimes it's more polite just not to mention—"

"It's one of those sex things, right? Chains and Speedos? You gotta hand it to that Anderson lady, flights with her are a lot more interesting that with the nuns or the squids, though don't sell those nuns short; they can really cut up when you get them away from the Vatican. Sort of like letting a slingshot loose after you pull it back extra far, if you know what I mean."

Buck was rescued from another feeble attempt at social networking by an incoming message from the home base. The pilot raised his hand and lowered his head a bit in the universal signal for "Don't bug me, I'm on the phone."

"Miss Anderson," he said through the overhead speakers. "Your boss wants to talk to you. Maybe you want to come up here. He says it's important."

"What, and break my leg? I don't see you walking around this damn helicopter in spike heels! Put him over the intercom. I'm not moving."

"He says it's kind of personal," said the pilot after a short negotiation.

"Personal? In his unsanitary dreams! You tell that little Vienna sausage that I'll have him up on sexual harassment charges so fast his ears will pop if he says one more personal thing to me about any of my—"

"Okay, okay, here he comes," he said flicking a switch and filling the room with an Icelandic rant that, by the sound of it, had already ramped up to nine point oh on the Freud-Britney hysteria scale.

"Hanna, you plastic-cow-uddered, public-error-prone, blond female-person!" screamed the intercom, in Icelandic. "Those people you filmed at the Coors Around-the-World-for-No-Good-Reason Regatta are impostors! That Laaka Nuuke condemned-refuse-vehicle wasn't the winning boat, you—you—you—"

"Guy says you're an impostor," whispered Gunner to Buck, by way of translation.

"There are plenty worse things," whispered Buck, defensively. Actually, being an impostor would be kind of an improvement. Impostors tended to be competent, well dressed, and well organized, with clearly thought-out contingency plans.

"It was too the winner!" Hana screamed back, in Icelandic. "The first boat is always the winner! Any stunted-individual-whose-brain-has-been-made-feeble-by-compulsive-self-stimulation knows that!"

"She's vouching for your *bona fides*," the pilot whispered, jerking his eyebrows up twice in the universal signal for "Please congratulate me for this rather strained but mannishly salacious double-entendre."

"It's nice to be appreciated," replied Buck, suddenly self-conscious about just how wide an angle of the passenger's forward view he must be taking up with his Speedoed butt.

"That's because they cheated!" screamed the intercom, in Icelandic. "There was no Laaka Nuuke in the beginning! Ask anyone, even the most pigment-depleted, silicone-burdened, avian-brained—"

"Something about the natural course of marital affections, I think," offered the pilot, who was having a little trouble picking the allegations out of the abuse.

"So we're off the hook, then?" asked Buck, relieved.

Gunner pulled his mouth down and shoulders up in the universal sign for "How the hell would I know?"

"Just because you and your dishonest-wager-brokering-associates bet on a losing boat doesn't give you the right to deny these courageous competitors, who have tirelessly hypertrophied their muscular bodies to glistening perfection, their rightful place in the annals of the Coors—" she began, in Icelandic.

"She likes your bodies," warned the pilot.

"I was afraid of that," admitted Buck.

"Will you shut up!" bellowed the intercom, in Icelandic. "I don't care who won that (untranslatable) race or what happens to anybody's body. What I'm calling about is a million times more important than any of that! A billion times even! In fact, this could be the biggest story in the entire history of Iceland!

"The Hekla volcano is about to blow, and according to the guys who are supposed to know, this is going to be the big one, the one that splits the country in two, if there is any country left afterwards. And of all of the reporters in the world it happens that it is you, Hana Anderson, God help us, who are the only one in a helicopter close enough and big enough to get there and get the last of the geothermal plant workers out alive. Now put an icicle in your (untranslatable) long enough to get this story! Do you understand, person-with-estrogen-poisoned-brain?"

"Of course I do, individual-with-pitifully-hypoplastic-midline-structures," she responded, in Icelandic. "I understand that I'll be picking up my Pulitzer Prize wearing my Medal of Honor and you'll be sweeping up after the party. So go eat your (untranslatable) out!

"Pilot!" she screamed, in English. "To Hekla! Top speed! And turn off that damn intercom!"

"Well?" said Buck as the pilot banked the Chinook sharply left.

"Looks like we got our wish," said Gunner.

"I was afraid of that, too," said Buck, knowing that he would hear the grizzly details soon enough.

CHAPTER 38

THERMAL

For untold generations it had been customary for the occasional schoolchild, after dozing bleary-eyed for months in front of a map of the world, to ask his or her teacher whether North and South America had broken off from the coasts of Europe and Africa and floated like big hunks of pond scum to their present positions in the west. After all, the kid would argue, the shapes fit together like in a puzzle (don't they?) and in puzzles this is never an accident. At that point, according to established protocol, the teacher must smack the kid's knuckles with a ruler for asking such a stupid question and order him or her back to memorizing dates of battles and declinations of subjunctive tenses.

From time to time, intellectually undisciplined or recalcitrant adults would also stumble upon the same observation but usually would have enough sense to keep their mouths shut about it. Occasionally, though, some wag would publish a cartoon map with the Atlantic snipped out and the continents all snuffled up together in an obscene display of geographical copulation. But as titillating as these images might be for the lower classes, they did little to advance the progress of geophysical thought. Any serious scientist knew he would be expelled from his profession in ridicule if he entertained any explanation for the continental mirror-symmetry other than that God, while otherwise admirably omnipotent, had found Himself on the first day with a rather limited selection of cookie cutters.

But then, all of a sudden, it was true. Not only was it true, but everybody knew it was true. So nowadays schoolteachers, by and large, no longer rap knuckles in response to children's intuitive understanding of plate tectonics. They are allowed to explain that, yes, Johnnie, you are right; we all really are living on a thin, brittle sheet of pond scum tossed on a turbulent sea of molten rock, so hot your skin vaporizes into smoke before you can touch it and so powerful and fickle that every speck of planetary life could be extinguished in an instant by one of its monstrous, flatulent eructations.

And yes, the continents are drifting apart like leaves on a stream, but they are also crashing into one another like great, flat, sumo wrestlers, with the loser being pushed down into a bubbling cauldron of lava to be burnt back into the elemental ash of creation. The teacher then may smile to herself with the satisfaction of knowing that tonight, when the lights go off in Johnnie's bedroom, the little blighter will be wishing that he had had his knuckles rapped instead of having the awful truth set loose upon his terrified imagination.

Conversely, if there is any common theme in the accelerating cacophony of assertions we call 'scientific progress,' it may be found in the following axiom: *The truth value of a proposition does not contribute positively to its believability.* Who would believe that the earth itself is bursting along a seam that runs around the world from pole to pole, that currents of magma welling up from the core are prying the east from the west as molten goo from the depths of Hades explodes relentlessly into our fragile little biosphere through this widening crack? Who would want to believe? Johnnie, is that you whimpering?

So, in the ordinary navigation of daily life, it is accepted practice to know, intellectually, that some horrifying fact is indisputably true and still not believe a single word of it. For example, it is assumed that one will thoroughly process a National Geographic fold-out of a spread-eagled Earth, pared open like a poisoned apple, with arrows and captions indicating the unstoppable plume of life-snuffing lava aimed directly at one's very feet, and yet still carry around a mental cartoon of our planet as a big clod of dirt, lolling like a marble through space, with nothing more frightening inside than a bunch of creepy earthworms.

Lucky thing, for our emotional denial mechanisms anyway, that the Mid-Atlantic Ridge is hidden away, deep on the ocean floor. Otherwise, it would serve up a daily reminder of our fragility, transience, and insignificance—a few other things we choose to know but not believe. Having it right there in your face would be like waking up every morning next to the grim reaper, having breakfast with your pall bearers, and riding to work in your hearse. It could get to you after a while.

Unless you were Icelandic. Then, of course, you would be used to it. After all, the island of Iceland is the only part of the Atlantic rift line that isn't buried under tons of water. In Iceland, creation isn't a myth; it is happening right in your face. The crust of the Earth is being made anew, right before your eyes, replacing landscape being lost in the collision of continents half a world away. It is beautiful, in a way, if you survive it. And if you are Icelandic, that's not always a given.

Because every now and then, when it's time for the Earth Mother to deliver up a spanking new Manhattan-sized piece of steaming real estate, even the Icelanders figure it's smarter to run than to watch. Used to be you could count on about a minute's warning before your local volcano blew its top off and you with it, but thanks to modern vulcanologic monitoring techniques, warnings of major conflagrations now come much earlier. Like an hour. When you're lucky.

"The Hekla volcano is one of our most obnoxious," said the pilot. "Dozens of major eruptions since anyone started counting. Sits right on the crack, you know. It spits to the east, you've got more Europe. It spits to the west, there's more North America. It spits straight up, well, that's when it really gets mad. Like now."

"So, let me guess," said Buck. "We are flying to safety full throttle in the opposite direction."

Gunner knew he wasn't serious. "Still a few operators left at the geothermal plant there. They pare down to a skeleton crew when the windows start rattling or the tea leaves look funky. Now its time for the rest of them to abandon ship, too."

"We going to drop these civilians off first?" asked Buck, nodding back into the passenger area.

"Maybe if it were the month for squid or the month for nuns, but this is the month for news and KICE is buying the gas. Daring rescues are news. So, once again, we are simultaneously the news team and the news. You know there is no bigger news for the news media than stuff about the news media. Especially stuff that makes them look good. Got to have the camera crew and the talent. You want me to drop you and your people off? Better decide quick. Not too many amenities around here."

"Let me talk with them," said Buck, walking back through the bucking helicopter. There was major turbulence in the air now.

"Apparently we are on our way into an exploding volcano," he said, leaning in between Ali and Petal. "Want to bail?"

"Is it warmer there?" asked Ali, shivering in his Speedo.

"Considerably," calculated Buck.

"How come?" asked Petal.

"News team needs to film itself rescuing some folks stuck there."

"Black tie or resort casual?" asked Petal, smoothing her hair.

"Kevlar. Asbestos optional," said Buck. "Is that a yes, then?"

"Of course, Buck," she said. "I can tell you want to go, and you were so nice about all the mushing and everything. Just see if you can get us something nice to wear for the camera. A little less décolleté, perhaps?"

Buck made his way back to Gunner.

"We're in. Got some extra clothes on board?"

"Check that locker in the back. Supposed to be cold weather gear for the nuns in there, but you know how they are. Get to partying all the way back to the Vatican and then 'forget' to change back into the nun getup. God knows what is back there now. You are welcome to it, whatever it is. Otherwise, looks like you are stuck bartering for sweaters with the film crew."

Buck gave his friends a thumbs up on his way back to the clothes locker. It would be nice to slip into something cozy from Patagonia. Something sturdy from REI. Something flannel from LL Bean. Something quilted from Campmor. Something black from the Vatican?

The locker did have copious quantities of heavy cloth stuffed into it, all of it jet black except for some stiff, white collars and a few muslin items of unidentifiable utility. Luckily, even though there was a certain monotony of style, there was a large selection of sizes, and Buck was able to collect perfect ensembles for the three of them, right down to sturdy shoes and appropriate accessories.

"Is that the Kevlar or asbestos?" asked Ali, as Buck returned with an armful of habits.

"Meet Your Maker After Six Wear," explained Buck. "Wool/nettle blend, by the feel of it. Warm, though."

"You guessed my size!" said Petal, impressed. "You are such a rascal! Here, help me with this head thing. And stockings with seams! Very sexy. And this doohickey, does it go this way or the other way?"

"Not unlike a dishdasha, really," said Ali, admiring himself. "Very nostalgic. I don't suppose there were any sandals back there? Probably not practical here anyway. These shoes will be fine, and I like a little heel. They don't make me look fat, do they?"

Everyone agreed that Ali looked stunning and not a bit fat once they found the right belt. Buck was tempted to skip the wimple, but he knew his ears would freeze without it. Hana called her makeup artist over to put the finishing touches on Petal, whose complexion had gotten much too dark from all that mushing, even with the sun so low. And the cameraman caught it all, knowing that the universe would grind itself into dust before this scene would ever be repeated.

The sound man pulled the cork out of a bottle of vodka with his teeth and spat it at the bulkhead, Russian-style. By tradition, the pilot got the first pull, but was too busy wrestling the chopper to put much of a dent in it. Buck wasn't permitted to take a pass, but managed to keep his mouthful on the small side.

At first he thought that there had been some mistake—maybe the word 'vodka' in Icelandic looked dangerously similar to "helicopter fuel' in Russian. Or maybe it was good luck to have what the helicopter was having, out of solidarity with your vehicle, like eating oats with your horse. Or maybe it was actually just awful. Anything was possible. Everyone else seemed to be enjoying it, though, so maybe it was just Buck. He didn't like the taste of jackfruit in lighter fluid, either.

Hana was standing on her seat now so that her interpretation of the Icelandic national anthem (Ó, guð vors lands! Ó, lands vors guð! Vér lofum þitt heilaga, heilaga nafn! Úr sólkerfum himnanna hnýta þér krans—) could be heard above a soccer discussion between the key grip and the best boy, who were rolling on the floor ironing out a fine point. Ali and the makeup man were making eyes and the pilot was screaming into the intercom for everyone to sit down and shut up like they always do whenever the party finally starts getting good.

In other words, it was a pretty mellow scene right up to the time Gunner dropped them below the clouds and filled the forward view with an incandescent curtain of liquid rock and the cabin with a thunderous roar like the inside of Niagara. A blast of superheated air pitched the nose up thirty degrees and sucked lift from the rotors like soda through a straw. Steaming bullets of semisolid lava shot through one side of the bulkhead and out the other leaving trails of smoke in their wake. Gunner struggled to control yaw as the earth spun faster beneath them and the chopper slid like an ice cube down a thermal incline too steep to fight.

And in the final seconds Buck, who had seen this movie before, managed to gather his two friends in a bear hug and topple them all into a crate of Styrofoam cups bearing the logo of last year's Coors Invitational Isafjordur to Isafjordur Great Circle Around the World from Pole to Pole Regatta. It was dark and it was soft in there. Just the place for the end of the world

CHAPTER 39

LYKILORO

"You guys okay in there?" asked Gunner. Blood ran down his arm as he stirred in the styrofoam, looking for survivors like they were prizes in the cereal. Pretty soon the styrofoam started to stir back, and three heads popped to the surface.

"You okay?" asked Petal, looking at his face.

"Yeah, must have bumped my nose," said Gunner. "It's nothing. Sorry to get blood on you."

"Yeah, but is everybody else dead?" asked Ali, gaping at the inert bodies strewn about the cabin.

"Dead drunk," answered Gunner, helping Petal climb out. "As usual. Good thing, too, or they'd really be in the way."

"So we didn't crash after all?" asked Buck, pulling himself and then Ali out of the crate.

"Let's just call it a hard landing," said Gunner. "Anyone who can stand is standing and the aircraft can take off again, probably. Start using the "C" word, and we'll be filling out forms for months. You want to quibble about semantics?"

"Not me," said Buck. "Personally, I hate those timid, limp-wristed landings. Give me a nice, firm, definitive landing any day. One that really lets you know you've landed, right down deep in your tailbone."

"You sure you're okay?" asked Petal. There really was a lot of blood around and it was still pouring out of Gunner's nose faster than he could wipe it away. "Here, tilt your head back and pinch like this."

"No, no, no," said Ali, moving her out of the way. "You've got to lean forward so you don't choke on the stuff. Yeah, like that. And we need something cold. Buck, get us some ice. They've got to have ice here. It *is* Iceland, right?"

Buck knew exactly how to get the gangway down and was back in a minute with a coronet full of snow. Pretty soon there was a lot of red slush on the deck and Buck was running back for more.

"Listen, we don't have time to waste on this nosebleed," said Gunner. "We've got to get whoever is left at the power plant on board and get the hell out of here before this volcano blows up!" He tried standing up but choked on blood running down his throat.

"Ali, you stay here and take care of Gunner," said Buck, helping the pilot into his seat. "Petal and I will collect the workers. And if any of the crew wakes up, don't let them wander off, okay? Just tell them to stay here and film each other." He grabbed Petal's hand and headed for the gangway. He stopped abruptly at the opening and called back in afterthought.

"Gunner," he said. "Say again how many people we are looking for and where they might be."

"Dispatcher couldn't say. Nobody answering the phone up there. Look for a building with windows, all the rest are just for machines. And the guy in charge is Dr. Lykiloro—Netfang Lykiloro. Kind of a wild man. You know the type—all brains, no sense. He'll be there if anyone is. Just don't get him talking. No, forget that. He'll be talking. Just don't listen to him. Pick him up and carry him out if you have to. And get on the intercom to notify anyone else up there. And hurry, this place is not long for this continent!" Just then the cabin shook with the impact of a huge explosion that lurched the helicopter sideways, pellets of smoking gravel raining down on the roof above them.

Buck and Petal paused at the exit to get their bearings while the volcano shower quickly petered out. The air was thick with smoking ash that smeared what dirty light trickled in from the dimming sun, but the horizon glowed orange with a hellish incandescence that seethed deep into the infrared. And in silhouette ahead loomed a monumental structure of pipes and stacks that looked like something Thor had stuck together back when he was in diapers and left to melt in front of the fire.

"Dumb place for a factory if you ask me," said Petal, lifting her skirts as she ran. "Especially with all of the empty real estate around here." She was right. This was the middle of nowhere and the only structure in sight appeared to be teetering on the brink of Hades.

"Must have made sense when they built it," said Buck, trying to imitate her skirt technique. The power plant was about five hundred yards up the rise ahead, and Buck figured he'd be lucky if his habit didn't trip him up at least once along the way. "Back when it was just a hot spot in the ground where they could tap into free energy."

"Free energy, huh?" she said, panting. "My uncle gave me a free car once. It blew up, too. Isn't there somebody's law about free stuff always blowing up?"

"Ought to be," allowed Buck. "But you got to admit that it sounds good in theory. Most of the mass of the Earth is really hot, just not at the surface. So you go to where the Earth's crust is thin, like here, and you've got a practically limitless source of heat that you can use to boil water to run turbines that make electricity. All without burning a drop of oil or polluting the atmosphere in any way. Great, eh?" Clouds of yellow smoke, reeking of brimstone, choked them as they ran.

"Until it blows up, you mean," said Petal, uninspired by the concept. As far as she was concerned, geothermal energy had made a bad first impression and would probably never get over it.

"I don't think it's the power plant's fault that the volcano is blowing up," insisted Buck, suppressing inner acknowledgement of the fact (which was obvious to both of them) that, on this point at least, he really didn't know what the hell he was talking about. In his defense, however, it should be pointed out that after one has publicly espoused a particular opinion for a sufficient period of time, it becomes nearly impossible for one to change one's mind on the issue, even when confronted with evidence as tangible as volcanoes blowing up in one's face.

"I think we may be quibbling over semantics again," said Petal. "Point is that no matter how free the energy is around here, it sure is ruining the ambiance."

Remembering how cold she had been not that long ago, Petal was not about to jettison any now-too-hot habits, but she did have her blouse open down to her Speedo. Buck, not one to quibble, also unbuttoned as much as he dared as they approached the entrance to the plant, a massive set of stainless steel doors, twelve feet high.

Just inside was a cavernous and deserted atrium of glass and chrome and volcanic rock, three stories high. The air was dry and hot, easily over ninety, and flecked with floating ash. Banks of lights on a schematic of the facility behind a huge reception desk all blinked furiously red, and some sort of siren, like a chorus of the damned in their final throes of torment, screamed over loudspeakers from all around them.

Buck ran to the map, squinted at the Icelandic script for a moment, and then pointed to the staircase on the left.

"Lykiloro. Third floor. Let's go!"

They were sweating like boxers when they burst through the director's door, their eyes at first scoured blind by sweat and darkness. They held each other, vertiginous, as the scene before them quickly attained visibility.

This room was an observation deck that overlooked the volcano. The back wall was entirely of glass, some forty feet wide and twenty tall, looking at this moment like a private screening of *The Birth of Hell*. Fountains of boiling rock shot skyward, filling the frame, and billows of exploding gas hammered against the pane. And in the center, standing on a massive desk, was Netfang Lykiloro, feet wide apart, head thrown back, pelvis thrusting a luminous Stratocaster toward the window in a wild riff of blood-curdling chords, heretofore unplayable by the human hand.

Lykiloro was nude but for his cowboy boots, jockeys, guitar, and headphones. His hair, which under other circumstances would have hung down to mid-back, now was electrified into a blond, dandelion Afro that sparked with static and undulated with his ecstasy. His skin was as translucent as parchment, stretched tight on a six-foot scaffolding, making him look like an anatomist's animation of a human body with all its fat cells removed.

"Listen!" Buck said, holding up his hand and staring intently. But Petal needed no such instruction; she was as transfixed as he was by the raw, auditory emotion that was pounding through every cell of their being.

The music was so pure and tight that it seemed at first to come from some single unearthly voice, calling from another dimension. But with concentration, Buck began to dissect its complexity, layer upon layer. Now he could see the graphical displays on the amplifiers at Lykiloro's feet, the needles on sound meters, the sine waves on oscilloscopes, the Fourier transforms on computer screens. These visual clues helped him isolate the auditory inputs in his head, to follow its message back to its source.

"Hear it?" asked Buck, holding Petal tightly with one arm and conducting with the other. "There! That's the heat signature of the volcano—listen as that fountain of lava shoots up. And there! That's the temperature fluctuation. They move together but they are subtly different. And that's the pressure wave; and those are the sub-audible groanings of the Earth's core itself, translated to human frequencies. And watch his hands, the guitar isn't making notes, he's got it programmed to manipulate the inputs from the volcano. He's orchestrating the energy of the Earth itself, erupting here in every frequency of the mechanical and electromagnetic spectra. He is translating the Earth's cry, its agony of birth, into the language of human emotion. Have you ever felt anything like this, Petal? Anything this powerful?"

Petal was beyond words, incapable of answering or even comprehending speech. She moved with Lykiloro, her knuckles white, gripping the neck of her air Stratocaster. She strained with him, drawing out one vibrato torrent of high energy photons after another, without a pause for breath. She was the sorcerer's apprentice now, commanding the fiery powers of planetary creation vastly beyond the human scale. Her life was complete, transcendent, a handful of atoms on the verge of vaporization.

Buck felt himself falling after her, after them, losing the will to consciousness, the will to exist apart from the core of the planet. The temperature in the room was in the one-teens now. Cracks darted like snakes across the glass. The floor heaved, then stumbled, now tilting steeply toward the window. And yet the two played on, Lykiloro and Steele, coaxing the volcano, calling the beast from its lair in its own voice. They would all die there in one mighty crescendo of fire, and it would be soon. It would be now.

Buck could feel his grip slipping. He was paralyzed by the sound, drawn toward the glass, ready to rejoin the Earth, when some automatic impulse, some last survival spasm threw him across the desk collapsing Lykiloro in a flying tackle. The man weighed next to nothing, and despite his struggles Buck had him under one arm, and then Petal under the other, and he was running with them, a super-human effort, out of his mind, deaf to their screaming, impervious to their clawing, leaping down stairs, racing down the heaving gravel toward the helicopter, its rotor spinning, its wheels desperate to leave the ground, with them or without them, as the Earth rose up in rage to swallow the men who had dared to steal its strength.

CHAPTER 40

BARGAIN

"So, Mr. Lykiloro, how do you feel having just been rescued from an exploding volcano by the courageous and heroic KICE Action News team?" Hana jabbed at his face with the microphone, her eyes locked on the camera, her grin engraved in stone.

"Rescue, you say?" he said, shading his eyes against the lights. "Kidnapping is more like it! Violation of human rights! Tramplin' of civil liberties! Involuntary transportation of miners across state lines for media purposes! You never read the Geneva Convention? The Magna Carta? My people are going to sue your people back to the Stone Age! Do you hear me, woman? Are you in there? Blink twice if you can hear me."

"Cut that," she said to the camera, without the tiniest shift of expression. "Take Two. Mr. Lykiloro, how does it feel being face to face with a volcano just before it burns you alive, when you don't have the slightest inkling that the courageous and heroic KICE Action News team is about to risk their very lives to rescue you."

"Orgasmic!" he shouted, gripping the microphone. "It feels totally orgasmic! It feels like every orgasm in creation were all soaked in tequila and ignited simultaneously, with time standing still and the volume turned up to max and—"

"Cut that," she said to the camera. "We can't say orgasmic on the air, can we?"

"Of course not, Hana," came the reply over the intercom. "You know it's on the list. You want me to read you the list again, Hana?"

"Take Three," she said, knowing that he lived to read her that list. "Mr. Lykiloro, how do you feel knowing that, rightly or wrongly, others will surely blame you for the horrible deaths of dozens of your employees, incinerated to a crisp while you were prancing half-nude on your desk in some sort of lascivious stupor, playing some sort of perverted guitar—"

"Elated!" he screamed into the mike. "They all deserved to die! Mindless robots! Zombies! Anencephalic androids! Vaporize them all! Melt them into puddles! Their incestuous rodent families, too. Rid the Earth of their saprophytic, sniveling, brain dead—"

"Hana, you moron!" bellowed the intercom. "All the employees are fine. He sent them home yesterday with full pay! Any investigative reporter worth their makeup would have dug that little fact up before interviewing—"

"Take Four," she said, her pupils dilating a nearly undetectable notch. "Mr. Lykiloro, how do you feel watching your career and credibility completely destroyed by this humiliating repudiation of everything you have stood for your entire life, this ironic mockery of the geothermal energy concept itself, now proven conclusively to be a fraud and a folly?"

"Ecstatic!" he cheered, jumping and flapping his arms. "Euphoric! Like winning every lottery in the world all at once! Like being King of the Universe! Like—"

"Seat belts, everyone!" came Gunner's voice over the loudspeakers. "Rough air ahead."

Everyone scrambled for seats as the helicopter bucked and rolled. Lykiloro ended up between Buck and Petal, with Hana gratifyingly far removed. Once buckled in, Lykiloro's mania seemed to evaporate and he looked like any other college professor in jockeys and boots.

"Buck Planck," said Buck, holding out his hand. "And this is Petal. Petal Steele."

"Netfang Lykiloro," he said. "Pleased to meet you. And thanks for pulling me out back there. I must have gotten a little carried away. Tough to leave before the climax, you know."

"Tougher afterward, sometimes." Conscious of his propensity for sappiness, Buck tried to limit such philosophical recapitulations to particularly close brushes with death.

"Point well taken," said Lykiloro, the very picture of civility and temperance. "Although I am embarrassed to say that at the time, with passion in control of reason, there was little chance that any effort on my part would have torn me away without your help. And you will forgive my little histrionic indulgences with the media, won't you? In my experience, the only way to handle them is to go over the top. If you try to be reasonable, they blow what you say into something monstrous. If you outdo them, they ignore you. It's the only reliable way to get them out of your hair."

"Seems to be working," said Buck, just able to see Hana's fretful pout up in the front row. Maybe this guy wasn't really such a madman, after all. He had to know a thing or two about geothermal energy, not to mention geo-symphonic orchestration. Sure, boots and jockeys might be a little eccentric, but Buck had always seemed to attract eccentrics, or maybe it was the other way around.

"I owe you two a great debt," said Lykiloro, his eyes politely resting on each of them in turn. "But I suppose with your vows of poverty and chastity—"

Petal, suddenly aware that her barely Speedoed cleavage was flagrantly exceeding this season's limits, clutched at her bodice and clenched tight her knees. She smiled wanly at Lykiloro, the sharp image of her recent enslavement to Pan at the volcano's edge smearing quickly into an indistinct fog of remorse and dread, as even the most vivid of dreams must do. But even after this transcendent and degrading experience had become but a troubling gap in her memory, she still remained wary of Lykiloro and the aura of malevolent and contagious insanity that swirled around him like a cloud of gnats, just below the level of resolution.

"Don't mention it, Netfang," said Buck, amicably. "Just part of the job. But I think you may have gotten the wrong idea about us being religious people. I mean we're definitely spiritual, I think, but it wouldn't be honest to call ourselves exactly religious, especially in regards to the poverty and chastity part—not that we aren't, exactly, but frankly not on purpose, which is what is supposed to count, isn't it, or am I way off base here, Petal?"

Petal's head was still a murky pool of conflicted biologic imperatives obscured by a haze of semi-suppressed guilt and semi-sublimated terror. Lykiloro reeked of rut and sulfur, and only the restraint of seat belts could contain the simultaneous forces of repulsion and attraction that raged chaotically within his sphere. She opened her mouth to speak, but the words clotted in her throat. She swallowed hard and shook her head, hoping Buck would understand. But, then again, how could he when she could not?

"I understand completely," said Lykiloro, as if to discipline her for presuming that her thoughts were private. "Spirituality. Religiosity. The inner world of complexity. The outer shell of appearance. These rarely have anything to do with one another, do they? We are so quick to confuse meaning with desire, purpose with gratification. Isn't that true Ms. Steele?"

Petal averted her eyes and nodded. She tried not to think, fearful of opening a crack to his insistent probing. She would build a firewall around her mind. She would huddle deep inside herself, ready with a stake that could be plunged into his heart or her own.

"Right-o," said Buck, jauntily. "Couldn't have put it better myself!" What good fortune to come across a true intellectual just when some heavy thinking needs to get done for the planet. You don't reach this level of discourse down at the tractor pull, that's for sure, or even at those black tie society benefits. Now if he could just ingratiate himself enough with Lykiloro, the energy part of their dilemma might just get solved before the helicopter touched down.

Petal was suffocating. Lykiloro was a vortex, warping space, consuming every molecule of oxygen, sucking all matter and volition into the voracious pit of his three-dimensional incarnation strapped shoulder to shoulder against her. His voice was like poisonous syrup seeping through her pores, its viscous evil choking the gears of her will.

"You know," Buck continued, "we were hoping you might tell us a bit about geothermal energy. We've got this little assignment that has to do with replacing fossil fuel and reversing global warming. It's due in ninety days, and, I'm afraid we're kind of stuck at this point."

"No problem, Buck," said Lykiloro. "I can get you all the energy you want right out of the ground. Here in Iceland we have more than we can use. Every building in the country is heated with geothermal. It's simple; all you have to do is warm up water at one of the volcanic hot spots and then pump it around. It even keeps snow off the roads, all for free. Or you can boil water into steam and spin a turbine to make electricity. Electricity is so cheap up here that we practically give it away.

"You know how aluminum is made? You dig up a mountain of Australian dirt—bauxite ore to be exact—and then you blast it with huge amounts of electricity. If they did this in Australia then aluminum would cost as much as gold. But you can put all that dirt in boats and spend all the money and oil it takes to ship it to Iceland, half a world away, and we can smelt it into aluminum for next to nothing. So even with all that extra cost, aluminum is so cheap that don't think twice about tossing a beer can away, unless you are worried about your landfill or something.

"Only problem with electricity is that it's tough to ship over long distances and it doesn't keep well—electricity goes bad faster than herring—you've got to use it as soon as you make it. So now we are taking all this free geothermal electrical energy and storing it as hydrogen. It's easy to make hydrogen, and the stuff lasts forever if you bottle it up tight. And when you burn it all you get is energy and water. Totally pollution-free. Not a carbon atom in sight.

"And you can turn the hydrogen back into electricity any time you want in a fuel cell—a simple, low-tech device with no moving parts. Oil-industry propagandists would have you believe that fuel cells are exotic, unproven, and expensive. Fact is, they were invented almost two hundred years ago, have been running submarines and space ships for years, and are cheap compared to oil when anyone other than the oil industry does the arithmetic. Those guys have a way of not counting the cost of pollution, wars, and carbon dioxide when they do the math.

"And here's a cool thing about running your car with a hydrogen fuel cell. While it is sitting around waiting for you to go somewhere, which is most of the time, there is a tiny amount of hydrogen that evaporates from your tank. Instead of just wasting this, your fuel cell could make it into a little electricity which you could sell back to the electric company. This doesn't seem like much, but if most people had hydrogen cars, it would be enough to replace all the coal and oil and nuclear power plants in your country—in anybody's country. Think of it, all that pollution, all the CO_2, all the strip mining, and all the nuclear waste, all the oil wars would just come to an end, just from cars sitting in their driveways. Ironic, isn't?

"No wonder this is so threatening to the ruling classes. Their authority, after all, depends on profits from polluting technologies, technologies that are dying and deserve to die. They will be swept away by a revolution. Their degenerate power will be replaced by a power that is clean and pure and one with Nature. And those men of courage who join this revolution will stand triumphant as leaders of a new era for Man and the Earth. Men and women, I should say, after what we three have been through together."

Petal cringed at the cold touch of his mental caress. She looked at her hands, expecting to see the blood of the innocent mixed with the blood of the guilty, both justly spilt in the cause of a righteous revolution.

"But what's the downside, Netfang," asked Buck, casually. "There must be a cost to geothermal energy. After all, we just witnessed the destruction of a huge and expensive power plant. What about all the resources and carbon dioxide that will be expended to replace it? What about all the people whose homes will be without heat or electricity because of this eruption? Not to mention all the people who could have been killed on the spot, including you and me and Petal.

"And what I hear is that these eruptions happen all the time, but nobody can say exactly when—our warning systems are still too crude. Isn't that the worst kind of predictable unpredictability? Shouldn't we admit that there are places on the Earth that people should just stay away from? We know where the geologically unstable places are, why not live somewhere else?

"But that's the bargain, isn't it Netfang. You don't find all this free geothermal energy anywhere except where the earth's crust is thin, where there is so much heat and pressure and poisonous gas built up just below the surface that the puny works of men are obliterated in an instant. You can't find just a little geothermal energy, can you? It doesn't come in a steady flow on a human scale. It's something for nothing until the bill for everything comes due. And then it's Hell to pay. Isn't that the deal, Netfang?"

"Well," Lykiloro intoned, pulling at his beard. "I suppose that, in the end, there is always a debt to be paid. But if you look closely at the winners in this world, you'll find they always manage to find someone else to pay it."

Petal fought to keep her head up, her spine rigid, her mind focused. She was alert now. For an instant something had flashed before her eyes, half hidden in the seamless net of Lykiloro's persuasion. He had tried to palm it, to rush it by unseen. But it was there. His intrinsic weakness, born with him at the beginning of time. It was their only route of escape, but a certain one. She smiled to herself. She was strong now.

"Mr. Lykiloro," she said, now able to return his stare, unflinching and unafraid. "I found your music quite compelling. Hypnotic, even. How tragic for it to be lost in the volcano."

"Please call me Netfang, Petal," he said, seemingly amused by her audacity. "I'm glad you liked it. Only those with the most sensitive spirits appreciate its meaning. But don't worry, nothing was lost. I knew that this composition would be the culmination of my life's work. The last minutes of the Hekla volcano, its final screams of death and rebirth, transformed into the language of the soul of Man. I made sure it was recorded, transmitted to my associates in Reykjavík."

"What a relief," she said, her eyelids closing an imperceptible notch. "Do you think we could hear some of it?"

"You mean now?" he said, squirming a little.

"Why not? This is the electronic age," she said, loosening her seat belt and standing up. "Anyone lend us a laptop?" she called to the KICE staff. Soon a battered SmakBook was passed back to her.

"Shouldn't be too hard for your friends to send us a copy," she said handing it to him.

He paused for a moment as if to consider options and then pecked at a few keys. The computer completed its ineffable ruminations in less than a minute and then there it was, right there on the screen with its innocuous file name. A hyperlink to madness made manifest. The piper's song that leads souls to the pit. A digital sword in a stone of code that no mortal could ever wield. The gods have nothing to fear from children playing with lightning bolts. There is no risk in playing it now. It could only cement the deal.

He gripped the computer, still uncertain of her gambit. She took it from him and smiled.

"It's kind of noisy in here for music. Do you mind if I just make a copy? Then we can appreciate it better later." She looked up into his suspicious face while she typed a few lines.

"Well—"

"Since, as you say, we saved your life," she said. "And you owe us a debt."

"Well, yes, I did say that. And the composition is meant to be heard, after all. But only in the right setting, of course."

"Then it's a bargain," she said, her finger plunging the key so intriguingly called Enter, sending the file to the Earth Rescue website. Siverth and Ole would know exactly what to do—how to turn this potion of Satanic seduction into an elixir of Earthly emancipation.

Petal felt as if she had just pulled a straight jacket off her soul, had just left Bedlam for Zen, had just traded chaos for clarity. Power was now in balance. The fragile barrier between good and evil intact once again.

"So now we are even, Mr. Lykiloro," she announced loudly enough for Buck to know she was addressing him, too. "You owe us nothing, and we owe you nothing. Our bargains have been fulfilled and our bargaining is now over. That's the rule, isn't it? We have to enter into a bargain of our own free will, don't we? Well, Mr. Planck and I choose not to accept any of your offers, whatever they may be. And if you will excuse us, we have some vows of chastity and poverty to discuss back in the Styrofoam."

And with a toss of her coif, she stood, took Buck's hand and led him back to the crate where they laughingly found themselves deep in their cups together.

CHAPTER 41

SPHINX

"Buck! Petal! I know you two are in there!" hollered Ali, perched on the edge of the crate. "Whatever you're doing, knock it off 'cause here I come!"

He scanned the churning Styrofoam surface for the calmest spot and vaulted in, trying for his best cannonball. It wouldn't have been such a bad entry if the helicopter hadn't been landing on the tarmac a little too hard at just the wrong time, bouncing the crate and its contents a foot into the air.

"Watch your foot!" squealed Petal's voice, close but invisible in the dim, swirling whiteness.

"How can I watch my foot when all I can see is cups?" he answered. "And watch your elbow!"

"Whose elbow?" asked Buck. "And be careful with that knee!"

"Ali, wouldn't you be more comfortable back in the cabin?" asked Petal. "Not that you aren't welcome here, of course, but it's just that Buck and I had just about gotten—"

"Please, no details! Believe me, I'd much rather be talking to that most intelligent and dangerously cute make-up guy, but your pilot friend insisted that I join you ASAP, whatever that is, and keep my mouth shut because of a little problem with the airport swarming with Smokeys, whatever they are. Can you imagine that? Telling the Sultan of Yomamah to keep his mouth shut? Well, I never!"

"What's a Smokey, Buck?" asked Petal, imagining yet another unhealthy variant of volcanic vomitus. As attached as she was to Mother Earth, Petal was getting about tired of Her lobbing lava in everybody's direction.

"Generic term for someone in authority whom you respect but whose attention is currently unwelcome," said Buck. "Usually not considered offensive unless you happen to be the Smokey. In this case probably referring to immigration officials, military police, INTERPOL, Vatican gendarmerie, or the Yasser Ibahb Knife and Gun Club, unless there are other uniformed organizations after us I don't know about."

"But we haven't done anything wrong!" protested Petal. "Is it some kind of crime nowadays to save the world? To write news articles? To help rich people make more money? To—"

"Steal nuclear weapons?" interjected Buck.

"Extort the US government?" hissed Ali.

"Impersonate a celibate?" continued Buck.

"Accessorize after the fact?" wondered Ali. "Or is it before?"

"I don't care which it is!" insisted Petal. "I refuse to act like some kind of criminal. I plan to hold my head up high and just tell those Smokeys in no uncertain terms that—"

"Whatever you do, keep your heads down and mouths shut," came Gunner's urgent whisper from the surface above them. "And don't breathe so much for a while until we can take the top off this crate again."

With a resounding clunk of wood on wood, their hiding place became totally dark and much too still. Nobody dared waste any breath arguing or questioning or even speculating. Being still was using air enough.

With a roar of engine noise, the crate lurched up, tilted ten degrees, and then began sliding and turning, much too fast. Buck recognized this as familiar forklift behavior, but Petal and Ali could only imagine that they were now in the jaws of a fire-breathing dragon that was giving them a good shake before swallowing them whole. Their ignorance was actually to their advantage, because had they had Buck's imagination, over-fertilized by years of one disaster after another, they would be conjuring up destinations for malicious forklifts that were much more horrible than the intestinal tracts of mythical lizards with glandular problems.

And if any of them had ever harbored secret doubts about the noxious effects of CO_2 before hopping into that crate, they had been thoroughly disabused of them now. As counterintuitive as it may seem, one's sense of impending suffocation is much less stimulated by a falling concentration of oxygen than it is by a rising level of CO_2. Even a few extra percentage points are enough to turn the most unflappable yogi into a clawing maniac. And so it was inside this crate, panic and carbon dioxide rapidly replacing oxygen and equanimity. Lucky thing that there was no apparently advantageous position in their smothering darkness, or the trio would have had to contend with an unwelcome pop quiz in Philosophy of Ethics on top of their final exam in Physiology of Hypoxia.

And then with a lurch, a flip, a thud, and a crash, they found themselves sprawled on the ground in a pile of cups and lumber, sucking down the most delicious atmosphere they had ever consumed, without the slightest embarrassment about their greedy excess.

"Welcome aboard the *Sphinx*," said the backlit form looming above them. "Any friend of Arni Gunnarsson is a friend of ours. I understand you three are traveling invisible class. Good choice for the young adventurer who values his privacy. Economical, too, if you don't mind skipping a few amenities. Like air. Feel that? We've just cast off. The authorities can't touch you now, even if they do figure out where you went."

Petal accepted his outstretched hand and struggled to her feet, smoothing her skirt and buttoning her blouse. Ali and Buck helped each other to get up and get presentable, swatting at the sprinkling of Styrofoam bits that clung to their habits like electrified snow.

"Buck Planck," he said shaking the guy's hand. Most rational people would have been a little slower with their real names in a situation like this, but Buck was a guy who found reassurance in his own knee-jerk assumption of good will in his fellow man. For him, preemptive sincerity had always been a talisman against bad luck and dirty dealings—and if you are going to rely on a talisman, you might as well pick one that works.

"And this is Petal Steele and Ali bin Said," pronounced Buck, preempting all around. "Awfully nice of you to give us a lift. That little business with the authorities back there was just an unfortunate misunderstanding. We really aren't bad people, I assure you."

"That I can see," he said. "Olaf Tórshavn, Captain of the *Sphinx*. Come, let's go to the bridge. It's much more comfortable there."

If Tórshavn wasn't a devoted student of Verne then he was living proof of the spontaneous reincarnation of fictitious characters. A tall thin man with meticulously trimmed beard and crisp navy uniform, Tórshavn carried himself like the commander-in-chief of his own nation-state. His ship, even down here in the hold, had the elegant Art Deco flow and detail of a time-encapsulated *Nautilus*. Petal and Ali were open-mouthed at the scene, and Buck was afraid they would start pumping Tórshavn for the name of his decorator before they had even determined whether the *Sphinx* was sailing on or below the ocean's surface.

As they reached the top of the spiral staircase it became clear that the answer was neither. This was the bridge, with the First and Second Officers at their stations in the center and a 360-degree view fore and aft, port and starboard. A view of nothing but an infinity of empty space.

"Where are we?" asked Petal, to anyone who might have a clue.

Tórshavn regarded her with a tolerant, fatherly smile and motioned her to the aft window. There, thousands of feet down, she could barely see the tiny city of Reykjavík, perched on the edge of the island of Iceland like a colorful fleck of lichen clinging to a hunk of newly minted rock.

The bridge was quiet enough to hear your heart beat. There was no sense of motion, no vibration, no sub-audible throb of distant machinery. The officers stood at parade rest, as unblinkingly still as mannequins. In all, it felt like a museum diorama after hours, waiting for opening time when schoolchildren would once again swarm against the glass, eager to view this re-creation of a scene that had never really existed.

"Is this a movie?" asked Petal.

"A dirigible," answered Tórshavn. "A flying machine."

Buck was craning his neck to see what he could of the superstructure of the craft that must be supporting them from above.

"Hydrogen or helium?" he asked.

"Hydrogen, of course," Tórshavn answered. "We drop by Iceland regularly to fill up. They hardly know what to do with all of their electricity, you know. So now they are turning it into hydrogen to run their cars and float airships like the *Sphinx*."

"How do you turn electricity into hydrogen?" asked Petal, vaguely recalling that electricity had something to do with electrons and hydrogen had something to do with protons. But then, her college course in Physics for Gossip Columnists was a long time ago and things could have changed considerably since then.

"Nothing to it," replied Tórshavn. "You just mix electricity with water and there you have it, ready for the gas station, or the dirigible station in our case."

"So are you part of the Icelandic Air Force or something?" asked Ali, a little nervously.

"Heavens no!" he said. "Can't you tell a Faroe Islander from an Icelander? I'd be careful about that, if I were you. It is quite a sensitive issue for some people around here."

"Sorry," said Ali. "I know what you mean; we've got the same problem where I come from. And while you are forgiving me, I'll have to admit I don't exactly know where the Faroe Islands are. Near Tahiti, right?"

"Not exactly. We're about 300 miles east of Iceland and 400 miles west of Norway and 200 miles north of Scotland. Ideal spot, really. As the realtors say, it's location, location, location."

"So you're with the Faroe Island Air Force, then?" asked Ali.

"Of course not, Mr. Said! Whatever would we want with an Air Force? It might be different in your part of the world, but if we put a bunch of our twenty-somethings into expensive warplanes they would be bound to start a war with somebody, probably right after the season's first soccer match. No, the *Sphinx* is proud to be the flagship of the Faroe Island Airborne Advertising Company. There's also the *Amenhotep*, the *Tutankhamun*, the *Nefertiti*, the *Cleopatra* and three more ships under construction. We are in great demand all over the world, you know. They have advertising where you come from, Mr. Said?"

"We're more into haggling, actually, but we understand the concept. How do you advertise from up here, anyway? Loudspeakers?"

"Don't be silly, that would be totally obnoxious. Hardly anything worse than noise pollution, in my opinion. One kid on a moped can wake up a thousand people on his way home from the mosh pit, or wherever it is that they go night after night. Ought to be a bounty on mopeds is what I say, and weed eaters, and leaf blowers. Chain saws, too, for that matter. What, they can't put mufflers on those things? My Mercedes has a thousand times more horsepower and you can hardly hear it running. I think that people who like to make noise in public are by definition anti-social and should be lobotomized. And if that doesn't fix them, castrated.

Take their appendix out, too. Whatever it takes. And I'm not the only one who feels this way, believe you me."

"I know I do," agreed Ali. "Personally, I think you are being too easy on them. Where I come from, somebody starts shooting off their AK 47 in the living room just because he likes the sound of it, well, we just take the guy out back and—"

"So, exactly what medium do you use for your advertising?" asked Petal stepping between them. Sometimes, some people's compulsive honesty needs to be tempered with a little compulsive mouth shutting.

"Why, sky writing, of course!" replied Tórshavn. "Let me show you. Now, what is your name again, young lady?"

"Petal. Petal Steele, but remember, we're trying to cool it."

"Ahh, that's right. So watch out the aft window." He busied himself with a keyboard at one of the consoles.

At first nothing seemed to be happening other than a slight dimming of the ambient light. Petal couldn't make out any detail of the world below them—from their vantage point the ocean appeared to stretch on forever. Iceland was now a little smudge loitering off near the horizon beneath a few cirrus clouds. There was no way to guess the ship's altitude or speed, but its position was no problem—they were considerably above the middle of nowhere.

Buck gave her a little nudge and pointed a finger upward. The cloud that had been shading their eyes now had taken on distinct edges. Tilting her head to the left, Petal could now see that it formed a gigantic letter "C." Soon thereafter followed a couple of "O's", a perfectly formed "L," a bit of a space, and then the expected "IT."

As the message floated off away from them (or, more accurately, they away from it) its edges seemed only to get sharper and its opacity greater—nothing like the immediate fuzz-out that you expect from the usual skywriter's scrawlings. Tórshavn had dropped their altitude a bit to give them a better perspective on what appeared to be a permanent (and, if not ironic, at least gratuitous) exhortation to the North Atlantic Ocean to "COOL IT."

"That's amazing," marveled Buck. "How do you keep the smoke from dispersing? There must be plenty of wind up here."

"Smoke is obsolete, Mr. Planck," he said. "Old technology. Very polluting. Our letters are constructed entirely of ice crystals, nothing but pure water."

"Like jet contrails, then?" asked Buck. "You usually don't see those below 26,000 feet. Are we really up that high?"

"Not nearly, but we could be if you want. Letters look kind of small when you write at that altitude, though. But don't forget, jets aren't trying to make contrails. In fact, there are a lot of people with nothing better to do who complain bitterly about them. Visual pollution, they say. Defacing the sky. The lunatic fringe even claims that contrails are evidence that the CIA is spraying chemicals out of airplanes to make them stupid, but frankly, I think there are much more likely explanations for their stunted mental states."

"But don't people complain about being told to "COOL IT" or "EAT MORE POSSUM" while they are trying to enjoy their sunsets?" asked Ali, always the advocate for the little guy and his simple pleasures.

"Do they complain about the Eiffel Tower? The Pyramids? The Hoover Dam? About any awe-inspiring human endeavor? Of course they do! So what? Who cares? You can't complain about people complaining. It's one of life's few inexhaustible pleasures. Personally, I love to complain. Nobody listens, and I don't blame them—I wouldn't listen either if I were them."

"How big can you make these letters, anyway?" asked Petal, half-imagining her *Times* column in a font that stretched from Greenwich Village to the Bronx.

"Ahh! I'm glad you asked. The *Sphinx* is equipped with the most advanced aero-typographic technology. Just watch." He pecked away at his console a bit and then beckoned them to join him at the starboard window.

Silently, a small dirigible appeared above them and moved away, powered by its own propeller. Then there was another, and another, and a dozen more, all in a line. Although it was too small to see, it became clear that they were supporting some sort of cable strung between them. Buck motioned to the port window opposite them, where now was visible an identical line of drones drifting off into the distance.

With a flourish worthy of a Moses conducting the Philharmonic, Tórshavn swept his arms in a wide arc. The invisible line connecting all of the little airships became suddenly white and began a mile-wide brushstroke of pristine snow. After a minute it was clear that this would be a "C" of epic proportions, one that could be read from the moon.

"Are you pumping water out there?" asked Buck, marveling at the scale of this engineering feat.

"We can when we need to," answered Tórshavn. "All of our power comes from hydrogen fuel cells that make water as a byproduct, so we have plenty to paint with when the humidity gets low. But usually there is enough water vapor out there to precipitate electrostatically and polymerize catalytically. In other words, you just need a little electricity and some rudimentary typing skills and you can print in any font you like up to two kilometers tall. We favor Times New Roman, but some of our clients are less conservative and will splurge on Verdana. Arabic script can be a little tricky, of course, especially if it's windy."

"But what if you were trying to get a suntan?" complained Ali, looking down at the ocean, which now sported a definite "COO" written in shadow on its otherwise blemishless surface. Ali was always a little over-sensitive about gratuitous comments regarding Arabic script, which he considered the very pinnacle of intuitive legibility, especially when compared to, say, Hindi-Urdu, for example. Petal thought he was just being a pill, but Buck thought he might be onto something.

"Good observation," said Tórshavn, taking no offense. "When the Faroe Island Airborne Advertising Company strategically places a "BLOAT LESS WITH BLATT'S BREW" overhead, it can take pride in the fact that it is not only helping the populace below avoid embarrassing borborygmal flatulence, but also skin cancers and premature wrinkles."

"And increase the Earth's albedo at the same time," mused Buck.

"The Earth's libido?" asked Petal, ears perked. She had always chosen Dom Pérignon over Blatt's before, but maybe she would reconsider.

"Reflectivity," said Buck. "The sun's energy is almost totally absorbed by dark surfaces like the ocean, and almost entirely reflected back into space by white stuff like clouds and snow. These letters are not only cool, but they are cooling the Earth at this very minute."

"I know, I know," said Tórshavn. "I've heard that criticism for years. 'Changing the climate,' 'bringing on another Ice Age,' 'meddling with Mother Nature,' 'blah, blah, blah.' Well, let me tell you, our people have studied this and the effect of our messages on global temperatures is a wash, just like any cloud cover. Sure, sun energy is reflected away from the Earth during the day, resulting in cooling—but at night, heat energy from the ground is reflected back downward instead of escaping into space, resulting in warming. Anybody who has camped under the stars knows how much colder it gets on a clear night than a cloudy one. Same deal with banners for LARRY'S LANDMINES or INSCRUTABLE ESCROW INC. 'Warming, cooling, warming, cooling.' Argue all you want. Just leave us out of it. We're neutral on the issue."

"Just how long do these messages hang around, anyway?" asked Buck.

"Depends on how much you want to pay," said Tórshavn. "But, to be honest, longer lasting letters don't really cost us more. It's just a matter of turning the dial here."

"So might you be able to paint a solid, mile-wide swath, the first part of which might last twelve hours and the final part of which might disappear after an hour or so?" asked Buck, squinting off at the sun, now touching down ever so gently on the horizon.

"Sure. No problem. But why on Earth would you want to do that?" asked Tórshavn.

"Oh, I don't know," he said, gathering Petal's half-manacled hands in his. "Just wondering."

And Petal was wondering, too, but mostly about what had gotten into Buck as she felt her feet leave the floor and her lips press to his and her breath squeezed away. Maybe it was all that talk about Blatt's. Maybe it was the beautiful sunset and its now orange COOL IT logo. Maybe it was the next stage in their growing relationship sneaking up on them as silently as a dirigible. Whatever it was, she wasn't about to talk about it. She may not keep her mouth shut, but she definitely wasn't going to talk about it.

CHAPTER 42

WORK

"Siverth, you've got to eat something. Remember that time out on the ice? You don't want that to happen again, do you?"

This time Siverth actually stopped what he was doing and looked up, his eyes vaguely focused on some distant point in space and time. Happen again? Happen again? What he would give to make that happen again. Was there anything the mortal imagination could conjure that might surpass that time out on the ice? If starving would rewind time, then should he ever eat another bite?

But then, what of Her charge to him? What of his responsibility? He should be ashamed of himself for being tempted by personal ecstasy when Her mission required his full commitment. He would eat, he would breathe. It was Her will.

"You're right, Ole. What have you got?"

Ole, encouraged by any glimmer of rationality from his obsessively oblivious friend, zipped open a heated carrier.

"Well, we've got Peloponnesian, Amish, and Rarotongan. I suggest the Rarotongan today. The iguana is fresh."

"These are pizzas again, right?" asked Siverth, looking disappointed.

"Of course they're pizzas!" said Ole. "You know the cover. Nuuk's Finest Everything-But-Italian Pizza. It's perfect, I can walk into any building in town and nobody suspects a thing—unless I start walking into other restaurants, that is. So eat, already. What difference does it make that it's flat and round? You want raw goat? You've got your Peloponnesian. Nettles? That's your Amish. Me, I'm having iguana. Don't worry; it doesn't really taste like chicken. More like rattlesnake, only gamier."

Siverth picked at the Cook Island classic, avoiding bits that looked too much like feet. He had to admit it wasn't anything like chicken. It wasn't much like food, either, but in his half-starved state, any semblance of nutrition brought a roar of approval from his desperate metabolic control centers. He finished the Polynesian pie and moved on to the Proto-Greek. He even drank some Soyuz Sunrise from his canteen. Color returned to his lips. He sat back in his chair and looked around, clear-eyed for once.

"What day is it, anyway?" he asked. Holed up as they were in the basement of KNUK-TV, he was denied even the meager diurnal cues the Greenland sun offered up this time of year.

"Wednesday, Siverth. Nearly midnight. You've been at this forever. You don't eat. You don't sleep. The only time you talk is to send me on some scavenger hunt or another. Ten broken cell phones. Air conditioner remote control. Angora sweater theft deterrence tag. Robot vacuum cleaner motor. Not that I mind, mind you. Happy to help save the world or whatever we're doing. But all I want to know is one thing, Siverth. And that is, what the hell are we doing? I mean, really, is that too much to ask?"

"Of course, Ole. Sit down. You need to know all of this in case something happens to me anyway."

Ole aligned his chair so he could see all three monitors and still reach the Amish, which wasn't that bad if you had enough beer. God only knew how the Amish choked it down.

"First, the password is your birthday plus the current date plus the lottery number from exactly two years ago. Got that? It changes every day at 12:01am, not before. Next, here is how to find the coordinates of all the nukes. CTL+M puts them on a map, like this."

A map of Greenland appeared on the center screen, with a handful of red dots scattered over the interior in what appeared to be a random pattern.

"All the bombs are still on sleds?" asked Ole.

"Right. Continuously moving. Safer than stashing them under the bed somewhere."

"And the Americans, what do they know?" asked Ole.

"They know their nukes are missing and being auctioned off on eBay and that they are way behind on their bidding. Other than that, they seem to be clueless. They've got their people crawling all over Greenland, but also over every other land, too. There's no indication that they suspect us over places like Canada or North Korea or Chuuk."

"Still makes me nervous," said Ole. "You sure they don't have nuke detectors in space?"

"Apparently not," said Siverth. "But that's why we've got the diversion. Here, if you press CTL+D you can see all the decoy sleds." The map lit up with thousands of green dots. "Everybody in Greenland with a sled—meaning just about everybody in Greenland—is out mushing old transmissions, boat anchors, or scrap iron around. That was the easiest recruiting job I ever had. Any excuse is good enough to get out and mush, but National Mush Metal for Your Mother Month was perfect. Thank your brother upstairs for that one, Ole."

"He's happy to help. By the way, he wants to know if you need more bandwidth." Ole's older sib was head of engineering at the station and was indispensable in covering up their radio and internet transmissions. He had lots of great spare electronics down here in the storeroom, too.

"We're fine on bandwidth so far," said Siverth. "What would be nice to have is some heat in this place."

"Different kind of engineering, apparently," said Ole. "You want bandwidth, we got bandwidth. You want heat. Rub sticks together. A metaphor for modern life, don't you think?" Ole commonly got this way after too much Amish. Siverth let it slide. He would never touch an unmixed metaphor.

"Next, the website," said Siverth, firing up the other panels. "Here you can see the cash flowing in as everybody in the world bids against the US government for the nukes. Astounding, isn't it? You would think that there would be at least one person left on their side. But again, that was then.

"And on this screen is the money going out to Chill the Anthropocene projects. This is all on auto-pilot; you don't have to worry about it. The computer picks a smart person who stakes his or her reputation on the results of each grant. Other smart people are selected to judge the results. Somebody is bound to figure out how to game this to their advantage, but it's worth making a few crooks happy just to keep the process moving."

Ole propped his jaw closed. Never had he seen this kind of money spent on anything other than what the Orwellians in the Pentagon would term "Defense."

"Now, listen carefully, Ole, because now we have to discuss the most important project of all—the art—the Work—our Work—our Masterpiece. No one in the history of the world—including me—has ever attempted an artistic endeavor of such magnitude before. Never has an artist set out to reach every individual on the planet, to find a way into their hearts of hearts to transform each one—to conscript them into service of a cause so compelling, so consuming, that trivial concerns about race, religion, and historical grievance are at once forgotten.

"A piece of art so powerful that it transforms humanity into what it imagines itself to be. One that frees each soul to embrace what it knows is imperative for the species. One that makes us all see ourselves and one another in a light that has never shone before, but one that we instantly recognize as pure and true—a light that exposes our beauty and forgives our ugliness, but that also sears away the spores of selfishness that are the origin of every evil. This is what great art should be, Ole. This is what our art will be.

"I have been consumed by this Work since that day on the ice. It has already grown astonishingly huge and complex, with hundreds of individual parts, each of which must be revealed with the utmost subtlety and orchestrated with the most sensitive touch. Our timing must be impeccable. Much, much more remains to be done, but its first movement is now ready. We are waiting for a sign that the time has come—a signal to set it all in motion, to set it free to do its work in the world.

"But first I need your validation, Ole. You have always been my anchor, my grip on reality. I am counting on you to look at this work honestly, objectively. Tell me if you think I'm insane. I can take it."

Ole was always telling Siverth that he was insane, but this time he would withhold judgment until he had made a thorough, professional assessment. As an impartial juror he would instruct himself to disregard the artist's long history of lunacy, delusion, and wholesale abrogation of reason. He would cast aside political prejudices and critique the project with an open mind, on its aesthetic and intellectual merits alone. He would be brutally honest with Siverth, as usual. And Siverth would ignore him, as usual.

Siverth centered Ole in front of the three screens. He pointed out the controls. He explained how each image, each sound would be revealed over time and place. He urged him to imagine the piece playing out in its intended cadence and apologized for the artificial but necessary compression required for this presentation. He asked if he was comfortable, if he needed a glass of water, did he have to pee. He wanted nothing to distract Ole's attention. Siverth eventually quit twittering and pushed the button. The screens and speakers slowly came to life.

Time must have passed, it always does—but just how much was impossible to say. Someone outside of the room could have told you, unless they had been comatose or in some kind of a trance. It would have to be a pretty special trance, though. Even the most absorbed trancers can somehow tell when the evening is up and it's time to go home.

But for Ole and Siverth there was no time. Or time had stopped. Or time had become sound. Or they had become time. Or sound. Or everything.

Sometimes the brain mobilizes every resource into an activity so important that insignificant details such as time and space are totally ignored. Procreation of the species, for example, merits a few seconds worth of such all-consuming intensity from time to time. Siverth's goal, as an artist, was to capture this human capacity for complete physical and spiritual transcendence, to expand it, to prolong it, and to focus it on something much more crucial than the mere replication of more *homo whatever* units.

Survival of the Earth itself was at stake here. Human individuals had not originally been programmed to care about this issue, one way or another. Originally, it had been none of their business. But over the centuries they had unwittingly made it their business, and now it was the responsibility of great art to make them care. To care as much as they did about their next internal squirt of dopamine and what it would take to get it.

This, the greatest work of art ever imagined, would have to entice even the least curious intellect, gently coax its defenses down, and engulf it within an orgasmic transformation so overwhelming as to render it unrecognizable to itself. It would have to sweep through the collective human imagination at the speed of thought, evoking a quantum evolutionary leap of consciousness as breathtaking as the invention of speech itself. History, thereafter, would explain the discontinuous trajectory of civilization in terms of *pre* versus *post* the Work. The Work that they were experiencing now.

The screens eventually became black and still. The last hypnotic reverberations of Lykiloro's symphonic acid trip had faded away. Yet Ole and Siverth sat staring but not seeing, as if in the dreamless sleep the brain employs to shore itself against insanity. Was Siverth not insane? Was everything they were doing not totally insane? Was every human thought, every human action just as insane? Neither of them moved. They didn't speak. They didn't even think. They were beyond thought now, or at least incapable of it.

Until the ring of the phone jerked them back to linear reality. Ole picked it up, listened a minute and set it down.

"Turn on the news, Siverth," he said softly. "Something important about today's Brazilian moon shot."

Siverth fiddled with the console and sat back. The talking heads were talking in Greenlandic-dubbed Portuguese with English-as-a-third language subtitles. They left the sound off. Any sound was offensive after what they had just experienced.

There was the Earth as backdrop, at first a shaky smudge, madly rushing away from the rocket's blast, and then forming itself into its iconic blue-green arc floating calmly in the blackness. There, you could see the unmistakable profile of the South American continent, and now the North American one, and now the Atlantic, as the full, round sphere of the globe began to look small and vulnerable. And now Northern Europe—but wait! What is that? Is it a camera trick? No, it is really there, out over the ocean where nobody could see it. How could this be? Is it a cloud? No, it has to be smoke from the Hekla volcanic eruption. As impossible as it may seem, the Earth must be sending a message, but to whom, and what could it mean? Judge for yourself. Here, we'll focus in on it for you.

And there it was, written in Times New Roman, all caps bold, a crisp white on a sparkling blue background:

COOL IT

Siverth looked at his friend. Ole had not yet delivered his critique. He had not yet made his psychiatric diagnosis. He had not reacted at all except to answer the phone, and then as if in a fugue. He just sat there staring at the image of the Earth. An Earth crying out to be heard. Crying out for help.

"Do it."

"What?" asked Siverth, barely able to hear him.

"Do it. Do it now, Siverth. Reach every one of them. All seven billion. Squeeze them by their hearts until they see. It is Her will. You know it is Her will."

And with the grave determination that precedes every irrevocable gamble, Siverth sent his finger plunging firmly into *Enter*, and the Earth plunging into a future imaginable only to the certifiably insane.

CHAPTER 43

SVALBARD

"More lemonade, ma'am?"

"No, thank you, Sunleif. It really is delicious, but I think this will be quite enough."

"Towels? Magazines? Another pillow for your deck chair?"

"No, thanks. I'm as comfy as can be. You are much too kind."

"And you, sirs, can I get you anything? Anything at all?"

"Not us. We're fine. Don't need a thing."

"Wax the shuffleboard?"

"Not yet. Still waxy."

"Hats? Sunscreen? Fans?"

"Got plenty. Doing great. We'll be sure to ring if we can think of anything."

"You sure, now?"

"We're sure, Sunleif. Why don't you take a break yourself? You've done a terrific job. We're not used to such great service."

"How about a radio? DVD player?"

"Nothing, Sunleif. Just a little time to talk among ourselves. Alone."

"Oh. I see."

"Don't hurt his feelings. He's such a sweet boy."

"I didn't mean it like that, Sunleif. We love having you around. It's just that we've got a little business stuff to talk about, and you know how tedious that can be. Business? Well, the, uh, nun business, of course. You know, returns on vestments, ecclesiastical equities, liturgical litigations, papal prospecti, Pontifical Power Points—all a big snore, really. Put you right to sleep. So why don't you go check on some of the other passengers and we'll give you a—"

"But there are no other passengers, Sister Buck, sir."

"No matter, why don't you—"

"There have never been any other passengers."

"What? That's surprising. Anyway, we shouldn't keep you from your other duties. Hate to be an imposition—"

"But I don't have any other duties, Sister Buck."

"New on the job, eh? Well, I think you'll find that after you've been around a while you'll be entrusted with more and more—"

"Six years."

"Six years?"

"I've been Passenger Steward since the Sphinx was commissioned six years ago."

"And you've been waiting for your first passenger for six years?"

"Well, I don't just sit around and wait. I practice. I study. There is a curriculum, you know. The canon. A body of knowledge that the great stewards say is impossible to master in a single lifetime. But one can try."

"How come the Sphinx doesn't have passengers? The accommodations are stunning, the service is impeccable, and the food is superb. Doesn't make sense."

"Confidentially, I have wondered about that myself. On the surface, the problem would seem to be related to the fact that the Ticket Seller's position has never been filled. This observation raises certain questions of its own. Particularly suspicious, in my opinion, are large cash expenditures from the Director of Housekeeping's discretionary budget labeled 'Bribes and Coercions' that correspond exactly to mysterious disappearances of applicants for the Ticket Seller's position. But then again it could be the itinerary."

"The itinerary?"

"Where we go."

"That would be the itinerary, all right."

"Something wrong with the itinerary?"

"Itinerary is everything in the cruise business. That's why they say it's 'itinerary, itinerary, itinerary.'"

"No they don't. It's 'hype, hype, hype.' You can sell any godforsaken itinerary with enough hype. Don't they have tourists in Yomamah?"

"Of course we do!"

"There you are, then."

"You aren't implying—"

"By the way, where are we going?"

"We're going where we always go, not counting Iceland, but that's just to fill up with hydrogen. You see, we have a standing skywriting order. Gets a little monotonous, but it is steady work. In this business you want to minimize travel time between jobs, and if you can get a continuous stream of messages to write in one place, you can optimize your cost to expense ratio."

"Which is where we are going now? To the *Sphinx's* steady gig?"

"Right. Should be just about there. We'll start writing in a few minutes."

"But it's totally black out there. Don't you want to wait until the sun comes up to write in the sky?"

"That would be February fifteenth at this latitude."

"Yeah, but who's going to see it in the dark?"

"Pretty much everybody in Svalbard will see it. In fact, they set their alarms to see it. People who go on vacation have their neighbors email them pictures of it. The TV station runs it on delay for shift workers who can't get out. I'd say we have as close to 100% market penetration as you could get."

"Svalbard? We're going to Svalbard?"

"How come I've never heard of Svalbard?"

"Everybody's heard of Svalbard. That's where the Seed Vault is. Seeds from every plant in the world are frozen there, dug deep into the Spitsbergen Mountain. The facility is hardened against nuclear attack, rising sea levels, ice ages, plagues, cosmic rays and meteor impacts. This is the place to come when it's time to restart the planet after a major global torching."

"Just plants, though?"

"It's a start."

"What about the animals?"

"Going extinct by the hundreds as we speak. Massive die offs."

"No Animal Bank?"

"Nope."

"So they are all gone forever?"

"We've got pictures."

"Not the same."

"Pity."

"But exactly where is Svalbard, anyway?"

"Down there. You can start to make out the streetlights now. See? That's the financial district, and over there is Chinatown, the hospital is the building with the helipad—that's where I was born, right on the helipad—and to the left is the theater area and then restaurant row, and those red lights—"

"But it's pitch black out there—"

"Watch our stern. Okay, see? That's the signal. Here we go!"

"Wow!"

"Amazing!"

"Look at all those searchlights! All pointed up at us!"

"Actually, slightly behind us. From our vantage point the text is pretty hard to read, but since it is all in Norwegian you aren't missing anything."

"Read it to us, Sunleif. What does it say?"

"So far all we have written is 'Inge's breath was hot against my swollen—'"

"Who's Inge?"

"My swollen what?"

"What exactly are we advertising here?"

"Where did he say Svalbard was?"

"Why is it so dark here?"

"Let him talk! Let him talk!"

"Well, Inge, an attractive but intense neurosurgical resident, was engaged to be married to Thore, the brash but sensitive private detective, but her father, Trygve, the ruthless but insecure real estate magnate had promised Lodve, the unscrupulous but timid—"

"It's a soap opera!"

"I do not know the term. Is it English?"

"American. A soap opera is any overwrought episodic drama in which universally vindictive characters inflict endless streams of suffering upon one another to the rapt attention of scandalized audiences who then rush out and buy soap."

"Like a movie, Sunleif, but in installments. But this case in writing, like in a magazine. But in this case, in the sky."

"It does sound somewhat similar. Except that soap operas are about fictitious people, right?"

"Your Inge, and Thore and Trygve are real people, then?"

"Of course they are. You can meet them at supermarket openings and Independence Day picnics—if you are good at pushing to the front of a crowd."

"But couldn't those people just be actors?"

"Actors? I don't think so. Why would everyone in Svalbard care what a bunch of actors were doing? Not likely. Not likely at all."

"I'm sure you're right, Sunleif. Don't pay any attention to them. What does the writing say now?"

"Kind of hard to read while the *Sphinx* is turning around for its next pass, but it looks like: 'The prenup is void, Sigrun, because just before your *in vitro*, Steinar's hateful ex-wife, Magnhild, switched the—'"

"Soap."

"Soap."

"Ignore them, Sunleif. They know nothing of life and art. And why don't you be a dear and sit down and tell me all about this exciting Svalbard destination. We are going to land there, I presume, it being on our itinerary. Or our entire itinerary, it seems."

"Oh, yes, we stop for the night."

"Until February fifteenth?"

"No, just until morning. You'll love it here. Very cosmopolitan. Great nightlife."

"Figures."

"One would hope."

"Will you two please knock it off? It's dark, okay? Get over it."

"It's all right, Sister Petal. We don't mind being teased about the length of our nights. And don't forget, we get as much daylight as anyone, just mostly in the summer. Consequently, nobody appreciates the sun more than Svalbardans. And few understand it as well, either. That's what my father says, anyway. And he should know, too, he's a professor of solar engineering at the university."

"What did you say your last name was, Sunleif?"

"Solberg."

"So your father must be Magnus Solberg? He's famous."

"He was on *Time* with that Virgin Airline guy, right?"

"Solar power! That's the ticket!"

"This could be our big break!"

277

"You nuns interested in solar power, then?"

"Higher powers of all sorts. Ours is a very open minded order."

"Well, how about I call Mom and tell her to set three more plates for dinner? It would mean a lot to me if you could come. I really want them to meet my first passengers. And Dad could tell you all about his work. He keeps saying that solar power will save mankind once divine intervention makes them listen. I guess nuns can't guarantee divine intervention, though."

"We can always try."

"It's what we do."

"Sounds lovely, Sunleif."

"Great! It's settled then. I'll go make the arrangements while you get changed for dinner. But, then, do nuns change for dinner?"

"Well, Sunleif, there are certain things that are best left mysterious, don't you think?"

"Yes, ma'am. I understand completely."

CHAPTER 44

MAGNUS

"Doesn't anybody wear coats up here?" Petal asked, noting that all Sunleif and the cab driver had on were basketball shorts, Hawaiian shirts, and flip flops. Even though she had to admit that she wasn't the slightest bit cold in the back seat with Buck and Ali, just knowing they were now above the 80th parallel made her shiver in her habit. Actually, she didn't have the slightest idea what a parallel was or how many was too many, but she had come away from Buck's geography lesson with one insight: if they went any farther north they would run smack into that metal gizmo that holds the globe to the stand.

"Takes more than a coat to keep you alive out there at this time of year," said Sunleif. "So, why bother with coats? The hangar is warm, the cab is warm, the garage is warm, the house is warm. In fact, clothes themselves are entirely optional in Svalbard. As you may know, we have one of the largest nudist colonies in the world here in Longyearbyen, but I don't suppose you nuns are interested in that sort of thing."

"I don't know. Personally, I have a particular—" started Ali before he was cut off by elbows in his ribs.

"But don't worry, my parents are quite conservative. They always dress for dinner. My sister dresses, too, but weirdly, since she is fifteen. Let me ask you, are all the girls in the Vatican difficult at fifteen or is it just here? Even the girls my age are difficult here, but not nearly so difficult as the fifteen-year-old ones."

"They are difficult everywhere at fifteen, Sunleif," said Petal. "It's one of nature's universal constants, like gravitation and spam. My advice is not to confront them head on about anything. A glancing blow will hurt you less."

"Maybe you could also advise Magnus and Berit about this— that's my mother, Berit—they are having a lot of misunderstanding with Trina—that's my sister, Trina—mainly I think because they are not so hip. While, in my opinion, my parents are sufficiently cool, I will grant that they are less than adequately hip, at least insofar as fifteen-year-old Svalbardan girl culture is concerned."

"No problem, Sunleif," said Petal. "Right up our alley. Centuries of missionary work have made nuns particularly skillful at dealing with alien beings with baffling cultures and unknowable mental processes. This is why NASA has such a large nun department, because if there actually is any real estate out in space worth finding, somebody else is bound to have gotten there first. And whoever those space dudes are, you can bet that they are almost as difficult as your average fifteen year old girl."

Sunleif pressed his thumbprint into the cab's meter and held the door for the rest of them. The garage was toasty, but the surface of the vehicle shimmered with cold. Ali's finger stuck to the door frame as he got out, as if to an ice tray.

"Don't move, Sister Ali," he said. "Olaf, let me have your zapper."

The cabbie pulled something that looked like a stun gun out of his glove compartment. Sunleif pressed it against the metal near Ali's finger and pulled the trigger.

"Wow, thanks, Sunleif," said Ali, pulling his finger away from the now-warm metal. "I should have known better. Can't touch the outsides of cars where I come from, either."

"Really?" said Sunleif. "I would never have guessed Rome was that cold." He led the way up a narrow stairway to the main floor.

"Will you shut up, Ali," whispered Petal. "We're supposed to be nuns!"

"Don't be so up tight!" he whispered back. "What do you know about nuns, anyway? And how come we can't go to the nudist colony?"

"Why can't we just tell the truth?" whispered Buck. "I thought that you were the one who—"

"Are you kidding?" hissed Petal. "And queer our best shot at solar power?"

"Watch it!" said Ali.

"Sorry. Just an expression. You use it."

"Only lovingly. And you've got to earn it first, dearest. Or do you have credentials I don't know about?"

"Well if I did, I certainly wouldn't—"

"Knock it off, both of you," said Buck. "Just calm down and let me do the talking?"

"No way!" said Petal. "I'll do the talking!"

"I'll talk all I want to!" said Ali. "And I'm not going to be pushed around by a couple of hopeless homophobes in dresses!"

"Who's a homophobe?" protested Petal. "I was your girlfriend! We were going to get married!"

"Aw, Ali," said Buck. "You know I'm not a homophobe. You know I'm not an anything-phobe. Come on, let's not fight."

"Yeah, Ali," said Petal. "Group hug?"

"Okay, okay," he conceded. "Group hug."

"Mom and Dad, I want you to meet my new friends and very first passengers, Sister Petal and Sister Ali and Sister Buck."

"Why are they doing that?" asked Mrs. Solberg, smoothing her apron.

"Are they cold?" asked Magnus.

"No it's just a nun thing, Mom. It's as cold in Rome as it is here, you know."

"Rome is nowhere near as cold as Svalbard, walrus brain," came a little voice from inside the house. "You'd think you'd pick up a little geography, working on a blimp."

"That's Trina," offered Sunleif to the trio, who were now looking embarrassed to have been caught doing the ice-core-hut-group-jump hug when they should have been on their best behavior. "She can't tell a blimp from a dirigible, even if you've told her a hundred times."

"We are pleased to make yours acquaintances," said Mrs. Solberg carefully, with a glance to her husband for approval of her English. "Sunleif has told us so much about yous alls."

"They're blimp riders, Mom," came Trina's voice from her bedroom. "Not his fiancées!"

"Well, whatever you are, please come in out of the cold and be welcomed to our's humble home," said Mrs. Solberg with a sweeping gesture.

"It's hotter out there than it is in here," said Trina's voice. "You'd think that a family that is supposed to be into energy would have enough sense to turn the thermostat in the garage down a little. Give the planet a break, for once."

"Magnus Solberg," he said three times, very softly and with a little bow, as the guests filed in and shook his hand.

Professor Solberg was indeed a conservative looking guy. Each hair of his crew cut and beard was trimmed to exactly the same length. The ends of his bow tie precisely aligned with the loops. His creases were sharp, his shirt was crisp, and his shoes mirror-buffed. He controlled his personal space with precision and discipline. One could tell that his professional life would be as exacting and regimented. But not, alas, his home life.

That such logical order would not naturally suffuse his own domicile was a constant source of puzzlement to him. What had happened? Trina had happened, that's what. But not all at once. At first child number two looked to be as low maintenance as child number one. The first ten years were delightful. The next two, not so bad. Each of the following, logarithmically more chaotic.

It was as if his once sweet and precious little daughter had been replaced by a changeling bent on mocking his intellect with a continuous stream of insoluble koans, each one a hair trigger to its own improvised emotionally explosive device. It was as if her very mission in life was to prove that all of his assumptions were incorrect, all of his judgments faulty, and all of his observations flawed. It was as if she could see things about him that he could not see himself, defects that no friend or colleague or even his wife could see. Ignoring her would be easier, of course, if he could rid himself of the nagging suspicion that everything she said might actually be true.

Petal and Ali followed Sunleif and Mrs. Solberg into the kitchen to pretend to help with dinner, leaving the professor and Buck in the main living area, a huge rectangular room with a ceiling that sloped up over twenty feet on one long side. That wall was covered by velvet drapes so black they seemed to disappear.

"Strictly passive?" asked Buck, walking over to take a closer look.

"Sometimes I stand up to her, but she always makes me regret it."

"I meant the solar heating," said Buck.

"Oh, that," he said, relieved to be talking about something comprehensible. "No, strictly passive wouldn't be latitude appropriate. The windows behind the curtains there let the summer sunlight into the room until it's time to sleep, then we blacken them off and collect what we can into our hot water system. Photovoltaic conversion of light to electricity doesn't make so much sense up here where the energy density is low and what we need is heat anyway."

"Energy density?"

"Right. How intense the sun is in a certain area. Where you come from it's about 300 watts per square meter in the summer—"

"Rome, you mean?"

"Tidewater Virginia, somewhere between Newport News and Norfolk. With overtones of Manhattan, above 110th, of course. It's the long a's and the nasal n's. Uncommon combination."

"Impressive. I hadn't even said ten words."

"Nine. It's a gift. A curse maybe. Anyway, only a hobby. Most people find it off-putting, like I was guessing their weight—or worse."

"So you can tell we're not nuns, then?"

"You're not? Plenty of nuns from Norfolk. There are even limericks about them—or ought to be, anyway. Besides, you don't have to be a nun to dress like a nun. Look at Sunleif, he dresses like a Maui Globetrotter and he doesn't apologize."

"Very kind of you," said Buck. "But the fact is that we're kind of in disguise right now because—through no fault of our own, I assure you—a number of over-excitable organizations have gotten the entirely wrong idea of what we are up to—including, regrettably, my own country's government, whom I personally have served dutifully for many years, in spite of the fact that I may have not voted for—"

"So what are you up to?" asked Professor Solberg.

"Energy. Sustainable. Non-polluting. Carbon neutral. Carbon negative, if you've got it," whispered Buck, trying to keep Petal and Ali from overhearing. They would no doubt goof everything up, if that wasn't being too goofophobic.

"What about it?"

"We want it. We are looking for it. And when we find it, we need to get it."

"How much do you need?" asked the Professor.

"I figure about fifty terawatts," said Buck, reading his calculations off the back of an envelope.

"Fifty watts?" asked Solberg. "You need to run a light bulb?"

"No sir, fifty *terawatts*. That would be fifty times ten to the twelfth power watts, if my numbers are correct." He did the multiplication again, just to be sure.

"You need this for a microsecond or two? For some kind of laser experiment? A monstrous capacitor might be able to handle such a jolt." The professor was interested now. Rarely did he have the pleasure of thinking in terawatts outside of office hours.

"No, no. We need a constant, inexhaustible supply of power. Fifty terawatts year in and year out for the foreseeable future."

"But the entire human consumption of power can't be more than eighteen terawatts," said Solberg, now scribbling on an envelope of his own.

"I rounded up to twenty," said Buck. "The other thirty is for remediation, to repair the damage done by a civilization built by burning carbon and ignoring the consequences. It's going to take a lot of power to pull out all the CO_2 we've dumped into the atmosphere, no matter how we do it. So let's start with thirty terawatts for that and see how it goes—we should at least be able to turn back the clock two or three years for every year we do it. Maybe ten times that, if we're smart."

"Well, that gets you off the farm, anyway," said Solberg, chewing on his pencil. "The entire photosynthetic output of all the Earth's plants is only 75 terawatts and falling. You appropriate two thirds of that for your project and the world goes hungry."

"Okay," said Buck. "Scratch biofuels." He drew a line across his envelope.

"Likewise geothermal," said Solberg. "The total heat flux from the planet's core is barely 44 terawatts, and only a few percent of that is accessible."

"Suits me," said Buck. "I've about had my fill of volcanoes anyway."

"And don't get me started on nuclear," warned the Professor.

"Not tempted," said Buck. "As they say, nuclear power is like a TV dinner, poisonous and there's not enough of it."

"Exactly," said Solberg. "So we're down to solar."

"How about hydroelectric?"

"Dams are just another way of collecting solar energy. For example, Hoover Dam—which can give you a couple of thousandths of a terawatt on a good day—generates electricity by capturing some of the energy given up by water as it runs from a high place to a low place, energy that would otherwise have been lost as turbulence and heat. But it was the sun's energy that brought the water up to a high place in the first place, that gave it the additional potential energy it didn't have loafing around at sea level.

"Water is incredibly sticky, you know. You have to pull really hard to get a molecule of the stuff unstuck from a lump of it, and when it finally lets loose it comes flying off like a cork out of a wine bottle. In other words, you have to pump a lot of energy into water to turn it from a liquid into a gas—to evaporate it into water vapor.

"This energy stays in the water-as-a-gas until it condenses back into liquid water again, when it gives most of it back to the surrounding atmosphere as heat. But it keeps a little, stored in the momentum of the falling raindrop as it rushes from the cloud back to the sea. Most of that, too, is lost bouncing around on its way, but a tiny portion can be captured to make electricity—that is, if you think it's worth it.

"Putting up the Three Gorges Dam only gave the Chinese ten times more power than Hoover at a cost of thirty billion dollars and displacement of a million and a half people. And whether or not you think the environment is better off after this kind of monumental geologic face lift, there's nobody who will think so after the inevitable earthquake rips it apart along the seismic rift that runs right through it. Just putting that much water weight on an unstable zone can bring on a quake—it has at other dams.

"So what is hydroelectric power but just an incredibly inefficient way of collecting solar energy? The ocean absorbs pretty much all of the energy of sunlight that falls on it—not counting the tiny bit gobbled up by ocean plants—and converts it all to heat, increasing its temperature. That's where your energy is, Mr. Planck, just waiting for you to come get it.

"The earth absorbs 174 petawatts of power from the sun, that's 174, 000 terawatts, and your project only needs fifty. There's more than a fifty terawatt variability in the sun from day to day due to sunspots and other solar storms, so you could easily confiscate that amount without the Earth even noticing. What's more, as the world's humans do what they want with the twenty terawatts you give them they will convert it all to heat, which is where the sunlight would have ended up anyway if it had just fallen to the ground. And even if what you do with the CO_2 you take out of the air results in less heat in the atmosphere, you would only turn back the clock to the way it was in 1820 anyway, and things were pretty nice then with a little less heat all around.

"In other words, Mr. Planck, our species can take all the energy it wants to run its fancy civilization without doing the slightest harm to the environment. All you have to do is—"

"Magnus, don't bore our guest with work talk," called Mrs. Solberg from the dining room. "Come sit down. Dinner is finally ready."

Buck and the professor filed in and took their seats. Petal and Ali were fretting about what they would do if asked to say grace. Sunleif was proudly sawing at some creature's roasted appendage while Mrs. Solberg shoveled into a steaming pile of homogenized root vegetables. The seat allotted to Trina remained conspicuously empty.

"Where's Trina?" Magnus whispered to his wife.

"She and her friends are going to the Chill. They'll get something to eat there," answered Mrs. Solberg, smiling all around as if to short-circuit any controversy.

"What's the Chill?" asked Magnus.

"I thought you knew," she said. "Anyway Helga and Sigrid will be with her. They are both sensible girls."

"I don't know," said Magnus. "She's only fifteen and I worry about the pernicious effect that popular culture inevitably has on girls of her—"

"Oh, Magnus, let her be," pleaded Mrs. Solberg. "Oh, there's the bell. It must be them. I'll get it."

"I'll get it!" came Trina's voice from the other room. From the dining area they could hear sounds of running feet, opening doors, and suppressed squealing.

"Okay, we're leaving. Bye now."

"At least come in and meet our guests and give us a kiss," said Mrs. Solberg.

"Aww Mom!" said Trina from down the hall. Her protest sounded like it originated from conditioned reflex rather than from reasoned philosophy, and almost immediately there were sounds of three girls skipping down the hall to meet the grownups. The guests had their backs to the hall, but they could tell from the faces of Professor and Mrs. Solberg that the farewell ceremony would not go smoothly.

286

Buck's Mama had taught him, back in Newport News, always to stand when a lady enters the room—a behavior that proved to have one of the highest returns on investment of any of the cultural algorithms that had been swatted into him in childhood. Petal, being a woman, felt no such conditioned imperative, but as Buck stood, so did she, impelled by the even more powerful requirements of an insuppressible feminine curiosity.

Their simultaneous movements both startled and pleased each of them equally, and they paused on their way up to acknowledge their psycho-physical connection with a glance that became a look that was drawn out into a gaze. This intimate interlude might have gone unnoticed by bystanders at other social occasions—the escape from Pompeii, for example—but at this moment at the Solberg's dinner table it was about as conspicuous as a lightning bolt and as erotic as a—as a—well, you know.

Buck and Petal were jolted back to the world of ordinary reality by an abrupt and absolute silence erupting around them—an instantaneous cessation of giggling, skipping, carving, and serving. Breathing, too. And as they forced their eyes away from each other's and turned to face the girls, their breathing stopped, as well.

Standing there before them were three precocious teens, each carefully manifesting (through her posture and expression and hair and clothes and jewelry) her own personal interpretation of this particular instant's Svalbardan Girl Culture, just as you would expect. And as you would also expect, this culture would constitute a calculatedly shocking affront to the sensibilities of Global Adult Culture, evolving continuously to maintain the maximum tension of tolerance between the two barely co-existing worlds.

But what could not be expected, at least by the likes of Buck and Petal, was that each of the now-blond girls would be wearing not much more than a Speedo and a pair of handcuffs, severed at their middle link.

And even more unexpected, at least by the likes of Trina, Helga, and Sigrid, would be that as Buck and Petal reached up to cover their open mouths, their sleeves would pull away from their wrists, and expose handcuffs of their own—perhaps not as fashionable as Helga's or even Sigrid's, but still authentic enough for Mrs. Solberg to drop her steaming bowl of homogenized root vegetables directly onto the floor without anybody noticing.

CHAPTER 45

CHILL

Svalbardan taxis proved no more adept at accommodating parties of six than Manhattan taxis, so Ali ended up riding with Sigrid and Helga while Buck and Petal caught the next one with Trina. The mood in both of the cabs was still totally spooked out—in Svalbardan girl-terminology—and at first no one spoke.

Even though it had never actually been acknowledged that the Solberg's dining room floor was now covered with steaming homogenized root vegetables, Petal felt guilty about leaving without helping clean up. Buck also felt bad about leaving, but primarily because he had not quite found out how to provide the world with a limitless supply of environmentally safe energy. Ali felt bad, too, but largely because he had missed dinner and because everybody cool seemed to be wearing handcuffs except him.

But there was no question about leaving. From the start of the Great Silence when Buck and Petal stood staring at the girls, and the girls stood staring at Buck and Petal, and Magnus and Berit Solberg stood staring at each other, and Ali sat staring at the roast beast, it was clear that dinner, as a social bonding ritual, was officially over.

Not that there wasn't plenty of bonding and ritual going on. With liturgical slowness, Petal had taken Trina's hands in hers and raised them up above the girl's head, turning her, inch by inch in a circle, peering at every nuance of her affectations. And then Helga, just as excruciatingly slowly, soundlessly, clock-like. And then Sigrid, moving her slightly closer to the light for her enraptured and meticulous revelation. Standing back at last, taking in the three girls at once, Petal had said the only words that were left for her at that rarified point in space-time, "We should go."

Buck and Ali had been glad to let her do the talking. Something was happening up here at the top of the world that had something to do with them. Something deeper than coincidence, more significant than serendipity, and more subtle than divine intervention. Something that they had better know about, if they knew what was good for them.

And while it was clear that Trina and her friends must know more about this than Magnus or Berit, it was also clear that Tina and her friends were like distant ripples, carriers of a far-away signal that had become attenuated, embellished, and iteratively reinterpreted on the convoluted journey from its original source. Buck and Ali knew that there was only one person who could, by dead reckoning, navigate this darkness back to its heart. Who could follow the thread as it wound through the tangled knot of Svalbardan girl culture back to the cosmic puppet master who had spun it out from God knows where.

Petal.

But here was Ali in the back seat between Sigrid and Helga, everybody acting all spooked out and afraid to say anything. Modern life is full of compulsory uncomfortable silences like this, when strangers are randomly jostled into intimate—but thankfully fleeting—proximities. Some people rebel at this socially mandated elevator-autism, engendering camaraderie among fellow travelers along their journeys from Men's Slightly Better Sportswear to Discount Designer Misses, no matter how brief. Others resolutely pretend invisibility long after everyone else has acknowledged that the elevator is indeed stuck, the Earth's population has been raptured away, and they had better start figuring out just who is going to eat whom when.

After more than a few minutes on the road, Ali realized that this trip to the Chill was likely going to take more than just a few minutes. A respectful, polite silence was no longer appropriate. Even in this kind of situation. Even if this situation had a kind of. As the adult, it was Ali's responsibility to establish rapport with these members of the younger generation. Some area of common ground was needed. Something non-confrontational. Even trivial. Amusing if possible. Politically neutral.

"Remember that Seinfold episode where they drop the mashed potatoes on the floor and then everybody acts like it never happened?" he offered.

"Seinfold, Seinfold," pondered Helga, cocking her head and pulling at her chin. "He's that celebrity who just bought scholarships for a thousand Kenyan agronomy students, right?"

"No, no," said Sigrid. "He's the fund manager who just built that water purification plant in Haiti."

"No, you're thinking of the other one," objected Helga. "Seinfold is the investment banker who just saved a million children's lives with mosquito netting and malaria pills."

"I think you have him mixed up with that health plan CEO who donated his offshore accounts to cover the uninsured," said Sigrid.

"No," said Ali, "I meant the actor Seinfold, the one with all the cars. You know the story—right after he pays two million dollars for his last car, some derivatives dealer in Chicago spends two and a half on an even more luxurious one. Well, this makes Seinfold very depressed. Here he has spent all this money on a car and now the whole thing just seems tawdry and cheap. He can't eat. He can't sleep. He wonders whether life itself is worth living, whether there really can be any meaning in a world that is so patently unfair. But just when things look darkest for him he has a revelation.

"He realizes that he has been looking at his place in the world from the entirely wrong perspective. He realizes that there is no reason to despair just because someone, somewhere has bought a more expensive car than he has. He realizes that, with enough determination, there really is no limit to how much money you can spend on a car. That if you really put your heart into it, if you truly follow your dream, you can spend three or even four million on a car. And so he does. And for good measure, he tears down the apartment building next door to build a special garage, just for that one car. Inspiring story, don't you think?"

"Are you sure you aren't confusing him with that dot com dude who pretended to drop ten million on a lavish wedding but secretly spent it on refugee relocation?" asked Helga.

"I know that guy! You mean he just pretended to get married?" asked Ali, beginning to realize that he was way out of his league with these girls.

"No, he really did get married," she said. "A tasteful little ceremony at home. It was the extravagant waste that was faked. If you look carefully at the videos, you can tell that the guests getting off their private 797's on Necker Island were all computer generated."

"But the guy is loaded!" objected Ali. "Okay, I can imagine him giving some tiny percentage of his wealth to some pet project, just for show. I can even imagine him going nuts and giving his entire fortune to charity. But either way, why would he go to all that trouble to make people think he had squandered a king's ransom on some self-aggrandizing party?"

"Same reason Seinfold wants everyone to believe he has a three million dollar car, I guess," said Sigrid.

"Makes sense to me," agreed Helga. "Perfectly obvious."

It was hard for Ali to see the girls' faces in the dark of the cab's back seat, but he peered at them as intently as he thought he could get away with. From every outward appearance, they were typical teeny-bopper clones, with their regimented eccentricities and audacious conformities. Ali hadn't actually talked with girls of this age in more years than he cared to admit, but he did have a clear expectation of what it would be like—and talking with Helga and Sigrid was nothing like that. They were supposed to be confused, not confusing. They were supposed to be vapid, not convoluted. They were supposed to be boring, not challenging.

Ali figured that there were at least three possible interpretations of the preceding conversation:

1. These ignorant children have all their facts wrong.
2. These young adults know something I don't.
3. These kids are yanking my chain.

Each of these possibilities spawned subsets of corollary hypotheses and topics for further inquiry (Have I missed that much CNN? Are all fifteen-year-old girls this difficult? Does my chain really look that easy to yank?). Ali was contemplating the most incisive next gambit when the cab pulled up to the curb and the girls spilled out giggling.

They were in another Svalbardan heated, drive-through garage, but clearly one meant for high-volume industrial traffic. This looked more like the basement of a warehouse than the entrance to some wholesome teen canteen. Sigrid and Helga seemed excited to be here, though, and greeted Trina's cab with age-appropriate enthusiasm.

"Buck," he said, collaring Planck, who was trying to get his finger off the cab's door handle. "That guy with the jillion dollar wedding, was he faking it?"

"Faking what?" Buck tried to ask for the cabbie's zapper, but his Urdu was rusty and all he got was half of a sandwich. "Being an idiot? No, I think he really is an idiot. No law against being an idiot, though. On the other hand, there probably ought to be—for that kind of monumental idiocy, anyway—although the wording of the statute would have to be rather carefully—"

"Forget that idiot! You're missing the entire point! I'm telling you, Buck, pay attention here. There's more to this than meets the eye."

"This what?"

"This whole thing."

"Oh, that. Definitely. I couldn't agree more."

"Good," said Ali, relieved. "I was beginning to think it was just me."

Ali was right; there were a number of disconcerting aspects to the current situation. The girls had disappeared, for one. Buck had promised the Solbergs that he would keep an eye on them at the Chill, and even though it had been clear to everyone that this was like promising that it wouldn't rain, Buck had hoped that the girls might actually try not to get lost quite so immediately. Also, it would have been reassuring to see a sign or two on the walls, even in Norwegian—some indication that people were supposed to be down in this concrete cave at this hour. A little light would be nice, too. Even a bouncer. Even a cop.

Petal was waving from the top of a staircase. As they climbed toward her, noise from beyond an open door spilled down around them—sounds of shouting, laughter, and music. Music that made Buck's skin crawl and his heart race.

"Lykiloro!" he said. "Hear that, Ali? That's what he was playing when the volcano was exploding—in fact, that is the volcano exploding."

"Creepy, but you can dance to it. I'll give it a five," judged Ali. "So how do you know it's him anyway? Maybe all the bands up here sound like this."

"No way," said Buck. "Lykiloro's stuff may be hyper-processed and over-orchestrated, but it is pure volcano-gone-critical in every wavelength. You've got to risk your life just to get the basic ingredient for this mix. I'll bet nobody has ever gotten that close to the Earth spilling its guts with so much recording muscle, and probably never will. No, that's Lykiloro, all right. You can tell from its contagious lunacy."

"You're right; it does have a certain virulent prurience. Are you sure that young people should be listening to stuff like this?"

"Maybe we should go tell those teenagers to be more careful with their music," said Buck, walking past him.

"Exactly."

It was even darker in the Chill than in the garage, and the three of them stopped just inside the doorway to let their eyes accommodate. At first, all they could tell was that they were in a huge room on a landing about twelve feet above the main floor. It was too loud to talk and too dark to see, so they huddled and gaped while arriving groups of kids greeted them in Norwegian like they were part of the show.

And quite a show it was. Every flat surface in the cavernous warehouse served as a screen for the projected video stream— walls, crates, columns, ceiling, and floor. Until your brain pieced together the solid structures beneath the moving images and made some sense of the place's geometry, the effect was pretty vertiginous. After that, it was more like motion sickness.

There didn't seem to be a coherent theme to the visuals, except for the complete absence of Hollywood-inspired pop-culture iconography, all the more remarkable given the Chill's clientele. Natural scenes predominated, but more toward the hurricane, flood, earthquake, and plague end of the emotional spectrum, with more than a smattering of in-your-face liquid magma.

It looked like most of the warehouse's normal contents had been piled up against the walls to make space for the mass of kids writhing to Lykiloro's satanic aria, and scattered about the dance floor were a couple dozen makeshift tables, each with what looked like a floor lamp with a shade standing on it. Each table had six or eight kids sitting around it intently working their laptops, and each of these had six or eight friends crowding over his shoulder cheering him on. Buck figured that some kind of massive multi-player online computer game was in progress. Oddly, it looked like the people around the tables were talking to one another, in spite of the noise. Maybe everyone learned to read lips after a while up here.

Out of nowhere Trina and her friends were there pulling on their sleeves and motioning for them to follow. Helga used her superior weight to plow a groove through the crowd to the closest table. As the six of them stepped into the cone of light cast by the lamp on its center, the noise of the room abruptly stopped.

Buck looked up, expecting the crowd to be as startled as he was by the sudden silence, but out on the floor, the dancers' epileptic ecstasies did not miss a beat. It took a minute for Buck to realize that he had not entirely lost his hearing, for he was now able to perceive the normal-toned conversation of the people around the table. He felt like he was in a classroom with a silent movie being shown around him. Then he figured it out.

"What happened?" asked Petal, pounding the side of her head as if to get water out of her ears.

"Noise cancellation," answered Buck, pointing up at the lamp on the table. "Very directional, too. I'll show you."

He took her hand and together they took a giant step sideways out onto the dark area of the dance floor. The noise of the music and countless screaming teenagers was deafening. Quickly they jumped back into the acoustic safety of the soundless oasis near the table and waited for their ears to stop ringing.

"Isn't this the greatest Chill?" asked Trina jumping up and down like you're not supposed to do anymore when you are fifteen.

"Best I've ever been to," admitted Buck. "Tell me, Trina, this music—Lykiloro's stuff—have you kids been listening to it long?"

"Is that his name? Isn't he totally spooked out?" she said, clapping her hands. "I mean, can you believe what he does with your innards? You won't tell my parents, will you? They'll have us all checked for organ damage or something."

"Completely spooked, but when did you first hear this music, I mean this exact stuff?" Buck knew this wasn't really the most important question he had, but still he was curious.

"It's always new at the Chill, Sister Buck," she said. "That's what the Chill is, you know. That's what all the kids at the laptops are doing, looking for it."

"Looking for what?" asked Petal, peering over the shoulder of a girl in a tie-dyed Speedo with hair to match who was driving her twenty-inch MicBook SemiPro through what looked like architectural drawings for pre-war Berlin sewer renovations. Her friends were urging her to send what appeared to be Albert Speer's signature through a decryption program to see if anything was hidden inside it.

"Clues," she said. "Fragments. Latent images. Bits of code. Sometimes it's obvious—seven frames in correct order—other times it seems just like noise within the cosmic background radiation, but with enough computing power—a hundred laptops all running in parallel—you can pull it out—and when you do, it goes up on the screens right away, or into the audio stream."

"You know how to do all this?" asked Petal, who still found email intimidating.

"Some. But not like the big kids. Mostly you don't get good enough to drive until you're sixteen or so. This girl Olga on the Mic is only fourteen, but she's got a gift being dyslexic. Helps you concentrate, she says."

Just then it became pretty loud within their little cone of quiet. Olga had found something while sifting through a compilation of mutant amphibian genome sequences. The kids around her were so excited that Buck and Petal got pushed out to the edge of the sound barrier, where the adrenal-squeezing strains of Lykiloro's brain contagion were seeping through.

"Olga's got a visual!" screamed Trina, hugging them all. "Now she sends it up to the VJ for authentication. If it's the real stuff, he'll put it in the stream right away!"

Buck put his arm around Petal, ostensibly to keep her from being jostled out onto the dance floor, but really because the whole scene was starting to really spook him out. It was difficult to see her face because of the flamboyant folds of her coif. Buck had tried to get her to wear a more conservative, face-framing wimple like his and Ali's, but back in the freezing helicopter she was opting for the most cloth available. At the time it had seemed like a reasonable choice, jaunty without being risky. Now he wanted to push it away, to take in the fullness of her smile, to be reassured by her way of looking. He thought he might just bend down and untie the white linen bow beneath her chin and free her curls from their restraint, and maybe even sweep her onto the floor, abandoning themselves to Lykiloro's Geode to Pan, to be young again with her, with lifetimes ahead and nothing to lose.

Until every surface around them, walls and ceiling and floor, all shone with a new image stream. Ghostly white at first. Blowing snow across a faint horizon. And then in the distance a figure, barely visible, arms outstretched, head thrown back, mouth open in a scream. The camera zooms in slowly—it is a woman, nearly nude, her lithe body sheathed in a single sheet of thin, clinging cloth. Her bare feet hover over the surface of the snow—she glides above, never touching its surface. She reaches out to us with both hands, beseeching us, beseeching the world. And from her wrists dangle the broken chains of manacles that had dared contain her. The camera pans up. The woman is no longer screaming. She looks straight at the camera, at us, with a look beyond that of mortal experience.

The crowd is frozen in mid-breath. The VJ has cut the audio stream. The visual loops back once, then stops on the last frame. The woman's expression fills all of space. There is no longer any doubt in anyone's mind.

This is She.

CHAPTER 46

GORSKI

"Oh, there you are! We were worried we would have to tell Magnus and Berit we lost you at the Chill."

It was only after the crowd had left and the lights had gone up that Helga had spotted something suspicious under one of the tables. At first she had taken it for a pile of trash hiding from the dump, but sounds of snoring had made her wonder if it was really a pile of nuns catching up on Z's. Of course, there was always a chance that it was a pile of Rottweilers catching up on Z's, so she had poked it with a broom handle rather than her foot.

Buck's head popped out first, then Ali's. Then after disappearing again and a bit of whispering, the three of them emerged—Buck, then Ali, then presumably Petal. Helga figured it must be Petal, because she had been the only nun at the Chill with such a distinctive and flamboyant coif (the only other nuns at the Chill being Buck and Ali in their more forgettable wimples). But now Petal (if that is who she or he was) was also wearing a face scarf tied in the traditional Yomamah fashion (allowing only a tiny but still shockingly lascivious glimpse of passion-inflaming female nostril and iris) plus a pair of completely opaque Love Canal® sunglasses with lenses the size of dinner plates.

"Sorry to flake out on you," said Buck. "But folks our age are used to being in bed by October. Great Chill, though. Is everybody else gone?"

"Well, basically," said Helga. "Trina and Sigrid met a couple of boys. They're over there making spooky eyes at each other. Disgusting!"

"Shouldn't we be getting you girls home now?" asked Buck, wondering what time it must be.

"I'll say. If the cops catch us here, my dad will ground me for a million years."

"Cops?" asked Ali. "Dance clubs are illegal in Svalbard?"

"Don't be silly," she said. "This isn't a club. It's just a warehouse where someone sort of left the door open sort of by accident. That's the way the Chill works. Everything we need fits into backpacks—laptops, speakers, projectors and the quiet-spot units. When one of us finds an empty space big enough, then the texts go out and the Chill happens. The cops are never too far behind, though, so we had better beat cheeks out of here before they show up."

"Yeah, let's beat cheeks," agreed Ali, quickly incorporating the idiom. "I can't stand being grounded myself."

Petal accepted Buck's hand up, maneuvering to keep his bulk between herself and Helga.

"You okay, sister Petal?" she asked, wondering at the dramatic change in her appearance and demeanor.

"The dark hurts her eyes," explained Buck. "And the smoke."

"No one smokes here," said Helga. "That would be so un-Chilled."

"I mean the dust. The dust hurts her eyes. And her nose. Not the nostrils, just the top of her nose. And her lips, too. That's why the scarf. She'll be okay. Happens all the time. Where did you say Trina was?"

They followed Helga across the room to a dark alcove near the exit. Spooky eyes were in progress, but nothing an even the most unromantic chaperone couldn't overlook.

"Oh, there you are!" said Trina. "Come meet Ivan and Igor. This is their first Chill. I'm telling them all about it. Do any of you speak Russian?" Trina presented two clean-cut young men in Hawaiian shirts and basketball shorts. Their tattoos, though, were old Soviet Navy, freshly minted.

"Здравствуйте," said Igor.

"Как поживаешь?" asked Ivan.

"We're great," said Buck. "Do you guys speak any English?"

"Skoshi English," claimed Igor.

"Yeah, skoshi," agreed Ivan.

"That much?" said Buck. "Very good. Let's get these girls home before we all go to ground." He made the universal sign for 'Squad, move out.'

The eight of them were almost to the exit when the door burst open and a uniformed Longyearbyen City policeman burst in, visor down, Mace drawn.

"Don't move!" he commanded. "You are all under arrest for trespassing, disorderly conduct, and chilling without a license, so help me God. Hands on your heads."

"Is that you, Uncle Sven?" asked Trina, walking right up to him, hands on her hips.

"Trina?" he said, putting down his weapon. "What are you doing here? Does your mother know where you are?"

"Sure, but we were just leaving. Give us a lift? Taxis are tough at this hour."

"Well, I don't know," he said. "I'm on official police business now and this is a serious matter. Breaking and entering. Or is it entering and breaking? Or is it break dancing? I know what you kids have been up to. I watch TV, too, you know."

"Nothing's broken and the door was open. Besides, you wouldn't want us out on the streets, would you? And besides, it's late and Mom will ground us both if you don't get us home pretty quick. Now where is your car?"

"Not so fast, somebody's got to go to jail here, what about them?" he pointed his Mace at Ivan and Igor.

"Diplomatic immunity," said Trina. "Russian sailors. You don't want to start an international incident, do you? You know how they get—poisoned umbrellas, phone bugs, ICBMs."

Ivan and Igor knew enough to show their identification badges and smile submissively.

"That leaves you three nun people. I want to warn you that I have a number of unresolved issues from my childhood regarding nuns. Nuns and rulers, actually. Now, I know it's not fair to generalize, and it was a long time ago, and penmanship instruction must have changed a lot since then—but if any of you are carrying rulers I want you to throw them out on the floor there right now, no questions asked. Okay, I am closing my eyes and counting to three. Ready? One. Two. Three."

Petal and Ali were certain that they weren't carrying rulers, but they searched their pockets anyway, just in case. Ali found a handful of unpaid Vatican parking tickets, but nothing solid enough to rap knuckles with.

"Unarmed, eh?" said Officer Sven. "Good, then it's off to the slammer with you three. You can tell it all to the judge next week. I think he may be back next week."

"Моё судно на воздушной подушке полно угрей," said Buck.

"What's that?" asked Sven.

"Моё судно на воздушной подушке полно угрей," he repeated, tugging on Ivan's sleeve.

"Oh, he say them with us," said Ivan, nodding and smiling furiously.

"Давай поженимся," pronounced Buck, solemnly.

"Russian Navy Nuns, them," assured Ivan. "First Class."

"Well, that's just great for all of you, but what am I supposed to do now with nobody to arrest?" complained Officer Sven.

"I promise we'll get you some even better prisoners next time," said Trina. "Clean, polite, Norwegian-speaking pacifists. Quakers, maybe. Deal?"

"Yeah, maybe that would be better, anyway," he conceded.

"Of course it would," she said, shooing everyone outside to Sven's paddy wagon, parked illegally at the curb. Within minutes they were home, paddy wagons not obliged to pay attention to speed limits and traffic lights.

Berit and Magnus looked more relieved than angry as they helped the girls out of the back of the van. Buck smiled at them and waved, but it seemed that the Solberg's hospitality had entirely lost its warmth in the short time their guests had been off getting their child chilled and arrested until all hours of the very long night.

Even Ali was forced to admit that their chance at scoring a quick solar fix for their little problem (not to mention the Earth's big problem) here in Svalbard had indeed been queered beyond rectification, as it were. Hanging around greater metropolitan Longyearbyen waiting for things to warm up was just as likely to overshoot—in fact, if events at the Chill were any indication, it was about to get very hot around here, especially for anyone who looked as much like Petal as Petal did.

So, after a couple rounds of balloting, the three agreed unanimously that they should do exactly what they were currently being compelled to do—not because it was the easiest thing to do, not because they had no choice in the matter, but because it was the right thing to do.

Not that they knew exactly what it was they were being compelled to do. Ivan and Igor commanded about as much English as Buck did Russian (enough to get your nose broken in a bar) and weren't capable of communicating more than they were going to "Russian Boat." After everyone had had their turn at cocktail-party-class pantomime, Pidgin Pig Latin, and English Spoken Very Loudly, they decided to leave it at that. Russian boat. Could be worse. Couldn't it?

There was no heated garage filled with nurturing family members at the dock where Sven dropped them all off. In fact, he had barely slowed to twenty before he popped the door and announced that they were now leaving the Semi-Sovereign Geographic Entity of Svalbard and he hoped they had had a pleasant stay and please don't come again, thank you very much.

The five stood shivering in their civvies as the cold north wind came sweeping down on them from the pole, about two bus stops north. Ivan eventually got his bearings and led them running, arms flapping, down a darkened pier towards an even darker blob at its end. At full speed they charged up a gangplank and onto the deck of what must have been Russian Boat, unchallenged by guards or officials. Ivan yanked at a couple of locked doors as Igor did the same. They both took on a panicked look as more doors were tried and found unyielding.

An impromptu but heartfelt conference in epithet-laden Russian was then convened, punctuated by epithet-laden expressions of accusation, indignation, remorse, reconciliation, and, finally, resignation. It was a quintessential Russian moment. The two hugged each other tearfully. Had a bottle of vodka been present, it would have been toast.

"Prepare for music in face," advised Igor, helping everyone to straighten their uniforms into their most presentable configurations. He and Ivan squared themselves into military formation and marched the group forward towards a source of faint illumination and muffled voices. Pretty soon it was clear that they were approaching a large group of people engaged in something particularly disagreeable. And then there it was, the entire crew assembled on deck, being berated by their captain, standing above them at the railing of the bridge.

"Good for us," whispered Igor. "Everybody get music in face tonight."

"What's he saying," said Ali, running his finger over a bulkhead curiously.

"Boat no go," said Ivan. "No key."

"They lost the key to the boat?" asked Petal, secretly glad to hear that this sort of thing happened to other people, too.

"Hey, I know this boat," said Ali, who was now down on his knees inspecting a plaque. "I've got two of these—my everyday yachts. I save the big one for special occasions."

"Why would you want a Russian Navy boat?" asked Petal.

"Dutch," said Ali. "Von Guilders Shipyards. Six hundred fifty feet. Twin Caterpillar 3000HP diesels. Five Jacuzzis standard—mine have eight. Great speed, lousy mileage."

"So this isn't a military vessel then?" asked Petal.

"Hardly," answered Ali. "Though mine do have water balloon launchers we used to capture St. Tropez one summer. I think they put a ban on them after that."

"Ever lose the key?" asked Buck.

"All the time. All it takes is a penny behind the right fuse. Or a thousand *dungat* Yomamah coin. Whatever you've got. Then there are a couple of wires to cross and it fires right up."

"Excellent," said Buck. "Ivan, why don't you introduce us to your boss? Locksmiths from the Vatican here to save the day. Я мечтаю встретить девушку, с которой я мог бы прожить всю жизнь."

"Okay, I'm like, oh my God!" agreed Ivan, seeing an opportunity for happy ending music in face.

As Ivan elbowed a path through the crowd, the Captain's ranting became steadily louder until it abruptly stopped. All eyes turned to the trio of clerics being led toward the front. The Captain glared down at them, guards on either side of him readying their Uzis. You could have cut the tension with an ice saw.

"Хочешь на горшок," declared Ivan.

"Я так сильно скучал/а по тебе," answered the Captain. The crowd murmured in agreement and backed away, looks of admiration and astonishment on their faces. Not a word was spoken as the three climbed the stair to the bridge and approached the man in charge, a fit aristocratic sixtyish guy with a buzz cut and a square jaw.

"Buck Planck," said Buck, extending his hand. "У меня плохо с русским."

"Boris Gorski," he said, gripping it powerfully. "You speak English? My English is perfect. So is my Italian. For your friend, I

304

can speak Yiddish if he wants. My Yiddish is impeccable." He nodded toward Ali, who was trying not to roll his eyes.

"English would be great," said Buck

"You nun people have the key to my boat? How can that be? You had better have a good explanation if you know what is good for you," he said in a tone that made his guards lean their rifles closer.

"No, no, no," explained Buck, his friends huddling close behind him. "We don't know anything about your key. We just know how you can start your boat without it."

"And how would you know that?" he said, looming at them aggressively. His guards didn't need advanced language skills to know they should loom, too. "This is very suspicious. Spies in nun's clothing. What else do you think you know about me?"

"No, no, no, no," expanded Buck. "We don't know anything about your boat *in particular*. We just know about your boat *in general*."

"Your English is not very impeccable, is it?" asked Gorski. "Or are you playing with your words on purpose? Maybe you people have something to hide, eh?"

He leaned around Buck to inspect Petal, or at least her nostrils, which (because he was a man) he found unbearably provocative. He gave Ali the once over and then snorted dismissively.

"Listen, Bozo," said Ali, who could put up with a lot, but not being snorted at. "You want your boat started or not? And don't get on our case—we're just the messengers." He pointed at the sky and nodded. "It's not up to us what information comes down from You-Know-Whom."

Gorski rocked back on his heels, looking like he had been slapped in the face with a wet herring. His guards went pale and looked at each other for clues to protocol. Buck and Petal squinted and cringed. Ali jutted his chin defiantly. This was a pivotal moment.

"No one alive knows that name! Never did my sainted mother ever call me her Precious Little Bozo in the presence of another living person. It was our secret, the only true and perfect intimacy of my life, one that she carried to her grave in silence. Surveillance tapes prove it conclusively!"

"We are as in awe of these mysteries as you are, Mr. Gorski," said Petal. "How Sister Ali receives his knowledge is one of those things that must forever remain unknowable. We can only be grateful that he is among us now, for as short a period as that may be."

Ali didn't know what to make of Petal's gratuitous reference to the limits of his mortality, but took it as a coded message that his life now depended on bullshit and he had better make it good.

"Mr. Gorski," Ali said pontifically. "All of your secrets are safe with us. Our sojourn in this physical plane has one purpose, and one purpose only, a higher purpose, a purpose beyond ourselves, a purpose handed down from One more powerful than any of us—present company excepted, of course."

"And that purpose would be?" prompted Gorski.

Ali glanced at his friends for guidance in bullshit trajectory, but Buck's face seemed only able to communicate that he was about to fall from a great height, and Petal's dilating nostrils could be interpreted in a number of ways. Silently, the eternal cosmic struggle of survival, truth, and bullshit was re-enacted within the instant of their gaze.

"To help rich people make more money," declared Petal, her voice so pure, so true that any detector of lies, be it man or machine, would have immediately embraced her as the ultimate standard of reference.

"Hallelujah!" said Gorski, gripping Ali's shoulders in his hands and beaming into his face. "I have always been the most pious of persons, but until now have never found a prophet whose message resonated so perfectly with my spirituality. Come, my new counselor. Bring your friends; we have some talking to do. But first, some hot food and cold vodka. Then we cast off for home, my home and now your new home, Novaya Zemlya, the closest place to heaven on Earth."

CHAPTER 47

CONFESSION

"Don't you know who this guy is?" asked Buck, pacing back and forth the long way across Ali's stateroom. He figured they only had a few minutes before they were called to dinner and they had better get a few things straight.

"Of course I know who he is," said Ali, stretched out on the king-sized bed, admiring himself in the ceiling mirror. "Everybody knows who he is. Boris Gorski, AKA "Bozo" as we have discovered, one of the ten richest men in Russia—ultra-nationalist arms smuggler, sex trader, mafia don, election rigger, ego maniac, bad dresser, and now recently converted religious nut. Why?"

"This guy is a violent lunatic, Ali. He's paranoid and schizy and likely hopped on uppers. We're surrounded by a boatload of bloodthirsty morons on our way to the most uncivilized, radiation-poisoned spot on the planet. We have to be careful here—you can't just pretend to be Rasputin dispensing the voice of God, for God's sake."

"Why not? Rasputin did pretty well—in the short term anyway—and wasn't he pretending, too? In fact, aren't they all pretending? I've got holy men and psychics and necromancers and soothsayers of every imaginable variety on my payroll and I can tell you there is only one thing they all have in common—they're pretending. Good thing, too. Last thing you want around is somebody who actually believes he is the voice of God. That's when things really get homicidal."

"I'm not suggesting that you believe it, Ali. It's just that—"

"And what about Petal? How come she gets to be the Supreme Iconic Leader of some global Earth Goddess cult and nobody says anything, but the first time I get the slightest bit of attention—"

"Break my heart—the poor baby never gets any attention," said Petal, intently painting her nails over by the vanity. "You're the

Shah of Yomamah, Ali. You get more attention than the law should allow."

"That's Sultan. And I meant recently."

"And do you think I like being The Cyber Earth Mother or whatever the hell Siverth has got me cooked up to be on the Internet? Look, I was as shocked as you were by those videos at the Chill, or whatever the hell that event was. In fact, now that we are on the subject, I'd like to know just what the hell is going on with this whole—"

"Ты нужна мне, Зайчик мой!" came an impatient voice from outside their door.

"Dinner," said Buck. "And make it snappy."

Petal had Ali help her back into the face scarf and sunglasses as she flapped her wet nails in the air. This was definitely not her color, but it had been the only polish in the drawer that didn't glow in the dark. And since there was nothing about her ensemble that wasn't either black or white, she figured she could get away with Blood of Lenin Red just this once.

The guard led them single file through a series of long corridors and staircases. As he walked through the boat, Ali at first marveled at its familiarity but then began to find it depressing. The Von Guilders Shipyard must be stamping these babies out like Toyotas.

It used to mean something to drive a custom-built mega-yacht like this. Ownership would signify your membership in an exclusive global elite; it would authenticate your superior status within the very cream of the planet's most rapaciously self-aggrandizing barons of greed. Not just anyone was allowed to sadistically parade their mobile orgies of waste in front the starving masses, gawking hollow-cheeked from the shore. Only the revered and visionary leaders of the global economy had earned the right to that pleasure. And rightly so, for they were the chosen ones. Chosen by the Market. Chosen, anointed, deified, and indemnified—all by the all-knowing and all-powerful Market.

But now, it seemed that any coarse and simple ruffian could show up at Guilders, uninvited, and pull from his pockets the hope for clean water in Zaire, the solution to malnutrition in Haiti, the possibility for literacy in Sao Paulo, or the protection from malaria for all the world's children—spilling them out on the velvet tabletop in the form of blood-flecked diamonds, corruption-levered securities, and government-guaranteed extortions—and expect Von Guilders himself to usher him into this once genteel and intimate brotherhood of yachting sportsmen.

Not that these newcomers didn't have as much right to drive a mega-yacht as anybody. After all, they had worked as hard for their money as anybody, and the market had rewarded their dedication and skill and strength of character. They had earned their membership in Ali's club. So why did he feel such nausea at the thought of associating with them? Maybe it was just a bug. Maybe the seas had kicked up. He would get over it.

Entering the Captain's Mess, he automatically walked over to the head of the table and sat down. The lighting was abominably bright and there was some annoying balalaika music in the background. He reached under the table for the controls and softened the spots, brought up the indirects in a slightly pinker hue and spun through the canned stuff to a restful riff by Rachmaninoff, equalized down to Hypnosis Session volume. With a couple of twists he added five degrees to the temperature and ten to the humidity and dropped in a dollop of positive ions. He lowered the table height a bit to suit his taste and was about to dial up the wine list when Gorski strode into the room and skidded to a stop.

Gorski couldn't believe his eyes. Where was he? Certainly not where he had eaten every meal for the last month. Gone was the permanently harsh, convenience-store glare. Gone was that ever-repeating, obnoxious balalaika music. His room had been replaced by an otherworldly sphere of shadow and mystery—beckoning, enveloping, engulfing, and as irresistible as the songs of the Sirens.

The three were already here, seemingly motionless but slightly levitating. They must have opened a rift in the ectoplasmic ether, exposing a dimension beyond—he could hear its haunting music wafting through the wormhole. This must be a séance in progress. The female was conjuring up the spirit world—her hands hovering over the shifting table, her nails dripping blood of martyrs. He swallowed hard. He must not let them sense his fear.

"May I speak," he whispered softly.

Behind her sunglasses, Petal could study Gorski while appearing to be looking across the table at Buck, who had worked himself up into some kind of catatonic trance trying to catch her eye through her sunglasses. She could also see that Ali, having finally digested Buck's appraisal of Gorski's psychotic potential, had also switched on his deer-in-headlights auto-pilot program. That left her with the ball, sitting there with her nails hanging out to dry like some kind of zombie sleepwalker.

She could see the sweat beading on Gorski's forehead. She could hear the tremor in his voice. She could smell his panic. Now was the time to seize the superior position, to skewer his psyche like a pin through a bug. Otherwise, there would be no place of safety around this man.

"Yesss," she intoned in the droning, nasal voice one must use when communicating with the spirit world. "The eternal Baba Rum Das is here among us tonight and prepared to receive inquiries through Sister Ali bin Said as his medium. Please sit and state your name."

"Boris Ivanovich Gorski," he said hoarsely, choking back a gasp as he sat. They had done something to his legs. They were so swollen now that he had to force them under the table. He would have to bear it. A show of weakness would certainly render him unworthy of participation, and who could guess the limits of the wrath of the spirits.

"And your confession, Boris Ivanovich?" mooed Petal, projecting her voice like a ventriloquist onto Ali, whose lips, like with your better mediums, never moved once.

"My confession?" he squeaked, his legs now numb from compression and his nose tingling with ozone.

"Yesss, your confession," Petal said through Ali in a voice so convincing that it fooled Buck completely and Ali half way. "Baba Rum Das will impart the secrets of immense wealth only to those who have proven themselves worthy through a life of dedicated and wanton ruthlessness, of unflinching abuse of power, of insatiable hoarding of resources, and of meticulous abstinence from the sentimentality of human compassion. Are you such a man? Baba Rum Das demands an answer."

"Yes, yes, O Holy One!" exclaimed Gorski frantically. "You will never find a more merciless acquisitor, a more unrepentant acolyte of avarice, or a more malicious manipulator of men if you walk down Wall Street all day long. I, Boris Ivanovich Gorski, was born to this greatness. From childhood, it was I who poisoned the futures of everyone around me just in case they might surpass me. It was I who assassinated the characters of those who stood between me and my control of the secret police, and then assassinated what remained of them later. It was I who carved out a fortress of privilege inside the Kremlin and patiently constructed the traps that would capture the wealth of the Soviets as soon as it was released from its pretense of egalitarian Communism into the slathering jaws of Capitalist egoism.

"You must admit, O Powerful One, how deliciously sinister an accomplishment this was! From a country too poor to feed its own people I was able to wring billions and billions just for myself! Yes, I know many others have stolen fortunes as well, but none of them with such exquisite invidiousness, such blatant unbeneficence, such extravagant hubris. I am the one you seek, O Omniscient One."

"Perhaps," said Baba Rum Das from the other plane. "But we need details, man. Generalities just don't cut it out here in the ether."

"Okay, then, let's take it from the beginning. At first one must practice tirelessly to hone one's skills, not expecting any reward other than the personal satisfaction of mastery of one's craft. The Gulag, for example. Did we get rich from all that work? And the purges? We barely broke even. The systematic revocation of human rights? The elimination of privacy? Sunk costs, all of them. Necessary investments, to be sure, but nothing to take to the bank.

"But then came the miracle of Capitalism complete with its ready-made, Orwellian double-speak. Privatization—how sweet a word! The Free Market—how deliciously oxymoronic! Deregulation—hallelujah! And our utmost gratitude to you, O Omnipotent One, for you must have been Capitalism's Supreme Creator. Yes, this has been our payback time, long awaited and much deserved by all of us intrepid entrepreneurs.

"But you must grant us some credit, too. Did we not lure that simpleton American president into a spending contest that brought us oligarchs to power and squandered his country's power? Don't they still credit him with 'defeating Communism?' Doesn't that make you laugh up your cosmic sleeve? And then tricking them into taking our place as targets in the Afghanistan shooting gallery, and willfully sticking themselves to the tar baby in Iraq—were these not brilliant feats of political engineering? And were we surprised, then, when our oil became more valuable than gold? Even the rusting remnant of a moribund Soviet industry can pump

311

privatized oil out of the ground, for God's sake—but please forgive me if I blaspheme, O Pitiless One.

"And now that we have the resources we can aspire to an even higher level of economic artistry through our ever-expanding, vertically integrated, international network of émigré franchisees. Look in any major city—we are there whether you see us or not, championing the cause of *laissez faire* on behalf of free men of every nationality.

"Because freedom is all men really want, isn't it? Freedom to move huge blocks of heroin, for example. Freedom to cook up a vat or two of crystal meth. Freedom to help an impoverished Ukrainian schoolgirl advance her career in the sex trade. Freedom to sell guns to whoever might be encouraged to harbor a grievance. These are basic human rights we are talking about here—freedoms from meddling bureaucratic interference.

"Yes, those of us who have been blessed by good fortune keenly feel our responsibility to give back to our communities. I personally have devoted countless uncompensated hours to advocacy of our political ideals. If it were not for our tireless and unselfish grass roots involvement there would still be dozens of unmurdered reporters sticking their noses into places they didn't belong, not to mention countless television stations and publishers spewing all manner of anti-growth negativism. If it were not for our vigilant stewardship and constant pruning, naive and sentimental neo-socialist parties would proliferate like bunnies, clogging up the efficiencies that are so vital to success in today's competitive global marketplace.

"And speaking of stewardship, let's not forget that we are living in an era of unprecedented environmental crisis. The very biodiversity of our planet is threatened as thousands upon thousands of species go extinct, crushed under the boot of abrupt climate flux. Indeed, the imminent extinction of our own species is virtually guaranteed unless our production of foodstuffs is maintained without interruption—and it is obvious that the grain that grows in today's climate will wither in the climate of tomorrow.

"You may be surprised to know that there are over a million and a half distinct species of seed grains that botanists have identified. Amazing, isn't it, how creative nature can be when unfettered from government regulation. It is crucial that none of

312

these genetic marvels be lost—any one of them may prove to be the salvation of mankind in the unpredictable future.

"There are repositories of seed samples in various countries, but all of these collections are incomplete and vulnerable to destruction themselves. So starting in 2006, vacuum-sealed packets of every known seed variety have been methodically collected and stored in the Svalbard Gene Bank, a hardened facility dug hundreds of feet into the frozen mountain near Longyearbyen, safe from every conceivable catastrophe, both natural and man made— immune to nuclear war, asteroid impact, melting ice caps, plague, pestilence, and Martian invasion. This is truly the Doomsday Escape Pod—the last hope for our species when the hammer finally drops on our fragile planet.

"This month, the last known species on Earth was added to the collection. It was an unparalleled human accomplishment, a tribute to Man's capacity for survival. This is why we came to Svalbard. We had to be here."

"To celebrate it?" prompted Baba Rum Das.

"To steal it," said Gorski.

"And all the other seed banks around the world?" asked Baba.

"Alas, all lost in fires last night. An ironic coincidence. Somehow it turns out that the Earth's genetic future now belongs to me."

"Marvelous!" said Baba.

"I knew it would please you, O Great Individualist. So now that I have proven my worthiness to receive your advice, tell me, I beseech thee, that which I long to know—how is it that I can break out of the small time and start making the real money I so richly deserve?"

CHAPTER 48

ZEMLYA

"Don't you know where we are?" asked Buck, pacing back and forth the long way across the bedroom of their suite. "This island is in the middle of the Arctic Ocean—we can't just hitch hike out of here."

"So we hitch a ride on a yacht," said Ali, stretched out on the bed, admiring himself in the ceiling mirror. "We got here on a yacht, didn't we? There have got to be other yachts. I have lots of yachting friends; one of them will give us a lift."

"This is Novaya Zemlya," said Buck. "Nobody comes here on purpose except for Boris Gorski and his band of cutthroats. The place is one big nuclear garbage heap—it makes Chernobyl look like a health spa. The Soviets set off hundreds of atomic bombs up here, dumped thousands of tons of reactor wastes, and abandoned dozens of rotting nuclear subs and warships. Gorski deals bootleg plutonium and other dirty dope out of here to other bad guys all over the world. None of your yachting friends would be caught dead within a thousand miles of this place. And if Gorski hadn't made this whole building out of lead, we'd all be cooked by now."

"So if you're so smart with geography, you come up with a way out," said Ali. "And stop pacing—you're driving me crazy."

"I'm thinking, I'm thinking," said Buck, pacing.

"Or you, Petal," said Ali. "Why don't you come up with a plan? After all, it's your fault we're still here. If you hadn't given Gorski such great financial advice he would have gotten tired of us and sent us back home."

"Sent us to the bottom of the ocean is more like it," answered Petal, painting her toenails over by the vanity. She had chosen Fallen Comrade Pink, but it really didn't matter. Lead walls or not, every bottle in the vanity glowed in the dark. "Don't be such a ninny."

"Anyway, it's clear that if we can't break out of here we've got to talk our way out," declared Buck. "Petal, you start thinking of a way to convince Gorski to let us go. Ali, you start thinking up a way to convince the guards to smuggle us out."

"Gorski's forgotten about us," said Petal. "Or maybe he's off on a trip. It's been ages since he called for us. We'll be here forever if we wait for him."

"That's the dumbest idea I ever heard," said Ali. "The closest we get to a guard is to watch meal trays slide under the door. Who knows, maybe there aren't any guards. It could just be a robot out there."

"Okay then you two come up with an idea," said Buck, pacing.

"Here's one," said Ali. "Quit pacing before you drive me crazy."

"Here's another," said Petal. "Help me with the laundry. We'll never convince Gorski we are from another world in clothes that smell so much like this one."

*   *   *

Meanwhile, in their office three floors above, Ivan and Igor tended to the bank of computer servers that were their primary responsibility when they weren't otherwise assisting with special projects such as commandeering the world's genetic future or harvesting bricks of enriched uranium. Gorski would rather have had a more seasoned pair of criminals run this part of his business, but it was tough to find thugs above a certain age who knew how to send a billion slices of spam a second to every possible e-mail address in the universe, to steal every identity of every man, woman, and child who ever lived, to enslave every chip, to pilfer every account, divert every transfer, crash every credit card, and generally piss everybody off, all day, every day. And this was before they had lured your daughter into prostitution, hooked your son on gambling, sent your wife to collections, blackmailed you with kiddy porn, and given your PC the clap, just for fun.

All of which takes lots of smarts, lots of programming, and lots of equipment to set up, but once you get it running, there is little left to do but make sure you don't spill your Diet Stalin Cola into the hard drive. So, Ivan and Igor, being, by necessity, of that certain age, found plenty of motive and opportunity to partake of all of the pleasures of the Net while they weren't otherwise busy subverting it.

There was little that could escape the continual wheedling, skulking, and prying of their pernicious programs. Secret stuff was magnetic to them, more attractive by far than a flash of flesh above the knee. They could smell a snip of buried code ten million websites away, and wouldn't rest until they had sniffed it out and dug it up—a nugget as delicious as some other dog's bone.

Which was why their heads were totally spooked out by the Chill. Everything that they had seen and heard there had been ferreted out of the Web by mere kids on mere laptops armed with nothing but mere instinct. Ivan and Igor couldn't have missed something this big if it had been on line before. It had to have just come up while they were off stealing seeds. Or had they been scooped by a bunch of amateurs? They became obsessed with tracking every image, every text, and every audio that could possibly be linked to that intoxicating night. And the more obsessed they became with the quest, the more enraptured they became by the quarry.

They pieced more of Lykiloro's music together, bar by bar, hidden within readouts of Argentinean rain gauges and Holland Tunnel thermometers. They teased out haunting clips of Her gliding above the surface, beckoning and then disassembling into the white noise of the cosmos—frame by frame—tireless sifting Monte Carlo roulette monitors, Toyota robot welding cams, and Hubble spectrometer calibrations for precious bytes stashed deep within the chaff.

And all along the way, they found themselves directed, link by link, to Siverth-set web traps designed to re-educate them into a mindset of grassroots planet-saving and recruit them into an international conspiracy to divert the funds of waste and war into a massively-distributed invention machine for sustainable, non-polluting energy.

How the mysterious cult of She and the exponentially expanding energy-development community were related to each other was not at all apparent, but these two phenomena were the most explosive events the Web had ever endured, and many a substandard server had been trampled to death by their traffic. And as incongruous as the right-brained, amorphous, spiritual movement was with the left-brained, self-organizing, techno-financial organization, it was impossible to believe that She was not the prime mover of it all—a deduction not lost on the American military's security centers, frantic to snatch back their missing nukes without the humiliation of losing a bidding war on eBay.

"Wouldn't it be a superior thing if the massive loot we collect through Mr. Gorski's servers found its way to the most excellent and spooky Chill the Anthropocene for repair of the imperiled planet?" verbalized Ivan, knowing Igor had been thinking the same thing.

"For which we would be disemboweled with dull instruments if discovered," answered Igor, also stating the obvious. "But then we might be forever memorialized as the first Post-Communist Martyrs, which, if there really is another world, would certainly guarantee us a more than sufficient quantity of succulent young girlfriends, hopefully in Speedo bathing costumes."

"Irregardless of that," asserted Ivan, "it might be more prudent for us, in the current world, to place the diversion point of Mr. Gorski's fundage flow at a location less readily linked to our particular profit center—say, maybe at some post-laundry sequestration where it all entwines together into one huge, untraceable, electronic (and therefore massless) mass."

"Which would then liberate to the noble cause an even more massive mass of massless money, thus creating the classic win, win, win, lose scenario we studied at the Harvard Business School On Line," said Igor, holding his hand up for a well-deserved high-five. "Which, in turn, would render Mr. Gorski powerless to hunt us down and forcibly extract our spleens without benefit of anesthesia."

"Maybe we should not gamble our entire spleens on that particular assumption," observed Ivan, spreading out an actual pencil-on-brown-paper drawing he had prepared. Igor found the retro media too quaint by half, but appreciated the security concerns that motivated its use.

"You see, I have been planning the contingency of our escape from Novaya Zemlya for some time now. Of course, we could just wait until we are on a mission—let's say selling radioactive crap to sons in laws of heads of states, for example—and beg the Nebraskans for asylum, but I think you will agree that time has suddenly become of the essence and we should beat cheeks out of this pop stand, ASAP."

Igor was not so facile with business school jargon as Ivan, but knew a drawing of a submarine when he saw one.

"We are going to steal one of the submarines?" he asked.

"No one will even notice. They don't care about those subs anymore; the reactors have all been sold off," said Ivan.

"So how are we going to make it go?"

"There's diesel backup for the generators. We can get out of the harbor on battery power. Then once we are under way, we deploy the kites."

"What kites?" asked Igor.

"Ahhh, these kites," said Ivan, unrolling another sheet of paper with schematics of huge kites being launched with the help of smaller kites which had been boosted up by smaller ones yet. "As it turns out, many of the Ukrainian schoolgirls that Mr. Gorski has sponsored on their Tour of the Sex Capitals of the World would rather sew than tour, and these parabolic kites are not so difficult to construct with a few computer-generated templates. I have collected more than enough of them in the hold of the *Fred October* waiting for this very moment."

"Kites pull subs?" asked Igor, initially stumped by the problem of there being no wind under water.

"Sails pull boats," said Ivan, impatiently. "And kites are much better than sails. Sails require masts that add more weight. More weight means you need more sail, which means you need more mast, and then you have to deal with more weight. Sails were a stupid idea from the beginning and it's a wonder they worked at all. But kites add no weight at all when aloft and even reduce the weight of the boat by their upward pull. There's more wind up high, too, compared with near the surface. And there's no limit to the area of cloth that you can put up there. I'm telling you, Igor, this sub will be faster under kite power than it was under nuclear."

"Very spooky," agreed Igor.

"Not only that," said Ivan unrolling another bit of foolscap. "Unless we try to go under an icecap or something, we can cruise below the surface totally undetected. The kites are invisible to radar and will be too high up to be seen by someone on a boat."

"Massively spooky," said Igor, excited.

"And one other thing," said Ivan, leaning in close. "We're taking the seeds with us. Then we can be heroes in this world when we deliver them back into responsible hands. You won't need to wait for the next world for your share of girlfriends in Speedo costumes."

"Ivan, you are truly a genius. You have thought of everything," said Igor. "Food, too, I hope."

"I have stashed enough provisions to last five people six months."

"Five people?" said Igor, now worried. There wasn't a person on Novaya Zemlya that he would turn his back on besides Ivan.

"It will take that many to handle the boat," said Ivan. "But relax. We'll just bring those nun people along. Yes, I know you'll say that they are too stupid to be of any help—only one of them is barely literate, it seems. But sometimes it can be useful to have simple people around who aren't burdened down by agendas of their own. They'll take orders—nuns are pacifists. And besides, we don't want to do all the spiritual heavy lifting, do we Igor?"

Igor nodded in agreement and set to work writing code. It would only take him a couple of hours. He had the easy part—stealing Gorski's money would be a snap. It was Ivan's part that would be hard. The getting away with it.

CHAPTER 49

FRED

Everyone under the covers was cold and cranky when the knock came from the door. Even with the zero humidity of Novaya Zemlya it was taking longer than expected for the habits to dry, and Gorski's prisoner's quarters, while luxuriously appointed compared to more equatorial third world counterparts, were rather stingily heated. Petal was sandwiched between Ali and Buck, but her turn was almost up. Buck was fretting because the labels had said "Dry Clean Only" and any shrinkage could easily have strangulating consequences. Ali was more worried about the wrinkles. And all the while, yards of thick, black wool continued their dripping, dripping. dripping, like dueling metronomes, onto the linoleum floor of the cell.

"Вы очень красивы!" boomed a voice from the hall, followed by fists pounding on the door.

"He says for us to open up," translated Buck, hopping out of bed in his Speedo.

"Tell them to come back when we're receiving callers," said Ali.

"Don't you dare, Buck," said Petal. "That door is the only way out. Do what they say."

"Счастья и здоровья," Buck called, explaining to their visitors that, with all due respect, the ones on the outside of the door were the ones who were supposed to have the key.

There was rustling and murmuring followed by the noise of keys being tried in the lock, one by one. Buck armed himself with a shoe, but then thought better of it and decided to wait empty-handed at attention. Petal and Ali hid under the blankets. Long minutes passed before the door burst open and two uniformed men tumbled into the room. Buck was relieved to see that it wasn't anyone actually scary, just Ivan and Igor trying to be scary.

"Everybody freeze!" commanded Ivan. Both he and Igor could make their way pretty well through websites written in English, but their facility with the spoken language was strictly confined to random bits of oft-repeated Hollywood dialog.

"We're freezing, we're freezing!" called back Ali, hidden in the bedclothes. "So close the door, already! I swear, was everyone up here born in a barn or what?"

The Russians conferred briefly and then heaved a duffel onto the floor.

"Uniform body, please!" ordered Ivan, waving what he thought might pass a pistol but what anyone could see was a staple gun.

Buck cooperated with a perfect, irony-free, "don't shoot" posture—chin in, eyes wide, elbows bent, wrists dorsiflexed. Even the most subtle indulgence in irony, he knew from long experience, could easily be misinterpreted as sarcasm (if not ridicule) by those assigned by fate to the stressful role of captor. It was in the captive's best interest, Buck well appreciated, for one's captors to languish in a state of relaxed self-assurance. Captors with unresolved social hierarchy insecurities and assertiveness guilt, Buck knew first hand, were less likely to appreciate a little light-hearted kidding around and more likely to feel obligated to kick your butt. Furthermore, Buck understood clearly, captors least skilled in the butt kicking arts (we aren't saying any names here) were the most likely to botch the whole butt kicking transaction, resulting in an unnecessarily unpleasant experience for everyone involved.

In the duffel were three Russian Navy uniforms, winter issue, Seaman, First Class. Buck selected the XXL one and then stuffed the other two under the covers for his friends. In spite of the disadvantage of dressing in the dark under blankets, Petal was finished first.

"Pssst! Buck! Pass me the scarf and shades," she whispered, trusting that there would be a day someday when she could freely show her face, but knowing that this day was certainly not that day.

Ivan and Igor, striving for credibility in their roles as captors, grunted impatiently, shifting weight from foot to foot. Their plan had been for all the prisoners to change into their disguises while cowering in the middle of the room like Buck. They had not

322

allowed for the possibility that two of them might do it thrashing around under the covers.

Actually, they had never imagined that anyone might prefer to put their clothes on before they got out of bed—but they were willing to admit that they really didn't know much about how the rest of the world went about getting up in the morning and it wasn't worth embarrassing themselves by being parochial about it.

"The pants button in front," whispered Buck after Petal and Ali had lined up at attention next to him.

"Now you tell me," she said, worried more about how Fallen Comrade Pink was clashing with her insignia.

"At least my ankles aren't showing," hissed Ali.

Ivan paced back and forth in front of them as he had seen Patton do in the movie. He slapped his staple gun into his palm a few times and murmured a few words to Igor.

"Good," he pronounced, pulling Ali's cap down over his forehead from its previously more jaunty angle. "We go."

Ivan took the lead, pausing at the door to look both ways. Buck adopted a completely un-exaggerated "walk softly" gait behind him, with Petal attached to his coattails. Igor herded Ali along with waves of his weapon (a VCR remote, or maybe it was a BetaMax) and covered everyone's six.

They made their way silently down the hall and paused at the entrance to a formal foyer. On Ivan's signal, they rushed across its open area to a stairway down to the basement. Again, no guards. Then down another flight to a darkened vestibule with coarse-hewn tunnels running off in three directions. Ivan knew just where he was going, but, for the sake of the others, lit up a flashlight. His walk broke into a jog for what seemed like a mile.

"How are the boots?" asked Buck, by way of conversation. He thought 'Are you OK?' might sound a little too condescending.

"Very comfy," said Petal, not even breathing hard. "I miss my mukluks, though."

"What's with this guy?" puffed Ali. "We didn't even stretch. I tell you, somebody's going to pull a groin muscle."

Ivan skidded to a stop, holding his hand up as a signal for quiet. He listened for a minute, and then waved everybody on. They were in the open now, the gibbous moon illuminating a wide expanse of wooden decking. The ocean smelled close, but could only be seen as a tarry blackness smeared into a matching sky.

And then there it was, looming in front of them, its massive, evil bulk a rude disruption of the Earth's magnetic flux, an ugly warping of the local gravitational field, an unsightly stain on backdrop of the night. The *Fred October*.

The *Fred* rode higher at dock than its designers had intended, having been cannibalized of not only its atomic fuel, but of its entire reactor and all its munitions. Ivan urged them up a steep, makeshift gangplank that, despite its recent construction, seemed in danger of collapsing under their weight. Only when safe on the bridge was Buck able to take stock of what was apparently going to be their new home.

Decades of debris littered the deck—rusting machine parts the size of Volkswagens, rotting crates with unreadable markings, and leaking drums of unspeakable poisons. Up near the bow, though, under the beam of a loading crane, was a gleaming, new structure the size of a mobile home with welding equipment scattered around it. The longer Buck looked at it, the more convinced he became that it was, in fact, a mobile home—not a custom double-wide, but not a Katrina special, either. Whatever it was, it was an after market modification that would certainly void whatever meager warranty was left on the aging *Fred*.

Ivan pulled walkie-talkies out of his backpack and clipped one to each of their belts. He led the way down to the deck and positioned Ali and Petal on either side of the bow.

"You watch left and you watch right," he whispered, pointing off into the velvet blackness. "See something, then push button. Make quiet or get shot. Understand?"

Petal and Ali nodded vigorously and took their positions staring into nothingness. Ivan walked Buck over to the mobile home somewhat aft of the others.

"We call you, then you go up ladder and turn big wheel on top. Then you come down and pull lever. Remember, wheel first then lever second or you blow up. Understand?" Ivan had clearly put considerable work into practicing this speech and Buck wanted to give him a little positive feedback on grammar and pronunciation, but he decided just to nod instead.

Ivan ran back up to the conning tower and disappeared into the sub. Buck waved to Petal and Ali who were stomping their feet in the cold. He figured that there would be plenty of warning before anything happened and wasn't prepared when gangway started crumbling into the water. The *Fred* was moving—silently accelerating so smoothly that it could scarcely be perceived.

Petal and Ali figured it out, though, and scanned the darkness ahead intently. The moon peeked out of the clouds briefly, making it possible for Ali to see the dim outline of another massive form at least as big as the *Fred* nearly dead ahead.

"Allah, be merciful to batteries!" Ali pleaded, pushing furiously on his button. "Mayday! Mayday! Big thing in front! Major liability! Mayday!"

His message was acknowledged by a hard rudder starboard, sending the *Fred* gliding noiselessly past what had to be one of her mothballed sister ships.

"Ah? Pardon me?" said Petal into her walkie. "Unless you mean to run through this serious piece of something with lights all over it, I suggest you turn back a teeny bit the other way or maybe just stop and check the map or ask someone? Hello? Ivan? I'm not kidding about this. Do you hear me, Ivan?"

The *Fred* eased a notch to port, but not soon enough to avoid a nasty scratch along its side as it plowed by the last pier in the harbor. The moon shook off its clouds and lit up the empty ocean ahead. The sea was like glass, the wind at dead calm. It would have been a beautiful night but for the certainty of cold feet and the uncertainty of survival.

Buck's walkie buzzed once, sending him up the ladder of the mobile home. There was indeed a wheel up there, which when turned, rolled up the canvas that was covering the top and front of the structure. Too bad it was too dark to see inside.

Back on the deck he found the lever and pulled it back, setting off loud hissing noises like locomotives letting off steam. He didn't know what to expect, but figured that it wouldn't hurt to step back a ways, so he wandered over to Petal's station. She was dutifully standing watch over the featureless ocean, ready for the unexpected appearance of whales, subs, or emerging continents.

"Take a look at that," said Buck, tapping her on the shoulder.

She turned toward the metal box just behind her on the deck. From it was growing a huge towering blob, the shape of an inverted teardrop, now fifty feet tall.

"Looks like a weather balloon," she said.

"Only bigger," said Buck. "This is the kind you could circle the globe in."

As they watched, the hissing abruptly stopped and the balloon rose out of its container, trailing a huge expanse of cloth. In the dark they could just make out the four lines that ran back to the trailer from the contraption.

"More sky writing?" asked Petal.

"If I didn't know better, I'd say that was the biggest kite you've ever seen."

"But there's no wind," she said.

"There is up there," Buck said. "The balloon is dragging the kite up to where it's blowing fifty knots—maybe a hundred. Looks to me like we might be on the maiden voyage of the world's first recycled, long-distance, post-nuclear, submersible, carbon-emission-free, kite-powered U-boat. Very cool. Let's go congratulate Ivan and Igor."

"Don't rush the relationship," she said. "I think they're kind of new to the prisoner-taking scene."

"Debutantes," agreed Ali. "Be gentle, I think it's their first time."

"Okay, then, how about we beg forgiveness for coming in out of the cold?"

"That's better," she said. "But don't overdo it. Russians are very sensitive about irony, you know."

"And rightly so," agreed Buck, leading his friends back to the conning tower. "Ironic, isn't it?"

CHAPTER 50

IMPACT

"Eat or die, prisoners!" commanded Ivan, raising his glass.

"Sir, yes sir!" barked the prisoners in unison, raising theirs in formation.

Ali and Petal had outdone themselves on this meal. All it had taken was Igor's laptop and its Russian to English translation program. Before that, the menus had been more or less randomly generated by Buck's one hundred percent perfect score at misreading the labels on cans. It turned out that Buck's proficiency in the Russian language was entirely confined to phonetic recapitulations of unsolicited bar room confrontations that he had accumulated over the years. The Cyrillic alphabet was Greek to him. Greek in a mirror.

And it didn't help that all the food on the sub was Russian Navy issue from the Soyuz Sunrise era. Fortunately, each can bore a collectable work of Socialist Realism Art (none of that more-military-than-thou, stencil-on-olive-drab, American K-ration boorishness) depicting the next patriotic theme on some conscripted artist's non-negotiable list. Unfortunately, (as Buck learned quite late) the assumption that there was a relationship between the image on the label and the contents of the can proved to be entirely fallacious.

For example, a container bearing an inspirational scene of two sunburned young women in head scarves—their sleeves rolled over bulging biceps, one wholesome but nubile creature on a stepladder picking an apple, the other, fecund with fruit, hugging an overflowing basket, both obviously nearing simultaneous orgasm with the Fatherland's Five Year Plan—would be filled with tuna. Another can, sporting an iconic image of Vladimir Lenin in chin-jutting profile—his knee deeply bent climbing a steep dune of decapitated aristocracy, his arm raised defiantly before him thrusting forth a cup of tea—would be filled with lard.

Meal preparation (the responsibility of prisoners, according to the Geneva Convention) was therefore, at first, significantly more creative than anyone had intended. Rutabagas in Chocolate Pudding. Shad Roe avec Tajik Tang. Donuts Fried in Borsht. Ox Tail with Dentifrice Glacé.

Ivan and Igor assumed that these were delicacies that they should be getting used to, now that they had burned every bridge that could carry them back to their mama's home cooking. But some Western tastes are more easily acquired than others (Dolly Parton versus Matzo Balls in Laundry Soap, for example) and eventually Igor took Buck aside with the intent of negotiating a temporary suspension of the Geneva Convention until the prisoners could learn a few Russian recipes—such as these on this lap top, for instance.

Buck soon realized that all it took was ALT+E on Igor's MacSki to get as good an English translation as you might expect after midnight on Christmas Eve when your kid's ten speed is still in the box, your brain is mired in eggnog, and the instructions direct you to "Caution: Inversion sprocket A or C w/wo bearings ring please immediately, if Auto Rised!"

Immediately everything made sense. Sort of. The kitchen contingent still had to translate the Russian-to-English translation into English. "Coagulated Flightless Aviary Ovum," while not particularly appetizing, was pretty clear. "Tincture of Olfactory Embryonic Stamen" remained unidentifiable, even after opening. But at least the cooks could be confident they were navigating through the right phyla, if not genus and species. Meals became edible. Dinners became tolerable. And some, as tonight's, even enjoyable.

"To freedom!" toasted Ivan, standing at the head of the table, surveying his domain with satisfaction. The captain's mess of the *Fred October* had probably been quite impressive in its day, and probably would still hold a certain retro kitsch for those who thought rust was cute. But even the most jaded QEIII veteran would have to admit that the accommodations were beyond spacious, the ride was silky smooth, and the utter silence delicious.

"To prisonerhood!" toasted Petal, who had grown to appreciate the pragmatic simplicity of the *Fred*'s unique feudal hierarchy. They were prisoners. What's the matter with that? They were well treated. Their rightful access to mail, counsel, and the

Red Cross were not (in theory) being abridged, not to mention those of *habeas corpus* and *qui mihi fatigo*. Exhausting interrogation sessions had been forgone completely. Their labor was fairly compensated, paid in the barter currency of Russian Adolescent Language lessons and equal turns at driving the *Fred*.

Nobody was better at driving the *Fred* than Igor, but, then again, there was hardly anyone on the globe better than Igor at *Massive Frag and Mutilation, Intergalactic Mutant Command*, or *Mary's Sweet Little Pony* (played under a different pseudonym) either. Even though it was Ivan who had modified the Nintendo Wiu to control the kite (altitude, pitch, yaw, angle of attack) and the *Fred* (depth, rudder, auxiliary power, brake, radar) through a collection of motion sensors sewn into a special pilot's jumpsuit, it was Igor who was the acknowledged master of its execution

In fair weather with calm seas, the designated pilot would literally be snoozing in an armchair while the rest of the crew sat chatting on the deck, pretending to catch some rays (sunrise still being months away.) On stormy days, however, the crew would defer to Igor who would amaze them with gymnastic routines worthy of the Russian Olympic Weasels Down Your Pants Team—and all without the benefit of any performance enhancing drug save for the occasional Yuri Gagarin No-Nap Cap they had found stashed in the Captain's sock drawer. He was an inspiration to them all, that Igor.

"To ultimate rehabilitation and parole!" toasted Ali, who was willing to go along with just about anything he couldn't come up with an alternative for—but only to a point. It was important, he felt compelled to reiterate, to stay focused on the mission's goals rather than on its methods. One must not lose sight of our objectives, he would remind them, by an over-preoccupation with process. Satisfied that he had made his point, he drained his glass and sat down, hoping that this time someone would actually explain to him just what the hell they were doing on this submarine.

"To the East!" toasted Buck, looking around expectantly.

Petal's fork stalled in front of her mouth. What was he driving at? The emergence of Asian market supremacy? The withering of Occidental hegemony? The triumph of the yin over the yang? The direction the boat was pointing?

Clearly they were going east. They had gingerly traversed the strait between Bolshevik Island and October Revolution Island into the Laptev Sea without running into a single hard part of Severnaya Zemlya. They had chosen to skirt the Anzhu Islands to the north to avoid the notorious Lyakhovsky Island pirates that Igor had heard about (or maybe read about in a comic.) They were well on their way to Wrangel Island and the Chukchi Sea. Alaska would then be just around the corner. Civilization. The Rule of Law. Retail. Satellite Internet Uplink. Decisions would have to be made.

To that end, it occurred to Petal, it would be nice to know what was going on in the world right about now. At one time, she had been one of those people who had CNN (sound off, captions on) constantly streaming in every room—vacations in Tahiti not excepted. But somewhere along the way—perhaps on the ice between Nuuk and Ittoqqortoormiit—she had become one of those people who couldn't stand those other people. She could no longer imagine voluntarily relinquishing control of her consciousness back to Popular Culture Corporate Command. She counted herself one of the lucky few who ever pull themselves out of the Public Prioritizing Processor onto hidden and protected oases of individual rationality.

Why would she ever again agree to spend more of her attention on celebrations of Brad and Angelina's exhibitionist excesses than on acts of compassion or on appreciation of the spiritual elegance of physical reality? Why, indeed? But could it be that once back in the real world she might not be given the option to agree or not, that the Mega-Pow-R-Flushing Action of the media torrent would sweep up her mind along with everyone else's and whoosh it down the dark sewer of consumer-cash effluent, narcotized by mass-produced, brain-numbing trivia and shunted sanitarily away from ideas that might slow the efficient grinding of the status quo?

She looked at Buck from the corner of her eye. She found herself appreciating him more all the time. What had first appeared to be a minor but annoying character flaw—that goofy obliviousness of those-who-just-don't-get-it—she now understood to be a rare and admirable attribute—a complete immunity to bullshit.

330

He had grown up in the same Pre-Packaged Peer-Pressure-Cooked Culture as she had and yet had never been captured by it. While she had been squandering her spleen on society gossip, caught up in the self-referential self-indulgences of the self-important, Buck had been giving his all where he was needed most, doing what one man could do for another man when it really mattered. He had been able to keep his priorities straight, in spite of the relentless indoctrination of a synthetic society bent on marginalizing anyone who would not be plasticized. And she—she had become a Captain in the Collaborationist Propaganda Machine.

Could he see that she was different now? Could he forgive her past complicity in the Evangelism of Systematic Selfishness that had brought the Earth so close to the brink of self-destruction? Could he appreciate her emerging humanity? Could he ever trust her? Could he ever love her?

She took off her sunglasses and pulled down her scarf. She wanted nothing between them now. She was proud of who she was. She would never hide again.

Despite the laws of physics, Buck could feel her gaze. Its intensity froze him in mid-toast, glass raised. All other eyes were on him, too, expecting him to continue with a casual bit of conventional optimism appropriate to the occasion.

He turned slightly, before he knew it—an instinctive reflex to a cherished voice calling from the distance. And when he saw her face looking at him now in that way that was so surprising yet so familiar, more intimate in that public place than at any time they had been alone, with that questioning look that erased all doubts, he forgot completely what he had started to say, what he had been thinking about, and even where he was. He was speechless, yet welling up inside him were all the words that he couldn't have spoken before, all the feelings that his unrooted life had denied to him, all of the dreams that he had not allowed himself to dream.

He lowered his glass and faced her, pushing back his chair. She was standing now, too, her cap off, her hair, longer now, tumbling around her face. She was reaching out to him as they stepped together into the open, to a place where they could finally embrace unencumbered by malicious concepts that had restrained them more completely than had their cuffs of steel, now peeking conspicuously from their sleeves.

Ivan dropped his fork. Igor dropped his jaw. They were transfixed by the sight of Petal's face, hidden from them up until now. This was the face that had been projected on every surface at the Chill. This was the face that now filled the internet. This was the face that had changed their lives. This was the face that was changing the world.

She had been there with them all along! What could that possibly mean? Had they—Ivan and Igor—somehow been chosen—guided by some higher power to this unlikely point in the drama of Mankind? What was intended for them? What parable was being acted out here on the *Fred* tonight that would be retold in liturgy for millennia to come? The Prisoners Embrace Their Captors? The Prisoners Slay Their Captors? What was really happening here? They both jumped to their feet, their faces as white as ghosts. Ali jumped up, too startled by their panic.

And standing like that, all together, was probably a fortunate thing, as everything in the Captain's Mess not bolted to the bulkhead suddenly became a projectile, launched by its inertial mass towards the bow, in the instant that the *Fred October* plowed full speed into something very massive and very solid right in the middle of the East Siberian Sea.

CHAPTER 51

POW

The failing lights of the *Fred* flickered in synchrony with the wail of her sirens, the percussion of exploding rivets, and the hiss of escaping steam. Jets of freezing brine spurted from the bulkheads, spraying the crew still sprawled in a pile on the deck. A meniscus of seawater crept up the gangway into the mess, faster than the entangled sailors could wiggle away from it.

"To the bridge!" shouted Buck, hauling Petal and then Ali to their feet. Igor and Ivan were doing pretty well getting upright on their own, despite the recently-airborne Tofu in Aspic that was over-lubricating their efforts.

This was one of those ideas that sounds good but feels bad, since it meant running into the rising water instead of away from it—entering your internal alarm systems into a shrieking competition with the *Fred*'s. Survival instinct can be as stubborn as a three year old when treated like that, and Buck felt the expected pull of resistance from Petal's hand in his when he took the lead toward the rapidly sinking bow.

"Quick, the ladder is just ahead! We can make it! Hold tight to one another!" Buck did not look back at her face. There was no time for indecision. Fear in her eyes might easily melt his resolve.

They were chest deep in water now, struggling against the surge. They could feel the bow tilting downward, but this did nothing to speed their progress forward, but only reduced their traction on the deck.

"Is everybody with us?" cried Buck, unable to pause his pulling to count heads.

"Yes! Yes! Da! Da!" they called back.

The lights flared bright and then went dark for good. Petal gasped. Ali prayed. Igor whimpered. Ivan pushed harder from the back of the chain. Buck made one more super-human lunge and grasped the ladder with one frozen fist. Pulling with all of his strength, he was barely able to get Petal positioned on the ladder before the water reached their heads. She scrambled up as fast as she could, weighed down by the wet uniform and the numbing cold.

"Buck! The hatch! It's locked or something! Which way does this thing turn? Clockwise looking up or clockwise looking down?" She was leaning hard into the wheel above her but nothing budged. Buck had shoved Ali up the ladder behind her, so now he couldn't reach the hatch to help—and Ali, well, he was Ali.

"Clockwise is clockwise looking up, down, or sideways, Petal!" Ali shouted over the screams of Igor and Ivan below, who in their panic of impending asphyxiation had forgotten what little New York Society Column English she had taught them and had regressed to Russian baby talk, reciting the kind of prayers that atheists devise in foxholes.

"So quit being such a woman and just open the damn hatch!" Ali hollered, crowding up the narrow shaft. There were only a few inches of air space left for those below them.

"Oh, so now one's sexual orientation is completely voluntary, is it?" she said turning away from her task to give him the look he deserved. "And just how would you suggest I go about resigning from my womanhood? You think I should join some twelve-step program that meets at the Y every night or maybe one of your posh rehabs full of court-ordered celebrities. Can I wean my self down or just go cold turkey? There must be a gum I can chew when the craving to be a woman again gets too much to handle. Bitch-o-rette, is that what they call it, Ali? Maybe you could use a big fat stick of that right about now. I tell you, of all the sexist—"

Igor and Ivan and Buck had their heads wedged as far up the ladder shaft as their shoulders and Ali's butt would allow, and the water had already risen above their ears. Every one of them was screaming his version of "Counter-clockwise!" as loud as he could, which rendered their messages completely unintelligible, even if they had been right. It was looking like their collective goose had been cooked (or drowned, or frozen, whatever) when a deafening sound of metal on metal boomed from all around them and the *Fred* lurched skyward, water draining away from them as if they were pasta in a colander.

They clung to the ladder, shivering but not risking a word. Sometimes, in dramatic moments like this, all it takes is one flippant remark to cue the frayed elevator cable to snap the rest of the way or the monster to vault back up, not really dead.

"Whew, that was close!" whispered Ali, finally.

"Shhh!" spewed the rest of them in unison, as the hatch burst open and a flashlight blinded them from above.

"Put your hands up or be shot!" came the command, finally in English after what sounded like English, only backward.

"With all due respect," began Ali. "One can hardly put one's hands up when one is clinging to a ladder for dear life. Let's be reasonable about—"

"We surrender! We surrender!" shouted everyone else, in all available dialects. Buck gave Ali a shove to demonstrate that it wasn't all that hard to raise at least one of your hands and still hold on, temporarily at least.

"Come out immediately!" ordered the heavily-accented voice from above. "No sudden moves! Hands up! No funny business!"

The five of them clambered up through the hatch and stood surrounded by a contingent of armed and uniformed men. Their obvious leader, the short one with the rococo outfit—death's head insignia, jodhpurs, jackboots, and riding crop—stood at attention before them. He queried in a few unidentifiable languages, shaking his head in dismay at everyone's blank stare.

"So it has to be English, then?" he said. "You Russians are so parochial. We North Koreans are all expected to speak Russian, of course, but do any of you bother to learn Korean? No, not one. Year after year in our country, every schoolchild in every village wasting hour after hour of their precious lives drilling in your degenerate language, but could you even come up with a single ambassador who understands ours? Never! Do you wonder why our Glorious Leader and Eternal Father, Premier Kim Chi Kim, has now commanded us to forget every word of the Russian language, under penalty of death?"

Ali almost never answered questions from nosy strangers, except for rhetorical ones posed for pompous effect. These, he almost never passed up.

"Funny you should mention that, because we were just trying to forget a few things ourselves," he said. "Did he tell you how to go about it? I mean, there must be a trick—it seems the harder I work on forgetting something, the harder it gets to forget."

"Have you tried the penalty of death part?" replied their captor, helpfully.

"No, do you think it would help?"

"Can't hurt. And here's something not to forget. As Commander in Chief of the *SS Waba Ti Li*, I, Captain Kim Kal Bi hereby declare you prisoners of war of the Republican People's Democracy of Korea. You have the right to be tortured, humiliated, and confined without charges for now and forevermore, so help you God. Any questions?"

"Prisoners of war? Doesn't there have to be a war first?" asked Buck, ignoring numerous precedents from past administrations that everyone was trying to forget. "North Korea isn't at war with Russia, is it?"

"It is now," answered Captain Kim. "Given your country's wanton and unprovoked attack against a helpless Korean fishing vessel innocently minding her own business out here in international waters."

Buck looked up to see that the *Fred* was now being hoisted out of the water by one of the biggest destroyers he had ever seen. There appeared to be a nasty scratch on the warship's paint where the *Fred* had crumpled her nose.

"But, Captain Kim," implored Buck. "We can explain. It was just an accident. An honest mistake. A fender bender. Happens all the time. I'll call State Farm first thing in the morning. They give me bulk rate on fender benders."

"That's what they said in the Gulf of Tonkin," replied Kim. "Remember?"

"Don't remind me. I had almost forgotten."

"Well, don't. And don't forget who it was who started this whole Stalinist thing in the first place, and who it was who would get all huffy anytime anybody didn't want to play along, and now that everybody has mortgaged their Stalin-R-Us franchises up the wazoo, who it is who is acting like they are too good for the suckers out in the boondocks left holding the bag," warned Kim.

"Times change," pleaded Buck. "God knows, we all miss Stalin, but after a while people just get tired of purges and secret police. It's like hemlines, right, Petal?"

"Absolutely," she assured him. "Up and down. But don't get discouraged, pretty soon Stalinism will be back and North Korea will be the world's fashion leader. No need to go to war about it. It's inevitable. Like death and taxes."

"We don't have taxes in North Korea. Taxes stifle the entrepreneurial spirit."

"Okay, death and spam then."

"No spam either," he said. "Penalty of death. Don't knock it. It works."

"You're really set on this war thing, aren't you?" asked Petal, realizing that argument was futile.

"It's what we do," said Kim, sweeping his arm to encompass the whole of his warship. The *Fred*'s conning tower was now at the level of its deck and a gangplank was being extended to them. "Besides, you don't really think that any of this is up to us, do you?"

"And just whom might it be up to?" asked Petal.

"The Glorious Father and Eternal Leader of the Republican People's Democracy of Korea, Premier Kim Chi Kim, of course."

"Well, maybe we can talk some sense into him," said Petal, pushing her way onto the gangplank. "After a hot shower, of course."

"That would not be very likely," said the captain, following close behind her. "No one has spoken in that manner to the Premier for quite some time now."

"And why not?" asked Petal, getting tired of protocol.

"He's been dead for nearly forty years."

CHAPTER 52

PEACE

Everyone in Pyongyang said it was unseasonably warm for this time in the season. They would always say this whenever the weather was just miserably cold instead of bitterly cold. They had been saying this in Pyongyang for thousands of years, and would likely continue to say this for thousands of years to come, whenever the weather was good enough just to be miserable. They would say this passing one another on the street or waiting in shops or standing in lines—quietly, of course, now that any reference to global warming was forbidden, under penalty of death.

The Republican People's Democracy of Korea had never been a major contributor to climate change—even the Eternally Glorious Leader of the Fatherland, Premier Kim Chi Kim, would have admitted that. However, as a major international power, it had every right to be, and—once the international capitalist anti-Korean conspiracy had finally been overcome—would proudly demonstrate its capacity to be.

Any reference, therefore, to allegations that global warming may or may not be happening, or could or could not be related to activities that the RPDK might or might not be doing or be capable of doing now or in the future were obviously unpatriotic and derogatory in nature (*vis à vis* the RPDK and its leadership) and thus demoralizing to the national will and thus rightfully punishable by death. That's why when everyone said it, as they always did, they would say it quietly.

"What gives?" complained Ali. "We sail south for days and all it gets is colder. I'll bet this place is colder than Greenland. I'll bet it's even colder than Svalbard, if thermometers go that low."

As expected, one of the guards poked him with a rifle to discourage unauthorized conversation. Over the days of their confinement they had determined that a poke in the ribs was a small price to pay for a break in the tedium. But tedium would have been a welcome emotion compared to what they were feeling now on this forced march through the snow, trudging from where their so-called personnel carrier had gotten stuck to their destination up ahead—the Republican People's Democratic Interrogation Center and Death Camp Complex.

"It's the humidity," said Buck, trying hard to stay in step with his shorter comrades so their leg irons wouldn't jerk.

"It's the pajamas," countered Petal, trying not to complain. She knew that almost everybody in this country who wasn't in the military had it worse than she did. Good thing almost everybody in this country actually was in the military.

"Do you think that now we'll finally get some proper prison clothes?" asked Ali. Even though he could happily spend days at home in his pajamas, he was one of those people whose nightmares invariably feature arriving at some state function in his Nick and Nora's. He particularly hated this red pair with the drop seat. In the world of pajama humiliation fantasies, drop seats soundly trumped tabby feet, not even counting the teddy bears in fire engines.

"Just so they don't blindfold us again," said Buck. "I hate that."

The ride from the docks to the Interrogation Center would have been nauseating enough without the blindfolds—bouncing in the back of a truck with splintered seats and shredded shocks—but hours of lurching in the dark had left them all totally carsick. Buck hated to be carsick even more than he hated to be blindfolded. His nightmares, of course, invariably featured both.

But, on the other hand, nausea does get one's mind off of food—a topic that had recently attained top-of-mind status within the group. Apparently, Korean naval destroyers were expected to catch their own dinners, and Captain Kim's crew had been conscripted from cohorts who had never once caught a fish. Despite the assertion that necessity will (by necessity) invariably give birth to invention, in this case the magical motivator of hunger (contrary to aristocratic myth) could not conjure up the ability to wring food from a fished-out sea.

Calories had been so chronically scarce on the SS *Waba Ti Li* that her crew even found the *Fred*'s ancient rations appealing—too good to share with POWs, who were compelled to order from the spa menu. Ivan and Igor had seemed happy enough with the brig's

Gruel à la Grease, but then, after Buck's cooking, they considered anything an improvement. Buck and Petal had choked it down, just to keep their strength up. Ali had gone on a hunger strike until he realized that gruel was as good as it got on a Korean Navy budget cruise.

The Interrogation Complex just ahead appeared to be one huge concrete cube, squatting at stool in a putrid puddle of frozen mud. While its architect had obviously exercised great utilitarian restraint in its design, he had indulged himself here and there with a few creative flourishes that exploited the natural beauty of protruding rebar, rust stains, and structural cracks.

Guards in earmuffed caps shooed the chain gang through a narrow door for people cut into a massive one for tanks. Inside was a courtyard the size of Wrigley Field suitable for various military high jinks on a massive scale. On the far end, a marching band was goose-stepping to some Korean brand of Sousa. Closer by, along the left wall, a firing squad was reloading between customers. Over to the right, new recruits in civilian clothes were being berated for taking so long to be old enough for the draft. And all the while, stinging shards of blowing snow pelted the prisoners, piercing their flimsy pajamas like salted buckshot.

The POWs had little time to enjoy the scene. New escorts relieved the old and double timed them to what looked like an entrance to a storm cellar, with sloped double doors opening onto a dark staircase, steeply down. Dim bulbs in cages barely illuminated wet concrete steps—treacherous enough for people not wearing leg irons. Igor whimpered. Ivan whispered something that sounded reassuring but seemed to make things worse. Everyone else gritted their teeth.

The smell of must and coal and rot got thicker as they descended flight after flight. Then the moaning started, far off in the dark below. First just one voice, then two, but as they got closer it became a chorus of moaning, a moaning of people who had been moaning for such a long time they didn't have much moaning left in them. It was a moaning that was as pitiful as it was horrifying.

The hall at the bottom of the stairs was a little brighter—too bad because you really didn't want to see into the cells that lined either side. Bearded men in rags hung from shackles, pleading with the entourage as it shuffled by. Startled rats darted into the shadows. Well-worn instruments of torture lay scattered about, waiting for the next shift of interrogators to clock in. By this time, Ivan was whimpering, too.

The guard at the front paused for no apparent reason other than to relish the ambiance and to make creepy faces at his charges. He slapped his billy-club into his palm a few times and barked an order at Ali, who shrugged and cringed, waiting to be clobbered. He leered at Petal and poked Buck in the ribs, acting more belligerent all the time. Things looked like they were about to get nasty when the door at the far end of the hall suddenly opened, flooding the dungeon with light.

The guard snapped to attention and shot one final glare at the prisoners before he waved them forward, swinging his truncheon impatiently. Ali, point man of the chain gang, pulled them all ahead at a triple time shuffle. Any place was better than this place. It had to be.

The lighted area beyond the door turned out to be an elevator, an industrial one big enough for a truck. It was a relief to be closer to the twentieth century than the thirteenth, but a little disconcerting to see that none of the guards dared to get in with them. The door slammed shut and the cab lurched up (better than down, five to zero) with a deafening sound of grinding gears and scraping metal (worse than total silence, four to one) and the smell of smoking Bakelite (better than leaking gasoline, three to two). The light flickered off (God damn it!) and then back on (thank you, God!) in a random pattern that maximized panic. When the cab finally froze in place with a dying clunk, everyone inside was relieved, even though they were apparently stuck in an elevator about as far from Otis as you could get and still be within the Earth's atmosphere.

The prisoners were just about ready to start singing Kum Ba Ya and confessing long-repressed embarrassments when the door jerked open onto an elegant 21st century executive conference room, done to the nines in cherry and Steuben. Tasteful blinds encouraged glimpses of the sky through towering windows on three sides while obscuring the odious landscape below. Faint whiffs of sandalwood and distant chords of a chamber orchestra wafted their way on an artificial breeze. The deeply polished table was set for six, with water glasses and three-ring binders placed before high-backed, leather chairs. This could be the boardroom of some extravagant financial conglomerate in modern day Dubai—or even New York City in the good old days, before they had pissed it all away.

And standing before them, smiling a face full of teeth, his arms open wide in welcome, was a short, round guy in Elton John glasses, an Armani Mao jacket, and an Eraserhead haircut. He skittered on his Beatle boots barely able to contain his excitement, almost falling on the polished marble floor.

"Yes, please come in, this is the place. I hope you didn't have any trouble with the address. I can't tell you how many ambassadors end up at the Republican People's Democratic Indoctrination Center instead. The ideograms are almost identical except for that little doohickey where the guy's *ule* is. And not that they don't enjoy a little indoctrination before getting down to the tough work of international diplomacy—heaven knows we could all use some, now and then. But with busy schedules nowadays, who can find the time?

"But listen to me, going on about nothing. Please come in and have a seat. I hope you don't mind that I took the liberty of deciding on the shape of the table. I know how important these details can be in delicate negotiations, and we certainly can have the whole room redone if you insist, but I just hate delays, and being a decisive man of action I just couldn't help myself. I'm sure you are all the same way or you wouldn't have risen to the top of the Soviet diplomatic corps and be here at this dramatic time in history negotiating the fates of two great warrior nations."

The trio indulged themselves in a millisecond of gaping. Sensing that a particularly pivotal moment had just winked into existence, Ali stepped forward to grasp it before it slipped away. This was easy for him. He was now in his natural element. He needed no rehearsal for this role of a lifetime.

"That's Russian now," corrected Ali, pouring himself a glass of water and holding it up to the window. Drifting particles of rust and silt twinkled in the sunlight.

"Pardon?" asked their host.

"No more Soviet Union," Ali said. "Russia is the brand now. Going forward, the C-levels calculated that it would wrongside the demographic if we failed to drill down to our core constituency, so we outsourced our saprophytic subsidiaries and looped back to a holistic, cradle to grave approach with a leaner, hungrier, hyper-tasking organization. Without the fat, you can score all the low hanging fruit without cooking the books, if you know what I mean. By the way, you got anything to eat around here?"

"Afraid not. You'll want to save your appetite for the state dinner anyway. The traditional thousand courses with a toast between each one. You'll never make it if you start with a full stomach, take it from me."

"And when does that start?" asked Ali.

"As soon as we sign the armistice. Don't worry, we can white out 'Soviet' and put in 'Russian' if you want. After all, I owe you one for conceding the shape of the table."

"Great," said Ali, ignoring the distressed expressions on his friends' faces. "Why don't we deep six the mumbo jumbo, cut to the bottom line, and John Hancock this thing? Where do we sign?"

"Heavens no!" said their host, looking horrified at the prospect. "We have hours and hours of tough negotiations ahead of us. Let's just roll up our sleeves and get down to some hard-nosed arm wrestling. But first, I must warn you that you will find me a formidable adversary—I have been preparing for this moment my entire life."

"A short time out while I confer with my delegation, please," said Ali holding up his hand and huddling his team over by the window.

"Will somebody please tell me what the hell is going on here," whispered Petal, grabbing Ali by the ear.

"He thinks we are Russian ambassadors," said Buck.

"In pajamas?" asked Petal.

"Look at how he's dressed," said Ali. "Diplomats always dress funny. Ever been to the UN? Scots in kilts. French in berets. Americans in cowboy boots. All acting like they've got the one true God-given culture, no matter how bizarre and arbitrary. Just act proud of your pajamas. He'll never know the difference."

"And we're at war? I mean Russia and North Korea?" asked Petal.

"That's what Captain Kim said," replied Buck. "And we started it."

"So let's finish it so we can eat," said Ali. "With a thousand courses, there's got to be at least one that's decent."

"But this is ridiculous," said Petal, knowing that she really shouldn't protest good fortune too much. "We're prisoners of war, not Ambassadors from the Kremlin!"

"Which is not as big a distinction as you might think," said Ali. "And I wouldn't push it, if I were you. The more important question is who is surrendering to whom."

"Well, if we can pretend to be Ambassadors in pajamas, I suppose we can pretend to know who won the war," proposed Buck, feeling his way through the unfamiliar landscape of bullshit. Everyone looked at him in disbelief, even Ivan and Igor, who didn't understand a thing other than that they were not yet chained up in the dungeon. On the other hand, no one had a better strategy. It would have to be a bluff. The delegation reconvened at the table.

"Thank you for your patience," said Ali. "We may now begin the formal negotiations. Your credentials, please, sir."

Blood appeared to drain out of Buck's face and into Petal's. They knew they should trust Ali with this. He was the head of state, after all. What did they know about what went on behind closed doors when crowds of reporters were bivouacked outside, poised to tell a breathless world what fate had been chosen for it by those powerful men in funny outfits just beyond the keyhole? Certainly Ali had been party to dozens of such war-ending and war-making confabs. But couldn't he have thought of a better opening gambit?

"Well, of course, strictly speaking, protocol does stipulate an exchange of credentials at this point, but since every sentient person on the planet must certainly recognize the face of Premier Kim Man Doo, Dutiful Son and Heir for Life of The Eternal Father of the Glorious Fatherland, Kim Chi Kim, His Will Be Done (Ret.), we may, in the interest of time, just stipulate our *bone fides* and move on to the business at hand, if you don't mind."

"We are willing to so stipulate," conceded Ali, making a mark in his notebook, just to keep track of concessions.

"Good then!" said Man Doo, rubbing his hands together. "Now, let's take these points in turn," he said, starting from the top of page one. "Border Issues."

"Do we share a border?" said Ali. "I thought there was China in between."

"You're absolutely right!" said Man Doo, checking that one off. "See, this is not that hard. Okay, next topic is 'Hostages'."

"Even swap," said Ali, his fist coming decisively down on the table. "One for one."

"Not so fast!" said Man Doo. "What if there are some left over on one side or the other? You know, like in musical chairs."

"Shoot them?" offered Ali.

"Come now," pleaded Man Doo. "The whole world is watching. How about universal repatriation? It's option 'a' right there. You can just put a check mark in the box."

"Universal repatriation it is," agreed Ali, checking it off. "Red Cross supervised?"

"I'm afraid that bird's not on our radar. You see, the RPDK is like a well-oiled machine—you get a lot of NGO visiting firemen in country and through-put of deliverables goes south pronto," said Man Doo. "Let's just trust each other on this one."

"You promise, now?" asked Ali.

"On my honor."

"We'll give you that one, then."

"Excellent!" said Man Doo. "Now, for the tough one. Reparations."

"I'll need to touch base with my people about that off-line," said Ali. "A little pre-preparation to get our ducks in a line."

"Certainly."

Ali reconvened his team off to the side.

"Will somebody please tell me just what the hell is going on?" said Petal again.

"We're winning," said Ali.

"How can you say that? You're the one making all the concessions!"

"Banking them," he assured her.

"Okay, Ali, I give up. You're winning. So what did you want to talk to us about?"

"Nothing," he said, waving his hands like he was having some kind of disagreement. "This is just part of the Kabuki dance. Act a little more argumentative, will you? That's right. Now insistent. Perfect. Indignant now. Nice. A touch of petulance. Not that much. Now pout a little. More lip. Excellent. Now on my count, hopeful resignation. One, two, three! Good, now a little smile cementing our solidarity. *Finis!*"

"Our delegation is ready, Premier Kim," said Ali, returning them to the table. "And in the interest of time, why don't we fast track the horse trading and operationalize this puppy before the grass under it gets too long."

"I like your 360 degree thinking on this," said Man Doo, trying not to look like he was having the time of his life. "I'll tell you what. I've got a piece of paper here with a number on it. You know the drill." He slid it across the table like a faro dealer.

Ali tilted his head to peek under the corner. He frowned.

"We're talking billions or trillions here?" he asked.

"Trillions of course."

"Just checking. And I'm thinking Euros, right."

"Certainly not dollars," answered Kim.

"That's a lot of Euros," whistled Ali. "Your people all good with this?"

"In this town, I'm the man," said Man Doo.

"Well, Premier Kim, you're about the toughest negotiator we've ever gone to the mat with. And while your numbers push the envelope of our comfort level, in the interest of time, I'm going to pull rank on my associates and walk the plank alone on this one. You've got yourself a deal." He stood and shook the Premier's hand and beamed at him in admiration.

"Pleasure doing business with you," said Man Doo, now standing over Ali's shoulder pointing out the places he needed to initial. "All the rest here is just boiler plate—disclaimers of implied disingenuity, amortization of fictitious capital, saponification of leveraged liability, blah blah blah—the suits can give it a legal scrub later. But first, a toast."

He raised his glass to them. The rest stood and raised theirs to him. Rays from the setting sun sent rusty rainbows darting around the room, like frugal fireworks commemorating this fateful day.

"To peace and prosperity for both of our great nations!" cried Man Doo.

"To peace!"

"Da!"

"To prosperity!"

"Da!"

"And many happy returns!"

CHAPTER 53

REVOLUTION

"A toast! To the Fatherly Glory of the Eternal Leaderland!" called Premier Kim, leaning on his plate for balance. They were barely out of the teens and he was already looking rocky.

Ivan and Igor were holding their own, though, thanks to a combination of lifelong practice, natural selection, and inducible hepatic enzymes. With each dedication they would snap to attention, salute the ranking officer, drain their glasses, and shout back the toast at maximum volume, trying to outdo one another.

"Doo Dah Fat Early Gorski of the Infernal Lederhosen!" they barked with glee.

Buck hadn't yet been able to get any of the traditional Korean spirit past his nose, thanks to a combination of an intact sense of smell, a personal aversion to poisoning, and an innate distrust of any drink distilled from tires. As a result, every time he would try to toss a glass down his gullet, his wrist would suddenly spasm, shooting the shot over his shoulder onto the slippery floor beyond.

Ali was abstaining, too, but for other reasons. As a veteran of countless armistices, he knew that deliberations like this were never over until they were over, and even then, were never really over, fat lady singing or not. He would need his wits about him the entire evening, for it was always at occasions featuring a thousand toasts that cease fires invariably quit ceasing, thereby guaranteeing permanent employment for diplomats and massive hangovers for everyone else.

Petal was entirely sober, too, thanks to her innate (but inexplicable) immunity to the laws of pharmacology. Good thing, too, because over the years she had actually developed a certain fondness for traditional Korean Yuk Chuk, especially the post-Chernobyl vintages. And like Premier Kim, she preferred hers with a dash of chili pepper oil so concentrated that stray drops of the stuff had perforated the boardroom table and lay smoking on the floor.

Her style was to politely wait until Kim had finished his toast and brought his glass to his lips and then, in a motion too fast for the eye to see, have her glass empty and back on the table before he had even finished his first sip. And yet never did she exhibit the slightest disinhibition of superego, expansion of self-regard, or distortion of risk-benefit calculation characteristic of those who purposefully dissolve their neurons in dry cleaning fluid.

Buck inspected the floor behind her for clues. Dry. Ditto for under her chair. He watched her hands close up; looking for the poorly executed false half-pass, Jimmy Wilson feint, or reverse thumb palm. Every move was flawless. She was a Houdini, this Petal, or maybe she was just legit. Spooky, either way. He regarded her with astonishment. Was that a little wink? Or maybe just the light.

"Another toast!" shouted Premier Kim, sloshing his upraised glass. "To the Glorious Eternal Father of the Eternal Glorious Eternal Eternal Eternal—" and with a tremendous crash he plunged forward into a steaming tureen of Terrapin in Turpentine.

"Doo Dah Goriest Internal Bother—" began the Russians, who were now standing at attention on the table, arms extended in salute.

"Will you two please shut up," interrupted Ali, just about sick of toasts.

As if on cue, the door to the kitchen opened and, instead of another course of Pickled Pig's Pineal, in strode Captain Kim Kal Bi from the *SS Waba Ti Li*.

"So, did he buy it?" said Kal Bi.

"No, I think he just passed out," said Ali, feeling for a pulse in the Premier's carotid.

"No, I mean did he buy the bit about you being the Russian ambassadors?"

"You were the one who set him up for that?" asked Ali. "Why?"

"You don't think any Koreans really want a war, do you?" asked Kal Bi. "Other than the Premier, of course."

"Well, I don't—"

"And can you imagine the trouble we'd be in if we let the Premier ever meet with a real Russian ambassador?"

"You could have at least clued us in ahead of time," said Ali.

"And give up my plausible deniability? You talk like you never had a boss."

"Well, actually—" Ali started.

"Besides, you are obviously a very accomplished team, and if you could pretend to be Russian sailors, you could pretend to be Russian ambassadors."

"You could tell we weren't Russian sailors?"

"You don't even speak Russian."

"I mean, besides that."

"Well, there's also the matter of her," said Kal Bi, clicking his heels and giving a respectful little bow in Petal's direction. "You must know as well as anyone that there isn't a computer, cell phone, TV, or billboard in the world that doesn't have her face on it. Luckily, the Premier assiduously avoids the decadent Western media and wouldn't know Mick Jagger from Mickey Mouse."

"My face?" asked Petal, incredulous.

"None other," said Kal Bi, peering at her, close up from different angles. "And don't be so coy; your publicity budget has got to be bigger than our GNP. This kind of celebrity doesn't just happen by accident."

"But, I never—"

"Save it. I don't even watch TV and I recognized you right out of that silly kite-sub. What I didn't understand until tonight was just how big you really are."

"Well, I do have a certain following in the Manhattan society gossip crowd," started Petal.

"Enough!" said Kal Bi, losing patience. "Don't you realize what you have done?"

"Negotiated the latest Russo-Korean armistice?" she ventured. "Earned you trillions in reparations? Or was it the other way around?"

"Behold!" said Kal Bi, opening the blinds with a flourish. Below them was a view of the compound and beyond. The scene had changed substantially since their arrival. A full on Chill was now in progress.

Throngs of townspeople were streaming in and out of the compound on foot or perched on liberated military vehicles, crowding around charcoal grills and kegs of beer. The marching band was now up on a makeshift stage it shared with some long-haired dudes with electric guitars. A sea of joyous citizens of the now-former RPDK undulated to the music, hands above their heads, each wrist dangling an iconic handcuff and sawed-off chain.

Soldiers were tossing clothes and food out of windows to the people below. A bulldozer was pushing a huge pile of weapons into a pit. Members of the firing squad had taken off their coats to warm prisoners who had been waiting their turns. In fact, it was difficult to tell soldier from civilian any more, if the distinction still existed at all.

Every concrete wall, the very embodiments of totalitarian repression, glowed with projected images of forests and fields, oceans and skyscapes—as if seen by a bird lazily gliding past the parallels, oblivious to the senseless boundaries of men. And every few minutes the camera would seem to zoom in on something—at first a lone speck in the distance which then grew bigger and bigger until it filled the entire surface, the image of a woman, floating in the swirling ether, her hands outstretched, beseeching the people of the world to care. Now. Finally. Once and for all.

"Siverth," said Petal.

"Siverth," agreed Buck.

"Where does this all leave you, Captain?" asked Ali.

"Out of a job if I'm around when he wakes up," said Kim. "But until officially relieved of my commission, I remain Captain of the *Waba Ti Li*. I figure it's time for a nice long cruise. You folks want to join me?"

"Prisoner class?" asked Ali.

"VIP class," said Kim, smiling and shaking hands all around. "In thanks for all you have done for our Glorious Fatherland."

CHAPTER 54

QUADRUPED

The *SS Waba Ti Li* was bound to be gone before they could make it to the docks. The traffic was insane, what with all of the parading and joy riding and generalized chilling going on, and by the time the team's pajamas had been exchanged for warmer duds (RPDK Special Forces, Class A, Dress Uniform, Dirty, Lost in Laundry) there wasn't a single vehicle left unliberated from the compound. Calling a cab was out (taxi drivers were not allowed to know the location of the compound, under penalty of death) so the escape was stalled until Captain Kim could scroll through every number in his cell phone and find a relative with enough gas for the trip. Finally, success. Sort of.

"Please meet my most honorable second cousin Officer Kim Jangeo Tang, Tenth District Quadrupedal Unit, a great humanitarian and dedicated public servant," said the captain, bowing to the driver of what looked like an ambulance that was very near to needing one itself.

Everybody bowed and shook hands in turn with Tang, an elderly guy dressed in what looked like scrubs that were begging to be scrubbed. He smiled back a bunch of gaps, excited to be of help and not the least bit apologetic for being clueless about what was going on. The Captain called shotgun and climbed in as the ancient vehicle started up with the sound of a bushel of beer cans being heaved into an empty dumpster.

The back door of the van was held shut with a clothes hangar—an ingenious device to be sure, but no match for Buck's technical experience. Wisely, he held on to this universal hominid tool, afraid he might need it when it was time to get the door open again.

Out on the street it had been dark as sin, but inside the van it was as dark as the inside of a cow. Crowded, too, with a full load of massive and smelly official business already on board.

"Watch it!"

"Is that you?"

"Not now, Buck!"

"Will you please?"

"Приятно познакомится!"

"Anybody got a light?"

Somehow Ivan had ended up in possession of a Zippo (another archetypal hominid tool) which bore the inscription:

Come on down to the 37th Parallel, Big Boy!
Madam Cherry Blossom's Number One Chinese Laundry
(Formerly Madam Cherry Blossom's
Number One Whorehouse)
(Same girls!)

He claimed he had found it in his uniform, but he probably had lifted it from the snoozing Premier's pocket. Without a thought to the overpowering smell of gasoline in the back of the van, he fired the lighter up, seeking illumination but more nearly achieving immolation.

"Put that thing out!" screamed Buck, clapping it shut. "Are you nuts?"

Ivan whimpered, partly from the horror of realizing how close he had come to blowing everybody up, but also from the horror of realizing that, besides them, this van was full of quadrupeds. Big ones. Hairy ones. Live ones.

If it hadn't been so noisy back there one would have been able to narrow down the list of possible quadruped candidates from their characteristic growls and snuffles—and even if one had never actually stopped to listen to a panda before, one would have found it's unfamiliar utterances more reassuring than, say, those of a mountain lion.

But as the van bounced down the mountain road it was hard to hear anything over what sounded like a wrecking crew on the roof with a dozen jackhammers. And as frightening as this was to the bipedal contingent, it was even more arresting to the quadrupedal, who, even if not inherently polite or shy, were nonetheless well behaved as a byproduct of being just as frozen in terror.

"Did you just see what I just saw?" asked Ali in a quivery voice, just audible above the din.

"Not likely," answered Petal without guilt, considering his snotty comment about feminine concepts of clockwise and counter-clockwise and the thoroughly documented male ability to stare into the refrigerator for an hour without seeing the jar of Bouquet Garni that we bought at that pretentious kitchen store last year when they didn't have what we were really looking for.

"Well, then, what did you see?" asked Ali, from somewhere in the noisy blackness.

"Did I say I saw something?" asked Petal, back-pedaling. "All I said was that whatever it was that you might have thought you saw, compared to whatever it was that I might have thought I saw, wasn't likely to bear any—"

"I'll tell you what I saw," yelled Buck, stepping verbally between them. "Dogs."

"Big dogs?"

"Big dogs."

"In cages?"

"No cages."

"Biting dogs?"

"Eating dogs."

"Did he say 'petting dogs'?"

"I think he said 'eighty dogs'."

"Around here there are dogs you feed and dogs you eat. I think these are the latter."

"Did he say ladders?"

"I think he said 'Labradors'."

"Dogs are pets. You can't eat pets!"

"Don't be a snob! They have different social norms here!"

"How about rabbits? We've got rabbits you pet and rabbits you eat. If you are into that sort of thing, that is."

"Petting?"

"Eating."

"Who isn't into eating?"

"Do eating dogs bite?"

"I know I would, if I were one."

"To them, you might be one."

"One what?"

"One something to eat."

"Dogs are pets, they don't eat people!"

"We're not talking about petting dogs; we're talking about eating dogs."

"So dogs here have different social norms, too?"

"Sure they do, dogs are very strict about social contracts."

"Are we talking Old or New Testament contracts?"

"I don't eat dogs and they don't eat me. That's fair, right?"

"Who said anything's fair? It's dog eat dog out there."

"I think we should let these dogs go."

"But malnutrition is a big problem here."

"We should keep our nose out of it."

"So that's your nose? I wish you would!"

"I want these dogs out of here now!"

"This is turning into a Pandora's can of worms!"

"I'm closing my eyes and counting to three. I better not see any dogs when I open—"

"You can't see any dogs now."

"You don't have to see a dog to know it's there."

"These dogs have been very nice so far. I think we should rescue them."

"I hate dogs."

"I love dogs."

The van, which had heretofore been mostly airborne as it launched from pothole to pothole, now seemed to be attempting a maneuver better suited to strictly land-based vehicles—a left turn. A detailed analysis of the physics of the situation is best left to the advanced reader, but basically this complex event involved a bad mix of centrifugal forces, centers of gravity, and oxcart-optimized road design. And so, as if in one of those slow motion, multi-angle, endlessly repeated action sequences, the van lifted its wheels as if to pee, teetered uncertainly for a moment, and then decisively flopped over onto its side.

In an instant the back of the van became an (unopened) Pandemonium's Box. All social contracts were rendered null and void. Man's best friend or Man's next dinner—predator, prey, pet, or problem—it hardly mattered any more. The only thing that mattered was getting that door open. Now.

Buck knew it was all up to him. After all, he was the guy with the coat hanger and the training to use it. Wallowing on his back in a washing machine of unwashed dogs, he poked and pried at what should have been the latch—to no avail, until an impatient nip at his nether regions boosted his motivation and rammed his shoulder square into the door. With a bang the rusty hinges popped free, spilling the contents of the van onto the blacktop and bringing a conclusive end to any moral dilemmas surrounding Man's relationship to Dog.

"Did you see the size of those dogs?"

"Thank God they're gone."

"But what will become of them?"

"Someone will care for them."

"Or eat them."

"Shut up!"

Buck was busy helping Tang and the Captain out of the cab. Astoundingly, no one was hurt, and, apparently, not all that surprised. This must not have been the first time the van had assumed this position. The Captain peeled a few bills off a roll for his cousin and rejoined his group. Tang and the Tenth District Quadrupedal Unit were on their own now.

"Soldiers, listen up. We've got us an extreme situation here with ongoing ambiguation of civil command structure. Stick to the shadows and avoid confrontation with non-uniformed personnel who may be engaged in unauthorized chilling activities," he ordered. "We should be able to hold our own against ad hoc chilling units—who tend to be poorly disciplined and inappropriately euphoric—but if an act of heroism is required, please be prepared to die with honor for your country."

"You mean your country," said Ali, whose list of things worth doing for the sake of honor definitely did not include dying.

"Do you not wear the uniform of the RPDK Special Forces, soldier?" snapped the Captain, appalled at the insubordination.

"Actually, I do," admitted Ali, brushing dog hairs off of his insignia. "And it looks like I outrank you, Captain."

"Well, maybe technically speaking," the Captain allowed, counting Ali's stripes.

"Good. So you take point, Captain, and we'll stick to the shadows and avoid confrontation with non-uniformed personnel."

"Aye, sir," he saluted and trotted off double time toward the docks with his team in tow.

The *SS Waba Ti Li* was indeed nowhere to be seen by the time they reached the water's edge. In its place was a flotilla of ramshackle sampans all lashed together for a party. Weathered fishermen were gathered in a circle playing music on traditional *hae gum* and *senap, tanso* and *kayagum*. Despite the ancient origin of their instruments, the music they were producing was eerily Lykiloro-like.

"What are those guys playing?" asked Ali, not quite believing his ears.

"Never heard it before," said Kim. "Ordinarily, the only music permitted would be one of Our Eternal Leader's posthumous compositions, invariably variations on the Gilligan's Island theme song. This one is just as creepy but much more compelling. Grows on you, doesn't it?"

"Definitely infectious," admitted Ali, concerned that the tune would confiscate even more mental real estate than Gilligan's had when it set up permanent residence in his head. "I just hope it's curable."

"Buck," whispered Petal. "Is there any more culturally isolated guy on the planet than a North Korean sampan driver? If Siverth has got them playing Lykiloro, what is the rest of the world like now?"

"I hope we have a chance to find out," he said. "I don't think we're going to get very far in any of these boats."

The Captain peeled a few wrinkled bills off of his wad and pressed them into the hand of the alpha sampan male.

"Yo, brah," he said in Korean. "Any of you dudes seen a destroyer around here? A grey one about yea big with a Russian submarine hanging off the side? Hard to miss, really."

Blank stares gave way to expressions of recognition as enough bills changed hands to jar such obscure memories into consciousness. A few more, and seats were being prepared for six passengers in one of the less tippy-looking boats. In the darkness, the surface of the water was practically invisible, and pushing away from the dock felt like untethering from the Mir and drifting off into deep space.

The porter whistled a tune that was about as close as you could get to Lykiloro and still only use your mouth. Ali gritted his teeth and hummed some obnoxious disco song in defense. The Captain bummed Ivan's Zippo and started flashing Morse code into the inky void. Petal said nothing, but found Buck's hand and held it tight.

"I was wrong about these boats," Buck said. "Very seaworthy. Maybe we should rent one when we get home. Take a little moonlight sail on a summer night—that would be romantic, wouldn't it, Petal?"

"Let's do that, Buck," she said, smiling up at him. "But why wait for summer? We should have all this wrapped up in about ninety days. Let's do it then."

"Kind of cold to sail in December," he said, holding her close.

"I certainly hope so," she said. "Or we'll have to do this all over again."

"Not that it has been all bad," he ventured.

"No. Not all bad at all."

CHAPTER 55

PLAN

The SS *Waba Ti Li* really wasn't that hard to find—that is, if you knew where to look and happened to have a few special sampan driving skills—skills you couldn't get at MIT or Harvard Business School, by the way. The Captain tipped the driver generously—the service had been impeccable, and the value of the North Korean Wont was now a complete mystery. The Captain had a feeling they wouldn't be worth anything outside the erstwhile RPDK, and in the end he tossed the whole wad to the driver with a flourish.

The *Waba Ti Li's* first officer had been a little sheepish about leaving the dock without the Captain, but was eventually commended for his initiative in protecting RPDK property during a time of civil unrest (mass euphoria officially being considered the most dangerous form of unrest). The rest of the crew were also given medals, promotions, and raises in pay—or at least promises thereof. Spirits were high all around when the RPDK Special Forces Expeditionary Force (i.e. the two Americans, two Russians, and one Sultan) under command of Captain Kim Kal Bi, convened in the officers' mess, freshly showered and free of dog hair. Too bad there still wasn't any food.

"Do you think we might want to make a plan sometime soon?" ventured Buck after the Captain's tenth toast. All they had to drink was Boris's 'It Can't Be Beet' Juice (From Concentrate) pillaged from the *Fred*, and nobody (except maybe Igor) could choke down another swallow.

The Captain gaped in surprise. Plans, even when they weren't secret (which was essentially never) were always generated at the highest levels of the RPDK leadership (Premier Kim Man Doo channeling Premier Kim Chi Kim over a bottle of Yuk Chuk) and never shared with Navy Captains or other such rank and file. The closest he ever got to a plan was when he received his orders.

Certainly plans weren't the sort of thing that a rag tag bunch of foreigners would have a hand in making, especially during national emergencies.

The Captain considered himself a great leader, but had never imagined himself as a planner. He was suspicious of the role and not a little insecure about it. There was something onanistic about making your own plans—if you did it, you definitely wouldn't talk about it in mixed company. Besides, what if everybody made their own plans? Then what would happen?

On the other hand, it didn't take a rocket scientist (or even a political scientist) to tell that the whole ludicrous concept of the RPDK had become history (and ancient history, at that) literally overnight, just like everyone always knew it inevitably must. There had never been a logical reason for anyone in the country to give a flying rip about what the brain-dead Kim Man Doo thought about what the thoroughly-dead Kim Chi Kim thought about anything, as if either of them had ever thought about anything but themselves anyway. All it took was a little playful nudge for the entire RPDK auto-repressive, self-delusional, mass-hysterical, totalitarian-justifying, paranoid worldview to collapse into oblivion, just like a bad dream does on your way to brush your teeth. The nightmare was over. The future was a blank slate. Hopefully, a bright blank slate.

But, then again, personally, he was out of a job. Furthermore, there was no reason to expect he would be treated sympathetically by the new regime, however nebulous their apparent politics. He didn't need remonstrations to give up his save-the-world fantasies, or even his save-the-country fantasies.

He had brought this international band of escapees to the *Waba Ti Li* so that he, himself, might escape. So that he might start a new life, not transplant his old one. So why did he so reflexively recoil at the prospect of autonomy? How could he be so fearful of not being told what to do? How much damage had a life of authoritarianism done to his spirit? Could he ever repair it? Could he ever be truly free? He would have to try. He would have to believe.

"Yes, a plan," he started. "There has to be a plan. But, you know, even not planning is a plan, really. So it's not like we don't actually have a plan already, though it may not necessarily be the best one, I admit."

He was floundering, and everyone knew it. They also knew that the next phase of Kim's rebirth would be a delicate one, now that the Captain's fragile and distorted ego had been laid bare. This brought out Petal's most nurturing instincts and Buck's most supportive reflexes. As for Ali—well, he was Ali.

"It's a place to start," encouraged Buck, hoping to help him make a tiny first step. "Right now our plan is to have another toast out here in the harbor. Let's drink to that. The beginning of our plan!"

The Captain nodded slowly, processing the novel concept that a plan was something that might be fashioned incrementally, rather than received fully formed. There apparently was a process with a starting point. He was already feeling a little less guilty about his total planlessness.

"Exactly," affirmed the Captain. "Just what I was saying. We must start our plan from where we are. It's the only way."

"With all due respect," interjected Ali. "As the Supreme Omnipotent Potentate of one of your major international geopolitical entities, I think I speak with a certain level of expertise when I say that a plan must begin with its objectives. First you determine what you want to accomplish, then you work back to where you are, not the other way around."

The Captain looked questioningly at Buck and Petal, who looked annoyingly at Ali, who looked smug in the assurance that his thesis was irrefutable. But being right is not the same as being helpful, especially when the probability of reaching unanimity of life goals within any group (no matter how small) is about as small as you can get without being zero.

"And, furthermore," he continued, ignoring his friends' disapproval, "I think it should be clear from the outset that certain people have greater responsibilities and resources than other people, and consequently should have greater authority in the planning process."

"That does it, Hookie!" said Petal, reaching across the table and grabbing him by the ear. The Captain gasped. His long-held beliefs about the ultimate futility of the democratic process and its inevitable decline into chaos and violence were once again being graphically validated.

"You are the last guy who should be pulling rank around here!" she said. "Greater responsibilities! That's rich. The only responsibility you have is for plotting the single most heinous act of terrorism in history! And what could you possibly have as a goal for us? Let me guess. Elect you as Pope? Wash your Mercedes? Certainly not save the planet. I vote that Ali's right to vote be revoked for the duration, or at least until we have time to thoroughly paddle his bottom."

"Time out, you two," said Buck. "No need to get physical. Aren't our goals perfectly clear? We've got ninety days to fix global warming and find a planetary power source that's clean and inexhaustible, all the while keeping the oil burners burning until their hardware can be converted. Of course it would be nice to have the nukes somewhere safe and all those governments not mad at us. And then there's the Publisher. Oh, and Judge Glashaus. Not to mention our friends Siverth and Ole—"

All of this was just about too much for the Captain, who was just about to impose martial law when Ivan stood at attention and saluted.

"Request permission to request plan goal," he said, eyes fixed at a spot three inches above the Captain's head.

"Granted."

"Respectfully request permission to submit proposal that plan goal be dinner." He walked over to a map of the world with North Korea as its center. "Here!"

The Captain peered beneath Ivan's finger.

"Tokyo?"

"Tokyo."

"Good plan," said Buck.

"Da," said Igor.

"It's unanimous," said Petal.

"What's wrong with Chinese?" asked Ali. "It's cheaper and closer and they do take-out and I love those little white cartons with the wire handles—"

"Forget it, Ali," said Buck. "We've got a plan and it's dinner in Tokyo."

"But the Chinese are really tight with us Arabs. In fact, if anybody hates the West more than we do it's the Chinese. Why, I wouldn't be surprised if they were in on—"

"Request permission to stuff a sock in Mr. bin Said's mouth," said Petal.

"Denied," said the Captain, finally making his mind up about his own personal plan goals. "A world where the voice of dissent is stifled is not a world worth saving. And since we are apparently out to build a better world we will treat Mr. bin Said's opinions with respect. We may ignore him, of course, when he is full of crap, but we will do it with respect."

The Captain pulled himself up tall. He had faced his greatest personal challenge and he had prevailed. He was now a free man. A leader of free men. He was captain of his own fate. He now had a goal, a plan. Dinner in Tokyo. Save the planet. One thing at a time.

CHAPTER 56

CHINESE

Turns out that Ali had been right all along about dinner in Tokyo. Even at the *L*'s top speed, cocktail hour would have had to last three days. That might have been okay for some people, but these people had no cocktails. So, astoundingly, the plan-goal's direction got bent ninety degrees without the slightest harm being done to the democratic process and only a minimum of gloating from Ali. The Captain remembered a great little place for Chinese in Dalian. It was unanimous. A short hop across the Yellow Sea and they would be done with the *Fred*'s museum-class rations forever.

Even Ivan, as champion of the original plan-goal, took no personal offense at its modification. He had heard of Dalian. From the beginning of history there had been so many Russians living there that critics complained you could taste it in the food. For Ivan, going to Dalian for Chinese was like a New Yorker going to Texas for Mexican—maybe not authentic, but definitely better. Igor remained noncommittal. For him, *Fred* rations would always be just fine.

Buck and Petal chafed a little at the delay in getting to Tokyo, even though they were as hungry as anyone. They were desperate to make contact with Siverth and Ole, cut off from them since Greenland. The artists had obviously been busy, as evidenced by the now ubiquitous Cult of Petal, which was insidiously tie-dyeing the very fabric of society from Svalbard to Pyongyang. More importantly, Buck and Petal needed to catch up with Chill the Anthropocene, the global re-engineering network funded by stolen nukes and Boris Gorski's ill-gotten gains. Also, a little news from home would be nice; reassurance that Western civilization had not completely collapsed while they had been underground in the East.

It was doubtful that Siverth's email address would work anymore, given the security deep freeze he must be hiding in, but it was all they had to go on. Unfortunately, the *Waba Ti Li*, like every other RPDK facility, was forbidden to access to the Internet under penalty of death. It did have a semaphore, a Morse code key, and a radio cemented to one station—WPDK ("All Kim Chi, all the time!") whose format did not yet include truth, news, or sports. Buck thought they might be able to find an Internet Café in Dalian, but Petal doubted they would be able to tell 'Send' from 'Delete' on a Chinese keyboard. No, they would just have to wait for Tokyo, the epicenter of the wired world.

Everyone was out on deck with their chopsticks when the GPS said they were nearing Dalian Harbor. Unfortunately, they couldn't see a thing, and it wasn't because it was night. There actually would have been a reasonable amount of daylight right then at forty degrees north had the sun's rays been able to penetrate the airborne cesspool of smog that had become permanently puddled, a mile deep, on top of the Chinese subcontinent.

The Chinese, long famous for their meticulous craftsmanship, exquisite aesthetics, intellectual sophistication, and impeccable manner, had in a few short decades also become absolute masters at cramming their own personal space full of toxic excrement. No other society could even hope to match their expertise in the art of mass ecological suicide. With the cultural discipline that had earned them the admiration of all other societies, the Chinese had collectively risen above selfish, petty concerns of individual survival, allowing them to work tirelessly toward the systematic conversion of their entire homeland into one reeking cloaca of industrial filth.

With patriotic pride and clockwork regularity, the Chinese would celebrate the startup of yet another maximum-polluting, coal-fired power plant, yet another province-raping hydro-electric monstrosity, yet another radiation-spewing nuclear abomination, and yet another uncountable swarm of inhumane sweatshops.

And who did the Chinese have to thank for this national psychosis of self-mutilation? The Communists? No, not this time. All the credit goes to another cult—the Industrialists. The Industrialists: improving standards of living by destroying quality of living, offering freedom from the land through slavery to the machine, and promising wealth for the lucky through impoverishment of everyone.

Was it the ideology of Marx, Lenin, or Mao that made the Industrialist the only truly free man in China? Hardly. For that kind of dogma you'll have to have to re-read your Ayn Rand, your Milton Friedman, your Ronald Reagan. Then you will understand how the New China was able to rise above the rest of the bleeding-heart liberal world and claim the status of Laissez Faire Industrial Utopia of the Universe.

Over the centuries, China had subjugated herself to warlords, to emperors, to Red Guards, and Cultural Revolutionists. She had survived each of these abusive relationships, recovering just enough strength in between to embrace her next sadistic and exploitative master. Until this final one, this most masochistic and degrading acquiescence of a great people to an evil idea—a voluntary submission to bondage so suffocating that death was now imminent. Death by industry. Genocide by progress. Strangulation by the invisible hand of the market.

"This stinks," said Petal.

"Did somebody step in something?" asked Ali.

"Maybe we should pick another city," offered Buck. "One without a sewage problem."

"They're all like this now," said the Captain. "You're just spoiled from being in North Korea. You'll get used to it. Pretty soon you won't be able to smell a thing."

"Or breathe," said Ali.

"We'll be quick. Just long enough to pick up some Chinese food."

"Maybe I'm not so hungry, after all," said Petal.

"Come on, be brave. There's the dock up ahead."

Through the opaque cloud of industrial flatus appeared the outline of a man-made shoreline just up ahead. Destroyers pull a lot of draft, and the Captain was a little surprised that the bridge hadn't started nagging him about getting too close to the shallows. He checked with the first mate through his headset. Still plenty room to the bottom. This was definitely not a pier or a dock in any harbor.

Relying on a Korean GPS was always a mistake because of the RPDK policy restricting its accuracy to plus or minus a hundred kilometers. This was great at discouraging disgruntled citizens from leaving the country, but kind of tough when you were trying to drive a boat in the dark. The *Waba Ti Li* must still be way out in the Yellow Sea. But what was this in front of them?

Drivers of destroyers tend to fall into two categories—ones that plow right over stuff in their way and ones that realize that no matter how big you are, some whacko with a death wish can always hurt you worse. How these two types sort by IQ, voting record, and longevity is pretty dramatic, but best left to another treatise. Suffice it to say, Captain Kim Kal Bi had been so appalled by the Florida recount decision that he had left his Mensa yoga class early to go get organically drunk.

"Let's take the launch over and check this out," he said after making it clear to his first mate that protecting RPDK property was one thing, but leaving the Captain to be fumigated in the Yellow Sea was something entirely different. The *Waba* had better be there when they got back; that's all there was to it.

The landing launch was actually quite luxurious as military vehicles go, designed by the Premier himself to impress visiting dignitaries—if ever there had been a dignitary who would agree to visit. The seats were done in red and white tuck and roll to match the Corvette Elvis had driven in *Viva Elizabeth City, New Jersey*. In fact, the interior was completely authentic down to fuzzy dice and a furry rear view mirror warmer. The exterior boasted twelve coats of hand-rubbed, candy-apple pink with traditional flame motif and mock side exhausts. Its machine gun turret might have been a little anachronistic, but definitely was something Elvis would have added had it been an option from Chevrolet that year.

"Nice ride," said Ali, wondering if his hot pink yacht would clash.

"Cop magnet," said Kal Bi. "This rig can't go slow enough to stay under the limit." He opened the glove box for Ali. It was crammed with speeding tickets.

"My Mandarin is kind of rusty, but by the look of these I'd say they've got warrants out for your arrest in most of the coastal provinces."

Ali knew that the Chinese had quit granting diplomatic immunity to anybody after their UN Ambassador was arrested for blowing off his ten thousandth parking ticket. This was something of a record for a guy who never went anywhere except by subway, and had earned him a certain celebrity status within diplomatic circles. But the NYPD had been in one of its humorless funks right about then, chafing under a mayor whose presidential aspirations pivoted on his ability to protect New Yorkers from the threat of expired parking meters. Of course, every political action creates an unequal and opposite over-reaction, and the ripples of this little display of mayoral manhood continued to expand like tsunamis long after his career had moved into its inevitable influence-peddling phase.

"'Zero tolerance'," said the Captain. "Latest self-delusion in law enforcement. Some bozo consultant from New York made a fortune pitching it around here. About as hard as handing out wine to winos, I figure."

"We're in the wrong business," said Ali.

"I'll say."

As the launch got closer it became clearer that this was not Dalian, or any other Chinese city on the map. That's not to say it wasn't Chinese, or that it wasn't a city, or that there couldn't possibly be a map of the place. It just that whatever this place was, it definitely wasn't what anyone would call 'on the map.'

First of all, unlike just about any other Chinese city, it was new. That's not to say it wasn't a mess, because it was definitely that. Or that it was high tech, because it was definitely not. It was the kind of low-tech, overcrowded mess that springs up overnight on any semi-flat sliver of land surrounding cities like Mumbai, Lagos, or São Paulo. This had to be the outskirts of somewhere. But where?

Captain Kal Bi found a free tie up for the launch and gave some final instructions to the sailors who would stay to defend it. After a series of wooden ramps took them about forty feet above sea level, the six of them found themselves in a typical bare-dirt shantytown like any other, with one exception. There was no dirt.

That's not to say it wasn't dirty. There was hardly a surface that wasn't covered with grime. It's just that the whole place seemed to be built on a single, absolutely flat slab of concrete. The crush of human activity pushed right up to the edge, which, without so much as a guardrail, plunged straight down into the sea. This edge disappeared off into the haze in either direction, as straight as the horizon.

"Flatland," explained Kal Bi, back from a quick discussion with an old woman in a stall selling ginseng and pirated DVD's. Who knows, the ginseng may have been pirated, too—the whole place had a distinctly pirate feel about it. Every building, every vehicle, and every bit of visible infrastructure looked like it had been made out of spliced-together pieces of stuff that had been sawed off of some poorly-guarded counterpart elsewhere. Flatland was obviously home to the world's most righteous recyclers or its most compulsive kleptomaniacs. Either way, the *L*'s expeditionary force looked completely out of place in uniforms that were internally consistent, let alone identical to one another.

"Have you seen anyone with matching shoes?" asked Petal. "Very hot. Paris is bound to pick this up. Watch the runways next season—nothing will match. I'll bet they won't even sell you two of the same shoe by spring."

Buck hadn't noticed. He was too busy trying to understand the social dynamics of their situation. Even though they looked as alien as aliens standing in this teeming center of urban squalor, no one was paying attention to them, one way or another. In a place like this you would expect to be mobbed by street urchins, panhandlers, and first-tier entrepreneurs of all types. Where were the local toughs, the logo purse pushers, the Andean flute players? Something was definitely weird here.

It felt like they had arrived at a street theater way before the show, that the city wasn't yet open for visitors—that they were welcome to hang around if they wanted, but if they expected to be hustled or have their pockets picked, they would just have to come back later.

"I think you may be projecting," said Ali. "Other than you and me, I'll bet there's not a soul within a hundred miles with any fashion sense. No offense, Buck. Anyway, let's eat. I'm starving." His nose had, as predicted, succumbed to such olfactory fatigue that he couldn't smell a thing.

They walked a while down the edge of the city so they could keep an eye on a direct route back to the launch, but there didn't seem to be any restaurants in this part of town. The Captain conferred with a fellow in a shop that seemed to be offering acupuncture or tattoos or pain or maybe some combination thereof.

"Just a few blocks inland," he reported. "Great food, reasonable prices, local ambiance."

"Should we drop breadcrumbs?" asked Petal, a little skeptical about the translation of the word 'block.' How could there be blocks when the roads didn't stay straight for more than a yard and weren't as wide as an alley?

"Don't worry," said Ali. "I have an unerring sense of direction. We just figure where the sun is now, and then—well, I guess you can't see the sun, can you? Captain, you have a compass?"

The Captain indicated that hand-held compasses had been categorically forbidden in the RPDK for obvious reasons, but that he had a really great one bolted to the bridge of the *Li.*

Looking excited, Igor fished something from his pocket and held it up. It was a compass, all right, and even though it had gone through the laundry, the needle still moved if you tapped it just right. The problem was that its original purpose was to bribe the astonishingly venal and easily amused physician targets of the Kuak Pharmaceutical Company ("Patient going south? Give 'em Expensacillin!) with a compass that had all four directions labeled 'E'.

"In theory, this should be better than nothing," said Buck. "Keep your eye on the needle, Igor. We'll be counting on you."

The team plunged ahead into the warren of huts, lean-tos, yurts, and unnamable structures made of blue tarp, scrap fiberboard, and corrugated tin. After six (or was it seven) obligatory ninety degree course changes, the architecture became more substantial, but not particularly more inspiring—a three-story structure on the verge of falling down having even less aesthetic appeal than a one-story one. Finally they came to a little open area and their apparent destination, a traditional building that looked as if it had been lifted as a unit from some condemned Chinese town.

"Just like the guy said," announced Kal Bi, striding ahead. Igor, afraid to look up from his compass, tripped on the verge and pitched headlong through the door, sprawling face down on the floor.

By the time the rest of the group had gotten him onto his feet and dusted him off, their eyes had become accustomed to the dim interior. The one big room didn't seem to have any of the trappings of a restaurant. What it did have, though, was a dozen armed men, standing around them in a circle.

"Looks like you boys are in a heap of trouble now," said one of them in Chinese.

"Is he the one taking our order?" Ali whispered to Kal Bi.

"He's the one giving us orders," said the Captain, embarrassed to have been led into such an obvious ambush.

"We got no choice now 'cept to take you to see The Man," continued the *de facto* leader.

"We're going to see The Man," translated the Captain.

"And The Man doesn't like cops or tax men poking around his turf."

"Good news," translated Captain. "The Man is our kind of man!"

CHAPTER 57

CHUCKY

"Buck," said Petal as they were being marched through the alleyways of Flatland by yet another band of armed men. "What do you think it says about our relationship that someone or other is always taking us prisoner?"

Buck wasn't afraid to talk about relationships. He was a sensitive kind of guy. He would tell you flat out when he thought a relationship was "okay." Under special circumstances he might even confide that a particular relationship was "special." But as for questions about the causal relationship between unrelated, unintended life events and the unknowable machinations of the collective unconscious, well, you might as well be talking about the emperor's new clothes.

"I mean, think about it," she said, as one of their captors nudged her on with his AK47, "Endgame in Eden, Grandma's gang, the Coeur d'Alene police, Yasser Ibahb, Boris Gorski, one Premier Kim or another, and now The Man. You don't think we're getting co-dependent or anything, do you?"

She did have a point. Unfortunately, it was lost on Buck, who by that time was way behind on his Sunday supplements. He figured that whatever she was talking about must have something to do with the social sciences, which, as he understood them, had something to do with making excuses for bad behavior. Right then, the only thing that he felt co-dependent about was lunch. And the only thing prisonerhood had to do with this was that it was currently in the way.

"I read that captives eventually start developing emotional bonds with their captors," continued Petal. "But how can we be expected to do that when there's so much turnover at the top?"

She was right. Modern life had become much too frenetic for stable, long-term attachments, even ones as inherently cohesive as the prisoner/imprisoner relationship. Maybe that explained why

Buck had remained single all these years. But, then again, this was probably just an excuse for bad behavior.

"To be honest, I think we have to share some of the blame," she continued. "If we weren't always in such a big rush to escape, there might be time for our captors and us to transcend each other's dominant paradigms, to nurture our congruencies, and to till our entrenched positions with ploughshares beaten from the swords of our prejudice."

Even for Petal, this was laying it on a bit thick. Lack of lunch was likely making her delirious. These wispy New York types were great in the sprints but they didn't carry enough in reserve. Great Grandma Planck could have trudged across the steppes for weeks without getting wiggy, but then again she was what you would call a 'big-boned' kind of woman. Petal would be okay once she got some carbs or oxidants or acai or whatever it was that New Yorkers would agree to eat these days.

"From now on Buck, let's commit to building meaningful relationships with our captors—our hierarchical group leaders, if you will—let's set aside our competitiveness, our resentments, our—"

Something was clearly going on here. Buck searched the faces of his compatriots for clues. Igor and Ivan were looking stupefied. Ali was looking amazed. The Captain had that eager, wide-eyed look parents get when their kid is three letters away from winning a spelling bee. He was even doing that circular "keep it rolling" thing with his index fingers and nodding encouragingly.

"—petit bourgeois notions of inherent class incompatibility, our inculcated fear of the Other, our oppressive capitalist—"

By this time Buck couldn't help but notice that their guards—all ten or so of them—were crowded around Petal, hanging on every word. It wasn't clear that they understood what she was saying, but the sound of her voice had mesmerized them like a piper.

"—obsessions, our unjustifiable unilateralism, our cultural hegemonic compulsions, our—"

The Chinese guys had stowed away their weapons and were shushing each other to be quiet. Even their leader had given up the hope of control, and was leading by walking backward, just so he could hear her, too.

"—pervasive personal insecurities, all of which together comprise the age-old and seemingly impenetrable barrier to species-wide human intimacy, obstacles which, when objectively examined, prove to be as ephemeral, as imaginary, as easily dispelled as—"

The group spilled out into a courtyard. At one end was the first reasonably modern building they had seen in Flatland. Standing in front of it was a bearded guy in a black tee shirt and jeans, flanked by a dozen lieutenants. This had to be The Man.

Petal, realizing that they had arrived, abruptly stopped talking. The guards pulled themselves out of their trances just enough to escort their prisoners across the open space in some semblance of order.

The Man stepped forward to meet them. He was young and tall and buff, the kind of guy more likely to be called 'The Man' in Silicon Valley than in some outlaw Chinese ghetto. His teeth were just imperfect enough to be real. Every hair had been freshly trimmed. His shirt was right out of the box. His jeans had a crease that was sharp enough to be dangerous. These clothes had to be custom made—you couldn't just go and buy stuff without logos like this right off the rack anymore.

"Charlton Chinn," he said in Midwestern, news-anchor English. He extended his hand to Petal. "Please call me Chucky. Sources say you are The One."

He peered at her close up, as if she might be just a convincing hologram.

Petal gave a little nod of acknowledgement. It was the kind of nod that in other circumstances might have communicated, "Yes I am the Pope, but why don't we just skip the formalities out here in the lifeboat?"

Chinn, perceptively, took it to mean, "Although I may be some hitherto unknown form of supernatural being, I humbly defer to your superior status here in this realm, and, until such time that I choose to vaporize you and your entire species, I will treat you as an equal because I can easily see why they call you The Man."

"Petal," she said, shaking his hand. "Petal Steele."

"Charming," he said. "The infosphere is careful only to reveal your first name. Shall I?"

"Yes," she said, blushing a little. "I would prefer it that way, if you wouldn't mind."

"Of course, Ms. Steele—"

"Petal. Please."

"Petal, of course. It is an honor to welcome you and your associates to Flatland. I hope you don't mind, but I took the liberty of preparing lunch. American okay? The Chinese around here isn't all that good. Entirely too Russified, if you know what I mean."

Each of them shook hands with The Man as they filed up the stairs. Each in turn was encouraged to call him Chucky and to try to think of some wish he might fulfill. The Man was a prince. You could tell it in fifteen seconds. A prince of yet another armed principality somewhere not on the map.

The building looked like a grove of cement trees, each one six feet in diameter, each separated from its neighbor by an equal expanse of glass. The interior was cool but bright. The air was light and crisp, scrubbed free of the pollution stench outside. The ceilings were high, the interior walls stark and unadorned. The floor was concrete as well, but polished like marble and covered, in part, with traditional Chinese rugs. This was a place of taste, of strength, of planning. Like the Man, it exuded an air of understated elegance and restraint. This had to be Flatland's center of power.

A conference room table had been set for lunch. The space was simple, utilitarian. There were no ostentatious corporate frills, no gratuitous displays of executive privilege. The chairs were rosewood, but straight-backed and unpadded. The table itself, concrete with a glass-like sheen.

After a light salad of avocado, basil, and tomato there was a cold leek and potato soup garnished with green onion and a Parmesan crouton. Because it was only lunch, the entrée was small—a petite, chicken-fried steak and green beans sautéed with chipotle and almonds. To finish, there was a fluffy lichee sorbet and traditional green tea. Alcohol was never mentioned. Tobacco, inescapable everywhere else in China, was unthinkable. The after-meal drink was water, clear and pure in its carafe.

Parenthetically, it should be noted here that even though the concept of Heaven is now widely accepted to be an archaic and primitive fantasy, its reality can become undeniable by the end of a truly civilized lunch. The entire contingent pushed back, satiated, atheists no more.

The Man proved to be an impeccable host, skillfully drawing out those guests who were most likely to feel socially insecure. He engaged Igor and Ivan in Russian, effortlessly providing concurrent translation for the rest of the group. He could tell without asking that Captain Kal Bi would prefer to converse in English and to avoid political topics. He encouraged Ali to flame a little and didn't challenge the glaring contradictions in his idiosyncratic narrative. He and Buck hit it off famously, each having earned advanced degrees in civil engineering from rival universities. They agreed to spend more time talking about concrete later, while the others were napping.

But with Petal, he was different. While at every turn of the conversation he masterfully created opportunities for her to express herself, he seemed incapable of asking her a direct question. And she, unsure about the underpinnings of his deference, remained attentive and engaged, but nearly silent throughout. She knew that until she could finally get a handle on the mythology that Siverth and Ole had fabricated around her image, she had better be as noncommittal as possible.

But even the most neutral of her comments seemed to make him catch his breath. And even though he was skillful at hiding it, every utterance she made would send a subtle wave of hypnotic bliss across his face—just as it had for the soldiers of his militia.

She realized that Siverth and Ole must be using her voice as well as her image in their pervasive program of global hypnosis The infosphere had to be full of it now, no doubt infused with the hallucinogenic absinthe of Lykiloro's music and who-knows-what other subliminal narcotic. Whatever she would want to say, she had better not say it until she was sure she knew what She would say.

After lunch a nap sure sounded good, but nobody wanted to miss anything so they all tagged along behind Buck and Chinn, pretending to be interested in concrete.

"I guess all civil engineers are in love with the stuff, but I'll have to admit I never met anyone who was quite as besotted as I am," said Chucky, leading them down another twisting Flatland alley. "I got a toy truck on my first birthday. I guess most boys do. But for me it must have been a religious experience. From then on, there was never any doubt about the focus of my life."

"Concrete will do that to you," agreed Buck. "My parents wanted me to be a doctor, but I couldn't see the point—where's the concrete?"

"Exactly. There must be something genetic or at least hard-wired about the lust for cement—there have been people like us in every generation, going back thousands of years. You know, the Romans were nuts about concrete. There are major structures they built entirely under water that are still as strong as anything we have today. Amazing!"

"And yet, for something so ancient and apparently mundane, the chemistry is quite sophisticated," said Buck, recalling those exciting afternoons back in Materials Science lab.

"Absolutely fascinating," agreed Chinn. "But let's not bore the rest of the group. Let me show you something I'm sure everyone will find interesting—the secret of Flatland itself."

Ears perked up at this prospect, although Buck was still eager to discuss the effect of aluminum silicates on the calcium oxide crystal lattice structure.

"Please meet Chiang Kai Chinn," said Chucky, leading the way through a nondescript doorway into a small courtyard that seemed to be part of a family residence. Chiang was a skinny man in his sixties with a scraggly white beard. At least three generations of his lineage peeked through surrounding windows at the visitors. Chucky introduced each of them in turn, allowing plenty of time for bowing all around. Turns out that in Flatland, if you're not a Chinn or a Chin you are probably a Chen or a Trotsky, everybody being more or less related to everyone else.

"Chiang is a typical resident of Flatland. He may have other sources of income, but he is primarily an artisan. And you can see what a magnificent job he is doing on this piece of work."

He swept his arm to encompass the whole courtyard, but the primary object of interest was sitting in a scaffolding right in the middle—a massive concrete cylinder.

The thing looked much like a piece of urban sewer pipe about six feet long and six feet across, but attached to its outer surface at the north, south, east, and west positions were walls that ran from top to bottom, sticking out about three feet. The entire piece was glazed, just like the conference room table—its surface smooth and hard.

"Thousands of families in Flatland produce these units in their homes. It is a simple process that requires only basic tools and materials, but takes considerable attention to detail. The dimensions of the unit are easy to assure, since everyone uses standardized templates and molds, but making sure that the final surface finish is free of holes and cracks requires the eye of a craftsman. Chiang and his sons have never had a piece rejected."

He led them out a back alley to another unmarked door.

"Ready?" he asked.

Without waiting for a reply he led them through it and out into the open. At first it looked like they were back at the waterfront where they started, but soon it became clear that they were on the edge of a massive series of lagoons, each one many acres in size, connected by locks and bristling with cranes and other heavy equipment.

"You're building ships here?" asked Buck, knowing he was missing something.

"Better than," said The Man. "It's more obvious if we look from over there."

They walked a hundred yards or so to the edge of what looked like a huge pit dug in the ocean. Sixty feet down, gangs of workers were piecing together concrete units identical to Chiang's, producing a matrix of vertical tubes connected by their side walls and stacked one on the other.

"Concrete is actually quite light—considering how strong it is—and once you figure out how to make it non-porous, you could easily build boat hulls out of it. What we are building here, though, is much more useful than a boat. We're building more Flatland.

"Imagine taking an empty water glass and turning it upside down. If you balance it carefully and lower it into a sink of water, air will be trapped inside, and if the size and weight of the glass is right, the glass will float. Let's say you tie dozens of water glasses together and turn them all upside down as a unit—well now you have a floating platform. Take a look down there. Pretty soon we will have a huge honeycomb that is stronger than steel and impervious to seawater. All we have to do is pour a concrete slab on top of it, make it all airtight and we've got ourselves another five acres of Flatland."

"Shell has had floating concrete oil platforms in the Bering Sea for twenty years," said Captain Kim. "Great places to stop for lunch, if you have something to trade. Usually they'll take a few bottles of Yuk Chuk, especially if they're low on diesel."

"And those platforms were twenty years old when Shell bought them from Exxon," said Ali, who kept track of such things.

"Exactly," said The Man. "And if you pull them out of the water now they will look exactly as they did the day they were made, plus a few barnacles. That's the beauty of this technology. It's simple. It's proven. It's durable. And it's scaleable—we can make as big a piece of real estate as we want, just by adding more of the units made in every Flatlander's back yard."

"So let me get this straight," said Ali, looking down into the construction area. "Once the tubes in this big pit are stacked up to there, you put a slab on them, just like we are standing on. Then what?"

"We let water into the pit—it's a lock, really—to float the platform. Then tugboats can take it to wherever we want the new waterfront to be and we hook it up to the existing platforms. Then we pump the water out of the lock here and start building the next platform."

"What about waves?" he asked. "Why doesn't everything bounce around and bump together?"

"Excellent question," said the Man. "Want to try that one, Buck?"

"That's why they leave the tubes open on the bottom, rather than sealing the whole thing up like a glass ball," said Buck. "A wave passing through the ocean is a line of higher pressure followed by one of lower pressure. The air trapped in and around the tubes will be compressed by the rising pressure, absorbing the energy as heat rather than transmitting it to the surface of the platform and pushing it up. So, instead of bobbing like a cork, the platform rides as smooth as a hydrofoil."

"If you say so," said Ali, jumping up and down a few times, trying to convince himself he wasn't really on dry land. "I'd still worry about tsunamis."

"No problem out here. In international waters, a tsunami is just a ripple," said Chinn. "It only does damage where the water gets shallow."

"Got to hand it to you Chucky," said Ali, one potentate to another. "This is a pretty nice set up. You got your own little offshore tax haven with waterfront property on demand and everybody pulling together like one big happy family. What's the catch? Come on, you can tell me. Everybody's got problems."

"Did I say we didn't have problems?" said Chinn. "We've got plenty of problems. And there's one problem that is so tough that it might just be the end of Flatland. One that, to be honest with you, I was hoping you and Ms. Steele might just help me solve, given your current, ahh, extra-national perspective, as it were."

"And what problem is that?" asked Ali.

"Power," he answered. "You know, energy. It takes a ton of it to run this place and it is getting harder to come by all the time."

"Yeah, we know," said Ali.

"Welcome to the club," said Buck.

"Da," said Ivan.

"Da, da," said Igor.

"Us, too," said Captain Kim.

"Chucky, I think we have you covered on that," said Petal. "If you give us about ninety days."

CHAPTER 58

PLOT

"Did you find him?" asked Chinn as he brought in a fresh pot of tea for his guests.

"No trouble finding him," said Buck, looking up from his computer screen. "He's everywhere."

"This is amazing," said Ali, pecking away at the computer at the next desk. "Every page on the Internet links to Siverth Narup in one way or another. Chill the Anthropocene scientific projects. Cult of Petal mystical weirdness. Saving the planet with A-bombs on eBay. Pissing off everybody in power and recruiting everybody else. Convincing your left brain and enchanting my right. Seducing my yin and conquering your yang. Inside and out, top to bottom, Siverth Narup has a lock on the infosphere, just like you said."

"And where did he get these clips of me speaking?" asked Petal, peering at her screen, one desk down. "I never said any of that stuff. In fact, I don't remember saying anything on camera."

"Synthesized," said Buck. "It's not that hard once you have someone's voice signature. There's an art to it, for sure, but Siverth's a great artist, you have to admit that."

"So you found him, then?" asked Chinn.

"No, and I didn't really expect to. He's got every military and intelligence outfit in the world looking for him. He's dug in deep. What we really need is a way to help him find us."

"Not so fast," said Ali. "All those guys with guns are looking for us, too. You can't just go firing off emails with our address on it—even if it's an address that isn't on the map."

"And we certainly can't risk bringing any trouble to Flatland," said Petal.

"But there's no way we are going to get this global disaster averted by ourselves. Siverth has got the whole world working on it, one way or another. We've got to tap into that, to put it together, to make it work. Siverth is counting on us for that. We have to make contact with him. That's all there is to it."

"So you have to make him see you without the authorities seeing you," said Chinn. "You need both visibility and anonymity. You need to hide in plain sight. Sounds like you need a city, a big city."

"Tokyo!" cried Ivan jumping up from his computer where he and Igor were playing Massively Brutal Renegade Philatelist. As always after he said anything, the rest of the group were left wondering whether he was just pretending to speak English or whether he was just pretending not to speak English. Either way, it seemed like a good idea.

"Tokyo!" agreed Buck. "Here's what we do. The Captain, with the help of Ivan and Igor, pulls some kind of stunt in Tokyo that gets the media's attention for a few minutes. That will guarantee that Siverth will be watching. Then we stage a Petal sighting somewhere in the city. Everybody will think it's just like all the others on the internet—everybody but Siverth, that is, who will know that it is the real thing and not another of his artistic creations. He'll draw the logical conclusion that both events are connected, and will know he can contact us through the Captain."

"This stunt, as you put it," said the Captain. "It better not be too expensive. As you know we are acutely broke and low on gas, at that."

"But don't forget," said Ali. "You and Ivan and Igor are international heroes for recovering the stolen seed bank. All we need is a little advance work and the entire city will be at the harbor welcoming the *Waba Ti Li* as it steams in, triumphant. Imagine what the Japanese government might pay (under the counter) for the honor of being entrusted with the very survival of the human species. Imagine the photo opportunities as the *Fred October* and its precious cargo is lowered into the arms of the incumbent party, whichever one that might be. Play this one right and we can fill your tank and have change left over."

"Okay, but how are we going to do this advance work?" asked Captain Kim. "None of us has any connections to the media, do we?"

Buck and Ali looked at Petal. The Captain obviously didn't know who he was dealing with.

"Piece of cake," she said, sitting down at a keyboard. "Captain, give me the earliest date we can get there. Figure in the tides, too. High tides are better for harbor shots—covers up the water stains. A full moon rising in the evening would be nice, but not essential. Ali, check out all competing media events we need to avoid—baseball games, elections, soap opera conclusions, you know the drill. Buck, Google Earth the city for a Petal sighting site. Top of a public building maybe. Not too high, though. And Chucky, help me launder these emails so they can't be traced back here. I'm sure you've got that figured out."

Chinn smiled back in amazement. He had assumed that supernatural protectors of Mother Earth would be smart, but had never imagined they would be cunning. It made him proud. It gave him hope. The world might just make it after all.

"No problem," he said. "And let me help with the dates— there are a few unlucky numbers and astrological signs you'll want to avoid."

"Okay," said Buck. "But don't draw this out too long. Remember, we only have ninety days."

CHAPTER 59

FISHING

"How do I look?" asked Petal, twirling around on her toes.

"Beautiful," said Buck, meaning it. "I love you in Earth tones."

"I'm talking about the disguise, silly. Is it convincing or not? I'm supposed to be a Japanese fisherman, not beautiful."

"Sorry then, you flunk. You look exactly like a beautiful Japanese fisherman."

"And you look exactly like a handsome Japanese fisherman," she said, holding him close for a long moment.

"Petal?" asked Buck. "When this is all over, do you think that maybe we could, you know—if everything turns out okay and all, that is—we could sort of, you know, get together, I mean—"

"Not ready yet?" asked Ali, barging into their cabin. "I tell you, if heteros weren't so sappy and over-sexed, they might get something done now and then. Get your mind off the opposite gender and you free up ninety percent of your brain for useful work. That's why gays are so creative, you know. There are scans that prove it."

"Sorry, Ali," said Petal. "We must have lost our heads for a minute."

"It won't happen again," promised Buck, pulling on his cap.

"I should hope not," he said. "Let's go, everyone is waiting. By the way, you don't think this kimono makes me look dumpy, do you?"

"Not at all, Ali," said Petal. "Melts the pounds right off."

"I thought you might be working out behind our backs," said Buck.

"Stay off of calendars, though," said Petal as they walked onto the deck. "We're still under cover."

The yellow moon was nearly full, flashing like a semaphore through speeding clouds as black as the beyond. Captain Kim was waving furiously for them to come to the rail. The seas and wind would not pause for long. The fishing boat would pass along side the *Li* for just a moment. The infiltration team must be waiting at the bottom of the ladder. The three of them would have to get it right the first time.

"Anybody here speak Japanese?" asked Ali as they clung to the rungs, swinging in the darkness. A faint flicker from a single lantern winked in the distance.

"Sorry."

"Nope."

"The Japanese all speak English, right?"

"Of course they do. First thing they learn in fisherman school."

"It's your contact, Petal; didn't you tell them we needed an English speaking fishing boat?"

"You mean a contact of my contact's contact. And I told him we needed an Arab-speaking fishing boat, for added security."

"Petal, I don't know why anyone would join a cult about anyone as full of it as you are."

"Wasn't my idea. I don't do cults. And I certainly wouldn't join one that would have me as their leader. Besides, cult leaders are supposed to be full of it. Did you ever hear of one that wasn't?"

"Of course not. The term 'cult' is inherently pejorative. Nobody in a cult thinks they are in a cult. It's only people outside the cult that think they're in a cult."

"You've got too many pronouns in the air."

"You know what I mean. If you're outside the cult you automatically think everybody in the cult is full of it, including the cult leader. If you didn't, then you'd be a fool not to join up, since cults always have so much cool stuff to offer. All I'm saying is that nobody in their right mind would join your cult because you are so obviously full of it. And it is 'Arabic-speaking boat' and you know it."

"I'd join her cult. Full of it, half-full of it, or half-empty of it."

"Why, that's the sweetest thing I've ever heard!"

"There you go again! See what I mean? I think this whole hetero thing is a cult. A mind-erasing, zombification cult. You two are so full of it you can't even tell who's full of it any more."

"I think he's full of it, don't you?"

"No. I think his problem is a failure to appreciate Siverth's ironic use of the term 'cult.' By calling it the 'Cult of Petal' from the beginning, he has preempted accusations that it really is a cult or that it is primarily concerned with worship of Petal, per se. 'Petal,' in this context, is an metaphor, a concept. In this way, Petal personally is excused from the individual infallibility and omniscience invariably demanded of cult leaders. She may be full of it or not, as she wishes, as long as she allows her image to personify a spiritual and intellectual ideal."

"That is the sweetest thing I ever heard. I think."

"Sappy hetero rationalization."

"Get ready! Here's the boat! Jump on three! One!"

"All at the same time?"

"Won't we land on top of one another?"

"Two!"

"I think we should take turns."

"Shouldn't we have discussed this?"

"Three!"

In less time than it takes to describe it, Petal and Ali found themselves safely in the arms of stout young fishing lads and Buck found himself tangled in a pile of smelly old fishing nets.

"Below decks, quickly, please!" said somebody, and they all scurried down into the hold, a surprisingly comfortable area clearly intended for transporting VIPs rather than fish.

"I'm Ikeo Yoshimura," said the guy in charge, sticking out his unweathered hand. "Tokyo AP bureau chief. Call me Isaac."

"Petal Steele, *New York Times*," she said, extending hers. "This is Buck Planck, World Disaster Mitigation, and Ali bin Said, Sultan of Yomamah. Thanks for helping out."

"My pleasure. Thanks for the exclusive. Our mutual friend gave me the ground rules. We'll be playing it close to the vest for a while, I hear."

"Mum for the next ninety days, then it's all yours," she said.

"Fair enough," he said. "And you three better keep mum if we get stopped by the Coast Guard. Unfortunately, they don't take bribes in Japan."

"And the country works?" asked Ali. "Astounding!"

"Actually makes things simpler," he said. "All of that pretending not to be offering a bribe and pretending not to be accepting a bribe while pretending not to be negotiating the details of the bribe got so time consuming that everyone here just agreed that everyone eventually would be bribing everyone else anyway so we might as well just call it even and forget the whole damn Kabuki dance."

"You think they could make an exception in our case, since we're from out of town?" asked Ali. "I feel kind of guilty breaking the law without at least offering a bribe. It just doesn't seem right."

"Perfectly understandable," said Yoshimura. "There's an online form for that. We have an online form for everything. Just go to *gaijinbribes.gov* and do what the cute cartoon character says. Be sure to print the receipt, though. Tributes, extortions, and embezzlements are deductible, but there's a nice little tax credit for bribes."

"Thanks for the tip, Isaac," said Buck, "But we've got bigger problems than income taxes. First of all, we have no income. Second of all, if we get lost in Tokyo, no one else will either."

"Yeah, I get your drift. Don't suppose any of you speak Japanese, just for starters?"

"Sorry."

"Nope."

"*Un peu.*"

"Don't worry; I'll tag along with you. This city can be kind of intimidating if you aren't a Harajuku schoolgirl."

"Much appreciated," said Buck. "We'll need some help staying under cover until the Petal sighting. I was thinking Tokyo Station for that. Sound okay?"

"Excellent choice. Great visibility. Maximum crowd density. Press pass gets us to the platform on top. Wait till the spotlights come on and they'll see her a mile away. Then we make a quick costume change and disappear onto a commuter train. Thousands of them go through there every day."

"Good," said Petal. "So we have the *Waba Ti Li* arriving at ten and the seed bank ceremony at noon. The evening news talking heads will be milking this to death when I do my materialization thing at the train station. It will be easy to copy the sightings Siverth created for the internet—they are all pretty much the same—crowded urban area, mysterious woman in Speedo strikes some beatific but beseeching pose from an unlikely elevated spot and then vanishes, followed by general pandemonium."

"I don't get it," said Ali. "These Siverth spots aren't just computer generated shorts. Those people in Rio and Moscow and Cape Town and Mumbai all swear that they saw you—there are hundreds of interviews on line. Half of them even claim their bunions were cured. But Siverth can't be going all over the world setting up hologram projectors, can he? He's supposed to be in hiding."

"We're in hiding, too," said Buck. "And we've managed to log a few miles. Also, Siverth's got lots of friends. Maybe they are doing the site work."

"Got to hand it to the guy," said Ali. "This is his masterpiece."

"Not to mention Chill the Anthropocene," said Petal. "Isaac, have you ever heard of that one?"

"You're joking," he answered.

"No. It's a real thing. Siverth Narup is behind it, too."

"You're pulling my leg," said Yoshimura. "Of course I've heard of it. Everybody in the world has heard of it. In Tokyo, it's hard to hear of anything else. There's a new startup every hour that has to do with energy, the environment, or one Earth science or another. Unemployment is in negative digits here. People are working a second job just to be part of it. The yen are flowing like tsunamis. I can't believe you didn't know."

"We've been a little out of touch recently," she said.

"That's an understatement," said Yoshimura. "You guys must have been in comas. But more about that later. What I really want to know is how can Narup be in charge of all this. I'll grant that he's a great artist, but this CTA thing is moving unimaginable amounts of money into the most advanced technologies all over the globe, ignoring every government's attempt to control it. Even if it doesn't save the planet, it is already the biggest worldwide economic event since they invented wampum. If this is what artists do then I'm buying me a beret."

"CTA is set up to be kind of self-organizing," said Buck, not really remembering how the programs were put together. "Panels review proposals and make grants. You know, like that."

"But somebody ultimately has got to be in charge. Somebody has got to make the big decisions when all the R and D is in. Who's got the ball here? Who's gonna be the number one guy? Who puts it all together?"

"I guess that'll be us," said Buck, spreading his hands and looking from Petal to Ali and back.

"Once we do a little homework," said Ali.

"But don't worry, Isaac," said Petal. "After all, we've got ninety days to figure it out."

CHAPTER 60

TOKYO

"Shouldn't we be changing into something more appropriate?" asked Petal as they made their way through the crowd on the docks. After all, even though they were now quite invisible among the pre-dawn catchers and cookers of fish, their ultimate destination was one of the most stylish and sophisticated urban areas in the world. Besides, with all of this unplanned-for public attention, she was starting to feel a little self-conscious in her baggy fisherman's outfit, and, despite Buck's ever-more-biased appraisals, not a little unbeautiful. One might temporarily tolerate being temporarily unbeautiful, thought Petal, especially if one is invisible. But being conspicuously unbeautiful was totally intolerable, no matter how temporarily. Even worse was being conspicuously unbeautiful on purpose—except perhaps as part of some theatrical teenage petulance, and Petal had long since recovered from that kind of craziness.

"Not at all," said Isaac. "We'll blend right in. You'll see."

A cab was waiting for them off in the shadows near a warehouse. Nearly invisible itself at first, it acknowledged their approach with a quick flash of running lights. Couldn't really be a cab then, could it, sensing their approach in the dark at that distance? But, then, this was Japan, wasn't it—where everything was completely wired and the rest was completely weird.

"Harvey Nakata," said Isaac by way of introduction as they all piled into the ersatz cab. "Visual Content Section Chief."

"Photographer," said Harvey, waving from behind the wheel. Harvey was dressed in traditional village blacksmith attire. Sort of. More precisely, his outfit appeared to be a modern interpretation of village blacksmith garb designed by someone whose only knowledge of village blacksmiths was from a previous designer's interpretation, who in turn knew nothing of villages or blacksmiths other than from a prior generation of purely speculative designers.

Which is to say that Harvey really didn't look anything like a blacksmith except to culturally savvy urban moderns, meaning everyone in Tokyo with the exception of Buck.

"Natty threads," complimented Petal. "Awesomely smithy."

"Thanks," said Harvey. "Love the nautical look. A little photorealistic, but very *avant garde* this month."

"Isaac's final touches," admitted Petal. "A true artist."

"Why he's the boss," agreed Harvey, pulling the car smoothly into barely moving traffic.

"This a hybrid?" asked Buck, impressed with the absolute silence within their vehicle.

"Electric," said Isaac patiently. People who were so behind about CTA shouldn't be assumed to know anything at all about modern life. "Plug in. Actually, plug ins don't really plug in anymore, they charge through an induction plate on the bottom. Whenever you park or are stalled in traffic you can charge up from plates in road if you want. With a little planning, though, you can do it cheaper off-peak or from your own solar or wind."

"Gas that expensive now?" asked Ali.

"Not really. When you count all the so-called hidden costs of wars, pollution, and climate change, fifty dollars a gallon is still a bargain. No, people are converting to electric for the same reason they do just about everything—because it's the thing to do.

"Remember back when gas went up to four bucks and nobody bought SUVs anymore? Was this because everybody in the country simultaneously sat down with a calculator and discovered that their gas budgets had just reached some universal physical limit, like the speed of light or the mass of the proton? Of course not. The extra money they begrudgingly stood to spend on gas was piddling compared to what they were gleefully dumping on ostentatious adornments for their monstrously shiny alter-egos. SUVs were shunned for a much more compelling reason than market forces or global altruism. The sudden death of the SUV was due entirely to the fact that, all of a sudden, buying an SUV was just not the thing to do anymore."

"Everybody in Tokyo went out and bought a new car?" asked Ali scanning the traffic.

"Nah," said Isaac. "They converted their old ones. Only takes a couple hours to yank out that disgusting gasoline engine and bolt in a clean power chain. Get some lunch and a haircut and come back to a car that's a hundred times better."

"That must be expensive," said Ali, looking for the catch. "What if you can't afford to convert?"

"Don't be silly," said Isaac. "It's free, just like your colonoscopy and your vaccinations. The voters decided that they'd rather not breathe carbon monoxide or ruin the planet anymore so they just voted it in. You'd be surprised how much your government can afford once the oil companies are off the dole. Factor in the real costs of gasoline and the conversion pays for itself. All you have to do is ignore the usual chorus of corporate-sponsored whining—'freedom of choice,' 'Big Brother' 'socialism,' 'market interference'—all driven by first-quarter-profit myopia and the fact that some people can't stand it when government does something good for people. Hide the whole project in your defense budget and you'd have America converted before Congress wakes up from the vote."

"But what about the guy who refuses to convert?" asked Ali, desperate. "The internal combustion engine is intrinsic to our heritage—it's the cornerstone of modern culture. Sure, it's smelly and wasteful and poisonous, but then aren't we all? The oil-burning car is more than just an obsolete way to get around; it is the defining icon of our species, a symbol of all that makes us truly human. You can't just make people give up their gasoline. It's like making them give up their booze or their religion. It's just not—not—American!"

"Americans are famous for making people give up all kinds of stuff. But, yes, there are some holdouts to conversion. You are allowed to burn gasoline if you want, you just have to clean up your own mess—just like you have to pick up your own dog's poop. See that bozo in the Hummer over there? He's still guzzling."

Definitely a Hummer, thought Ali, with the ton of chrome trim every combat-hardened GI must have for protection on the battlefield or at the mall. But it did look kind of dorky with that home freezer strapped to its roof.

"Scrubber," explained Isaac. "Got to back-flush it every night, and then you've got another disposal problem on your hands. But the real oil addicts don't seem to mind. It's like cigarettes. Even at a hundred dollars a pack, they still sell plenty of them."

"But how are you making all this electricity?" asked Buck, hoping that their search might be over.

"Well, that's the rub," said Isaac. "Still mostly carbon. Coal, gas, and oil. Maybe a third is from hydro and renewables. Somebody needs to make a breakthrough here. A lot of publicity about space mirrors and cold fusion, but I'm convinced the oil companies sponsor these fantasies just to make sustainable solutions seem far-fetched. I'm counting on Chill the Anthropocene to get us something clean."

"Us, too," said Petal.

"I thought Japan was heavy into nuclear," said Buck.

"That was back when it was still cool to dump your trash in somebody else's living room. In fact, until recently, the most important part of a modern business plan was how your company was going to trick the public into paying its dumping bills. But as soon as the guys who generate radioactive trash were held responsible for dealing with their mess, all of a sudden they didn't want to run reactors anymore. Nuclear power was always a Ponzi scheme and everybody knew it.

"Let's say you run your hair dryer today on electricity from a wind farm. Once you send in your ten yen then you are done— you've paid your fair share of the equipment and labor required to make the power and get it to you. But if you use nuclear-generated electricity you are incurring a debt that never gets paid off, a forever mortgage with escalating interest that you pass to your children and theirs for the next fifty thousand years. You might as well get out of the shower and call up your neighbor and say 'hey, why don't your grandkids come over here and dry my hair for me?'

"It seems laughable now that corporations were able to muscle governments all over the world into subsidizing nuclear plants in spite of their multiple fatal flaws—you can't clean up their pollution, there's not enough uranium to go around, and they breed terrorists like flies. So, how many fatal flaws does it take to kill this nuclear vampire, anyway, once and for all?

"But then again, it wasn't logic or rationality that finally drove a stake through its carcinogenic heart here in Japan. It was the people's change of heart. Something happened that, all of a sudden, made it unthinkable for them to disrespect the Earth anymore. All of a sudden, ruining the planet became something that just wasn't done."

"And how did such a massive brain shift happen?" asked Petal. "What caused it?"

"Beats me," said Isaac. "A lot of weird things are going on all at once these days, and if you can figure out how the cause and effect arrows go then please let me know. It's just too simple to credit Siverth Narup and Chill the Anthropocene and even—with all due respect, ma'am—the Cult of Petal.

"Who knows, maybe all these things are happening just because after ten thousand years of irresponsible behavior the human race has finally decided to grow up. Maybe Siverth Narup is just doing what all brilliant artists do, pointing out what we should already have seen—what we would all eventually see—and making the inevitable happen. Who's to say that if Siverth Narup had decided to get drunk instead of doing whatever it is he is doing, some Peruvian artist wouldn't have gone on to create the Cult of Pedro at the very same moment—just because the time was right— just because the conditions of the universe made it impossible for it not to happen?"

"You a Calvinist, Isaac?" asked Ali. "I have to tell you that I find this predestination stuff a little depressing. Why try at all if everything is inevitable?"

"Taoist," he answered. "And it's not that the Universe is predestined, it's that it's non-linear, complex, emergent, self-organizing. It's always been that way and always will. Everything depends on everything else. And everything depends on every animate and inanimate thing in the universe working its little heart out at whatever it is supposed to be working on. Including us."

"Inspiring," said Buck, but then he was the kind of guy who wasn't truly happy unless he was working his heart out on something—and usually something huge and noble and hopelessly futile. "Looks like everybody in this city is doing just that."

It was true. It was barely sunup and already crews of workers were swarming in and out of buildings and up and down their sides, too.

"Part of the No Photon Left Behind Project," said Isaac. "Which is actually a consortium of hundreds of little projects all funded by CTA—that's Chill the Anthropocene to you. The idea is to use every ray of light to its full advantage. Mostly that means covering horizontal surfaces with gardens and vertical ones with photovoltaic panels. But there are also light-guides that illuminate interior spaces and thermal traps for heating."

"Excellent," said Buck. "I hate wasting energy."

"Exactly," said Isaac. "But there's more than just electromagnetic energy being wasted out there—think of all the mechanical energy. In the next hour we'll have ten million people walking to work on those streets, throwing away energy with every step. Why not turn it into useful work?

"See how the sidewalk is darker in front of that department store? It's a generator. People unconsciously congregate there because the sidewalk is softer, it gives a little when they step. And each little give is mechanical work that can be used to generate power. So the store owners win twice by making its sidewalk more comfortable to walk on. More people pause to look in their windows and they help power their building with free electricity."

"Roadways have this, too?" asked Buck.

"Roadways are even better," said Isaac. "Electric cars recapture mechanical energy when they brake, but they still lose a lot into the road. Be there with your generator when the semi-trailers come down a hill and you've got yourself a Niagara's worth of energy free for the taking."

"Breakfast?" called Harvey, pulling into an unmarked break in the sidewalk the size of a single car.

"Starved," said Petal, hopping out first. A quick glance at the passing crowd had convinced her that Isaac was right—they were going to fit right in here. She stood patiently studying the Tokyo street scene, while everyone else climbed out and Harvey pressed a thumbprint into a meter, quickly lowering the cab into some automated parking mechanism below street level.

Petal had always appreciated the highly developed Japanese sense of style, but she knew there was no national monopoly on preoccupation with appearance. Whether crushed by poverty, dazed by chaos, or smothered by authoritarian repression, the human spirit will find a way to validate—no, to create—its own self-image through subtle manipulations of dress, manner, and personal aura. It will find its way to its own style.

In fact, it seems like the more primitive the circumstances, the more sophisticated the individual's stylistic creativity. A Maori shaman has just as highly developed sense of style as a Parisian courtier or a gangsta rapper. He is just attempting to construct a different self-image. Just how the human spirit comes to imagine its particular avatar of self is the ultimate mystery pursued by advertisers, psychoanalysts, and demagogues since the beginning of civilization. And it was mystifying Petal at this very moment.

She tried to make generalizations about the hundreds of people streaming by on their way to work this sunny morning. At first it was tough to find any unifying characteristic, except for the absolute perfection of everyone's appearance, no matter how dirty or disheveled. That and the fact that they were all dressed as agrarian peasants. Sort of.

Milk maids. Plowboys. Millers. Weavers. Masons and carpenters. A smattering of barbers and shopkeepers, but mostly front line, pulling-the-tuber-from-the-Earth-class subsistence frontiersmen. No financial derivatives marketing analysts. No esoteric issue legislative lobbyists. No masters of the universe.

Yet every shred of faded homespun was meticulously draped, every fanciful smudge of artificial dirt carefully applied. Mud on boots never flaked off. Nobody stank. Everyone's teeth were perfect.

And all of them were talking, but none of them to each other—murmuring in quiet conversation with their cell phone partners, be they inches or miles away. No electronics were visible. In fact, no artifacts of the last two centuries could be discerned anywhere in the crowd—except for one. Handcuffs.

A length of chain dangled from every sleeve. Metal flashed from every wrist. This was the one universal. No one would be seen on the street in Tokyo without cuffs. Not these days.

Of course, not all the cuffs were identical. Petal supposed that if she could get up close she would find them all subtly different, in the way every stylistic element continuously mutates and evolves. Many appeared to be standard issue, like Petal's and Buck's, but some had grotesquely wide bands, others exaggeratedly long chains. Some were spiked with barbs, others encrusted with broken glass, but most variations served to soften the metaphor with iridescent colors, gemstones, and organic materials. Some folks sported both cuffs on one wrist; some cuffs had migrated to neck or ankle.

Isaac and Harvey pulled up their sleeves when they caught her staring.

"I guess we know where this one got started," said Isaac with a little bow. Theirs were relatively flat and linked like Rolex bands.

The chains had shrunk to vestigial remnants, and there was a faint LED glow beneath their gunmetal surface. "Although I guess yours aren't wired, are they?"

He held out his wrist for inspection. "Every cuff you see out there is part of the network. The cheaper ones are just phones and messaging devices. The expensive ones have more gizmos and computing power—mine takes care of my insulin and blood pressure. The girls' do their birth control. The medicines work better going through your skin instead of your stomach anyway, and the cuff orders refills for you when it starts getting low.

"The cuff calls in if your heart rhythm gets funky or your vital signs sag, and the medics scoop you up on the first bounce. Of course, the cuffs are a boon to retail—you just pick up whatever you want in a store and walk out—the transaction is handled automatically and the store gets paid immediately. The kids have hundreds more things they do with them. Every day I hear about some new trick, but my guess is that most of those programs wouldn't even run if you're over twenty."

Petal pulled her cap down over her forehead and her scarf up over her mouth. People were looking at them now, but with more curiosity than disapproval. The problem was that their costumes had been selected for their ability to fool the Coast Guard, not for their creative adherence to the strict but rapidly shifting rules of urban fashion. Within this sea of archetypal agrarian peasants on their way to their accounting jobs, Petal and her friends were looking a little too literal.

What saved them was the fact that even though their outfits appeared authentic, they themselves didn't. The fact that none of them looked the slightest bit like fishermen conjured around them an air of high art rather than of low class. The crowd, which would have been forced by class and convention to find real fishermen invisible, was thus encouraged to twitter and gawk in expanding waves around the daring gaijin in their midst.

Of course it helped that Harvey's blacksmithy appearance was stolidly conventional, which allowed him to assume the role of escort for this clutch of eccentric but trend-setting rock star equivalents. Ali and Buck followed Petal's example, hiding their faces while being led through the crowd. Flashbulbs would have been popping if there still had been such things. Instead, the excitedly curious took clips with their cuffs, using the same unobtrusive gesture as one uses to look at one's watch.

Isaac hurried them into the restaurant where a waiting maitre d' swished them into a private booth, curtained off with hanging beads. There they could be hidden in shadow while still able to survey the passing scene.

"Didn't fit in quite as well as I had hoped," said Isaac. "This fashion scene baffles me. Every time I come downtown I'm more out of it."

"I told you, boss," said Harvey. "You can look like a fisherman but only in a certain way."

"What way is that?"

"It's a visual thing, boss," said Harvey. "You know it when you see it."

"You mean you know it when you see it. I obviously don't know squat when I see it. I thought we looked great."

"You do look great. You just don't look like you are supposed to look. To be honest, boss, even on the docks you didn't fool anybody."

"But nobody there paid any attention to us. They never looked twice."

"That's because down on the docks they don't care what anyone looks like," said Harvey. "You could have been dressed as the Dowager Empress and no one would have cared—unless you were spooking the price of fish, that is. Up here it's just the opposite. Everyone is totally obsessed with how you look and couldn't give a rip about the price of fish."

"It would be nice not to draw so much attention," said Petal.

"Until it's time to draw everybody's," added Buck.

"And then we really need to get invisible to escape," said Ali.

"Not a problem," said Harvey. "Chanel is across the alley. They owe me—I do their fashion layouts. Plenty of time after breakfast to get some new duds. Might be kind of pricey, but sometimes you have to pay whatever it takes to be completely inconspicuous.

"In the meantime let's eat," he said, opening the menu. "I'm starving. You might want to try this new item. Seems to be in all the hot places these days. Some sort of health drink. They call it Soyuz Sunrise."

403

CHAPTER 61

CHANEL

"Ready for a little shopping?" asked Harvey, putting down his chopsticks.

"Absolutely!" said Petal.

"Of course!" said Ali.

"Guess so," said Buck. They had been eating for an hour but he couldn't be sure he had consumed any actual food. *Sun Baked Fillet of Baby Basil. Desalinated Infusion of Virgin Soy. Rarified Air Puffed Hydroponic Krill. Cloned Collagen Monolayer Sashimi. Precipitates of Amino Acid Emulsion. Bipolar Ice Core Aqua, 60/40 Blend.* And, of course, Soyuz Sunrise, served warm in its original carton.

"Who's buying?" asked Isaac.

"Associated Press, of course," said Harvey. "Don't be a Scrooge, boss. This is the biggest story of the century. You don't want to look like some kind of rube, do you?"

"That's not what we're trying to look like?"

"Or a curmudgeon, either."

"Okay, okay. You're the visual content guy. Lead the way. Just don't tell my wife I went to Chanel without her."

After a few rounds of lively but inconclusive bowing with the proprietor, his wife, the chef, and the wait staff, they were able to extricate themselves to the alley out back.

"Nice restaurant, except for all the babies," said Ali, who had always wondered why children couldn't just play among themselves somewhere out of earshot until they were eighteen. After that they would be allowed to join adult society, if they could be quiet about it.

"No babies in there," explained Isaac. "Part of the cuff's population control function. Every hour or so it counters that little voice in your head that's all the time whispering 'Let's breed! Let's breed!' with the universal nonverbal rebuttal, the voice of an insistent infant. Very effective. So-called unplanned pregnancies are way down."

"Wouldn't a nice, quiet jolt of electricity work just as well? Certainly not all of us are at risk for breeding. Why should everybody have to listen to bawling rug rats?"

"Would-be aunties and grandmas are the world's greatest threat to population control, second only to can't-wait-to-be uncles and grandpas. Knock some sense into them and maybe the Earth will have a chance."

"No such thing as a screaming-kid noise-cancellation program for the rest of us?" asked Ali.

"Black market, maybe," answered Isaac. "But clearly anti-social and ought to be illegal. Something I would expect from one of those 'wishful-thinking-only' anti-contraception cults, though why promoting over-population could ever be considered religious is beyond me. Personally, I could never understand why people choose omnipotent deities who are so hung up about rubbers, especially with so many more heinous evils in the world begging for divine intervention."

"I don't think it's rubbers, per se, that have all the Almighties' shorts in a bunch," opined Ali. "After all, holy beings have been weird about sex since long before there were any Trojans. It's like their most common personality trait. Must have something to do with living in the non-material plane. When you don't have an *ule* yourself it's tough not to get peevish when everybody else is getting it on with theirs."

"*Ule* envy," agreed Isaac. "Ironic fate for Creators of the Universe."

"They have no One but themselves to blame."

"Amen," said Isaac. "In my opinion, when they pass the plate in church you should be able to put in a dollar or take out a rubber. That would send the right message."

"Small compensation for all those centuries of anti-sex, pro-breeding indoctrination," said Ali. "By the way, I hope your local Cult of Petal has its head on straight about this."

"Definitely pro-love and anti-proliferation," said Harvey. "As you will plainly see once we enter the modern world of Tokyo retail." He held a door open for them, one that was usually reserved for VIP's by appointment only.

They found themselves in a private dressing area that, luckily, was now unoccupied. This was a place where the over-moneyed classes might meet with their personal shoppers, have a few drinks, drop a small fortune, and slip away without revealing to the gawking public their tastes in studded bustiers, cleavage-enhancing jocks, and Mickey Mouse garter belts.

Next to the bar, directly in front of an overstuffed loveseat, was a mannequin wearing what must have been the last customer's final selection, now awaiting packaging and delivery. The gown was a traditional Cinderella design, long and silvery and light as air. But there was something startling about it, something that you could only see if you looked carefully and moved slowly. The material shimmered, reflecting ambient light back in waves and sparkles, except from a handful of perspectives, each only milliseconds of arc in width. From these fleeting vantage points the material of the gown became totally transparent, revealing tantalizing glimpses of the woman beneath, completely nude except for her Speedo.

"Great effect," said Ali, circling the mannequin. "Very sexy. Except for the Speedo part."

"Ahh, that's where you will be soundly outvoted by popular opinion," said Harvey, clearly the authority on current fashion. "While urban business attire must strictly conform to the modest conventions of an imagined agrarian peasantry, beneath every sack cloth tunic now lurks the seething sexuality of a Speedo.

"And within the otherworld of after-hours Tokyo, from the dimly lit jazz clubs to the frantic rave Chills, the heady sensuality of the Speedo becomes more overtly revealed, elaborated, and celebrated. At this time in history, there is no greater erotic titillation than to imagine—let alone get a peek at—a feminine form ensheathed beneath her kimono in the primary-colored nylon of a Speedo."

"Except for maybe a masculine form in a Speedo," offered Ali.

"You may have something there," agreed Harvey.

"We should do some pictures later," suggested Ali.

"You're on," said the photographer.

"Much later," said Petal. "We need to be getting clothes on right now, not the other way around. Is someone going to bring us stuff to try on in here, or do we have to go out there?"

She nodded at the door that, even though unmarked, clearly led to the public retail area, where any ragamuffin could wander in off the street and blow a king's ransom on a pair of satin stilettos with matching bag.

"We go," said Harvey. "Be brave, stick close, and stay alert. If you straggle or appear weak, you'll be cut off from the group in a minute. The floorwalkers hunt in packs out there. Everyone got a buddy? Watch each other's six. Okay, on my count—three—two—one—shop!"

The unit moved out in tight formation, Harvey at point, Isaac holding up the rear. They hugged the wall as long as they could, using Buck's mass on the inner flank to shield Petal in the middle. They made up for their conspicuousness with an air of official intimidation—bystanders took them for a battalion of plainclothesmen on their way to a major bust, and instinctively scurried off to other departments where collateral damage would be confined to their credit balance.

It was only when Harvey paused to reconnoiter that the rest of them had a chance to appreciate the true grandeur of the scene. Chanel Tokyo was modeled after Eiffel's *Le Bon Marché* in Paris, with a towering central atrium lit by a giant stained glass dome some twelve floors up. Diners looked tiny beneath a full-grown mango tree in the center, which in turn was dwarfed by the extravagance of open space above it.

Perhaps in December this expanse would be filled with decorations commemorating Christmas, Hanukkah, Kwanzaa, Bodhi Day, or Eid al-Adha, but now it was dominated by a single artistic installation. Simple in design, subtle in message, exquisite in execution, and gigantic in scale, it filled all available space between the mango and the dome—one unimaginably huge green bubble.

"When it comes to bubbles, the Japanese have always been way ahead of the Americans," explained Harvey. "Tulip bubbles, South Sea Island bubbles, gold bubbles, Beanie Baby bubbles, dot com bubbles—the West has nothing on the Japanese. We had our real estate bubble twenty years before yours—same thing exactly. Only took us a decade to dig out of it, but then again we didn't use the occasion to give rich people seven hundred trillion dollars just to keep them from pouting. We spent our money on jobs so people could pay off their debts. And did America think they could learn something from our experience? No-o-o. Couldn't do that.

408

Creating jobs would be socialism. Not like bailing out the bankers who caused the whole—"

"Forget about that," said Buck. "It's a joke, right? The green bubble."

"It's art," said Harvey. "Art can communicate lots of things. Some of them are funny, some poignant. Some profound, some flippant. But the greatest works of art—in my opinion, of course—are the ones that communicate the most complex of human concepts within the simplest of physical forms."

"Whatever," said Buck. Right now he was more interested in determining the direction in which the modern world was hurling itself, *vis-à-vis* the cosmic toilet, than he was in predicting who or what would make it to the Met.

"But what is it driving at? What does it mean? I mean literally, now, Harvey. Simple declarative sentences. Art for engineers, okay?" He wasn't going to let go of this.

Petal and Ali thought Buck was being intentionally dense. Some men will stop at nothing to get out of shopping. So it's a green bubble? So what? Next week a blue bubble. Who gives a rip? It's just some department store prop, not the golden plates of Mormon.

"Look around you, Buck," said Harvey, swinging his arm to encompass not only the visible space but the whole of Tokyo and, by extension, the entire intelligent world. "Everything is green now, in one way or another. Every shopper you see is working for a company that has been smart enough to steer itself into the flow of green yen now surging through the country in exponentially increasing volumes. A lot of it is CTA money furiously circling the globe in search of the greenest place to grow. But the rest of it is homegrown dough that in the past would have been happy fattening itself up in some self-indulgent mutual fund or snoozing safely in a cozy municipal bond.

"You remember the time, long ago, when money took pride in dog-like loyalty to its owner? This was its *raison d'être*, after all. Back then money was made of metal, paper, and ink. You could hold it, protect it, pet it—and in turn it would serve you and you alone.

"But there is no money like that anymore. Sure, some people still carry bills and coins around and we indulge their quaint little rituals. But this is not real money. Real money has completely dematerialized. It resides nowhere, wandering the ethereal cloud of electromagnetic code that wraps the Earth like a second atmosphere. It is owned by no one—merely herded by hungry custodians who suck sustenance from its teats as it lumbers from one cyber-refuge to another, circling the planet over and over, hour after hour, without a moment for self-reflection.

"So should it be a surprise that money would undergo this crisis of conscience? From its modern vantage point it can clearly see that its survival depends on the survival of human civilization, not on the survival of a single person or even a single country. Without civilization, money would not only lose its supreme position as God of Modernity, it would wither into irrelevance. It would go extinct. Money has got to be green now. It is fighting for its life."

"A compelling metaphor, Harvey, if a little over-anthropomorphized," said Buck. "But what I really want to know is what this gigantic green bubble is doing in the middle of this department store."

"I'm getting there. A bubble, of course, is an economist's metaphor. But, let's face it, for all its pretense of being a science, the field of economics is nothing more than a hodge-podge of folk psychology translated into intentionally confusing academic jargon. Look at any economic theory and you will find that, at its core, it is based on some completely unsubstantiated speculation about the mental and emotional processes of some hypothetical buyer and seller, of which there never seems to be a single living example.

"Take for example the concept of a 'bubble.' It's not like these are rare or inconsequential events. The history of nations can pivot on bubbles growing and bubbles bursting. So wouldn't it be fair to ask our most esteemed economic advisors to explain what causes a bubble? And shouldn't we expect their answers to be based on some objective scientific principles? Some quantitative equations? A testable hypothesis maybe? A little data? Huh?

"'Exuberance.' That's what they'll say. 'Optimism.' I kid you not. This is what the Chief Senior Economist for the Bank of the Universe or the University of the Bank will whisper secretly to his Premier or President or Ayatollah across a polished desk as their country teeters on the brink of economic self-annihilation.

"Of course, on the way up it would have been the good kind of exuberance, the right variety of optimism. A demonstration of the people's faith in the fundamental principles of a free market. Consumer confidence. It would be plotted on a graph. They would have nodded with self-satisfaction.

"On the way down, though, in the free fall after the bubble has burst, the whole mess will be blamed on the wrong kind of exuberance—'over-exuberance' is the scientific term—and a pernicious, 'unjustified' optimism that had infected the market like some plague of madness, converting the rational agents of their theoretical society into a slathering herd of lunatics."

"Yes, but—"

"I know. I know. You want to know why there is a green bubble filling up this immense space."

"Right."

"Well, I'll tell you. Because it's funny. And sad, in a way, too. And wise, really. You see, not that long ago the people of Japan were in despair. Times were bad. Everyone was in debt. The country was in decline. The Earth was decaying and no one thought there was anything that could be done.

"But now, we are on our way up. The people are optimistic. Everyone is working together now, for the Earth. There is no unemployment—even people who don't need the money are working two jobs just because it is the right thing to do. But they don't complain—it makes them feel good to do it.

"And the extra money they make, well, some of it goes into green investments but they spend plenty of it, too—because they feel they deserve it, because they are working so hard and are doing the right thing. So, of course, the economy is booming. Look at all these people in this ridiculously expensive store! See how happy they are shopping for green stuff they don't really need.

"The people are exuberant. You can feel it, can't you? Even though CTA hasn't really solved the big problems—energy, climate, the environment—we are optimistic. No, we are more than optimistic. We are certain. We are certain enough to bet our fortunes on it. To bet our futures on it.

"But is this the exuberance people feel as they begin a new millennia of prosperity, as they collect their reward for finally getting it right? Or is it a manic, delusional over-exuberance, frantically inflating a bubble that is about to burst? Is there a way to tell the difference, except in retrospect? Maybe there really is no difference. Think about that.

"And what could you do about it, anyway? Is there any way to intervene in the world economy that might deflect its trajectory toward the boom and away from the bust? Maybe, if it is true that the entire course of economic history actually does pivot on the emotional state of the man in the street, then the right piece of art at the right place at the right time might just be the most effective intervention possible—more important than any coercion the Fed or the World Bank or the IMF could ever concoct.

"So that's why there's a green bubble in the middle of this store. It's a joke, you see. But it's also a talisman and an affirmation. It is saying that because we can laugh at our good fortune by calling it a bubble, it can't really be a bubble. It is saying that if anyone calls it a bubble we won't let it be one. We have preempted the bubble by facing up to it—by having it in our face. The bubble cannot sneak up on us because it is right in front of us."

Buck looked at Petal and then at Ali. They were all thinking the same thing.

"Siverth."

"He's here."

"He's everywhere."

CHAPTER 62

HOLOGRAM

Petal felt much better now that no one was giving her more than a second glance. It was nice to be fitting in. Granted, she might still be blatantly non-compliant in critical areas of bodily dimension and genetic underpinning, but at least she was conventionally dressed.

Not that conventionality was all that easily attained or inconspicuity all that cheap. In fact, they had to shop especially hard to find Chanel outfits that were truly inconspicuous and not merely "understated." It had taken Harvey's personal connections and a healthy gratuity for them even to be shown the special collection reserved for rich people who might, temporarily, for their own reasons, wish to appear truly inconspicuous rather than, as usual, obviously posing as inconspicuous.

Chanel, understandably, would have to charge a bit more for this extra subtlety, the sum total of which would precipitate a rather alarming case of either heartburn or coronary ischemia in Isaac when he was presented the bill. The Personal Shopping Assistant, rigorously trained at Institut Haute Pasteur, was ready with an ampoule of *Chanel No. Code 500*—a proprietary mixture of aspirin, nitro, Maalox, and gin—which had him up and staggering to the door under his own power in no time.

So, as Petal walked down the street in her not-unstylish but certainly-not-daring ancient-Japanese-peasant knockoff, she felt a true solidarity with all the other urban professional women crowding the sidewalk. Shoulder to shoulder, murmuring quietly into their invisible cell connections, competently balancing the demands of family, career, and responsible world citizenship, making their way to depositions, acquisitions, exhibitions or even less agrarian situations, they seemed to radiate an aura of barely-contained excitement, of adventure and anticipation. The atmosphere crackled with their energy. Electrochemical energy. Animal magnetic energy. Sexual energy.

Scientists must have devices that measure this sexual energy field—who knows, maybe they even have transformers that charge batteries off of it. Certainly, they must have theorems, equations, and hypotheses to spare—perhaps even entire textbooks, graduate programs and institutes dedicated to the topic. After all, we are talking about one of the fundamental forces of nature here, not some academic curiosity like dark matter, light matter, dozen matter, or whatever. Chanel obviously had their top R and D guys studying their brains out on it. How else could they have produced the garment she was wearing, with its imaginary peasant exterior and its sexual field transmitter/receiver interior?

She knew there was something weird about it as soon as she saw it on the rack—that is, in addition to how it looked, of course. First of all, even though its fabric was supposed to simulate some rough-woven linen or hemp, it was really quite soft to the touch— luxurious enough to make its silk lining seem like an unnecessary extravagance. Once inside it, though, Petal became convinced that there must also be some high-tech middle layer with a chip, if not a mind, of its own.

The insides of dresses are not supposed to be fresh. Friendly, maybe, in a sisterly kind of way. Silently conspiratorial even. But certainly not forward. Not like this dress. And, from looks on faces, every other dress in the Ginza.

In the dressing room she had jumped out of it as soon as she had put it on and felt around inside of it with her hand. Nothing. The salesgirl had given her a knowing look, assuring her that all was as intended and that she would get used to "Active Matrix Foundation" in no time. Well, it had been some time, and she sure as hell wouldn't be getting used to *this* any time soon.

Not that it was unpleasant. Or unwelcome, even. Just a little distracting trying to pay attention to one's business with all that going on down there all the time. And rather disconcerting, too, it being so sneaky about everything. You couldn't really catch it at it even if you reached in there real fast or peeked down the neckline real quick. It was like your refrigerator light that way.

After a while she figured it must have something to do with her Speedo. Separate the dress from the Speedo and they both behaved. Get them together and the mischief wouldn't quit. Could these women walking to work with that look on their faces all be wearing Speedos underneath? And the occasional grumpy looking one—was she the only woman wearing satin and lace?

Petal was supposed to be the fashion maven, how had all of this happened without her knowing? Was this all Cult work, or was it some breakthrough CTA energy project? Or maybe a monumental piece of Siverth Narup underwear performance art? Perhaps they could stop at a nail place for a couple of hours of girl talk that would straighten all of this out. Certainly out of ninety days they could make a little time for that.

"Hey, hold up!" said Ali. "That's the *Waba Ti Li.*"

They stopped and peered through a store window. There on a hundred screens was Captain Kim shaking hands with an official in morning coat and top hat. The *Fred October* was being lowered to the dock in the background. Igor and Ivan were signing autographs for screaming schoolgirls. Here on the street, cheering sporadically broke out in response to what must have been inspiring pronouncements by microphoned commentators. Customers inside were clapping each other on the back and shaking hands all around.

"Great day for Japan," said Isaac.

"Makes you proud," agreed Harvey.

"I'll bet it'll be a national holiday from now on," said Isaac. "This month needs another holiday."

"What are you talking about?" asked Ali. "So your country got handed some hot seeds? Big deal. We did all the work."

"Shut up, Ali," said Petal. "You haven't done any work since—since—now that I think of it, I don't think you've ever done any work."

"Besides, matters of national pride almost never make any sense," said Buck. "I bet Yomamah has plenty of completely incomprehensible holidays."

"Watch it," he warned. "You can only criticize holidays in countries that separate church and state, as you would say—or at least pretend to, which would be more accurate. Since we in Yomamah are above such hypocrisy, we freely admit that all national commemorations are religious and vice versa and therefore are immune to all criticisms of irrationality."

"So you get to criticize our National We've Got All the Seeds Day," said Isaac, "and we aren't allowed to criticize your—your—"

"Eid ul-Egg," prompted Petal. "How about that one, Ali? All I remember is crawling over dunes blindfolded all day. And this was supposed to be some kind of festive occasion? That one made no sense at all."

"Careful," he said. "A most holy celebration of the day Sheik Wad ei Said, after wandering lost in the desert for a month, came upon a perfectly formed egg. This, of course, was an instruction from Allah to eviscerate the tribe of Hippites to the north, which, of course, Wad arranged without hesitation or anticipation of personal gain.

"In return, Allah rewarded Wad with a fortune in semi-precious leveraged mortgage derivative guarantees which sustained him and his people for all the days of their lives. Every year the people of Yomamah gleefully anticipate the ritual in which we crawl through the desert one half hour for each day Wad spent wandering."

"And the blindfolds?" asked Isaac.

"Wouldn't want to find an egg," said Ali. "Hippites have nukes now."

"Perfect sense," conceded Buck, abruptly terminating the discussion with an upheld hand. "Look, there, behind Captain Kim. What's happening?"

At first it was barely visible, even on the huge screen right in front of them. Off in the distance, a shimmering, like heat over a mirage. The crowd on the dock saw it before the camera crew or dignitaries did. There was an audible collective gasp, then complete silence, and then a roar of cheering. The camera pulled back from the puzzled celebrities and jerked skyward. There it was, hovering over Tokyo harbor, now as sharp and clear and solid as the *Waba Ti Li* itself.

Petal held her breath as she watched her holographic image, hundreds of feet tall, look down upon the people of Tokyo—beckoning, beseeching, but above all, approving. Her hair was loose, snowflakes blowing through it. Her cheeks were red against the cold. Her eyes calm but pupils wide. The apparition scanned the city below her and stopped to stare right at the camera—a stare that could only be taken as a warning.

And then, with a start, the towering figure stood up tall, looking quickly around. She held up her hands as if to push something away, a look of alarm on her face. And then she was gone.

The camera panned back immediately, searching for a trace. And then there they were, speeding in from all sides. Black attack helicopters, no insignias on any of them, their searchlights probing the space where Petal's hologram had been, finding only emptiness and each other. Frustrated, the war machines fanned out, skimming the tops of Tokyo buildings, their blinding lights and oppressive roar burying the city beneath a smothering blizzard of intimidation and fear.

The screens went blank for a moment and then all of them began running the same official message. Even without translation the message was clear. "This is an emergency. Go to your assigned area. Do not use your phones. Await orders." Sirens erupted all over the city, their wails harmonizing in the wind.

"Off the street," said Isaac, herding them toward the store's entrance.

"Door's locked," said Harvey, leaning against it. "It's automatic."

The people on the street were running now. There was fear on their faces, but they were all totally silent. Some were helping old people, but most were moving as individuals, determined to get to their personal safe havens in the quickest but most orderly fashion.

Harvey tried the next door down, one he had just seen someone enter. Locked.

"The door recognizes you by your cuff," he said. "Lets in the locals and those with high authorization status. Outsiders are out of luck."

"You guys not local enough?" asked Ali, amazed. How many tribes could there be in Tokyo?

The street had emptied out. Except for an old couple from Florida in Bermudas puzzling over a map, there was not another soul in sight. Helicopters popped above the horizon four blocks to the south, sweeping streets with their searchlights. Sirens loudened from the north. They had better move now and they had better move quick.

"Subway!" shouted Isaac, sprinting for the stairs.

The station was packed with people who had been caught waiting when the trains shut down, but instead of milling around and feeding each other's hysteria, they were all sitting quietly on the ground in neat rows with their identification papers in their hands.

"Follow me," Isaac whispered, making his way to the far end of the platform which looked like a dead end, except if you were a train. He fumbled with a ring of keys on a chain, finally producing one that he held up for inspection.

"Wish us luck," he said. "This was supposed to help us escape from the main station. Let's hope it works here."

He jiggled the rusty lock for a minute, then leaned his shoulder into the stubborn door. It opened with a complaining squeak.

"Maintenance passageway, I think," he explained. "We can walk to Tokyo Station from here and be right on schedule. It's only a mile or two away. We can't go wrong."

"Unless we get lost," said Harvey. "Some of these old tunnels just connect to older tunnels that only connect to abandoned tunnels. You got a map, boss?"

"Maps are for tourists," he said disdainfully. "I have an unerring sense of direction. Trust me."

And with a flourish he reached in and flipped the light switch. One dim bulb flickered in the distance for a moment and then went dark. Behind them a bullhorn blared orders in Japanese. Petal stopped at the threshold.

"I wonder what Petal would do in a situation like this?" she thought to herself. The answer was obvious. Nodding to the men, she strode past them into the darkness.

CHAPTER 63

ZOMBIES

"What do you suppose that was all about?" asked Petal, holding tight to Buck's shirttail in the dark.

"Depends on which that you are talking about, doesn't it?" answered Ali, clinging tight to the hem of her dress. "If you mean the four hundred foot 3-D movie of you making spooky eyes at the people of Tokyo, I don't think it was a sign from Allah, if you know what I mean. A billboard from Siverth, maybe. A jalapeño pizza nightmare, even more likely."

"That's not what I meant, and you know it," she said. "What I'm talking about is this big emergency. The helicopters. The lockdown. The instant martial law. All because of a picture of me? What's that all about?"

"Does seem weird," said Buck, holding on to Harvey's collar. "I thought they loved you here."

"Nothing weird about it," said Harvey, clenched tight to Isaac's coat. "Of course they love you here, Petal. They're ga-ga about you. You are their true hero—their spiritual leader. Their entire lives have changed since you started showing up. You have made reverence for the Earth a matter of personal pride. You have given them the courage to fight for justice for the biosphere against the entrenched forces of consciencelessness. You have made it cool for them to align their lives with nature. You have given them hope for a better world, Petal. No exaggeration."

"Me?" she asked. "Really, I haven't done anything—"

"Don't be so modest," he said. "Now, of course, having everybody love you can be a pretty dangerous thing. Not only will everybody hate you for it, some of them will get positively homicidal. But that's just people—you expect that sort of thing from them. They're only human, right? The real problem is with the zombies."

"You still have zombies in Japan?" asked Ali, trying to remember the last time he saw a zombie, even in a movie. Ten years? Fifteen? He figured all of them must be retired by now, feet up in nursing homes, reminiscing about the great brains of yesteryear.

"Of course we do," answered Harvey. "They're everywhere. They walk the Earth day and night, oblivious to borders, indifferent to laws, police, and military might, driven by their mindless compulsion to consume everything in their path."

"Zombies?" said Ali, incredulous.

"He's not talking about the same kind of zombies you're talking about," said Isaac, leading their way through the tunnel by the light of his cuff's luminous dial.

"There's kinds of zombies?" asked Ali.

"He's only speaking metaphorically," explained Isaac. "That's the problem with speaking metaphorically, Harvey. No one knows what the hell you're talking about."

"I say if the metaphor fits, wear it," said Harvey. "Besides, I think they really are zombies. Otherwise they would think, wouldn't they? Isn't that what zombies do, unthinkingly pursue some unholy abomination, damn the consequences?"

"He's talking about corporations, Ali," said Isaac. "He calls them zombies. It gets the department in no end of trouble."

"What else would you call them?" asked Harvey. "A zombie is born when the law allows the corporation to 'incorporate.' 'Incorporate' means get inside a corpse. And by law this animated corpse has all the individual, God-given rights of any living human being—the right to privacy, the pursuit of happiness, free speech—the whole nine yards. The problem is that society only works when individual rights are balanced with social responsibility, a concept that requires the moral judgment of actual intelligent human beings."

"But, Harvey," objected Ali. "Corporations are made up of human beings. People who join a corporation are just as moral and intelligent as anybody else."

"Ahh, that's the next step in the zombification process. The zombie corporation is driven by one and only one irresistible compulsion—to consume human lives and human wealth. So the first thing that happens when a normal person takes a job in a corporation is that he gets bitten on his neck—"

"That's vampires, Harvey," said Isaac.

"Metaphorically speaking. The new hire then becomes a zombie himself, mindlessly shoveling human lives into the slathering corporate maw. Now here is the tricky part. When the corporate man goes home at night he reassumes the form of a real human being—one with all the normal feelings of right and wrong, of guilt and pride—but with only a dimly veiled memory of what he has done in his zombified state.

"A sparrow falls from its nest, and the after-hours corporate man feeds it with a dropper. Girl Scouts come by with cookies, he pays with a bill and waves off the change. His neighbors don't suspect a thing. 'A quiet man,' one will report. 'Always kept his yard neat,' another will testify. He might even get a 'pillar of his community' or two. But the next day, when the corporation reels him back in, his human parts get shut back down. He becomes part of the conscienceless corporation once again.

"Does the corporation feel guilt for destroying the environment? How about poisoning baby's milk? Assassinating union leaders? Stealing pensions? Corrupting the political process? Scuttling economies? Overthrowing democracies? Bankrolling juntas? Of course not. The corporation is a corpse, not a human. It has no human emotions. It is incapable of remorse or guilt or compassion.

"But what about the corporate man at his desk, signing off orders, preparing reports, updating spreadsheets? Does he feel guilt? Does he feel responsibility?

"Of course not. He isn't at fault. He's just one small mindless part of the soulless corporation. His job is to do his job or lose his job. It is not his job to feel. His conscience is clear. The corporation has removed it, along with the rest of his humanity."

"But what does this have to do with the helicopters, the emergency—" started Petal.

"It's obvious, Petal," he said. "The corporations hate you. They fear you. You oppose them. You expose them."

"Me?" she asked. "But, really, I haven't—"

"Of course you have, and bless you for it," he insisted. "Because of you, the zombified worker at her desk is fighting her way back to consciousness. Your image in the sky opens her eyes to the blood on her hands. It makes her see that when she looks up the chain of command, to the very pinnacle of her corporation, there are only people like herself there, zombified and stripped of their personhood, mindlessly serving something that has no physical existence at all—the evil assertion that nothing matters except profit.

"And when she passes others in the hall, she can see that they have seen it, too, even if they are afraid to admit it where they might be overheard. And in their meetings they may give each other knowing looks while they subtly subvert the most egregious of their corporation's atrocities. And after work, they join CTA projects or take to the streets or go to a Chill knowing that they have found a bigger purpose in life than feeding profit to an invisible zombie who will ultimately consume them all."

"But Harvey," said Ali. "Look at all these high-tech companies working on energy and environmental projects for Chill the Anthropocene. They've got to be making a profit. They're not evil, are they?"

"Of course not," said Harvey. "Those are admirable companies."

"So how do you tell the difference?"

"Can you tell the difference between art and pornography?"

"Sure. Easy."

"Same way," said Harvey.

"So shutting down the city was a corporate thing, not a government thing?" asked Petal.

"Governments, corporations—these distinctions are just for show, you know that. Governments exist primarily to funnel public money into corporate hands and secondarily to funnel corporate debt into public hands. When it comes to displays of physical force, the corporations like to use their own guys for small jobs like disappearing labor organizers and to contract out the big jobs like wars and police actions to their government partners.

"Look, your government has a legitimate beef with you guys for stealing their nukes and getting the world to outbid them on eBay. Can you blame them? The corporations have a legitimate gripe about you guys subverting their workforce and seducing their customers. And remember, the corporations don't belong to any country—they are just as entangled with one government as another. Therefore, our government is just as pissed at you as yours is.

"I hate to say it, but you guys better get used to it—everybody in the world may love you, but you've got nowhere on Earth to go."

CHAPTER 64

TUNNEL

"Wish us luck," said Isaac, as he plunged his key into a door that, with luck, should lead them directly into Tokyo Station.

"Good luck to us!" everyone cooperated, even though none of them actually believed that the complex flow of human history might pivot on whether one wished good fortune upon one's self or not. In fact, at least one of them was suspicious that auto-induction of fortuity might actually constitute a violation of some basic law of nature, resulting in a penalty somewhere in between the mandatory sentences imposed for stepping on a crack and breaking a mirror.

He turned key with a satisfying clunk and leaned his shoulder into the door. Push as he might, though, it wouldn't budge.

"Let me have a try at that," said Buck, never having met a door he couldn't unstick. After a few embarrassingly futile lunges, he tried fiddling with the key again. No luck.

"Maybe if we all push," said Harvey.

"I could give it a karate kick," volunteered Ali.

"A running start might do it," offered Buck

"I feel lucky today," said Petal, pushing them aside and stepping up to the door as if it were Excalibur in the stone. "Sometimes intractable problems like this yield to a more feminine touch."

Carefully positioning herself with knees slightly bent and shoulders back, she took a deep breath, grasped the knob with both hands, and pulled the door wide open, smooth as butter, to reveal a young couple in the middle of taking a shower.

Everybody screamed, of course, as is customary on occasions of accidental shower interruption, but, because it was Japan, the couple skipped the part where they fall all over each other scrambling for towels to cover their nudity. Instead, with the authority that comes from being obviously in the right (even if obviously nude) they inquired, in formal Japanese, just what the hell all these people were doing in their bathroom.

This was a good question, especially from their point of view. The corollary question—just what the hell their bathroom was doing in an abandoned Tokyo subway maintenance tunnel—was also a good one, even if it could not be asked with quite as much righteous indignation as the first.

As for Isaac and Harvey, this was evidently not the first time in their careers that they had found themselves in places that nobody but they thought they had any business being, because without missing a beat they both had produced their press credentials—overly official-looking laminated placards packed with shields, seals, calligraphy, and holographic images of themselves, the Prime Minister, the Emperor, and his dog. Luckily, this time their media mojo was working, and within minutes a potentially explosive bathroom situation was transformed into a quite congenial, if impromptu, tea ceremony.

Toshiko Watanabe and his lovely wife Yuki actually turned out to be quite appreciative of the opportunity to entertain guests in their home. They had both grown up in neighborhoods where friends who just happened to be passing by would drop in for a chat, neighbors would knock on each other's doors on the flimsiest of pretexts, and folks would sit out on the front steps with a beer whenever the evening was fine. But ever since they had moved to their new place in the tunnels, all that had changed.

When you live in the tunnels, nobody is ever just walking by—present company excepted, of course. Maybe you have a neighbor, maybe not. You'd never know. And as for inviting people over, well, even though living in the tunnels is nothing to be ashamed of, it can get kind of embarrassing when guests suddenly succumb to acute claustrophobia and have to be rushed to the surface. Apparently, even people who are quite skillful at suspending their fear of being buried alive during rush hour commutes can get unexpectedly wiggy during an entire dinner without windows. People who live on a fault line get nervous without a visible exit strategy. After a while, you just quit having company.

This is just temporary, of course, until tunnel living gets more popular. Pretty soon it will be positively stylish, and friends will be

426

coming by all the time just to hang in the digs of the real fashion leaders underground. It's just a matter of time.

For one, tunnel living makes perfect ecological sense. Why clog up open urban space with a bunch of residential buildings? By all rights, everything above ground should be part of the public sphere. And it's healthier, too, with the natural protection from cosmic rays and neutrino storms you get from fifty feet of bedrock over your head. And that's not even counting the complete control of atmospheric purity you have when you don't have to worry about a bunch of polluted air sneaking in through the cracks all the time.

Then there's the security. Nobody climbing in the windows and taking your stuff, that's for sure. Plus the quiet. Here you are in the middle of the city and are you listening to a domestic spat every evening at eleven, a bachelor party every night at two, a garbage truck every morning at four, or one siren or another every ten minutes? No. You're listening to a pin drop every night in your dreams.

Of course, the biggest attraction of tunnel living is economic. First of all, think of all the money you won't spend painting the outside of your house, tunnels, by their topological nature, not actually having any outside to paint. And the insulation—unsurpassed, summer and winter. Property taxes—well, you can't get lower than zero, can you?

Okay, we admit that property taxes are totally unpredictable and for no good reason might jump from something reasonable to a high multiple of one's entire life earnings overnight. But then you could say that about property values themselves, couldn't you? Which, I guess, is the only reason why anybody would be stuck down in a miserable hole like this in the first place.

Let's be honest about this real estate thing, shall we? How did it come to this? If you think way back, you'll remember that once upon a time people could afford to buy a place. Not right away, of course, but if both of you worked, plus maybe a little extra on the side, and saved up, and got some help from the parents, you could get a little studio walk-up in a not-too-dangerous part of town. Then, as your equity grew and your career advanced, you would trade up to a roomier flat in a tonier neighborhood, and before you were too old to enjoy it, a house of your own.

A real home of your own. A place of sanctuary for your family. A protected refuge of constancy and safety within a threatening and erratic world of change. Your own piece of the planet—not a big piece, but your piece and you owned it.

But somehow something happened to this setup without anybody asking anybody if it was okay. At first it seemed like nothing too out of the ordinary—prices go up a little faster than inflation—hey, that's supply and demand—what are you going to do about that? And you've got your little piece of it which is going up, too—can it be all bad?

But then, as if emboldened by the discovery of how easy that was, prices took a little bigger jump, and, getting away with that, another and then another. Soon the numbers were clicking as fast as the pump filling up your SUV. It became a thing of wonder, like a comet or aurora, awesome but benign and even a source of pride, in a way, as the market heaped riches upon the smallest apartment owner on up.

The conventions of polite conversation expanded to include mandatory observations about housing prices in addition to the weather, accompanied by low whistles and politically neutral superlatives. Words like "unbelievable" and "incredible" became divorced from their literal (but, ironically, more apt) definitions, turning into expressions of amazed approval for this most remarkable of natural phenomena.

That is, of course, unless you happened to be somebody who needed a place to live. Someone who found themselves working at a job that paid for work done rather than for position held. Someone who could add. Someone who, because of some quirk of personality, was uncomfortable with an outgo an order of magnitude greater than income.

Upon these people it finally dawned that, invisible or not, somebody had to have a hand in this, and that hand was already way up their dress. It was one thing to be buffeted by earthquakes and tidal waves (though even those could have been prepared for better) but it was entirely another thing to be jerked around by an arbitrary, intensely scrutinized, and highly regulated human artifice such as finance.

And soon thereafter even the once ebullient homeowners became aware that what they had thought was their family's legacy was now just a chip in someone else's high stakes bluff, a pawn to be sacrificed in a grand global gambit, a joke that after the shards of bursted bubble finally settled would end up being entirely on them.

But by that time it was too late. The sirens were already going off, the blue lights spinning. Doors lovingly painted pierced by nails bearing notices. Furniture carefully polished streaked by rain in the street. Futures guaranteed now futures revoked. Good faith with a smirking face. Social contracts for suckers only. Every man for himself. Women and children last.

But wait! What is that? Off in the distance, a glimmer of hope, galloping towards us at breakneck speed. Will we be rescued in time? What will it take for them to pull us out of this quicksand? How can we possibly repay these valiant rescuers? Whatever it takes— now is a time for bold action, not the time for timid quibbling. Things couldn't be worse, right?

Fear not, drowning middle class schmuck, the pin-striped knights had said. We will save you from this crisis of liquidity which has caused you to wet your pants. We will save you from this crisis of confidence that bankers no longer have in one another. We will save you from prices too high and prices too low and all that wealth that seems to have left your accounts and be hiding somewhere until we call ollie ollie income free.

You see, all that has to be done is for this paper to have this signature—yes, right there. And this bill a certain number of votes—oh, that's quite enough, thank you. And that tiny clause in that oppressive regulation—we've drawn a red line through it for you—that's better. And this one. And that one. Ahh! See how smoothly it's running again. See how much confidence we have now. Sure it was a lot of money, but after all it was only taxpayer's money. What were they going to do with it anyway? Pay teachers? Welfare mothers? How much money do they need anyway? Nothing compared to what we bankers need to restore our confidence.

Did I hear grumbling there in the back? You didn't get what you wanted? Aren't property values pumped back up to where no one can afford them? Wasn't that the greatest good for society? Wasn't that the best use you could have made of your next generation's GNP?

And besides, you can always go live in the tunnels, now, can't you?

CHAPTER 65

STATION

"You sure this doesn't lead to somebody's bathroom?" asked Isaac, his hand on the knob.

Toshiko assured him that the map they had followed was the most highly rated bootleg underground blueprint on the internet, and it obviously indicated that the door they were about to open led straight into Tokyo Station, guaranteed. What it didn't indicate, worryingly, was the only door they actually knew existed—the one in the back of Toshiko's shower stall. But, while perhaps morally equivalent, sins of omission are always easier to forgive than sins of commission, and they all agreed that even the lowest internet blueprint bootlegger deserved the benefit of the doubt once in a while. So, confident or not, they were going with this map, this door, right now.

Now was time to make their move. Behind the ramen stand on Platform Sixteen would be a staircase that would take them to the roof of Tokyo Station. The spotlights would be on by now. Rush hour would be reaching its peak. The city would be watching. The world would be watching. Siverth would be watching. All they had to do was get on TV.

They had spent the afternoon monitoring the situation on the Watanabes' television. Astoundingly, the talking heads had barely mentioned the state of emergency, making oblique references to 'commuter delays' as if a water main had sprung a leak. If a Godzilla-sized Petal had taken on a flotilla of attack helicopters in Tokyo Harbor, it had somehow escaped notice of the television news establishment. History, just hours old, was already being rewritten.

"What gives, Isaac?" Ali had protested. "You guys call yourselves newsmen? Where's all that great footage we saw earlier? The choppers. The Petal monster. The cowering populace. All of it cut out! And I thought you had a free press here. This is worse than in Yomamah!"

"It is free, usually," said Isaac. "Sure, I've seen pressure put on editorial comment before, but never overt censorship like this. Petal must have totally freaked the godfather CEO/politicos into playing the national security card. I always say you can tell who's in power by who decides what's an emergency.

"I'll bet there are men in black in the newsroom right now, monitoring every monitor, protecting the country from Cult of Petal aggression. The state of emergency may have been called off in the streets, but as of now it's got the media locked down tight."

"But we're counting on TV coverage of the stunt we are about to pull right now," said Petal. "If we don't get air time then Siverth won't know we are here and we're back to square one."

"Nobody can cover this up, Petal," said Buck. "Thousands of people will see you and immediately tell everyone they know. This is going to be news. You here in person. Not a projected hologram. The real you."

"I've got a cameraman out in front waiting to broadcast live, Petal," said Isaac. "They showed you this morning live. They'll get it through."

"If they won't show a four hundred foot Petal swatting helicopters at a Presidential photo op, why would they show a five foot ten one with her hand out at the railroad station?" asked Petal. "And come on, Isaac, we both know that remote feeds have a built in delay so they can bleep out unscripted nipples and doo-doo words. The men in black weren't paying attention this morning, but you can bet they are now. This is looking bad."

"Let's stick with our plan," said Isaac. "I've got faith in my people."

"We've come this far," agreed Buck.

"Worst that can happen is that we get arrested," said Ali. "Or assassinated."

"Censor it, Ali," said Harvey. "Or I'll get the cameraman to shoot your bad side."

So they had watched Captain Kim get his share of face time, praising the Japanese people for their advanced state of agrarian (at least in fashion) consciousness and their generous (if unoffered) stewardship of the world's agricultural future. Leaders of the majority party, the minority party, and all twelve lunatic fringe parties took turns taking credit for the whole wholesome spectacle. Baseball scores were then tallied. The weather was revealed. Consumer products were extolled. It was time.

Buck, Petal, Ali, and Harvey now were crowded behind Isaac in the tunnel leading to Tokyo Station. Toshiko had retreated to safety back in the darkness. On Isaac's count the operation would begin. It was now or never.

One, two, three!

They leaned on the door as one, half-expecting it to be stuck. Instead, it swung easily away, tumbling them through the doorway onto a tile floor right in back of twenty men standing at a urinal.

"Take your time," said Buck.

"Passing through," said Ali.

"Press corps," said Harvey.

"Platform 16?" asked Petal.

"Let me see that map," said Isaac.

This being Japan, they skipped the part where everybody screams about there being a person of one sexual orientation in the same room with people of another sexual orientation who are doing something as unrelated to sexuality as taking a leak. Instead everybody shrugged it off as not nearly as great an indignity as standing twenty to a urinal in the first place.

Turns out this men's room belonged to Subway Platform 116, which was about as far from Subway Platform 16 as you could get without having to take a subway to get there. Not that they minded the idea of walking, in fact they found it positively recreational to be ambulating in an environment where you could actually see where you were going. What they minded was not being able to walk at all—not with all these people jammed in here. Shut down the trains for two hours and you can pretty much count on there being an extra two hours' worth of commuters packed into the terminal, a terminal that was jam packed in the best of times.

"Now what?" asked Petal, looking out over the sea of cheek to jowl humanity.

"I guess we'll just have to wait our turn," said Buck.

"Wait our turn?" said Ali. "We don't have a turn, Buck. Nobody has a turn here. This is every man for him or herself. Honestly, sometimes I wonder why you haven't starved to death by now."

"And just what are you suggesting, Ali? Brute strength?" asked Petal.

"I practically have a black belt in karate, you know," he answered.

"Ali, how would kicking some poor commuter make any more room in here?" she asked. "Honestly, sometimes I wonder why you haven't been deposed or something by now."

"Nobody kick anybody," said Isaac searching furiously through his coat pockets. "Here it is. Okay, everybody line up behind me again. Harvey, you ready?"

"Yeah, boss. Got mine. On your count."

"Okay. Three!"

Isaac and Harvey began blowing on whistles and waving one of their laminated placards, this one clearly possessing more mojo than any trumped-up press credential. Immediately, everyone in the crowd stopped talking and sat on the ground, identification cards in hand.

"This trick could come in handy in New York," observed Petal, picking her way gingerly across the platform.

"New Yorkers would just whistle back at you," said Buck. "If you were lucky."

"Hey Harvey, just who are we pretending to be?" asked Ali, knowing that whoever it was must have a lot more clout than your average Middle Eastern potentate.

"Don't ask," said Harvey. "It's too embarrassing."

The crowd was back on their feet seconds after the five of them had passed, acting like nothing remarkable had transpired. Nobody pulled any alarms or showed the slightest resentment. The charade had worked like a charm and had been well worth whatever embarrassment they ought to have felt but didn't.

Pedestrian traffic was moving pretty fast through the main corridor now, so the team stowed its whistles and placards and returned to looking anonymous. Good thing, too, because the place had suddenly gotten thick with police who might not be so impressed with impersonations of nameless embarrassing entities.

Pretty soon the corridor fed everyone onto a mechanical sidewalk. The Japanese, masters at moving massive clumps of people from here to there with speed and efficiency, are also masters at mass marketing. This was the perfect opportunity to do both, so the captive pedestrians were treated to TV news projected

434

onto the walls of the corridor. To prevent neck strain and motion sickness, the images traveled along the wall at the same rate as the horizontal escalator. Commuters could either look at TV or look at the guy's head in front of them. Reading a book was out—it was too crowded for that.

The *Waba Ti Li-Fred October* seed ceremony was being replayed *ad nauseam*, interrupted by thirty second animated spots of cute, unrecognizable, primary-colored animals selling cute, unrecognizable, primary-colored products. Petal was becoming mesmerized by the repetitive loop of Captain Kim talking Japanese-dubbed Korean and cute animals talking Japanese-dubbed cute animal over and over as the endless corridor flowed sleepily by them.

"Buck!" she cried, perking out of her stupor. "Look at that!"

"I'm trying not to look," said Buck. "I've seen it a dozen times and I still can't tell what they're selling. It does kind of make you want one, though, whatever it is."

"Not the ad," she said. "The news clip. Watch over Captain Kim's shoulder when they shove the mike at him. Wait now, here it comes. There! See it? Just three or four frames worth but enough to register. I'm sure it had been blanked out entirely earlier this afternoon."

"No doubt about it," said Buck. "That was you all right."

"Hot dog!" said Isaac. "I knew some treasonous newsperson would get around to threatening national security sooner or later. What'd I tell you?"

"Makes you proud," said Ali. "I wish the press in Yomamah would defy me like that sometimes. Show a little gumption."

"Maybe it would help if you updated your sentencing guidelines," said Petal. "As I recall, the last time you did that was in the Iron Age, right?"

"When men were men," said Ali. "World's been going downhill ever since."

"There it is again!" said Harvey, pointing at the moving TV image. "Six frames this time. Somebody on the inside is giving us the signal. We better get this thing done before the Smokeys pick this up and black out the whole station. Come; make your way over to the left. Platform 16 is right at the end of the conveyor."

There was no ramen stand on Platform 16 but there was a Colonel Sanders-san Kentucky Fried Rice trolley in its stead. By that time, no one was in the mood to quibble about bootleg maps or bad directions or the impermanency of landmark fast food establishments. There was a door behind the greasy chopstick and that was good enough for them.

This was a staircase, all right, and well lit if unmarked. The team powered up it, flight after flight, without another person in sight. Panting, they paused at the final landing, the low ceiling sloping toward a metal door, this one finally labeled.

"Roof access," read Isaac out loud. "Emergency Only. Alarm Will Sound."

"Does our plan have alarms sounding?" asked Ali.

"Our plan has all Hell breaking loose," answered Petal, unselfconsciously stripping down to her Speedo. "Wish us luck."

"Good luck to us," they answered, meaning it this time.

"And give 'em Hell," said Buck, sweeping her into his arms in one smooth and impulsive gesture. Someday they would find a private place to kiss.

"Be right back," she said, when finally released. "Don't go anywhere."

"Sure you don't want company?" he asked.

"Ruin the effect."

"Okay, on three."

"Three!"

A blast of frigid air swept through the open door. All was empty space beyond it except for a narrow catwalk with a way-shorter-than-code railing. Spotlights reached up from below, washing out the city in the distance. She stepped forward into the wind.

Petal stood tall, as she had done on the ice. She held out her hands as Siverth had directed. She imagined the faces of the people who were counting on her. She looked at their mental images with encouragement and solidarity.

The sirens began immediately, first from within the building and then from every direction below. And then there was shouting—one or two voices at first and then groups of voices and then the voice of a stadium when the home team wins the big one.

And then there was that other sound, the one from this morning. Helicopters. A dozen of them, closing in, their searchlights panning the building for a moment before they all locked on Petal.

And then the gunfire.
And then she was down.

CHAPTER 66

POLICE

It's tough to beat the speed of sound—unless you are a bullet. That never kept Buck from trying, though, and he was hurtling through the air himself by the time the second unmistakable muzzle flash had erupted from the gunships' turrets. Calculating in mid leap that the politeness of taking a bullet for Petal might be totally negated by the rudeness of squashing her flat, Buck managed to roll ninety degrees at the last moment and land on his side next to her. Momentum thus dissipated, he gingerly threw his bulk over her at the apex of his first bounce.

Shards of concrete and brick rained around them as projectiles strafed the spot where she had just stood. The low ironwork railing deflected a few but could not be trusted to stand up to many more. For now, though, hiding in its shadow was better than squinting into the searchlights, and both of them hugged the ground as well as each other.

"Petal! Petal! Where are you hit?" shouted Buck above the din of gunfire, engines, sirens, and bullhorns.

"I'm not hit, are you hit?"

"I'm not hit. I thought you were hit. You went down."

"I do that whenever people shoot at me. It's kind of embarrassing, really. Happens sometime when I laugh too hard or see blood. Especially my own."

"Cataplexy," said Buck. "Nothing to be ashamed of—just a little inherited autonomic hypersensitivity. No doubt an evolutionary advantage in prehistoric times."

"Prehistoric?"

"Now, too, I guess."

"Let's leave, Buck. It hurts my feelings when people try to kill me."

"Ali!" shouted Buck to the team inside the door. "Take off your tunic and throw it over the side. No arguing. Ready? You ready, Petal? Wait till I say go, okay? Ali? On my count. One. Two. Throw!"

Ali's garment flew out the doorway and off into space, tumbling like a person falling from the catwalk. The searchlights locked on the shape as it dropped into the darkness and gunfire exploded anew from all directions.

"Go!" commanded Buck, launching both of them back through the doorway in one superhuman lunge. Someone slammed the door, which immediately rang with the impact of machinegun fire.

"You're not hit!" cried Harvey, helping her up. "Can you walk?"

"I'm okay," she said. "Tweaked my ankle a little."

"Follow me!" ordered Isaac. "Quickly!"

"Roger that," she said, powering down the stairs two at a time like a man. Buck and Ali were close behind carrying her clothes. Even she didn't want to take the time to get dressed. There was bound to be a place to hide for a minute on one of the floors below.

Three landings down and still no exit from the stairway.

Fourth landing—nothing.

Fifth landing—Police! Sidearm drawn.

Everyone froze—speechless at first.

"Press Corps! Press Corps!" Isaac and Harvey called out. The policewoman ignored them, transfixed by the image of Petal before her.

"You are—you are—you are—" she said, wavering her gun in the general direction Petal's navel.

"Petal Steele," she answered.

"You are—you are—She?"

"Yeah, I guess I'm her, alright," admitted Petal.

"You are—hurt?" the officer asked, her English slurred with adrenalin.

"Skinned my knees," Petal said, brushing off her abrasions. "Twisted an ankle. Nothing really. Thanks for asking. You okay?"

The policewoman was definitely not looking all that okay. Her skin had turned from flushed to pale to cyanotic. Her balance had gotten iffy and her breathing ragged. Sweat dripped from her nose. She lowered her gun and wiped her face with her sleeve.

"Law says arresting officer be responsible for prisoner safety," she said slowly. "To me, you are suffering trauma and shock and cold. Therefore, I order you immediately official protective covering." She holstered her gun and steadied herself against the wall with a hand.

"It is kind of chilly in this Speedo," she admitted, rubbing her arms. "I've got some clothes here somewhere, though."

"Not official," she said. "Law says official covering."

With that the officer dropped her utility belt to the ground and began unbuttoning her uniform. Hanging each layer carefully on Harvey's outstretched arm, she peeled down to a Speedo the exact color of Petal's.

"These are official protective coverings," she said. "You must put on now."

Petal quickly dressed in the officer's uniform, right down to utility belt. Buck handed Petal's outfit to the cop, who nodded in appreciation and zipped herself in.

"Regulations say gun must stay in holster always except for emergency," said the officer, who had perked up remarkably once in Petal's dress. "Do not take out."

"Yes, officer," said Petal, stuffing stray hairs inside her cap. "I never touch guns. You never know where they've been."

"Also, prisoners must not speak," she warned. "Law says."

Petal nodded. An orderly society depends on respect for law.

"Now we go," said the now expensively but inconspicuously dressed police officer. "Follow closely and do not speak."

They tiptoed down another couple of flights, stopping at her signal. Here was a door leading into a passageway for ducts and pipes. There was only room enough to enter single file, and the officer led the way. A few yards in, she stopped to peer through a grating in the wall. The rest of them crowded around to look, too.

Their vantage point was about twenty feet above the floor of a vast open area, the junction of a half dozen major corridors routing pedestrians to and from train platforms. People were hurrying as fast as they could, some running, everyone in a state of alarm as rumors of the violence outside spread through the crowd.

Suddenly, all movement stopped. The commuters were frozen in place, watching the first news clips come up on the ubiquitous television screens. There She was, standing peacefully on the ledge, softly lit from below, with the majestic building and the night sky behind her. She reached out with her hands and looked directly into the camera with the Look—the Look that by now had found its way into the heart of every man, woman, and child on Earth.

And then there were the helicopter's darting searchlights, panning and then homing in on Petal's brave but horrified face. And then the gunfire. And then She was gone.

The crowd screamed as one, with the shriek of a huge, wounded animal. Destinations and deadlines were now irrelevant. People stood immobilized by shock and disbelief. Some crumpled to the ground holding their faces.

A man in uniform appeared on the screens. He was obviously giving orders, not reporting news. The crowd fell silent.

"Homeland Security," explained Isaac. "Reminding everyone of their legal duty to cooperate with authorities in the apprehension of foreign provocateurs who threaten the public order, blah, blah, blah."

The crowd then burst into applause, cheering. Those on the ground jumped up and hugged strangers next to them.

"He says that a notorious foreign agent had attempted to evade arrest by faking her own death, but is believed to be alive and at large," translated Isaac.

At that point the screens jumped to video feeds of SWAT teams in urban camo storming Tokyo Station. The crowd became agitated again, clumping into small groups, calling out to one another. Then the impossible happened.

"What are they doing down there," asked Petal, her nose pressed to the grate.

"I don't believe it," said Ali.

"It's like they have rehearsed this," said Buck.

"This sort of thing doesn't go on in Japan," insisted Isaac.

"Well, we're looking at it," said Petal.

"And I'm here without my camera," said Harvey.

Below them the transformation was nearly complete. Every woman in the station had stripped down to her Speedo. Short and tall, fat and thin, dark and fair—all of them stood proud in their regal nylon vestment. Street clothes had been neatly folded into shopping bags and handed to men for safe keeping. All eyes were now on the passageway that led from the street. No one moved.

Then there they were, the SWAT teams with their automatic weapons, rushing into from the far end of the huge room and then stopping—stopping and staring and not knowing what to do. Soon their leaders were on their phones trying to convince central command that they weren't hallucinating.

"All of the station is like this now," said the policewoman. "This is our time to go."

She led them quickly down the stairs, pausing briefly at door behind Colonel Sanders-san.

"Hold tight my arm here," the policewoman instructed Petal. "Walk fast. Look only ahead. I will guide. You others, hold up press identification. Stay close."

The entourage strode boldly into the cavernous hall. The space was eerily silent. It felt like they were in some future re-enactment of today's momentous event. Hundreds of people, standing motionless, half of them practically nude in their Speedos, the other half holding shopping bags and pretending not to notice. And on all sides SWAT teams nervously awaiting instruction.

Petal followed the policewoman's lead like a ballroom dancer, making her way through the crowd with an air of official determination. Soon it became clear that their destination was another maintenance door on the far side of the concourse. As long as the stalemate continued, their path would not need to cross a SWAT team barricade. They might just make it after all.

But then came the crackling boom of military bullhorns. Petal cringed but only allowed herself a sideways glance. The soldiers were in motion now, churning at the periphery of the crowd. The commuters there were apparently cooperating, but ever so slowly, provoking impatient nightstick pokes. There was no other resistance, no arguing. Every civilian remained totally silent throughout.

The barricades had reformed as gauntlets, two lines of soldiers between which each civilian was being herded one at a time for inspection and interrogation. This process looked like it could go on for hours before it was Petal's turn, and their destination was only a few minutes away. So far, so good.

But just when she allowed herself a breath of relief, she caught sight of streams of soldiers, dispatched in pairs, penetrating the crowd in precisely spaced rays. The commuters did their best to produce friction without violence, but the squads cut through the crowd like shuriken through tofu. Petal picked up their pace, risking appearance of desperation, but so did the SWAT team that was also bee lining their way to the same maintenance door. There was no way to get there first without running, and running was far from an option for anybody.

Petal stared straight ahead but could see the two soldiers rushing toward her, automatic weapons held over their heads. They were barking orders in Japanese, ever louder, ever angrier at being ignored. The door was almost in reach now, but they were not going to make it in time. She would not stop, though. She would not give in this time.

Her hand was on the knob. It turned easily. There was the sound of scuffling and shouting around her. She felt herself being pushed from behind. Looking back, she caught a glimpse of Harvey and Isaac waving press placards in the soldiers' faces.

"Run!" hissed the policewoman, slamming the door behind Buck and Ali. They were in another maintenance tunnel, this one straight and brightly lit. Petal found herself in a flat out sprint before she had a chance to question leaving Harvey and Isaac behind, and once it did come to mind she rationalized their desertion quickly. If anyone would come out on top it would be that pair of newsmen. They might just pull down a Pulitzer for it.

The tunnel ended at a loading dock for trucks, now deserted at this late hour. Astonishingly, there was no SWAT team barricade, just a single police cruiser sitting empty on the asphalt. Petal slowed to let the policewoman pass and then followed her to the patrol car.

"Key is electronic, on your belt," said the officer. "You must drive. Others in back seat." She held the door for Petal as Buck and Ali climbed in.

"Safe journey," she said through the window.

"You aren't coming with us?" asked Petal.

The officer said nothing, but backed away into the shadows, quickly becoming invisible.

The car leapt forward with a tap on the accelerator and screeched to a stop with a touch of the brakes.

"You okay with this car?" asked Buck.

"A bit friskier than my Priup," admitted Petal, now speeding down the truck access road. "Got any tips?" She slowed briefly at a stop sign and pulled into traffic.

"Just one," answered Buck diplomatically. "Unless you are a policeman, they expect you to drive on the left over here."

"Forget that," said Petal. "It's hard enough just dealing with a car that has its steering wheel in the wrong place."

CHAPTER 67

CLUB

"Petal, will you please drive on the right side of the road!" said Ali, his knuckles white from gripping the seat in front of him.

"I am driving on the right side of the road," she said, dodging another truck.

"I mean the correct side! The left side! The sidewalk! The subway! Anywhere there aren't trucks coming straight at us!" Ali covered his eyes.

"I'd be happy to drive, if you like," volunteered Buck. He was used to driving in countries that only had one side of the road to begin with and figured that a place with two or three could only be easier.

"Now how would that look?" she asked, straddling the center line. "Besides, you're supposed to be navigating. Find a way back to the *Waba Ti* so we can get the hell out of this crazy country."

"This is not that easy, Petal," said Buck, squinting out the window. "I can't see anything but neon and kanji. Or is it hiragana?"

"No maps back there?"

"I think one of those screens on your dash is a GPS," said Buck. "But don't look now."

"Don't look ever!" cried Ali, peeking through his fingers.

"Turn left, Petal. I think I saw some sailors going down that street."

Her left turn was perfectly executed if you don't count the news stand. Buck was right—three sailors were doing their best sailor walk down the half of the sidewalk not occupied by the police car.

"Pardon me, sirs," said Petal, leaning out the window. "You guys are sailors, right?"

"Taler du dansk?"

"I don't suppose any of you speak English?"

"Undskyld."

"Farsi?"

"Ét sprog er aldrig nok?"

"Buck, do you speak any languages?"

"Sounds Danish," he said. "All I can remember in Danish is *'Den dame betaler!'"*

"Jeg påskønner, hvad du gør for mig!"

"Vil du danse med mig?"

"Mit luftpudefartøj er fyldt med ål!"

The sailors opened the door and graciously escorted Petal out onto the sidewalk. They lined up at attention, saluted her smartly, and then marched her off down the street, arm in arm.

"Buck?" asked Ali. "How is it that the only Danish phrase you know is 'Take me to Tokyo Harbor'?"

"I never said that's what it meant. All I said was that it was the only one I knew."

"Well, that must be what Petal thought it meant, otherwise why would she be taking off with those three guys?"

"Dazzled by their uniforms?" offered Buck. "Mad at us for making fun of her driving?"

"You hetero's are so neurotic. It must get you into no end of trouble.

By the way, just what did that phrase mean?"

"Hell if I know. All I remember is that everyone cheers when they hear *'Den dame betaler!'* Probably something patriotic."

"What do you mean by 'everyone'?"

"Everyone in the bar."

"That's what I figured," said Ali. "We'd better catch up with them before she gets into trouble."

He grabbed the door handle and pushed. Nothing. Buck tried his side. No go.

"I can't believe it!" cried Ali. "We're locked in the back of a police car like a couple of prisoners! Get us out of here, Buck—you know how claustrophobic I am!"

"Ali, Police cars are specifically designed for claustrophobia. I've found even the most primitive ones to be virtually impossible to break out of. For example, there was this time in Karjackistan when seven of us—"

"This is Japan, Buck!" insisted Ali. "All their stuff is made in Japan—you know, plastic junk that breaks even when you don't want it to. You're the muscle guy. Give it a punch!"

Buck gave the windows a few solid kicks just to prove the futility of it.

"That was then, Ali," he said. "This is now. The Japanese don't make plastic junk anymore. They've lost their touch. We're stuck in here until Petal comes back with the key. Don't worry. It won't be long before she realizes we aren't right behind her."

Which would have been true if the three sailors had not been so engaging—each intent on impressing her with every English phrase they knew. Besides, Buck and Ali had to be right behind them—why wouldn't they be?

"Do you frequent this premises frequently?" asked Sailor Number One.

"My first time—you?" she answered.

"Our horoscopic signage is coincidental, no?" observed Sailor Number Two.

"I'm afraid all these signs are Greek to me," said Petal. "You can read them?"

"My hovercraft is full of eels," complained Sailor Number Three.

"Tragic," sympathized Petal. "Maybe we can help. Are we almost at the harbor?"

Of course, in retrospect, it was obvious that she should have checked to make sure that Buck and Ali actually were right behind them, smirking at her lame attempts at conversation, just as they had at her driving, which, under the circumstances really hadn't been all that bad—and certainly not bad enough to deserve blood-curdling screams. It was clear who owed whom an apology here, and who ought to be checking whether who was right behind whom or not.

Without breaking stride the sailors made a sharp turn through a door rimmed in neon kanji. They were well into the establishment's depths by the time Petal's eyes adjusted to the dark.

"*Den dame betaler!*" Sailors number One through Three called out in one voice.

Cheers rang out from every direction and what looked like a significant portion of the Danish Navy emerged from the shadows, slapping shoulders all around. Pretty soon they had all assembled in formation, right hands held high, each holding a small glass of clear liquid.

"*Den dame betaler!*" they saluted in unison, swallowing their drinks in one synchronized gulp. They all looked to her expectantly.

Petal fired hers down and turned the glass over on the back of her hand. Not a trace of a ring. There never was. The crowd cheered again.

"*Den dame betaler!*" came the call. All glasses up. Down. More cheers.

"*Den dame betaler!*" Again. And again. And again.

By this time Petal was getting seriously worried about Buck and Ali and the Danish Navy was getting seriously sloshed. A few more calls of "*Den dame betaler*" and the only ones standing were Petal and the bartender, a big-boned Nordic woman in yellow pigtails.

"Quite a performance, honey," she said in English. "Now what do you do, pick their pockets?"

"I beg your pardon," said Petal. "I'll have you know I am not a crook."

"Well, you're not a policewoman, either. That's obvious. So you'd better make good on this bill or I'm calling the cops. They put up with lots of crazy hookers in lots of crazy outfits, but I guarantee they won't be amused by you in yours."

"Hookers! Bill! These gentlemen were merely escorting me and my friends to Tokyo Harbor when for some inexplicable reason we ended up in here. You must have known that—they said it over and over. '*Den dame betaler!*' 'Take me to the harbor!'"

"That may be 'Take me to the harbor' where you come from, but in Denmark it's 'The lady is buying!'"

"You sure about that?" asked Petal, looking around for Buck's neck to wring.

"Positive."

"I guess that interpretation does possess considerable explanatory power, as Buck would say."

"The cash, Honey?"

"This is actually a borrowed outfit," started Petal, pulling at zippers. "I would be surprised if its owner carried all that much—"

Petal dumped the contents of her pockets onto the bar.

Mace. Gun. Makeup.

"Sorry," said the bartender. "Got to be cash."

Badge. Ticket book. Victoria's Secret receipt.

"Keep digging."

Blackjack. Tazer. Eyelash curler.

"Nope."

Radio. Key to patrol car. Hello Kitty nail file.

"Well, at least you have some collateral," she said, scooping up the key. "For until you work off the tab."

"Work off the tab?" asked Petal, looking around for Buck and Ali. Where were they? "Actually, we're in kind of a hurry here—"

"Good," she said. "I am, too. Nothing I like better than a motivated worker. Come, I'll put you in the lineup. The girls will show you the ropes—if they don't scratch your eyes out first. But you know the drill. I can tell you've been around the block a few times."

"Drill? Block? Ropes?" muttered Petal, wondering what kind of construction job she was getting into. "Maybe I could spare a few minutes to help with your interior design. Choose some swatches? Pin down the colors? Tweak the lighting?"

"Here we are," said the bartender, leading the way into a back room. "You get the last seat. The first seat goes to the highest earner, and don't be trying to sneak ahead if you know what's good for your health. Right girls?"

The score of women seated along the wall snarled briefly in agreement and went back to their gum, magazines, and nails. Petal considered introducing herself, shaking hands with each in turn, but quickly reconsidered and tiptoed over to an empty chair on the end.

Out of the corner of her eye she studied her compatriots. Immediately next to her was a blond Asian woman in an Alice in Wonderland dress, pinafore, and petticoat. Next to her was a red-haired African woman in a nurse's uniform, complete with white seamed stockings and red-crossed cap. There was a petite Kazakh milkmaid, an Amazonian Playboy Bunny, a corn-fed Kansas farm girl, and an Argentinean gaucho in pink spurs. Just when Petal was about to strike up a conversation with Alice on her right, a California drive-in waitress glided into the room on roller skates and plopped into the empty chair on her left.

"How come so slow?" she asked no one in particular. "What happened to all the Danish sailor boys?"

"Some bitch got them drunk, I hear," said a Transylvanian vampire girl.

"Won't be good for anything when they wake up," said a bespectacled Wall Street hedge fund girl.

"I hate it when they throw up and then come in here expecting sympathy. Pitooey!" said a tie-dyed hippie chick.

"And they were so cute," said a fetching Nazi SS trooper in jackboots and jodhpurs.

"Wait till I get my hands on the hussy who pulled that stunt," said an aging English schoolgirl in plaids. "I'll rip her eyelashes off!"

"I'll knock her right off her platforms!" said a deeply décolletaged accounts receivable reconciliation supervisor, swinging her calculator.

"I'll give her G-string a wedgie she'll never forget!" said a dungeon mistress in leather and grommets.

Petal could tell that this was a volatile situation that needed quick defusing before it went critical, hurting a lot of innocent (and relatively innocent) people in the process.

"Ladies," she said. "It's natural to feel anger and, yes, even fear in these times of grave economic crisis—and believe me, those of us down here on this end of the line feel it more deeply than anyone. And when emotions run this high, it is easy to lose sight of who we really are, in our heart of hearts, in our highest selves.

"Look at us. Are we not all women? Do we not have a higher calling, a noble mission, a sacred duty? Isn't it up to us to succor the suffering, to deliver the world from violence, to channel its resources into all that is nurturing? Do you not feel the power in this room—the power of creation, the power of passion, the power of love?

"I ask you, is there a greater concentration of feminine life force anywhere on the planet than in this room? Are we going to just let it slip away, like sand through an hourglass? Or are we going to stand up and seize it—grasp what is rightfully ours—and holding it high like the righteous sword it is, march out of this room to lead the rest of the women of this world—teach them what we above all women know best—the skill to wield this most awesome power. And to wield it in a way that leaves the Earth a better place and the men smiling in their sleep!"

All the women were standing now—erect, proud, ready. Never before had they seen their lives so clearly, their purpose more surely, their futures more certainly.

It was time now. Time to make it all happen. With a look of joyful determination on their faces, they gathered behind Petal and strode out of the room as one.

CHAPTER 68

FORTUNE

"Guys, I'd like you to meet my new friend Hjordis," she said opening the door without the slightest difficulty. So they had been napping all along, eh? You'd think they would have been the tiniest bit worried or at least curious enough to come looking.

The two men awakened with a start, hardly remembering where they were.

"Oh, Hi. Pleased to meet you," said Buck. He had a definite feeling that he and Petal were having some issues, but he couldn't recall if he was supposed to be mad or repentant, indignant or remorseful, conciliatory or assertive. He settled on baffled and optimistic, his default position.

"This really does look like a police car," said Hjordis, sliding in beside Petal. "You've got your shtick down pat, don't you girl?"

"Hjordis is going to show us the way to the harbor," said Petal, easing the cruiser off the sidewalk.

"Least I can do," said Hjordis, her intonation almost as subtle as a nudge and a wink. "After that performance back at the club."

"Club?" prompted Ali. "Performance?"

"Just girl stuff," said Petal. "At the girl's club. Hjordis is the owner."

"Or was," she said. "The girls just bought me out. Great price, too. Plenty enough to set me up in a cozy new, er, girls club back in Copenhagen. Don't get me wrong—I love Japan—but I miss the cold. It just doesn't get cold in Japan any more. Closest you can get to a good chill around here is reading a book in the meat locker. But even that is kind of lame since you don't get the wind. Turn at that next right there, honey, and keep to the left or you'll get us all killed."

Petal was getting the hang of this Tokyo driving. The key was to imagine yourself through the looking glass, as her new friend Alice had suggested. Too bad time was so short—she could have learned a lot more from those women. When all of this was over she would have to drop them a line. Every one of them had a heart of gold. People in the helping professions are always like that. Give you the shirts off their backs.

"That's the exit, honey. Yeah, the one with the little boat on it. What pier's your boat at?"

"Pier One," said Buck, remembering the TV coverage from that morning.

"Pier One is it now? Mighty fancy. Wait till I tell the other girls. They'll be green, they will."

"Hjordis," said Petal, pulling off the road under a sign that pointed to Pier One in a dozen languages. "That might turn out to be kind of embarrassing for a whole lot of people. Maybe we could work a deal to keep this little secret just between you and me."

"Well, I don't—"

"What say I give you this swell police girl fantasy limo, free for nothing? You'll have to get your own police girl costume."

"For sure?"

"Absolutely. As a token of our mutual trust and understanding, of course."

"You bet, Honey. Your secret's safe with me. As far as I know, you and I never met."

"You're a true friend, Hjordis," said Petal, jumping out to join Buck and Ali on the street. "As long as I live, I'll never remember you."

Hjordis took back the key as she slid into the driver's seat.

"Ditto here, whoever you are," she said and, spinning a squealing U turn, sped off into the night.

"This town is full of nice people," said Petal, striding off toward the pier. "Kind of sad to be leaving."

"Leaving?" said Ali. "You two talk like we have somewhere to go. What makes you so sure that the all-seeing eye of Siverth Narup wasn't just getting some no-seeing shuteye while we were pulling that mystical ledge-jumper stunt? And even if he did see it, what makes you so sure that his little brain will draw the connection between the *Tokyo Station Massacre* and the *Waba Ti Li Seed Party*? And if he does, what makes you think he can get some kind of message to us? And if he can, what makes you think he has the slightest idea what we should do that will make the slightest difference to the planetary melt down, let alone reverse global warming and save civilization from certain collapse when the oil runs out in ninety days? Huh? What makes you so sure?"

"Did you hear something, Buck?" asked Petal, trudging on through the dark.

"Sounded like a foghorn," he replied. "Maybe a gooney bird."

"More like goose farts on a muggy day."

"Just noise. Annoying, though."

"Okay, okay," said Ali. "Ignore me. Dismiss all rational discourse. Hide your Poly Esther rose-colored heads in the sand if you want. Just don't come whining to me when the Earth goes down the toilet and you're not ready."

"That's Pollyanna," said Buck. "And it's glasses."

"Whatever."

"You get ready to go down the toilet," said Petal. "Buck and I will be too busy cleaning up after you and your foolish fossil fuel friends."

Fortunately, Petal's uniform got them waved through a couple of security gates without having to resort to their nonexistent Japanese language skills. Finally there it was, the *Waba Ti Li* sitting unlit at the end of the pier. A velvet rope was draped across the gang plank, a souvenir of its fifteen minutes of fame. There were no guards. There was really nothing left to guard. Every porthole they could see was dark save one, way up near the bow.

Petal led them up onto the main deck. The vast expanse was deserted. The only sound was a sleepy lapping of waves. Long moon shadows sliced the ship like a wedding cake, opening sharp crevasses of blackness in its steel gray hull. They picked their way forward, keeping to the light until they were finally inside.

They made their way through empty gangways toward the captain's mess. They paused outside the doorway, listening. Nothing.

Buck pulled open the door. The place was empty except for the inert bodies of Igor and Ivan and Captain Kim Kal Bi sprawled on the deck. There were no signs of violence—except for that done to the eviscerated carcasses of several empty vodka bottles rolling with the swells at their feet.

Petal knelt next to Kal Bi, cradling his head in her hands. The others tended to Ivan and Igor.

"Captain Kim," she whispered softly. "Are you okay?"

His eyes fluttered open, closed briefly and then grew wide.

She watched as behind them the rickety existential scaffolding that separated rationality from superstition, faith from disbelief, and this world from the next—now thoroughly saturated with volatile spirits—was ignited by a spark of recognition. The whites of his eyes were already as red as flame. Smoke from his ears would be next.

"We are dead!" he finally managed in English. The Korean prologue had sounded considerably less upbeat. "We are all dead!"

"How do you feel?" she asked gently.

"Feel? Feel? I feel my head exploding!" he moaned, closing his eyes again and pressing his temples.

"Then you aren't dead, are you?" Petal pointed out. "Being dead doesn't hurt."

"It doesn't?" he asked, sneaking one eye open a little.

"Totally painless," she asserted. "Not particularly pleasant, mind you, but completely anesthetic. That's why hangovers are so reassuring."

"They are?" he asked, propping himself up on one elbow and regarding the mess in the Mess.

"Nothing like a good hangover to reaffirm one's connection to life," she said. "Now get yourself into that chair and I'll get you some water."

"I'm not dead? Then that means you're not dead," said Kal Bi, his synapses getting used to firing again. "But we saw you die. We saw them shoot you. We saw you fall from the roof. It was all on TV. It was horrible."

"That was the improv part of the gig," she said, helping him up. "Tough crowd, too. Even in Vegas they don't throw Gatling fire at you."

"When you died we didn't know what to do. So we got drunk."

"We see this," she said.

"So, what you are trying to say is that you're not dead?" asked Ivan, sitting down at the table. So he does speak English, after all. Or had he just memorized that from a particularly underabridged phrase book?

"Not in so many words," she said, pushing water on them. "But yes, alive to you three—that is, if you can keep a secret. I haven't decided if being alive to everybody in general is all that conducive to my longevity, if you know what I mean."

"Drink to that?" asked Igor, sensing from the conversation's tone that something conspiratorial was going on. Its content, though, remained to him unfathomable.

Kal Bi started looking around for something suitable to throw at him, but because he had to do it without moving his eyes, he soon gave up and nursed his water instead.

"Drink up," she said, filling his water glass. "Any food around here? We haven't eaten since breakfast, and I'm not sure you could call that food either."

"Might be," said Kal Bi, nodding at the mess at the far end of the table. "When you died, we sent out for vodka and they brought some Chinese with it."

"That's kind of weird. Then what happened?"

"We ate it."

"Figures," she said rummaging through a pile of little white cartons. There was a little rice left and, of course, the fortune cookie. Nobody was ever hungry enough to eat the fortune cookie. This time might be a first.

She cracked it open, not quite hungry enough to eat the slip of paper with its inevitably inscrutable but unignorable aphorism.

"2-25-33-N   129-33-05-W," she read out loud. "That's a fortune?"

Buck was on his feet by the final digit.

"Read that again," he said, going to the world map that covered the starboard bulkhead.

"2-25-33-N   129-33-05-W," she read again. "What kind of fortune is that?"

He squinted close at the map, running his finger left and right, then up and down. Finally it settled on a spot in the middle of the Pacific, a spot of blue in thousands of miles of nothing but blue.

"It's our fortune," he said, leaning hard on his digit to keep the *Waba Ti* from wiggling away beneath it.

"Siverth!" she cried, clinging hard to Buck's arm. "The message!"

"We sail on the tide!" exclaimed the Captain, joining them at the map.

"Are you all nuts?" said Ali, turning the slip of paper over in his hand. "This is just some typo or a UPN or some factory worker texting her boyfriend. What's with you people, anyway?"

"We're not dead yet!" called Ivan, standing at attention, glass raised.

"We drink!" called Igor, clicking his heels.

And they did.

CHAPTER 69

THE NUTTING ISLANDS

From Wikipedia, the free encyclopedia.

(Editor's Note: WikArbCom has classified this article as Moderately to Moderately-Severely Unwiki. While suitly emphazi, beta-admin cross-namespace redirects have triggered multiple flamewars, resulting in serious edit-creep and inexcisable link rot. Blue ink spills, disambiguation crashes, and sluggish data dumps have rendered its proseline hopelessly POV. Newbie warning: Level Three. Ed.)

The Nutting Islands, officially **The People's Democratic Kingdom of the Nutting Islands**, is an equatorial Pacific nation located approximately 2º25'33"N, 129º33'05"W. It is comprised of four main islands (The Big Island, The Other Big Island, The Other Big Island Number Two, and Scram—This Is O'ola's Island) and at least fifty other minor islands, atolls, seamounts, rock piles, sand dunes, coral reefs, and other occasionally dry patches in mid ocean.

HISTORY

Original Settlement:

The Nutting Islands are unique among the Pacific islands in that they appear not to have been originally settled by Pacific Islanders.

While study of the Nuttingese historical record is hampered by the lack of a written language, a confabulist oral tradition, and a deep cultural suspicion that history itself is bunk, there nonetheless emerges from it a clear image of an early people who inhabited the Islands long before the next early people got there. These proto-people (the *Nixohunes*) are invariably described as swarthy, resentful individuals of short stature who assume the role of trickster in the usual mythological claptrap manufactured on the spot for visiting anthropologists.

The current ethnic Nuttingese people (due to a deep cultural suspicion that white people with needles are up to no good) have not been genetically profiled using modern DNA mapping techniques. Therefore, their self-professed descendancy from the royal family of Nubian King Teharqa, who escaped via the subcontinent after his defeat by the Assyrians under Esarhaddon in 671 BCE remains less than thoroughly substantiated, if not patently ridiculous. However, it is obvious that they are awfully black, or at least used to be. (See below.)

European Discovery:

While it is speculated that the first European contact was made by the famously lost Spanish explorer Vasco Verammi in 1546 (journal entries considered by some historians as clearly describing The Other Big Island are interpreted by competing historians as clear references to Newark or perhaps Elizabeth City) the official, so-called European "discovery" (*editor's note: WMO Bias Alert: Text requires Wikification of white-male-oppressor POV*) was made by Captain Horatio Nutting of the *HMS Lassitude* in 1785. Blown off course by a freak storm, Captain Nutting apparently mistook the Nutting Islanders (who went by another name back then, of course) for an LLC of Amazonian realtors who had been principle beneficiaries of the collapsed Amazonian Real Estate Bubble of 1784. A stubborn man who never gave up a grudge (especially when it came to his IRA) Nutting proceeded to barge into King O'ola's palatial hut and demand either recompensation or satisfaction. He was promptly eaten.

Picking up the unmistakable scent of Englishman roasting on an open fire, Second-in-Command Nigel Jodhpur-Fly took about a second to command the HMS Lassitude to set immediate sail for ports elsewhere, unfortunately leaving Mrs. Forbearance Nutting fuming on the beach in her best Sunday go-to-meetin' outfit.

Mrs. Nutting, a woman of impenetrable Christian morality and indomitable survival instinct, quickly received from her Creator two divine insights that would prove to be the guarantors of her longevity. The first was the realization that these indigenous innocents could not technically be considered cannibals because they had not actually considered their dinner to have been human. The second was the realization that her life's true purpose was to bring to them civilization, Christianity, literacy, and a little taste of some really strange strange.

Modern History:

Early:

During the period 1784-1984 nothing much happened in the Nutting Islands that hadn't happened in the period 670 BCE-1784. This was largely owing to several unique features of Nuttingian geography:

It's out of your way.
It can be proven by direct observation that: Any line (AB) connecting any place anybody is (A) with any place anybody wants to go (B) will never intersect any of the Nutting Islands (N_{1-n}). Q.E.D.

You can't get there.
The Nutting Islands archipelago sits deep inside the Intertropical Convergence Zone, a fixed area of low atmospheric pressure in which the prevailing winds are zero. Sailors refer to this area as The Doldrums when they are in polite company.

You wouldn't want to, anyway.
Coincidentally, The Nutting group forms the central point of the Subtropical Pacific Gyre, a clockwise vortex of ocean currents maintained by the Earth's Coriolis force, opposing wind patterns at the gyre's boundaries, and the predictable behavior exhibited by excrement on inclined planes. Also referred to as The Great Pacific Garbage Patch, this area becomes the final resting place for every piece of semi-buoyant trash in the ocean. Every hour 17.8 trillion plastic bags are produced worldwide. It takes an average of 4.7 days for 80% of them to make their way to the ocean (the remaining 20% find other, more creative ways to screw up the environment). People who don't like colossal dunes of grime-caked plastic traditionally have not visited Nutting.

And if you did, they would eat you.
But only because you are sub-human. Nutting
Islanders are not cannibalistic.

Middle:

In the summer of 1982, while relaxing at a movie in the White
House screening room, United States President Ronald Reagan
suddenly experienced one of those brilliant flashes of insight
that occur in the minds of great thinkers only once or twice
every generation. Complex and seemingly insoluble dilemmas
concerning America's security, destiny, and corporate profits
had been nagging at him for days, keeping him awake hours at
a time every afternoon. But all at once, at a time when his
consciousness was ostensibly occupied elsewhere (some
speculate it was the scene in which the *Millennium Falcon*
approaches the planet Naboo) a vision appeared to The
President—a fully formed solution to America's intractable
problems and his own tenuous place in history—the Death Ray
From Space.

The Great Communicator had only to articulate this vision to a
grateful and inspired nation for every American of every party,
every creed, and every federal sub-contract to rally around
him in support. This was the American Century, and America
would have its Death Ray From Space.

Sure, it would be expensive—everything really valuable in life
is expensive, isn't it? Would it work? Would it work, you ask?
Was there ever anything that the American people had put
their Yankee ingenuity and strong backs and hard-borrowed
dollars up against that hadn't worked? The answer was
obvious. Within eighteen months, the first satellite had been
launched from Cape Canaveral.

The site of the first test was to be Bikini Atoll. There were two
main reasons for this selection. First, the poor bastards who
lived around there had already had their pants A-bombed off
all through the fifties and might not even notice. And second,
the name had come to The President in a vision (some
speculate it was during the opening scene of *Goldfinger*).

However, in 1984 there was no such thing as Google Earth and
computer chips were still being flaked from flint (the combined
US and USSR nuclear arsenals, for example, were controlled
by as much computing power as can now be found in a

modern Singing Trout Wall Plaque). The Death Ray From Space might have been going for Bikini, but what it got was Nutting.

The Top Secret Commission on Keeping Nutting Secret convened on The Other Big Island January 2, 1984. It took until August 18, 1987 for it to complete the process of hearings, petitions, examinations, interrogatories, depositions, inquisitions, extortions, and obfuscations required to produce its report, all 750,000 pages of it, which was finally placed on The President's desk the evening of December 24th.

Reagan found the Commission's report very disturbing. Just prior to its delivery, he had been deep in thought, contemplating the complex relationships among the various components of a new Munch-O-Matic Food Processor, which, along with the collapse of the Soviet Union, was to be his Christmas gift to Nancy that year. He had long given up on trying to put the thing together, something which had appeared so intuitive when demonstrated on TV, and was struggling to get the pieces back in the box when a UPS guy with a hand truck wheeled in the Commission's report.

By statute, all Commission Reports and other Important Paperworks of State must actually be placed on the President's desk to be considered legally delivered. This law is the basis of a loophole last used by President Abraham Lincoln, who had resorted to a self-induced sneezing fit to clear from his desk a unanimous Resolution of Congress informing the Southern States that if they really wanted to break it off it was okay with them because the relationship wasn't going anywhere anyway, and everybody needed some space to get their heads together before things got way too heavy.

Seven hundred and fifty thousand pages takes up a lot of room, especially when printed on twenty-five pound premium bond and hand bound in tooled Moroccan leather. Getting it all to fit on the desk was a major undertaking, in the process of which the constituent parts of the Munch-O-Matic, some of them razor sharp, were swept off the President's desk, spilling bearings and springs as they bounced around the Oval Office.

The President, in a rare episode of loss of cool, decided then and there that he'd be damned if he would read 750,000 pages worth of aboriginal whining about a little zap from a little Death Ray From Space when any red-blooded American would have been proud to have taken the same and more for his country. Furthermore, he'd be damned if he'd read the damn *Executive Summary*, either. Or the damn *Executive Summary Talking Points*. Or even the damn *Reader's Digest Condensed Cliff's Notes of the Executive Summary*. He didn't even read the goddamn *Bottom Line*. He just signed the damn thing. Signed it and ordered his secretary to get somebody from UPS to pick up the damn report and somebody from DARPA to pick up the damn Munch-O-Matic.

This little Yuletide drama was to have important consequences for the Nuttingese people, for had the Gipper's pen paused for even a moment, his eyes just might have picked up a crucial typographical error right above his signature—a simple transposition of "m" into "b"—just two keys west for an exhausted GS-2 clerk-typist anxious to get home in time to tie a bow on the almost-new crutch she had bought her boy for Christmas.

And so it was that instead of getting Big Number *million* dollars to keep their mouths shut about the whole Death Ray From Space thing—which itself would have been a lot of money for a people whose median annual income was approximately zero—the Nuttingese people became the recipients of Big Number *billion* dollars. But, even though the Government Accountability Office would generally classify an error of this magnitude as a "Big Typo," the distinction was completely lost on the Nuttingese, whose culture forbade anyone but the chief and his cronies from counting anything above three—as well as on the Americans, whose culture forbade anyone but the chief and his cronies from counting anything in the defense budget.

Late:

It is nearly unheard of for the receipt of Big Number million dollars by a small group of poor people not to be followed immediately by receipt of a grand scale, self-induced catastrophe, usually involving the simultaneous celebration of all seven deadly sins plus a couple dozen of slightly less lethal ones. And that's Big Number million dollars. For Big Number billion dollars, a disastrous, ugly, and embarrassing outcome is virtually guaranteed.

But the Nuttingese are an exceptional people, and O'ola was an exceptional leader.

(Editor's Disambiguation: Critical fact omission: Please note: This is not the same O'ola! Nuttingese kings are always named O'ola! Would it have been so hard for the author to have mentioned this at the beginning of the article and saved the reader the trouble of asking himself, "Hey, how can this O'ola character be eating Englishmen in 1784 and ripping off the American Taxpayer in 1987? Do all cannibals live this long? Maybe there is something to the consumption of human flesh, after all. No wonder it's taboo. What if everybody ate everyone else—then maybe everyone would live hundreds of years. But, then, wouldn't the planet get overrun with people, unless maybe the rate of eating people exceeded the rate…etc, etc."?! But no, he had to spew out O'ola after O'ola, sending readers running off in confused circles all over infospace. Pathetic. But I guess this is what you get if you let every idiot on Earth write stuff in your encyclopedia. Ed.) As was every O'ola before him and every O'ola to follow, because by tradition the Nuttingese people had always chosen as their king the most competent person in the nation and renamed him O'ola, which, translated loosely, means "most competent person in the nation." *(Editor's note: Sorry. Please disregard above. Ed.)*

For example, when the Top Secret Commission had convened on The Other Big Island January 2, 1984, it was O'ola that the Nuttingese people depended on to figure out just what the hell was going on. Hour after hour O'ola would sit on his throne saying nothing while pin-striped representatives of the Government of the United States of America would talk about Big Number dollars and then, hearing nothing but silence, would huddle, regroup, and return with Even Bigger Number. On the third day O'ola abruptly rose and walked out of the hut, leaving two of his most ferocious men to guard the door.

The crowd outside knew by the look on O'ola's face that the situation must be very grave indeed. They knew that in times of national crisis O'ola would seek the wisdom of counsel before making his final proclamation. They stood silently as he strode through the village, passing the huts of his advisors— the Promoter of War, the Fabricator of Currency, the Inciter of Spirits, the Witchdoctor General—but not stopping at any of them. The crowd held their collective breath. This must be the most serious emergency of all time. O'ola was going straight to the top. They watched him pause at the last hut in the village. He knocked. The door opened. Mrs. O'ola invited him in.

"America Men say their sky weapon hurt Nutting people. They want give us Big Number money so we don't stay mad," he explained.

"Many Nutting people hurt?" she asked.

"Not, I think," he said. "In fact, none, I think."

"Think more," she said. "No big hurt, no Big Number."

"In that case, what if all Nutting people hurt?" he said. "Then get really Big Number."

"O'ola think good now," she said. "Sky weapon hurt all Nutting people real bad."

"How we hurt? Better be good," he said. "Got to show America men."

"Look at us," she said, holding her arms wide, her uku-fiber pareo falling open. "We hurt bad, can't you see?"

"No," he admitted, admiring the inviting expanse of glistening skin. "You look good."

"Silly, O'ola," she said, "Sky weapon turn Nutting people white! Very bad! Very, very bad!"

"Yes!" cried O'ola, slipping her pareo to the ground. "Before sky weapon, Nutting people black as Nubians. Now look at us! Brown like mud! We so shame! Only big Big Number make us not mad forever. I go tell America Men right now!"

"America Men can wait," she said, slipping his pilau-feather cloak to the ground. "First we try out new skin."

Later:

In the ensuing years, O'ola, with the wise counsel of Mrs. O'ola, worked hard to make sure that Big Number money would not bring the curse of wealth to the Nutting people. Education, hard work, competence, and merit—that's what Big Money would bring. The University of the Nutting Islands grew to encompass the entire Other Big Island Number Two, with dozens of outreach campuses throughout the archipelago.

Modern day Nutting Islanders are now the best-educated people in the world, most having acquired at least one postgraduate degree at or beyond the Ph.D. level. Scientific topics tend to be the most popular, but it is considered *déclassé* to start one's post-doc in magnetic resonance crystallography, for example, before completing one's dissertation in Mesopotamian Cuneiform Syntax. MFA's are a toss off. MBA's are only for laughs.

Scholarly papers now pour out of its labs and libraries on every conceivable subject. There is only one problem. No one outside the Islands is allowed to read them.

This was the crux of the American settlement agreement. At the time, it had seemed like a reasonable stipulation. The Nutting people would get Big Number dollars. They could buy anything they wanted with it, ordered through and delivered by the US Post Office. In exchange, the Nuttingese would stay on their islands as they always had anyway and never talk to anyone from the outside, as they never had anyway. They wouldn't be prisoners, exactly—they just couldn't leave. And since the area is designated an Administrative Hassle Zone, no one from the rest of the world would ever bother to go there. The People's Democratic Kingdom of the Nutting Islands would remain in its own little world forever.

Which, to the credit of the Nuttingese people, has always been just fine with them.

CHAPTER 70

ADRIFT

Bulgogi Class destroyers such as the *Waba Ti Li* are designed for a crew of 250 men, optimally to be composed of 130 officers, 27 cooks, 12 barbers, 15 painters, 7 plumbers, and 50 human resource specialists. The day to day work of running the ship would be done by 19 enlisted men, of which at any time five would be expected to be in the brig for calling in drunk, four in sick bay for repetitive emotion injuries (see below), and seven in analysis for pre-traumatic stress syndrome. Which then would leave one guy per shift to sit in the engine room waiting for the captain to call down the tube "All ahead full!" so that he could push the "All Ahead Full button" and go back to watching Korean soap operas, each of which would be composed of one third wistful longing, one third uncontrollable weeping, and one third hair pulling.

But there was no time now for Korean soap operas on the *Waba Ti Li* (except for Ali, who watched under the covers when he was supposed to be asleep) since there were only six of them left to run the whole ship. There had been quite a few more sailors on the trip from Pyongyang to Tokyo (520 to be exact), but somehow for them "LIB" (Liberty) had stretched into "LOA" (Leave of Absence) which had evolved into "AWOL" (Absent Without Leave) which had escalated into "TBSOS" (To Be Shot On Sight) but with time would eventually mellow into "CRKS" (Celebrity Refugee Keynote Speaker).

So when it was time to weigh anchor, the only crew Captain Kim had left under his command consisted of two quasi-reformed Russian Mafiosi, one semi-repentant Arab potentate, one conscripted journalist/Earth Goddess, and one unjustifiably optimistic disaster guy. It would mean overlapping triple shifts for everyone (work four hours, sleep four hours, work four hours, etc. around the clock) (except for Ali who would work four hours, watch Korean soap operas four hours, sleep four hours, argue about how come he didn't show up for work four hours ago four hours, etc. around the clock) all the way from Tokyo (35°40'20"N, 139°49'48"E) to Wherever They Were Going (2°25'33"N, 129°33'05"W).

Fortunately, Captain Kim had been able to barter the seed bank for a full tank of gas and, at the last minute, a hold full of past-dates miso ramen and recalled Sake Tumi, a heavily caffeinated rice wine and high fructose corn syrup drink popular with teenagers that somehow had become contaminated with Phu Quoc fish sauce back at the factory.

Petal looked up from a huge pot of ramen she was cooking to see Buck coming up from the engine room covered in grease.

"How come you're the only one who comes up from the engine room covered in grease?" she asked. "There's nothing but buttons down there."

"Actually, if you look closely you'll find a couple of engines down there, too," he said, washing at a sink. "One of which has been cannibalized for parts to fix the one that's running, which itself is going to seize up pretty soon unless it gets a major overhaul. I don't read Korean very well, but by the logbook it looks like the last time that engine had any maintenance was before you were born."

"I hope you don't read women's ages very well either," she said. "Do you think it will get us to the number place?" she asked.

"You mean 2°25'33"N, 129°33'05"W?"

"Yeah, that place. You sure it doesn't have an easier name?

"Well, I don't know and I don't know," he said, plucking a noodle from the broth with chopsticks. "When that engine will burn out is anybody's guess, and every map we've got shows nothing but open ocean at 2°25'33"N, 129°33'05"W. No names anywhere."

"You think maybe Siverth has a boat meeting us there?" she asked. They had had this conversation a couple dozen times over the week that had passed since they left Tokyo. She wanted to see how many answers he could come up with. So far he had never repeated himself.

"Or a sub or a dirigible," he answered, "or maybe a new island is forming from a submerged volcano. In that case we could be the ones to name it. How about we call it "2°25'33"N, 129°33'05"W"? Or maybe "2-129" for short? Okay, we'll call it Petal's Island. No?

Well, we can decide when we get there. Which should be in about twenty-six hours, if the engine holds up. Anyway, what's for dinner?"

"Well, tonight we have ramen with Sake Tumi, ketchup, and pepper but this time no salt."

"Masterful," he said, savoring his sample. "Petal, you are a true culinary artist. Every night, a new gustatory adventure—and from such humble ingredients."

"Thanks, Buck. You really think so?"

"Sure I do. And everybody else appreciates it, too. It's not easy cooking for all these guys with nothing but ramen and Sake Tumi, even if it does have fish sauce in it."

"You're just being sweet," she said, turning to face him. According to the timer they had a minute and a half to sneak a kiss before the noodles were done. They had just about maneuvered themselves into the only anatomically feasible position that did not include death by scalding when there was a tremendous explosion followed by what sounded like your can and bottle recycling bin being tossed into a tree chipper. Then there was silence. Then there was smoke.

"Pull the alarm and get on deck!" said Buck. "And put on a lifejacket. I'll see what's going on."

"I'm going with you," she said, draining the noodles. Nothing worse than overcooked ramen. Buck pulled the alarm himself.

They bounded down the stairs to the engine room. The smoke was already dissipating. It was clear that there wasn't a major fire. The boat wasn't listing. In fact, the ship seemed eerily still. Maybe it wouldn't be so bad after all.

They passed through doors Petal had never opened and descended into the innards of the machine compartment. The odor of macerated metal and baked Bakelite hung in the air.

"There's your trouble," announced Buck, crouching next to a pile of rubble that looked like what CERN would get if they collided two Hummers at near-light speeds.

"Can you fix it?" asked Petal, knowing the question was ridiculous but trusting that Buck would take it as a compliment.

"Twelve men, a month, and about fifteen million in parts," he answered. "And the shop manual. Then, maybe."

"What about the good one?"

"This is the good one."

473

"What happened?" cried Captain Kim, running into the engine room, still in his pajamas.

"Da?" Ivan and Igor tumbled in, followed closely by Ali. As usual, nobody had followed emergency protocol. Nobody ever thinks emergency protocol applies to them.

"Main bearings seized, shaft snapped, engines kept spinning until the part still attached had flailed half the room to death. Good thing nobody was in here when it happened," Buck said, referring to himself with a shudder.

"Very unfortunate development," declared Kim, pacing through the debris. "Similar to accident aboard the gunship *Bi Bim Bap* in 1942. Drifted many months before being found. Sadly, all hands lost, but not before turning to cannibalism in the end."

"Disgusting," said Ali.

"Horrible," agreed Petal.

"Dinner?" asked Igor. So he spoke English, too. Or maybe not.

"Might as well," said Buck. "Nothing to do down here."

The men sat around the table after dinner looking at charts while Petal counted crates of ramen and did some back-of-the-envelope calculations. It would be a couple of weeks before she would have to start serving crew members for dinner—or maybe sooner if she ran out of ramen variations.

"We're really not that far from 2°25'33"N, 129°33'05"W," observed Captain Kim.

"How far is not that far?" asked Ali.

"Two hundred nautical miles," he said.

"Well, that's just great. We're only two hundred miles from a wet spot in the ocean that has nothing but water around it for a thousand miles in any direction," he said.

"Think we could rig a sail?" asked Petal. "Ivan and Igor are expert sail sailors."

"We're in the doldrums, Petal," said Buck.

"What's got into you two?" scolded Petal. "A little engine trouble and you throw in the towel? We've been through worse than this. Buck up, guys!"

"He means there's no wind, Petal," said Kim. "There's almost never any wind in the doldrums. Hence the name."

"You know I'd never give up," said Buck, holding her hand.

"Give up?" cried Ali. "Give up what? Give up risking death from cannibalism to drag our butts out to a fortune cookie typo in the middle of the Pacific? So we can save a world that never did anything for us in the first place but throw us into some sadistic survival-of-the-fittest evolutionary snuff drama? Give up? Am I allowed to give up? Nobody told me I could give up! Where do I sign up to give up?"

"I know you would never give up, Buck," she said, gazing into his eyes. "You're not that kind of guy."

"Well, I'm that kind of guy," said Ali, waving his hands trying to get their attention. He hated it when they ignored him. "Give me a white flag any day. In fact, I'm going out on deck right now and giving up to the first person I see."

"We can do it, Petal," said Buck. "Look at how far we have come. Who would have imagined a worldwide network of people dedicating themselves to saving the Earth, all because of you?"

"Mass hysteria is going to save the Earth?" asked Ali, pacing around and jumping up to their eye level. "Epidemic self-delusion? *Folie à deux x 109?* You two need your medication adjusted."

"Oh, Buck, you know I can't take credit for any of this," she said, putting her hands around his neck. "I owe everything to you. Before we met I was just another bubble-headed society columnist who thought that concern for the environment meant having the right interior decorator. Without you I'd still be one of those people who cared what The Publisher thought. Can you believe how silly we once were?"

"Once were?" howled Ali, standing on a chair. "Not like now, rationally planning how to save the planet while we drift forever in the middle of the ocean. I don't suppose either of you post-silly people has put any thought into getting us rescued. I mean, doesn't saving the world start at home, after all?"

"Petal, all the credit is yours," said Buck. "You have inspired millions. You have inspired me. There is no one I respect more than you."

"Okay you two," said Ali, looking desperate. "Time to snap out of it and get to work. Do you hear me? Blink twice if you hear me."

"Buck, do you really mean that?" said Petal, dissolving into his arms. "That's the nicest thing anyone has ever said to me."

"I'm going to count to ten now," said Ali. "And when I reach ten you both will wake up as if from a sound sleep, feeling refreshed and remembering nothing of—"

"There's something else I want to say."

"One, two—"

"What is it, Buck? What is it?"

"Three, four—"

"I love you, Petal."

"Five, six—"

"I love you, Buck."

"Seven, eight—"

"Will you marry me?

"Nine—"

"Yes!"

"Ten! Wake up!"

"Da! We drink!"

"We drink!"

"We drink!"

CHAPTER 71

ATOLL

"Catching anything?" asked Petal, handing him a glass of water. On principle, Buck wouldn't drink Sake Tumi. Actually, on about a dozen principles, not even counting the principal principle that it smelled of rotting fish.

But even a rotting fish would have been a welcome addition to the *Waba Ti's* Prix Fixe, which had been getting progressively more spa-like as time went on. Day after day the crew would take turns at the poles, but for all the fish they caught they might as well have been watching Korean soap operas under the covers with Ali. Buck took Petal's shifts for her—her skin couldn't stand that much sun and her temperament couldn't stand that little excitement. As a consequence, he had grown nearly as dark as a nut and almost as skinny as a rail, and only slightly less mad than a hatter.

Buck was sitting under a makeshift umbrella watching the lines. The sun burned down on them from directly overhead. There wasn't a cloud. There wasn't a breeze. The ocean was like a mirror. A mirror with acne.

"What's all that stuff out there?" she asked, leaning over the rail trying to identify the ocean's pockmarks.

"Plastic," he said. "From all over the world. Even though it doesn't feel like we are moving at all, the current has been sweeping us into some kind of massive graveyard for oceanic trash. Now, initially, you might not find this concept particularly appealing, but it's really quite interesting once you get over your outrage and disgust. Just think of the place as an archaeological site where you don't have to dig. After all, what is archaeology anyway, other than rooting around in other people's trash? Could anything be more disgusting than burrowing through a mountain of rotting garbage? How much nicer is this, where all of the artifacts of history are laid out right in front of you like sushi on a tray?

"Here, take a look at this yellow plastic ducky—it's not only iconically kitsch, it's ecologically famous. In 1992 about a jillion of these critters fell off a container ship on the way from Hong Kong to Tacoma. How deeply the people of Tacoma suffered the loss of their duckies is too tragic to relive, but what happened to the little guys themselves is the most heartwarming of stories. Sit down and I'll tell it to you. And keep an eye on that pole.

"You see, pretty soon thereafter, children all over the world were treated to the sight of yellow plastic bathtub toys arriving at their beaches, at first one at a time, and then by the hundreds, year after year after year. And, of course there were the ducky's friends, little green plastic frog and little red plastic truck. Jillions of them, too. It was like Christmas every day for the children of the world.

"And there were toys for the grownups, too, just to be fair. You had your plastic shopping bag, your plastic six pack holder, your plastic tampon deployment gizmo, and, if you were lucky, your plastic hypodermic syringe. Everybody likes something for nothing, right? All of a sudden, going to the beach was like going to Vegas, except that you always won.

"Looks almost new, doesn't it, even after decades in the ocean. People accuse these duckies of being non-biodegradable, but that's not exactly fair. The sun and the ocean eventually break them into little pieces and grind them into finer and finer bits of plastic sand. After a while, the particles get smaller than the eye can see.

"This is a sad thing, not only because everyone misses the sight of spunky little duckies bobbing on the waves, but as it turns out, little bits of plastic actually get more environmentally toxic the smaller they get.

"For example, ocean animals really couldn't care less if there are billions of plastic Extreme Mega-Concussion Energy Shock soda bottles floating on the surface. Hardly any creature big enough to swallow something that size is stupid enough to want to. So the junk travels the seas for years, soaking up the surface scum of dioxins and other unpronounceable oily toxins like a flotilla of sponges. That sounds like a good thing—sweeping the ocean clean of industrial poisons—right?

"Not so fast. The big floating hunks eventually get pulverized into micro-plastic bits that sink down to where there are micro-critters just dumb enough to eat anything that is slightly more

478

micro than they are. Gobbling plastic dust not only gives these tiny guys a massive stomach ache, it injects tons and tons of poisonous chemicals right into the very origin of the food chain, where they get exponentially more concentrated at every step up the ladder.

"So, by the time you tuck into the Healthy Choice Fresh Caught Wild Ocean Special at your local Michelin's Five Star, you can rest assured that you are treating yourself to the most potent distillate of all the industrial toxic waste the seven seas have to offer. Right there on your plate, self-righteously elbowing out that Unhealthy Choice Coronary Clogging T-Bone you would have rather ordered, squats a fishy sub-lethal dose of PCBs, mercury, organophosphates, and hundreds of other bio-accumulated—"

"So, what you're saying is you're not catching anything," said Petal.

"A little run of bad luck," admitted Buck. "Try jiggling that lure a little. Sometimes a woman's touch is all it needs."

Petal jigged the line most seductively but, astoundingly, there were no takers. Maybe if she gave it a bit more zig and a little less zag. Surely, fishermen must have worked out a foolproof technique for this millennia ago. If the *Li* hadn't been so electronically challenged they could have just skipped all this re-inventing the pole and Googled their way into a tasty tuna or two.

"Look at that one, Buck," she said, squinting at the horizon. "It must be an iceberg of plastic garbage."

Buck joined her at the rail with binoculars.

"It's a ship!" he hollered. "Coming right toward us. We're saved! Hot dog!"

"Looks kind of like a tugboat," said Petal, taking her turn with the binos. "Just what we need! Call the others. This is our lucky day!"

Within minutes the entire *Li* contingent was on deck waving white flags.

"Shouldn't we be planning the terms of our surrender?" asked Ali. "Reparations, tributes, ransoms, amnesties, repatriations—that sort of thing? I think we would be better off negotiating as a unit."

"We're not surrendering to anybody," said Petal. "We're just being rescued. That's a totally different thing."

"I thought we discussed this already," said Ali. "And you are waving a white flag."

"We're just waving," said Buck. "You're the one giving up."

"Ali, why don't you give up on this giving up thing and just keep your mouth shut until we figure out the situation," said Petal. "You can always surrender later. I don't think there is a penalty for late surrendering."

Pretty soon it was clear that pilot of the tug was heading right for them. They took turns scoping the guy out through the binos.

"Doesn't look like he's missed any meals," observed Ali.

"Maybe he'll invite us to dinner," said Buck.

"Do all three hundred pound bald guys smoke cigars?" asked Petal. "How does that work, anyway? Do cigars make your hair fall out which makes you depressed so you eat to cheer yourself up? Or does the sun on your scalp give you strange cravings for cigars and cheeseburgers?"

"Be nice," said Buck. "Big guys are sensitive about their size."

"And it is he who is rescuing us," said Captain Kim. "After all."

"He's got on some kind of lava-lava," said Ali, squinting through the lenses. "With suspenders."

"Maybe he's the super around here," said Petal. "Supers always wear suspenders and smoke cigars."

"Super?" asked Kim, wondering at the term.

"Superman?" asked Igor.

"Supersize?" asked Ivan, struggling with him over the binoculars.

"Superhero!" declared Igor, getting a glimpse.

They scrambled toward the bow and prepared to throw a line as the tug pulled up next to them. A couple of hand signals passed between the captains and pretty soon the *Li* was scooting along behind the little boat.

"There's something weird about that tug," said Petal. "There's no smoke or noise coming out of it. It doesn't—you know—stink."

"And how can it pull this big ship so fast?" asked Ali. "Look at our wake!"

"Never seen anything like it," allowed Kim, passing the binos to Buck. "Do you recognize the insignia?"

"Blue field with green dots," he observed. "No flag I've ever seen. Boat's name is something like *Nirub Bish*. Ring a bell, Petal? Sounds like a Bollywood movie star."

"No," she said, steadying the glasses against his shoulder. "But couldn't that be *N I Rubbish*?"

"A garbage scow!" cried Ali. "We're not being rescued, we're being refused! Carted off by a nuclear-powered trash truck to be flushed down some seamy equatorial toilet! We'll be lucky if they don't sell our organs and boil the scraps down into soap! Of all the people we could have surrendered to, you had to pick this guy? What's wrong with the Supreme Commander of NATO? The High Commission on Accounting Conventions? At least we would have decent accommodations at The Hague before our tribunal. But no, you had to surrender to the guy who's sweeping up!"

"You're right," said Buck. "I can see it now, N.I. Rubbish, no doubt about it. What is N.I.?"

"Who cares about the N.I. part?" whined Ali. "It's the rubbish part you should be worried about."

"You're the one who ought to be worried, Ali," said Petal. "All you self-important oil guys are about to wind up in the dustbin of history. If you're lucky, maybe the green world might let you sweep up."

"Quit fighting and check this out," said Buck, handing her the binos.

"Some kind of low island," she said.

"He's stopped," said Kim. "Looks like he's coming back here."

"This is just great!" said Ali. "A boarding party at our flanks and we stand here helpless—too stubborn to surrender but powerless to resist. We'll be cut to ribbons by their sabers!"

"What do you mean, powerless? This is a first class RPDK destroyer, after all," said Captain Kim. "We can fire up the big guns if you want to."

"No, we do not want to," said Petal. "Your boarding party is one hairless Santa with a stogie. Will you two get a grip?"

"I'll have you know I nearly have a black belt in *Qui Wut Fo*," said Ali, brandishing a fishing pole like a sword. "I, for one, will not go quietly into the compost."

"Ahoy, mates!" called the guy from the tug, now right beneath them. "You all look hungry. Luau tonight. Lots of food for everybody. You got about three hundred crew aboard, do you?"

"Just the six of us." said Petal. "But one's not hungry. The rest of us would be honored to attend."

481

"Only six of you left," frowned the guy. "Oh my! You have been drifting a long time. I trust there's been no cannibalism. Cannibalism is strictly forbidden in the Nutting Islands—or at least seriously frowned upon."

"No. No cannibalism yet," said Petal. "There were only six of us to start with. So that's where we are, Nutting Island?"

"Not exactly the Nutting Island," said the guy. "There are actually lots of islands in the Nutting chain back that way. This one isn't even an island—it's just an atoll."

"So it's us oilmen who will end up in the dustbin of history?" whispered Ali. "You greenies set out to save the world and look what you end up with."

"Nutting Atoll?"

CHAPTER 72

LUAU

"Captain Bufo?"

"Please call me Vita, Petal."

"Of course, Vita. I just wanted to say again how much we appreciate you saving our lives out there."

The rest of the *Waba Ti Li* contingent looked up from their plates and nodded agreement, being too polite to speak with their mouths full, but not quite polite enough to stop cramming food into them. The luau was in full swing now, with men standing around a steaming *imu*, women serving poi on ti leaves, girls dancing hula on a makeshift stage, and children playing tag on the grass. Most families sprawled on mats, but the guests of honor got to sit around a weathered picnic table. Captain Bufo, who might have been able to fit next to them a couple of hundred pounds ago, sat at one end in a lawn chair scaled up to his size.

"Don't mention it, Petal. That's my job, after all, sweeping up the flotsam. But I'll admit it's rare for the Department of Rubbish to get such a hefty hunk of flotsam in a single lump. And such heavily populated, military flotsam, at that. Anyway, I'm sure your country will be coming after you soon. Countries tend to have strong emotional attachments to their military flotsam."

"I'd be surprised if anyone from the RPDK is coming to get us," said Captain Kim, looking dejected. "Frankly, I'd be surprised if the RPDK even exists anymore."

"How sad to lose one's country," said Bufo. "Political or geologic?"

"Strictly political," said Kim.

"Oh, well, that's not so serious then," he said, leaning back in his chair. "Don't worry; you'll have a new political entity in place in no time. Why, I remember a seminar in Quantitative Revolutionary Dynamics where we calculated nation-state turnover times. Turns out that the interval between one tax-levying regime and the next is almost never more than thirty-six—"

"You took Quant Rev too?" asked Kim. "Tough elective. What's a sea captain like you doing taking upper-level, post-graduate seminars?"

"It sounds like I could ask you the same question."

"A lot of military officers have advanced degrees," said Kim. "Took me years of correspondence, but I finally got my Master's in Naval History."

"PhD in Political Science," said Bufo, giving him a thumbs up. "I figure as long as you are doing the masters you might as well go the whole way."

"So you used to be a professor or something?" asked Petal. "Sea captaining a second career?"

"Naw, Petal, Poli Sci was just for fun. A piece of cake really—it's not like it's a real science or anything. My professional degrees are in Oceanography, Marine Engineering, and Ecology. Those were the hard ones."

"You have PhDs in all those things?" asked Petal.

"Why, you don't think I look old enough?" Bufo laughed.

"What I mean is, don't people usually just finish one PhD and then call it a day?"

"Not in Nutting," he said. "Here everyone is always working on their next degree. It's part of the social contract. Continuous education isn't exactly compulsory, but if you drop out people wonder what's wrong with you. Retiring from your job is okay, but retiring from your education is definitely not. There's a lot to learn out there—even with a whole lifetime you couldn't learn it all."

"Great system," said Buck, marveling at the concept. "How did that come about? Strong teacher's union?"

"Wise leader," said Bufo. "Back in the seventies our country came into some money, and instead of blowing it on stuff, King O'ola invested it in education. He was an inspiration to all of us. As you can see, the Nutting people still aren't much interested in stuff."

Buck took another look at the whole scene. From the minute they landed, he had thought the place looked strange. So was this it, the general lack of stuff? Bufo was right, the Islanders didn't seem to have much in the way of possessions, but there was something stranger than that going on. Something subtle but deeply weird.

At first glance, the Nutting people seemed to be a typical Pacific Island subculture dependent upon subsistence fishing, small-scale agriculture, and a paternalistic public sector. But on closer inspection Buck could see that something very basic was conspicuously absent. Something crucial was missing from the picture. Some necessary condition of reality. Buck would have called it "entropy." Petal would have called it "dirt."

Everything in Nutting was clean, meticulously clean. There was not a speck of trash anywhere. There was not a coconut out of place. It wasn't the lack of stuff that was so weird about Nutting; it was the lack of mess.

Nothing on Nutting was fancy, mind you—a snapshot of the place would pass any National Geographic editor's Authentic Picturesque Ethnic Village filter. Dwellings were rough-hewn and painted in primary colors. Their designs were primitive, their executions crude. There was even the occasional well-placed rust stain here and there. But there was no grime, no disorder, no disarray. There was randomness, but the kind you get from a randomness generator. The longer Buck looked, the more he got the impression that Nutting was not so much a culture as a commemoration of one.

"Surely you must get the occasional person who would rather spend his life making money in the big world than collecting PhDs in paradise," said Petal.

"You know, that does happen, and more often than you might expect," said Bufo, leaning closer. "I think it must be a common genetic mutation. But it's not a problem, really. We just give kids like that a check and a ticket and then everyone's happy. Keeps the population stable and the Islands free of entrepreneurial types."

"But what about when they come back and start building condos all over the place?" asked Petal, still trying to understand how a society could be made up of under-acquisitive, over-educated rubbish collectors.

"They can't come back, Petal," explained Bufo. "It's part of the deal. Nobody comes to the Nutting Islands—except for folks like you, of course, who just stumble upon us."

"Why not?" she asked.

"Well, it's because officially we don't exist. It's the essence of the Nutting bargain. We get to live our lives exactly as we wish as long as we're invisible. The kids who leave are sworn to secrecy and are given plenty of incentive to keep their mouths shut. As far as the outside world knows, the Nutting Islands are just a figment of some drunken sailor's imagination. Look on any map. It will show nothing but open ocean at 2°25'33"N, 129°33'05"W."

Buck and Petal bolted upright. Kim and Ali dropped their forks. Igor and Ivan came to attention. Bufo looked puzzled at their reaction. His story made perfect sense to him.

"Do you know a guy named Siverth Narup?" asked Buck.

"The artist?" asked Bufo. "Of course. Avant garde Greenlandic performance-installation-videographer. My favorite piece was when he put a condom on the Eiffel Tower and—"

"No, he means do you personally know him yourself?" asked Petal.

"Personally, no," said Bufo. "But everybody in the Art History field knows about Siverth Narup. In fact, my own dissertation drew heavily on his early use of high explosives as a metaphor of post-modern—"

"He didn't call you?" asked Buck. "Send you an email?"

"We don't have email here. No outside calls, either. We do get regular mail, but it's kind of laundered to keep us out of sight. Post office box in Taiwan forwarded through Tunisia. Good for ordering reference works and correspondence courses."

Buck looked at Petal. Ali looked at Captain Kim. Igor and Ivan looked at their deserts. How come nothing was ever easy?

"I told you this was a wild goose chase," said Ali.

"What are you talking about?" said Petal. "Didn't you hear him say 2°25'33"N, 129°33'05"W?"

"So that's where we are. So what? That's where we were headed," said Ali. "Are you always surprised when you end up where you were headed?"

"But for there to be a place like this at those very coordinates has got to mean something," said Petal.

"How do you know there aren't places like this all over the Pacific?" he asked. "Since they're not on any maps, you'd have no way of knowing, would you? I'll bet the oceans are chockablock with invisible places. Pick coordinates out of a hat and you're bound to land on one."

"Ali?" asked Petal. "What do you think it would take to get you to shut up?"

"A check and a ticket?" he ventured.

"To the dump, maybe," she answered.

"To the dump," repeated Buck to no one in particular.

"Captain Bufo?"

"Call me Vita, Buck."

"Vita, you're in charge of the Department of Rubbish, right?"

"I'm the guy, all right. Passionate about rubbish."

"And you're devoted to education, right?"

"Only thing I'm more passionate about than rubbish."

"Well, how about helping with our educations?"

"Love to. Where would you like to start? Art History? Poli Sci?"

"Rubbish."

"Rubbish?"

"Rubbish."

CHAPTER 73

RUBBISH

"Class?"

"Yes, Professor Bufo!"

"I just wanted to say again how delightful it is to have students who are as enthusiastic about rubbish as you are."

Bufo placed his chalk in the tray and perched on an over-sized stool in front of the blackboard. Buck, Petal, and Captain Kim sat attentively at their desks. Ali slouched with chin on hand, daydreaming about the Polynesian hunk trimming bushes outside the window. Igor and Ivan snored softly. It had been a long morning, and they had barely scratched the surface of Introduction to Rubbish Theory. The board was covered with Vita's meticulous notes summarizing History of Rubbish Philosophy, Lecture One.

"The pleasure is all ours," said Petal. "You really make the subject come alive."

"I'll say," said Buck. "So many inspiring concepts."

"They boggle the mind," added Petal.

"Would hate to rush through," said Buck. "Without a chance to digest it all."

"Let it all sink in a bit," said Petal. "Sleep on it."

"Maybe this afternoon you could take us on a field trip," offered Buck. "Show us how it's really done."

"Some of us are more visual kind of learners," said Petal nodding at the Russians. "It might help to see the practical application of theory."

"An overview," said Buck. "The big picture."

Bufo beamed. He could have just received the Nobel Prize in Rubbishology.

"Excellent idea! Concurrent combination of the concrete and the conceptual! Praxis juxtaposed with principle! Let's go now!" he said. "I love your enthusiasm."

He led the way out of the one-room schoolhouse into the open air. It was bright and clear that morning, but cool and breezy under the manicured canopy of mango, guava, ficus, and palm. Curious Nutting Islanders in floral pareos giggled and gossiped as they passed, the bolder ones waving and blowing kisses. Most people were on foot, but many took advantage of the ubiquitous canvas-topped tricycles that seemed to be communal property. Bufo and his students climbed aboard an elongated golf cart on a path roughly parallel to the pedestrian walkway.

"I know I should walk more," said Bufo, patting his stomach. "But we are going all the way to seven."

"Seven?" asked Petal.

"Seven o'clock," he replied. "We're at about two fifteen now. The atoll is circular, after all. Every address has a radial dimension, too, when we need to be precise—but, to be honest, I can't remember ever needing to be precise in Nutting."

Gliding along at about ten miles an hour, they really couldn't tell they were moving around the circumference of a big annulus. From time to time the ocean would peek through the trees on their left, usually beyond a deep, white beach. Low hills stretched off to their right, the last remnant of a disappearing volcanic cone. Small fields of taro, rice, and cane nestled in the tropical forest. Clusters of simple houses seemed scattered at random, each with its own community structure that served simultaneously as schoolhouse, post office, swap meet, and clinic.

"Nice ride," observed Buck. "Everything around here electric? I haven't heard a single internal combustion engine since we arrived—even on your tug."

"Fuel cells," he replied. "We've got no truck with petroleum. Never touch the stuff."

"Hydrogen fuel cells?" asked Buck, surprised. "That's pretty high tech."

"You've got it backwards, Buck," he said. "Fuel cells are nineteenth century technology—so are batteries and electric motors. Much simpler than internal combustion engines. A fraction of the moving parts. Hardly ever wear out. Never need maintenance. Clean, silent, and they don't stink. Nobody would choose internal combustion if they were really given the choice."

"But aren't fuel cells too expensive to make?" asked Petal. "That's what the newspapers say, anyway. Every day."

490

"Only if you want a fuel cell that will burn petroleum, too. Fuel cells that only use hydrogen are cheap and easy to build. Always have been. I suppose if you can't imagine a world without petroleum you would insist on having a fuel cell that could use both fuels, but that would be like insisting that your lawn mower had to double as a toothbrush. Who would think that way?"

"I can think of a few," said Petal.

"But how do you make hydrogen around here—geothermal?" asked Buck.

"Nah," said Bufo. "The hot spot that created Nutting moved on millions of years ago. But hydrogen is a snap to make. I'll show you. This is the place."

Everybody climbed out onto the grass and looked around. This might be seven o'clock but it didn't look all that much different from any other o'clock they had seen on Nutting Atoll. They were on a little rise now, about fifty feet above the ocean. They had a fine view of a protected harbor which in turn connected to a canal that led to the atoll's watery interior. A dozen fishing boats bobbed at anchor and a few tugs were silently fuel-celling their way out to sea. Other than a concrete pier beneath them, there was no other sign of human industry.

"This is it?" asked Ali, who apparently had been expecting something more like Dubai, or at least Las Vegas.

"Well, it doesn't look like much on the outside," said Bufo. "But isn't that the way it should be?"

He led them into a hut that proved to be not much more than a vestibule for a staircase leading down.

"Nutting industry is all underground," he explained. "Actually, we don't really dig under ground—the water table is too close—we just cover all our factories over with dirt and grass and trees. Keeps the countryside beautiful and hardens the infrastructure against typhoons. Why countries would allow industry to take up good land where people could be living has always been a mystery to me."

They left the stairwell and filed onto a catwalk overlooking a huge room of pipes, pumps, tanks, and gauges. Workers in white jumpsuits stood around on the floor below. On one end a conveyor belt inched metal spheres the size of beach balls along at a lazy pace. Otherwise there was little movement and not much noise.

"Wow!" said Petal, whose idea of heavy industry was an office with two copying machines.

For Buck, however, the scene mainly rekindled his initial sense of strangeness about Nutting Atoll. Here was technology, to be sure, but the kind of retro technology that one might see in a forties *Flash Gordon* episode—and that would be the nineteen forties, to be perfectly clear. Here was something that Tom Swift might have put together from plans in the *Boy's Life* classifieds. With a little bit of Daddy Warbuck's cash, that is.

"Sweet, eh?" said Bufo, hooking thumbs into his suspenders. Bufo seemed to be the only Nutting Islander fat enough to need suspenders on his pareo.

"Maybe you could tell us more about how all this works," said Captain Kim. Already he was casing the joint for parts that might save the *Waba Ti Li* from whatever fate awaited flotsam drifting near 2°25'33"N, 129°33'05"W.

"With pleasure!" said Bufo, rubbing his hands. "That pipe over there brings in cold ocean water. Even at the equator, you don't have to drop a hose very deep to get water that's almost freezing. The other pipe brings in warm surface water, which around the equator never gets below the mid eighties. As you know, the ocean surface is a perfect collector for sun energy. A green plant might capture a few percent of it and a really good solar panel might get a quarter. But the ocean surface grabs almost every photon and converts one hundred percent of its energy into heat. It's a simple matter, then, to spin a turbine using the power of that temperature difference—that's the big cylinder over there—which in turn drives our electrical generator."

"Very cool," acknowledged Buck. "And the hydrogen?"

"Couldn't be simpler. Jam a couple of wires into water and turn on the current. It takes energy to break H_2O into hydrogen and oxygen—energy you get back as electricity from your fuel cell when you ask it to combine the hydrogen back with oxygen. Of course, hydrogen takes up too much room to store as a gas, so we cool it down and ship it around in thermos bottles—see them over on that conveyor belt? Any machine that wouldn't be practical to plug into the electric power grid—like a vehicle—makes its own electricity from a hydrogen fuel cell. Pick up a thermos or two when you are running low or have the Hydrogen Man deliver, just like they used to do with milk."

"But doesn't it take a lot of energy to cool hydrogen down to a liquid?" objected Ali, smelling either a rat or a violation of the Second Law of Thermodynamics.

"Sure it does, but we've got more energy than we can use," said Bufo.

"How much more?" asked Petal, trying not to look as excited as Buck.

"Well, Petal," said Bufo. "I can show you the math later, but let's put it this way. If you tried to compare the entire world's energy needs to the amount of sun energy captured by the ocean it would be like comparing a grain of sand to the Sahara Desert. You could run all of civilization on less energy than the normal minute to minute variation in light we get from the sun. In other words, humans could have all the energy they wanted and not even put a scratch in what's available. Humans could increase their energy consumption by a power of ten and it would still get lost in the noise of the sun."

"But surely there's a catch," objected Ali. "Some toxic effluent you're trying to hide."

"Well, the process does create a fair amount of fresh water as a byproduct," admitted Bufo. "Water condenses on cold surfaces, you know. But you couldn't really call it toxic since we drink it. I think it tastes a little flat, since it's essentially distilled water. Add back some trace minerals and it's just like the bottled stuff, except without the arsenic."

"How about thermal pollution?" insisted Ali, desperate. "All that cold water. It's got to poison the environment somehow."

"You're right, Ali, no heat engine is perfectly efficient—"

"I knew it!"

"And we do end up with a fair amount of cold seawater to dispose of in the end. I suppose we could just run it back to the appropriate depth, but instead we cool down our fresh water with it and raise strawberries and rainbow trout. Try that in Hawaii!" Bufo said proudly.

"But if this—this—this—" stammered Ali.

"Ocean Thermal Energy Conversion," prompted Bufo.

"Whatever. If a bunch of pumps and pipes could supply the world with a limitless supply of renewable, clean energy, how come you guys are the only ones to think of it?"

"We didn't think of it. We just looked it up. Machines that use differences in temperature to do useful work have been around since before elevators or typewriters or even oil wells. Ditto for hydrogen fuel cells and electric motors. This is not rocket science, as you can see. Nothing radioactive, no high temperatures, no high pressures, no exotic materials, no toxic chemicals."

"Okay, so you didn't think of it. But if it's such a good idea, how come nobody else is doing it?"

"No ocean in Detroit?" offered Bufo. "Too cold in Washington? Let's face it, Ali, the reason is historical, not logical or scientific. In the olden days, people got by burning renewables like wood and candles. It wasn't great, but energy wasn't the limiting factor in what they wanted to do, anyway. But then came the industrial revolution and people needed power to run their machines. Coal and oil were just sitting there for the taking. Burn them and you got energy out. It was a slam dunk. We were hooked. It seemed like a good idea at the time.

"Believe it or not, there was a day that it was considered okay to mutilate your landscape and indenture your lower classes digging coal, to invade other countries chasing their oil, and to poison everyone's air burning the stuff. There was a day that people thought fossil fuels would never run out. There was a day that people thought Somebody Else up there would clean up after us, would rescue us from ourselves. Maybe there are even a few of those people left. Hopefully nobody is listening to them much any more.

"Don't forget it's only recently that any Non-Nutting people have been looking for ways to kick the carbon habit. Too bad they are looking in the wrong places. What would lead them so astray? A couple of things.

"The first is the motivation to become 'energy independent.' If a country wants to quit being dependent on other countries for its energy, it starts looking for energy in its own back yard. What does it find there? Hydroelectric, wind, photovoltaic panels— which would be okay if they weren't such penny-ante power producers. So then your country gets desperate and starts pretending there is such a thing as 'clean nuclear' and 'clean coal' and is back mainlining toxic junk straight into its veins again. You can't look for ocean thermal energy in your backyard. Check out the map. There aren't any countries with equatorial oceans inside their borders. The oceans are international. Nations with nationalistic motives for developing alternative energy are blind to ocean thermal. It doesn't even appear on their list.

"The second thing that steers people away from ocean thermal energy is the Church of Competition. This religion is very permissive in a lot of ways. It doesn't really care how you treat other people. It doesn't really care how you think or act. But it is very strict about one thing—its first commandment. *You Shall Have No Other God Before Me.*

"To be competitive you have to have an edge over the competition. You have to deliver the goods at a lower cost. It's tough to beat the fossil fuel establishment at this game, because they have spent the last two hundred years perfecting ways to get the general public to pay their costs for them—cleaning up their mess and fighting their wars, among countless other subsidies. But even if the playing field was leveled, and every possible source of energy was lined up to compete for investors' money, ocean thermal would be disqualified before the contest even started. Why? Because of its blasphemy against the Church of Competition.

"How can you be competitive if you choose ocean thermal—a technology that is so low tech that anybody could copy it? Where is your edge? Better to put your research and development dollar into building a better photovoltaic panel. If you coax another few volts out of your design, then your company gets all the solar panel business—for a while, anyway, until your competitor discovers your secret, improves on it, and takes all your business for himself. Better yet, put your investment money into nuclear technology and let your government protect your technological edge for you under the guise of national security.

"The Church of Competition demands its sacrifices. The spirit of cooperation must be laid upon its altar. The blood sport of Winner-Take-All must be played for its amusement. There are no windfalls to be found in a technology that is already community property, and there is no place for community in the Congregation of the Big Win. As long as you let the Church of Competition choose the fate of your civilization on the basis of the short-term profits of individual investors you will never develop ocean thermal. It won't even make it to the menu.

"Ocean thermal energy has been there as long as the sun and the ocean. The technology for converting it into usable, transportable forms like electricity and hydrogen has been around since before your grandparents were born. Over the years there have been dozens of free thinking scientists and engineers that pointed this out to their leaders. But those leaders didn't have what it takes to understand. It takes a leader who thinks that allegiance to his country implies an allegiance to his planet. It takes a leader who thinks that the short run is the next quarter century, not the next quarter. And it takes a leader who might nail a letter on the door of the Church of Competition, demanding it cease and desist its mindless meddling in the future of Man."

"We got anybody like that?" asked Petal.

"Not so far," answered Buck. "But there is an election coming up."

"Better not get our hopes up," she said. "After all, we've only got ninety days."

CHAPTER 74

ARAGONITE

"But I digress," said Bufo leading his students back to the stairwell. "What we are really interested in is rubbish."

Petal was pulling on Buck's sleeve trying to start with a million questions about what they had just heard, Ali was arguing with Captain Kim about who could tell bullshit when he or she smelled it, the Russians were scribbling schematics in Cyrillic, and Buck was trying to get everybody to pay attention to the teacher.

"Now, remember, our little field trip is just an overview of the multifaceted and ever-fascinating field of rubbish, so don't expect to get a full appreciation of the scope of the subject until you have a few more semesters of concerted study under your belts. So where should we start today? The inner nature of rubbish? The creation of rubbish? The husbandry of rubbish? Its collection? Processing? Metamorphosis? Rebirth? " Bufo was rubbing his chin.

"Start at the end," Ali called out from the back. He didn't know how much more of this he could take. Petal jabbed him in the ribs.

"Excellent idea!" said Bufo. "If one starts at the end and works backwards, one can always keep one's goal in view. Thank you, Ali. You are an insightful as well as inquisitive student. I appreciate that. The other students should follow your example. Always question! Always innovate!"

"He's a natural, all right," said Petal. "We always figured he'd end up in rubbish."

"To start at the end, we'll have to take another ride," said Bufo, escorting them back into the stretch golf cart.

This time they set off down a path toward the island's center. It took about half an hour of gentle climbing to reach the top of the hill that formed the center of the atoll's ring. From this vantage point they could see all of the immense central lagoon and the several canals connecting it with the ocean. Maybe they were three hundred feet above sea level, probably less.

"As you have no doubt noticed, Nutting Atoll is nothing at all like any other atoll," started Bufo. "By definition an atoll is a ring of coral that remains after a volcanic island has eroded completely away. But Nutting Atoll was named by people who knew nothing at all about other atolls. All they knew is that it was one big donut of an island and that was good enough for them."

"And if it was good enough for them, it's good enough for us," said Ali.

"Well said, Ali," said Bufo. "The way I look at it, any island that ends up with a great big hole in its middle deserves to be called an atoll, no matter how it managed to get that way."

"What else are you going to call it?" agreed Petal. "A coral-less torus? A volcanut? An atolloid?"

"Exactly," nodded Bufo. "Now, in the unique case of Nutting Atoll, extensive geologic investigations—"

"Let me guess," interjected Ali, "led by PhD candidate in geology, Dr. Vita Bufo—"

"Precisely. Extensive geologic investigations conducted by my team demonstrated that Nutting Atoll was once a huge volcanic cone reaching ten thousand feet above the ocean's surface, its extinguished caldera containing one gigantic inland freshwater lake. Here, within the most isolated body of water in the ancient Pacific, evolved life forms found nowhere else. Strobo-luminescent anemone! Multi-marsupial amphibians! Hydrophobic trans-gendered sponges! Toothless anti-pelagic sharks! And carnivorous penguinoid ostriches! But, alas, eons of weather would eventually wear the fragile cone ever downward until, on one catastrophic day, the wall protecting this precious sanctuary would be breached, and a hungry, jealous ocean would gobble up the living treasures of Lake Nutting, leaving only their fossil remains behind."

"A sad day," murmured Ali, bowing his head. "How can one go on?"

"But, just beyond every tragedy, there always lies hope," said Bufo, pulling himself up. "Which brings us to the End of Rubbish, just where you asked me to start. And in this sense I also mean 'End' in the sense of the word 'Purpose' or 'Meaning.' What is the true destiny of rubbish? Its highest calling? Can you answer that, class? Ali?"

"To serve its fellow man?" he ventured.

"Exactly!" said Bufo, slapping him on the back. "Rubbish is destined to fulfill mankind's greatest needs. To satisfy Man's most noble desires. Which is, of course, in this case, the restoration of Lake Nutting!"

"With rubbish?"

"With rubbish," asserted Bufo. "I'll show you how."

Bufo drove their vehicle down to the lagoon's edge, near the mouth of the canal. Here was another nondescript entrance into a buried industrial complex next to a simple concrete dock. Tugboat traffic was heavy here. If you looked closely you could see that each arriving tug was pulling a long, mostly-submerged cylinder about a hundred feet long.

"The tugs sweep flotsam into those big plastic baggies and drag it to facilities like this one," he said, leading them into another underground mechanical room. "Here we reclaim some of it for our manufacturing—making more baggies for example—but mostly we just grind it into chunks to use as aggregate in the concrete—"

"More concrete!" moaned Ali. "Man's most noble desire is more concrete?"

"—that we are using to restore the once majestic cone of Nutting Atoll, which then, of course will be nothing at all like an atoll."

The operation taking place on the factory floor below them looked even lower tech than the ocean thermal one. Gigantic grinders, furnaces, and hoods predominated.

"So you are in the process of making a concrete replica of something that existed millions of years ago," asked Ali. "A ten thousand foot volcano with a lake on top of it."

"Well, we hate to call it a replica," admitted Bufo. "But we don't have the means of creating volcanic rock. Concrete is the next best thing."

"I think you'll be happy with concrete," said Buck. "Much more durable than volcanic."

"My feeling exactly," agreed Bufo. "Done right, it should last ten times longer than the original."

"I'm a big fan of concrete," said Buck.

"He could talk about it for hours," agreed Petal.

"He's the most concrete guy I know," said Ali.

Buck waved off the compliments and positioned himself right in front of the professor. From the look on his face, there was something more than professional curiosity at stake.

"Vita, may I ask where you are getting the cement for all this concrete?"

"Why, we make it ourselves, of course."

"If I promise not to give away your recipe, do you think you could show me the process?"

"Sure," said Bufo, appreciating the enthusiasm, "you can have the recipe. It's not ours anyway. I think this one's a couple hundred years old. Of course, the Romans had some pretty reliable—"

"Vita," said Buck. "I'm really interested in the way you do it. Just walk me through it, nice and slow."

"Well, like everybody else we start with limestone and then—"

"You have limestone around here? How could that be? The Nutting Islands are all volcanic. Limestone is sedimentary."

"Okay, technically you're right. Limestone is mostly calcite. What we use is aragonite. So like everybody we take the aragonite and then—"

"You mean calcium carbonate, right?"

"Of course. Calcite and aragonite are just different crystal forms of calcium carbonate. CaCO3. Same thing."

"So do you dig calcium carbonate out of your reef? Grind up oyster shells? Mine the ocean floor?" Buck knew he was on to something.

"Heaven's no!" said Bufo. "The reef is a precious natural resource. We are doing everything we can to preserve it. In fact, reefs all over the Pacific are endangered by rising acidity from higher levels of CO_2 in the atmosphere. Besides, there's not nearly enough coral to supply our project. Do you know how much concrete it takes to make a ten thousand foot cone?"

Buck counted to ten before asking the obvious.

"So, all this calcium carbonate? Where do you get it?"

"Simple," said Bufo. "Old technology. Calcium carbonate is nothing but calcium and carbon dioxide, after all. The ocean is full of dissolved calcium and it's full of dissolved CO_2. Ocean critters make their shells out of it—coral, pearls, barnacles, limestone—all are just calcium carbonate made by little water animals. Now we could just farm a bunch of barnacles and grind them up, but we're kind of in a hurry to restore Nutting Atoll, given that the ocean level is rising so fast and we Nutting Islanders, while we love the ocean, don't get me wrong, it's just that we prefer to sleep where it is dry, if you know what I mean."

"We know. It's one our favorite things, too," said Buck. "So exactly how does somebody who is not a little ocean critter make solid calcium carbonate out of liquid ocean water?"

"Piece of cake. Hard to avoid it, really. All it takes is a little electric current down a wire and the stuff cakes right on. At one time we thought we could grow our own beams this way, you know, mimic what the sea creatures do. Imagine a beam as strong as an oyster shell—those things are tough, let me tell you. But matching Mother Nature is always more difficult than you think—you see, ocean critters have this very tricky thing they do with proteins that gets the calcium carbonate molecules all packed together real tight. Makes their shells strong as iron. What we make is pretty hard—kind of a cross between coral and pearl—but nothing like oyster shell. I think we may be getting a little too much magnesium in the precipitate, probably brucite or dolomite—"

"Electrical current is all it takes to get solid calcium carbonate out of liquid seawater?" Buck wanted to be sure he had this right.

"Right. Totally low tech. A metal screen, electricity, seawater, and a few cranks and levers to scrape the stuff into a bucket. We are already pumping tons of seawater around at our ocean thermal plants, and, of course, we've got all the electricity we need for free. Getting calcium carbonate out of the ocean is the least of our problems, believe me. Restoring a ten thousand foot volcano, now that's an engineering problem worth talking about. Think of the shear stresses, not to mention compressive forces and seismic torque. Maybe later after rubbish class you and I could chat about—"

"And what if you didn't make cement out of this calcium carbonate and just piled it up on the ground, or filled in your lagoon with it? What if you filled in all the atolls in the Nutting Island chain and made islands out of them? What about that?" asked Buck, struggling to slow his thoughts.

"Well, you could do that if you wanted," said Bufo, pulling his chin. "But it wouldn't be so good."

"Why not?"

"It would only take a couple million years for them to wash away again. Concrete would last much longer."

"Okay, you win, concrete it is. But concrete is nothing but cement with a bunch of rocks and sand in it—what you call aggregate. You could make rocks and sand out of calcium carbonate, right?"

"Sure. That's what we do already. Our concrete is mostly calcium carbonate aggregate, plus our own proprietary blend of rubbish bits that gives it that special elasticity, its unique porosity, its matchless workability, its alluring fragrance—"

"And at the end of the project you've got a ten thousand foot pile of carbon dioxide locked up for ten million years. Carbon dioxide that once was dissolved in the ocean," said Buck.

"Sure, if you want to look at it that way," said Bufo.

"And since CO_2 in the ocean is in equilibrium with the CO_2 in the air, every molecule you take out of the ocean means one less molecule in the atmosphere, right?"

"Sure, Buck. Simple physics. Trivial, really. But we digress. What we are really interested in is rubbish, right?"

"Absolutely right," said Buck, slapping him on the back. "But this time we're going for the Holy Grail of rubbish. There's a pile of rubbish out there that's been growing since the day Man discovered fire, and with your help we are going to take it on, tear it down, and build a new world with it. Get ready, Vita, 'cause we are going to scrub the Anthropocene!"

CHAPTER 75

SLIP

"We've got it!" We've got it!" sang Buck as he hugged Petal off the ground and spun her around the hut.

Ali and Kim sat at the table with Ivan and Igor shuffling through the stacks of three by five cards they had generated over the course of the evening. Somehow the Russians' cards had gotten mixed in with rest and Kim was having difficulty telling which ones were hopelessly illegible, written in Cyrillic, or simply upside down.

"What are you two talking about?" asked Ali. "From where I sit, we haven't got squat."

"Are you kidding?" answered Petal, her hair flung wild by her spin. "In the same day we stumble upon enough clean energy to power the planet a thousand times over and a way to clean up the CO_2 littered by every bumbling biped back to before Raquel Welch could hold up a fur bikini. If that ain't squat, I don't know what is."

"Yeah, Ali," said Buck. "You saw Bufo's equipment. Any country in the world could be mass producing this stuff in a month. Imagine, the secret to a pollution free, hydrogen economy right in front of our noses all along."

"Did I miss something?" asked Ali. "Bufo's steam-powered magic wand that changes the world's umpteen jillion gasoline engines into hydrogen fuel cells before the oil dries up in ninety days? Get real.

"You know how the car makers are. They never do anything new without being forced to. They won't even do something new that makes sense to them until they have a gun to their heads. Remember seat belts? Pretty risky move for Detroit to install those babies. Could have brought the whole industry down. Had to pass a law to get them to do it. Heaven knows how they survived the trauma. Same for catalytic converters. Too expensive. People would just stop buying cars all together. Another law. Then they listened. But listen to consumers? That's not how it works in the car business. Well, by the time they see the gun this time, the trigger will already have been pulled."

"Okay, so it will take a while to get things rolling," said Petal. "But with Siverth's Chill the Anthropocene organization and the Cult of Petal network and everybody in the world pulling with us, I'm sure that—"

She looked up to see Vita Bufo standing in their doorway. Nutting dwellings didn't seem to come with doors, but visitors were always polite enough to knock anyway.

"Hope I'm not interrupting," he started. "But I thought you might be interested in this." He placed a pile of crumpled newsprint on the table.

"Came as packing material for a shipment of textbooks. The complete *Aztec Tax Code for Dummies* series, actually. We are not supposed to get newspapers at all or any other publication less than five years old—part of the Nutting Bargain, like I said. But every now and then something like this sneaks through. Orders are to turn it in right away, but under the circumstances I thought we could bend the rules a little."

They smoothed the scraps out on the table and tried to make sense of them. The *Tri-City Picayune Tribune* had been pretty thoroughly shredded, but with a little patience and the uncanny skills of Igor and Ivan, sizable blocks of text began to emerge. For most of an hour no one spoke. Eventually, everyone sat down in sober silence. Petal was the first to break it.

"How could things have gotten so rotten so quick?" she asked. "Has it been that long since we left New York?"

"The economy is really down the crapper this time."

"I always knew it was one big Ponzi scheme."

"Is that the same as a bubble?"

"A bubble on credit."

"Credit on steroids."

"There isn't any credit."

"You can't even buy credit."

"Credit has crunched."

"Who crunched the credit?"

"Poor people borrowing money."

"Middle men flipping speculations."

"Greedy profiteering."

"I thought profit was the point."

"Bankers not banking."

"Lenders not lending."

"Tell me again why they won't lend money?"

"There isn't any money, stupid. It's a recession."

"Where'd it all go?"

"Bonuses, I think."

"Bailouts."

"Entitlements."

"Boomers."

"X-ers."

"Y-ers."

"Elites!"

"Ignorami!"

"Unemployment through the roof."

"Nobody wants to work anymore."

"When did you ever work?"

"Worthless stocks."

"Corrections."

"Plunging property values!"

"Bargains."

"The climate is out of control."

"Was it ever?"

"But icebergs in Miami?"

"Proves there's no global warming."

"Hurricanes in London?"

"Al Gore's fault."

"Rush Limbaugh's."

"Bovine flatus."

"Sunspots."

"How would you like a nice punch in the nose?"

"You and whose over-extended army?"

"That's enough! All of you just calm down! We've got no time to fight, we've got to plan!"

Buck separated the most volatile combatants and issued three by fives to everyone.

"Ali's right," he started. "Civilization won't last a month without oil. Changing everyone over to hydrogen could take a year. We've got to make oil in the meantime, that's all there is to it. Vita, how about it? You said Nutting was petroleum-free. Certainly you must lubricate your machines with something. It can't be all whales and coconuts."

"Lubricant technology!" said Bufo, clasping his hands. "Fascinating field. A personal hobby of mine, actually. In fact, we have a contest here—Slipperiest of the Nuttings—where everybody gets on this big mat and—"

"But your machines, Vita," said Buck. "All those motors of yours. The bearings. You must use something?"

"The kukui nut has a fine oil, though tends to degrade at higher temperatures. The karumba berry holds up better, but has viscosity issues under pressure. Palm is hopeless and goes rancid. Bad for your heart, too, I hear. There are a dozen other tropical nuts, each with its own strength, but overall I think the best is kukui."

"So that's what you do for oil, squeeze nuts?"

"Nah," said Bufo. "Too much trouble. Those trees are a bitch to climb. A guy could break his neck. We just run off strings of carbon, hydrogenate the hell out of them, and call it a day. Kind of crude, but, hey, who's looking?"

"You are making hydrocarbon chains, is that what you said?" Buck couldn't believe his ears.

"No big deal," he said. "We got the process from Procter and Gamble. They use it to make Crisco, you know. Since we already have the hydrogen from our ocean thermal conversion and the carbon from our calcium carbonate production all it takes is energy to drive the reaction that sticks the two together. That we have plenty of, so we just bang these chains out using brute strength. With the right catalysts I'll bet we could increase the efficiency by an order of magnitude or two. Why do you ask? Planning to compete for slipperiest Nutting?"

"Thinking about getting into the oil business."

"About how much oil you thinking about making?" asked Bufo.

"I think a hundred and twenty million barrels a day would do it."

"Easier just to pump it out of the ground."

"Keep it under your hat, but the world's out in ninety days."

"And nobody's got a plan for that?"

"We do now."

"Love your enthusiasm."

506

"Yours, too, Vita."

"So where do we start?"

"I kinda need to talk with some of our people on this."

"Mail pickup's in about a month."

"No phones?"

"No phones."

"Email?"

"Nope."

"Radio?"

"Sorry."

"Maybe it doesn't matter. We don't exactly know where they are anyway."

"So, your people, how exactly do you get in touch with them?"

"Well, usually we pull a stunt big enough for the whole world to see and then our people find us."

"This could be a problem in Nutting. We're invisible, remember?"

Buck looked to his friends. They shuffled their feet. They fingered their three by fives.

"Smoke signals?" offered Petal

"Message in a bottle?" suggested Ali.

"Fix the *Waba Ti Li*?" posed Captain Kim.

Buck considered all of these and more. It took him most of a minute.

"Vita, how many of those big plastic baggies filled with hydrogen do you think it would take to get a Korean destroyer up to airline cruising altitude?"

"An unimaginably huge number."

"Well, then, what are we waiting for? Let's do it!"

CHAPTER 76

SIGNAL

"The tradition is hopelessly archaic, Captain."

"Suicidally outmoded."

"Lethally sentimental."

"Morbidly romantic."

"Masochistically exhibitionistic."

"Patriotically perverse."

"Really dumb."

"In other words, forget it. It's just a boat."

Intellectually, Captain Kim knew they were right, but in his heart he knew that, above all else, he was still the captain of the *Waba Ti Li*. It was his duty to go down with his ship—or in this case, up with it. It didn't matter that the Navy of the Republican Peoples' Democracy of Korea had ceased to exist. It was irrelevant that the entire concept of naval destroyers had become irrelevant. It was beside the point that her crew had deserted, her engines had blown, her guns rusted solid, and her toilets backed up. He didn't care that she didn't have a radio, CD, or air conditioning. For as long as either of them could remember, she had been his ship and he had been her captain. He would not leave her now.

He stood stoically by as Bufo's men swarmed over her like an army of leaf cutter ants. He cringed as cranes carried off every appendage that torches could amputate. He grew pale as she exsanguinated rivers of steel, copper, and iron into the hungry hoppers of the Nutting Island Recycling Unit. He blushed in shame as she was laid bare in front of his eyes. Within an hour she was stripped.

But, actually, she didn't look that bad naked. She was definitely more feminine without all those cannons poking out at their unmistakably phallic angles. Bufo's crew had even touched up her gray. She was positively buoyant with the ballast out of her bottom—though she would have listed a little had it not been for some discreet hydrogen uplift. It was like she was teetering on her first pair of heels after her first glass of bubbly. The grand old ship was now a princess debutante. She was ready to fly. Parental approval or not.

Dozens of plastic baggies, each hundreds of feet long, clustered at the ends of cables bolted to her hull. As each was inflated and deployed, the *Waba Ti* sat higher in the water until she seemed to skate on the surface like a bug. Thermoses of supercooled hydrogen sat on her deck, feeding the balloons through hoses running up the cables. Bufo himself made the last adjustment on the valve timers and switched on a bank of fans fixed to the bow. He scurried onto the gang plank to meet Kim striding toward him.

"Captain Bufo, if you will please step aside, I will now board my ship," said Kim, with a formal salute.

"Captain Kim," said Bufo politely, "if you are looking for your ship, I think you will find most of her down in the recycling area awaiting her next incarnation. What you see in front of you is a mere afterimage, the mist of her breath set loose on the wind. It is not her spirit. The spirit of the *Waba Ti Li* is destined for greatness, but it cannot be reborn unless you are alive. Don't chase this apparition. She may be pretty, but she is not your love."

Kim hesitated, searching Bufo's face and the faces of his friends. Finally, he relented.

"Captain Bufo, do what you must. I only ask that you be gentle."

"You'll be proud, Captain."

Bufo gave the signal and the lines were cast off. *The New Waba Ti Li* seemed to cling to the surface for one long moment more and then finally, with a flourish, leap a foot into the air. She paused there briefly as if getting used to her wings and then slowly began her ascent skyward.

At about five hundred feet a puff of smoke shot across her deck and a banner unfurled, the length of the ship and ten times as high. Its inspiring message:

LET'S DO IT!

A cheer broke out from the assembled multitude, one that didn't abate until the *Li* was just a speck against the deep blue dome of the Pacific sky.

"I sure hope that thing doesn't come down on us," said Ali.

"It shouldn't come down on anybody," said Bufo. "The winds are westerly and the fans should nudge out another tenth of a knot. There's nothing but open ocean ahead of her for thousands of miles. With the calculated rate of hydrogen leakage, she ought to settle back into the water well before she reaches Australia."

"Unless an airliner runs into it," said Ali.

"Planes are on the lookout for this sort of thing," said Petal. "All we need is one to get close enough for a few cell phone photos. Once they hit the internet Siverth will know it's us."

"Foolproof!"

"Exactly. What could go wrong?"

"Let's have lunch."

And dinner. And then breakfast. And lunch again. And a few more meals after that. Captain Kim spent his time scanning the sky and searching the horizon. Buck and Bufo studied engineering drawings. Ivan and Igor filled legal pads with Cyrillic scratchings. Petal and Ali debated the color of the big picture.

"The big picture is rosy," said Ali, "because Nutting is the perfect place for us to be when civilization collapses—self-contained, insulated, invisible. Even an atomic cloud would have trouble finding us here. I have to admit, stumbling onto this place was a stroke of luck."

"We didn't stumble on this place, we were sent here by Siverth. And we're not here to save our skins, you ninny—we're here to save the world. But I'll agree with you on one thing, if the big picture hasn't turned exactly rosy, it's definitely pinker than puce."

"Too much purple in puce. More pink would just make it look bruised."

"With all of the work ahead of us, I think we should go with a more metallic hue—something like Anodized Aluminum Areola. My cell phone was that color. I wonder what ever happened to my cell phone."

"Darling," said Ali. "Your cell phone has immolated itself on a pyre of unanswered voice mails. Don't you know they spontaneously ignite when you get over a thousand?"

"Do you think I will ever care about voice mails again?"

"Looking at you now, I sincerely doubt it."

Petal, as would any woman, instinctively glanced around for a mirror—that's another thing Nutting houses didn't seem to come with, mirrors. But even without one, she knew he was right.

No longer abused by stylists, Petal's hair now shone with the sun. Recovered from years of cosmetics, her skin beamed with pride and gratitude. Unbound from urbanity, her muscles stretched her tall and curved her full. Now her feet were wider, her nails stubbier, her hands tougher. She wasn't the same Petal. She never would be. No editor would ever trust her with a society page again.

"Thank you, Ali. That's the nicest thing you've ever said."

"Don't get mushy on me. Being less girlie doesn't make you more manly. In fact, the effect is quite the opposite."

"You think so?" she said, smoothing her pareo. Mrs. Bufo had taught her three hundred ways to tie it, but she never was sure she had it right. "I don't need a complete make over?"

"That would be a crime," he said. "Punishable by death. Death by curling iron. Death by mud pack. Death by dyeing."

"I'm sorry I called you a ninny," she said, hugging him.

"Well, don't be. I work hard at being one."

"Everybody quick!" called Buck from outside. "Come look at this!"

Buck passed the binos to Petal and pointed her in the right direction. The only thing Ali could make out with his naked eye was a shiny spot in the western sky. Kim was dancing around like a kid with an iPod and Bufo was racing off somewhere in his golf cart. Something big was indeed up.

"I know you are trying to get me to say that I see a battleship chasing a blimp just so everyone can have a good laugh," said Petal. "So, to show what a good sport I am, that's my final answer. A battleship chasing a blimp."

"We've seen that blimp before," said Ali, taking his turn with the binos. "Yeah, you can just about read the name on it—*The Sphincter.*"

"That would be *The Sphinx*, if you look closely," said Buck. "Olaf Tórshavn gave us a lift from Reykjavík to Svalbard aboard it. And I think if you look closely enough you will see that behind it is our very own *Waba Ti Li* in tow."

512

With the graceful precision characteristic of lighter than air craft, the Faroe/Korean flotilla slowly cruised over them, positioned itself over Nutting Atoll's central lagoon, and hung there. For the next hour the only action seemed to be the insistent LET'S DO IT ! gently undulating in the breeze.

"I guess now we just wait for the baggies to leak and the *Li* to settle down into the water," said Petal, stating the obvious feminine solution.

"Not as long as guys are involved," said Buck. "Here, look at the last window on the *Sphinx*."

Petal steadied the glasses against Buck. He was right. There it was. The typical guy solution to life's knottiest problems. Hang out of a window with a gun.

"Isn't this how the Hindenburg lost its health insurance?" asked Petal.

"Just one theory," said Buck. "Along with lightning, sabotage, wet paint, and bad driving."

"But, there's also a theory about hydrogen burning when you light it, right?"

"Widely accepted as having graduated from the class of 'theory' into the class of 'just about guaranteed'," granted Buck.

"Why not use a bow and arrow?" asked Petal. "A slingshot? A blowgun? Aren't they guy things, too?"

"The rule is you have to use the most monstrous tool available. Any wuss can hang a picture with a hammer—it takes a real guy to do it with a sledge. This is why arms control is such a good idea," said Ali.

"And why it never passes the Senate," said Buck.

"Maybe it would if they had other opportunities to be guys," said Petal, watching with horror as the guy in the *Sphinx* popped a cap into one of the *Li*'s baggies.

"Younger mistresses? Longer limos? Softer money?" offered Ali.

"You're right," she said, cringing as the shooter inched out on a strut for a better shot. "It's hopeless. Guys are totally out of control."

"I don't know," said Buck, projecting a nudge of body English at the Korean destroyer, which was now pitching bow down at an unhealthy ten degrees. "What if there was a counterbalance. Some force that made the yin as powerful as the yang. A long-awaited correction of mankind's disastrous experiment with guy hegemony."

"It would have to be huge," she said, wincing as another baggie went limp, lurching the *Li* back to an even keel. "Worldwide. Revolutionary."

"Something like the Cult of Petal, perhaps?" asked Buck, heaving a sigh of relief as the *Waba Ti Li* started its slow descent.

"If you two are doing this Vaudeville routine for my benefit, you're wasting your time," said Ali. "I don't care how much hype the Cult of Petal gets on the internet, there is no force of nature great enough to get guys to admit there is any other way but theirs. Especially when every once in a while they manage to get a hole in one."

And with that a cheer went up from every non-corner of Nutting Atoll as the *Waba Ti* and it's quintessential guy message settled sweetly down right in the center of the blue lagoon.

CHAPTER 77

ZIP

Despite all the overly conspicuous, meant-to-be-reassuring rituals of airline procedure ("wheels—check, engines—check, movies—check"), operation of flying vehicles remains to this day largely a matter of improvisation. For example, if one attempts to consult one's manual regarding disembarkation of passengers from dirigibles parked over bodies of water, one may find many helpful hints, but no universally applicable algorithm that lets your judgment off the hook.

Passengers of heavier-than-air craft will nearly all agree that the least harrowing part of their travel experience is the transition from seat to terminal (not counting the part when some bozo jerks his carry-on full of pennies out of the overhead bin directly onto your noggin). Not so with lighter-than-air. Unless you get that baby cinched down good and tight in a hangar with the doors closed, you are never quite sure exactly where you stand, *vis à vis* the tarmac. Exits over water are that much worse, with the added ups and downs intrinsic to the air/liquid interface. Methods utilizing elastic ladders, catamaran trampolines, slides, and pulleys have spawned handsome catalogs of patented devices, but none have as yet inspired the confidence of the traveling public.

Thus, even on this most tranquil day in the most tranquil of places, it was not obvious how the passengers of the *Sphinx* were going to get out. Lacking any means of communication with the ship, Bufo assumed that, as harbor master, the responsibility fell to him, and he had better get with it. First, he positioned four tugs below the dirigible, each at a corner of a fishing net they stretched as tight as they could. But the center of the net still rested in the water, which negated almost every benefit to those who might choose to jump. After a while it became apparent that this had indeed been an idea, just not a good one, and Bufo gave the order for the net to be stowed. But at that moment someone appeared at the exit door of the *Sphinx* and dropped an object into the net.

Buck and his friends were watching the whole thing from the highest point of the atoll's ridge, but from this distance it was hard to pick up much detail.

"I think they just threw Bufo a bottle of champagne," said Buck, squinting through the binos.

"I didn't know Bufo drank champagne," said Petal, realizing that was another thing Nutting houses didn't seem to come with, champagne. "Do you think it will help?"

"No, wait. It's a champagne bottle with a note in it. Hope it's in English. Or Nuttingese—maybe Olaf knows Nuttingese—it's got to be easier to learn than English—okay, they're giving each other the thumbs up. That's universal, right? Now they are lowering lines to the tugs. Good. Now the tugs are taking them to docks—four different docks—a little redundant—three would have been enough—no, I see what's up, Bufo is bringing the end of one of the lines up here in his cart. The other lines are being cinched in—see how the *Sphinx* is settling down? She'll be just about level with us in a minute."

Bufo's cart made its way slowly up the hill from the lagoon, laboring under the load of the cable (not to mention the load of Bufo). With Buck's help, he managed to wrap the line around a big ironwood tree and block the cart's wheels with boulders. They all then stood out on the edge of the rise and gave a team thumbs up to the *Sphinx*, riding there in mid air at the other end of the cable.

Instantly, a figure appeared in the doorway, gave a salute, and jumped.

"Oh my God!" cried Petal. "Is he nuts?"

"It's only a zip line, Petal," said Ali. "Tourists love them in Yomamah."

"Yeah, I know. But would any local get on one?"

"Are you kidding; you think we're nuts?"

"Here he comes!"

The physics of zip lines, on first glance, appears deceptively simple. As long as point A is higher than point B you would think that zipping down a line from A to B would be about as simple as falling off a dirigible. In reality, however, zip lines are made from real cables that really weigh something, and therefore form themselves into parabolic rather than straight lines. In other words, they sag in the middle—and the longer they are, the stronger they have to be, and the stronger they are, the heavier they are, and the heavier they are, and the more they sag.

This means that it is entirely conceivable that a timid zipper with insufficient momentum might find him or herself hopelessly 'stuck in the sag,' as they say in the zip line industry. Such a line-clogging event can have immediate negative repercussions on the franchisee's cash flow unless alternate tourist through-put pathways have been previously constructed. Attempts at clearing clogged lines are almost never cost effective and always more trouble than investing in a solid, reliable liability waiver form in the first place.

Whether this particular zipper had taken all of these factors into consideration or merely had no idea what he was doing was not evident in his technique, which basically consisted of flailing wildly with his arms and legs while screaming his head off. This method proved to be highly efficient at both conserving forward momentum and generating cardiac arrhythmias, and by the time he approached point B both he and everyone's heart rate were going like bats out of hell. Buck and the Russians were bowled completely over trying to catch the guy, but their efforts did scrub off enough energy for Bufo to grab him before he bounced off the tree.

"Welcome to Nutting Atoll," said Bufo with a salute. "Captain Vita Bufo, harbormaster, at your service."

"Olaf Tórshavn, Captain of the *Sphinx*, at your service," he saluted with one hand while straightening his tie with the other. "Nice work with the lines down there. Most ports are still unfamiliar with correct dirigible protocol."

"Our first time, actually," said Bufo. "And beautiful job with the *Waba Ti Li*— we thought we'd never see her again."

"Your chaps in that balloon? Well, you better give them a good talking to. Never saw such an unsafe configuration. No place for amateurs in aviation, in my opinion. If we hadn't come along, I don't know what would have happened to them."

"No one aboard. We sent it as some kind of signal. You'll have to ask—"

"Captain Tórshavn, how good of you to come," said Petal. Buck reached to shake his hand.

"Ms. Steele and Mr. Planck! This is getting stranger and stranger. What are you two doing here?"

517

"Didn't Siverth Narup send you for us when he saw the *Waba Ti Li* on the internet?" asked Petal.

"Of course not. I don't know any Siverth Narup. I'm here to deliver a passenger—and would have been here considerably sooner if I hadn't been dragging that damn battleship the last couple of days. And as for the internet, why would such a dumb stunt merit space on the internet?"

"A passenger?" asked Buck. "Maybe it's Siverth using another name. Artistic looking guy—wispy but intense?"

"Afraid not. Here she comes now, maybe she knows your friend Narup."

Another figure appeared in the *Sphinx's* doorway, this one about half the mass of Tórshavn. Buck and the Russians braced for another fast one, but this zipper clearly knew what she was doing, and with perfect zip technique (hand up, hips flexed, knees bent, mouth shut) she cruised in for feather-light landing. As soon as she hit the ground, she ran straight to Petal and jumped into her arms.

"I knew it was true! I knew it was true! Everybody said I was crazy, but I knew it was true!" squealed the girl.

"Trina! How did you find us? Are Sunleif and your parents with you?" Petal held her at arm's length to get a better look. Her outfit had morphed a bit since the Chill in Svalbard, no doubt the logical consequence of the global girl subconscious digesting Petal's disastrous materialization scene at the Tokyo train station.

Her Speedo had been Japonified with a few bits of Kanji and some stylized gunshot wounds, and her cuffs now sported some dangerous-looking shards. Her hair was nearly white except for a streak of crimson that left the disquieting impression that her scalp had been grazed by a bullet. A cardboard tag dangled by string from her left big toe. Each part of her ensemble worked perfectly with the rest to achieve the unadmitted goal of giving every member of the parental class an immediate heart attack.

"We met Trina when your steward invited us to his home for dinner," explained Buck to the puzzled Tórshavn. "Nice family."

"She's Sunleif Solberg's sister?" he asked, incredulous. "I thought she was some kind of heiress to be able to book a trip all the way here by herself. Dirigible cruising is quite competitive when you take the amenities into account, but it's still far from cheap."

"Where'd you get the cash for this, Trina," asked Petal. "Did Siverth Narup send it to you?"

"I just put it on Daddy's Visa," she said. "And who is Siverth Narup?"

"The best laid plans—" started Ali.

"Shut up, Ali," said Petal. "And how did you know to come here, Trina? I think that's the most important question."

"The fortune cookie, of course," said Trina, stamping her foot. Grownups could be so dense sometimes. "Helga and Sigrid and I were hacking into some old Tokyo rail station municipal bond records, you know, just after the helicopters mutilated your body with gatling fire, and of course we were so-o hungry and it didn't help that there was this annoying pop-up ad for the most excessively ordinary Chinese restaurant in Longyearbyen, so we were, like, Oh My God, was this a major clue or what? So, of course, what did we do? I mean, duhh—what else? We ordered, like every dish they had, which was massive given that your average Chinese menu has, what, like a thousand choices? Of course, it's really only about six things with lots of names—like who can tell the difference between Thousand Year Fortunate Emperor and Lucky Embryo Bird Taste? I mean really? You can't even tell by the writing on the boxes—I think they do that sloppy Chinese writing on purpose, don't you? Anyway, it was a mega-number of boxes— they totally filled up my entire bedroom. Just opening them all took an hour, and I'll have to tell you we were all about to puke before we had even tasted half of them. And so here we are lying there knowing our stomachs will be like totally bloated and fat forever, when Helga is, like, Oh My God, these people are so cheap that we order every dish on the menu and they only give us one lousy fortune cookie. Which is fine with me, because I never tasted one in my life that hadn't gone stale like a million years ago. But Helga is like, no-o you got to eat the fortune cookie or it will be bad luck until you completely die or something. And then she's like, what kind of fortune is this anyway? A bunch of numbers and letters—"

"2-25-33-N 129-33-05-W?" asked Petal.

"Something like that, so we Google it and, can you believe it, we get nothing! I mean, you could like drop your cat on the keyboard and Google would give you a couple million pages at least, but this one gets nothing! How spooky is that? So this is so spooky that I even tell my brother, who despite being a complete dweeb blimpmeister occasionally will know something completely obscure, like when the trash pickup is or how to run the dishwasher, so what do you think he says?"

"Nutting Atoll?" offered Petal.

"Nah, he says it's a place! Written in some sort of secret code for places. So then here we are."

"Amazing," said Petal.

"What's so amazing?" asked Ali. "You know that every fortune cookie since the beginning of time was made in the same dingy Hong Kong factory. So their fortune machine got stuck on 2-25-33-N 129-33-05-W. So what? I'll bet there are a jillion fortune cookies out there with the same message. Mark my words—next week the Nuttings will be crawling with even more nuts who think that fortune cookies are talking to them."

"Don't pay any attention to him, Trina," said Buck, seeing the look on her face. "You followed the numbers and found us, that's all that counts. What we really need to do is make sure that your parents know you're safe. It would be terrible for them to worry."

"Yeah, I guess you're right. I've never been this far from home before. I did go to Iceland once last summer with my family. They had water there that wasn't frozen. Pretty spooky. But I guess we're farther than Iceland now."

"Considerably."

"I'll just drop them a quick email."

"They don't have email here, Trina," said Petal. "Phones either. Maybe a postcard?"

"No email? What kind of place is this?" she said, rifling through her backpack. Out came a hot pink Hello Kitty laptop with Cult of Petal stickers all over it.

"Let's see here, looks like a pretty good satellite signal. Email downloads fine. I'll just send one to myself—see, mine works great. Maybe you've got your password wrong or something. Let's try a video call—hey! Sigrid, take a look! Now we know who's crazy, don't we?"

Trina spun the computer around on her knee with the practiced air of a Globetrotter with a ball. All of a sudden Petal was staring at Helga and vice versa, neither quite knowing what to say.

"Is that really you?" Helga finally managed.

"Sure is, Helga."

"Did it hurt when the gunships mutilated your body with gatling fire?"

"Not a bit," said Petal.

"And when you fell like a hundred stories to the street below?"

"Skinned my knee a little. But, Helga?"

"Yes, Petal?"

"Don't try it at home."

"Yes, ma'am. I sure won't."

CHAPTER 78

VMAIL

"Okay, let's do it!" shouted Petal above the others.

The room fell silent. Every bloodshot eye turned to her.

"We've been debating this for days. Stacks of legal pads filled. Hundreds of three by fives sorted. And that blackboard. All those arrows going every which way. What a mess. Now, I'm not saying that we shouldn't talk through our issues, or nurture consilience, or work out our insecurities or anything like that. But this is a crisis! Time is running out! We've dillied our last dally. Let's cut the chitchat, roll up our sleeves, and do it!"

"Do what?" asked Ali.

"Do it! You know, get on with it."

"And precisely which it should we get on with first?"

"I don't care. We've got a list of a hundred things that need doing. Just pick one in the middle and start on that one. They're all connected to one another anyway, right?"

"Isn't that precisely the problem?" asked Ali. "Everything depends on everything else. You can't just barge in before the groundwork has been done. The support elements have to be in place before an intervention can succeed. I know what I'm talking about—I've been in government all my life."

"So, no matter where we start, it won't work because we haven't done something else first?"

"Well, a real team player wouldn't put it that way," objected Ali. "But it is true that according to our interdependency diagrams, our plan has to be started up everywhere at once." He went to the blackboard to demonstrate how all of the arrows eventually led back to their origins.

"Baloney. You want to know what to do? Then I'll tell you what to do. What we do is call up Siverth Narup and ask him what to do, that's what."

"I think Siverth is depending on us to figure out what to do," said Buck. "From a technical standpoint anyway."

"And what makes you think it will be so easy calling up Siverth Narup?" asked Ali. "You want to launch the *Waba Ti Li into* space again?"

"No-o-o!" wailed Captain Kim, holding up his hands. Bufo's men had almost finished making her seaworthy, albeit not war worthy, once again.

"And don't forget what happened in Tokyo when the authorities caught up with us," said Ali. "As soon as we start firing off emails, somebody's army will triangulate our position and start firing bullets back in return. Or worse."

"But Siverth sent Trina down here for a reason—"

"Objection!" cried Ali. "Speculation stated as fact—"

"And the reason has to be for her to deliver that laptop." She pointed to the painfully pink plastic replica of Hello Kitty's hideous head, crammed full of high tech electronics. Its screen glowed blankly; its twittering torrent of teenage text now shunted to Trina's handheld, somewhere on its way back to Svalbard aboard the *Sphinx.*

"And since none of his stuff is coming in, he obviously intends for our stuff to be going out!"

"I agree with Petal," said Buck. "We've done our homework. We've rechecked all our calculations. We've got all the blueprints and engineering drawings ready to go. We're ready to pull the switch on this thing. We even know enough people in the right places to get it started. But Ali's got a point, too. Once we get on that internet, we had better be quick about it because we're bound to be spotted."

"So we get our act together, get on the net, get it done, and get off. Maybe if we're lucky, Siverth will see us before Interpol does. But once we're finished, we'd better get out of town quick," said Petal.

"Leave Nutting?" cried Ali. "But this is the greatest place in the world!"

"Another reason why it shouldn't be in the crossfire when we're in the crosshairs," said Buck. "Without these people the world is toast."

"And I'm already a little worried about that video session with Trina and Helga," said Petal. "Even with those girls sworn to secrecy, that bit of code is out there in the cyber-thicket, you can bet on that. Some face-recognition program is bound to troll it up soon. I say we strike tonight and sail in the morning."

"Wait! Wait! Aren't you forgetting the most critical thing?" said Ali. "Siverth is the one with the money. All these grandiose plans will take trillions in capital. Nobody's going to make a move until they have the cash in their hands. "

"Well, we're not in any position to be cutting checks," said Petal. "But we can get it all teed up and then when Siverth is on board he can start the cash flowing."

"Not good enough," said Ali. "Why would anyone even listen to us?"

"They wouldn't," said Buck. "But they will listen to Petal. Petal's got something more powerful than money."

"And what would that be?"

"She's got the people. Billions of them."

Ali had to admit that it might just play.

"We had better get this right the first time," he said. "There won't be any encores. We'll contact everybody by video email. Much more effective than text or audio. All the technical stuff can go as attachments. We'll get them all recorded and then send them as a block—that will minimize our exposure on the net.

"Buck, you script out all the messages. They've got to be imperative, explicit, and short. Petal, you print Buck's copy on cue cards and practice your spookiest expression. Kim, you and the Russians will build the set—Bufo can get us the materials. I'll take care of Petal's wardrobe and makeup and the special effects. Everybody got it? Okay, move!"

It only took a few hours to get ready for show time. Bufo wanted to stay and watch, but if the *Waba Ti Li* was to sail on the tide, he would need to supervise final preparations down at the dock. The Russians had done an amazing job painting an arctic landscape backdrop, and since they were still eager to help, Ali let them run the dry-ice fog generator and styrofoam-snowflake blizzard machine.

Petal's bloom of health had to go, but because there was no makeup around (another thing Nutting households didn't come with) they improvised with chalk dust and coconut oil. Getting her suitably cold wasn't a problem with all that dry ice around—they just had to be careful to keep chattering teeth from interfering with intelligible speech. Costume was easy—Speedo already on.

Every theatrical production must have its near fatal, last minute catastrophe just to keep everyone's adrenal glands squeezed down to raisins. It was two minutes before 'go live' when the laptop started whining about a low battery level. Since Trina had been understandably distracted at the time of her departure (one last hug from Petal swearing her to secrecy, one last holler from Tórshavn to hurry up, one last text to Helga regarding omg cn u blv it, one last email to her father pleading for leniency, and one last call to her mother insisting that she hadn't done anything with anybody) it was forgivable that she had run off with the charger in her backpack.

What wasn't forgivable was that with all their planning to satisfy the entire world's energy needs, no one had planned for the energy needs of this one little machine. Igor was quickly dispatched to the dock and struggled back with a transformer the size of an air conditioner—the closest thing Bufo could come up with at the last minute. Hooking it up without the requisite proprietary Hello Kitty Powder Puff Power Plug Adapter was a major hassle, finally requiring a soldering iron, two C-clamps, six feet of copper wire, and a yard of friction tape. In the end the little icon of Hello Kitty lapping up electrons from a saucer took the place of Hello Kitty suffering from the final stages of electron kwashiorkor, and all was ready to go again.

"Let's start with the easy ones first," said Buck, cuing the fog and snow. "Quiet on the set! On my count. One, two, three, talk!"

"Chucky," said Petal looking straight into the laptop's camera. "We need platforms, a lot of them. And we need you to make them in just about every country with a coastline, simultaneously, starting tomorrow. The attachments to this email will tell you all the details. And another thing, be a dear and watch over the money. All the numbers to the account are right there. Nothing there now, but will be soon. Take what you need. Others will be calling. Thanks, Chucky, you're the man."

"Cut!" cried Buck. "Excellent. You're on a roll. Now for this one you'll need to trade warmth for intimidation. Ready? Go!"

"Mr. Uberpipe, get all your boys at Daimler-Chrysler-Ford-GM together and listen carefully. You know your heads should be on stakes for crimes against the planet, but relax—we're not coming for you yet. In fact, this could be the luckiest day of your miserable little lives—all you have to do is open your eyes, join the human race, and cooperate for once and I'll hand you the bail-out of the century, right on a plate.

"First of all, you guys have built your last fossil-fired engine. Period. Next, check out the plans for the hydrogen fuel cell vehicles attached to this email. Look familiar? They've been in your safe for decades. Well, get started building them. And those electric cars? Make those, too. The numbers are all there. You may have to put on some extra workers to meet our requirements. Too bad, I know how you hate that.

"Finally, see the drawings for the ocean thermal conversion units? Pretty simple, eh? Not as complicated as an automatic transmission. You could bang those out by the thousands, right? Well, then, get with it. The production deadlines and delivery sites are all there. And none of that planned obsolescent, intentionally shoddy, wears-out-in-five-years kind of crap you're famous for. Make 'em like Model T's. Take some pride.

"This, of course, will make you a ton of money. You can even spin it to look like great humanitarians. I don't care about any of that. Have fun. Just one thing, though. Don't forget who's calling the shots from now on."

"Cut!" called Buck. "Inspired! Perfect! Keep it up. Next let's do Clinker and Wiremeter together—these coal and electric power guys are joined at the hip. One. Two. Three. Geev um!"

"Rex? Is that you, Rex Clinker, King of Coal? Get your buddy Otto Wiremeter over here and pay attention. You know who I am and who I represent, and I don't give a damn that you don't like any of us. Well, we don't much like what you've done to our planet either. But what say we not send you to the guillotine just yet because, with a little rehabilitation, you two might be of some use and maybe even redeem yourselves.

"First of all, your gang-rape of the countryside is over. Your mines are closed. Send the miners home. We've got plenty of healthier jobs for them. Coal power is done with, and so is your propaganda about 'clean coal,' whatever the hell that is.

"Otto, if your power plants can burn that hideously dirty coal, they can easily be converted to burn totally clean hydrogen. No more poisonous ash, no more acid rain, no more CO_2 —just pure water as a byproduct. You'll save a ton of money and everybody

527

will love you. I know it will be tough adapting to the new image, but with a few years of psychotherapy I'm sure you can do it. But we're not going to wait for you to you to want to change—you and your industry are changing today. Why? Because the people of the planet say so, that's why. And we are finally taking charge of this.

"Rex, all that monstrous equipment you've got ripping the tops off of mountains—we've got other plans for that. First, you can start by cleaning up your mess. Later, we've got enough infrastructure work to last you a hundred years. Your instructions are in the documents attached. They are very specific. You won't even have to think. Just sit back and get rich, because all of this will make you both an obscene amount of money. Not that you deserve it. Now, get busy!"

"Cut!" called Buck. "Masterful. Petal, you're a natural. Now the oil guys, Kelvin and Flare. And a one, and a two, and a three! Hit it!"

"Kelvin! Flare! All you oily Shell Exxon Mobile dudes! Now hear this! As of today you are no longer in the oil finding-drilling-pumping-business! All that oil under the ground is doing just fine right where it is, thank you, so forget about it. You are now in the energy distribution business, get it? Much easier, less risky, and more profitable for you anyway. All those tankers of yours—they'll still be carrying oil for now, but it will be green oil from our ocean thermal conversion rigs, not from your Earth-crust-sucking ones. Tell your guys on their North Sea platforms that we've got new assignments for them in the South Pacific. If they complain, have 'em call us.

"You've got a year before we phase out making green oil. That's plenty of time for you to convert oil distribution to hydrogen distribution and shut down those disgusting refineries. Let us know if any of your station operators miss smelling like gasoline. Not that we care, really. And we don't really care if you end up making a whole lot more money than you ever did, either. Just so you get on board and quit sabotaging the inevitable. Fossil oil is over. Get over it. Green oil is there to help you detox. You're welcome. Clean, renewable, carbonless energy is taking over. This is an offer you can't refuse. Petal out."

"Cut!" cried Buck. "Incredible! Just a few more easy ones. Ready? Go!"

"Horace Tick. You still running the EPA? Must be a record. Well it's your time to make history again. This time the heroic act will be doing your job. Why should you? Look out your window, Horace. See all those townspeople with pitchforks? Yeah, it does look like the crowd goes all the way to Georgetown. In kind of a nasty mood, too, wouldn't you say? What do they want, you ask? They want you to do your job, Horace, and I don't think they're going to be happy until you do.

"What's your job, you ask? Gee, Horace, look around on your desk, maybe there's a little laminated card with your job description. Never mind. We've got a list for you. Just follow it to the letter. And, no, your corporate cronies can't save you now.

"I know, it's kind of a long list. Job too big for you? Put on a few competent people to help you. Don't know any? Start with Loudon Stillwright in the basement; he'll give you some names.

"And, you have to admit, none of these things on this list are what real people would call work. The only work for you is signing your name, and I'll bet your secretary has a stamp for that. What's her name again? Brushmeat? Dear girl. Say hi to her for me.

"Yes, you're reading it right. No more nukes. Shut them down. Clean them up. And for God's sake get all that radioactive crap under lock and key somewhere. And Horace? Apologize to all those people who have had to live near those abominations all these years.

"Yes, Horace, CO_2 is a pollutant. Yes, I know it's natural. What isn't natural, Horace? It's a natural pollutant that is polluting the natural environment. Somebody's got to protect the environment. Why not the Environmental Protection Agency? Sounds like a natural. But don't worry, you won't have to work so hard on this, we've done all the work for you. Pretty soon without oil and coal there will be hardly anything for you to do about CO_2. In the meantime, just follow the instructions and start fining the pants off of the big CO_2 producers. Yes, I know they're your friends, but what are friends for if you can't use them?

"And Horace? Those fines? Just drop them into that Swiss bank account. The number is on the bottom of the page. See it there? And ditto for your last couple years' worth of kickbacks, bribes, honoraria, and so-called book deals, too. Okay?

"There's a lot more, I know, but you're a smart guy, you can read. We'll be looking for those checks in the morning. Have a good day. Ten four."

"Cut!" said Buck. "Beautiful! Keep going or take a break?"

"Let's do it!"

"These are easy ones, anyway. Ready, go!"

"Mr. Ferret. This is Ms. Steele regarding the article you commissioned us to do for the *Hedge Insider Daily*. Sorry for not getting back to you sooner, but, as you may have noticed, we've been kind of busy creating a global revolutionary network and dodging multiple assassination attempts. Not that we haven't been working tirelessly on your project. Quite the contrary. Day and night we have been consumed by the question 'What's a filthy rich investor to do? The planet is on the verge of ecologic-socio-politico-economic meltdown. The market has been exposed as a fraud and a delusion. The financial industry turned over to petulant toddlers. Wealth is winking out. Privilege bankrupt. Celebrity cancelled.'

"Well, Mr. Ferret your readers need not fret a minute longer. We have their inside scoop all done up with sprinkles in a sugar cone. The guaranteed hedge against collapse of civilization. All the details are attached to this email. Tell the Publisher there's plenty of room for everybody's money in this one, but hurry, because, as all of your readers know, the boldest investors always get the biggest piece. Just be sure all the transfers go to that Swiss account at the bottom of the page.

"And Mr. Ferret, would you be so kind as to put our fees into that account as well? No sense collecting them now when we could have ten times as much in ninety days.

"So bye now, and don't hesitate to call if we can help you and your investors with anything else in the future."

"Cut," said Buck. "Brilliant! Ready for Grandma Bootstrap? Here goes! Shoot!"

"Grandma? This is Petal. Long time no see. Just dropping you a line to see how things are going back in Coeur d'Alene. We're fine. Been doing a little traveling for work lately and we're looking forward to the holidays to relax—but who can really relax over the holidays with all the baking and decorating to be done, as I'm sure you know. Buck had a little cold for a while, but he's fine now. I swear, traveling is just so much trolling for viruses with all the sick people on planes nowadays.

"By the way, just thought you might be interested in something a little birdie told me. It's right on the attachment there. Scout's honor, it's true. Now wouldn't it be cool if Grandma's could get a head start on this? Have all your franchises ready to convert cars from internal combustion to hydrogen or plug in? The Japanese have it all worked out. Aren't they clever, those people? There's our friend Ike Yoshimura's email. Mention my name and he'll get his people to help you. But hurry; when this thing comes down, everybody will be doing it.

"So, ta ta, Grandma Bootstrap. Give our love to all the other Grandmas, too."

"Cut!" said Buck. "Very sweet. Is that a wrap?"

"Can we check in with Louise?"

"Sure. Send something to all the New Eden folks. Ready? You're on."

"Louise? Hi. This is Petal. And hi to Archie and Ephraim, too. Hope you all are doing well and busy getting ready for the collapse of civilization. Just one thought, though. We've got a little project going that you might be interested in. Tell your neighbors, too. This is perfect for any of your survivalist, utopian, millenarian, or whatever kind of groups you've got up there in the woods with you.

"Here's the offer, free for nothing. What each of you gets is a fifty acre floating platform in the tropics, complete with its own clean energy and fresh water. Great place to raise kids and a garden while you ride out the apocalypse.

"And you can feel good about yourself while you're doing it. Not only will you be making hydrogen and green oil for the world, you'll be scrubbing CO_2 out of the air and out of the ocean to make limestone, which you can use to build your own islands. And if civilization decides not to collapse anytime soon, you can go into real estate. Let's be honest, what better way is there to pass the time waiting for Armageddon than by working to prevent it?

"I know this is kind of sudden, but we could really use your help on this one. If having your own private paradise turns out not to work for you, you can always go back to swatting mosquitoes and tax collectors in Idaho. Drop this guy an email—Buck, give me

Chucky's email address—thanks—here it is. He'll tell you where to get aboard. Okay, bye for now."

"Cut. Excellent idea. Why didn't I think of that? Here, let me do a quick one. Am I on? You sure? Okay, hey Xuyen, Thanh, Tyrone and all the rest of you Nguyens! This is Buck, obviously. How's it in the Big Apple? All right! Okay, here's the deal. We have a little catering job maybe you would like to take on. Well, actually it's a big catering job. Get with this guy—here's his email—and he'll tell you how many meals for how many thousand people in how many thousand places over the world. You might have to get all the Nguyens in on this, now that I think of it. Oh, and the rent. I guess I'm a little late again. Don't worry though, I'll be back soon. Okay. Bye."

"Cut," said Petal. "Good thought. Food. I guess the platforms will need catering until they start growing their own."

"Got to eat," said Buck, rifling through his notes. "Oh no! We almost forgot Tórshavn! That would have been a disaster!"

"Forget Tórshavn," said Ali. "We've got energy and the atmosphere covered. This blimp idea of yours is redundant."

"No way. The climate system has so much momentum that even if we quit fossil fuels and scrub CO_2 and pull heat out of the ocean, global temperatures will continue to rise for decades. Tórshavn is our only hope. Here, put me on, I'll do this one.

"Olaf. Buck here. Nice of you to bring Trina and her laptop down. Listen. We need to commission the *Sphinx* and the rest of the Faroe Island Airborne Advertising fleet. In fact, we need just about every dirigible in the world and then some. See the plans on the attachment? What do you think?

"Yes, I know it's a big job, but it's got to be done and you're the guy to do it. You said you could put a mile-wide swath of contrail that disappears at nightfall. Well, take a look at the itineraries. You give us enough daytime cloud cover and we change the Earth's albedo right now. Reflect just a tiny portion of incoming sunlight back into space and we drop the planet's temperature in real time.

"Yes, I know you'll have to build more ships. We've accounted for that in the calculations. All the money you need is in a Swiss account. Our friend Chucky can get it out for you. The details are all there.

"And Olaf, we're counting on you. The whole world is counting on you."

"Cut!" cried Ali. "I thought you guys were going to make this quick! Send all those messages and let's get out of here."

Ivan and Igor shut down the Styrofoam blizzard and waved their hands wildly.

"Forget us don't!"

Buck herded them on camera and gave them the cue. Two simultaneous Slavic streams burst forth into the camera.

"They're recruiting every sex worker in six continents," Buck explained to Ali, "to sew kites for the platforms. What better way to move them into position?"

The Russians gave thumbs up when they were done, and Buck shut down the recording. Everyone gathered around the laptop. With great ceremony, Buck took Petal's finger and with it gently pressed *Send*. A Hello Kitty icon in a mail carrier's uniform went from leaning against the edge of the screen eating a donut to squatting down with as constipated an expression an icon could make without a mouth or eyebrows.

"It's working!" said Petal, jumping up and down with glee.

"Congratulations!" said Captain Kim, slapping Buck on the back.

"We drink! We drink!" shouted Ivan and Igor, dancing some kind of polka.

"Let's go! Let's go!" insisted Ali.

"Just a minute! Just a minute!" said Buck, peering at the screen, trying to make sense of Hello Kitty going postal.

"Tide's high! All aboard that's going aboard!" boomed Bufo's baritone from the doorway.

Bufo had always knocked before. He didn't this time. Nobody had seen him come to the door. It was dark. They were all over-stimulated and exhausted. No one saw exactly what happened when they all jumped at the sound of Bufo's voice. The only thing that they saw was the makeshift power cord jerking like a whip with the hot pink laptop clinging tightly to it, until the tip of Hello's chin came crashing into the steel transformer, transforming her bulbous computer head into an massive explosion of consumer electronic particles. A state of shock froze the room in place. The only movement was a wisp of smoke from Hello Kitty's smoldering remains, settling in a pile at their feet.

"Did she finish?" asked Petal.

"Finished or not, she's finished," said Ali, poking at the shards of immolated plastic and metal with his foot. "And unless somebody wants to say a prayer, I suggest we get out of Dodge before the shooting starts."

Ali was right. There was nothing left to do but go. Buck put his arm around Petal and led her out into the night. The moon was full again. There was even a breeze. The tide was high. They had done what they could. It was time for them to go.

CHAPTER 79

CONFRONTATION

"Catching anything?"

Buck looked up to see Petal standing there with a pitcher of lemonade. As usual, she was wearing a pareo that he had never seen before. As a going-away present, Mrs. Bufo had given her a collection that might go years without repeating. This time Petal had it tied in the Eight O'clock style—a precarious method considered scandalously risqué by the more conservative residents of Three O'clock. And, to be honest, it wasn't all that bad up in Three O'clock.

"Small ones, but really juicy," he said, rinsing off a strawberry and popping it into her mouth. "Corn coming in soon, too. Peas and tomatoes still going strong. You're not tired of these beans yet, are you?"

"I love everything you grow up here," said Petal, she said surveying the scene. With its instruments of violence gone, there was plenty of room for gardening on the deck of the *Waba Ti Li*. Everything was planted in elevated trays so that they could be taken below during bad weather—easier on the back for weeding, too. Scaffolding held up screens of various opacities to protect the crops from too much sun and spray. Cold water from the ocean thermal unit made plants from any latitude welcome. And, of course, if they needed a bit more sand, they could just make some.

Ivan and Igor had their farm on the deck below using sun piped in through light guides topside. There was plenty of electricity to power their grow bulbs, but unless the *Li* wandered close to the poles in the dark season, they would never need to use them. So far the Russians had produced four varieties of beets and six types of potatoes, which translated into eight varieties of borscht and twelve brands of vodka. Or was it the other way around?

Captain Kim was deliriously happy in his new persona of pacifist gentleman agrarian yachtsman. Dumping all those guns had taken a tremendous weight off his personality. All day long he would putter around his new machinery, adjusting the intakes, monitoring the exchangers, and tweaking the turbines. Hour after hour he would polish and swab the *Li*'s vast expanses of rustless metal, secretly delighted that he didn't have to share the fun with a bunch of ungrateful sailors.

The *Li*'s war to peace metamorphosis had also freed up lots of room for hydrogen storage. In a pinch, she could pull up her deep-water intake hose and run full speed on fuel cells for a week. But after the first couple of days sprinting away from Nutting, her throttle was cranked down to Slow, her auto-pilot set to Cruise, and her crew given orders to kick back and enjoy the ride. Their itinerary had them tracing a continent-size circle that straddled the equator, miles above the ocean floor. According to their maps and sextants (because that's another thing Nutting households didn't come with—electronics) they could do this forever without running into anything, except for maybe a whale, but even then, not all that hard.

Ali, surprising even himself, couldn't find enough hours in the day—what with decorating his humongous stateroom, producing each evening's theatrical production, and writing the Fossil-Free Floating Farm Cookbook. He even was getting along with everybody, and hardly ever mentioned the end of civilization or the obvious fact that they had failed to prevent it.

Buck drank a second glass of lemonade and sat down in the shade with Petal. As a joke, Bufo had planted a mango tree in a big tub amidships. They had laughed that it would take another fifteen years for it to bear fruit, and only then if they managed to find it a boyfriend. But now, sitting under it, listening to the quiet rustling of its leaves and the murmur of the ocean, that didn't seem so long to wait. What more could they ask for, they asked one another, except for the planet to have been saved so that every other pair of lovers in the world could have had a chance to sit under their own mango, hoping it found love.

Slowly but surely they had had to give up their save-the-world fantasies, smoldering on a pyre of Hello Kitty fragments and almost-sent emails. The deadlines had been missed. Christmas had come and New Years, too. They had toasted their valiant efforts

536

with strawberry champagne and kind-of caviar. They agreed, unspoken, to have no regrets, no remorse, and no mourning of what might have been. No one was to imagine the suffering and horror that must be happening now in the world beyond theirs. A world without energy. A world without civilization.

They would live out their lives within their own little floating civilization. In harmony with each other, the sun, and the planet. If they were to be the last, they would make history proud that way. It was the least they could do. It was the only thing they could do.

"Buck?" said Petal, stirring him from a little dream. "Is that a storm coming?"

He sat up and shaded his eyes with his hand. There was a thin band of white hovering over the eastern horizon.

"It is awfully weird," he said. "I'll get the glasses."

He was back in a minute with the binoculars. By that time the band had quadrupled in height.

"Some kind of weather," he said. "Totally white cloud, though. No sign of turbulence."

"Still, weird is bad," she said. "Let's call the others."

"Good idea. Maybe Kim has seen something like this."

Petal had them all on deck in short order. Each took his turn with the binos. A solid blanket of white now covered the eastern quarter of the sky.

"Atomic cloud?" asked Ali. "Do you think one of those bozos finally pushed the button?"

"If so, we're out of luck," said Buck. "We don't have any desks to hide under."

"They wouldn't dare!" insisted Petal. "After all the trouble we went to. Got to be a storm."

"Either way, we'd better start trucking the garden below decks," said Ali. "Or it will be potatoes and beets from now on."

"Da!" agreed Igor and Ivan.

"You mean, 'da, let's move the garden' or 'da, let's eat potatoes and beets from now on'?" asked Ali.

"Da!" they nodded eagerly.

"Wait!" said Kim, pointing at the cloud's advancing edge. "What's that?" He handed the glasses to Buck.

"Well, I'll be dipped!" he shouted, slapping everybody on the back. "We did it! The messages must have gotten out! The one to Tórshavn was the last one out and there he is! Do you know what this means! We did it! Look at that cloud. There must be a hundred dirigibles all in a row—each one painting a mile-wide swath—so Tórshavn must have built more ships. That means that money got into the bank account. That means everything else could be working, too! Hot dog in heaven!"

He and Petal broke into some sort of polka with Ivan and Igor. Kim and Ali slapped high fives. Everybody stuffed strawberries into their mouths and Igor ran off for a bottle of Wabichnya, aged one week. Eventually all six stood waving their pareos at the sky as the contrail front approached eleven o'clock high. Then the band of white just above them began to break up.

The party grew quiet as the empty spaces in the cloud started to make sense.

"WA?" read Petal. "He's going to spell *Waba Ti Li*, I'll bet you."

"WATCH," read Ali. "We're watching! We're watching!"

"WATCH OUT," read Buck.

"That's kind of ominous," said Petal. "Is that a scolding 'watch out' as in 'you'd better not pout'?"

"Or is it a 'duck quick' watch out?" asked Ali.

"Either way, we'd better watch out," said Buck, scanning the horizons for stuff to watch out for.

"Uh oh," he said. "Somebody coming."

He handed the binos to Kim and pointed east. Igor tugged at his Speedo and pointed south. Ivan poked his shoulder and pointed north. Ali was jumping up and down and pointing west.

"That's a ship, Buck!" screamed Ali. "A big, ugly, warship with guns and everything. It's huge! Do something!"

"They're all ships, Ali," said Buck. "United States Navy. And I think the best thing to do is look friendly. Well, maybe not that friendly."

Ali put his pareo back on. "Where are our white flags? I know, sheets! I'll get sheets! They're white. We can cut them up and—"

"Relax, Ali," said Petal. "Who would shoot at us? We don't have any guns. All we have are beans and strawberries."

"Beets!" added Ivan, raising the bottle of Wabichnya.

"Potatoes!" saluted Igor, wrestling it from him.

"Look sharp!" ordered Captain Kim, looking through the binos. "Prepare for visitors. To the helicopter pad!"

A helicopter had taken off from the carrier that was approaching from the east. The *Waba*'s crew had barely had time to scramble up to the pad and stow the paddle tennis net before the chopper touched down. Kim stood at attention in front of the others and raised his hand in salute.

Down the aircraft's ladder clambered two men loaded with video gear.

"You guys in dresses mind moving over that way a bit?" said the big one, arranging them in a cluster off to the side. "Back a little more."

"And ma'am, if you could move up front here—that's right—and turn slightly—good—eyes on the door over there—don't look at the camera—perfect!" He fussed around, getting her pareo straight, while his partner set up the tripod and fired up the microphones.

"Okay on the deck!" called the cameraman. On cue, a young dude in a Hawaiian shirt and shades came bounding down the stairs.

"Hold it!" said the cameraman, punching at some buttons. "Take two."

The dude sulked into the helicopter and then bounded back down the stairs. He strode directly up to Petal and swept off his sunglasses.

"Ms. Petal, I'd like you to meet the President of the United States of America."

"You're the President?"

"No, no, no. I'm only the advance guy, Justin Dime."

"Pleased to meet you," she said, extending her hand. "Petal, Petal Steele."

Justin started to kneel, but Petal wouldn't allow it. Eventually they just shook hands like there was nothing to it.

"Well," said Justin, putting his sunglasses back on and surveying the scene. Three US Navy destroyers and one aircraft carrier now loomed over them. "Looks like we don't have to worry about security."

"We won't worry if you won't," promised Petal.

"Here's the gig," said Justin. "I go back to the carrier and give the okay. Then Marine One hops over here with the President and his entourage. Guy will get out with a red carpet. You stand right here and it should unroll right up to you. Cameramen, be sure to get that shot from both angles—one in tight as the carpet snaps right at her feet—the other wide angle from over there. Now, Petal—I may call you Petal? Now Petal, just keep your eyes on the door the whole time, cause the snap is the President's cue to come down the stairs. I'm not going to tell you how to act or anything, but it should be 'Mr. President' at all times even if you voted for the other guy, even though I can't imagine how you could have."

"Mr. President it is, then," said Petal.

"Okay then, let's do it!" he said, and bounded back into the aircraft.

Nobody moved as they watched Dime's chopper touch down on the carrier and Marine One lift off. Helicopters create a lot of wash in general, and Marine One was famous for blowing everyone off the tarmac when landing. Its rotors were still whipping a mighty wind when the carpet snapped at Petal's feet. She stood at attention, looking straight ahead, but senses two through six reported that her pareo must now be somewhere far downwind. Eight o'clock had failed to hold. Speedo still hanging tough. Thank God. And then the carpet snapped.

A tall man in a dark suit appeared at the door, glanced around once, and then jogged down the stairs. He turned and waited for a statuesque woman to descend and held his hand out for her on the last step. Two girls followed, the older with a little camera, the younger in a Petal tee shirt, both with modest cuffs and chains. The family huddled at the base of the stairs, waiting for the rotors to be quiet. Then the President strode down the carpet.

"Ms. Steele, it is an honor to meet you," he said, extending his hand.

"The honor is all mine, Mr. President," she said, without a curtsey. "Please call me Petal."

"I want to tell you how much I admire your work. The scope of what you have achieved in just a few short months is truly astonishing—solving the global crises in climate, energy, and the economy in one bold stroke—but more important is how you have inspired the people of America—the people of the world—to honor the Earth. That's what I admire most."

"Why, thank you, Mr. President. That's the nicest thing anybody ever said to me."

"And I mean it, too, Petal," he said, finally letting go of her hand. "And Petal, just one more thing."

"Yes, Mr. President?"

"You think the girls could get an autograph?"

"Sure thing, Mr. President."

He gave a nod and the girls came running over with pens and books. While Petal was signing hers, the little one pulled up her tee shirt to show she was wearing the same color Speedo. The First Lady gave Petal a hug.

"Bless you, Petal."

The President and his family turned to wave at the top of the stairs. Petal waved back until the helicopter was way beyond waving range. But by that time everything was a blur. The chopper's wash had filled her eyes with tears.

CHAPTER 80

COEUR

It was cold that winter in Idaho, but it was a nice, steady kind of cold. Nothing like those freaky flash freezes of the last few years that would grab the state by its panhandle and smash it to smithereens when it wasn't looking. No, it was the kind of reliable, reasonable, negotiable cold like they had back in the forties—the 1840's, that is. Of course, everybody still complained about the weather—that was half the fun of winter—but nobody missed the sombreros and everyone was happy that the Earth was finally on the mend after that bad case of Anthropocene flu.

Judge Glashaus was even happy to be going to the courthouse today, even though it was Sunday and even though it wasn't really a courthouse anymore and even though he hated the name Coeur d'Alene Center of Conscience. Way too somber. Especially for days like today. They could easily change its name to Coeur d'Alene Center of Celebration for days like today. It wouldn't be that hard.

Sure, he couldn't help but be a little nostalgic for the old courthouse in all its historic grandeur—monoxide-spewing furnace, heat-bleeding windows, vast unusable spaces, and other such endearing touches characteristic of the Blight on the Landscape School of Architecture popular with the city's courageous but ecologically-clueless founders. Had the Committee for the Restoration of the Old Courthouse prevailed, the building would have been painstakingly returned to its original 1870 configuration, one that almost everyone at the time (other than the architect) thought was an abomination, an eyesore, and a damn waste of taxpayer's money. Instead, the old biddies would have to be content with "restoration through recycling," a concept which they considered not only incoherent but politically subversive in some indefinable kind of way.

Well, too bad about them, thought Glashaus, hopping on the bus. If they couldn't have fun on a day like today then they just must not like having fun. Because today was unarguably going to be the most fun day in the history of Coeur d'Alene, if not the entire Northern Idaho panhandle. If not the world.

Certainly, the eyes of the world would be upon Coeur d'Alene today. Dignitaries, celebrities, film crews, and groupies had been streaming in for days, filling up every hotel, timeshare, guesthouse, and spare room in the county. Fortunately, some other public servant would be dealing with security, crowd control, port-a-potties, and other logistical nightmares. All Glashaus would have to do was preside. And presiding is what he did best.

Admittedly, he didn't have much experience with this particular kind of presiding, but then again, who did? Performing a wedding would be a snap. Unveiling an artistic masterpiece—intuitive. Officiating abdication of a monarchy—a little dicey. Emceeing a Pan-Global Mega-Chill—kind of intimidating.

The Center's interior walls had been rolled aside to make room for the lucky thousands who had somehow scored admission passes. Glashaus nodded to familiar faces as he made his way down the aisle to the podium. A dimming of lights and the crowd settled down. Cell phones automatically switched to stun. Spotlights up. Main screen lit. Remote monitors live. Showtime.

"On behalf of the proud city of Coeur d'Alene, Idaho, United States of America, I welcome the people of the world to this historic event. Or maybe I should address you as Citizens of the New World—for every corner of our world is now starting anew, and each of you have earned the right to be addressed as Citizen.

"Mr. Siverth Narup was a Citizen of the New World back when most of us couldn't see farther than our own ethnic noses. Through his art he warned us, warned Mankind, to wake up. And once we were awake, he pleaded with us to grow up. Well, the fact that we are here today is proof that life has finally listened to art, and Mankind has finally come of age. It is my great honor to introduce to you, Mr. Siverth Narup."

Siverth took the stage. He was dressed as if he had just mushed in from Ittoqqortoormiit—his hair and anorak still glistened with snow.

"A mother does not forget the childhood of her child," he began. "No matter how much she is asked to forgive, she does not forget. No matter how great her hurt, her disappointment, her betrayal, she still will save the pictures, the letters, the mementos of those early years, those childish years of stubborn ignorance before her child knows enough to honor her.

"Our Mother kept those mementos. She left them out for all of us to see, but we were always too busy, too self-absorbed to notice. And when we did notice, we were too childish to care. Until we finally grew up. Then we could see what pain we had caused her and try to make amends.

"Today, I bring you our Mother's scrapbook. I give you *Mankind: The Baby Pictures.*"

The lights went down and the screen slowly brightened to scenes of Earth being born of interstellar dust. Wordlessly, the story of life itself was told. Millions of years of life passed before the Earth was finally ready for Mankind, years of constant turmoil and cataclysmic upheaval, climatic catastrophe and massive extinctions. The Earth and her Life could bear all of this. But it never had to bear the brutal hegemony of one species against all the rest. That would come later.

Then there were Man's first snapshots, with him all naked and vulnerable on a bear skin rug. At first, this new kind of life behaved like all the others—using energy of the sun no faster than green plants could turn it into food and shelter. Mankind was still kind of lovable in those days. At least he wasn't taking more than his share.

But then the terrible threes. Man found where Mother was saving old sunlight in the wood of trees and delighted in burning years of it away in an hour of fire. Burning became Man's defining act. Burning everything that would burn.

But that was not obnoxious enough—he had to build machines to help him burn more. Selfish, ravenous machines. Machines so greedy they demanded every ray of light the sun had ever shone—sunlight that our Mother had used to make the air safe for us, locking billions of tons of toxic CO_2 deep in the ground as coal and oil. In a minute, his machines would undo centuries of her nurturing and use that energy to make more rapacious machines.

But in the adolescence of Man, even that was not obnoxious enough. For his own self-aggrandizement, he would sicken the biosphere with indestructible poisons. He would despoil it with poisonous weapons of destruction. He would split the atom and send its vengeful pieces out to murder the future. Before Man could learn to control his own nature he had come close to destroying all of nature.

And then there appeared on the ice of the North a vision of a woman. A woman floating in the air, untouched by the cold but weighed down by the suffering of the planet. A woman whose pleading face would reach the heart of Man. Would bring him to his senses. Would make him grow up. Would make him into a man.

And as the camera draws back we see person after person in country after country waking up, growing up. People by the thousands, then millions, then billions. People giving of their time and hope and, yes, money. All with the same purpose—to save the planet. To stop their self-destructive ways. To undo the hurt they had done.

They would do it at first by doing less. By questioning their commitment to mindless consumption. By admiring the small more than the large. By making it last instead of getting it over. By choosing new ways over new things.

And they would do it not by asserting their dominion over the Earth, but their dominion over their machines. They would build a simple machine to harvest energy from the sun, waiting there on the surface of the sea. They would build a simple machine to bring the carbon back from the ocean and the air, turning it into land for people in need. And they would cool the feverish planet with clouds of their making, until her health was restored, and all was in balance, and the Anthropocene was over at last.

The camera pans to factories in every town, where once-idle workers make these machines from plans freely available to all. It sweeps over ports on every coastline where concrete is shaped into platforms that, linked together, make floating energy cities, pulled into place by kites. It focuses on fleets of dirigibles, carrying tanks of hydrogen from platform to coast, fueling everything from electric grids to cars and buildings.

And then the camera pulls back, farther and farther, until the wholeness of the Earth can be taken in all at once. A blue gem on an infinity of velvet. Unique. Irreplaceable. New again because of one thing. A change in the heart of Man.

Siverth's film was over. The screen was dark and the lights coming up. The audience sat stunned for a moment and then rose to their feet as one in applause. As loud as it was in the Center, you could still hear the crowd outside, cheering and hugging each other

546

in their parkas and mittens—as did those in pareos, kilts, and kimonos around every television that could find a plug.

Judge Glashaus was doing his best presiding, but the crowd was getting hard to preside. Netfang Lykiloro and his band were already tuning up on the back stage, and people were craning their necks to see. Better get this abdication over with while they could still sit still.

"Thank you Siverth, that was a work of genius. Promise that you will bring us *Mankind: The Productive Years* in a couple of decades.

"And, ladies and gentlemen, while we celebrate today Mankind's new respect for the Earth, let us also celebrate our new respect for one another. Growing into adulthood has given our species the wisdom to give up our battle against the elements and the skills to live in harmony with our ecosystem. But it has also given us the maturity to reject those who would lead us into conflict with one another.

"When we are in our most honest selves, we admit what cruelty we inflict in the name of tribe, nation, religion, and ideology. When we are in our most enlightened selves, we are ashamed of our concepts of class, our cravings for power, and our concentrations of wealth. When we are in our most developed selves, we do something. We act on what we know is right.

"Today, the brotherhood of Man will witness one such act. We will celebrate it, as we celebrate every act that seeks to erase discrimination, poverty, ignorance, and despair. Just as we celebrate every act that brings freedom, equality, and self-respect to a world that has suffered so long waiting for us to grow up.

"Ladies and gentlemen, I present to you Sultan Ali bin Said Andun, the Supreme Ruler of the Kingdom of Yomamah!"

Ali took the stage to a round of polite applause. He was dressed in his most conservative Supreme Ruler outfit. He looked a little nervous, which was so-o not him.

"The world is watching us today," he began, "because something has captured the world's attention. Something powerful. Something transformative. Something magical. It wasn't just an image or even just a message. It was something much more personal than that. Like a gift, but a gift that only someone who believes in you could give. A gift that made you believe in yourself. A gift that gave you courage.

547

"I was there, but I was one of the last to believe. No doubt there are many still out there who remain cynical and unmoved. We will be sad for them, but we will not let them stand in our way. We will not let them infect another generation with violence and hate. We know how to defeat these defeatists, those whose selfishness is so deep it cannot be cut out. We will ignore them. We will make them irrelevant. We will let them go.

"So, tonight I stand before you eager to become a Citizen of the New World. No longer will I be Sultan and Supreme Ruler of my country. No longer will anyone be Supreme Ruler of anyone in my country. Tonight, I do not abdicate my throne, but rather I retire it. There is no place for thrones now, even ceremonial ones. There is no place for rituals that place one man above another. We will no longer celebrate that embarrassment.

"Now we will make our own traditions. We will honor our own heroes. We will commemorate the erasure of boundaries, the amnesia of conquests, and the dissolution of hierarchies. We will lay wreaths on the graves of peacemakers, and name days after those who made us tell the truth about ourselves.

"In my hand is the official crown of the Kingdom of Yomamah. Don't worry, I'm not going to do anything tacky like step on it or throw it in the trash. It's going to the museum along with a lot of other fairly cool royal stuff which you can come look at when you visit our very friendly country, which I hope a lot of you do real soon. Not that we aren't doing well since the end of oil—let's face it, nobody beats our solar—but we do love those tourist dollars.

"In a few hours the men and women of Yomamah will go the polls for the first time in history. They will choose an interim president and delegates to a constitutional convention. Just like grown ups. Maybe in a few years I'll even run for office. Who knows? But until then, I'm happy just being one of you guys, Citizen of the New World."

This time the applause was more than just polite. The crowd went nuts for Ali. It was his finest hour. He took a few bows and threw a few too many kisses before someone escorted him to his seat next to Siverth on the stage.

"Nice work," whispered Siverth, above the roar of the crowd.

"You, too," whispered Ali. "A masterpiece."

"I mean it," said Siverth. "You guys saved the world."

"You're the one," protested Ali. "But tell me, whatever happened to all those nukes?"

"In the freezer. In the middle of Greenland the ice is two miles thick. We stuck them underneath it."

"How did you do that?"

"Easy. You put something hot enough on the ice and it will sink right through it. Water fills in above and freezes right away. Get yourself a fuel cell and some wire, put one of those atomic buggers in a block of concrete, and send the whole package on down. Do the math right and it makes it to the bedrock as the fuel runs out. Couldn't be simpler. Getting it back up is another thing, though."

"Excellent! And one other thing," said Ali, over the rising noise level. Lykiloro was struggling to find the right key for the Wedding March.

"What's that?" asked Siverth. Lykiloro had abandoned the concept of keys and charged ahead keyless into Mendelssohn's classic.

"How did you get those fortune cookies to us and to Trina Solberg?" The lucky couple had started down the aisle. The old tradition of sitting respectfully as they passed had been replaced by the new tradition of stomping your feet and hollering your lungs out.

"What fortune cookies?" asked Siverth. "And who is Trina Solberg?" Even Lykiloro's music was being drowned out by the roar of the crowd.

"I knew it!" screamed Ali. "I knew it! Everybody is nuts but me! But it really doesn't matter, now, does it?"

"What?" screamed Siverth, but it was impossible to hear anything but the sound of joy, released.

Glashaus was ceremoniously reading to the bride and groom, but the crowd knew all the lines and were reciting them at full volume, *Rocky Horror* karaoke style, in synchrony with his lips.

"Do you, Petal Steele, take this man, Buck Planck, to have and to hold, from this day forward, with no thought of *until* anything?"

"I do!" screamed every woman on every continent and energy platform on the planet.

"Do you Buck Planck, take this woman, Petal Steele, to have and to hold, from this day forward, because you are the luckiest guy in the world?"

"I do!" hollered men from every spot on the globe.

"You may now kiss!"

Pandemonium broke out as the suggestion was universalized across the entire biosphere and kissing replaced burning as Mankind's defining act—an act so consuming that hardly anybody noticed that beneath Petal's pareo was the swell of a new life, due to arrive in about ninety days.

THE END

ACKNOWLEDGMENTS

This book would not have been nearly as much fun without the entirely uncompensated advice and encouragement of a cast of characters as colorful as those who are part of Buck and Petal's lives. In no particular order, I would like to thank Doc Berry, Frank Tabrah, Karen Huffman, Dennis Mahaffay, Michael Fellmeth, David Collins, Julie D'Angelo, Jude Yablonsky, Ruth McGillion, Phil Olsen, Carole Wilcox, Patricia Prukop, Terri Bear, Maureen Schaeffer, my coach and mentor E. L. Rayner and a host of others too shy to be named.

My greatest appreciation, however, must go to Professor of Ocean Engineering Hans Krock, who, once given the chance, will actually save the planet.